The Fourth Inspector Morse Omnibus

The Inspector Morse novels

Last Bus to Woodstock
Last Seen Wearing
The Silent World of Nicholas Quinn
Service of all the Dead
The Dead of Jericho
The Riddle of the Third Mile
The Secret of Annexe 3
The Wench is Dead
The Jewel That Was Ours
The Way Through the Woods
The Daughters of Cain
Death is Now My Neighbour

Also available

Morse's Greatest Mystery and other stories
The First Inspector Morse Omnibus
The Second Inspector Morse Omnibus
The Third Inspector Morse Omnibus

The Fourth Inspector Morse Omnibus

The Way Through the Woods
The Daughters of Cain
Death is Now My Neighbour

Colin Dexter

MACMILLAN

The Way Through the Woods first published 1992 by Macmillan
The Daughters of Cain first published 1994 by Macmillan
Death is Now My Neighbour first published 1996 by Macmillan

This hardback omnibus edition first published 1998 by Macmillan
an imprint of Macmillan Publishers Ltd
25 Eccleston Place, London SW1W 9NF
and Basingstoke

Associated companies throughout the world

ISBN 0 333 73780 6

1 2 3 4 5 6 7 8 9

A CIP catalogue record for this book is available from
the British Library.

Typeset by SetSystems Ltd, Saffron Walden, Essex
Printed and bound in Great Britain by
Mackays of Chatham plc, Chatham, Kent

Not all the characters in these novels are wholly fictitious.

15408647

Contents

The Way Through
the Woods

To Brian Bedwell

The author wishes to record his gratitude to the authorities of both Wytham Woods and Blenheim Park for the information and help they so readily gave him. Also to Detective Inspector John Hayward, of the Thames Valley Police, and to Simon Jenkins, Editor of *The Times*.

Acknowledgements

The author and publishers wish to thank the following who have kindly given permission for use of copyright materials:

Extract from *A Portrait of Jane Austen* by David Cecil, published by Constable Publishers;

Extract from *The Rehearsal* by Jean Anouilh, published by Methuen London;

The Observer, for a quote by Aneurin Bevan © *The Observer*;

Faber & Faber Ltd for the extract from 'La Figlia Che Piange' in *Collected Poems 1909–1962* by T. S. Eliot;

Oxford University Press for the extract from 'AUSTIN, Alfred (1835–1913)' from the *Oxford Companion to English Literature* edited by Margaret Drabble (5th edition 1985);

Don Manley for the extract from the *Chambers Crossword Manual* (Chambers 1992);

Extract from *Marriage and Morals* by Bertrand Russell, published by Unwin Hyman;

Kate Champkin for the extract from *The Sleeping Life of Aspern Williams* by Peter Champkin;

Extract from *Further Fables of Our Time*, published by Hamish Hamilton, 1956, in the UK and Commonwealth and Simon and Schuster in the US. Copyright © 1956 James Thurber. Copyright © 1984 Helen Thurber.

The Observer, for a quote by Edwina Currie © *The Observer*;

Extract from *The Road to Xanadu* by John Livingston Lowes. Copyright 1927 by John Livingston Lowes. Copyright © renewed 1955 by John Wilbur Lowes. Reprinted by permission of Houghton Mifflin Co. All rights reserved;

Extract from *A. E. Housman: Scholar and Poet* by Norman Marlow, published by Routledge;

Faber & Faber Ltd for the extract from 'I Have Started to Say', *Collected Poems* by Philip Larkin;

Extract from *Half Truths One and a Half Truths* by Karl Kraus, published by Carcanet Press;

The University of Oxford for the extract from the Wytham Woods deed.

Every effort has been made to trace all the copyright holders but if any has been inadvertently overlooked, the author and publishers will be pleased to make the necessary arrangement at the first opportunity.

Maps of Wytham Woods and Blenheim Park drawn by Graeme James.

Weather and rain have undone it again,
And now you would never know
There was once a road through the woods
Before they planted the trees.
It is underneath the coppice and heath
And the thin anemones.
Only the keeper sees
That, where the ring-dove broods,
And the badgers roll at ease,
There was once a road through the woods.

From *The Way Through the Woods*
by Rudyard Kipling

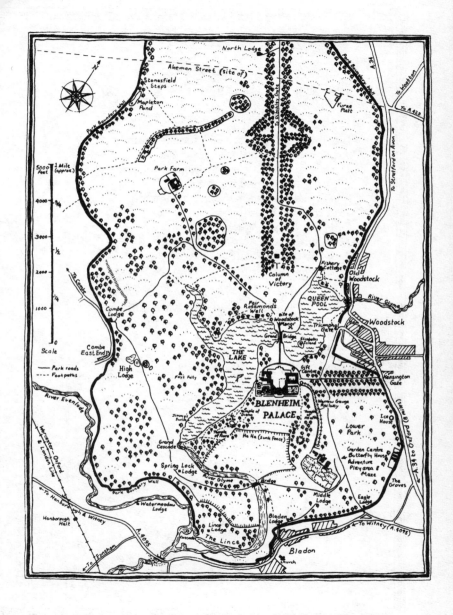

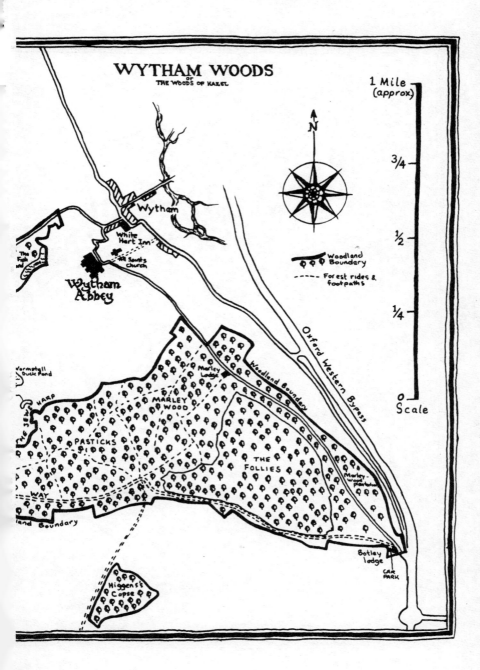

PROLEGOMENON

Though your sins be as scarlet, they shall be whiter, yea whiter, than snow.

(Isaiah, ch. i, v. 18)

Whereof one cannot speak, thereof one must be silent
(Wittgenstein, *Philosophical Investigations*)

'I MUST speak to you.'

'Speak on, my child.'

'I've not often come to your church.'

'It is not my church – it is God's church. We are all children of God.'

'I've come to confess a big sin.'

'It is proper that all sins should be confessed.'

'Can all sins be forgiven?'

'When we, sinful mortals as we are, can find it in our hearts to forgive each other, think only of our infinitely merciful Father, who understands our every weakness – who knows us all far better than we know ourselves.'

'I don't believe in God.'

'And you consider that as of any great importance?'

'I don't understand you.'

'Would it not be of far greater importance if God did not believe in *you*?'

'You're speaking like a Jesuit.'

'Forgive me.'

'It's not you – it's *me* who wants forgiveness.'

'Do you recall Pilgrim, when at last he confessed his sins to God? How the weight of the great burden was straightway lifted from his shoulders – like the pain that eases with the lancing of an abscess?'

'You sound as if you've said that all before.'

'Those self-same words I have said to others, yes.'

'Others?'

'I cannot talk of them. Whatever it is that men and women may confess to me, they confess – through me – to God.'

'You're not really needed at all, then – is that what you are saying?'

'I am a servant of God. Sometimes it is granted me to help those who are truly sorry for their sins.'

'What about those who aren't?'

'I pray that God will touch their hearts.'

'Will God forgive them – whatever they've done? You believe that, Father?'

'I do.'

'The scenes of the concentration camps . . .'

'What scenes have you in mind, my child?'

'The "sins", Father.'

'Forgive me, once again. My ears are failing now – yet not my heart! My own father was tortured to death in a Japanese camp, in 1943. I was then thirteen years old. I know full well the difficulties of forgiveness. I have told this to very few.'

'Have you forgiven your father's torturers?'

'God has forgiven them, if they ever sought His forgiveness.'

'Perhaps it's more forgivable to commit atrocities in times of war.'

'There is no scale of better or of worse, whether in times of peace or in times of war. The laws of God are those that He has created. They are steadfast and firm as the fixed stars in the heavens – unchangeable for all eternity. Should a man hurl himself down headlong from the heights of the Temple, he will break himself upon the law of God; but never will he break the universal law that God has once ordained.'

'You *are* a Jesuit.'

'I am a man, too. And all men have sinned and fallen short of the glory of God.'

'Father . . .'

'Speak on, my child.'

'Perhaps you will report what I confess . . .'

'Such a thing a priest could never do.'

'But what if I *wanted* you to report it?'

'My holy office is to absolve, in the name of our Lord and Saviour, Jesus Christ, the sins of all who show a true repentance. It is not my office to pursue the workings of the Temporal Power.'

'You haven't answered my question.'

'I am aware of that.'

'What if I *wanted* you to report me to the police?'

'I would be unsure of my duty. I would seek the advice of my bishop.'

'You've never been asked such a thing before?'
'Never.'
'What if I repeat my sin?'
'Unlock your thoughts. Unlock those sinful thoughts to me.'
'I can't do that.'
'Would you tell me everything if I could guess the reasons for your refusal?'
'You could never do that.'
'Perhaps I have already done so.'
'You know who I am, then?'
'Oh yes, my child. I think I knew you long ago.'

CHAPTER ONE

A perpetual holiday is a good working definition of Hell
(George Bernard Shaw)

MORSE never took his fair share of holidays, so he told himself. So he was telling Chief Superintendent Strange that morning in early June.

'Remember you've also got to take into consideration the time you regularly spend in pubs, Morse!'

'A few hours here and there, perhaps, I agree. It wouldn't be all that difficult to work out how much—'

'"Quantify", that's the word you're looking for.'

'I'd never look for ugly words like "quantify".'

'A useful word, Morse. It means – well, it means to say how much . . .'

'That's just what I said, isn't it?'

'I don't know why I argue with you!'

Nor did Morse.

For many years now, holidays for Chief Inspector Morse of Thames Valley CID had been periods of continuous and virtually intolerable stress. And what they must normally be like for men with the extra handicaps of wives and children, even Morse for all his extravagant imagination could scarcely conceive. But for this year, for the year of our Lord nineteen hundred and ninety-two, he was resolutely determined that things would be different: he would have a holiday away from Oxford. Not abroad, though.

He had no wanderlust for Xanadu or Isfahan; indeed he very seldom travelled abroad at all – although it should be recorded that several of his colleagues attributed such insularity more than anything to Morse's faint-hearted fear of aeroplanes. Yet as it happened it had been one of those same colleagues who had first set things in motion.

'Lime, mate! Lime's marvellous!'

Lime?

Only several months later had the word finally registered in Morse's mind, when he had read the advertisement in *The Observer*:

THE BAY HOTEL
Lyme Regis

Surely one of the finest settings of any hotel in the West Country! We are the only hotel on the Marine Parade and we enjoy panoramic views from Portland Bill to the east, to the historic Cobb Harbour to the west. The hotel provides a high standard of comfort and cuisine, and a friendly relaxed atmosphere. There are level walks to the shops and harbour, and traffic-free access to the beach, which is immediately in front of the hotel.

For full details please write to The Bay Hotel, Lyme Regis, Dorset; or just telephone (0297) 442059.

'It gets tricky,' resumed Strange, 'when a senior man takes more than a fortnight's furlough – you realize that, of course.'

'I'm not taking more than what's due to me.'

'Where are you thinking of?'

'Lyme Regis.'

'Ah. Glorious Devon.'

'Dorset, sir.'

'Next door, surely?'

'*Persuasion* – it's where some of the scenes in *Persuasion* are set.'

'Ah.' Strange looked suitably blank.

'And *The French Lieutenant's Woman*.'

'Ah. I'm with you. Saw that at the pictures with the wife . . . Or was it on the box?'

'Well, there we are then,' said Morse lamely.

For a while there was a silence. Then Strange shook his head.

'You couldn't stick being away that long! Building sand-castles? For *over a fortnight?*'

'Coleridge country too, sir. I'll probably drive around a bit – have a look at Ottery St Mary . . . some of the old haunts.'

A low chuckle emanated from somewhere deep in Strange's belly. 'He's been dead for ages, man – more Max's cup o' tea than yours.'

Morse smiled wanly. 'But you wouldn't mind me seeing his *birth*-place?'

'It's gone. The rectory's gone. Bulldozed years ago.'

'Really?'

Strange puckered his lips, and nodded his head. 'You think I'm an ignorant sod, don't you, Morse? But let me tell you something. There was none of this child-centred nonsense when I was at school. In those days we all had to learn things off by heart – things like yer actual Ancient Bloody Mariner.'

'My days too, sir.' It irked Morse that Strange, only a year his senior, would always treat him like a representative of some much younger generation.

But Strange was in full flow.

'You don't forget it, Morse. It sticks.' He peered briefly but earnestly around the lumber room of some olden memories; then found what he was seeking, and with high seriousness intoned a stanza learned long since:

> *'All in a hot and copper sky*
> *The bloody sun at noon*
> *Right up above the mast did stand*
> *No bigger than the bloody moon!'*

'Very good, sir,' said Morse, uncertain whether the monstrous misquotation were deliberate or not, for he found the chief superintendent watching him shrewdly.

'No. You won't last the distance. You'll be back in Oxford within the week. You'll see!'

'So what? There's plenty for me to do here.'

'Oh?'

'For a start there's a drainpipe outside the flat that's leaking—'

Strange's eyebrows shot up. 'And you're telling me *you're* going to fix *that*?'

'I'll get it fixed,' said Morse ambiguously. 'I've already got a

bit of extra piping but the, er, diameter of the cross-section is . . .
rather too narrow.'
'It's too bloody *small*, you mean? Is *that* what you're trying to
say?'
Morse nodded, a little sheepishly.
The score was one-all.

CHAPTER TWO

Mrs Austen was well enough in 1804 to go with her husband
and Jane for a holiday to Lyme Regis. Here we hear Jane's
voice speaking once again in cheerful tones. She gives the news
about lodgings and servants, about new acquaintances and
walks on the Cobb, about some enjoyable sea bathing, about a
ball at the local Assembly Rooms
(David Cecil, *A Portrait of Jane Austen*)

'IF I MAY SAY SO, sir, you really are rather lucky.'
The proprietor of the only hotel on the Marine Parade pushed
the register across and Morse quickly completed the Date – Name
– Address – Car Registration – Nationality columns. As he did
so, it was out of long habit rather than any interest or curiosity
that his eye took in just a few details about the half-dozen or so
persons, single and married, who had signed in just before him.
There had been a lad amongst Morse's fellow pupils in the
sixth form who had possessed a virtually photographic memory
– a memory which Morse had much admired. Not that his own
memory was at all bad; short term, in fact, it was still functioning
splendidly. And that is why, in one of those pre-signed lines,
there was just that single little detail which very soon would be
drifting back towards the shores of Morse's consciousness . . .
'To be honest, sir, you're *very* lucky. The good lady who had
to cancel – one of our regular clients – had booked the room as
soon as she knew when we were opening for the season, and she
especially wanted – she *always* wanted – a room overlooking the
bay, with bath and WC *en suite* facilities, of course.'
Morse nodded his acknowledgement of the anonymous
woman's admirable taste. 'How long had she booked for?'
'Three nights: Friday, Saturday, Sunday.'

Morse nodded again. 'I'll stay the same three nights – if that's all right,' he decided, wondering what was preventing the poor old biddy from once more enjoying her private view of the waves and the exclusive use of a water-closet. Bladder, like as not.

'Enjoy your stay with us!' The proprietor handed Morse three keys on a ring: one to Room 27; one (as he learned) for the hotel's garage, situated two minutes' walk away from the sea front; and one for the front entrance, should he arrive back after midnight. 'If you'd just like to get your luggage out, I'll see it's taken up to your room while you put the car away. The police allow our guests to park temporarily of course, but . . .'

Morse looked down at the street-map given to him, and turned to go. 'Thanks very much. And let's hope the old girl manages to get down here a bit later in the season,' he added, considering it proper to grant her a limited commiseration.

'Afraid she won't do that.'

'No?'

'She's dead.'

'Oh dear!'

'Very sad.'

'Still, perhaps she had a pretty good innings?'

'I wouldn't call forty-one a very good innings. Would you?'

'No.'

'Hodgkin's disease. You know what that's like.'

'Yes,' lied the chief inspector, as he backed towards the exit in chastened mood. 'I'll just get the luggage out. We don't want any trouble with the police. Funny lot, sometimes!'

'They may be in your part of the world, but they're very fair to us here.'

'I didn't mean—'

'Will you be taking dinner with us, sir?'

'Yes. Yes, please. I think I'd enjoy that.'

A few minutes after Morse had driven the maroon Jaguar slowly along the Lower Road, a woman (who certainly looked no older than the one who had earlier that year written in to book Room 27) turned into the Bay Hotel, stood for a minute or so by the reception desk, then pressed the Please-Ring-For-Service bell.

She had just returned from a walk along the upper level of Marine Parade, on the west side, and out to the Cobb – that great granite barrier that circles a protective arm around the harbour and assuages the incessant pounding of the sea. It was not a happy walk. That late afternoon a breeze had sprung up from the south, the sky had clouded over, and several people now promenading along the front in the intermittent drizzle were struggling into lightweight plastic macs.

'No calls for me?' she asked, when the proprietor reappeared.

'No, Mrs Hardinge. There's been nothing else.'

'OK.' But she said it in such a way as if it weren't OK, and the proprietor found himself wondering if the call he'd taken in mid-afternoon had been of greater significance than he'd thought. Possibly not, though; for suddenly she seemed to relax, and she smiled at him – most attractively.

The grid that guarded the drinks behind reception was no longer in place and already two couples were seated in the bar enjoying their dry sherries; and with them one elderly spinster fussing over a dachshund, one of those 'small dogs accepted at the management's discretion: £2.50 *per diem*, excluding food'.

'I think I'll have a large malt.'

'Soda?'

'Just ordinary water, please.'

'Say when.'

' "When"!'

'On your room-bill, Mrs Hardinge?'

'Please! Room fourteen.'

She sat on the green leather wall-seat just beside the main entrance. The whisky tasted good and she told herself that however powerful the arguments for total abstinence might be, few could challenge the fact that after alcohol the world almost invariably appeared a kinder, friendlier place.

The Times lay on the coffee table beside her, and she picked it up and scanned the headlines briefly before turning to the back page, folding the paper horizontally, then vertically, and then studying one across.

It was a fairly easy puzzle; and some twenty minutes later her not inconsiderable cruciverbalist skills had coped with all but a couple of clues – one of them a tantalizingly half-familiar quotation from Samuel Taylor Coleridge – over which she was still frowning when the lady of the establishment interrupted her with the evening's menu, and asked if she were taking dinner.

For a few minutes after ordering Seafood Soup with Fresh Garden Herbs, followed by Guinea Fowl in Leek and Mushroom

Sauce, she sat with eyes downcast and smoked a king-sized Dunhill cigarette. Then, as if on sudden impulse, she went into the glass-panelled telephone booth that stood beside the entrance and rang a number, her lips soon working in a sort of silent charade, like the mouth of some frenetic goldfish, as she fed a succession of 20p's into the coin-slot. But no one could hear what she was saying.

CHAPTER THREE

Have you noticed that life, real honest-to-goodness life, with murders and catastrophes and fabulous inheritances, happens almost exclusively in the newspapers?

(Jean Anouilh, *The Rehearsal*)

MORSE found his instructions fairly easy to follow. Driving from the small car park at the eastern end of Marine Parade, then turning right, then left just before the traffic lights, he had immediately spotted the large shed-like building on his left in the narrow one-way Coombe Street: 'Private Garage for Residents of The Bay Hotel'. Herein, as Morse saw after propping open the two high wooden gates, were eighteen parking spaces, marked out in diagonal white lines, nine on each side of a central KEEP CLEAR corridor. By reason of incipient spondylosis, he was not nowadays particularly skilled at reversing into such things as slanting parking bays; and since the garage was already almost full, it took him rather longer than it should have done to back the Jaguar into a happily angled position, with the sides of his car equidistant from a J-reg Mercedes and a Y-reg Vauxhall. It was out of habit as before that he scanned the number plates of the cars there; but when about a quarter of an hour earlier he'd glanced through the hotel register, at least *something* had clicked in his mind.

Now though? Nothing. Nothing at all.

There was no real need for Morse immediately to explore the facilities of Room 27, and the drinks-bar faced him as he turned into the hotel. So he ordered a pint of Best Bitter, and sat down in the wall-seat, just by the entrance, and almost exactly on the same square footage of green leather that had been vacated ten minutes earlier by one of the two scheduled occupants of Room 14.

He should have been feeling reasonably satisfied with life, surely? But he wasn't. Not really. At that particular moment he longed for both the things he had that very morning solemnly avowed to eschew for the remaining days of his leave: cigarettes and newspapers. Cigarettes he had given up so often in the past that he found such a feat comparatively simple; never previously however had he decided that it would be of some genuine benefit to his peace of mind to be wholly free for a week or so from the regular diet of disasters served up by the quality dailies. Perhaps that was a silly idea too, though . . .

His right hand was feeling instinctively for the reassuring square packet in his jacket pocket, when the maîtresse d'hotel appeared, wished him a warm welcome, and gave him the menu. It may have been a matter of something slightly more than coincidence that Morse had no hesitation in choosing the Seafood Soup and the Guinea Fowl. Perhaps not, though – and the point is of little importance.

'Something to drink with your meal, sir?' She was a pleasantly convivial woman, in her late forties, and Morse glanced appreciatively at the décolletage of her black dress as she bent forward with the wine list.

'What do you recommend?'

'Half a bottle of Médoc? Splendid vintage! You won't do much better than that.'

'A bottle might be better,' suggested Morse.

'A bottle it shall be, sir!' – the agreement signed with mutual smiles.

'Could you open it now – and leave it on the table?'

'We always do it that way here.'

'I, er, I didn't know.'

'It likes to breathe a little, doesn't it?'

'Like all of us,' muttered Morse; but to himself, for she was gone.

He realized that he was feeling hungry. He didn't often feel hungry: usually he took most of his calories in liquid form; usually, when invited to a College gaudy, he could manage only a couple of the courses ordained; usually he would willingly exchange an entrée or a dessert for an extra ration of alcohol. But this evening he *was* feeling hungry, quite definitely; and just after finishing his second pint of beer (still no cigarette!) he was glad to be informed that his meal was ready. Already, several times, he had looked through the glass doors to his left, through to the dining-room, where many now sat eating at their tables, white tablecloths overlaid with coverings of deep maroon, beneath the subdued lighting of crystal chandeliers. It looked inviting. Romantic, almost.

As he stood by the dining-room door for a moment, the maîtresse was quickly at his side, expressing the hope that he wouldn't mind, for this evening, sharing a table? They had quite a few non-residents in for dinner . . .

Morse bade the good lady lose no sleep over such a trivial matter, and followed her to one of the farthest tables, where an empty place was laid opposite a woman, herself seated half-facing the wall, reading a copy of *The Times*, an emptied bowl of Seafood Soup in front of her. She lowered the newspaper, smiled in a genteel sort of way, as though it had taken her some effort to stretch her painted lips into a perfunctory salutation, before reverting her attention to something clearly more interesting than her table companion.

The room was almost completely full, and it was soon obvious to Morse that he was going to be the very last to get served. The sweet-trolley was being pushed round, and he heard the elderly couple to his right ordering some caramelized peaches with nuts and cream; but – strangely for him! – he felt no surge of impatience. In any case, the soup was very soon with him, and the wine had been there already; and all around him was goodwill and enjoyment, with a low, steady buzz of conversation, and occasionally some muted laughter. But the newspaper opposite him, for the present, remained firmly in place.

It was over the main course – his only slightly after hers – that Morse ventured his first, not exactly original, gambit:

'Been here long?'

She shook her head.

'Nor me. Only just arrived, in fact.'

'And me.' (She *could* speak!)

'I'm only here for a few days . . .'

'Me, too. I'm leaving on Sunday.'

It was the longest passage of speech Morse was likely to get, he knew, for the eyes had drifted down again to the Guinea Fowl. Stayed on the Guinea Fowl.

Bugger you! thought Morse. Yet his interest, in spite of himself, was beginning to be engaged. Her lower teeth – a little too long maybe? – were set closely together and slightly stained with nicotine; yet her gums were fresh and pink, her full mouth undoubtedly attractive. But he noticed something else as well: her mottled, tortoise-shell eyes, though camouflaged around with artificial shadow, seemed somehow darkened by a sadder, more durable shadow; and he could see an intricate little criss-cross of red lines at the outer side of either eye. She might have a slight cold, of course.

Or she might earlier have been weeping a little . . .

When the sweet-trolley came, Morse was glad that he was only halfway down the Médoc, for some cheese would go nicely with it ('Cheddar . . . Gouda . . . Stilton . . .' the waitress recited); and he ordered Stilton, just as the woman opposite had done.

Gambit Number Two appeared in order.

'We seem to have similar tastes,' he ventured.

'Identical, it seems.'

'Except for the wine.'

'Mm?'

'Would you, er, like a glass of wine? Rather good! It'll go nicely with the Stilton.'

This time she merely shook her head, disdaining to add any verbal gloss.

Bugger you! thought Morse, as she picked up *The Times* once more, unfolded the whole broadsheet in front of her, and hid herself away completely – together with her troubles.

The fingers holding the paper, Morse noticed, were quite slim and sinuous, like those of an executant violinist, with the unpainted nails immaculately manicured, the half-moons arching whitely over the well-tended cuticles. On the third finger of her left hand was a narrow-banded gold wedding ring, and above it an engagement ring with four large diamonds, set in an unusual twist, which might have sparkled in any room more brightly lit than this.

On the left of the opened double-page spread (as Morse viewed things) her right hand held the newspaper just above the crossword, and he noticed that only two clues remained to be solved. A few years earlier his eyes would have had little trouble; but now, in spite of a sequence of squints, he could still not quite read the elusive wording of the first clue, which looked like a quotation. Better luck with the other half of the paper though, held rather nearer to him – especially with the article, *the quite extraordinary article*, that suddenly caught and held and dominated his attention. At the foot of the page was the headline: 'Police pass sinister verses to Times' man', and Morse had almost made out the whole of the first paragraph –

> THE LITERARY correspondent of *The Times*, Mr Howard Phillipson, has been called upon by the Oxfordshire police to help solve a complex riddle-me-ree, the answer to which is believed to pinpoint the spot where a young woman's body

– when the waitress returned to the table.
  'Coffee, madame?'
  'Please.'
  'In the bar – or in the lounge?'
  'In the bar, I think.'
  'You, sir?'
  'No. No, thank you.'
  Before leaving, the waitress poured the last of the Médoc into Morse's glass; and on the other side of the table the newspaper was folded away. To all intents and purposes the meal was over. Curiously, however, neither seemed over-anxious to leave immediately, and for several moments they sat silently together, the last pair but one in the dining-room: he, longing for a cigarette and eager to read what looked like a most interesting article; wondering, too, whether he should make one last foray into enemy territory – since, on reflection, she really did look rather attractive.
  'Would you mind if I smoked?' he ventured, half-reaching for the tempting packet.
  'It doesn't matter to me.' She rose abruptly, gathering up handbag and newspaper. 'But I don't think the management will be quite so accommodating.' She spoke without hostility – even worse, without interest, it seemed – as she pointed briefly to a notice beside the door:

IN THE INTEREST OF PUBLIC HEALTH, WE RESPECTFULLY REQUEST YOU TO REFRAIN FROM SMOKING IN THE DINING AREA. THANK YOU FOR YOUR CO-OPERATION.

Bugger you! thought Morse.

He'd not been very sensible though, he realized that. All he'd had to do was ask to borrow the newspaper for a couple of minutes. He could *still* ask her, of course. But he wasn't going to – oh no! She could stick her bloody paper down the loo for all he cared. It didn't matter. Almost every newsagent in Lyme Regis would have a few unsold copies of yesterday's newspapers, all ready to be packaged off mid-morning to the wholesale distributors. He'd seen such things a thousand times.

She'd go to the bar, she'd said. All right, *he* would go to the lounge . . . where very soon he was sitting back in a deep armchair enjoying another pint of bitter and a large malt. And just to finish off the evening, he told himself, he'd have a cigarette, just one – well, two at the very outside.

It was growing dark now – but the evening air was very mild; and as he sat by the semi-opened window he listened again to the grating roar of the pebbles dragged down by the receding tide, and his mind went to a line from 'Dover Beach':

But now I only hear its melancholy, long withdrawing roar.

Much-underrated poet, Matthew Arnold, he'd always thought.

In the bar, Mrs Hardinge was drinking her coffee, sipping a Cointreau – and, if truth be told, thinking for just a little while of the keen blue eyes of the man who had been sitting opposite her at dinner.

CHAPTER FOUR

The morning is wiser than the evening.
(Russian proverb)

MORSE rose at 6.45 the following morning, switched on his room-kettle, and made himself a cup of coffee from one of the several sachets and small milk-tubs provided. He opened the curtains and stood watching the calm sea, and a fishing boat just leaving the Cobb. Blast! He'd meant to bring his binoculars.

The gulls floated and wheeled across the esplanade, occasionally hanging motionless, as if suspended from the sky, before turning away like fighter-aircraft peeling from their formation and swooping from his vision.

The sun had already risen, a great ball of orange over the cliffs to the east, over Charmouth – where they said someone had discovered a dinosaur or a pterodactyl, or something, that had lived in some distant prehistoric age, some figure with about twelve noughts after it. Or was it twenty?

Deciding that he really ought to learn more about the world of natural history, Morse drained his coffee and without shaving walked down to the deserted ground floor, out of the hotel, and left along Marine Parade – where his search began.

The newsagent on the corner felt pretty sure that he *hadn't* got a previous day's *Times*: *Sun*, yes; *Mirror*, yes; *Express*, yes . . . but, no – no *Times*. Sorry, mate. Turning left, Morse struggled up the steep incline of Broad Street. Still out of breath, he enquired in the newsagent's shop halfway up on the left. *Telegraph*, *Guardian*, *Independent* – any good? No? Sorry, sir. Morse got another 'sir' in the newsagent's just opposite – but no *Times*. He carried on to the top of the hill, turned left at a rather seedy-looking cinema, then left again into Cobb Road, and down to the western end of Marine Parade – where a fourth newsagent was likewise unable to assist, with the chief inspector reduced in rank to 'mate' once more.

Never mind! Libraries kept back numbers of all the major dailies; and if he were desperate – which he most certainly *wasn't* – he could always go down on his knees and beg Mrs Misery-guts to let him take a peek at her newspaper. If she'd still got it . . . Forget it, Morse! What's it matter, anyway?

What's *she* matter?

Strolling briskly now along the front, Morse breathed deeply on the early-morning air – cigarettes were going to be *out* that day. Completely out. He had, he realized, just walked a sort of rectangle; well, a 'trapezium' really – that was the word: a quadrilateral with two parallel sides. And doubtless he would have told himself it wouldn't be a bad idea to brush up on his geometry had he not caught sight of a figure in front of him, about two hundred yards distant. For there, beneath the white canopy of the buff-coloured Bay Hotel, with its yellow two-star AA sign, stood Mrs Hardinge, Mrs Crabcrumpet herself, dressed in a full-length black leather coat, and searching in a white shoulder-bag. For a purse, probably? But before she could find it she raised her right hand in greeting as a taxi drew up along the lower road, its driver manoeuvring 180 degrees in the turning area, then getting out and opening the near-side rear door for the elegant, luggageless woman who had just walked down the ramp. Morse, who had stopped ostensibly to survey the ranks of fruit machines in the Novelty Emporium, looked down at his wrist-watch: 7.50 a.m.

The ground floor was still deserted, and as yet no delicious smell of fried bacon betrayed the opening of the hostelry's daily routine. Morse passed by the giant potted-palm, passed by the statue of a maiden perpetually pouring a slow trickle from her water-jug into the pool at her feet, and was starting up the stairs when his eye fell on the reception desk to his right: a jar of artificial flowers; a tray of mineral water; a yellow RNLI collecting box; and below a stack of brochures and leaflets – the hotel register. He glanced around him. No one.

He looked swiftly along the linear information once again:

3.7.92 – Mr and Mrs C A Hardinge – 16 Cathedral Mews, Salisbury – H 35 LWL – British – Rm 14

It had been the Oxfordshire letter-registration, LWL, which had caught his eye that previous evening. Now it was something else: that C. It was her all right though, for he'd seen the room number on her key-ring at dinner. And frowning slightly as he mounted the stairs, he found himself wondering how many married women were unable to write out the accepted formula for their wedded state without getting the wrong initial. Perhaps she was only recently married? Perhaps she was one of those liberated ladies who had suddenly decided that if only *one* initial were required it was going to be hers? Perhaps ... perhaps they weren't 'Mr and Mrs' at all, and she had been momentarily confused about what names they were going under *this* time?

The latter, he thought – a little sadly.

Breakfast (8.45 a.m.–9.30 a.m.) was for Morse a solitary affair, yet he was finding it, as ever, the biggest single joy of any holiday. After some Kellogg's Corn Flakes and a mixed grill, he strolled along the edge of the sea once more, feeling pleasantly replete and (he supposed) about as content as he was ever likely to be. The weather forecast was good, and he decided that he would drive out west to Ottery St Mary and then, if the mood took him, north up to Nether Stowey, and the Quantocks.

As he reached the second-floor landing after his return to the hotel, Room 14 was almost directly in front of him; and with the door slightly ajar, as one blue-uniformed room-maid came out with a hoover, he could see another maid inside the room replenishing the sachets of coffee and tea and the little tubs of milk. He took his chance. Knocking (not too hesitantly), he put his head round the door.

'Mrs Hardinge in?'

'No, sur.' She looked no more than eighteen, and Morse felt emboldened.

'It's just that she promised to keep yesterday's newspaper for me – we had dinner here together last night. *The Times*, it was.'

The maid gave Morse a dubious look as he cast a swift glance over the room. The bed nearer the window had been slept in – the pillow deeply indented, a flimsy black negligée thrown carelessly over the duvet. But had *Mr* Hardinge slept in the other? The bed could have been made up already, of course ... but where was his case and his clothes and his other impedimenta?

'I'm afraid there's no newspaper as I can see 'ere, sur. In any case, I wouldn't—'

'Please, please! I fully understand. I mean, if it's not in the waste-paper basket ...'

'No, it's not.'

'There'd be another basket, though? In the bathroom? It's just that she *did* say ...'

The young girl peered cautiously round the bathroom door, but shook her head.

Morse smiled affably. 'It's all right. She must have left it somewhere else for me. Probably in *my* room. Huh! Sorry to have bothered you.'

Back in Room 27, he found his own bed made up, the floor hoovered, and his coffee cup washed and placed upside-down on its matching saucer. He stood for several minutes looking out at the sea again, telling himself he must re-read *The Odyssey*; and soon, almost unconsciously, finding himself smoking one of his forbidden cigarettes and wondering why the brown leather suitcase he had just seen lying closed on the set of drawers in Room 14 bore, in an attractive Gothic script, the gilt letters 'C S O'. The only thing he knew with such initials was Community Service Order – but that seemed wholly unlikely. Must be *her* initials, surely. But whatever the C stood for – Carole? Catherine? Claire? Celia? Constance? – it was going to be obvious even to an under-achiever in the new seven-year-old reading tests that the

O didn't stand for 'Hardinge'. It may reasonably have been the lady's surname before she got married. But the case was a new one – a very new one . . .

So what, Morse! So bloody *what*!

He sat down and wrote a note.

Dear Mrs H, I shall be most grateful if you can save yesterday's Times for me. Not the Business/Sport section; just the main newspaper – in fact I only really want to look at the bit on p. 1 (and probably a continuation on an inside page) about the 'Sinister Verses' article. Your reward, which you must accept, will be a drink on me at the bar before dinner, when I promise to adhere religiously to every one of the management's ordinances.

Room 27

Leaving this innocent, if rather pompous, communication with the proprietor, Morse walked along to the private garage, pondering the reason why the female half of Room 14 had not made use of car H 35 LWL instead of ordering a taxi. Pondering only briefly though, since he thought he now knew why Mrs C. Something (Hardinge?) had been acting so strangely. Well, no – not 'strangely', not if you looked at it from *her* point of view. Forget it, Morse! Get your road atlas out and trace the easiest route to Ottery St Mary.

Soon the Jaguar was on its way, with the sun growing warmer by the minute, and hardly a cloud in the bluest of skies. By the time he reached Honiton, Morse had almost forgotten the rather odd fact that when he had looked just now around the other cars in the hotel's garage, there had been no sign whatsoever of any vehicle with the registration H 35 LWL.

CHAPTER FIVE

Extract from a diary dated 26 June 1992 (one week before Morse
had found himself in Lyme Regis)

Words! Someone – a Yank I think – said you can stroke people
with words. I say – sod words! Especially sod the sight of
words. They're too powerful. 'Naked's powerful. 'Breasts' are
powerful. Larkin said he thought the most splendid verb in the
language was 'unbutton'. But when the words are a joke? Oh
God, help me! Please God, help me! Yesterday Tom wrote me
a letter from his new house in Maidstone. Here's part of what
he wrote

> I've got a pair of great tits in the garden here. Now don't
> you go and think that when I look down from my study
> window with the binocs you bought me there's this
> bronzed and topless and vastly bosomed signora
> sunning herself on a Lilo. No! Just a wonderfully
> entertaining little pair of great tits who've taken up
> residence – a bit late aren't they? – in the nesting-box we
> fixed under the beech tree. Remember that line we
> learned at school?
> Tityre tu patulae recubans sub tegmine fagi . . .

Those are Tom's words. Wouldn't you think that any normally
civilized soul would be delighted with the thought of those
little blue black white yellow birds (my speciality!!) slipping
their slim little selves into a nesting-box? Wouldn't you think
that only a depraved and perverted mind would dwell instead
upon that picture of a woman on a sunbed? Wouldn't you
think that any sensitive soul would rejoice in that glorious
Virgilian hexameter instead of seeing another 'tit' in the opening word? Christ, it was only a pun wasn't it! The Greek term
is 'paronomasia'. I'd forgotten that but I just looked it up in
my book of literary terms. And still the words follow me.
Looking through the p's I found 'pornography' again. Words!
Bloody hell. God help me!

'Common subjects of such exotic pornography are
sadism, masochism, fetishism, transvestism, voyeurism
(or scoptolagnia), narcissism, pederasty, and necrophilia.
Less common subjects are coprophilia, kleptolagnia, and
zoophilia.'

Should it be a fraction of comfort that my tastes don't yet run
to these last three 'less common' perversions – if that's the
right word. What does the middle one mean anyway? It's not
in Chambers.

(Later) Dinner in SCR very good – 'Barbue Housman'. I phoned
C afterwards and I almost dare to believe she's really looking
forward to next weekend. I just wish I could go to sleep and
wake up on the 3rd. But I seem to spend half my time wishing
my life away. I have drunk too much. Oh God, let me sleep
well!

CHAPTER SIX

... and hence through life
Chasing chance-started friendships
(Samuel Taylor Coleridge,
'To the Revd George Coleridge')

IN MID-AFTERNOON Morse looked back on his Coleridge pil-
grimage with considerable disappointment.

Half a dozen miles west of Honiton he had turned left off the
A30 for the little market town of Ottery St Mary. Parking had
proved a virtually insuperable problem; and when he finally got
to the Information Office he learned only that 'Coleridge was
born here in 1772 at the Rectory (gone), the tenth child of The
Revd J. Coleridge, vicar 1760–81, and master of the Grammar
School (gone). The rapidly growing family soon occupied the old
School House (gone) . . .'. St Mary's was still there though, and
he walked around the large church consulting some printed notes
on 'Points of Interest', fixed to a piece of wood shaped like a
hand-mirror. He began to feel, as he read, that it was high time
he re-familiarized himself with 'corbels' and 'mouldings' and

'ogees'; but it was something of a surprise that the author of the notes appeared never to have heard of Coleridge. Indeed it was only by accident that as he was leaving the church he spotted a memorial plaque on the churchyard wall, with a low-relief bust of the poet beneath the outspread wings of an albatross.

An hour and a half later, after a fast drive up the M5, Morse was equally disappointed with the village of Nether Stowey. 'The small thatched cottage, damp and uncomfortable' wherein Coleridge had lived in 1796 was now enlarged, tiled, and (doubtless) centrally heated, too. More to the point, it was closed to the public – on Saturdays; and today was Saturday. Inside the church the leaflet available for visitors ('Please take – quite free!') was a singularly uninformative document, and Morse felt no inclination to heed the vicar's exhortation to join the church fellowship – 'emphasis ever on joyous informality'. He put 50p in a slot in the wall and joylessly began the drive back to Lyme Regis.

Perhaps Strange had been right all along. Perhaps he, Morse, was the sort of person who could never really enjoy a holiday. Even the pint of beer he'd drunk in a rather dreary pub in Nether Stowey had failed to satisfy, and he didn't really know what he wanted. Or rather he did: he wanted a cigarette for a start; and he wanted something to engage his brain, like a cryptic crossword or a crime – or the previous day's issue of *The Times*. But there was something else too, though he was hardly prepared to admit it even to himself: he would have wished Mrs Hardinge (or Mrs Whatever) to be beside him in the passenger seat.

A voice in his brain told him that he was being quite extraordinarily foolish. But he didn't listen.

At 3.45 p.m. he parked the Jaguar in the hotel garage: only three other cars there now – none of the three with the Oxon registration.

At the Corner Shop on Marine Parade, he succumbed to two temptations, and resisted a third. He bought twenty Dunhill International, and a copy of *The Times*; but the magazine with the seductively posed, semi-clad siren on its glossy cover remained on the top shelf – if only because he would be too embarrassed and ashamed to face the hard-eyed man behind the counter.

Back in the hotel, he took a leisurely bath and then went down to the residents' lounge, where he unfolded the cover from the full-sized billiard table, and for half an hour or so pretended he was Steve Davis. After all, didn't *The Oxford Companion to Music* devote one entire page to 'Mozart on the Billiard Table'? Morse, however, was unable to pot virtually anything, irrespective of angle or distance; and just as carefully as he had unfolded the cover he now replaced it, and returned to his room, deciding (if life should allow) to brush up on his cuemanship as well as on that glossary of architectural terms. This was exactly why holidays were so valuable, he told himself: they allowed you to stand back a bit, and see where you were going rusty.

It was whilst lying fully clothed on his single bed, staring soberly at the ceiling, that there was a knock on the door and he got up to open it. It was the proprietor himself, carrying a Sainsbury's supermarket carrier bag.

'Mrs Hardinge wanted you to have this, Mr Morse. I tried to find you earlier, but you were out – and she insisted I gave it to you personally.'

What was all this to Morse's ears? Music! Music! Heavenly music!

Inside the carrier bag was the coveted copy of *The Times*, together with a 'Bay Hotel' envelope, inside which, on a 'Bay Hotel' sheet of note-paper, was a brief letter:

For 27 from 14. I've seen a paperback called The Bitch by one of the Collins sisters. I've not read it but I think it must be all about me, don't you? If I'm not at dinner I'll probably be in soon after and if you're still around you can buy me a brandy. After all these newspapers do cost honest money you know!

For Morse this innocent missive was balm and manna to the soul. It was as if he'd been trying to engage the attention of a lovely girl at a dinner party who was apparently ignoring him, and who now suddenly leaned forward and held her lips against his cheek in a more than purely perfunctory kiss.

Strangely, however, before reading the article, Morse picked up the bedside phone and dialled police HQ at Kidlington.

CHAPTER SEVEN

I read the newspaper avidly. It is my one form of continuous fiction

(Aneurin Bevan, quoted in *The Observer*, 3 April 1960)

POLICE PASS SINISTER VERSES TO TIMES' MAN

THE LITERARY correspondent of *The Times*, Mr Howard Phillipson, has been called upon by the Oxfordshire police to help solve a complex riddle-me-ree, the answer to which is believed to pinpoint the spot where a young woman's body may be buried.

The riddle, in the form of a five-stanza poem, was sent anonymously by a person who (as the police believe) knows the secret of a crime which for twelve months has remained on the unsolved-case shelves in the Thames Valley Police HQ at Kidlington, Oxfordshire.

'The poem is a fascinating one,' said Mr Phillipson, 'and I intend to spend the weekend trying to get to grips with it. After a brief preliminary look I almost think that the riddle has a strong enough internal logic to be solvable within its own context, but we must wait and see.'

According to Detective Chief Inspector Harold Johnson of Thames Valley CID the poem would fairly certainly appear to have reference to the disappearance of a Swedish student whose rucksack was found in a lay-by on the northbound carriageway of the A44, a mile or so south of Woodstock, in July 1991. Documents found in the side-panels of the rucksack had identified its owner as Karin Erikksson, a student from Uppsala, who had probably hitchhiked her way from London to Oxford, spent a day or so in the University City – and then? Who knows?

'The case was always a baffling one,' admitted DCI Johnson. 'No body was ever found, no suspicious circumstances uncovered. It is not unknown for students to be robbed of their possessions, or lose them. And of course some of them run away. But we've always thought of this as a case of potential murder.'

At the time of her disappearance, Miss Eriksson's mother informed the police that Karin had phoned her from London a week or so previously, sounding 'brisk and optimistic', albeit rather short of cash. And the Principal of the secretarial college where Karin was a student described her as 'an attractive, able, and athletic young lady'. Since the discovery of the rucksack, no trace whatever has been found, although senior police officers were last night suggesting that this new development might throw fresh light on one or two possible clues discovered during the earlier investigation.

The poem in full reads as follows:

Find me, find the Swedish daughter –
Thaw my frosted tegument!
Dry the azured skylit water,
Sky my everlasting tent.

Who spied, who spied that awful spot?
O find me! Find the woodman's daughter!
Ask the stream: 'Why tell'st me not
The truth thou know'st – the tragic slaughter?'

Ask the tiger, ask the sun
Whither riding, what my plight?
Till the given day be run,
Till the burning of the night.

Thyme, I saw Thyme flow'ring here
A creature white trapped in a gin,
Panting like a hunted deer
Licking still the bloodied skin.

With clues surveyed so wondrous laden,
Hunt the ground beneath thy feet!
Find me, find me now, thy maiden,
I will kiss thee when we meet.

A. Austin
(1853–87)

The lines were typed on a fairly old-fashioned machine, and police are hopeful that forensic tests may throw up further clues. The only immediately observable idiosyncrasies of the typewriter used are the worn top segment of the lower-case 'e', and the slight curtailment of the cross-bar in the lower-case 't'.

'To be truthful,' admitted Chief Inspector Johnson, 'not many of my colleagues here are all that hot on poetry, and that's why we thought *The Times* might help. It would be a sort of poetic justice if it could.' Final word with Mr Phillipson: 'It might all be a cruel hoax, and the link with the earlier case does appear rather tenuous, perhaps. But the police certainly seem to think they are on to something. So do I!'

Morse read the article at his own pace; then again, rather more quickly. After which, for several minutes, he sat where he was, his eyes still, his expression quite emotionless – before turning to the back page and reading the clue he hadn't quite been able to see the evening before:

''Work without hope draws nectar in a—' (Coleridge) (5).

Huh! If the poem was a 'riddle', so was the answer! A quotation from Coleridge, too! Half smiling, he sat back in his chair and marvelled once more at the frequency of that extraordinarily common phenomenon called 'coincidence'.

Had he but known it, however, a far greater coincidence had already occurred the previous evening when (purely by chance, surely?) he had been ushered into the dining room to share a table with the delectable occupant of Room 14. But as yet he couldn't know such a thing; and taking from his pocket his silver Parker pen, he wrote 'I' and 'V' in the empty squares which she had left in S-E-E – before reaching for the telephone again.

'No, sir – Superintendent Strange is still not answering. Can anyone else help?'

'Yes, perhaps so,' said Morse. 'Put me through to Traffic Control, will you?'

CHAPTER EIGHT

*Extract from a diary dated July 1992 (one day before Morse
had found himself in Lyme Regis)*

I must write a chapter on 'Gradualism' in my definitive
opus on pornography, for it is the gradual nature of the
erotic process that is all important, as even that old fascist
Plato had the nous to see. Yet this is a factor increasingly
forgotten by the writers and the film-directors and the
video-makers. If they ever knew it. 'Process' is what it
should be all about. The process typified in the lifting of a
full-length skirt to a point just above the ankle, or the first
unfastening of a button on a blouse! Do I make things clear?
Without the skirt, what man will glory in the ankle? Without the blouse, what man will find himself aroused by the
mere button? Nudity itself is nothing: it is the intent of
nudity which guarantees the glorious engagement. Never
did nudity in itself mean very much to me, even when I
was a young boy. Never did I have any interest in all those
Italian paintings of naked women. Likewise it seems to me
that few of our licentious and promiscuous youth take overmuch notice of the women who flaunt their bodies daily in
the tabloid press. Such young men are more interested in
back-page soccer stories. Is there a moral here?

I've just read through all that shit I've just written and it
makes me sound almost sane. Almost as if I'd laugh out-
right at any quack who suggested that I ought to go along
and see somebody. But in truth there's not much to laugh
about considering the wreck I've now become – I've always
been perhaps. These others are bloody lucky. Christ, how
lucky they are! They have their erotic fancies and imaginings
and get their fixes from their filthy mags and porno flicks
and casual sex. But me? Ha! I study those articles in the
quality press about the effects of pornography on the sex-
crime statistics. That's what the civilized sex maniacs do.
Does then pornography have the effect that is claimed? I
doubt it. Yet I wish it did. Yes! Then almost everyone would
be committing some dreadful sex-offence each day. I know –

of course I do! – that such a state of affairs wouldn't be all that bloody marvellous for the goody-goody girls who've been guarding their virginity. But at least I would be normal! I would be normal.

Come on Time! Hurry along there! It is tomorrow that I see her and I can hardly wait to watch the hours go by. Why do I wait? Because although I have never really loved my wife (or my children all that much) I would sacrifice almost everything in my life if by so doing I could spare her the despairing humiliation of learning about my own shame.

(Later) I picked up The Guardian in the SCR and read about a Jap who murdered a young model and feasted off her flesh for a fortnight. They didn't keep him in jail very long because he was manifestly crackers. But when they transferred him to a loony asylum he kicked up such a fuss that they didn't keep him there long either. Why? Because the authorities became convinced that he was normal. After they'd let him go he said to a newspaper reporter: 'My time in the mental ward was like Hell. Everyone else in there was real crazy, but the doctors saw that I wasn't like the rest of them. They saw I was normal. So they let me go.' I wasn't too upset about what this weirdo said. What really upset me was what the reporter said. He said the most distressing aspect of this strange and solitary cannibal was the fact that he really believed himself to be normal! Don't you see what I'm saying?

CHAPTER NINE

And I wonder how they should have been together!
(T. S. Eliot, *La Figlia Che Piange*)

HE MADE his way from the dining-room to the bar. The meal had been a lonely affair; but Morse was never too worried about periods of loneliness, and felt himself unable to appreciate the distinction that some folk made between solitude and loneliness. In any case, he'd enjoyed the meal. Venison, no less! He now ordered a pint of Best Bitter and sat down, his back to the sea, with the current issue of *The Times*. He looked at his wrist-watch, wrote the time (8.21) in the small rectangle of space beside the crossword, and began.

At 8.35, as he struggled a little over the last two clues, he heard her voice:

'Not finished it yet?'

Morse felt a sudden rush of happiness.

'Mind if I join you?' She sat down beside him, to his right, on the wall-seat. 'I've ordered some coffee. Are you having any?'

'Er, no. Coffee's never figured all that prominently in my life.'

'Water neither, by the look of things.'

Morse turned towards her and saw she was smiling at him.

'Water's all right,' he admitted ' – in moderation.'

'Not original!'

'No. Mark Twain.'

A young bow-tied waiter had brought the coffee, and she poured an almost full cup before adding a little very thick cream; and Morse looked down at those slim fingers as she circled the spoon in a slow-motion, almost sensual stir.

'You got the paper?'

Morse nodded his gratitude. 'Yes.'

'Let me tell you something – I'm not even going to ask why you wanted it so badly.'

'Why not?'

'Well, for one thing, you told me in your note.'

'And for another?'

She hesitated now, and turned to look at him. 'Why don't you offer me a cigarette?'

Morse's new-found happiness scaled yet another peak.

'What's your name?' she asked.

'Morse. They, er, call me Morse.'

'Odd name! What's your surname?'

'That *is* my surname.'

'As well? Your name's Morse Morse? Like that man in *Catch 22*, isn't it? Major Major Major.'

'Didn't he have *four* Majors?'

'You read a lot?'

'Enough.'

'Did you know the Coleridge quotation? I could see you looking at the crossword last night.'

'Hadn't you got the paper twixt thee and me?'

'I've got X-ray eyes.'

Morse looked at her eyes, and for a few seconds looked deeply *into* her eyes – and saw a hazel-green concoloration there, with no sign now of any bloodshot webbing. 'I just happened to know the quote, yes.'

'Which was?'

'The answer was "sieve".'

'And the line goes?'

'Two lines actually, to make any sense of things:

"Work without Hope draws nectar in a sieve,
And Hope without an object cannot live."'

'You *do* read a lot.'

'What's your name?'

'Louisa.'

'And what do you do, Louisa?'

'I work for a model agency. No, that's wrong. I am a model agency.'

'Where are you from?'

'From a little village just south of Salisbury, along the Chalke Valley.'

Morse nodded vaguely. 'I've driven through that part once or twice. Combe Bissett? Near there, is it?'

'Quite near, yes. But what about you? What do *you* do?'

'I'm a sort of glorified clerk, really. I work in an office – nine-to-five man.'

'Whereabouts is that?'

'Oxford.'

'Lovely city!'

'You know Oxford?'

'Why don't you buy me a large brandy?' she asked softly in his ear.

Morse put the drinks on his room-bill and returned with one large brandy and one large malt Scotch. Several other couples were enjoying their liqueurs in that happily appointed bar and Morse looked out from the window at the constantly whitening waves before placing the drinks side by side on the table.

'Cheers!'

'Cheers!'

'You're a liar,' she said.

The three words hit Morse like an uppercut, and he had no time to regain his balance before she continued, mercilessly:

'You're a copper. You're a chief inspector. And judging from the amount of alcohol you get through you're probably never in your office much after opening time.'

'Is it *that* obvious – I'm a copper, I mean?'

'Oh no! Not obvious at all. I just saw your name and address in the register and my husband – well, he happens to have heard of you. He says you're supposed to be a bit of a whizz-kid in the crime world. That's all.'

'Do I know your husband?'

'I very much doubt it.'

'He's not here—'

'What are *you* doing in Lyme?'

'Me? I dunno. Perhaps I'm looking for some lovely, lonely lady who wouldn't call me a liar even if she thought I was.'

'You deny it? You deny you're a copper?'

Morse shook his head. 'No. It's just that when you're on holiday, well, sometimes you want to get away from the work you do – and sometimes you tell a few lies, I suppose. Everyone tells a few lies occasionally.'

'They do?'

'Oh yes.'

'Everyone?'

Morse nodded. 'Including you.' He turned towards her again, but found himself unable to construe the confusing messages he read there in her eyes.

'Go on,' she said quietly.

'I think you're a divorced woman having an affair with a married man who lives in Oxford. I think the pair of you occasionally get the opportunity of a weekend together. I think that when you do, you need an accommodation address and that you use your own address, which is not in the Chalke Valley but in the Cathedral Close at Salisbury. I think you came here by coach on Friday afternoon and that your partner, who was probably at some conference or other in the area, was scheduled to get here at the same time as you. But he didn't show up. And since you'd already booked your double room you registered and took your stuff up to your room, including a suitcase with the initials "C S O" on it. You suspected something had gone sadly wrong, but as yet you daren't use the phone to find out. You had no option but to wait. I think a call did come through eventually, explaining the situation; and you were deeply disappointed and upset – upset enough to shed a tear or two. This morning you hired a taxi to take you to meet this fellow who had let you down, and I think you've spent the day together somewhere. You're back here now because you'd booked the weekend break anyway, and your partner probably gave you a cheque to cover the bill. You'll be leaving in the morning, hoping for better luck next time.'

Morse had finished – and there was a long silence between them, during which he drained his whisky, she her brandy.

'Another?' asked Morse.

'Yes. But I'll get them. The cheque he gave me was more than generous.' The voice was matter-of-fact, harder now, and Morse knew that the wonderful magic had faded. When she returned with the drinks, she changed her place and sat primly opposite him.

'Would you believe me if I said the suitcase I brought with me belongs to my mother, whose name is Cassandra Samantha Osborne?'

'No,' said Morse. For a few seconds he thought he saw a sign of a gentle amusement in her eyes, but it was soon gone.

'What about this – this "married man who lives in Oxford"?'

'Oh, I know all about him.'

'You *what*?' Involuntarily her voice had risen to a falsetto squeak, and two or three heads had turned in her direction.

'I rang up the Thames Valley Police. If you put any car number through the computer there—'

'—you get the name and address of the owner in about ten seconds.'

'About *two* seconds,' amended Morse.

'And you did *that*?'

'I did that.'

'God! You're a regular shit, aren't you?' Her eyes blazed with anger now.

'S'funny, though,' said Morse, ignoring the hurt. 'I know *his* name – but I still don't know *yours*.'

'Louisa, I told you.'

'No. I think not. Once you'd got to play the part of Mrs Something Hardinge, you liked the idea of "Louisa". Why not? You may not know all that much about Coleridge. But about Hardy? That's different. You remembered that when Hardy was a youth he fell in love with a girl who was a bit above him in class and wealth and privilege, and so he tried to forget her. In fact he spent all the rest of his life trying to forget her.'

She was looking down at the table as Morse went gently on: 'Hardy never really spoke to her. But when he was an old man he used to go and stand over her unmarked grave in Stinsford churchyard.'

It was Morse's turn now to look down at the table.

'Would you like some more coffee, madame?' The waiter smiled politely and sounded a pleasant young chap. But 'madame' shook her head, stood up, and prepared to leave.

'Claire – Claire Osborne – that's my name.'

'Well, thanks again – for the paper, Claire.'

'That's all right.' Her voice was trembling slightly and her eyes were suddenly moist with tears.

'Shall I see you for breakfast?' asked Morse.

'No. I'm leaving early.'

'Like this morning.'

'Like this morning.'

'I see,' said Morse.

'Perhaps you see too much.'

'Perhaps I don't see enough.'

'Goodnight – Morse.'

'Goodnight. Goodnight, Claire.'

When an hour and several drinks later Morse finally decided to retire, he found it difficult to concentrate on anything else except taking one slightly swaying stair at a time. On the second floor, Room 14 faced him at the landing; and if only a line of light had shown itself at the foot of that door, he told himself that he might have knocked gently and faced the prospect of the wrath to come.

But there was no light.

Claire Osborne herself lay awake into the small hours, the duvet kicked aside, her hands behind her head, seeking to settle her restless eyes; seeking to fix them on some putative point about six inches in front of her nose. Half her thoughts were still with the conceited, civilized, ruthless, gentle, boozy, sensitive man with whom she had spent the earlier hours of that evening; the other half were with Alan Hardinge, Dr Alan Hardinge, fellow of Lonsdale College, Oxford, whose young daughter, Sarah, had been killed by an articulated lorry as she had cycled down Cumnor Hill on her way to school the previous morning.

CHAPTER TEN

Mrs Kidgerbury was the oldest inhabitant of Kentish Town, I believe, who went out charing, but was too feeble to execute her conceptions of that art

(Charles Dickens, *David Copperfield*)

WITH A sort of expectorant 'phoo', followed by a cushioned 'phlop', Chief Superintendent Strange sat his large self down opposite Chief Inspector Harold Johnson. It was certainly not that he enjoyed walking up the stairs, for he had no pronounced adaptability for such exertions; it was just that he had promised his very slim and very solicitous wife that he would try to get in a bit of exercise at the office wherever possible. The trouble lay in the fact that he was usually too feeble in both body and spirit to translate such resolve into execution. But not on the morning of Tuesday, 30 June 1992, four days before Morse had booked into the Bay Hotel . . .

The Chief Constable had returned from a fortnight's furlough the previous day, and his first job had been to look through the correspondence which his very competent secretary had been unable, or unauthorized, to answer. The letter containing the 'Swedish Maiden' verses had been in the in-tray (or so she thought) for about a week. It had come (she thought she remembered) in a cheap brown envelope addressed (she *did* almost remember this) to 'Chief Constable Smith (?)'; but the cover had been thrown away – sorry! – and the stanzas themselves had lingered there, wasting as it were their sweetness on the desert air – until Monday the 29th.

The Chief Constable himself had felt unwilling to apportion blame: five stanzas by a minor poet named Austin were not exactly the pretext for declaring a state of national emergency, were they? Yet the 'Swedish' of the first line combined with the 'maiden' of the penultimate line had inevitably rung the bell, and so he had in turn rung Strange, who in turn had reminded the CC that it was DCI Johnson who had been – was – in charge of the earlier investigations.

A photocopy of the poem was waiting on his desk that day when Johnson returned from lunch.

It had been the following morning, however, when things had really started to happen. This time, certainly, it *was* a cheap brown envelope, addressed to 'Chief Constable Smith (?), Kidlington Police, Kidlington' (nothing else on the cover), with a Woodstock postmark, and a smudged date that could have been '27 June', that was received in the post room at HQ, and duly placed with the CC's other mail. The letter was extremely brief:

Why are you doing nothing about my letter?
Karin Eriksson

The note-paper clearly came from the same wad as that used for the first letter: 'Recycled Paper – OXFAM ● Oxford ● Britain' printed along the bottom. There was every sign too that the note was written on the same typewriter, since the four middle characters of 'letter' betrayed the same imperfections as those observable in the Swedish Maiden verses.

This time the CC summoned Strange immediately to his office.

'Prints?' suggested Strange, looking up from the envelope and note-paper which lay on the table before him.

'Waste o' bloody time! The envelope? The postman who collected it – the sorter – the postman who delivered it – the post room people here – the girl who brought it round – my secretary . . .'

'*You*, sir?'

'And me, yes.'

'What about the letter itself?'

'You can try if you like.'

'I'll get Johnson on to it—'

'I don't want Johnson. He's no bloody good with this sort of case. I want Morse on it.'

'He's on holiday.'

'First I've heard of it!'

'You've been on holiday, sir.'

THE WAY THROUGH THE WOODS

'It'll have to be Johnson then. But for Christ's sake tell him to get off his arse and actually *do* something!'

For a while Strange sat thinking silently. Then he said, 'I've got a bit of an idea. Do you remember that correspondence they had in *The Times* a year or so back?'

'The Irish business – yes.'

'I was just thinking – thinking aloud, sir – that if you were to ring *The Times*—'

'Me? What's wrong with *you* ringing 'em?'

Strange said nothing.

'Look! I don't care what we do so long as we do *something* – quick!'

Strange struggled out of his seat.

'How does Morse get on with Johnson?' asked the CC.

'He doesn't.'

'Where is Morse going, by the way?'

'Lyme Regis – you know, where some of the scenes in *Persuasion* are set.'

'Ah.' The CC looked suitably blank as the Chief Superintendent lumbered towards the door.

'There we are then,' said Strange. 'That's what I reckon we ought to do. What do you say? Cause a bit of a stir, wouldn't it? Cause a bit of interest?'

Johnson nodded. 'I like it. Will *you* ring *The Times*, sir?'

'What's wrong with *you* ringing 'em?'

'Do you happen to know—?'

'You – can – obtain – Directory – Enquiries,' intoned Strange caustically, 'by dialling one-nine-two.'

Johnson kept his lips tightly together as Strange continued: 'And while I'm here you might as well remind me about the case. All right?'

So Johnson reminded him of the case, drawing together the threads of the story with considerably more skill than Strange had thought him capable of.

CHAPTER ELEVEN

Nec scit qua sit iter
(He knows not which is the way to take)
(Ovid, *Metamorphoses II*)

KARIN ERIKKSON had been a 'missing person' inquiry a year ago when her rucksack had been found; she was a 'missing person' inquiry now. She was not the subject of a murder inquiry for the simple reason that it was most unusual – and extremely tricky – to mount a murder inquiry without any suspicion of foul play, with no knowledge of any motive, and above all without a *body*.

So, what *was* known about Miss Eriksson?

Her mother had run a small guest-house in Uppsala, but soon after the disappearance of her daughter had moved back to her roots – to the outskirts of Stockholm. Karin, the middle of three daughters, had just completed a secretarial course, and had passed her final examination, if not with distinction at least with a reasonable hope of landing a decent job. She was, as all agreed, of the classic Nordic type, with long blonde hair and a bosom which was liable to monopolize most men's attention when first they met her. In the summer of 1990 she had made her way to the Holy Land without much money, but also without much trouble it appeared, until reaching her destination, where she may or may not have been the victim of attempted rape by an Israeli soldier. In 1991 she had determined to embark on another trip overseas; been determined too, by all accounts, to keep well clear of the military, wherever she went, and had attended a three-month martial arts course in Uppsala, there showing an aptitude and perseverance which had not always been apparent in her secretarial studies. In any case, she was a tallish (5 foot 8½ inches), large-boned, athletic young lady, who could take fairly good care of herself, thank you very much.

The records showed that Karin had flown to Heathrow on Wednesday, 3 July 1991, with almost £200 in one of her pockets, a multi-framed assemblage of hiking-gear, and with the address of a superintendent in a YWCA hostel near King's Cross. A few days in London had apparently dissipated a large proportion of her English currency; and fairly early in the morning of Sunday, 7 July, she had taken the tube (perhaps) to Paddington, from where (perhaps) she had made her way up to the A40, M40 – towards Oxford. The statement made by the YWCA superintendent firmly suggested that from what Karin had told her she would probably be heading – in the long run – for a distant relative living in mid-Wales.

In all probability K. would have been seen on one of the feeder roads to the A40 at about 10 a.m. or so that day. She would have been a distinctive figure: longish straw-coloured hair, wearing a pair of faded-blue jeans, raggedly split at the knees à la mode. But particularly noticeable – this from several witnesses – would have been the yellow and blue Swedish flag, some 9 inches by 6 inches, stitched across the main back pocket of her rucksack; and around her neck (always) a silk, tasselled scarf in the same national colours – sunshine and sky.

Two witnesses had come forward with fairly positive sightings of a woman, answering Karin's description, trying to hitch a lift between the Headington and the Banbury Road roundabouts in Oxford. And one further witness, a youth waiting for a bus at the top of the Banbury Road in Oxford, thought he remembered seeing her walking fairly purposefully down towards Oxford that day. The time? About noon – certainly! – since he was just off for a drink at the Eagle and Child in St Giles'. But more credence at the time was given to a final witness, a solicitor driving to see his invalid mother in Yarnton, who thought he could well have seen her walking along Sunderland Avenue, the hornbeam-lined road linking the Banbury Road and the Woodstock Road roundabouts.

At this point Johnson looked down at his records, took out an amateurishly drawn diagram, and handed it across to Strange.

'That's what would have faced her, sir – if we can believe she even got as far as the Woodstock Road roundabout.'

With little enthusiasm, Strange looked down at the diagram and Johnson continued his story.

Karin could have gone straight over, of course – straight along the A40, a road where it would be very much easier for a hitchhiker to get a lift than along the motorways and dual-carriageways she'd already negotiated successfully. In addition, the A40 would lead pretty directly towards the address of her third cousin, or whatever, near Llandovery. But it had not seemed to the detectives who considered the matter that she had taken the 'Witney' option – or the 'Wolvercote' – or the 'City Centre' one; but had taken the road that led to Woodstock . . .

CHAPTER TWELVE

Sigh out a lamentable tale of things,
Done long ago, and ill done
(John Ford, *The Lover's Melancholy*)

AT ABOUT 7.15 (Johnson continued) on the sunny Tuesday morning of 9 July 1991, George Daley, of 2 Blenheim Villas, Begbroke, Oxon, had taken his eight-year-old King Charles spaniel for an early-morning walk along the slip-road beside the Royal Sun, a roadside ale-house on the northern stretch of the A44, a mile or so on the Oxford side of Woodstock. At the bottom of a hawthorn hedge, almost totally concealed by rank cow-parsley, Daley had spotted – as he claimed – a splash of bright colour; and as he ventured down, and near, he had all but trodden on a camera before seeing the scarlet rucksack.

Of course at this stage there had been no evidence of foul play – still wasn't – and it was the camera that had claimed most of Daley's attention. He'd promised a camera to his son Philip, a lad just coming up for his sixteenth birthday; and the camera he'd found, a heavy, aristocratic-looking thing, was a bit too much of a temptation. Both the rucksack and the camera he'd taken home, where cursorily that morning, in more detail later that evening, he and his wife Margaret had considered things.

'Finders keepers', they'd been brought up to accept. And well, yes, the rucksack clearly – and specifically – belonged to someone else; but the camera had no name on it, had it? For all they knew, it had no connection at all with the rucksack. So they'd taken out the film, which seemed to be fully used up anyway, and thrown it on the fire. Not a crime, was it? Sometimes even the police – Daley had suggested – weren't all that sure what should be entered in the crime figures. If a bike got stolen, it was a crime all right. But if the owner could be persuaded that the bike hadn't really been stolen at all – just inadvertently 'lost', say – then it didn't count as a crime at all, now did it?

'Was he an ex-copper, this fellow Daley?' asked Strange, nodding his appreciation of the point.

Johnson grinned, but shook his head and continued.

The wife, Margaret Daley, felt a bit guilty about hanging on to the rucksack, and according to Daley persuaded him to drop it in at Kidlington the next day, Wednesday – originally asserting that he'd found it that same morning. But he hadn't really got his story together, and it was soon pretty clear that the man wasn't a very good liar; and it wasn't long before he changed his story.

The rucksack itself? Apart from the pocket-buttons rusting a bit, it seemed reasonably new, containing, presumably, all the young woman's travelling possessions, including a passport which identified its owner as one Karin Eriksson, from an address in Uppsala, Sweden. Nothing, it appeared, had been tampered with overmuch by the Daleys, but the contents had proved of only limited interest: the usual female toiletries, including toothpaste, Tampax, lipstick, eye-shadow, blusher, comb, nail-file, tweezers, and white tissues; an almost full packet of Marlboro cigarettes with a cheap 'throwaway' lighter; a letter, in Swedish, from a boyfriend, dated two months earlier, proclaiming (as was later translated) a love that was fully prepared to wait until eternity but which would also appreciate a further rendezvous a little earlier; a slim money-wallet, containing no credit cards or travellers' cheques – just five ten-pound notes (newish but not consecutively numbered); a book of second-class English postage-stamps; a greyish plastic mac, meticulously folded; a creased postcard depicting Velasquez's 'Rokeby Venus' on one side, and the address of the Welsh relative on the other; two clean (cleanish) pairs of pants; one faded-blue dress; three creased blouses, black, white, and darkish red . . .

'Get on with it,' mumbled Strange.

Well, Interpol were contacted, and of course the Swedish police. A distraught mother, by phone from Uppsala, had told them that it was very unusual for Karin not to keep her family informed of where she was and what she was up to – as she had done from London the previous week.

A poster ('Have you seen this young woman?') displaying a blown-up copy of the passport photograph had been printed, and seen by some of the citizens of Oxford and its immediate environs in buses, youth clubs, information offices, employment agencies, those sorts of places.

'And that's when these people came forward, these witnesses?' interrupted Strange.

'That's it, sir.'

'And the fellow you took notice of was the one who thought he saw her in Sunderland Avenue.'

'He was a very good witness. Very good.'

'Mm! I don't know. A lovely leggy blonde – well-tanned, well-exposed, eh, Johnson? Standing there on the grass verge facing the traffic ... Bit odd, isn't it? You'd've thought the fellow would've remembered her for *certain* – that's all I'm saying. Some of us still have the occasional erotic daydream, y'know.'

'That's what Morse said.'

'Did he now!'

'He said even if most of us were only going as far as Woodstock we'd have taken her on to Stratford, if that's what she wanted.'

'*He'd* have taken her to Aberdeen,' growled Strange.

The next thing (Johnson continued his story) had been the discovery, in the long grass about twenty yards from where the rucksack had been found – probably fallen out of one of the pockets – of a slim little volume titled *A Birdwatchers' Guide*. Inside was a sheet of white paper, folded vertically and seemingly acting as a bookmark, on which the names of ten birds had been written in neat capitals, with a pencilled tick against seven of them:

HOBBY ✓
RED KITE
LESSER SPOTTED WOODPECKER
BEARDED TIT ✓
CORN BUNTING ✓
TREE PIPIT ✓
REDSTART ✓
NIGHTINGALE ✓
GRASSHOPPER WARBLER ✓
NUTHATCH

The lettering matched the style and slope of the few scraps of writing found in the other documents, and the easy conclusion was that Karin Eriksson had been a keen ornithologist, probably buying the book after arriving in London and trying to add to her list of sightings some of the rarer species which could be seen during English summers. The names of the birds were written in English and there was only the one misspelling: the 'breaded tit' – an interesting variety of the 'bearded plaice' spotted fairly frequently in English restaurants. (It had been the pedantic Morse who had made this latter point.)

Even more interesting, though, had been the second enclosure within the pages: a thin yellow leaflet, folded this time across the middle, announcing a pop concert in the grounds of Blenheim Palace on Monday, 8 July – the day before the rucksack was found: 8 p.m.–11.30 p.m., admission (ticket only) £4.50.

That was it. Nothing else really. Statements taken – inquiries made – searches organized in the grounds of Blenheim Palace – but . . .

'How much did Morse come into all this?' asked a frowning Strange.

Johnson might have known he'd ask it, and he knew he might as well come clean.

CHAPTER THIRTEEN

He that reads and grows no wiser seldom suspects his own deficiency, but complains of hard words and obscure sentences, and asks why books are written which cannot be understood
(Samuel Johnson, *The Idler*)

THE TRUTH was that Morse had *not* figured on the scene at all during the first few days of the case – for it was not a case of homicide; and (as was to be hoped) still wasn't. Yet the follow-up investigations had been worrying, especially of course the steadily growing and cumulative evidence that Karin Eriksson had been a responsible young woman who had never previously drifted into the drink-drugs-sex-scene.

Only after the case had grown a little cold had Morse spent a couple of hours one afternoon with Johnson, in that late July, now a year ago – before being side-tracked into a squalid domestic murder out on the Cowley Road.

'I reckon he thought it all a bit – a bit of a joke, sir, quite honestly.'

'Joke? *Joke*? This is no bloody joke, Johnson! Like as not, we shall be opening a couple of extra lines on the switchboard once these bloody newspapers get hold of it. It'll be like an air disaster! And if the public come up with some brighter ideas than the police . . .'

Johnson gently reminded him: 'But it's *your* idea, sir – this business of sending the letters to *The Times*.'

'What did you mean – about Morse?' asked Strange, ignoring the criticism.

'What I meant, sir, is that he, well, he only skipped over the details with me, and he sort of said the first things that came into his head, really. I don't think he had time to think about things much.'

'He'd have *ideas* though, wouldn't he, Morse? Always did have. Even if he'd been on a case a couple of minutes. Usually the wrong ideas of course, but . . .'

'All I'm saying is that he didn't seem to take the case at all seriously. He was sort of *silly* about things, really—'

Strange's voice sounded suddenly thunderous: 'Look here, Johnson! Morse may be an idiot, you're right. But he's never been a fool. Let's get *that* straight!'

For Johnson, the differentiation between what he had hitherto regarded as virtual synonyms – 'idiot' and 'fool' – was clearly beyond his etymological capacities; and he frowned a guarded puzzlement as his superior officer continued:

'Some people are occasionally right for the wrong reasons. But Morse? He's more often than not wrong for the right reasons. The *right* reasons . . . you understand me? So even if he sometimes drinks too much . . .'

Johnson looked down at the file in front of him: he knew, alas, exactly what Strange was saying. 'Would you rather Morse took over the case, sir?'

'Yes, I think I would,' said Strange. 'So would the CC, if you must know,' he added cruelly.

'So when does he get back from leave . . .?'

Strange sighed deeply. 'Not soon enough. Let's see what happens with this newspaper angle.'

'He's pretty sure to see it – if they print it.'

'What? Morse? Nonsense! I've never seen him reading anything. He just spends half an hour on the crossword, that's all.'

'Ten minutes – last time I watched him,' said Johnson honestly,
if somewhat grudgingly.

'Wasted his life, Morse has,' confided Strange, after a pause.

'Should've got married, you mean?'

Strange began to extricate himself from his chair. 'I wouldn't
go as far as that. Ridiculous institution – marriage! Don't you
think so?'

Johnson, himself having married only six months previously,
forbore any direct response, as Strange finally brought his vertebrae to the vertical, from which vantage point he looked down
on the papers that Johnson had been consulting.

'Isn't that Morse's writing?' he queried presbyopically.

Yes, it was Morse's handwriting; and doubtless Johnson
would have preferred Strange not to have seen it. But at least it
would prove his point. So he picked out the sheet, and handed it
over.

'Mm.' Chief Superintendent Strange held the piece of paper at
arm's length, surveying its import. Unlike Morse, he was an
extremely rapid reader; and after only ten seconds or so he
handed it back to Johnson: 'See what you mean!'

Johnson, in turn, looked down again at the sheet Morse had
left him – the one he'd found on his desk that morning a year ago
now, when Morse had been transferred to what had appeared
more urgent inquiries:

I never got to grips with the case as you know but I'd have
liked answers to the following half-dozen qq:
(a) Had Daley or his missus owned a camera themselves?
(b) What was the weather like on Tuesday 9th July?
(c) 'It's striped: what about ze panties?' (5)
(d) What's the habitat of 'Dendrocopus Minor'?
(e) What beer do they serve at the Royal Sun (or at the White
     Hart!)?
(f) What's the dog's name?

Strange now lumbered to the door. 'Don't ignore all this
bloody nonsense, Johnson. That's what I'm telling you. Don't take
too much notice of it; but don't *ignore* it, understand?'

For the second time within a short while the etymological
distinction between a couple of unequivocal synonyms had

completely escaped Inspector Johnson's reasonably bright but comparatively limited brain.

'As you say, sir.'

'And, er, and one other thing . . . the wife's just bought a new dog – little King Charles, lovely thing! Two hundred pounds it cost. Pisses everywhere, of course – and worse! But it's, you know, it's always glad to see you. More than the wife sometimes, eh? It's just that we've only had the bloody thing a fortnight, and we still haven't christened it.'

'The dog's name was "Mycroft". Good name – be a good name for *your* dog, sir.'

'Imaginative, yes! I'll, er, mention it to the missus, Johnson. Just one little problem, though . . .'

Johnson raised his rather bushy eyebrows.

'Yes. She's a *she*, Johnson!'

'Oh.'

'Anything else Morse said?' pursued Strange.

'Well, yes. He, er, thought – he said he had a gut-feeling—'

'Huh!'

'—that we'd been searching for a body in the wrong *place*.'

'In Blenheim, you mean?'

Johnson nodded. 'He thought we ought to have been looking in Wytham Woods.'

'Yes. I remember him saying that.'

'Only after we'd drawn a blank in Blenheim, though.'

'Better wise after the event than never.'

Augh, shut up! Johnson was becoming a little weary of all the innuendos: 'If you recall, sir, it wasn't just Morse who was in favour of a wider operation. But we hadn't got the personnel available for a search of Wytham Woods. You said so. I came to ask you myself.'

Strange was stung into retaliation. 'Look, Johnson! You find *me* a body and I'll find *you* all the bloody personnel you need, all right?'

It was the chicken-and-egg business all over again, and Johnson would have said so – but Strange was already guiding his bulk downstairs, via the hand-rail on the HQ wall.

CHAPTER FOURTEEN

Only the keeper sees
That, where the ring-dove broods,
And the badgers roll at ease,
There was once a road through the woods
            (Rudyard Kipling, *The Way Through the Woods*)

IT WAS to be Morse's last breakfast at the Bay Hotel, that morning of Monday, 6 July 1992, six days after the long meeting just recorded between Strange and Johnson at Kidlington HQ in Oxfordshire. He would have wished to stay a further couple of days – but there were no vacancies; and, as the proprietor reminded him, he'd already had more than his share of luck.

As he waited for his mixed grill he re-read the article, again high-profile page-one news – the article promised the previous Friday by Howard Phillipson, literary editor of *The Times*:

A PRELIMINARY ANALYSIS

INTEREST in the 'Swedish Maiden' verses printed in these columns last week (Friday, July 3) has been sweeping this newspaper's offices, but I am myself now somewhat more diffident than I originally was about solving the fascinating riddle-me-ree presented by the five stanzas. I had earlier assumed that there might well be sufficient 'internal logic' in the information received by the Thames Valley Police to come to some firm conclusions. I am no longer so strongly of this opinion.

Only with considerable hesitation therefore do I offer my own amateurish analysis of the riddle, in the fairly certain knowledge that very soon the cryptologists and cabbalists, criminologists and cranks, will be making their own considerably more subtle interpretations of these tantalizing lines.

For what it is worth, however, I suggest that the parameters of the problem may be set, albeit rather vaguely. In modern mathematics (as I understand the situation) pupils are asked, before tackling any problem: 'What roughly do you think the answer might be? What sort of answer might you logically expect?' If, say, the problem involves the speed of a supersonic jet flying the Atlantic, the answer is perhaps unlikely to be 10 m.p.h., and any pupil coming up with such an improbable answer is advised to look back through his calculations and find out where he might have dropped a couple of noughts. If we are set to discover the time taken by those famous taps to fill the family tub, the answer is still rather more likely to be ten minutes than ten hours. Permit me then to make a few general comments on what would appear to be the sort of solution we might expect. (The verses are reprinted on page 2.)

Clearly the poem is cast in a 'sylvan' setting: we have 'woodman'; 'stream'; 'riding' (sic!); 'Thyme flow'ring; 'trapped'; 'hunted deer'; etc. There will be no prizes, I realize, for such an analysis, but the neglect of the obvious is always the beginning of unwisdom.

The setting of some wood or forest therefore must be our donné, and my suggestion to the Thames Valley CID would be to concentrate their doubtless limited resources of man-power within two of the local areas which seem to hold the greatest promise: the forested area around Blenheim Palace, and the Wytham Woods – the latter becoming increasingly famous for its fox and badger research.

Let us now turn to the more specific import of the stanzas. The speaker of the poem, the 'persona', is clearly no longer a living being. Yet her dramatic message is quite unequivocal: she has been murdered; she has been drowned (or perhaps just dumped) in one of the lakes or streams situated in the wood(s); if such waters are searched and dredged her corpse will be found; finally the police may have been (somewhat?) remiss in not pursuing their inquiries with rather greater perseverance.

What can be gathered from the nature of the verses themselves? Their composer is certainly no Herrick or Housman, yet in terms of technical prosody the writer is more than competent. Vocabulary ('tegument', 'azured', etc.) is more redolent of the Senior Common Room than the Saloon Bar; and the versification, punctuation, and diction, all point to a literate and well-read man – or woman! Can anything more specific be said about the writer? For some while, as I read and re-read the verses, I toyed with the idea of their author being a relative of the dead girl. The reason for my thinking was the continued emphasis, throughout the poem, of the 'find me' motif; and I was reminded of the Homeric heroes of the *Iliad* where death in battle was a fully expected and wholly honourable end – but where the most terrible fate of all was to die unrecognized, unburied, *unfound*, in some unknown and far-off land. Is the poem then above all a desperate cry for the Christian burial of the body? This would be most understandable. We have seen in recent years so many tragic instances (in the Middle East, for example) where the simple return of a dead body has paved the way for some peace initiative.

But I no longer believe this to be the case. My firm conviction now is that the verses have been sent to the police by a person for whom the period – now a year – between the murder of Karin Eriksson and the present time has become an intolerable Hell. A person who is very near to breaking point. A person who wishes the crime at last to be uncovered, and who is now prepared to pay the penalty. In short, the murderer!

Dare I go any further? I learned two further (hitherto unpublished) facts from Detective Chief Inspector Johnson. First, that the letter-writer was able to spell, correctly, the not very easy or obvious 'Eriksson'; second, that the writer was aware of the previous Chief Constable's surname, but not that of the current incumbent. On the old adage then that one might just as well be hanged for a sheep as a lamb, I reckon the murderer to be male; to be between thirty and thirty-five years old; to have a degree in English literature; to have lived until about six or nine months ago in Oxfordshire; to have revisited the scene of his crime during the last month, say, whilst staying at one of the more upmarket hostelries in Woodstock, Oxon.

I rest my case, m'lud!

'Hi!' she said. 'Mind if I join you?'

'Please do,' said Morse, carefully mounting the last segment of his fried egg on the last square of his fried bread.

'You ever read about cholesterol?' Her voice was very cultured, the two 't's of her simple question affectedly exaggerated.

Morse swallowed his latest mouthful and looked at the slim,

expensively dressed woman who now sat opposite him, ordering black coffee and a croissant – nothing more.

'They say we've all got to die of something.' He tried to make it sound reasonably cheerful.

'Ridiculous attitude!' The lips, expertly outlined in some pale crimson shade, looked severe, yet the grey eyes in the delicate, oval face might almost have been mocking him.

'I suppose it is,' he said.

'You're overweight anyway, aren't you?'

'I suppose so,' he repeated lamely.

'You'll have high blood pressure in your mid-fifties – unless you're there now? Then you'll probably have a stroke in your early sixties; and like as not die of a heart attack before you're seventy.' She had already drained her coffee cup, and held up an elegant, imperious hand to the waitress. 'What's your job?'

Morse sighed, and considered the last piece of toast in the rack. 'I'm a policeman, and I come from Oxford, and I'm on holiday here until about ten o'clock this morning. I'm single and maybe I'm not much of a catch, but if I'd known I was going—'

'—going to meet a beautiful girl like me! Surely you can be more original than that?' The eyes were mocking him again.

Morse took the toast and started buttering it. 'No, I can't. I can't do much better than that.'

'Perhaps you underrate yourself.'

'What about you? What do you do?'

'Why don't *you* tell *me*. You're a policeman, you say?'

For half a minute or so Morse looked at her, cocking his head slightly to the right. Then he gave his judgement: 'You're a beautician, possibly a dietitian too, which you probably spell with a "t" and not a "c"; you're in your late twenties, and you went to school at Cheltenham Ladies'; you're married but you sometimes leave off your wedding ring – like now; you're fond of pets but you tend to think children are something of an exaggerated pastime. And if you come for a walk with me along the prom, I'll try to fill in a few more of the details as we go along.'

'That's much better.'

'Well? How did I do?'

She smiled and shook her head. 'Is your name Sherlock Holmes?'

'Morse.'

'Am I *that* transparent?'

'No. I, er, saw you come in with your husband last night – when you went straight to bed and he—'

'He stayed at the bar!'

'We had one or two drinks together, and I asked him who the beautiful woman was—'

'And he said, "That's not a beautiful woman: that's my wife!"?'

'Something like that.'

'And he talked about me?'

'He talked nicely about you.'

'He was drunk.'

'He's sleeping it off?' Morse pointed to the ceiling.

She nodded her dark curls. 'So he won't mind much if you take me on that walk, will he, Mr Morse? When you've finished your toast, of course. And wouldn't *you* spell dietitian with a "t"?'

CHAPTER FIFTEEN

At the very smallest wheel of our reasoning it is possible for a handful of questions to break the bank of our answers
(Antonio Machado, *Juan de Mairena*)

ON THE same morning that Morse was packing his single suitcase ('On the day of their departure guests are respectfully requested to vacate their rooms by 10.30 a.m.') Sergeant Lewis knocked on Johnson's door, soon seating himself opposite the chief inspector, and beside Sergeant Wilkins.

'Good of you to spare a few minutes.'

'If I can help in any way . . .' said Lewis warily.

'You know Morse better than most.'

'Nobody knows him all *that* well.'

'You've got a reasonable idea how his mind works though.'

'He's got a strange sort of mind—'

'Not many'd disagree with you.'

'He's good at some things.'

'Such as?'

'He's not bad at catching murderers for a start.'

'And you do realize the odds are we're trying to catch another murderer now, don't you, Sergeant?'

'If it *is* murder.'

'Did Morse think it was murder?'

'As I remember, sir, he was only on it with you for a day or so.'

'Less than that.' (Wilkins had made his first contribution.)

'You're following this – this newspaper business, I presume, Lewis?'

'Everybody reads *The Times* before the *Sun* now.'

'What do you make of this?' Johnson handed a photocopy of Morse's 'half-dozen qq.' across the desk.

Lewis looked down at the list and smiled. 'Bit of a joke – some of this, isn't it?'

'Take my advice, Lewis, and don't try telling that to the Super!'

'I don't know the answer to any of 'em,' admitted Lewis, 'except (e) – well, part of (e). It's a "Morrell's" pub, the Royal Sun. I've bought quite a few pints there, I reckon.'

'What, for Morse, you mean?'

'Who else?'

'But has he ever bought *you* any, Lewis? That's the real question, eh, Wilkins?'

The two men sniggered. And suddenly Lewis hated them both.

'What about the White Hart?' continued Johnson.

'Lot of "White Harts" about.'

'Yes, we know that!' Johnson gestured to Wilkins, the latter now reading from his notes: 'Headington, Marston, Wolvercote, Wytham, Minster Lovell, Eynsham . . .'

'I expect Morse could probably add to the list,' ventured Johnson.

Lewis, determining henceforth to be as minimally helpful as possible, made only a brief comment: 'She'd've got past the first two.'

Johnson nodded. 'What about Eynsham and Minster Lovell? Just off the A40, both of them – if she ever travelled along the A40, that is.'

Lewis said nothing.

'What about the other two: Wolvercote and Wytham? Which would you put your money on?'

'Wytham, I suppose.'

'Why's that?'

'The woods there – easy enough to hide a body.'

'Did you know that Morse asked the Chief Super about a search of Wytham Woods last year?'

Lewis did, yes. 'Only after the search in Blenheim didn't come up with anything.'

'Do you know how big Wytham Woods *is*, man?'

Lewis had a good idea, yes. But he merely shrugged his shoulders.

'Why would Morse be interested in the dog?'

'Don't know. He told me once he'd never had any pets when he was a lad.'

'Perhaps he should get one now. Lots of bachelors have dogs.'

'You must suggest it to him, sir,' replied Lewis, with a note of confidence in his voice, and a strange exhilaration flooding his limbs, for he suddenly realized that it was Johnson who was on the defensive here, not himself. They were trying to pick his (Lewis's) brains because they were envious of his relationship with Morse!

'What about the camera?' continued Johnson.

'You can ask the Daleys, can't you? If they're still there.'

'Odd question though, wouldn't you say?'

'I just don't know, sir. I think Morse told me he had a "Brownie" given him once, but he said he never really understood how to work it.'

Sitting back in an almost relaxed manner now, Lewis looked down at the questions again. 'Should be easy to check on (b) – about the weather . . .'

Again Johnson waved a hand, and Wilkins consulted his notes: 'According to Radio Oxford . . . the ninth of July . . . "Dry, sunny, seventy-two to seventy-four degrees Fahrenheit; outlook settled; possibility of some overnight mist".'

'Nice, warm day, then,' said Lewis blandly.

'What about (c)?'

'Crossword clue, sir. He's pretty hot on crosswords.'

'What's the answer?'

'No good asking me. Sometimes I can't even do the *Mirror* coffee-break one.'

'"Ze-bra" – that's the answer.'

'Really? Well, that's another one crossed off.'

'What about this "Dendrocopus Minor"?' There was a note of exasperation in Johnson's voice now.

'Pass,' said Lewis with a gentle smile.

'For Christ's sake, man, we're on a potential *murder* inquiry – not a bloody *pub*-quiz! Don't you realize that? As a matter of fact it's the Lesser something bloody Woodpecker!'

'We learn something new every day.'

'Yes, we do, Sergeant. And I'll tell you something else, if you like. Its habitat is woodlands or parklands and there are a few pairs nesting in Wytham!'

Lewis's new-found confidence was starting to ebb away as Johnson glared at him aggressively. 'You don't seem all that anxious to help us, Sergeant, do you? So let me just tell you why I asked you along here. As you probably know, we're starting searching Blenheim all over again today, and we're going to search and search until we're blue in the bloody face, OK? But if we still don't find anything we're going to hand over to Morse – and to *you*, Sergeant. I just thought you might like to know what we're *all* up against, see?'

Lewis was conscious of a sinking sense of humiliation. 'I – I didn't know that, sir.'

'Why should you? They don't tell even you everything, do they?'

'Why might they be taking you off?' asked Lewis slowly.

'They – "they" – are taking me off because they don't think I'm any fucking good,' said Johnson bitterly as he rose to his feet. 'That's why!'

CHAPTER SIXTEEN

Between 1871 and 1908 he published twenty volumes of verse,
of little merit
('Alfred Austin', *The Oxford Companion to English Literature*,
edited by Margaret Drabble)

MORSE was spending the last three days of his West Country holiday at the King's Arms in Dorchester (Dorchester, Dorset). Here he encountered neither models nor beauticians; but at last he began to feel a little reluctant about returning to Oxford. On the Wednesday he had explored Hardy's Dorchester on foot (!) a.m., and spent the whole p.m. in the Dorset County Museum. Nostalgic, all of it. And when finally he returned to 'the chief 'hotel in Casterbridge' he sat drinking his beer in the bar before dinner with the look of a man who was almost at ease with life.

On the Thursday morning he drove out through the country-side that provided much of the setting for *Tess of the d'Urbervilles*, along the A352 to the east of Dorchester, following the Vale of the Great Dairies, past Max Gate and Talbothays towards Wool. As he was driving through Moreton, he wondered whether there was any follow-up to the Phillipson analysis (there had been no mention in the Tuesday or Wednesday editions), and he stopped and bought the last copy of *The Times* from the village news-agent's. The answer was yes – yes, there was; and he sat for a while in the sunshine beside the wall of the cemetery containing the grave of Lawrence of Arabia, reading the long letter which (as with succeeding letters) now found its place naturally in the newspaper's correspondence columns:

From Professor (Emeritus) René Gray

Sir, My mind, doubtless like the minds of many of your regular readers, has been much exercised these past few days following the publication (July 3) of the letter received by the Thames Valley Police. I beg the courtesy of your columns to make one or two observations.

This is not a poem by Alfred Austin, though the words 'A. Austin' appear beneath it. The name 'Austin' does not seem to refer to a make of motor car: 'A'-registration Austins date from 1983–84, and there is no resemblance between this date and those given in brackets. The dates given are not Austin the poet's dates. He was born in 1835, and died in 1913. There is a remote possibility that the last two digits of his birth-date have been trans-posed for some reason, but the death-date is plainly wrong. Dying in 1913, he was 78 years old at the time of his death. By a strange coincidence the transposition of these digits gives us the '87' which is writ-ten here. I conclude that the dates are not all they seem, and most likely constitute the key to the cypher.

The figures do not appear to give geographical co-ordinates. They do not match the format of Ordnance Survey co-ordinates, and they are not co-ordinates of latitude and longitude, since Great Britain lies between the 50th and 60th lines of latitude and between the longitudes 2°E and 10°W.

We are left with six digits which somehow must give the clue to the interpretation of the words of the message. I have not been able to work out the cypher. I have tried the first word, followed by the eighth, followed by the fifth after that (giving either 'Find ... my ... the ... skylit', or 'Find ... frosted ... skylit ... me'). I have re-transposed the sequences of digits, to no better effect. I have tried lines, first words of lines, last words of lines. I have taken the digits in pairs, i.e. as 18, 53 (or 35) and 87 with the same result. I have alternated the beginnings of the lines with the ends of the lines, and vice versa.

I have simplified the expression '1853–87' by interpreting the hyphen as a minus sign. The answer, '1766', does not produce any happier result. The only sensible word produced is yielded by taking letters in that sequence in the first line, thus giving 'F-i-s-h;, but the message does not continue. (A red herring, possibly!)

There are a large number of other combinations and permutations, but no method other than trial and error for seeing whether any make any sense.

The overriding advantage of the mechanical method of deciphering is that the poem itself does not have to make sense; a random sequence of words would fulfil exactly the same purpose of concealing the message. Hence odd words such as 'tiger' need not fall into the category of important words at all: in its place, 'chairman' or 'post-box' would do equally well; these words meet the requirements of the metre, but would not be included in the deciphered message. Likewise, the upper case 'T' in the middle of line 13 is not significant. The fact that the poem does make some kind of sense in places thus merely adds to the bafflement.

If this line of thinking is correct, it does not matter what the poem says, or what it means. What is needed is the services of a skilled cryptographer.

Yours faithfully,
RENÉ GRAY,
137 Victoria Park Road,
Leicester

Morse read the letter once only, and decided to wait until his return to the King's Arms (where he had the two earlier cuttings) in order to have a more careful look at the good professor's analysis and suggested methodology. He sounded an engaging sort of fellow, Gray – especially with that bit about the 'chairman' and the 'post-box'.

Back in Dorchester that afternoon, Morse went into the public library and looked up 'Austin' in *The Oxford Companion to English Literature*. He'd heard of Austin the poet – of course he had; but he'd never known anything much about him, and he was certainly unaware that any poem, or even line, produced by the former Poet Laureate had merited immortality.

From the library Morse walked on to the post office, where he bought a black and white postcard of Dorchester High Street, and stood for an inordinate length of time in the queue there. He didn't know the price of the stamp for a postcard, and didn't wish to waste a first-class stamp if, as he suspected, the official tariff for postcards was a few pence lower. It was, he realized, quite ridiculous to wait so long for such a little saving.

But wait Morse did.

Lewis received the card the following morning, the message written in Morse's small, neat, and scholarly hand:

> Mostly I've not been quite so miserable since last year's holiday, but things are looking up here in D. Warmest regards to you (and to Mrs Lewis) – but not to any of our other colleagues. Have you been following the Swedish lass? I reckon I know what the poem means. Definitely home Sat.
>
> M

This card, with its curmudgeonly message, was delivered to police HQ in Kidlington – since Morse had not quite been able to remember Lewis's Headington address. And by the time it was in Lewis's hands, almost everyone in the building had read it. It might, naturally, have made Lewis a little cross – such contravention of the laws of privacy.

But it didn't. It made him glad.

CHAPTER SEVENTEEN

Extract from a diary dated Friday, 10 July 1992

Please God let me wake from this dream! Please God may she not be dead! Those words – the ones I so recently wrote – for them may I be forgiven! Those terrible words! – when I disavowed my love for my own flesh and blood, for my own children, for my daughter. But how could I be forgiven? The fates decree otherwise and ever have so decreed. The words may be blotted out but they will remain. The paper may be burned in the furnace but the words will persist for evermore. Oh blackness! Oh night of the soul! Throw open the wide door of Hell, Infernal Spirits, for it is I who approach – all hope of virtue, all hope of life abandoned! I have reached the Inferno and there now read that grim pronouncement of despair above its portal.

I am sunk deep in misery and anguish of mind and spirit. At my desk I sit here weeping bitter tears. I shout Forgive me! Forgive me! And then I shout again Forgive me! Everyone forgive me! Had I still belief in God I would seek to pray. But I cannot. And even now – even in the abyss of my despair – I have not told the truth! Let it be known that tomorrow I shall once more be happy – some of tomorrow's hours will bring me happiness again. She is coming. She is coming here. She herself has arranged and organized. She it is who has wished to come! For my sake is this? Is this for my need – my grief's sake? Yet such considerations are of minor consequence. She is coming, tomorrow she is coming. More precious to me is that woman even than the mother who suffers all that pain . . .

(Later.) I am so low I wish I were dead. My selfishness my self-pity is so great that I can have no pity for the others – the others who grieve so greatly. I have just re-read one of Hardy's poems. I used to know it by heart. No longer though and now my left forefinger traces the lines as slowly I copy it out:

I seem but a dead man held on end
To sink down soon ... O you could not know
That such swift fleeing
No soul foreseeing –
Not even I – would undo me so.

I never really managed to speak to you my daughter. I never told you my darling daughter because I did not know – and now you can never know why and can never understand.

I have reached a decision. This journal shall be discontinued. Always when I look back on what I have written I see nothing of any worth – only self-indulgence – theatricality – over-emotionalism. Just one plea I make. It was never forced or insincere or hypocritical. No, never!

But no more.

CHAPTER EIGHTEEN

A 'strange coincidence' to use a phrase
By which such things are settled now-a-days
(Lord Byron, *Don Juan*)

CLAIRE OSBORNE turned right from the A40 down into Banbury Road, knowing that she would have to drive only three or four hundred yards along it, since she had received a detailed map through the post. She was a little surprised – a lot surprised – when she spotted, on her right, the Cotswold House, a considerably more striking and attractive building than the 'suburban, modern, detached,' blurb of *The Good Hotel Guide* had led her to expect. She experienced an unexpected feeling of delight as she parked her Metro MG (what a disaster not taking that to Lyme!) on the rusty-red asphalt in front of the double-fronted guesthouse, built of honey-coloured Cotswold stone in the leafy environs of North Oxford.

Flower-baskets in green, red, purple, and white hung all around her as she rang the bell at the front door, on which a white notice announced 'No Vacancies'. But Claire had earlier found a vacancy, and booked it: a vacancy for two.

The door was opened by a tall, slim man, with a shock of prematurely grey hair, black eyebrows, a slightly diffident smile, and a soft Irish brogue.

'Hello.'

'Hello. My name's Mrs Hardinge, and I think you'll find—'

'Already found, Mrs Hardinge. And I'm Jim O'Kane. Now do come in, won't you? And welcome to the Cotswold House.' With which splendid greeting he picked up her case and led her inside, where Claire felt immediately and overwhelmingly impressed.

Briefly O'Kane consulted the bookings register, then selected a key from somewhere, and led the way up a semi-circular staircase.

'No trouble finding us, I trust?'

'No. Your little map was very helpful.'

'Good journey?'

'No problems.'

O'Kane walked across the landing, inserted a key in Room 1, opened the door, ushered his guest inside, followed her with the suitcase, and then, with a courteous, old-world gesture, handed her a single key – almost as if he were presenting a bouquet of flowers to a beautiful girl.

'The key fits your room here *and* the front door, Mrs Hardinge.'

'Fine.'

'And if I could just remind you' – his voice growing somewhat apologetic – 'this is a non-smoking guest-house . . . I *did* mention it when you rang.'

'Yes.' But she was frowning. 'That means – everywhere? Including the bedrooms?'

'Especially the bedrooms,' replied O'Kane, simply if reluctantly.

Claire looked down at the single key. 'My husband's been held up in London—'

'No problem! Well, only *one* problem perhaps. We're always a bit pushed for parking – if there are *two* cars . . .?'

'He'll have his car, yes. But don't worry about that. There seems to be plenty of room in the side-streets.'

O'Kane appeared grateful for her understanding, and asked if she were familiar with Oxford, with the North Oxford area. And Claire said, yes, she was; her husband knew the area well, so there was no trouble there.

Wishing Mrs Hardinge well, Mr O'Kane departed – leaving Claire to look with admiration around the delightfully designed and decorated accommodation. *En suite*, too.

O'Kane was not a judgemental man, and in any case the morality of his guests was of rather less importance to him than their comfort. But already the signs were there: quite apart from the circumstantial evidence of any couple arriving in separate cars, over the years O'Kane had observed that almost every wedded woman arriving first would show an interest in the in-house amenities and the like. Yet Mrs Hardinge(?) had enquired about none of these . . . he would have guessed too (if asked) that she might well pay the bill from her own cheque-book when the couple left – about 50 per cent of such ladies usually did so. In the early days of his business career, such things had worried O'Kane a little. But not so much now. Did it matter? Did it really matter? Any unwed couple could get a *mortgage* these days – let alone a couple of nights' accommodation in a B & B. She was a pleasantly spoken, attractive woman; and as O'Kane walked down the stairs he hoped she'd have a happy time with that Significant Other who would doubtless be arriving soon, ostensibly spending the weekend away from his wife at some Oxford conference.

Oxford was full of conferences . . .

Claire looked around her. The co-ordinated colour scheme of décor and furnishing was a sheer delight – white, champagne, cerise, mahogany – and reproductions of late-Victorian pictures graced the walls. Beside the help-yourself tea and coffee facilities stood a small fridge, in which she saw an ample supply of milk; and two wine glasses – and two champagne glasses. For a while she sat on the floral-printed bedspread; then went over to the window and looked out, over the window-box of busy Lizzies, geraniums, and petunias, down on to the Banbury Road. For several minutes she stood there, not knowing whether she was happy or not – trying to stop the clock, to live in the present, to grasp the moment . . . and to hold it.

Then – her heart was suddenly pounding against her ribs. A man was walking along the pavement towards the roundabout. He wore a pink, short-sleeved shirt, and his forearms were bronzed – as if perhaps he might recently have spent a few days beside the sea. In his left hand he carried a bag bearing the name of the local wineshop, Oddbins; in his right hand he carried a bag with the same legend. He appeared deep in thought as he made his way, fairly slowly, across her vision and proceeded up towards the roundabout.

What an amazing coincidence! – the man might have thought had she pushed open the diamond-leaded window and shouted 'Hi! Remember me? Lyme Regis? Last weekend?' But that would have been to misunderstand matters, for in truth there was no coincidence at all. Claire Osborne had seen to that.

There was a soft knock on her door, and O'Kane asked if she – if either of them – would like a newspaper in the morning: it was part of the service. Claire smiled. She liked the man. She ordered *The Sunday Times*. Then, for a little while after he was gone, she wondered why she felt so sad.

It was not until just before 9 p.m. that Dr Alan Hardinge arrived – explaining, excusing, but as vulnerable, as loving as ever. And – bless him! – he had brought a bottle of Brut Imperial, *and* a bottle of Skye Talisker malt. And almost, *almost* (as she later told herself) had Claire Osborne enjoyed the couple of hours they'd spent together that night between the immaculately laundered sheets of Room 1 in the Cotswold House in North Oxford.

Morse had arrived home at 2.30 p.m. that same day. No one, as far as he knew, was aware that he had returned (except Lewis?); yet Strange had telephoned at 4 p.m. Would Morse be happy to take on the case? Well, whether he would be happy or not, Morse was *going* to take on the case.

'What case?' Morse had asked, disingenuously.

At 5 p.m. he had walked down to Summertown and bought eight pint-cans of newly devised 'draught' bitter, which promised him the taste of a hand-pulled, cask-conditioned drop of ale; and two bottles of his favourite Quercy claret. For Morse – considerably out of condition still – the weight felt a bit too hefty; and outside the Radio Oxford building he halted awhile and looked behind him in the hope of seeing the oblong outline of a red double-decker coming up from the city centre. But there was no bus in sight, so he walked on. As he passed the Cotswold House he saw amongst other things the familiar white sign 'No Vacancies' on the door. He was not surprised. He had heard very well of the place. He wouldn't mind staying there himself.

Especially for the breakfasts.

CHAPTER NINETEEN

I like to have a thing suggested rather than told in full. When every detail is given, the mind rests satisfied, and the imagination loses the desire to use its own wings

(Thomas Aldrich, *Leaves from a Notebook*)

STRANGE had been really quite pleased with all the publicity. Seldom had there been such national interest in a purely notional murder; and the extraordinary if possibly unwarranted ingenuity which the public had already begun to exercise on the originally printed verses was most gratifying – if not as yet of much concrete value. There had been two further offerings in the Letters to the Editor page in the Saturday, 11 July's issue of *The Times*:

From Gillian Richard

Sir, Professor Gray (July 9) seems to me too lightly to dismiss one factor in the Swedish Maiden case. She is certainly, in my view, alive still, but seemingly torn between the wish to live – and the wish to die. She has probably never won any poetry competition in her life, and I greatly doubt whether she is to be found as a result of her description of the natural world. But she is *out* there, in the natural world – possibly living rough; certainly not indoors. I would myself hazard a guess, dismissed by Professor Gray, that she is in a *car* somewhere, and here the poem's attribution (A. Austin 1853–87) can give us the vital clue. What about an A-registration Austin? It would be a 1983 model, yes; and might we not have the registration number, too? I suggest A 185 – then three letters. If we suppose 3=C,

8=H, and 7=G (the third, eighth, and seventh letters of the alphabet), we have A 185 CGH. Perhaps then our young lady is languishing in an ageing Metro? And if so, sir, we must ask one question: who is the owner of that car? Find her!

Yours etc.,
GILLIAN RICHARD,
26 Hayward Road,
Oxford.

From Miss Polly Rayner

Sir, I understand from your report on the disappearance a year ago of a Swedish student that her rucksack was found near the village of Begbroke in Oxfordshire. It may be that I am excessively addicted to your own crossword puzzles but surely we can be justified in spotting a couple of 'clues' here? The '-broke' of the village name is derived from the Anglo-Saxon word 'brok', meaning 'running water' or 'stream'. And since 'beg' is a synonym of 'ask', what else are we to make of the first three words in line 7: 'Ask the stream'? Indeed, this clue is almost immediately confirmed two lines later in the injunction 'ask the sun'. 'The Sun' is how the good citizens of Begbroke refer to their local hostelry, and it is in and around that hostelry where in my view the police should re-concentrate their enquiries.

Yours faithfully,
POLLY RAYNER,
President,
Woodstock   Local   History
Society,
Woodstock,
Oxon.

That was more like it! Strange had earlier that day put the suggested car registration through the HQ's traffic computer. No luck! Yet this was just the sort of zany, imaginative idea that might well unlock the mystery, and stimulate a few more such ideas into the bargain. When he had rung Morse that same Saturday afternoon (he too had read the postcard!) he had not been at all surprised by Morse's apparent – surely only 'apparent'? – lack of interest in taking over the case immediately. Yes, Morse still had a few days' leave remaining – only to the Friday, mind! But, really, this case was absolutely up the old boy's street! Tailor-made for Morse, this case of the Swedish Maiden . . .

Strange decided to leave things alone for a while though – well, until the next day. He had more than enough on his plate for the minute. The previous evening had been a bad one, with the City and County police at full stretch with the (virtual) riots on the Broadmoor Lea estate: car-thefts, joy-riding, ram-raids, stone-throwing ... With Saturday and Sunday evenings still to come! He felt saddened as he contemplated the incipient break-down in law and order, contempt for authority – police, church, parents, school ... Augh! Yet in one awkward, unexplored little corner of his mind, he knew he could *almost* understand some-thing of it all – just a fraction. For as a youth, and a fairly privileged youth at that, he remembered harbouring a secret desire to chuck a full-sized brick through the window of one particularly well-appointed property ...

But yes – quite definitely, yes! – he would feel so very much happier if Morse could take over the responsibility of the case; take it away from his own, Strange's, shoulders.

Thus it was that Strange had rung Morse that Saturday afternoon.

'*What* case?' Morse had asked.

'You know bloody well—'

'I'm still on furlough, sir. I'm trying to catch up with the housework.'

'Have you been drinking, Morse?'

'Just starting, sir.'

'Mind if I come and join you?'

'Not this afternoon, sir. I've got a wonderful – odd, actually! – got a wonderful Swedish girl in the flat with me just at the moment.'

'Oh!'

'Look,' said Morse slowly, 'if there *is* a breakthrough in the case. If there *does* seem some reason—'

'You been reading the correspondence?'

'I'd sooner miss *The Archers*!'

'Do you think it's all a hoax?'

Strange heard Morse's deep intake of breath: 'No! No, I don't. It's just that we're going to get an awful lot of false leads and false confessions – you know that. We always do. Trouble is, it makes us look such idiots, doesn't it – if we take everything *too* seriously.'

Yes, Strange accepted that what Morse had just said was exactly his own view. 'Morse. Let me give you a ring tomorrow, all right? We've got those bloody yoiks out on Broadmoor Lea to sort out . . .'

'Yes, I've been reading about it while I was away.'

'Enjoy your holiday, in Lyme?'

'Not much.'

'Well, I'd better leave you to your . . . your "wonderful Swedish girl", wasn't it?'

'I wish you would.'

After Morse had put down his phone, he switched his CD player on again to the Immolation Scene from the finale of Wagner's *Götterdämmerung*; and soon the pure and limpid voice of the Swedish soprano, Birgit Nilsson, resounded again through the chief inspector's flat.

CHAPTER TWENTY

When I complained of having dined at a splendid table without hearing one sentence worthy to be remembered, he [Dr Johnson] said, 'There is seldom any such conversation'

(James Boswell, *The Life of Samuel Johnson*)

IN THE small hours of Sunday, 12 July, Claire Osborne still lay awake, wondering yet again about what exactly it was she wanted from life. It had been all right – it usually was 'all right'. Alan was reasonably competent, physically – and so loving. She liked him well enough, but she could never be in love with him. She had given him as much of herself as she could; but where, she asked herself, was the memorability of it all? Where the abiding joy in yet another of their brief, illicit, slightly disturbing encounters.

'To hell with this sex lark, Claire!' her best friend in Salisbury had said. 'Get a man who's interesting, that's what I say. Like Johnson! Now, he was interesting!'

'*Doctor* Johnson? He was a great fat slob, always dribbling his soup down his waistcoat, and he was smelly, and never changed his underpants!'

'Never?'

'You know what I mean.'

'But everybody wanted to hear him *talk*, didn't they? That's what I'm saying.'

'Yeah. I know what you mean.'

'Yeah!'

And the two women had laughed together – if with little conviction.

Alan Hardinge had earlier said little about the terrible accident: a few stonily spoken details about the funeral; about the little service they were going to hold at the school; about the unexpected helpfulness of the police and the authorities and support groups and neighbours and relatives. But Claire had not questioned him about any aspect of his own grief. She would, she knew, be trespassing upon a territory that was not, and never could be, hers . . .

It was 3.30 a.m. before she fell into a fitful slumber.

At the breakfast table the following morning she explained briefly that her husband had been called away and that there would be just her: coffee and toast, please – nothing more. A dozen or so newspapers, room-numbered in the top-right corner, lay in a staggered pile on a table just inside the breakfast room – *The Sunday Times* not amongst them.

Jim O'Kane seldom paid too much attention to the front page of the 'Sundays'; but ten minutes before Claire had put in an appearance, he'd spotted the photograph. Surely he'd seen that young girl before! He took *The Sunday Times* through to the kitchen where, under the various grills, his wife was watching the progress of bacon, eggs, tomatoes, mushrooms, and sausages. He pointed to the black and white photograph on the front page:

'Recognize her?'

Anne O'Kane stared at the photograph for a few seconds, quizzically turning her head one way, then the other, seeking to assess any potential likeness to anyone she'd ever met. 'Should I?'

'I think *I* do! You remember that young blonde girl who called – about a year ago – when we had a vacancy – one Sunday – and then she called again – later – when we hadn't?'

'Yes, I do remember,' Anne said slowly. 'I *think* I do.' She had been quickly reading the article beneath the photograph, and she now looked up at her husband as she turned over half a dozen rashers of bacon. 'You don't mean . . . ?'

But Jim O'Kane *did* mean.

*

Claire was on her last piece of toast when she found her hostess standing beside her with the newspaper. 'We pinched this for a minute – hope you didn't mind.'

'Course not.'

'It's just that' – Anne pointed to the reproduction – 'well, it looks a bit like a young girl who called here once. A young girl who disappeared about a year ago.'

'Long time, a year is.'

'Yes. But Jim – my husband – he doesn't often forget faces; and I think,' she added quietly, 'I think he's right.'

Claire glanced down at the photograph and the article, betraying (she trusted) not a hint of her excitement. 'You'd better tell them – the police, hadn't you?'

'I suppose we should. It's just that Jim met one of the men from CID recently at a charity do, and this fellow said one of the biggest problems with murders is all the bogus confessions and hoax calls you always get.'

'But if you *do* recognize her—'

'Not one hundred per cent. Not really. What I do remember is that this girl I'm thinking of called and asked if we'd got a room and then when she knew what it would cost she just sort of . . . Well, I think she couldn't afford it. Then she called back later, this same girl . . .'

'And you were full?'

Anne O'Kane nodded sadly, and Claire finished a last mouthful of toast. 'Not always easy to know what to do for the best.'

'No.'

'But if your husband knows this CID man he could always just, you know, mention it unofficially, couldn't he?'

'Ye-es. Wouldn't do any harm. You're right. And he only lives just up the road. In one of the bachelor flats.'

'What's his name? Lord Peter Wimsey?'

'Morse. Chief Inspector Morse.'

Claire looked down at her empty plate, and folded her white linen table napkin.

'More toast?' asked Anne O'Kane.

Claire shook her head, her flawlessly painted lips showing neither interest nor surprise.

CHAPTER TWENTY-ONE

It is only the first bottle that is expensive
(French proverb)

CLAIRE OSBORNE had discovered what she wanted that same morning. However, it was not until the following morning, 13 July (Sunday spent with Alan Hardinge), that she acted upon her piece of research. It had been terribly easy – just a quick look through the two-inch-thick phone-book for Oxford and District which lay beside the pay-phone: several Morses, but only one 'Morse, E.' – and the phone number, to boot! Leys Close, she learned from the Oxford street-map posted on the wall just inside the foyer, looked hardly more than two hundred yards away. She could have asked the O'Kanes, of course ... but it was a little more exciting not to.

It was another fine sunny morning; and having packed her suitcase and stowed it in the boot of the Metro, and with permission to leave the car ('Shouldn't be all that long,' she'd explained), she walked slowly up towards the roundabout, soon coming to the sign 'Residents Only: No Public Right of Way', then turning left through a courtyard, before arriving at a row of two-storey, yellow-bricked, newish properties, their woodwork painted a uniform white. The number she sought was the first number she saw.

After knocking gently, she noticed, through the window to her left, the white shelving of a kitchen unit and a large plastic bottle of Persil on the draining board. She noticed, too, that the window directly above her was widely open, and she knew that he must be there even before she saw the vague silhouette behind the frosted glass.

What the hell are you doing here? – is that what she'd expected him to say? But he said nothing as he opened the door, bent down to pick up a red-topped bottle of semi-skimmed Co-op milk, stood to one side, inclined his head slightly to the right, and ushered her inside with an old-world gesture of hospitality. She found herself in a large lounge with two settees facing each other, the one to her left in a light honey-coloured leather, to which Morse pointed, and in which she now sat – a wonderfully soft and comfortable thing! Music was playing – something with a sort of heavyweight sadness about it which she thought she almost recognized. Late nineteenth century? Wagner? Mahler? Very haunting and beautiful. But Morse had pressed a panel in the sophisticated bank of equipment on the shelves just behind the other settee, a smaller one in black leather, in which he seated himself and looked across at her, his blue eyes showing a hint of amusement but nothing of surprise.

'No need to turn it off for me, you know.'

'Of course not. I turned it off for *me*. I can never do two things at the same time.'

Looking at the almost empty glass of red wine which stood on the low coffee table beside him, Claire found herself doubting the strictly literal truth of the statement.

'Wagner, was it?'

Morse's eyes lit up with some interest. 'It does show some Wagnerian harmonic and melodic traits, I agree.'

What a load of crap, the pompous oaf! Blast him. Why didn't he just *tell* her? She pointed to the bottle of Quercy: 'I thought you couldn't cope with two things at once?'

'Ah! But drinking's like breathing, really. You don't have to think about it, do you? And it's good for you – did you know that? There's this new report out saying a regular drop of booze is exceedingly good for the heart.'

'Not quite so good for the liver, though.'

'No.' He smiled at her now, leaning back in the settee, his arms stretched out along the top, wearing the same short-sleeved pink shirt she'd seen him in the previous Saturday. He probably needed a woman around the house.

'I thought you were supposed to wait till the sun had passed the yard-arm, or something like that.'

'That's an odd coincidence!' Morse pointed to *The Times* on the coffee table. 'It was in the crossword this morning: "yard-arm".'

'What is a yard-arm, exactly?'

Morse shook his head. 'I'm not interested in boats or that sort of thing. I prefer the Shakespeare quote – remember? That line about "the prick of noon"?'

'"The bawdy hand of the dial is now upon the prick of noon"?'

'How on earth did you know that?'

'I once played the Nurse in *Romeo and Juliet*.'

'Not the sort of thing for a schoolgirl—'

'University, actually.'

'Oh. I was never on the boards much myself. Just the once really. I had a line "I do arrest thee, Antonio." For some reason it made the audience laugh. Never understood why . . .'

Still clutching her copies of the previous day's *Sunday Times* and the current issue of *The Times*, Claire looked slowly around at the book-lined walls, at the stacks of records everywhere, at the pictures (one or two of them fractionally askew). She especially admired the watercolour just above Morse's head of the Oxford skyline in a bluey-purple wash. She was beginning to enjoy the conversational skirmishing, she admitted that; but there was still something *irritating* about the man. For the first time she looked hard, directly across at him.

'You're acting *now*, aren't you?'

'Pardon?'

'You're pretending you're not surprised to see me.'

'No, I'm not. I saw you sitting outside the Cotswold House yesterday; smoking a cigarette. I was walking down to Cuttes-lowe for a newspaper.'

'Mind if I smoke now?'

'Please do. I've, er, stopped myself.'

'Since when?'

'Since this morning.'

'Would you like one?'

'Yes, please.'

Claire inhaled deeply, crossed her legs as she sat down again, and pulled her Jaeger skirt an inch or so below her knees.

'Why didn't you say hello?' she asked.

'I was on the opposite side of the road.'

'Not very pally, was it?'

'Why didn't you say hello to me?'

'I didn't see you.'

'I think you did, though.' His voice was suddenly gentle and she had the feeling that he knew far more about her than he should. 'I think you saw me late Saturday afternoon as well – just after you'd arrived.'

'You *saw* me? You saw me when you walked by with your booze?'

Morse nodded.

Blast him! Blast him! 'I suppose you think you know why I've come here now.'

Morse nodded again. 'It's not because I'm psychic, though. It's just that Jim, Mr O'Kane, he rang me yesterday . . .'

'About this?' She held up the newspapers.

'About the girl possibly calling there, yes. Very interesting, and very valuable, perhaps – I don't know. They're going to make a statement. Not to me though, I'm on holiday. Remember?'

'So it's a bit of a wasted journey. I was going to tell you—'

'Not a wasted journey – don't say that!'

'I – I kept thinking about the girl – all day yesterday . . . well, quite a few times yesterday . . . You know, her calling there and perhaps not having the money and then—'

'How much does a single room cost there now?'

'I'm not sure. And you're acting again! You know perfectly well I booked a *double*, don't you? A double for two nights. You asked O'Kane – you nosey bloody parker!'

For several seconds Morse seemed to look across the room at her with a steady intensity. 'You've got beautifully elegant legs,' he said simply; but she sensed that her answer may have caused him a minor hurt. And suddenly, irrationally, she wanted him to come across the room to her, and take her hand. But he didn't.

'Coffee?' he asked briskly. 'I've only got instant, I'm afraid.'

'Some people prefer instant.'

'Do you?'

'No.'

'I don't suppose I can, er, pour you a glass of wine?'

'What on earth makes you suppose that?'

'Quite good,' she commented, a minute or so later.

'Not bad, is it? You need a lot of it though. No good in small quantities.'

She smiled attractively. 'I see you've finished the crossword.'

'Yes. It's always easy on a Monday, did you know that? They work on the assumption that everybody's a bit bleary-brained on a Monday morning.'

'A lot of people take *The Times* just for the crossword.'

'Yep.'

'And the Letters, of course.'

Morse watched her carefully. 'And the Letters,' he repeated slowly.

Claire unfolded her own copy of *The Times*, 13 July, and read aloud from a front-page article:

CLUES TO MISSING STUDENT

BOTH *The Times* offices and the Thames Valley Police are each still receiving about a dozen letters a day (as well as many phone calls) in response to the request for information concerning the disappearance a year ago of Karin Eriksson, the Swedish student who is thought to be the subject of the anonymous verses received by the police and printed in these columns (July 3). Chief Superintendent Strange of Thames Valley CID himself believes that the ingenious suggestions received in one of the latest communications (see Letters, page 15) is the most interesting and potentially the most significant hitherto received.

'You must have read that?'

'Yes. The trouble is, just like Mr and Mrs O'Kane said, you can't follow up everything. Not even a tenth of the things that come in. Fortunately a lot of 'em are such crack-pot...' He picked up his own copy and turned to page 15, and sat looking (again) at the 'ingenious suggestions'.

'Clever – clever analysis,' he remarked.

'Obviously a very clever fellow – the one who wrote that.'

'Pardon?' said Morse.

'The fellow who wrote that letter.'

Morse read the name aloud: 'Mr Lionel Regis? Don't know him myself.'

'Perhaps nobody does.'

'Pardon?'

'See the address?'

Morse looked down again, and shook his head. 'Don't know Salisbury very well myself.'

'It's *my* address!'

'Really? So – are you saying *you* wrote this?'

'Stop it!' she almost shrieked. '*You* wrote it! You saw my address in the visitors' book at Lyme Regis, and you needed an address for this letter, otherwise your – your "ingenious suggestions" wouldn't be accepted. Am I right?'

Morse said nothing.

'You *did* write it, didn't you? *Please* tell me!'

'Yes.'

'Why? Why go to all this silly palaver?'

'I just – well, I just picked someone from the top of my mind, that's all. And you – you were there, Claire. Right at the top.'

He'd spoken simply, and his eyes lifted from her legs to her face; and all the frustration, all the infuriation, suddenly drained away from her, and the tautness in her shoulders was wonderfully relaxed as she leaned back against the soft contours of the settee.

For a long time neither of them spoke. Then Claire sat forward, emptied her glass, and got to her feet.

'Have you got to go?' asked Morse quietly.

'Fairly soon.'

'I've got another bottle.'

'Only if you promise to be nice to me.'

'If I tell you what lovely legs you've got again?'

'*And* if you put the record on again.'

'CD actually. *Bruckner Eight.*'

'Is *that* what it was? Not all that far off, was I?'

'Very close, really,' said Morse. Then virtually to himself: for a minute or two, very close indeed.

It was halfway through the second movement and three-quarters of the way through the second bottle that the front doorbell rang.

'I can't see you for the minute, I'm afraid, sir.'

Strange sniffed, his small eyes suspicious.

'Really? I'm a little bit surprised about that, Morse. In fact I'm surprised you can't see *two* of me!'

CHAPTER TWENTY-TWO

In a Definition-and-Letter-Mixture puzzle, each clue consists of a sentence which contains a definition of the answer and a mixture of the letters

(Don Manley, *Chambers Crossword Manual*)

THERE WERE just the two of them in Strange's office the following morning, Tuesday, 14 July.

It had surprised Strange not a little to hear of Morse's quite un-equivocal refusal to postpone a few days of his furlough and return immediately to HQ to take official charge of the case; especially in view of the latest letter – surely the break they'd all been hoping for. On the other hand there were more things in life than a blonde damsel who might or might not have been murdered a year ago. This bloody 'joy'(huh!)-riding, for a start – now hitting the national news and the newspaper headlines. It all served, though, to put things into perspective a bit – like the letter he himself had received in the post ('Strictly Personal') that very morning:

To Chief Superintendent Strange,
Kidlington Police HQ

Dear Sir,
It is naturally proper that our excellent whodunnit writers should pretend that the average criminal in the UK can boast the capacity for quite exceptional ingenuity in the commission of crime. But those of us who (like you) have given our lives to the detection of such crime should at this present juncture be reminding everyone that the vast majority of criminals are not (fortunately!) blessed with the sort of alpha-plus mentality that is commonly assumed.

Obviously if *any* criminal is brought to book as a result of the correspondence etc. being conducted in sections of the national press, we shall all be most grateful. But I am myself most doubtful about such an outcome, and indeed in a wider sense I am very much concerned about the precedent involved. We have all heard of trial by TV, and we now seem to be heading for investigation by correspondence column. This is patently absurd. As I read things, the present business is pretty certainly a hoax in any case, with its perpetrator enjoying himself (or I suppose herself?) most hugely as various correspondents vie with one another in scaling ever steeper and steeper peaks of interpretive ingenuity. If the thing is *not* a hoax, I must urge that all investigation into the matter be communicated *in the first instance* to the appropriate police personnel, and most certainly not to radio, TV, or newspapers, so that the case may be solved through the official channels of criminal investigation.

Yours sincerely,
Peter Armitage
(former Assistant Commissioner, New Scotland Yard)
PS I need hardly add, I feel sure, that this letter is not for publication in any way.

But this must almost certainly have been written before its author had seen the latest communiqué from the most intrepid mountaineer so far: the writer of the quite extraordinary letter which had appeared in the correspondence columns of *The Times* the previous morning.

Strange now turned to Lewis. 'You realize it's the break, don't you?'

Lewis, like every other police officer at HQ, had read the letter; and, yes, he too thought it was the break. How else? But he couldn't understand why Strange had asked him – *him* – along that morning. He was very tired anyway, and should by rights have been a-bed. On both Saturday and Sunday nights, like most officers in the local forces, his time had been spent until almost dawn behind a riot-shield, facing volleys of bricks and insults from gangs of yobbos clapping the skidding-skills of youths in stolen cars – amongst whom (had Lewis known it) was a seventeen-year-old schoolboy who was later to provide the key to the Swedish Maiden mystery.

'Lewis! You're listening, aren't you?'

'Sorry, sir?'

'You do *remember* Morse belly-aching about transferring the search from Blenheim to Wytham?'

'Yes, sir. But he wasn't on the case more than a day or so.'

'I know that,' snapped Strange. 'But he must have had some *reason*, surely?'

'I've never quite been able to follow some of his reasons.'

'Do you know how much some of these bloody searches cost?'

'No, sir.'

Nor perhaps did Strange himself, for he immediately changed tack: 'Do you think Morse was right?'

'I dunno, sir. I mean, I think he's a great man, but he sometimes gets things awfully wrong, doesn't he?'

'And he more often gets things bloody *right*!' said Strange with vehemence.

It was an odd reversal of rôles, and Lewis hastened to put the record straight. 'I think myself, sir, that—'

'I don't give a *sod* what you think, Sergeant! If I want to search Wytham Woods I'll bloody well search 'em till a year next Friday if I – if *I* – think it's worth the candle. All right?'

Lewis nodded wordlessly across the table, watching the rising, florid exasperation in the Super's face.

'I'm not sure where I come into all this—' he began.

'Well, I'll tell you! There's only one thing you can do and I can't, Sergeant, and that's to get the morose old bugger back to work here – smartish. I'm under all sorts of bloody pressure . . .'

'But he's on holiday, sir.'

'I *know* he's on bloody holiday. I saw him yesterday, drinking shampers and listening to Schubert – with some tart or other.'

'Sure it was *champagne*, sir?'

But quietly now, rather movingly, Strange was making his plea: 'Christ knows why, Lewis, but he'll always put himself out a bit for you. Did you realize that?'

He rang from Morse's own (empty) office.

'Me, sir. Lewis.'

'I'm on holiday.'

'Super's just had a word with me—'

'Friday – that's what I told him.'

'You've seen the letter about Wytham, sir?'

'Unlike you and your philistine cronies, Lewis, my daily reading includes the royal circulars in *The Times*, the editorials—'

'What do I tell the Super, sir? He wants us – you and me – to take over straightaway.'

'Tell him I'll be in touch – tomorrow.'

'Tell him you'll ring, you mean?'

'No. Tell him I'll be back on duty tomorrow morning. Tell him I'll be in my office any time after seven a.m.'

'He won't be awake then, sir.'

'Don't be too hard on him, Lewis. He's getting old – and I think he's got high blood pressure.'

As he put down the phone, with supreme contentment, Lewis knew that Strange had been right – about Morse and himself; realized that in the case of the Swedish Maiden, the pair of them were in business again – w.e.f. the following morning.

In his office, Strange picked up the cutting from *The Times* and read the letter yet again. Quite extraordinary!

From Mr Lionel Regis

Sir, Like most of your other correspondents I must assume that the 'Swedish Maiden' verses were composed by the person responsible for the murder of that unfortunate young lady. It is of course possible they were sent as a hoax, but such is not my view. In my opinion it is far more probable that the writer is exasperated by the inability of the police to come anywhere near the discovery of a *body*, let alone the arrest of a murderer. The verses, as I read them, are a cry from the murderer – not the victim – a cry for some discovery, some absolution, some relief from sleepless, haunted nights.

But I would not have written to you, sir, merely to air such vague and dubious generalities. I write because I am a setter of crossword puzzles, and when I first studied the verses I had just completed a puzzle in which the answer to every clue was indicated by a definition of the word to be entered, and also by a sequenced *anagram* of the same word. It was with considerable interest therefore – and a good measure of incredulity – that I gradually spotted the fact that the word WYTHAM crops up, in anagrammatized form, in each of the five stanzas. Thus: THAW MY (stanza 1]; [stre]AM WHY T[ell'st] (stanza 2); WHAT MY (stanza 3); [s]AW THYM[e] (stanza 4); and [no]w THY MA[iden] (stanza 5).

The occurrence of *five* such instances is surely way beyond the bounds of coincidence (I have consulted my mathematical friends on this matter). 'Whytham', I learn (I am not an Oxford man), is the name of some woods situated to the west of Oxford. If the verse tells us anything then, it is surely that the body sought is to be found in Wytham Woods, and it is my humble suggestion that any further searches undertaken should be conducted in that quarter.

Yours,
LIONEL REGIS,
16 Cathedral Mews,
Salisbury.

Like Lewis, Strange remembered exactly what Morse had said on his postcard: 'I reckon *I* know what the poem means!', and he pushed the newspaper aside, and looked out across the car park. 'Lionel Regis, my arse!' he said quietly to himself.

CHAPTER TWENTY-THREE

On another occasion he was considering how best to welcome the postman, for he brought news from a world outside ourselves. I and he agreed to stand behind the front door at the time of his arrival and to ask him certain questions. On that day, however, the postman did not come

(Peter Champkin,
The Sleeping Life of Aspern Williams)

WEDNESDAY, 15 July, was never going to be a particularly memorable day. No fire-faced prophet was to bring news of the Message or the name of the One True God. Just a fairly ordinary transitional sort of day in which events appeared discrete and only semi-sequential; when some of the protagonists in the Swedish Maiden case were moved to their new positions on the chessboard, but before the game was yet begun.

At a slightly frosty meeting held in the Assistant Chief Constable's office at 10.30 a.m., the Swedish Maiden case was reviewed in considerable detail by the ACC himself, Chief Superintendent Strange, and Detective Chief Inspectors Johnson and Morse. General agreement was reached (only one dissident voice) that perhaps there was little now to be gained from any prolongation of the extensive and expensive search-programme on the Blenheim Palace Estate. The decision was reported too, emanating from 'higher authority', that Morse was now i/c and that Johnson would therefore be enabled to take his midsummer furlough as scheduled. Such official verbiage would fool no one, of course – but it was possibly better than nothing at all.

Amongst the items reviewed was yet another letter, printed that morning in *The Times*:

From Mr John C. Chavasse

Sir, The Wood (singular not plural please) at Wytham is a place most familiar to me and I suspect to almost all gener- ations of young men who have taken their degrees at Oxford University. Well do I remem- ber the summer weekends in the late 40s when together with many of my fellow undergraduates I cycled up through Lower Wolvercote to Wytham.

In lines 14 and 15 of the (now notorious!) verses, we find 'A creature white' (*sic*) 'Trapped in a gin' (*sic*), 'Panting like a hunted deer' (*sic*). Now if this is *not* a cryptic reference to a gin-and-whatnot in that splendid old hostelry in Wytham, the White Hart –

then I'm a Dutchman, sir! But I am convinced (as an Englishman) that such a reference can only serve to corroborate the brilliant analysis of the verses made by Mr Lionel Regis (Letters, July 13).

Yours faithfully,
JOHN C. CHAVASSE,
21 Hayward Road,
Bishop Auckland.

Around the table, 'Mr Lionel Regis' looked slightly sheepish; but not for long, and now it was all an open secret anyway. He realized that there would be little he could do for a day or so – except to reread all the material that had accumulated from the earlier inquiries; to sit tight; to get Lewis cracking on the admin; and perhaps to try to think a bit more clearly about his own oddly irrational conviction that the young student's body *would* be found – and found in Wytham Wood(s). There *was* that little bit of new evidence, too – the call from the O'Kanes. For if their memories served them to any degree aright, then Karin Eriksson had at some point gone *down* the Banbury Road from the roundabout; it was the testimony of the man who had been waiting for a bus there that Sunday noon-time which should have been given credence – not that of the man who had driven along Sunderland Avenue.

Such and similar thoughts Morse shared with Sergeant Lewis in the early afternoon. Already arrangements were well in hand for the availability of about twenty further members of various local forces to supplement the thirty due to be switched immediately from Blenheim. One annoying little hold-up, though. The head forester at Wytham, Mr David Michaels, was unfortunately away that day at a National Trust conference in Durham. But he was expected home later that night, his wife said, and would almost certainly be available the following morning.

Things *were* moving, that afternoon. But slowly. And Morse was feeling restless and impatient. He returned home at 4 p.m., and began typing a list of gramophone records . . .

Before leaving him the previous Monday, a quarter of an hour after Strange's inopportune interruption, Claire Osborne had asked him to send her his eight Desert Island Discs and the versions he possessed of the Mozart *Requiem*. It was high time she started to improve her mind a bit, she'd said; and if Morse would promise to try to help her...? So Morse had promised, and reiterated his promise as he'd kissed her briefly, sweetly, fully on the lips, at her departure.

'You do know my address, I think?' she'd shouted from the gate.

Morse was still not *quite* sure of numbers seven and eight as he sat and slowly typed his list that afternoon.

A quarter of an hour or so before Morse had begun his labour of love, Philip Daley swaggered loutishly out of his class-room in the Cherwell School, just along the Marston Ferry Road in North Oxford. Only two more days to go! Roll on! School would be finishing on the 17th and he couldn't wait to get shot of it. Shot of it for good and all! His dad (his dad's own words) didn't give a fuckin' toss, though his mum (as he knew very well) would have been glad if he could have settled down to schoolwork and stayed on in the sixth form and maybe landed up with a decent job and all that bullshit. But other thoughts were uppermost in his bitterly discontented mind as he walked up the Banbury Road that afternoon. At lunch-time he'd asked one of the girls from his class, the one with the blouseful, whether she'd go with him to the end-of-term disco; and she'd said he must be bloody jokin' and anyway she'd already got a feller, 'adn't she? Soddin' cunt! As he walked up to the shops he crashed his fist against some ancient wooden fencing there: fuck it, fuck it, *fuck* it! Just wait till Friday, though. He'd show the fuckin' lot of 'em.

It was at 7.15 p.m., twelve hours after reaching HQ earlier that day, that Lewis sat down at his home in Headington to his beloved eggs and chips.

Blast him! thought Claire, as she turned first to one side and then the other in her bed that night. She could not understand at all why he was monopolizing her thoughts – but he was. And blast that other copper – that fat slob of a man who'd stood there talking to him on the doorstep for almost a quarter of an hour. She'd have had to leave very soon anyway, she realized that. But it had meant there had been no time to develop that little passage of intimacy between them . . . and now, and again, and again, he was passing through her mind. Bloody nuisance, it all was! Only temporary, she trusted – this inability to sleep, this inability to thrust him from her thoughts. She just hoped she'd get a letter from him in the *next* post, that's all. He said he'd write; he'd promised; and she'd been looking out eagerly for the postman.

On that day, however, the postman did not come.

CHAPTER TWENTY-FOUR

The Grantor leaves the guardianship of the Woodlands to the kindly sympathy of the University . . . The University will take all reasonable steps to preserve and maintain the woodlands and will use them for the instruction of suitable students and will provide facilities for research

(Extract from the deed under which Wytham Wood was acquired by the University of Oxford on 4 August 1942 as a gift from Col. ffennell)

MANY Oxonians know 'Wytham' as the village on the way to the wood. But Morse knew the spot as the village, situated on the edge of the wood, which housed the White Hart Inn; and he pointed lovingly to the hostelry the next morning as Lewis drove the pair of them to their meeting with the head forester.

'Did you know,' asked Morse (consulting his leaflet) 'that in the parish of Wytham, a large part of it covered with woods, the ground rises from the banks of the Thames – or "Isis" – to a height of 539 feet at Wytham Hill, the central point of the ancient parish?'

'No, sir,' replied Lewis, turning right just after the pub into a stretch of progressively narrowing roadway that was very soon marked by the sign 'Private Property: University of Oxford'.

'You don't sound very interested—'

'Look!' shouted Lewis. 'See *that*?'

'No!' In his youth Morse had almost invariably been the boy in the group who missed out; whilst his schoolmates were perpetually spotting birds' eggs, the blue flash of kingfishers, or gingery foxes momentarily motionless at the edge of cornfields, the young Morse had seldom seen anything; the old Morse had seen nothing now.

'What exactly *was* the cause of all the excitement, Lewis?'

'Deer, sir. Roe-deer, I think. Two of them, just behind—'

'Are they different from normal deer?'

'I don't reckon you're going to be too much help in this neck of the woods, sir.'

Morse made no comment on such a nicely turned phrase, as Lewis drove half a mile or so further, with an area of fairly dense woodland on his left, until he reached a semi-circular parking lot, also on his left. 'Cars must be left at one of the two car parks shown on the plan,' the map said; and in any case a locked barrier across the road effectively blocked further progress to motor vehicles. Lewis pulled the police car in beside an ancient, rusting Ford.

'Good to see some people care, sir,' ventured Lewis, pointing to an RSPB sticker on one side window and a larger 'Save the Whale' plea on the other.

'Probably here for a snog under the sycamores,' Morse replied cheerfully.

A low, stone-built cottage stood thirty yards or so back on the further side of the track. 'That must be where Mr Michaels lives, sir. Nice view – looking right across there to Eynsham.'

'C'mon,' said Morse.

It was just past the barrier, which they negotiated via a kissing-gate, set in its V-shaped frame, that the two detectives came, on their left, to a large clearing, some 100 yards square, with fir-saplings planted around the fenced perimeter, in which was set a whole complex of sheds and barns, built in horizontally slatted wood, with piles of spruce- and fir-logs stacked nearby, and with several tractors and pieces of tree-felling machinery standing beside or beneath the open-fronted barns.

From the furthest shed a figure walked down the slope to greet them – a man of about fifty or so, blue-eyed, closely bearded, and little short of six foot – introducing himself as David Michaels, the head forester. They shook hands with the man, Morse being careful to keep slightly behind Lewis as a black and white dog, bounding energetically after his master, sought to introduce himself too.

In the forester's hut, Michaels briefly described the lay-out of the woods (plural!), referring repeatedly to the four Ordnance Survey maps on the inner wall, themselves pinned together in a large oblong to give a synoptic view of the whole area under the forester's charge. There was a University Committee, the policemen learnt, administering Wytham Woods, to whom he (Michaels) was personally responsible, with a University Land Agent acting as Executive Officer; and it was to the latter that the police would need to apply formally. Permits to walk in the woods (this in answer to Lewis) were issued, on request, to any resident teachers or administrators in the University, and of course to any other citizen, Town or Gown, who was able to provide adequate cause, and no criminal impediment, for wishing to visit the area.

Morse himself became more interested when Michaels moved closer to the maps and expanded on the woods' main attractions, his right forefinger tracing its way through what (to Morse) was a wonderfully attractive-sounding catalogue: Duck Pond; The Follies; Bowling Alley; Cowleaze Copse; Froghole Cottage; Hatchett Lane; Marley Wood; Pasticks; Singing Way; Sparrow Lane . . . almost like the music of the woods and birds themselves.

But as he watched and listened, Morse's heart was sinking slightly lower. The woodlands were vast; and Michaels himself, now in his fifteenth year there, admitted that there were several areas where he had never – probably *would* never – set foot; parts known only to the badgers and the foxes and the deer and the families of woodpeckers. Yet somehow the mention of the woodpeckers appeared to restore Morse's confidence, and he gratefully accepted the forester's offer of a guided tour.

Lewis sat on the floor in the back of the rugged, powerful, ineffably uncomfortable and bouncy Land Rover, with Bobbie, the only dog allowed in the woods. Morse sat in the front with Michaels, who spent the next ninety minutes driving across the tracks and rides and narrow paths which linked the names of his earlier litany.

For a while Morse toyed with the idea of bringing in the military perhaps – a couple of thousand men from local units, under the command of some finicky brigadier sitting in Caesar's tent and ticking off the square yards one by one. Then he put his thought into words:

'You know I'm beginning to think it'd take an army a couple
of months to cover all this.'

'Oh, I don't know,' replied Michaels. Surprisingly?

'No?'

Patiently the forester explained how during the summer
months there were dozens of devotees who regularly checked the
numbers of eggs and weights of fledglings in the hundreds of
bird-boxes there; who laid nocturnal wait to observe the doings
of the badgers; who clipped tags and bugging devices to fox-
cubs; and so many others who throughout the year monitored the
ecological pattern that Nature had imposed on Wytham Woods.
Then there were the members of the public who were forever
wandering around with their birdwatchers' guides and their
binoculars, or looking for woodland orchids, or just enjoying the
peace and beauty of it all . . .

Morse was nodding automatically through much of the recital,
and he fully took the point that Michaels was making; he'd
guessed as much anyway, but things were clearer in his mind
now.

'You mean there's a good deal of ground we can probably
forget . . .'

'That's it. And a good deal you can't.'

'So we need to establish some priorities,' Lewis chirped up
from the rear.

'That was the, er, general conclusion that Mr Michaels and
myself had just reached, Lewis.'

'Eighteen months ago, all this was, you say?' asked Michaels.

'Twelve, actually.'

'So if . . . if she'd been . . . just *left* there, you know, without
trying to hide her or anything . . .?'

'Oh yes, there probably wouldn't be all that much of her still
around – you'll know that better than most. But it's more often
"found in a shallow grave", isn't it? That's the jargon. Not
surprising though that murderers should want to cover up
their crimes: they often dig a bit and put twigs and leaves
and things over . . . over the top. But you need a spade for
that. In the summer you'd need a *sharp* spade – and plenty
of time, and a bit of daylight, and a bit of nerve . . . They tell me
it takes a couple of sextons about eight hours to dig a decent
grave.'

Perhaps it was the crudity and cruelty of the scene just

conjured up which cast a gloom upon them now – and they spoke no more of the murder for the rest of the bumpy journey. Just about birds. Morse asked about woodpeckers, and Michaels knew a great deal about woodpeckers: the green, the great-spotted, the lesser-spotted – all had their habitats within the woods and all were of especial interest to birdwatchers.

'You interested in woodpeckers, Inspector?'

'Splendid birds,' muttered Morse vaguely.

Back in the hut, Morse explained the limitation of his likely resources and the obvious need therefore for some selective approach. 'What I'd really like to know is this – please don't feel offended, Mr Michaels. But if *you* wanted to hide a body in these woods, which places would come to mind first?'

So Michaels told them; and Lewis made his notes, feeling a little uneasy about his spelling of some of the names which Morse had earlier found so memorable.

When twenty minutes later the trio walked down towards the police car, they heard a sharp crack of a gun.

'One of the farmers,' explained Michaels. 'Taking a pot at some pigeons, like as not.'

'I didn't see any guns in your office,' commented Lewis.

'Oh, I couldn't keep 'em *there*! Against the law, that is, Sergeant.'

'But I suppose you must have one – in your job, sir?'

'Oh yeah! Couldn't do without. In a steel cabinet in there' – Michaels pointed to the low cottage – 'well and truly locked away, believe me! In fact, I'm off to do a bit of shooting now.'

'Off to preserve and maintain some of the local species, Mr Michaels?'

But the degree of sarcasm behind Morse's question was clearly ill-appreciated by the bearded woodsman, who replied with a decided coolness: 'Sometimes – quite often – it's essential to keep some sort of stability within *any* eco-system, and if you like I'll tell you a few things about the multiplication-factor of one or two of our randier species of deer. If I had my way, Inspector, I'd issue 'em all with free condoms from that white machine in the gents at the White Hart. But they wouldn't take much notice of me, would they?' For a few seconds Michaels' eyes glinted with the repressed anger of a professional man being told his job by some ignorant amateur.

Morse jumped in quickly. 'Sorry! I really am. It's just that as I get older I can't really think of killing things. Few years ago I'd have trodden on a spider without a thought, but these days – I don't know why – I almost feel guilty about swatting a daddy-long-legs.'

'You wouldn't find *me* killing a daddy-long-legs!' said Michaels, his eyes still hard as they stared unblinkingly back at Morse's. Blue versus blue; and for a few seconds Morse wondered what exactly Michaels *would* kill ... and would be killing now.

CHAPTER TWENTY-FIVE

For wheresoever the carcase is, there will the eagles be gathered together

(*St Matthew*, ch. 24, v. 28)

REGIS'S (Morse's) cracking of the Swedish Maiden verses had sparked off a whole series of letters about the Great Wood at Wytham. But only one of these letters was to be published by *The Times* that week – the latest in a correspondence which was gripping the interest of that daily's readers:

From Stephen Wallhead, RA

Sir, It was with interest that I read what must surely be the final analysis of the Swedish Maiden affair. I had not myself, of course, come within a mile of the extraordinarily subtle interpretation (Letters, July 13) in which Wytham Woods are suggested – surely *more* than suggested – as the likeliest resting-place of that unfortunate girl. My letter can make only one small addendum; but I trust an interesting one, since the injunction 'Find the Woodman's daughter' (1. 6 of the verses) may now possibly be of some vital significance.

An oil-on-canvas painting, *The Woodman's Daughter*, was worked on by John Everett Millais in 1850–51. It depicts the young son of a squire offering a handful of strawberries to the young daughter of a woodman. Millais (as always) was meticulous about his work, and the whole picture is minutely accurate in its research: for example, we know from the artist Arthur Hughes that the strawberries in the boy's hand were bought at Covent Garden in March 1851!

The background to this picture shows a woodland area with a clear perspective and a distinctive alignment of trees, and in my view it is at least a possibility that even allowing for decades of cutting-down and replantation the original site could be established. But here is the point, sir! From the diary of one of the artist's friends, Mrs Joanna Matthews, RA, we learn as follows: 'Millais is hard at work painting the background of his picture from nature in *Wytham Wood*' (my italics). Could not such a background point the place where the body is to be found? And may we not further infer that our murderer has not only an intimate knowledge of the woods themselves but also of the Pre-Raphaelite painters?

Yours faithfully,
STEPHEN WALLHEAD,
Wymondham Cottage,
Helpston, Lincs.

Early on the morning of Friday, 17 July, this letter had been seen by Strange, Morse, Lewis, and most of the personnel on duty at Thames Valley HQ. But not by everyone.

'Just tell me exactly what the 'ell we're supposed to be looking for!' Constable Jimmy Watt complained to his colleague, Constable Sid Berridge, as the two of them halted for a while, side by side, in the riding between Marley Wood on their right and Pasticks on their left.

Seventeen of them, there were, working reasonably scientifically through this particular stretch. Watt had been seconded only that day, taken (quite willingly) off traffic duties, while Berridge had already spent the earlier part of his week in Blenheim. And, in truth, their present duties were unwelcome to neither of them, for the temperature was already warm that morning, the sky an almost cloudless Cambridge blue.

'We're looking for a condom, Jimmy – preferably one with a handful of fingerprints on it—'

'Wha'? Bloody year ago?'

'—so's Morse'll be able to discover which 'and he pulled it on with.'

'We used to call 'em "french letters" in my day,' said Watt, with a hint of nostalgia in his voice.

'Yeah. Things change, though.'

'Yeah! Some of us missed out a bit, don't you reckon? The way some of these young 'uns . . .'

'Yeah.'

'Who'd you wanna go in *there* with, though?' Watt pointed to his left, to the dense patch of forestation nearby.

Berridge rose to the challenge: 'Brigitte Bardot? Liz Taylor? Joan Collins? Madonna? Me next-door-neighbour's wife—'

'In *there*, though?'

Berridge decided to scale down his previous decision: 'Perhaps not . . . Perhaps only the woman next door.'

It had been an hour earlier, at 8.30 a.m., that a member of the Wytham Trust had addressed their party, and explained why Pasticks could be a reasonably safe each-way bet for a site where a body may have lain undisturbed for a longish time. Why? Well, most people would think that the cutting-down of trees and the selling of the wood to wholesale dealers was invariably going to be a profitable undertaking. Not so! The expense of hiring men to saw down trees, to trim the fallen timber, then to transport and treat it, and finally to sell it to furniture dealers, or fencing designers, or the rest – such expense would always be considerable. And the Trust had long since agreed that it could do little better than see the whole business of thinning the woods, etc., as, well, as tit-for-tat: *they* would pay nothing for the cutting-back of the various copses and spinneys; and in turn the wood-cutters and carters would receive the proceeds from the tens of thousands of assorted tree-trunks that were annually removed from Wytham Woods. But occasionally there was a bit of a hiccup in the system – when, for example, a few of the areas of reforestation were not quite ready for such biennial decimation; when the thinning of a particular area ought, for whatever reason, to be delayed for a couple of years.

Such a situation had in fact arisen the year before in the very latest plantation (1958–62) – a mixed hardwood affair of Norwegian spruce, oak, beech, red cedar – in the area called Pasticks. And that wouldn't be a bad place to leave a body! The trees there allowed in very little light; and in the middle of it all were three or four old spinneys that had existed even before the Enclosure Acts. Dense places. Double-dense.

For Berridge and Watt the task certainly looked uninviting. From any point some two or three yards within the wood it seemed almost as if a curtain had been drawn in front of them, cutting them off from any further investigation, with the leafless horizontal and perpendicular branches of the trees there forming a sort of blurring criss-cross mesh of brown across their vision.

It was a good many hours later, at 3.55 p.m., that the deeply and progressively more pessimistic pair of constables heard a shout of triumph from somewhere to their left. A body had been found; and very soon each wing of the search-party had enfolded the scene like the wings of a mother-bird protecting her young.

The foxes had already been there – often enough by the look of it – and the badgers, and the birds of the air . . . for the bones of what appeared to be a single human being had been dragged apart there – in some cases seemingly removed – from their familiar configuration. Yet not so far removed as to render the pristine pattern unrecognizable. A femur still lay in its approximately normal relationship to its pelvis; a few ribs still in roughly parallel formation above it; a shoulder bone in a vaguely formal relationship with the vertebrae; and the vertebrae themselves about two or three feet separated from a comparatively small and badly savaged skull; not far from which was a faded, tasselled neck-scarf, still boasting its original colours – the twin proud colours of the Swedish national flag.

CHAPTER TWENTY-SIX

Science is spectrum analysis: art is photosynthesis
(Karl Kraus, *Half Truths One and a Half Truths*)

WORD quickly spread and the verdict in all quarters was the same: here he was – only a couple of days into the investigation, only one day into the search, and eureka! Clever bugger, Morse!

A bit lucky, perhaps. Could have been another week before they'd found her if they'd started at the other, the western, side of the woods.

'Touch nothing!', 'Keep your distance!' had been the orders of the day; and it had been around an unmolested, untrodden area of four or five square yards of woodland, carpeted with a thick, darkish-brown pile, that a rather irregular cordon had been drawn.

Morse had arrived on the scene within twenty minutes, and now stood there silently, not venturing beyond the waist-high red and white tape, his eyes recording the evidence before him. He saw the dislocated pattern of the bones; the scattered, residual clothes; and especially he saw the tasselled scarf beside the horridly damaged head. It reminded him of something from a DIY manual, in which various arrows point from the outer-lying parts towards a putative centre, giving instruction for the assemblage of the purchase: 'Bring this part into *there*; attach this part to *that*; connect *here*; it will fit, all of it, if only you take your time, read the instructions carefully, and know that you are going wrong if more than gentle force is required for the final assembly.' Occasionally Morse moved his weight slightly on the packed twigs and spindles beneath his feet; but still he said nothing. And the others standing there were silent too, like awkward mourners at a funeral.

Lewis, busily negotiating that afternoon with the University authorities, would not be with him. But neither of them, neither Morse nor Lewis, would be of much use at this stage. It was Max who was going to be the important personage, and Max had already been informed, was already on his way; Max who ten minutes later made his lumbering progress across the crackling bracken, and stood wheezing heavily beside Morse.

Silently, just as Morse had done earlier, the hump-backed surgeon surveyed the sorry sight which lay at the foot of an evergreen of some sort, the lower branches leafless, brittle, dead. If any attempt had been made to conceal the body, it was not now apparent; and disturbingly (as others had already noticed) a few of the major bones, including the whole of the lower left arm, had been carried away somewhere – to some den or earth or sett. From the look of it the clothes were slightly better preserved than the body: several strips of stained white, and substantial remnants of what looked like blue jeans, perhaps; and some yellow-ish, straw-coloured hair still gruesomely attached to the skull.

But Morse hadn't kept his eyes long on the skull . . .

'This what you've been looking for, Morse?'

'Yes. I think that's her.'

'Her?'

'I'm certain it's a "her",' said Morse with finality.

'Do you know the last words my old mother said? She'd been baking earlier in the day – the day she died. Then she was taken to her bed, but she still wanted to see how the fruit cake was doing. And it was flat. The bloody thing forgot to *rise*, Morse! And she said, "You know, life's full of uncertainties." Then she closed her eyes – and died.'

'It's the girl,' repeated Morse simply.

Max made no further comment, staring guardedly on as Morse nodded to the scenes-of-crime officer and the police photographer, both of whom had been standing waiting for some while. If there was anything of any import there that Morse should have seen, he was not aware of it; but he still felt nervous about the patch of ground, and instructed both to keep as far as possible from the grisly finds.

After a few minutes of photographic flashing, Max stepped rather gingerly into the area, hooked a pair of ancient spectacles around his large ears, looked down at the scattered skeleton, and picked up a bone.

'Femur, Morse. *Femur, femoris*, neuter. The thigh bone.'

'So?'

Max placed the bone down carefully and turned to Morse. 'Look, old friend, I don't very often ask you for any forensic guidance, but just for once give me a little advice, will you? What the hell am I supposed to do with this bloody lot?'

Morse shook his head. 'I'm not sure.' But suddenly his eyes glowed as if some inner current had been activated. 'I knew she'd be here, Max,' he said slowly. 'Somehow I *knew* it! And I'm going to find out who murdered our Swedish Maiden. And I want you to help me, Max! Help me paint a picture of what went on in this place.'

The almost Messianic fierceness with which Morse had enunciated these words would have affected most people. But not Max.

'You're the artist, dear boy: I'm just a humble scientist.'

'How long will you be?'

'Looking at the bones, you mean?'

'And the clothes . . . and the underclothes.'

'Ah, yes! I remember. You've always had an interest in underclothes.' He consulted his watch. 'Opening time at six? I'll see you in the upstairs bar at the White Hart—'

'No. I've got a meeting back at HQ at half-past six.'

'Really? I thought *you* were in charge of this case, Morse.'

There were the four of them again: the ACC, Strange, Johnson, and Morse; and for the latter, naturally, congratulations were generous. For Johnson, however, there were very mixed feelings: Morse had come up with the girl's body in a couple of days, whilst he had come up with nothing in a twelve-month. That was the simple truth of the matter. It was good for the *case*, of course; but not much good for his own morale or his rating amongst his colleagues, or for his wife . . . or indeed for his newly acquired mother-in-law. But when, an hour later, the meeting broke up, he shook Morse's hand and wished him well, and almost meant it.

After the ACC and Johnson had left, Strange in turn wished Morse continued success, observing that now Morse had come up with a body, all that remained for him was to come up with a murderer, so that he, Strange, would be able to get a nice little report and send it to the DPP. No problems! Then they'd kick the smart-alec defence lawyers up the arse, and stick the bugger who did it in the nick for the rest of his natural. Put a rope round his bloody neck, too, if Strange had *his* way.

'Just as well we didn't hang the Birmingham Six,' said Morse quietly.

CHAPTER TWENTY-SEVEN

It was a maxim with Foxey – our revered father, gentlemen – 'Always suspect everybody'

(Charles Dickens, *The Old Curiosity Shop*)

ON THE following morning, Saturday, 18 July, Morse appeared, as Lewis saw things, somewhat distanced, somewhat reserved. It was customary for the chief to start, if not always to continue, any case with a surfeit of confidence and exuberance, and doubtless that would soon be the way of things again; just not for the moment.

'Not really all *that* much to go on there, sir.' Lewis nodded to the two red box-files on the table.

'I've done my homework too, you know.'

'Where do we start?'

'Difficult. We ought really to wait till we hear from Max before we do too much.'

'All this DNA stuff, you mean?'

'DNA? He doesn't know what it *stands* for!'

'When's the report due?'

'Today some time, he said.'

'What's that mean?'

'Tonight?' Morse shrugged. But he suddenly sat forward in the black leather chair, appeared to sharpen up, took out his silver Parker pen, and began making a few minimal notes as he spoke:

'There are several people we've got to see pretty soon.'

'Who are you thinking of, sir?'

'Of whom am I thinking? Well, number one, there's the fellow who found the rucksack – Daley. We'll go through his statement with a nit-comb. I never did like the sound of him.'

'You never met him, did you?'

'Number two. There's the YWCA woman who spoke with Karin before she left for Oxford. She sounds nice.'

'But you never—'

'I spoke to her on the phone, Lewis, if you must know. She sounds nice – that's all I said. You don't *mind*, do you?'

Lewis smiled to himself. It was good to be back in harness.

'Number three,' resumed Morse. 'We must have a long session with that Wytham fellow – the Lone Ranger, or whatever he's called.'

'Head forester, sir.'

'Exactly.'

'Did you like *him*?'

Morse turned over the palm of his right hand, and considered his inky fingers. 'He virtually told us where she was, didn't he? Told us where *he* would hide a body if he had to . . .'

'Not likely to have told us if he'd put it there *himself* though, surely? Self-incrimination, that!'

Morse said nothing.

'The witnesses who said they saw her, sir – any good going back over them?'

'Doubt it, but . . . Anyway, let's put 'em down, number four. And number five, the parents—'

'Just the mother, sir.'

'—in Uppsala—'

'Stockholm, now.'

'Yes. We shall have to see her again.'

'We shall have to *tell* her first, surely.'

'If it is Karin, you mean?'

'You don't really have much doubt, do you, sir?'

'No!'

'I suppose you'll be going there yourself? To Stockholm, I mean.' Morse looked up, apparently with some surprise. 'Or you, Lewis. Or *you*!'

'Very kind of you, sir.'

'Not kind at all. Just that I'm scared stiff of flying – you know that.' But the voice was a little sad again.

'You all right?' Lewis asked quietly.

'Shall be soon – don't worry! Now, I just wonder whether Mr George Daley's still working on the Blenheim Estate.'

'Saturday, though. More likely to be off today.'

'Yes . . . And his son – Philip, was it? – the lad who had a short-term birthday present of a camera, Karin Eriksson's camera. He was still at school last year.'

'Probably still is'

'No – not precisely so, Lewis. The state schools in Oxfordshire broke up yesterday, the seventeenth.'

'How'd you know that?'

'I rang up and found out. That's how.'

'You've been having a fair old time on the phone!' said Lewis happily, as he got to his feet – and went for the car.

As he drove out along the A44 to Begbroke, Lewis's eyes drifted briefly if incuriously to his left as Morse opened an envelope, took out a single handwritten sheet of A4, and read it; not (in fact) for the first, or even the fourth, time:

Dear Chief Inspector,

    V m t f y l and for your interesting choice of records.

    It would make a good debate in the Oxford Union – 'This

house believes that openness in matters of infidelity is preferrable to deception.' But let me tell you what you want to know. I was married in '76, divorced in '82, remarried in '84, separated in '88. One child, a daughter now aged 20. Work that out, clever-clogs! As you know I consort fairly regularly with a married man from Oxford, and at less frequent intervals with others. So there! And now – Christ! – *you* come along and I hate you for it because you're monopolizing my thoughts just when I'd told myself I was beyond all that nonsense.

I write for two reasons. First to say I reckon I've got some idea how that young girl who monopolizes *your* thoughts may have come by a bit of cash. (Same way I did!) Second to say you're an arrogant sod! You write to me as if you think I'm an ignorant little schoolgirl. Well let me tell you you're not the only sensitive little flower in the whole bloody universe. You quote these poets as if you think you're connected on some direct personal line with them all. Well you're wrong. There's hundreds of extensions, just like in the office I used to work. So there!

Please write again.

Dare I send you a little of my love? C.

Morse hadn't noticed the misspelling before; and as he put the letter away he promised himself not to mention it . . . when he wrote back.

'I'm still not quite sure why we're interviewing Mr Daley, sir.'

'He's hiding something, that's why.'

'But you can't say *that*—'

'Look, Lewis, if he's *not* hiding something, there is not much reason for us interviewing him, is there?'

Lewis, not unaccustomedly, was bewildered by such zany logic; and he let it go.

Anyway, Morse was suddenly sounding surprisingly cheerful.

CHAPTER TWENTY-EIGHT

Be it ever so humble there's no place like home for sending one
slowly crackers

(Diogenes Small, *Obiter Dicta*)

GEORGE DALEY, on overtime, was planting out flowers in the
Blenheim Garden Centre when he looked up and saw the two
men, the shorter of them flashing a warrant card briefly in front
of his face. He knew what it was all about, of course. *The Oxford
Mail* had been taking a keen interest in the resurrected case; and
it would be only a matter of time, Daley had known, before the
police would be round again.

'Mr Daley? Chief Inspector Morse. And this is Sergeant Lewis.'

Daley nodded, prodded his splayed fingers round a marigold,
and got to his feet. He was a man in his mid-forties, of slim build,
wearing a shabby khaki-green pork-pie hat. This he pushed back
slightly, revealing a red line on his sweaty forehead.

'It's that thing I found, I suppose?'

'Those things – yes,' said Morse carefully.

'I can only tell you the same as I told 'em at the time. I made a
statement and I signed it. Nothin' else as I can do.'

Morse took a folded sheet of A4 from his inside pocket, opened
it out, and handed it to Daley. 'I'd just like you to read this
through and make sure it's – well, you know, see if there's
anything else you can add.'

'I've told you. There's nothin' else.' Daley rubbed a hand
across an unshaven cheek with the sound of sandpaper on wood.

'I'd just like you to read it through *again*,' said Morse simply.
'That's all.'

'I shall need me specs. They're in the shed—'

'Don't worry now! Better if you give yourself a bit of time. No
rush. As I say, all I want you to do is to make sure everything's
there just as you said it, nothing's been missed out. It's often the
little things, you know, that make all the difference.'

'If there was anythin' else I'd've told the other inspector,
wouldn't I?'

Was it Lewis's imagination, or was there a momentary glint of
anxiety in the gardener's pale eyes?

'Are you in this evening, Mr Daley?' asked Morse.

'Wha' – Saturday? I usually go over the pub for a jar or two at the weekends but—'

'If I called at your house about – what, seven?'

George Daley stood motionless, his eyes narrowed and unblinking as he watched the two detectives walk away through the archway and into the visitors' car park. Then his eyes fell on the photocopied statement once more. There was just that one thing that worried him, yes. It was that bloody boy of his who'd fucked it all up. More trouble than they were worth, kids. Especially *him*! Becomin' a real troublemaker he was, gettin' in all hours – like last night. Three bloody thirty a.m. With his mates, he'd said – after the end-of-term knees-up. He'd got a key all right, of course, but his mother could never sleep till he was in. Silly bitch!

'Where to, sir?' queried Lewis.

'I reckon we'll just call round to see Mrs Daley.'

'What do you make of Mr?'

'Little bit nervous.'

'Most people get a bit nervous with the police.'

'Good cause, some of 'em,' said Morse.

Lewis had earlier telephoned Margaret Daley about her husband's whereabouts, and the woman who opened the door of number 2 Blenheim Villas showed no surprise. She appeared, on first impressions, a decided cut or two above her horticultural spouse: neatly dressed, pleasantly spoken, well groomed – her light brown hair professionally streaked with strands of blonde and grey.

Morse apologized for disturbing her, looked around him at the newly decorated, neatly furnished, through-lounge; offered a few 'nice-little-place-you-have-here' type compliments; and explained why they'd called and would be calling again – one of them, certainly – at seven o'clock that evening.

'It was you, Mrs Daley, wasn't it, who got your husband to hand the rucksack in?'

'Yes – but he'd have done it himself anyway. Later on. I know he would.'

The shelves around the living area were lined with china ornaments of all shapes and sizes; and Morse walked over to the shelf above the electric fire, and carefully picked up the figure of a small dog, examining it briefly before replacing it on its former station.

'King Charles?'

Margaret Daley nodded. 'Cavalier King Charles. We had one – till last February. Mycroft. Lovely little dog – lovely face! We all had a good cry when the vet had to put him down. Not a very healthy breed, I'm afraid.'

'People living next to us have one of those,' ventured Lewis. 'Always at the vet. Got a medical history long as your arm.'

'Thank you, Lewis. I'm sure Mrs Daley isn't over-anxious to be reminded of a family bereavement—'

'Oh, it's all right! I quite like talking about him, really. We all – Philip and George – we all loved him. In fact he was about the only thing that'd get Philip out of bed sometimes.'

But Morse's attention appeared to have drifted far from dogs as he gazed through the french windows at the far end of the room, his eyes seemingly focused at some point towards the back of the garden – a garden just over the width of the house and stretching back about fifty feet to a wire fence at the bottom, separating the property from the open fields beyond. As with the patch of garden in the front, likewise here: George Daley, it had to be assumed, reckoned he did quite enough gardening in the course of earning his daily bread at Blenheim, and carried little if anything of his horticultural expertise into the rather neglected stretch of lawn which provided the immediate view from the rear of number 2.

'I don't believe it!' said Morse. 'Isn't that *Asphodelina lutea*?'

Mrs Daley walked over to the window.

'There!' pointed Morse. 'Those yellow things, just across the fence.'

'Buttercups!' said Lewis.

'You've, er, not got a pair of binoculars handy, Mrs Daley?'

'No – I – we haven't, I'm afraid.'

'Mind if we have a look?' asked Morse. 'Always contradicting me, my sergeant is!'

The three of them walked out through the kitchen door, past the (open) outhouse door, and on to the back lawn where the daisies and dandelions and broad-leaf plantain had been allowed a generous freedom of movement. Morse himself stepped up to

the fence, looking down at the ground around him; then, cursorily, at the yellow flowers he had spotted earlier, and which he
now agreed to be nothing rarer than buttercups. Mrs Daley
smiled vaguely at Lewis; but Lewis was now listening to Morse's
apparently aimless chatter with far greater interest.

'No compost heap?'

'No. George isn't much bothered with the garden here, as you
can see. Says he's got enough, you know . . .' She pointed vaguely
towards Blenheim, and led the way back in.

'How do you get rid of your rubbish then?'

'Sometimes we go down to the waste disposal with it. Or you
can buy those special bags from the council. We *used* to burn it,
but a couple of years ago we upset the neighbours – you know,
bits all over the washing and—'

'Probably against the bye-laws, too,' added Lewis; and for
once Morse appeared to appreciate the addendum.

It was Lewis too, as they were leaving, who spotted the rifle
amid the umbrellas, the walking sticks, and the warped squash
racket, in a stand just behind the front door.

'Does your husband do a bit of shooting?'

'Oh *that*! George occasionally . . . yes . . .'

Gently, for a second time, Lewis reminded her of the law's
demands: 'Ought to be under lock and key, that. Perhaps you'd
remind your husband, Mrs Daley.'

Margaret Daley watched them through the front window as they
walked away to their car. Just a bit of a stiff-shirt, the sergeant
had been, about their legal responsibilities. Whereas the inspector
– well, he'd seemed much nicer with his interest in dogs and
flowers and the decoration in the lounge – *her* decoration. Yet
during the last few minutes she'd begun to suspect her judgement a little, and she had the feeling that it would probably be
Morse who would be returning that evening. Not that there was
anything to worry about, really. Well, just the one thing, perhaps.

In spite of that day being Saturday – and the first of the holidays
– Mrs Julie Ireson, careers mistress at the Cherwell School,
Oxford, had been quite willing to meet Lewis just after lunch;
and Lewis was anxious to get the meeting over as soon as

possible, for he was desperately tired and had been only too glad to accept Morse's strict directive for a long rest – certainly for the remainder of the day, and perhaps for the next day, Sunday, too – unless there occurred any dramatic development.

She was waiting in the deserted car park when Lewis arrived, and immediately took him up to her first-floor study, its walls and shelves festooned with literature on nursing, secretarial courses, apprenticeship schemes, industrial training, FE's, polys, universities . . . For Lewis (whose only career advice had been his father's dictum that he could do worse than to keep his mouth mostly shut and his bowels always open), a school-based advice centre for pupils leaving school was an interesting novelty.

A buff-coloured folder containing the achievements of Philip Daley was on the table ready for him. Non-achievements rather. He was now just seventeen years old, and had officially abandoned any potential advancement into further education w.e.f. 7 July – the previous day. The school was prepared to be not over-pessimistic about some minor success in the five GCSE subjects in which, the previous term, he had tried (though apparently not over-hard) to satisfy his examiners: English; Technical Drawing; Geography; General Science; and Communication Studies. Over the years, however, the reports from his teachers, even in non-academic subjects, had exhibited a marked lack of enthusiasm about his attitude and progress. Yet until fairly recently he appeared not to have posed any great problem to the school community: limited, clearly, in intellectual prowess; limited too in most technical and vocational skills; in general about average.

Current educational philosophy (Lewis learned) encouraged a measure of self-evaluation, and amongst other documents in the folder was a sheet on which eighteen months previously, in his own handwriting, Philip had filled in a questionnaire about his six main 'Leisure Interests/Pastimes', in order of preference. The list read thus:

1   Football
2   Pop music
3   Photography
4   Pets
5   Motorbikes
6   TV

'He can spell OK,' commented Lewis.

'Difficult to misspell "pets", Sergeant.'

'Yes. But – well, "photography" . . .'

'Probably had to look it up in the dictionary.'

'You didn't like him?' said Lewis slowly.

'No, I'm afraid I didn't. I'm glad he's gone, if you must know.'

She was younger than Lewis had expected: perhaps more vulnerable too?

'Any particular reason?'

'Just general, really.'

'Well, thanks very much, Mrs Ireson. If I could take the folder?'

'Any particular reason you want to know about him?'

'No. Just general, really,' echoed Lewis.

He slept from 6.30 that evening through until almost ten the following morning. When he finally awoke, he learned there had been a telephone message the previous evening from Morse: on no account was he to come in to HQ that Sunday; it would be a good idea, though, to make sure his passport was in order.

Well, well!

CHAPTER TWENTY-NINE

Every roof is agreeable to the eye, until it is lifted; then we find tragedy and moaning women, and hard-eyed husbands
                    (Ralph Waldo Emerson, *Experience*)

IT WAS two minutes to seven by the Jaguar's fascia clock when Morse pulled up in the slip-road outside number 2 Blenheim Villas. He was fairly confident of his ground now, especially after reading through the folder that Lewis had left. Certain, of course, about the electric fire in the Daleys' main lounge; almost certain about the conversion of the old coal-house into a utility room, in which, as they'd walked out to the garden, he'd glimpsed the arrangement of washing-machine and tumble-drier on newly laid red tiles; not *quite* so certain about the treeless back garden though, for Morse was ridiculously proud about never having

been a boy scout, and his knowledge of camp-fires and cocoa-
barbecues, he had to admit, was almost nil.

For once he felt relieved to be on his own as he knocked at the
front door. The police as a whole were going through a tough
time in public esteem: allegations of corrupt officers, planted
evidence, improper procedures – such allegations had inevitably
created suspicion and some hostility. And – yes, Morse knew it –
he himself was on occasion tempted to overstep the procedural
boundaries a little – as shortly he would be doing again. It was a
bit like a darts player standing a few inches in front of the oche
as he threw for the treble-twenty. And Lewis would not have
brooked this; and would have told him so.

In the lounge, in a less than convivial atmosphere, the Daleys sat
side by side on the settee; and Morse, from the armchair opposite,
got down to business.

'You've managed to go through the statement again, Mr Daley?'

'You don't mind the wife being here?'

'I'd prefer it, really,' said Morse innocently.

'Like I said, there's nothin' as I can add.'

'Fine.' Morse reached across and took the now rather grimy
photocopy and looked through it slowly himself before lifting his
eyes to George Daley.

'Let me be honest with you, sir. It's this camera business that's
worrying me.'

'Wha' abou' i'?' (If the dietitian sometimes had paid over-nice
attention to her dental consonants, Daley himself almost
invariably ignored them.)

Morse moved obliquely into the attack: 'You interested in
photography yourself?'

'Me? Not much, no.'

'You, Mrs Daley?'

She shook her head.

'Your son Philip is though?'

'Yeah, well, he's got fairly interested in it recently, hasn't he,
luv?' Daley turned to his wife, who nodded vaguely, her eyes on
Morse continuously.

'Bit more than "recently", perhaps?' Morse suggested. 'He put
it down on his list of hobbies at school last year – early last year
– a few months before you found the camera.'

'Yeah, well, like I said, we was going to get him one anyway, for his birthday. Wasn't we, luv?' Again, apart from a scarce-discernible nod, Margaret Daley appeared reluctant verbally to confirm such an innocent statement.

'But you've never had a camera yourself, you say.'

'Correck!'

'How did you know the film in the camera was finished then?'

'Well, you know, it's the numbers, innit? It tells you, like, when you've got to the finish.'

'When it reads "ten", you mean?'

'Somethin' like that.'

'What if there are twelve exposures on the reel?'

'Dunno.' Daley appeared not to be at all flustered by the slightly more aggressive tone of the question. 'It was probably Philip as said so.' Again he turned to his wife. 'Was his ten or twelve, luv? D'you remember?'

Morse pounced on the answer: 'So he had a camera *before*?'

'Yeah, well, just an el cheapo thing we bought him—'

'From Spain.' (Mrs Daley had broken her duck.)

'Would you know how to get the film *out* of a camera, Mr Daley?'

'Well, not unless, you know—'

'But it says here' – Morse looked down at the statement again – 'it says here that you burnt the film.'

'Yeah, well, that's right, isn't it, luv? We shoulda kept it, I know. Still, as I said – well, we all do things a bit wrong sometimes, don't we? And we said we was sorry about everything, didn't we, luv?'

Morse was beginning to realize that the last three words, with their appropriate variants, were a rhetorical refrain only, and were not intended to elicit any specific response.

'Where did you burn it?' asked Morse quietly.

'Dunno. Don't remember. Just chucked it on the fire, I suppose.' Daley gestured vaguely with his right hand.

'*That's* electric,' said Morse, pointing to the fireplace.

'And we got a grate for a coal-fire next door. All right?' Daley's voice was at last beginning to show signs of some exasperation.

'Did you have a fire that day?'

'How the 'ell am I supposed to remember *that*?'

'Do *you* remember, Mrs Daley?'

She shook her head. 'More than a year ago, isn't it? Could you remember that far back?'

'I've not had a coal-fire in my flat for fifteen years, Mrs Daley. So I could remember, yes.'

'Well, I'm sorry,' she said quietly, 'I can't.'

'Did you know that the temperature in Oxfordshire that day was seventy-four degrees Fahrenheit?' (Morse thought he'd got it vaguely correct.)

'Wha'! At ten o'clock at night?' Clearly Daley was losing his composure, and Morse took full advantage.

'Where do you *keep* your coal? Your coal-house has been converted to a utility-room – your wife showed—'

'If it wasn't here – all right, it wasn't *here*. Musta been in the garden, mustn't it?'

'What do you burn in the garden?'

'What do I burn? What do I *burn*? I burn bloody twigs and leaves and—'

'You haven't got any trees. And even if you had, July's a bit early for leaves.'

'Oh, for Christ's sake! Look—'

'No!' Suddenly Morse's voice was harsh and authoritative. '*You* look, Mr Daley. If you do burn your rubbish out there in the garden, come and show me where!' All pretence was now dropped as Morse continued: 'And if you make up any more lies about *that*, I'll bring a forensic team in and have 'em cart half your lawn away!'

They sat silently, the Daleys, neither looking at the other.

'Was it you who got the film developed, Mr Daley? Or was it your son?' Morse's voice was quiet once more.

'It was Philip,' said Margaret Daley, finally, now assuming control. 'He was friendly with this boy at school whose father was a photographer and had a dark-room an' all that, and they developed 'em there, I think.' Her voice sounded to Morse as if it had suddenly lost its veneer of comparative refinement, and he began to wonder which of the couple was potentially the bigger liar.

'You must tell me what those photographs were.' Morse made an effort to conceal the urgency of his request, but his voice betrayed the fear that all might well be lost.

'He never kept 'em as far as I know—' began Daley.

But his wife interrupted him: 'There were only six or seven out of the twelve that came out. There was some photos of birds – one was a pinkish sort of bird with a black tail—'

'Jay!' said Daley.

'—and there was two of a man, youngish man – probably her boyfriend. But the others, as I say . . . you know, they just didn't . . . come out.'

'I must have them,' said Morse simply, inexorably almost.

'He's chucked 'em out, surely,' observed Daley. 'What the 'ell would he keep 'em for?'

'I must have them,' repeated Morse.

'Christ! Don't you understand? I never even *saw* 'em!'

'Where is your son?'

Husband and wife looked at each other, and husband spoke: 'Gone into Oxford, I should think – Sa'day night . . .'

'Take me to his room, will you?'

'We bloody *won't*!' growled Daley. 'If you wanna look round 'ere, Inspector, you just bring a search-warrant, OK?'

'I don't need one. You've got a rifle behind the front door, Mr Daley, and it's odds-on you've got a box of cartridges somewhere lying around. All I need to do to take your floorboards up if necessary is to quote to you – just *quote*, mind – Statutory Instrument 1991 No. 1531. Do you understand? The pair of you? That's *my* only legal obligation.'

But Morse had no further need for inaccurate improvisations regarding the recently enacted legislation on explosives. Margaret Daley rose to her feet and made to leave the lounge.

'You won't search Philip's room with *my* permission, Inspector. But if he has kept them photos I reckon I just might know . . .'

Morse heard her on the stairs, his heart knocking against his ribs: Please! Please! Please!

No word passed between the two men seated opposite each other as they heard the creak of floorboards in the upstairs rooms. Nor was much said when Margaret Daley returned some minutes later holding seven coloured prints which she handed to Morse – wordlessly.

'Thank you. No others?'

She shook her head.

After Morse was gone, Margaret Daley went into the kitchen where she turned on the kettle and spooned some instant Nescafé into a mug.

'I suppose you're out boozing,' she said tonelessly, as her husband came in.

'Why the 'ell didn't you tell *me* about them photos?'

'Shut up!' She spat out the two words viciously and turned towards him.

'Where the 'ell did you find 'em, you—'

'Shut up! And listen, will you? If you must know, I've been looking in his room, George Daley, because if we don't soon get to know what's goin' on and do something about it he'll be in bloody jail or something, that's why! See? There were twelve photos, five of the girl—'

'You stupid bitch!'

'Listen!' she shrieked. 'I never gave him *them*! I've hidden 'em; and now I'm gonna get rid of 'em; and I'm not gonna show 'em to you! You don't give a sod about anything these days, anyway!'

Daley walked tight-lipped to the door. 'Stop moaning, you miserable cunt!'

His wife had taken a large pair of kitchen scissors from a drawer. 'Don't you ever talk to me like that again, George Daley!' Her voice was trembling with fury.

A few minutes after hearing the front door slam behind him, she went upstairs to their bedroom and took the five photographs out of her underwear drawer. All of them were of Karin Eriksson, nakedly or semi-nakedly lying in lewdly provocative postures. She could only guess how often her son had ogled these and similar photographs which he kept in a box at the back of his wardrobe, and which she had discovered when spring-cleaning his room the previous April. She took the five photographs to the loo, where standing over the pan she sliced strip after strip from the face, the shoulders, the breasts, the thighs, and the legs of the beautiful Karin Eriksson, intermittently flushing the celluloid slivers down into the Begbroke sewers.

CHAPTER THIRTY

A man's bed is his resting-place, but a woman's is often her rack

(James Thurber, *Further Fables for Our Time*)

THE AMBULANCE, its blue light flashing, its siren wailing, finally pulled into the Casualty Bay of the John Radcliffe 2 Hospital at

9.15 p.m. The grey face of the man hurriedly carried through the automatic doors on a stretcher – the forehead clammy with sweat, the breathing shallow and laboured – had told its immediate story to the red-belted senior nurse, who straightaway rang through to the medical houseman on duty, before joining one of her colleagues in taking off the man's clothes and fastening a hospital gown around his overweight frame. A series of hurried readings – of electrocardiograph, blood pressure, chest X-ray – soon confirmed the fairly obvious: a massive coronary thrombosis, so very nearly an immediately fatal one.

Two porters pushed the trolley swiftly along the corridors to the Coronary Care Unit, where they lifted the heavy man on to a bed; around which curtains were quickly drawn, and five leads connected to the man's chest and linked to monitors, which now gave continuous details of heart rhythm, blood pressure, and pulse rate, on the screen beside the bed. A very pretty, slightly plump young nurse looked on as the houseman administered a morphine injection.

'Much hope?' she queried quietly a minute or two later, as the two of them stood at the central desk, where the VDU monitors from each of the small ward's six beds were banked.

'You never know, but . . .'

'Quite a well-known man, isn't he?'

'Taught me as a student. Well, I went to his lectures. Blood – that was his speciality, really; and he was a world authority on VD! Police get him in all the time, too – PMs, that sort of thing.'

The nurse looked at the monitor: the readings seemed significantly steadier now, and she found herself earnestly willing the old boy to survive.

'Give him some Frusemide, Nurse – as much as you like. I'm worried about all that fluid on his lungs.'

The houseman watched the monitor for another few minutes, then went over to the bed again, where the nurse had just placed a jug of water and a glass on the bedside locker.

After the houseman had left, Nurse Shelick remained beside the sick man's bed and looked down at him with that passionate intensity she invariably felt for her patients. Although still in her twenties, she was really one of that old-fashioned school who believed that whatever the advantages of hyper-technology, the virtues of simple human *nursing* were almost as indispensable.

She laid the palm of her right hand across the wet, cold brow, and for the next few minutes wiped his face gently with a warm, damp flannel – suddenly aware that his eyes had opened and were looking up at her.

'Nurse?'

'I can hear you – yes?'

'Will you . . . will you . . . get in touch . . . with someone for me?'

'Of course! Of course!' She bent her right ear towards the purple lips, but without quite making out what he was saying.

'Pardon?'

'Morse!'

'I'm sorry. Please say it again. I'm not quite sure—'

'Morse!'

'I still . . . I'm sorry . . . please.'

But the eyes of the man who lay upon the bed had closed again, and there was no answer to her gently repeated queries.

The time was 11.15 p.m.

The head forester's beautiful young wife was also in bed at this time. She too lay supine; and still lay supine, wakeful and waiting, until finally at 11.35 p.m. she heard the front door being opened, then locked, then bolted.

In spite of four pints of Burton ale and two whiskies at the White Hart, David Michaels knew that he was very sober; far *too* sober – for there was something sadly amiss when a man couldn't get drunk, he knew that. After cleaning his teeth, he went into the bedroom, shed his clothes swiftly, and slid under the light-weight duvet. She always slept naked, and after their marriage he had followed her example – often finding himself erotically aroused not so much by the fact or the sight of her nakedness as by the very thought of it. And now as he moved in beside her in the darkened room, he knew that she was suddenly and wonder-fully necessary once more. He turned his body towards her and his right hand reached gently across her and fondled her breast. But with her own right hand she grasped his wrist, and with surprising strength moved it from her.

'No. Not tonight.'

'Is there something wrong?'

'I just don't want you tonight – can't you understand?'

'I think I understand all right.' Michaels' voice was dull and he turned to lie on his back.

'Why did you have to tell them?' she asked fiercely.

'Because I know the bloody place better than anyone else, that's why!'

'But don't you realize—?'

'I had to tell them something. God! Don't you see that? I didn't *know*, did I?'

She sat up in bed and leaned towards him, her right hand on the pillow beside his head. 'But they'll think *you* did it, David.'

'Don't be so stupid! I wouldn't be giving them information if it was *me*. Can't you see that? I'm the very *last* person they're going to suspect. But if I hadn't agreed to help . . .'

She said nothing more; and he wondered for a while whether it would be sensible to go down and make a couple of cups of piping-hot coffee for them, and then perhaps turn on the bedside lamp and look upon his lovely bride. But there was no need. Seemingly Cathy Michaels had accepted the logic of his words, and her mind was more at ease; for she now lay down again and turned towards him, and soon he felt the silky caress of her inner thigh against him.

CHAPTER THIRTY-ONE

The background reveals the true being of the man or thing. If I do not possess the background, I make the man transparent, the thing transparent

(Juan Jiménez, *Selected Writings*)

IT WAS rather like trying to see the answer to a tricky crossword clue, Morse decided, as at 11 o'clock that same night he sat in his North Oxford lounge, topping up his earlier libations with a few fingers of Glenfiddich, and looking yet again at the photographs that Margaret Daley had given him. The closer he got to the clue – the closer he got to the photograph – the less in fact he saw. It was necessary to stand away, to see things in perspective, to look *synoptically* at the problem.

As he had just considered the photographs, it was the man

himself, pictured in two of them, who had monopolized his interest: a small- to medium-sized man, in his late twenties perhaps, with longish fair hair; a man wearing a white T-shirt and faded-blue denims, with a sunburnt complexion and the suggestion of a day's growth of stubble around his jowls. But the detail was not of sufficient definition or fidelity for him to be wholly sure, as if the cameraman himself – or almost certainly the camera*woman* – had scarcely the experience needed to cope with the problems of the bright sunlight that so obviously pervaded the garden in which the snaps had been taken. But although Morse knew little (well, nothing) about photography, he was beginning to suspect that there might be slightly more competence in the arrangement of the 'subject' in relation to the 'background' than he'd originally supposed.

The man had been photographed at an oblique angle across the garden, with a house clearly shown to the left of the figure: a three-storey, rosy-bricked house, with a french window on the ground floor, slightly ajar, with another window immediately above it, and one above that, all painted white, and with a black drain-pipe reaching down to ground level; and to the figure's right a smallish tree of some sort with large curly leaves, unidentifiable to Morse who knew little (well, nothing) of such things. But there was even more to learn. Clearly the photographer had been kneeling down, or sitting down, to take the shots, for the man's head showed some way above the line of the garden wall, which rose clearly behind the shrubs and foliage. Even more to learn though! – Morse decided, as he studied the background yet again. The roof-line of the house stretched away in a slightly convex curve (as it appeared) above the man's head, and then was cut off in the middle of the top of the photograph; but not before suggesting that the house could be one of a terrace, perhaps?

It was amazing, Morse told himself, how much he'd managed to miss when first he'd considered the photographs; and with the strange conviction that there would certainly be a final solution to the mystery if only he looked at it long enough, he stared and stared until he thought he could see two houses instead of one, although whether this was an advance in insight or in inebriation, he couldn't be sure. So what, though? So what if it *were* part of a terrace? The number of three-storeyed, red-bricked terraces in the UK was myriad; and just in Oxford alone it must be . . . Morse shook his head and shook his thoughts. No. It was going to be almost impossible to locate the house and the garden; so the only thing left was the young man's face, really.

Or was it . . .?

Suddenly an exciting thought occurred to him. A straight line could be seen as a curve, so he'd been supposing, either because the camera had looked at it in a particular way, or because in a larger view the line began to bend in a sort of rounded perspective. But such explanations were surely far less probable than the utterly obvious fact that was staring him, literally *staring* him, in the face; the fact that the roof-line of the terraced houses which formed the backdrop here might *look* as if it was curving in a convex fashion for one supremely simple and wholly adequate reason: it *was* curving!

Could it be . . .? Could it be . . .? Did Morse, even now, think he *knew* where it was? He felt the old familiar tingle across his shoulders, and the hairs at the nape of his neck were suddenly erect. He rose from his armchair and went over to his bookshelves, whence he extracted the thick Penguin *Oxfordshire*, in the 'Buildings of England' series; and his right hand shook slightly as he traced 'Park Town' in the index – page 320. On which page he read:

Laid out in 1853–5. This was North Oxford's first development, built on land originally intended for a workhouse. The trust created for its developments promised elegant villas and [Morse's eyes snatched at the next word] terraces. What it became is this: two crescents [the blood tingled again] N and S of an elliptical central garden, with stone frontages in late-classical style, and bricked at the rear [!] with attractive french windows [!] leading on to small walled [!] gardens.

Phew!

Ye gods!

Bloody hell!

If he were so disposed (Morse knew) he could go and identify the house at that very moment! It *must* be in Crescent S – the sunshine would rule out Crescent N; and with that tree with its big, furry, splayed (beautiful!) leaves; and the drain-pipe, and the windows, and the wall, and the grass . . .

As he sat down again in the black leather settee, Morse's face was betraying a high degree of self-gratification – when the phone rang. It was now a quarter to midnight, and the voice was a woman's – husky, slightly timid, north-country.

She identified herself as Dr Laura Hobson, one of the new girls in the path labs; one of Max's protegées. She had been working late with Max – on Morse's bones – when just before 9 p.m. she'd found him lying there on the floor of the lab. Heart attack – severe heart attack. He'd been unconscious most of the time since they'd got him to hospital ... but the sister had rung her (Dr Hobson) and the possibility was that he (Max) had been trying to ask for him (Morse) – if he (Morse) knew what she (Dr Hobson) was trying to say ...

Oh dear!

'Which ward's he in?'

'Coronary Care Unit—'

'Yes! But *where*?'

'The JR2. But it's no good trying to see him now. Sister says—'

'You want to bloody *bet*?' snapped Morse.

'Please! There's something else, Inspector. He'd been working on the bones all day and—'

'Bugger the bones!'

'But—'

'Look. I'm most grateful to you, Dr, er ...'

'Hobson.'

'... but please forgive me if I hang up. You see,' suddenly Morse's voice was more controlled, more gentle, 'Max and I – well, we ... let's say we don't either of us have too many friends and ... I want to see the old sod again if he's going to die.'

But Morse had already put down the phone, and Dr Hobson heard nothing of the last five words. She too felt very sad. She had known Max for only six weeks. Yet there was something basically kindly about the man; and only a week before she'd had a mildly erotic dream about that ugly, brusque, and arrogant pathologist.

At least for the present, however, the pathologist appeared to have rallied quite remarkably, for he was talking to Nurse Shelick rationally, albeit slowly and quietly, when he learned of his visitor; and threatened to strike the houseman off the medical register unless Morse (for such it was) were admitted forthwith.

But one patient newly admitted to the JR2 had not rallied that night. Marion Bridewell, an eight-year-old little West Indian girl, had been knocked down by a stolen car on the Broadmoor Lea estate at seven o'clock that evening. She had been terribly badly injured.

She died just after midnight.

CHAPTER THIRTY-TWO

And Apollo gave Sarpedon dead to be borne by swift companions, to Death and Sleep, twin brethren, who bore him through the air to Lycia, that broad and pleasant land

(Homer, *Iliad*, xvi)

'How ARE you, old friend?' asked Morse with spurious cheerfulness.

'Dying.'

'You once told me that we're all moving towards death – at the standard rate of twenty-four hours *per diem*.'

'I was always accurate, Morse. Not very imaginative, agreed; but always accurate.'

'You've still not told me how—'

'Somebody said . . . somebody said, "Nothing matters very much . . . and in the end nothing really matters at all".'

'Lord Balfour.'

'You always were a knowledgeable sod.'

'Dr Hobson rang—'

'Ah! The fair Laura. Don't know how men ever keep their hands off her.'

'Perhaps they don't.'

'I was thinking of her just now . . . Still have any erotic daydreams yourself, Morse?'

'Most of the time.'

'Be nice – be nice if she was thinking of me . . .'

'You never know.'

Max smiled his awkward, melancholy smile, but his face looked tired and ashen-grey. 'You're right. Life's full of uncertainties. Have I ever told you that before?'

'Many a time.'

'I've always . . . I've always been interested in death, you know. Sort of hobby of mine, really. Even when I was a lad . . .'

'I know. Look, Max, they said they'd only let me in to see you if—'

'No knickers – you know that?'

'Pardon? Pardon, Max?'

'The bones, Morse!'

'What about the bones?'

'Do you believe in God?'

'Huh! Most of the *bishops* don't believe in God.'

'And you used to accuse *me* of never answering questions!'

Morse hesitated. Then he looked down at his old friend and answered him: 'No.'

Paradoxically perhaps, the police surgeon appeared comforted by the sincerity of the firm monosyllable; but his thoughts were now stuttering their way around a discontinuous circuit.

'You *surprised*, Morse?'

'Pardon?'

'You *were*, weren't you? Admit it!'

'Surprised?'

'The bones! Not a *woman's* bones, were they?'

Morse felt his heart pounding insistently somewhere – everywhere – in his body; felt the blood sinking down from his shoulders, past his heart, past his loins. *Not a woman's bones* – is that what Max had just said?

It had taken the hump-backed surgeon some considerable time to say his say; and feeling a tap on his shoulder, Morse turned to find Nurse Shelick standing behind him. 'Please!' her lips mouthed, as she looked anxiously down at the tired and intermittently closing eyes.

But before he left Morse leaned forward and whispered in the dying man's ear: 'I'll bring us a bottle of malt in the morning, Max, and we'll have a wee drop together, my old friend. So keep a hold on things – please keep a hold on things! . . . Just for me!'

It would have been a joy for Morse had he seen the transient gleam in Max's eyes. But the surgeon's face had turned away from him, towards the recently painted, pale green wall of the CCU. And he seemed to be asleep.

Maximilian Theodore Siegfried de Bryn (his middle names a surprise even to his few friends) surrendered to an almost totally welcome weariness two hours after Chief Inspector Morse had left; and finally loosed his grip on the hooks just after three o'clock that morning. He had bequeathed his mortal remains to the Medical Research Foundation at the JR2. He had earnestly wished it so. And it would be done.

Many had known Max, even if few had understood his strange ways. And many were to feel a fleeting sadness at his death. But he had (as we have seen) a few friends only. And there was only one man who had wept silently when the call had been received in his office in Thames Valley Police HQ at Kidlington at 9 a.m. on Sunday, 19 July 1992.

CHAPTER THIRTY-THREE

What is a committee? A group of the unwilling,
picked from the unfit, to do the unnecessary
(Richard Harkness, *New York Herald Tribune*, 15 June 1960)

SUNDAY is not a good day on which to do business. Or to expect others to be at work – or even to be out of bed. But Dr Laura Hobson was out of bed fairly early that morning, and awaiting Morse at the (deserted) William Dunn School of Pathology building at 9.30 a.m.

'Hello.'

'Hello.'

'You're Inspector Morse?'

'Chief Inspector Morse.'

'Sorry!'

'And you're Dr Hobson?'

'I am she.'

Morse smiled wanly. 'I applaud your grammar, my dear.'

'I am not your "dear". You must forgive me for being so blunt: but I'm no one's "luv" or "dear" or "darling" or "sweetheart".

I've got a name. If I'm at work I prefer to be called Dr Hobson; and if I let my hair down over a drink I have a Christian name: Laura. That's my little speech, Chief Inspector! You're not the only one who's heard it.' She was smiling sufficiently as she spoke though, showing small, very white teeth – a woman in her early thirties, fair-complexioned, with a pair of disproportionately large spectacles on her pretty nose; a smallish woman, about 5 foot 4 inches. But it was her voice which interested Morse: the broad north-country vowels in "luv" and "blunt"; the pleasing nairm she had – and perhaps the not unpleasant prospect of meeting her sometime orver a drink with her hair doon . . .

They sat on a pair of high stools in a room that reminded Morse of his hated physics lab at school, and she told him of the simple yet quite extraordinary findings. The report on which Max had been working, though incomplete, was incontestable: the bones discovered in Wytham Woods were those of an adult male, Caucasian, about 5 foot 6 inches in height, slimly built, brachycephalic, fair-haired . . .

But Morse's mind had already leaped many furlongs ahead of the field. He'd been sure that the bones had been those of Karin Eriksson. All right, he'd been wrong. But now he *knew* whose bones they were – for the face of the man in the photograph was staring back at him, unmistakably. He asked only for a photocopy of Dr Hobson's brief, preliminary report, and rose to go.

The pair of them walked to the locked outer door in silence, for the death of Max was heavy on her mind too.

'You knew him well, didn't you?'

Morse nodded.

'I feel so sad,' she said simply.

Morse nodded again. ' "The cart is shaken all to pieces, and the rugged road is at its end." '

She watched him, the slightly balding grey-haired man, as he stood for a few seconds beside his Jaguar. He held the photocopied report in his left hand, and raised it a few inches in farewell. She relocked the door, and walked thoughtfully back to the lab.

*

Morse wondered about driving up to the JR2, but decided against it. There was little time anyway. An urgent meeting of senior police officers had been summoned for 11 a.m. at the HQ building, and in any case there was nothing he could do. He drove along Parks Road, past Keble College, and then turned right into the Banbury Road. He had a few minutes to spare, and he took the second right turn now, and drove on slowly into Park Town, driving clockwise along the North Crescent, and along the South Crescent ... There would be little chance of doing much that day though, and in any case it would be better to postpone things for twenty-four hours or so.

Senior personnel from both the City and the County Forces were meeting at a time of considerable public disquiet – and criticism. Hitherto the impression had been abroad that known ringleaders were joy-riding and shop-ramming almost with impunity; and that the police were doing little to check the teenage tearaways who were terrifying many sections of the community on the Broadmoor Lea estate. There was little justification for such a view, since the police were continually finding themselves hamstrung by the refusal of the local inhabitants to come out and name names and co-operate in seeking to clean up their crime-ridden neighbourhood. But the death of Marion Bridewell had changed all that.

During this Sunday, 19 July, major decisions were taken, and their immediate implementation planned: a string of arrests would be made in a co-ordinated swoop the following morning, with special sittings of magistrates' courts scheduled for the following two evenings; council workmen would be sent in during the next few days to erect bollards and to construct sleeping-policeman humps across selected streets; police presence on the estate during the next week would be doubled; and a liaison committee of police officers, local head-teachers, social workers, and church ministers would be constituted forthwith.

It was a long and sometimes ill-humoured meeting; and Morse himself contributed little of any importance to the deliberations, for in truth his mind was distanced, and only once had his interest been fully engaged. It had been Strange's inveterate cynicism about committees which had occasioned the little contretemps:

'Give us a week or two at this rate,' he growled, 'and we'll have a standing committee, a steering committee, an *ad hoc* committee – every committee you can put a name to. What we should be doing is hitting 'em where it hurts. *Fining* 'em; fining their dads; docking it off their dads' wages. That's what I reckon!'

The Chief Constable had agreed quietly. 'Splendid idea – and the new legislation, I think, is going to be a big help to us. But there's just one snag, isn't there? You see, a good many of these young lads haven't *got* any fathers, Superintendent.'

Strange had looked disconcerted then.

And Morse had smiled his second smile of the day.

CHAPTER THIRTY-FOUR

The newly arrived resident in North Oxford is likely to find that although his next-door neighbour has a first-class degree from some prestigious university this man is not quite so clever as his wife

(*Country Living*, January 1992)

MORSE was on his own when finally, in mid-morning the following day, he drove down to Park Town, this time again slowly circling the two crescents on either side of the elliptical central garden, well stocked with trees and flowering shrubs. There were plenty of parking spaces, and after his second circuit he pulled in the Jaguar along the south side and walked past the fronts of the dozen Italianate properties which comprised the attractive stone-faced terrace. At the eastern end he turned down an alleyway, and then into the lane, about three yards wide, which ran behind the properties. To his right the continuous brick wall which protected the small back gardens was only about five feet in height, and he realized that it would not even be necessary to enter any of the gardens to find the one he was looking for. It was all childishly easy – no Holmesian intellect needed here; indeed a brief Watsonian reconnoitre would have established the spot almost immediately. Thus it was that after only a couple of minutes Morse found himself leaning over the curved coping-stones of the westernmost property, and finding the details on his photographs so easily matchable here: the configuration of the black drain-pipes, the horizontal TV aerial, and then, crucially, the tree upon whose lower bough a child's red swing was now affixed. At the left of the garden, as Morse observed it, was a wooden garden seat, its slats disintegrating; and he felt thrillingly certain that it was from this seat, in this very garden, that someone – and most probably Karin Eriksson herself – had taken the two photographs of the fair-headed, bracycephalic, slimly built . . . what else had Dr Hobson said? He couldn't remember. And it didn't matter. Not at all.

He walked to the imposing front door of the end property, designated 'Seckham Villa' by a small plaque on the right-hand wall of the porch; and below it, three bells: second floor Dr S. Levi; first floor Ms Jennifer Coombs; ground floor Dr Alasdair McBryde. An area clearly where D.Phils and Ph.Ds proliferated. He rang the bottom bell.

The door was opened by a tallish, heavily bearded man in his mid-thirties, who studied Morse's authorization cautiously before answering any questions. He was over from Ostrylia (he said) with his wife, to pursue some research project in micro-biology; they had been in the flat since the previous August, and would be returning home in two weeks' time; he'd learned of the property from a friend in Mansfield College who had been keeping an eye open for suitable accommodation the previous summer.

The previous August . . .

Was this to be Morse's lucky day?

'Did you know the people – did you *meet* the people who were here before you?'

'Fried not,' said the Australian.

'Can I – have a quick look inside?'

Rather unenthusiastically, as it seemed, McBryde led the way into the lounge, where Morse looked around the rather splendid, high-ceilinged room, and tried to attune his senses to the vaguest vibrations. Without success. It was only when he looked out through the french window at the sunlit patch of lawn that he felt a frisson of excitement: a dark-haired little girl in a pink dress was swinging idly to and fro beneath the tree, her white ankle-socked feet just reaching the ground.

'Your daughter, sir?'

'Yeah. You got any kids yourself, Inspector?'

Morse shook his head. 'Just one more thing, sir. Have you got your book, you know, your rent-book or whatever handy? It's important I get in touch with the, er, people who were here just before you last year . . .'

McBryde stepped over to an escritoire beside the french window and found his Property Payment book, the legend 'Finders Keepers' on the cover.

'I'm not in arrears,' said McBryde with the suggestion of his first smile.

'So I see. And I'm not a bailiff, sir,' said Morse, handing back the book.

The two men walked back towards the entrance, and McBryde knocked very gently on the door to his right, and put his ear to the panel.

'Darling? Darling?'

But there was no reply.

At the front door Morse asked his last question.

'Finders Keepers – that's the Banbury Road office, is it?'

'Yeah. You off there now?'

'I think I'll drop in straightaway, yes.'

'Is your car parked here?'

Morse pointed to the Jaguar.

'Well, I should leave it here, if I were you. Only five minutes' walk, if that – and you'll never park in North Parade.'

Morse nodded. Good idea. And the Rose and Crown was just along in North Parade.

Before leaving Park Town however, Morse strolled across into the central oval-shaped garden separating the Crescents, where he read the only notice he could find, fixed to the trunk of a cedar tree:

THIS GARDEN, LAID OUT CIRCA 1850, IS MAINTAINED BY
THE RESIDENTS FOR PLEASURE AND PEACE. PLEASE
RESPECT ITS AMENITIES. NO DOGS, BICYCLES, BALL
GAMES, OR TRANSISTORS.

For a few minutes Morse sat on one of the wooden seats, where someone had obviously not respected the amenities, for an oblong plate, doubtless commemorating the name of a former inhabitant, had been recently prised from the back. It was a restful spot though, and Morse now walked slowly round its periphery, his mind half on Max's death, half on the photographs taken in the back garden of the ground-floor flat at Seckham Villa.

As he turned at the western edge of the garden, he realized that this same Seckham Villa was immediately across the road from him, with the maroon Jaguar parked just to the left of it. And as once again he admired the attractive frontages there, he suspected perhaps that a heavily bearded face had suddenly pulled itself back behind the rather dingy curtains in the front room of Seckham Villa, where Mrs Something McBryde lay suffering from goodness knows what. Was her husband slightly more inquisitive than he'd appeared to be? Or was it the Jaguar – which often attracted some interested glances?

Thoughtfully Morse walked out of Park Town, then left into the Banbury Road. Finders Keepers was very close. So was North Parade. So was the Rose and Crown.

CHAPTER THIRTY-FIVE

Doing business without advertising is like winking at a girl in the dark. You know what you are doing, but nobody else does
(Stewart Henderson Britt, *New York Herald Tribune*, 30 October 1956)

AFTER two pints of cask-conditioned ale in the Rose and Crown, Morse walked the short distance to Finders Keepers, where he was soon ushered through the outer office, past two young ladies busy with their VDUs, and into the inner sanctum of Mr Martin Buckby, the dark, smartly suited manager of Property Letting Services. It was fairly close to lunch-time, but the manager would be only too glad to help – of course he would.

Yes, his department was responsible for letting a good many of the Park Town properties, most of which had been converted from single homes into two, sometimes three, flats and were more often than not let out to graduates, occasionally to students. Naturally the accommodation varied, but some of the flats, especially those on the ground floor – or first floor, as some of them called it – were roomy, stylish, and well maintained. The letting year usually divided itself into two main periods: October to June, covering the academic year at Oxford University; and then June/July to the end of September, when very frequently various overseas tenants were interested in short-term leases.

Advertisements for the availability of such accommodation were regularly placed in *The Oxford Times*; and occasionally in *Property Weekly*. But only advertised once, for the flats were almost invariably snapped up straightaway. Such adverts gave a brief description of the property available, and the price asked: about £200–£250 a week for a short-term let (at current rates) and slightly less, proportionately, for a long-term let. Business, in the first instance, was usually conducted by phone, often through agents; and someone – either the client himself or a representative of an agency – would go along to view the property ('Very important, Inspector!') before the paperwork was completed, either there in the firm's offices or, increasingly now, directly by fax interchange with countries overseas. A deposit would be lodged, a tenancy agreement signed, a reference given – that was how it worked. There was no *guarantee* of bona fides, of course, and basically one had to rely on gut-reaction; but the firm experienced very few problems, really. When the client was due to move in, a representative would go along to open the property, hand over keys, explain the workings of gas, electricity, stop-cocks, central heating, fuses, thermostats, everything, and to give the client a full inventory of the property's effects – this inventory to be checked and returned within seven days so that there could be no subsequent arguments about the complement of fish-knives or feather pillows. The system worked well. The only example of odd behaviour over the previous year, for example, had been the overnight disappearance of a South American gentleman who had taken his key with him – and absolutely nothing else. And since, as with all short-term lets, the whole of the rental was paid in advance, as well as an extra deposit of £500, no harm had been done there – apart from the need to change the lock on the front door and to get a further clutch of keys cut.

'Did you report that to the police, sir?'

'No. Should I have done?'

Morse shrugged.

He had a good grasp now of the letting procedure; yet his mind was always happier (he explained) with specific illustrations than with generalities; and if it were proper for him to ask, for example, what Dr McBryde was paying for the ground-floor flat at Seckham Villa . . .?

Buckby found a green folder in the filing cabinet behind him and quickly looked through it. 'Thirteen hundred pounds per month.'

'Phew! Bit steep, isn't it?'

'It's the going rate – and it's a lovely flat, isn't it? One of the best in the whole crescent.' Buckby picked out a sheet from the folder and read the specification aloud.

But Morse was paying scant attention to him. After all, that was the manager's job, wasn't it? To make the most of what Morse had seen with his own eyes as a pretty limited bit of Lebensraum, especially for a married couple with one infant – at least one infant.

'Didn't you just say that the maximum for a short-term let was two hundred and fifty pounds a week?'

Buckby grinned. 'Not for *that* place – well, you've seen it. And what makes you think it's a *short*-term let, Inspector?'

The blood was tingling at the back of Morse's neck, and subliminally some of the specifications that Buckby had recited were beginning to register in his brain. He reached over and picked up the sheet.

Hall, living room, separate dining room, well-fitted kitchen, two bedrooms, studio/study, bathroom, full gas CH, small walled garden

Two bedrooms . . . and a sick wife sleeping in one of them . . . studio . . . and a little girl sitting on a swing . . . God! Morse shook his head in disbelief at his own idiocy.

'I really came to ask you, sir, if you had any record of who was living in that property last July. But I think – I *think* – you're going to tell me that it was Dr Alasdair McBryde; that he hasn't got a wife; that the people upstairs have got a little dark-haired daughter; that the fellow probably hails from Malta—'

'Gibraltar, actually.'

'You've got some spare keys, sir?' asked Morse, almost despairingly.

In front of Seckham Villa the Jaguar sat undisturbed; but inside there were to be no further sightings of Dr McBryde. Yet the little girl still sat on the swing, gently stroking her dolly's hair, and Morse unlocked the french window and walked over the grass towards her.

'What's your name?'

'My name's Lucy and my dolly's name's Amanda.'

'Do you live here, Lucy?'

'Yes. Mummy and Daddy live up there.' Her bright eyes lifted to the top rear window.

'Pretty dolly,' said Morse.

'Would you like to hold her?'

'I would, yes – but I've got a lot of things to do just for the moment.'

Inside his brain he could hear a voice shouting, 'Help, Lewis!' and he turned back into the house and wondered where on earth to start.

CHAPTER THIRTY-SIX

Nine tenths of the appeal of pornography is due to the indecent
feelings concerning sex which moralists inculcate in the young;
the other tenth is physiological, and will occur in one way or
another whatever the state of the law may be

(Bertrand Russell, *Marriage and Morals*)

LEWIS arrived at Seckham Villa at 2.15 that afternoon, bringing with him the early edition of *The Oxford Mail*, in which many column-inches were devoted to the wave of car crime which was hitting Oxfordshire – hitting the national press, too, with increasing regularity. Everyone and everything in turn was blamed: the police, the parents, the teachers, the church, the recession, unemployment, lack of youth facilities, car manufacturers, the weather, the TV, the brewers, left-wing social workers, and right-wing social workers; original sin received several votes, and even the Devil himself got one. Paradoxically the police seemed to be more in the dock than the perpetrators of the increasingly vicious crimes being committed. But at least the operation that morning had been successful, so Lewis reported: the only trouble was that further police activity in Wytham Woods was drastically curtailed – four men only now, one of them standing guard over the area cordoned off in Pasticks.

The temporarily dispirited Morse received the news with little surprise, and briefly brought Lewis up to date with his own ambivalent achievements of the morning: his discovery of the garden wĕre in all probability Karin Eriksson had spent some period of time before she disappeared; and his gullibility in allowing McBryde – fairly certainly now a key figure in the drama – more than sufficient time to effect a hurried escape.

At the far end of the ground-floor entrance passage, fairly steep stairs, turning 180 degrees, led down to the basement area in Seckham Villa, and it was here that the first discovery was made. The basement comprised a large, modernized kitchen at the front; and behind this, through an archway, a large living area furnished with armchairs, a settee, coffee tables, book-shelves, TV, HiFi equipment – and a double bed of mahogany, stripped down to a mattress of pale blue; and beside the bed, a jointed series of square, wooden boards, four of them, along which, for the length of about ten feet, ran two steel rails – rails where, it was immediately assumed, a cine-camera had recently and probably frequently been moving to and fro.

Morse himself (with Lewis and one of the DCs) spent most of his time that afternoon in this area, once the fingerprint men, the senior scenes-of-crime officer and the photographer had com-pleted their formal tasks. Clear fingerprints on the (unwashed) non-stick saucepan and cutlery found in the kitchen sink would doubtless match the scores of others found throughout the flat, would doubtless be McBryde's, and (as Morse saw things) would doubtless advance the investigation not one whit. No clothing, apart from two dirty pairs of beige socks found in one of the bedrooms; no toiletries left along the bathroom shelves; no videos; no correspondence; no shredded letters in either of the two waste-paper baskets or in the dustbin outside the back door. All in all it seemed fairly clear that the flat had been slimmed down – recently perhaps? – for the eventuality of a speedy get-away. Yet there were items that had *not* been bundled and stuffed into the back of the white van which (as was quickly ascertained) McBryde had used for travelling; and cupboards in both the ground floor and the basement contained duvets, sheets, pillow-cases, blankets, towels, and table-cloths – clearly items listed on the tenant's inventory; and the kitchen pantry was adequately stocked with tins of beans, fruit, salmon, spaghetti, tuna fish, and the like.

Naturally however it was the trackway beside the basement double bed which attracted the most interest, much lifting of eyebrows, and many lascivious asides amongst those investiga-tors whose powers of detection, at least in this instance, were the equal of the chief inspector's. Indeed, it would have required a man of monumental mutton-headedness not to visualize before him the camera and the microphone moving slowly alongside the mattress to record the assorted feats of fornication enacted on that creaking charpoy. For himself Morse tried not to give his imagination too free a rein. Sometimes up at HQ there were a few pornographic videos around, confiscated from late-night raids or illegal trafficking. Often had he wished to view some of the crude, corrupting, seductive things; yet equally often had he made it known to his fellow officers that he at least was quite uninterested in such matters.

In a corner of the kitchen, bundled neatly as if for some subsequent collection by Friends of the Earth, was a heap of old newspapers, mostly the *Daily Mail*, and various weeklies and periodicals, including *Oxford Today*, *Oxcom*, *TV Times*, two RSPB journals, and the previous Christmas offers from the Spastic Society. Morse had glanced very hurriedly through, half hoping perhaps to find the statutory girlie magazine; but apart from spending a minute or so looking at pictures of the black-headed gulls on the Loch of Kinnordy, he found nothing there to hold his interest.

It was Lewis who found them, folded away inside one of the free local newspapers, *The Star*. There were fourteen A4 sheets, stapled together, obviously photocopied (and photocopied ill) from some glossier and fuller publication. On each sheet several photographs of the same girl were figured (if that be the correct verb) in various stages of undress; and at the bottom of each sheet there appeared a Christian name, followed by details of height, bust, waist, hips, dress- shoe- and glove-measurements, and colour of hair and eyes. In almost every case the bottom left-hand picture was of the model completely naked, and in three or four cases striking some sexually suggestive pose. The names were of the glitzy showgirl variety: Jayne, Kelly, Lindy-Lu, Mandy ... and most of them appeared (for age was not given) to be in their twenties. But four of the sheets depicted older women, whose names were possibly designed to reflect their comparative maturity: Elaine, Dorothy, Mary, Louisa ... The only other information given (no addresses here) was a (i), (ii), (iii), of priority 'services', and Lewis, not without some little interest himself (and amusement), sampled a few of the services on offer: sporting-shots, escort duties, lingerie, stockings, leather, swim-wear, summer dresses, bras, nude-modelling, hair-styling, gloves. Not much to trouble the law there, surely. Three of the girls though were far more explicit about their specialisms, with Mandy listing (i) home videos, (ii) pornographic movies, (iii) overnight escort duties; and with Lindy-Lu, pictured up to her thighs in leather boots, proclaiming an accomplished proficiency in spanking.

And then, as Morse and Lewis were considering these things, the big discovery was made. One of the two DCs who had been given the job of searching the main lounge above had found, caught up against the top of one of the drawers in the escritoire, a list of names and addresses: a list of clients, surely! Clients who probably received their pornographic material in plain brown envelopes with the flap licked down so very firmly. And there, fourth from the top, was the name that both Morse and Lewis focused on immediately: George Daley, Blenheim Villas, Begbroke, Oxon.

Morse had been delighted with the find – of course he had! And his praise for the DC had been profuse and (in Lewis's view) perhaps a trifle extravagant. Yet now as he sat on the settee, looking again at the unzippings and the unbuttonings of the models, reading through the list of names once more, he appeared to Lewis to be preoccupied and rather sad.

'Everything all right, sir?'

'What? Oh yes! Fine. We're making wonderful progress. Let's keep at it!'

But Morse himself was contributing little towards any further progress; and after desultorily walking around for ten minutes or so, he sat down yet again and picked up the sheet of addresses. He would have to tell Lewis, he decided – not just yet but . . . He looked again at the seventeenth name on the list: for he was never likely to forget the name that Kidlington HQ had given him when, from Lyme Regis, he'd phoned in the car registration H 35 LWL:

Dr Alan Hardinge.

He picked up the pictures of the models and looked again through their names and their vital statistics and their special proficiencies. Especially did he look again at one of the maturer models: the one who called herself 'Louise'; the one who'd had all sorts of fun with her names at the Bay Hotel in Lyme Regis; the woman who was photographed here, quite naked and totally desirable.

Claire Osborne.

*

'Pity we've no address for – well, it must be a modelling agency of some sort, mustn't it?'

'No problem, Lewis. We can just ring up one of these johnnies on the list.'

'Perhaps *they* don't know.'

'I'll give you the address in ten minutes if you really want it.'

'I don't want it for myself, you know.'

'Of course not!'

Picking up his sheets, Morse decided that his presence in Seckham Villa was no longer required; and bidding Lewis to give things another couple of hours or so he returned to HQ, where he tried her telephone number.

She was in.

'Claire?'

'Morse!' (She'd recognized him!)

'You could have told me you worked for an escort agency!'

'Why?'

Morse couldn't think of an answer.

'You thought I was wicked enough but not quite so wicked as that?'

'I suppose so.'

'Why don't you get yourself in your car and come over tonight? I'd be happy if you did . . .'

Morse sighed deeply. 'You told me you had a daughter—'

'So?'

'Do you still keep in touch with the father?'

'The father? Christ, come off it! I couldn't tell you who the father *was*!'

Like the veil of the Temple, Morse's heart was suddenly rent in twain; and after asking her for the name and address of the modelling agency (which she refused to tell him) he rang off.

Ten minutes later, the phone went on Morse's desk, and it was Claire – though how she'd got his number he didn't know. She spoke for only about thirty seconds, ignoring Morse's interruptions.

'Shut up, you silly bugger! You can't see more than two inches in front of your nose, can you? Don't you realize I'd have swapped all the lecherous sods I've ever had for you – and instead of trying to understand all you ask me – Christ! – is who fathered—'

'Look, Claire—'

'No! *You* bloody look! If you can't take what a woman tells you about herself without picking over the past and asking bloody futile questions about why and who he was and—' But her voice broke down completely now.

'Look, please!'

'No! You just fuck off, Morse, and don't you ring me again because I'll probably be screwing somebody and enjoying it such a lot I won't want to be interrupted—'

'Claire!'

But the line was dead.

For the next hour Morse tried her number every five minutes, counting up to thirty double-purrs each time. But there was no answer.

Lewis had discovered nothing new in Seckham Villa, and he rang through to HQ at 6 p.m., as Morse had wished.

'All right. Well, you get off home early, Lewis. And get some sleep. And good luck tomorrow!'

Lewis was due to catch the 7.30 plane to Stockholm the following morning.

CHAPTER THIRTY-SEVEN

To be buried while alive is, beyond question, the most terrify- ing of those extremes which has ever fallen to the lot of mere mortality

(Edgar Allan Poe, *Tales of Mystery and Imagination*)

THE DEATH of Max was still casting a cloak of gloom round Morse as he sat in his office the following morning. During the previous night his thoughts had been much preoccupied with death, and the mood persisted now. As a boy, he had been moved by those words of the dying Socrates, suggesting that if death were just one long, unbroken, dreamless sleep, then a greater boon could hardly be bestowed upon mankind. But what about the body? The soul might be able to look after itself all right, but what about the physical body? In Morse's favourite episode from *The Iliad*, the brethren and kinsfolk of Sarpedon had buried his body, with mound and pillar, in the rich, wide land of Lycia. Yes! It was fitting to have a gravestone and a name inscribed on it. But there were those stories that were ever frightening – stories about people prematurely interred who had awoken in infinite and palpitating terror with the immovable lid of the coffin only a few inches above them. No! Burning was better than burying, surely ... Morse was wholly ignorant of the immediate procedures effected once the curtains closed over the light-wooded coffins at the crematoria ... like the curtains closing at the end of *Götterdämmerung*, though minus the clapping, of course. All done and finished quickly, and if somebody wanted to sprinkle your mortal dust over the memorial gardens, well, it might be OK for the roses, too. He wouldn't mind a couple of hymns either: 'The day thou gavest', perhaps. Good tune, that. So long as they didn't have any prayers, or any departures from the Authorised Version of Holy Writ ... Perhaps Max had got it right, neatly sidestepping the choice of interment or incineration: the clever old sod had left his body to the hospital, and the odds were strongly on one or two of his organs giving them plenty to think about. Huh!

Morse smiled to himself, and suddenly looked up to see Strange standing in the doorway.

'Private joke, Morse?'

'Oh, nothing, sir.'

'C'mon! Life's grim enough.'

'I was just thinking of Max's liver—'

'Not a pretty sight!'

'No.'

'You're taking it a bit hard, aren't you? Max, I mean.'

'A bit, perhaps.'

'You seen the latest?'

Strange pushed a copy of *The Times* across the desk, with a brief paragraph on the front page informing its readers that 'the bones discovered in Wytham Woods are quite certainly not those of the Swedish student whose disappearance occasioned the original verses and their subsequent analysis in this newspaper. (See Letters, page 13).'

'Anything to help us there?' asked Morse dubiously, opening the paper.

'Scraping the barrel, if you ask me,' said Strange.

Morse looked down at page 13:

From Mr Anthony Beaulah

Sir, Like the text of some early Greek love-lyric, the lines on the Swedish student would appear to have been pondered over in such exhaustive fashion that there is perhaps little left to say. And it may be that the search is already over. Yet there is one significant (surely?) aspect of the verses which has hitherto received scant attention. The collocation of 'the tiger' with 'the burning of the night' (lines 9 and 12) has indeed been commented upon, but in no *specific* context. In my view, sir, one should perhaps interpret the tiger (the cat) as staring back at drivers in the darkness. And the brilliantly simple invention which has long steered the benighted driver through the metaphorical forest of the night? Cat's eyes!

I myself live too far away from Oxford to be able to test such a thesis. But might the police not interpret this as a genuine clue, and look for some stretch of road (in or around Wytham?) where cat's eyes have recently been installed?

Yours
ANTHONY BEAULAH,
Felsted School,
Essex.

'Worth getting Lewis on it?' queried Strange, when Morse had finished reading.

'Not this morning, sir. If you remember he's, er, on his holidays.' Morse looked at his wrist-watch. 'At this minute he's probably looking out of the window down at Jutland.'

'Why didn't *you* go, Morse? With all these Swedish blondes and that . . .'

'I thought it'd be good experience for him.'

'Mm.'

For a while the two were silent. Then Strange picked up his paper and made to leave.

'You made a will yet, Morse?'

'Not much to leave, really.'

'All those records of yours, surely?'

'Bit out of date, I'm afraid. We're all buying CDs now.'

'Perhaps *they'll* be out of date soon.'

Morse nodded. Strange was not in the habit of saying anything quite so perceptive.

CHAPTER THIRTY-EIGHT

Men are made stronger on realization that the helping hand they need is at the end of their own right arm

(Sidney J. Phillips, speech, July 1953)

ON THE forty-kilometre bus ride from Arlanda airport southwards towards Stockholm, Lewis enjoyed what for him was the fairly uncommon view of a foreign country. After a while the tracts of large pine and fir woods changed to smaller coppices and open fields; then farmhouses, red, with barns that were red too, and a few yellow, wooden, Dutch-roofed manor houses, just before the outskirts of Stockholm, with its factories and tidy, newish buildings – and all so very clean and litter-free. In wooded surroundings within the city itself, three- and four-storeyed blocks of flats took over; and finally the end of the journey, at the Central Station terminal.

Lewis had never studied a foreign language at school, and his travel abroad had hitherto been restricted to three weeks in Australia, two weeks in Italy, and one afternoon in a Calais supermarket. The fact that he had no difficulty therefore in summoning a taxi was wholly due to the excellent English of the young driver, who soon brought Lewis into the suburb of Bromma – more specifically to an eight-storey block of white flats in Bergsvägen.

The Stockholm CID had offered to send one of its own men to meet him, but Lewis had not taken advantage of this when he'd arranged the details of his visit the previous morning. Seldom was it that he could assert any independent judgement in an investigation; and here was his chance.

The entrance hall was of polished pink granite, with the long list of tenants' names displayed there:

ANDREASSON	8A
ENGSTRÖM	8B
FASTÉN	7A
OLSSON	7B
KRAFT	6A
ERIKSSON	6B

Sixth floor!

Lewis felt excited at the sight of the name; it was almost as if ... as if he felt he was going to make some significant discovery.

The door, bearing the name-plate ERIKSSON, was opened by a woman in her mid-forties, of medium height, plumply figured, hazel-eyed, and with short, brownish-blonde hair.

'Mrs Eriksson?'

'Irma Eriksson,' she insisted as he shook her hand, and entered the apartment.

The small hallway was lined with cupboards, with what looked like a home-woven mat on one wall and a large mirror on the other. Through the open door to the right Lewis glimpsed a beautifully fitted kitchen, fresh and gleaming, with a copper kettle and old plates on its walls.

'In here, Mr Lewis.' She pointed smilingly to the left and led the way.

Her English was very good, utterly fluent and idiomatic, with only a hint of a foreign accent, just noticeable perhaps in the slight lengthening of the short 'i' vowels ('Meester Lewis').

The place was all so *clean*; and so particularly clean was the parquet flooring that Lewis wondered whether he should offer to take off his shoes, for she herself stood there in her stockinged feet as she gestured him to a seat on a low, brown-striped settee.

As he later tried to describe the furnishings to Morse, he felt more conscious than anything about the huge amount of stuff that had been packed into this living room: two coffee tables of heavy, dark wood; lots of indoor plants; groups of family portraits and photographs all around; dozens of candle holders; a large TV set; pretty cushions everywhere; vases of flowers; a set of Dala horses; two crucifixes; and (as Lewis learned later) a set of Carl Larsson prints above the bricked fireplace. Yet in spite of all the clutter, the whole room was light and airy, the thin curtains pulled completely back from the south-facing window.

Conversation was easy and, for Lewis, interesting. He learned something of the typical middle-class housing in Swedish cities; learned how and why the Erikssons had moved from Uppsala down to Bergsvägen almost a year ago after ... after Karin had, well, whatever had happened. As Lewis went briefly through the statement she had made a year ago, Irma Eriksson was watching him closely (he could see that), nodding here and there, and at one or two points staring down sadly at a small oriental carpet at her feet. But yes, it was all there; and no, there was nothing she could add. From that day to this she had received no further news of her daughter – none. At first, she admitted, she'd hoped and hoped, and couldn't bring herself to believe that Karin was dead. But gradually she had been forced to such a conclusion; and it was better that way, really – to accept the virtual certainty that Karin had been murdered. She was grateful – how not? – for the recent efforts the English police had made – again! – and she had been following the newspaper correspondence of course, receiving cuttings regularly from an English friend.

'Can I get you coffee? And a leetle Swedish schnapps, yes?'

When she went out to the kitchen, Lewis could scarcely believe that it had been himself who had answered 'yes' to the first, and 'yes' to the second. So often in his police career he'd prayed for Morse to be on hand to help him; but not now. He stood up and walked slowly round the room, staring long at some of the photographs; and especially at one of them: at three young ladies standing arm in arm, dressed in Swedish national costume.

'Ah! I see you've found my beautiful daughters.'

She had moved in silently, and now stood beside him, still in her stockinged feet, some five or six inches shorter than the six-foot sergeant; and he could smell the sweet summer freshness of her, and he felt an unfamiliar tic in a vein at his right temple.

'Katarina, Karin, Kristina.' She pointed to each in turn. 'All of them better looking than their momma, no?'

Lewis made no direct reply as he still held the framed photograph. So much alike the three of them: each with long, straight gold-blonde hair; each with clear-complexioned, high-cheekboned faces.

'That's Karin – in the middle, you say?' Lewis looked at her again, the one who was looking perhaps just a little more serious than her sisters.

Momma nodded; then, unexpectedly, took the photograph from Lewis's hands and replaced it – with no explanation for her slightly brusque behaviour.

'How can I help you any more?' She sat cross-legged opposite Lewis in an armchair, tossed back her small, squat glass of schnapps, before sipping the hot, strong coffee.

So Lewis asked her a lot of questions, and was soon to be forming a much clearer picture of the daughter about whom her mother spoke so lovingly now.

Karin had been a reasonably clever girl, if occasionally some-what idle; she had left her secondary school in Uppsala at the age of eighteen, with good prospects before her; attractive, *very* good at swimming and tennis; and with a series of badges and diplomas from school societies and guides' groups for birdwatching, orienteering, rock-climbing, judo, embroidery, and amateur musicals. It was just after she had left school that Irma's husband, Staffan Eriksson, had moved in with a darkly seductive brunette he had met on a business trip to Norway and, well, that was about it really. She uncrossed her legs and looked over at Lewis with a gentle smile.

'Another schnapps?'

'Why not?' said Mr Lewis.

Katarina (Irma Eriksson resumed), the eldest daughter (should it be 'elder' now, though?), was married and working with the European Commission in Strasbourg as an interpreter; the youngest (younger) daughter, Kristina – still only eighteen – was in her last year of schooling, studying social sciences. She was living at home, there in the flat, and if Mr Lewis would like to see her . . .? If Mr Lewis were *staying* in Stockholm?

The troublesome tic jerked in Lewis's temple once more, as he turned the conversation back to Karin.

What was Karin *like* – as a person? Well, her mother supposed she would call her 'independent' – yes, above all, independent. The summer before she'd gone to England, she'd spent two months on a kibbutz near Tel Aviv; and the year before that she'd joined a group of enthusiastic environmentalists in the Arctic Circle. But she was never (for the first time Irma Eriksson had seemed to struggle with her English vocabulary) she was never an 'easy' young girl. No! That wasn't the word at all! She was never the sort of girl who went to bed, you know . . .?

'Was she – do you think she was a virgin, Mrs Eriksson?'

' "Irma", please!'

'As far as you know . . . Irma?'

'I'm not sure. Apart from the trouble in Israel, if she had sex with anyone it would be with someone she liked. You know how I mean, don't you?'

'She was fond of birdwatching, you said?' Lewis was losing his way. (Or was he?)

'Oh, yes! Never did she go out on any holiday or walk without taking the binoculars.' (The idiom was breaking down – just a bit.)

There was just the one thing left now which Morse had asked

him to confirm: the passport and the work-permit procedures for a young lady like Karin.

No problem. For the first time Lewis thought he saw the underlying grief behind the saddened eyes, as she explained that Sweden did not belong to the EC; that all Swedish nationals needed to apply for work-permits in the UK if they proposed to stay for any length of time; that even for au pair work it was wholly prudent to do so. But Karin had not applied for such a permit; she gave herself only three weeks in the UK; and for this, her Swedish passport, valid for a ten-year period, would have been sufficient.

Lewis was suddenly aware that if there *had* been anything mildly flirtatious in the woman's manner, the situation had now changed.

'You kept Karin's passport, didn't you?' she continued quietly.

Lewis nodded, and his slight frown prompted her quick explanation:

'You see, I suppose we hoped she might – if she were still alive – she might apply for a new passport – if she'd *lost* it. Do you see . . .?'

Lewis nodded again.

'And she hasn't, has she, Mr Lewis? So!' She got up briskly, and put her feet into a pair of black, semi-heeled shoes. 'So!'

'I'm afraid we can't bring you any hopeful news – not really,' said Lewis, himself now rising to his feet.

'It's all right. I knew from the start, really. It's just . . .'

'I know. And thank you. You've been very helpful. Just one more thing – if I could just *borrow* a photo of the three girls . . .?'

As they stood in the hallway, Lewis ventured a genuine compliment:

'You know, I always envy people like you, Mrs – Irma – you know, people who can speak other languages.'

'We start learning English early though. In the fourth grade – ten years of age. Well, I was twelve myself, but my daughters all learn from ten.'

They shook hands, and Lewis walked down to the ground floor, where he stood for several minutes beside a play area surrounded by a low palisade of dark brown wooden slats – not a potato-crisp packet in sight. It was early afternoon now on a beautiful summer's day, with a cloudless blue sky and a yellow sun – like the colours of the flag on the rucksack found at Begbroke, Oxfordshire.

Standing on her high balcony, Irma Eriksson watched him go. As soon as he had disappeared into the main thoroughfare, she stepped back into her flat and let herself into the rear bedroom, where the ensuing conversation was held in Swedish:

'Was he intelligent?'

'Not particularly. Very nice though – *very* nice.'

'Did you ask him to bed with you?'

'I might have done if *you* hadn't been here.'

'Do you think he suspected anything?'

'No.'

'But you're glad he's gone?'

Irma Eriksson nodded. 'Shall I get you coffee?'

'Please!'

When her mother had left, the young lady looked at herself in the long wall-mirror in the shaded room, deciding that she was looking tired and dark around the eyes. Yet had Lewis seen her there that afternoon he would have been impressed by her pale and elegant beauty; would have been struck immediately too by a very close likeness to the photograph of the student found in the rucksack at Begbroke, Oxfordshire.

CHAPTER THIRTY-NINE

In a world in which duty and self-discipline have lost out to hedonism and self-satisfaction, there is nothing like closing your eyes and going with the flow. At least in a fantasy, it all ends happily ever after

(Edwina Currie, *The Observer*, 23 February 1992)

ALAN HARDINGE had gained a first in both parts of the Natural Sciences Tripos at Cambridge; had stayed on in that university for a Ph.D.; then done two years' research at Harvard before being elected in 1970 to a fellowship at the 'other place'. A year later he had courted a librarian from the Bodleian, had married her six months later, subsequently siring two offspring, both girls: the one now in her second year at Durham reading Psychology;

the other dead – killed nineteen days earlier as she cycled down
Cumnor Hill into Oxford.

He had not been wholly surprised to receive the phone call
from Chief Inspector Morse that morning of Tuesday, 21 July,
and a meeting was arranged for 2 p.m. the same day, in
Hardinge's rooms overlooking the front quad of Lonsdale
College.

'What does your wife know about your interests in Seckham
Villa?'

'Nothing. Absolutely nothing. So *please* can we keep Lynne –
my wife – out of this? She's still terribly upset and nervy – God
knows what . . .'

Dr Hardinge spoke in disjunct bursts, punctuated by the
equivalent of verbal dashes. He was a smallish, neat man, with
crinkly grey hair, darkly suited still in high summer, when many
of his colleagues were walking along the High in T-shirts and
trainers.

'I can't promise that, of course—'

'Don't you see? I'd do anything – anything at all – to see
that Lynne's not hurt. I know it sounds weak – it *is* weak – it's
what we all say – I know – but it's true.' From his hunched
shoulders Hardinge's face craned forward like that of an earnest
tortoise.

'Know this man?' Morse handed across one of the photographs
taken in the garden of Seckham Villa.

Hardinge took a pair of half-lensed spectacles from their case;
but appeared not to need them, glancing for only a second or two
at the photograph before handing it back.

'James – or Jamie? – Myton. Yes, I know him – knew him –
sort of jack-of-all-trades really.'

'How did you get to know him?'

'Look – it'll be better if I tell you – about myself – I think it
will.'

Morse listened with interest, and with no moral reproof, as
Hardinge stated his apologia for a lifetime of sexual adventurism.

As a boy a series of older women had regularly intruded
themselves into his dreams, and he had readily surrendered
himself, *almost* without guilt, into the sexual fantasies he found
he could so easily conjure up for himself – fantasies in which
there were no consequences, no disappointments. In his twenties
he would willingly have preferred – *did* prefer – to watch the
pornographic films and videos that were then so readily available.

Then he'd met Lynne – dear, honest, trusting Lynne – who would be utterly flabbergasted and so hurt and ashamed if she even began to suspect a fraction of the truth. After his marriage, though, his fantasies persisted; grew even. He was experiencing a yearning for ever greater variety in his sexual gratification, and this had gradually resulted in a string of rather sordid associations: with private film clubs; imported videos and magazines; live sex-shows; 'hostess' parties – for all of which he'd become a regular and eager client. The *anticipation* of such occasions! The extraordinarily arousing words that became the open sesame to such erotic entertainments: 'Is everybody known?'

'And that's what happened regularly at Seckham Villa?'

'Fairly regularly – seldom more than five or six of us – usually people we'd met once or twice before.'

Morse watched the middle-aged, dapper deceiver, leaning forward all the time, with his aquiline cast of feature, his pale complexion, his slightly pernickety enunciation. He felt he should have despised the man a little; but he couldn't do that. If Hardinge were a bit of a pervert, he was an extraordinarily honest one; and with his faded, watery eyes he looked rather tired and rather lost; weak, and not pretending to be strong.

'You're not a "medical" doctor, sir?' asked Morse when the carnal confessions were complete.

'No. I just wrote a Ph.D. thesis – you know how these things are.'

'On?'

'Promise not to laugh?'

'Try me.'

'"The comparative body-weight of the great tit within the variable habitats of its North European distribution".'

Morse didn't laugh. Birds! So many people in the case seemed interested in birds . . .

'*Original* research, was that?'

'No other kind, as far as I know.'

'And you were *examined* in this?'

'You don't get a doctorate otherwise.'

'But the person who examined you – well, he couldn't know as much as *you*, could he? By definition, surely?'

'*She*, actually. It's the – well, they say it is – the *way* you go about it – your research; the way you observe, record things, categorize them, and then draw some kind of conclusion. Bit like your job, Inspector.'

'All I was thinking, sir, is that it might not have been difficult for you to fabricate a few of the facts . . .'

Hardinge frowned, his head moving forward on his shoulders once more. 'I am *not*, Inspector, fabricating anything about Seckham Villa – if that's what you're getting at.'

'And you first met Claire Osborne there.'

'She told you that was her name?'

'"Louisa Hardinge", too.'

Hardinge smiled sadly. 'Her one and only tribute to me! But she loves changing her name – all the time – she doesn't really know who she is . . . or what she wants, Inspector. She's a sort of chameleon, I suppose. But you'll probably know that, won't you? I understand you've met her.'

'What *is* her name?'

'Her birth-certificate name? I don't really know.'

Morse shook his head. Was there *anyone* telling him the truth in this case?

'She never went to Seckham Villa herself – as far as I know,' resumed Hardinge. 'I met her through an agency. McBryde – you've spoken to him? – through McBryde. They give you photographs – interests – you know what I mean.'

'Measurements?'

'Measurements.'

'And you fell for her?'

Hardinge nodded. 'Not difficult to do that, is it?'

'You still in love with her?'

'Yes.'

'She with you?'

'No.'

'You'll have to give me the address of the agency.'

'I suppose so.'

'How do you manage to get all the stuff without your wife knowing?'

'Plain envelopes – parcels – here – to my rooms. I get lots of academic material delivered here – no problem.'

'No problem,' repeated Morse quietly, with some distaste in his voice at last, as the authority on the great tits wrote down a brief address.

Hardinge watched from his window as the chief inspector walked along to the Porters' Lodge beside the well-watered, weedless lawn of the front quad. He'd seemed an understanding man, and Hardinge supposed he should be grateful for that. If he'd been a little brighter, perhaps, he would have asked one or two more perceptive questions about Myton, though. Certainly Hardinge knew amongst other things the TV company the lecherous cameraman claimed to have worked for. Yet oddly enough the chief inspector had seemed considerably more interested in Claire Osborne than in the most odious man it had ever been his, Hardinge's, misfortune to encounter.

CHAPTER FORTY

Then the little Hiawatha
Learned of every bird its language,
Learned their names and all their secrets
(Henry Wadsworth Longfellow, *The Song of Hiawatha*)

THAT afternoon PC Pollard was completely 'pissed off' with life as he later reported his state of mind to his Kidlington colleagues. He'd spoken to no one for more than two hours, since the two fellows from the path lab had been along to examine the cordoned-off area, to dig several spits out of the brownly carpeted earth where the bones had lain, and to cart them off in transparent polythene bags. Not that they'd said much to him when they had been there just after lunch-time: the sort of men (Pollard had little doubt) with degrees in science and bio-chemistry and all that jazz. He appreciated the need for such people, of course, although he thought the force was getting a bit too full of these smart-alecs from the universities. He appreciated too that it was important to keep people away from the scene of the crime – if it *was* a crime. Exactly who these people were though, he wasn't sure. It was a helluva way from the car park for a couple to carry a groundsheet for a bit of clandestine sex; and they wouldn't go *there*, surely? He'd seen a few birdwatchers as he'd been driven along; but again, not *there*. Too dark and the birds couldn't *fly* in there anyway; it'd be like aeroplanes flying through barrage-balloon cables.

The afternoon was wearing tediously on, and for the ump-teenth time Pollard consulted his wrist-watch: 4.25 p.m. A police car was promised up along the Singing Way at 5 p.m.; with further instructions, and hopefully with a relief – unless they'd decided to scrub the whole thing now the ground had been worked over, now the first excitement was over.

4.45 p.m.

4.55 p.m.

Pollard folded away his copy of the *Sun* and picked up the flask they'd given him. He put on his black and white checkered cap, and walked slowly through the woodland riding, wholly unaware that a tiny white-fronted tree-creeper was spiralling up a beech tree to his left; that a little further on a lesser-spotted woodpecker was suddenly sitting very still on a short oak branch as the crunching steps moved alongside.

Another pair of eyes too was watching the back of the shirt-sleeved constable as he walked further and further away; the eyes of a man who made no movement until the woodland around was completely still again, with only the occasional cries of the birds – the thin 'tseet-tseet' of the tree-creeper, and after a while the high 'qui-qui' of the woodpecker – to be heard in that late, still, summer afternoon. For unlike Constable Pollard this man knew much about the woods and about the birds.

The man made his way into the area behind the cordoned square, and, leaning forward, his eyes constantly fixed to the ground, began to tread slowly, as systematically as the terrain would allow, for about twenty yards or so before turning and retracing his steps along a line four or five feet further into the forest; repeating this process again and again until he had covered an area of roughly fifteen yards square. Once or twice he picked up some object from the densely matted floor, only to throw it aside immediately. Such a pattern of activity he repeated on the left-hand side of the cordoned area – into which he ventured at no point – working his way patiently along, ever watchful, ever alert, and occasionally freezing completely like a statue-waltzer once the music has abruptly stopped. In this fashion he worked for over an hour, like an ox that pulls the ploughshare to the edge of the field, then turns round on itself and plods a parallel furrow, right to left . . . left to right. Boustrophedon.

It was just after 6 p.m. when he found it. *Almost* he had missed it – just the top of the black handle showing. His eyes gleamed with the elation of the hunter pouncing on his quarry; but even as he pocketed his find his body froze once more. A rustle . . . nearby. Very near. Then, just as suddenly, he felt his shoulder muscles relax. Wonderfully so. The fox stood only three yards in front of him, ears pricked, staring him brazenly in the eye – before turning and padding off into the undergrowth, as if deciding that this intruder, at least, was unlikely to molest its time-honoured solitary territory.

The police car was very late ('Traffic!' the driver said) and the four of them – the three at the vehicular access points to the woods, and Pollard himself – couldn't alas be relieved until 7 p.m. Priority was still with the joy-riding kids, and no one seemed to know *who* was in charge of things there anyway: Sergeant Lewis had buggered off for a skiing holiday in Sweden – Christ! – and Chief Inspector bloody Morse was temporarily 'unavailable', probably in a pub. Pity the walkie-talkie wouldn't function a bit better, probably all those bloody trees, eh?

The tree-creeper was gone, and the lesser-spotted woodpecker was gone, as Pollard plodded reluctantly back to his post.

And something else was gone too.

CHAPTER FORTY-ONE

Little by little the agents have taken over the world. They don't do anything, they don't make anything – they just stand there and take their cut

(Jean Giraudoux, *The Madwoman of Chaillot*)

WHETHER the agency was very busy, or whether the phone was out of order, or whether someone just didn't want to speak to him, Morse couldn't know. But it was 4.30 p.m. before he finally got through, and 5 p.m. before, crawling with the other traffic, he finally pulled into the small concreted parking area of the Elite Booking Services in Abingdon Road. The establishment (as it seemed to Morse) should ideally have been a glitzy, marble-and-glass affair, with a seductive and probably topless brunette contemplating her long scarlet fingernails at reception. But things were not so.

The front room of the slightly seedy semi-detached property was so cluttered with file-cases and cardboard boxes that room could be found for only two upright chairs – for the two women

proprietors: one, very large, and certainly ill-advised to be wearing a pair of wide, crimson culottes; the other rather small and
flat-chested, black-stockinged and minimally skirted. Both were
smoking menthol cigarettes; and judging from the high-piled
ashtrays around the room, both were continuously smoking
menthol cigarettes. Instinctively Morse felt that the latter (if
either) would be the boss. But it was the large woman (in her late
twenties?) who spoke first:

'This is Selina – my assistant. I'm Michelle – Michelle Thompson. How can I help you?'

The smile, on the rounded dimpled cheeks, seemed warm
enough – attractive even – and Morse, reluctantly taking Selina's
seat, asked his questions and received his answers.

The agency was the receptor, the collator, and the distributor
of 'information', from all quarters of the country, which might be
of interest and use to assorted businesses, ranging from TV
companies to film producers, clothes designers to fashion organ-
izers, magazine editors to well, all right, purveyors of rather less
salubrious products. In its Terms and Conditions contracts, the
agency dissociated itself officially, legally, completely, from any
liability arising from the *misuse* of its services. When a particular
client hired a particular model, such a booking was made with
the strict proviso that any abuse of contractual obligation was a
matter to be settled between model and client – never model and
agency. But such trouble was rare – very rare. McBryde had been
a client for about two years: a very *good* client, if full and prompt
payment were the criterion – 80 per cent of the negotiated fee to
the model; 20 per cent to the agency.

Each spring a Model Year Book was produced; there were
always new models, of course, and always new clients – with
new, differing interests. But one of the Terms and Conditions
('Terribly important, Inspector!') was that any information originally divulged *to* the agency concerning individual models, and
any information subsequently learned *by* the agency about the
activities of either clients or models, would always remain a
matter of the strictest confidentiality. Must still remain so now,
unless, well . . . But at least the inspector could understand that
once trust was gone . . .

'And that's why you never contacted the police?'

'Exactly,' asserted Ms Thompson.

The link with the YWCA in London was very simple. The
woman the police had earlier interviewed, Mrs Audrey Morris,

was her sister. On the Friday before Karin had hitch-hiked to Oxford, Audrey had phoned to say that they had a young Swedish student with them who was down to her last few pennies; that the YWCA had given her a ten-pound note from the charity fund; that Audrey had written out the name, address, and telephone number of the Elite agency, and assured Michelle that the young lady was shapely, *very* photogenic, and probably sufficiently worldly-wise to know that a suitable session with a photographer might well work wonders for an impoverished pocket.

'You work on Sundays?'

'Sunday's a good day for sin, Inspector. And we had a client willing and waiting – if she came.'

'And she came?'

'She rang us from a call-box in Wentworth Road in North Oxford and Selina here went up in the Mini to fetch her—'

Morse could contain himself no longer. 'Bloody hell! Do you realize how much time and trouble you could have saved us? No wonder we've got so much unsolved crime when—'

'What *crime* exactly are we talking about, Inspector?'

Morse let it go, and asked her to continue.

But that was about it – little more to say. Selina had brought her there, to Abingdon Road: attractive, bronzed, blonde, full-figured, skimpily dressed; with a rucksack – yes, a red rucksack, and with very little else. The client from Seckham Villa had been on the look-out for such and similar offerings. A phone call. A verbal agreement: £100 for a one-hour session – £80 to the girl, £20 to the agency.

'How did she get up to Park Town?'

'Dunno. She said she'd walk up to the centre – only five minutes – and get a bite to eat. Didn't seem to want much help. Independent sort of girl.'

So that was that. At least for the present.

Before he left Morse asked to look through the current Model Year Book, a thick black-covered brochure from which, fairly certainly – or from a previous edition of which – the selected photocopies found at Seckham Villa had been taken. The photographs were all in black and white, but in this edition Morse could find neither Claire nor Louisa amongst the elegant ladies in their semi-buttoned blouses and suspendered stockings. No Karin either among the Ks: just Katie, and Kelly, and Kimberly, and Kylie . . .

'If I can take this?'

'Of course.'

'And I may have to bother you again, I'm afraid – with my sergeant.'

As Morse was leaving the phone rang and Selina made forward as if to take the call. But the senior partner picked up the receiver first, placed her hand over the mouthpiece, and bade her visitor farewell. Thus it was Selina the Silent who accompanied the chief inspector to the door, and who, a little to Morse's surprise, walked out with him to the Jaguar.

'There's something I want you to know,' she said suddenly. 'It's not important, I know, but . . .'

Unlike the Cockney ancestry of her partner's speech, the vowels here were curiously curly: the vowels of Oxfordshire and Gloucestershire.

'I picked her up, you see. She was a lovely girl.'

'Yes?'

'Don't you see? I *wanted* her, Inspector. I asked her if she would see me – afterwards. I've got plenty of money, and she'd got . . . she'd got nothing.' A tear, soon to roll slowly down the thin cheek, had formed in the right eye of Selina, the sleeping, weeping partner of the Agency.

Morse said nothing, trusting that for once his instincts were right.

'She said "no",' continued the woman simply. 'That's what I want you to know really: she wouldn't have done . . . *some* things. She just *wouldn't*. She wasn't for sale – not in the way most of them are.'

Morse laid a hand on a bony shoulder, and smiled at her understandingly, hoping that he'd assimilated whatever it was she'd wanted to tell him. He thought he had.

As he drove away, Morse could see the mightily dimensioned Michelle still busily engaged with the needs of another client. She was certainly the dominant partner in the business; but he wondered who might be the dominant partner in the bed.

He was not back in Kidlington HQ until a quarter to seven, where he learned that some directive was needed – pretty soon! – about the personnel in Wytham Woods. Was the police team there to be disbanded? On the whole Morse thought it was becoming a waste of time to maintain any further watch. But logic sometimes held less sway in Morse's mind than feeling and impulse, and so he decided that perhaps he *would* continue with it after all.

He drove out of the HQ car park and turned on the radio; but he'd just missed it – blast! – and he heard the signing-off signature-tune of *The Archers* as he headed towards Oxford, wondering how much else he might have missed that day.

Turning right at the Banbury Road roundabout he continued down to Wolvercote and called in at the Trout, where for more than an hour he sat on the paved terrace between the sandstone walls of the inn and the low parapet overlooking the river: drinking, and thinking – thinking about the strangely tantalizing new facts he was learning about the death of the Swedish Maiden.

Lewis rang at 10.15 p.m. He was back. He'd had a reasonably successful time, he thought. Did Morse want to see him straightaway?

'Not unless you've got some extraordinary revelation to report.'

'I wouldn't go quite so far as that.'

'Leave it till the morning, then,' decided Morse.

Not that any decision Morse made that night was to be of very much relevance, since the routines of virtually every department at police HQ were to be suspended over the next three or four days. Trouble had broken out again at Broadmoor Lea, where half the inhabitants were complaining bitterly of under-policing and the other half protesting violently about police over-reaction; council workmen there were being intimidated; copy-cat criminality was being reported from neighbouring Bucks and Berks; another high-level two-day conference had been called for Thursday and Friday; the Home Secretary had stepped in to demand a full report; and the investigation of a possible crime committed perhaps a year earlier in either Blenheim Park or Wytham Woods or wherebloody-ever (as the ACC had put the case the following morning) was not going to be the number-one priority in a community where the enforcement of Law and Order was now in real jeopardy.

CHAPTER FORTY-TWO

To some small extent these Greek philosophers made use of observation, but only spasmodically until the time of Aristotle. Their legacy lies elsewhere: in their astonishing powers of deductive and inductive reasoning
(W. K. C. Guthrie, *The Greek Philosophers*)

LEWIS'S report from Sweden had been far more interesting, far more potentially suggestive, than Morse could have hoped. The flesh was being put on the bones, as it were – though no longer those particular bones which had been discovered in Pasticks. The thoughts of others too appeared to be shifting away from any guess-work concerning the likeliest spot in which to dig for the Swedish Maiden, and towards the possible identity of the murderer who had dug the hole in the first place – his (surely a 'he'?) interests, his traits, his psychological identikit, as it were. Especially the thoughts behind the latest letter to *The Times*, which Morse read with considerable interest on the morning of Friday, 24 July.

From the Reverend David M. Sturdy

Sir, Like so many of your regular readers I have been deeply impressed by the ingenuity expended by your correspondents on the now notorious Swedish Maiden verses. All of us had hoped that such ingenuity would eventually reap its reward – especially the wholly brilliant analysis (July 13) resulting in the 'Wytham hypothesis'. It was therefore with much disappointment that we read (Tuesday, July 21) the findings of the police pathologist in Oxford.

I cannot myself hope to match the deductive logic of former correspondents. But is it not profitable to take a leaf out of Aristotle's book, and to look now for some *inductive* hypothesis? Instead of asking what the original author intended as clues, we should perhaps be asking an entirely different question, viz., what do the verses tell us about the person who wrote them, especially if such a person were trying to conceal almost as much as he was willing to reveal.

Two things may strike the

reader immediately. First, the archaisms so prevalent in the verses ('tell'st', 'know'st', 'Whither', 'thy', 'thee', etc.) which strongly suggest that the author is wholly steeped in the language of Holy Writ. Second, the regular resort to hymnological vocabulary: 'The day thou gavest, Lord, is ended' (i. 11); 'As pants the hart for cooling streams' (l. 15); 'When I survey the wondrous cross' (l. 17) – all of which seem to corroborate the view that the author is a man *regularly* conditioned by such linguistic influences.

May I be allowed therefore to put two and two together and make, not a murderer, but a minister of God's church? May I go even further? And suggest a minister in the Church of Rome, where the confessional is a commonplace, and where in rare circumstances a priest may be faced with a grievous dilemma – the circumstances, say, when a sinner confesses to an appalling crime, and when the priest may be tempted to compromise the sacred principle of confidentiality and to warn society about a self-confessed psychopath, especially so if the psychopath himself has expressed a wish for such a course of action to be pursued.

Might it not be worthwhile then for the Thames Valley CID to conduct some discreet inquiries among the RC clergy within, say, a ten-mile radius of Carfax?

Yours truly,
DAVID M. STURDY
St Andrew's Vicarage,
Norwich.

This letter was also read by Inspector Harold Johnson on holiday with his wife on the Lleyn Peninsula in North Wales. The small village store was not in the habit of stocking *The Times*, but he had picked up a copy on a shopping trip to Pwllheli that morning, and felt puzzled by the reference to 'the findings of the police pathologist in Oxford'. Not just puzzled, either; a whole lot *pleased*, if he were honest with himself. It wasn't very specific, but it must surely mean that the girl still hadn't been found. They'd found some *other* poor sod. Huh! That must have shot bloody Morse in the foot. Shot him up the arse if Strange had his finger on the trigger. He was reading the letter again quickly as his wife was arranging the supermarket carrier bags in the boot of the Maestro.

'What are you smiling at, darling?' she asked.

*

On Broadmoor Lea, the erection of bollards and concrete blocks, the construction of humps across the streets, and the simpler expedient of digging several holes to the depth of several feet – these activities had put a virtual stop to any possibility of further joy-riding. All a bit makeshift, but all quite effective. There was revulsion too at the young girl's death. And more public co-operation. The police were winning. Or so it appeared. Marion Bridewell had been knocked down by a car (a shiny new BMW stolen from High Wycombe) with four youths inside. The car itself had been abandoned on the neighbouring Blackbird Leys estate, but a good many of the local inhabitants knew who one or two of them were; and some few bystanders, and some few indeed who had earlier applauded the teenagers' skills, were now semi-willing to testify to names and incidents. Earlier that week fourteen youths and two men in their early twenties had been arrested on the estate, and charged with a variety of motoring offences; six of them were still sitting in the cells. There would very soon be four more of them – the BMW four; and looking at things from the point of view of both the City and the County Constabularies, it was fairly certain that normal police duties could be resumed almost immediately.

The following day, Saturday 25 July, Philip Daley had caught the bus into Oxford at 11 a.m., and his mother had watched him disappear up to the main road before venturing quietly, fearfully, into his bedroom with the hoover. The red-covered pocket diary she'd given him for Christmas had remained unused in his drawer until earlier that month, when the entries had started. The first had been on Saturday the 4th, the writing cramped and ill-fitted into the narrow daily space:

> Another tonight. Wow!!! What a squeeler what a bute. I never been so exited before.

And then the last, a fortnight later:

> Finish Finis End! We never meant it none of us. The screems sounded just like the tires but we never meant it.

Margaret Daley looked down again at the date, Saturday, 18 July. Her heart was sinking again within her, and in her misery she wished that she were dead.

CHAPTER FORTY-THREE

It is not the criminal things which are hardest to confess, but those things of which we are ashamed

(Rousseau, *Confessions*)

MRS MARGARET DALEY pulled her white Mini into the tarmacadamed area ('For Church Purposes Only') just above St Michael and All Angels at the northern end of the Woodstock Road in Oxford – a white, pebble-dashed edifice, with a steeply angled roof surmounted, at the apex of the gable, by a small stone cross. Although she was not a regular worshipper – once a month or so, with the occasional Easter or Whitsun or Christmas service – Margaret's face was not unfamiliar there, and on the morning of Sunday, 26 July, she exchanged a few semi-smiling greetings; a few only, however, for the congregation was thin for the first Holy Mass at 8 a.m.

The car was George's really, but so often he used the Blenheim Estate van for getting around that it was almost always possible for her to have the prior call; and especially so on Sunday mornings. There had been very few cars on the road as she had driven down the dual-carriageway to the Pear Tree roundabout – her mind deeply and agonizingly preoccupied.

It had begun two years earlier, when George had bought the video; a bit surprising in any case, because he was no great TV addict, preferring a pint in the Sun most evenings to a diet of soaps. But he *had* bought a video machine; and soon he'd bought a few videotapes to go with it – the highlights of great sporting occasions, mostly: England's 1966 victory in the World Cup; Botham's miracles against the Australians; that sort of thing. The machine had been a rather complex affair, and from the outset there had been a taboo on anyone else manipulating it without his lordship's permission and supervision. It was *his* toy. Such possessiveness had irked young Philip a little, but the situation had been satisfactorily resolved when the lad had been presented with a small portable TV of his own on his fifteenth birthday. But in spite of his growing collection of tapes, her husband seldom actually watched them. Or so she'd thought. Gradually, however, she'd begun to realize that he *did* watch them – when she was away from the house; and particularly so on the regular occasions she was out, twice a week: aerobics on Tuesdays; WI on Thursdays. It had been one Tuesday night when she had been feeling unwell and flushed that she had left the class early and returned home to find her husband jumping up from his seat on the floor beside the TV screen, hurriedly flicking the 'Stop' switch on the video, turning over to the ITV channel, and taking out the tape. The next day, when he was at work, she had managed, for the first time, to get the wretched thing working – and had witnessed a few minutes of wholly explicit and (to her) monstrously disgusting pornography. She had said nothing though; had still said nothing.

But other things were fitting into place. About once every three weeks a brown, plain A4 envelope would be found among George's limited mail, containing, as she'd guessed, some sort of magazine of about thirty or forty pages. Often the post would arrive before George left for work; but she had taken the next opportunity of a later delivery partially to steam open the flap on such a communication, and to discover more than sufficient to confirm her suspicions. But again she'd said nothing; had still said nothing; and would still say nothing. For although it was half of her trouble, it was the half of her trouble that she could the better bear . . .

Perhaps things were slightly easier as she followed the Order of Mass that early Sunday morning, glancing the whiles around her at the familiar stations of the cross as she sat in a pew at the rear of the church. She knew next to no Latin herself – only what she had learned as a young girl from the RC services in the Douay Martyrs' Secondary School in Solihull. But especially had she then loved the sound of some of the long words they'd all sung: words like 'immolatum' from the *Ave Verum Corpus* – a serious-minded word, she'd always thought, sort of grand and sad and musical with all those 'm's in it. Although she'd never really known what it meant, she felt disappointed that they'd got rid of most of the Latin and gone for a thin kind of Englishness in the services; felt this disappointment again now as the Celebrant dismissed them:

'The Mass is ended. Go in peace.'

'Thanks be to God,' she'd replied, and waited in her place – until only one other solitary soul lingered there, still kneeling, head bowed, in one of the side pews.

After a few mild exhortations in the porchway to his departing flock, Father Richards re-entered the church; and as he did so Margaret Daley rose and spoke to him, requesting a confessional hearing at one of the appropriate times: Saturdays, 11–12 a.m.; 5.30–6.15 p.m. Perhaps it was the earnestness of her manner, perhaps the moist film of her incipient tears, perhaps her voice – unhappy, hesitant, and trembling . . . But whichever, it mattered not. Father Richards took her gently by the arm and spoke quietly into her ear.

'If it will help, my child, come now! Let Christ, through His cross and through His resurrection, set you free from all your sins!'

It was not in the normal confessional box at all; but in a small study in the Manse behind the church that Father Richards heard as much as Margaret Daley felt willing to tell him. But even then she lied – lied when she said she had gone into her son's bedroom to collect his dirty washing, lied about her deepest and most secret fears.

Twice, surreptitiously, Father Richards had looked down at his wrist-watch as he listened. But he refrained from interrupting her until she had told him enough, until he thought he understood enough. The burden of her sin was heavy; yet even heavier (he sensed it) was her guilt at prying into the affairs of others; her anguished conviction that it was precisely *because* of her prying, *because* of her snooping, that there had been such terrible secrets to discover. Had she *not* done so . . . *the secrets themselves might not have existed*. This was her punishment. Oh God! What could she do?

For a while Father Richards offered no words of consolation; it was important, he knew, for the waters to be drained from the poisoned cistern. But soon – soon he would speak to her. And so it was that he sat and waited and listened until she was dry-eyed again; until her guilt and humiliation and self-pity were for the moment spent. She may have told him a lot or a little, he wasn't sure; but she had told him enough, and now it was time for him to speak.

'You must talk to your son, my child, and you must feel able to forgive him; and you must pray to God for guidance and strength. And this I promise – that I too will pray to God for you.' Momentarily there was a twinkle in the old priest's eyes. 'You know, with the two of us praying for the same thing, He might just listen a little bit harder.'

'Thank you, Father,' she whispered.

The priest placed his hand gently on hers, and closed his eyes as he recited the absolution: 'May God Almighty have mercy on you, forgive your sins, and lead you in the paths of righteousness.'

An 'Amen' was called for, but Margaret Daley had been unable to enunciate a single word, and now walked out of the Manse, and fiddled in her handbag for the car keys. The Mini was the only car remaining on the parking area, but another person was standing there, probably waiting for a lift, it seemed; the person who had been kneeling in the church after everyone else had gone; a person who now turned round and looked into Margaret's face – then looked past her face, unrecognizing, and turned away. The look had lasted but a second, yet in that second Margaret Daley's scalp had thrilled with sudden fear.

CHAPTER FORTY-FOUR

Impressions there may be which are fitted with links and which may catch hold on each other and render some sort of coalescence possible

(John Livingstone Lowes, *The Road to Xanadu*)

ON THE morning of Monday, 27 July, Morse and Lewis were back in business at Kidlington HQ: Lewis (at Morse's insistence) once more going through his Swedish trip in meticulous detail – especially through the furnishings and the photographs on view in Irma Eriksson's living room; and Morse (as always) seeking to convince himself that there was probably some vital clue he'd already missed; or, if not *missed* exactly, some clue whose true significance had hitherto eluded him. Since early that morning he had, as it were, been shaking the atoms laterally in the frying pan, hoping that a few hooks and eyes might link together and forge some new chain of thought; a new *train* of thought ... train *spotting* ... *bird*-spotting ... birds ... yes, birds (like dogs!) had figured all over the place so far, especially the lesser-spotted woodpecker – 'spotted' (that word again!) – yet still the link refused to make itself. He considered once again Karin's list of hopefully-soon-to-be-identified British birds, and realized that as yet he had made no contact with the woman who lived down near Llandovery ... the home of the red kites ... Llandovery, out into Wales along the A40 ... A40, the third of the possibilities ... the third of the roads that led off from the Woodstock Road roundabout. Inspector Johnson had done his pedestrian best with the road out to Blenheim Park; and he himself, Morse, had done his (equally pedestrian?) best with the road posted down to Wolvercote and Wytham. But what if *both* of them had been wrong? Morse had reread the statement made by Mrs Dorothy Evans (not an aunt, it appeared, but some second or third cousin, twice or thrice removed) in which she'd affirmed quite simply that Karin Eriksson had never visited her, never even telephoned her at that time; in fact had not seen 'little Karin' since that now largish girl was ten years old. No! The solution to the murder lay there in Oxford, in the environs of Oxford, Morse was convinced of that.

At 10.30 a.m. he decided that he had to speak to David Michaels once more; the man who had pointed the way – almost literally so – to the body found in Pasticks; the man who knew the woodland ridings out at Wytham better than almost any man alive.

From the very roundabout where Karin Eriksson might well have made her fatal decision, Lewis drove down through the twisting road of Lower Wolvercote, past the Trout Inn, and then up the hill towards Wytham village.

'What exactly *is* a handbrake-turn?' Morse had asked suddenly.

'Don't you know – really?'

'Well, of course, I've got a vague idea ...'

'Just a minute, sir. Wait till we're round this next bend and I'll show you.'

'No! I didn't—'

'Only a joke, sir.'

Lewis laughed at his chief's discomfiture, and even Morse managed to produce a weak smile.

The police car drove up to the T-junction at Wytham village, turned left, then immediately right, past the dovecote in the car park of the White Hart, then right again into the lane that led up into Wytham Woods. On a gate-post to the right was fixed a bold notice, black lettering on an orange background:

> **WYTHAM AMATEUR**
> **OPERATIC SOCIETY**
> *presents*
> **THE MIKADO**
> BY
> **GILBERT & SULLIVAN**
> Thursday July 30th, Friday
> July 31st, & Saturday August 1st
> **TICKETS £3.50**
> (Senior Citizens & Children £2.50)

'The wife's very fond of Gilbert and Sullivan. Far better than all your Wagner stuff, that,' ventured Lewis.

'If you say so, Lewis.'

'Full o' tunes – you know what I mean?'

'We don't go in for "tunes" in Wagner – we go in for "continuous melody".'

'If you say so, sir.'

They drove up to the semi-circular clearing at the edge of the Great Wood.

'We did it at school. I wasn't in it myself, but I remember, you know, everybody dressing up in all that oriental clobber.'

'*The Mikado*, you mean? Oh, yes. Well done!'

Morse seemed for a while almost half asleep, as Lewis stopped the car and looked across at the stone cottage where Michaels lived.

'We're in luck, sir.' Lewis wound down his window and pointed to the forester, a rifle under his right arm, its barrel tilted earthwards at 45 degrees, the black and white Bobbie happily sniffling the route ahead of him.

'Start the car up again, Lewis,' said Morse very quietly.

'Pardon?'

'Back to the village!' hissed Morse.

As the car momentarily drew alongside, it was Morse's turn to wind his window down.

'Morning, Mr Michaels. Lovely morning!'

But before the forester could reply, the car had drawn away; and in his rear-view mirror Lewis could see Michaels standing and staring after them, a look of considerable puzzlement on his face.

They were almost the first customers in the White Hart, and Morse ordered a pint of Best Bitter for himself.

'Which would you prefer, sir? We've got—'

'Whatever the locals drink.'

'Straight glass or handle?'

'Straight. Optical illusion, I know, but it always looks as if it holds more.'

'Both hold exactly—'

But Morse had turned to Lewis: 'You'd better not have too much. You're driving, remember.'

'Orange juice – that'll be fine, sir.'

'And, er . . .' Morse fiddled in his trouser pockets. 'I don't seem to have any coins on me. I'm sure the landlord doesn't want to change a twenty this early in the day.'

'Plenty of change—' began the landlord, but Morse had turned to the wall with his pint and was studying a medieval map of the old parishes around Wytham . . .

At the time Morse was lifting his first pint, Alasdair McBryde was standing beside reception at the Prince William Hotel in Spring Street, just opposite Paddington railway station. After leaving Oxford – with what a frenetic burst of mental and physical energy! – he had driven the swiftly, chaotically loaded van via the M40 up to London, where he'd parked it in a lock-up garage off the Seven Sisters Road before taking the tube, and a suitcase, to Paddington – to the Prince William. It gave him considerable confidence that he could, if necessary, be standing in front of the departure board of the mainline BR station within one minute of stepping outside this hotel – or if need be by *jumping* outside it, for the sole window of his *en suite* bedroom was no more than six feet above the pavement.

The hotel proprietor was a small, perpetually semi-shaven Italian who spent half his working hours at reception studying the racing columns of the *Sporting Life*. He looked up as McBryde took out his wallet.

'You stay another day, Mr Mac?'

'Mc' had been the only part he could read of the semi-legible scrawl with which his guest had signed the register. And there was no typed name on any cheque to help; no cheque at all – just the two crisp twenty-pound notes he received each day for the following night's B & B, with the repeated injunction (as now) from Mr Mac: 'Give the change to the breakfast girl!' Not a big tip though, for the daily rate was £39.50.

Soon Luigi Bertolese was again reading through the runners in the 2 p.m. at Sandown Park, and looking especially at a horse there named 'Full English', with some moderate form behind him. He looked down too at one of the twenties, and wondered if the Almighty had whispered a tip in his ear.

'So you see, old friend? You *see*?' Morse beamed hugely as he finished his second pint. 'It was all due to *you*. Again!'

Lewis *could* see: for once was able to see perfectly clearly. And this for him was the joy of working with the strange man called Morse; a man who was somehow able to extricate himself from the strait-jacketing circumstances of any crime and to look at that crime from some exterior vantage point. It wasn't fair really! Yet Lewis was very proud to know that he, with all his limitations, could sometimes (as now) be the catalytic factor in the curious chemistry of Morse's mind.

'You having any lunch, sir?'

Morse had been talking for half an hour or so, quietly, earnestly, excitedly. It was now 12.15 p.m.

'No. Today I'll take my calories in liquid form.'

'Well, I think I'll get myself—'

'Here!' Morse took the precious twenty-pound note from his wallet. 'Don't go mad with it! Get yourself a cheese sandwich or something – and another pint for me.' He pushed his glass across the slightly rickety table. 'And get a beer-mat or something and stick it under one of these legs.'

For a few seconds as he stood at the bar Lewis looked back at his chief. Several other customers were now seated around, and one youth looked almost embarrassingly blissful as he gazed into the bespectacled eyes of the rather plain young woman sitting beside him. He looked, Lewis decided, almost as happy as Chief Inspector Morse.

CHAPTER FORTY-FIVE

His addiction to drinking caused me to censure
Aspern Williams for a while, until I saw as true
that wheels must have oil unless they run on nylon
bearings. He could stay still and not want oil, or
move – if he could overcome the resistance
(Peter Champkin, *The Waking Life of Aspern Williams*)

IN HER laboratory, Dr Laura Hobson had now begun to write her
report, after resuming her analysis of the Wytham bones. Not
really 'resuming' though, for the bones had hardly left her over
the weekend. Quite early on she'd spotted the slight groove on
the lower-left rib: it might have been the sharp incision of a
rodent's tooth, of course; but it looked so distinctive, that thinly
V-shaped mark. It was almost as if someone had deliberately
made a notch in the rib – with a knife or similar instrument. It
might be important? But no, that was the wrong way of looking
at things. It *might* be important – no question mark; and Laura
was oddly anxious to score a few Brownie-points on her first real
inquiry. In any case she'd very much like to ingratiate herself a
little with the strange policeman who had monopolized her
thoughts these last few days. It was odd how you couldn't shake
someone out of your mind, however hard you tried. And for
Laura that weekend Morse should, she felt, have been reported
to the Monopolies' Commission . . .
    Once more she studied the scene-of-crime photographs, and
she could identify quite easily the bone that was engaging her
interest now. It had obviously lain *in situ* – not disseminated as
so many of the others; and she felt fairly certain that the incision
which her patient investigation had revealed was unlikely to
have been caused by the tooth of some wild creature, tearing
away a morsel from the still-fleshed bones. *Could* the notch have
been caused by a knife, she wondered: after all, she was working,
was she not, upon a *murder*? So if it wasn't the foxes or the
badgers or the birds . . . Again she adjusted the focus of the
powerful microscope upon the top of the rib-bone, but she knew
there could never be any *definite* forensic findings here. The very
most she would suggest in her report was that the marked

incision made slantwise across the top of the bottom-left rib-bone might possibly have been caused by some incisor tooth, or more probably some sharp implement – a knife, say. And if it *were* a knife that had been driven through the lower chest, it could well be, probably *was*, the cause of death. The body would have bled a good deal, with the blood saturating the clothing (if any?) and then seeping into the soil beneath the body; and not even the intervening months of winter, not even the last of the leaves and the accumulating débris from the growth all round, would ever completely obliterate such traces. That angle, though, was being pursued in the University Agricultural Research Station (coincidentally situated out at Wytham) and doubtless she would be hearing something soon. So what, though? Even if there were clear signs of blood to be found there, at the very most *she* would have a blood group, and *Morse* would be able to assume that the body had been murdered *in situ*. Big deal.

Morse! She'd heard he was a bit of a stickler for spelling and punctuation, and she wanted to make as good an impression as she could. Halfway down the first page of her report she was doubtful about one word, and spying a *Chambers Dictionary* on Max's shelves she quickly looked up the spelling of 'noticeable'.

It was the *Pocket Oxford Dictionary* that was being consulted (over 'proceeding') by another report-writer that afternoon, in the Thames Valley Police HQ. Orthographic irregularities were not an uncommon phenomenon in Lewis's writing; but he was improving all the time, and (like his chief) was feeling very happy with life as he transcribed the full notes he had taken on his Swedish investigation.

At 4 p.m., Mrs Irma Eriksson knocked lightly on the door of her daughter's bedroom, and brought in a tray carrying a boiled egg and two rounds of buttered toast. The flu had been virulent, but the patient was feeling a good deal better now, and very much more relaxed.

As was her mother.

At 6.45 p.m. the first – well, the first serious – rehearsal was under way for *The Mikado*. It was quite extraordinary, really, how much local talent there always was; even more extraordinary was how willingly, eagerly almost, this local talent was prepared to devote so much of its time to amateur theatricals, and to submit (in this instance) to the quite ridiculous demands of a producer who thought he knew – and in fact *did* know – most of the secrets of pulling in audiences, of ensuring laudatory reviews in the local press, of guiding the more talented vocalists into the more demanding rôles, and above all of soothing the petty squabbles and jealousies which almost inevitably arise in such a venture.

Three hours, his wife had said – about that; and David Michaels had been waiting outside the village hall since 9.30 p.m. It wasn't all that far from home – back down the lane, past the pub, then right again up the road into the woods – little more than a mile, in fact; but it was now beginning to get really dark, and he was never going to take any chances with his lovely wife. His talented wife, too. She'd only been a member of the chorus-line in the Village Review the previous Christmas; but it had been agreed by all that a bigger part would be wholly warranted in the next production. So she'd been auditioned; and here she was as one of the three little Japanese girls from school. Nice part. Easy to learn.

She finally emerged at 10.10 p.m. and a slightly impatient Michaels drove her immediately along to the White Hart.

'Same as usual?' he asked, as she hitched herself up on to a bar stool.

'Please.'

So Michaels ordered a pint of Best Bitter for himself; and for his wife that mixture of orange juice and lemonade known as 'St Clements' – a mixture designed to keep the world's bell-ringers in a state of perpetual sobriety.

An hour later, as he drove the Land Rover back up to the cottage, Michaels felt beside the gear-lever for his wife's hand, and squeezed it firmly. But she had been very silent thus far; and remained so now as she tucked the libretto under her arm and got out, locking the passenger door behind her.

'It's going to be all right, is it?' he asked.

'Is *what* going to be all right?'

'What do you think I mean? The Mickadoo!'

'Hope so. You'll enjoy *me*, anyway.'

Michaels locked his own side of the Land-rover. 'I want to enjoy you now!'

She took his hand as they walked to the front porch.
'Not tonight, David. I'm so very tired – please understand.'

Morse too was going home at this time. He was somewhat over-beered, he realized that; yet at least he'd everything to celebrate that day. Or so he told himself as he walked along, his steps just occasionally slightly unbalanced, like those of a diffident funambulist.

Dr Alan Hardinge decided that Monday evening to stay in college, where earlier he'd given a well-rehearsed lecture on 'Man and his Natural Environment'. His largely American audience had been generously appreciative, and he (like others that evening) had drunk too much – drunk too much wine, had too many liqueurs. When at 11.30 p.m. he had rung his wife to suggest it would be wiser for him to stay in his rooms overnight, she had raised not the slightest objection.

Neither Michaels, nor Morse, nor Hardinge, was destined to experience the long unbroken sleep that Socrates had spoken of, for each of the three, though for different reasons, had much upon his mind.

CHAPTER FORTY-SIX

A fool sees not the same tree that a wise man sees
(William Blake, *The Marriage of Heaven and Hell*)

WEDNESDAY, the 29th July, was promising to be a busy day; and so it proved.

Inspector Johnson had returned from his holiday the day before, and was now au fait with most of the latest developments in the Swedish Maiden case. At 9.30 a.m. he girded his loins – and rang Strange.

'Sir? Johnson here.'

'Well?'

'I've been sorry to read things haven't worked out at Wytham—'

'Yes?'

'It's just that if you'd be prepared to give me the chance of some men in Blenheim again—'

'*No* chance. Don't you realize that while you've been lying bare-arsed on the beaches we've had all these bloody joy-riders—'

'I've read all about it, sir. All I was thinking—'

'Forget it! *Morse* is in charge now, not you. All right, he's probably making a bloody mess of it. But so did *you!* And until I give the say-so, he's staying fully in charge. So if you'll excuse me, I've got a train to catch.'

Morse also had a train to catch and left on the ten o'clock for London, where Lewis had arranged for him to meet a representative of the Swedish Embassy (for lunch), and the supervisor of the King's Cross YWCA (for tea).

For Lewis himself, after seeing Morse off at Oxford railway station, there were a great many things still to be done. Preliminary inquiries the previous day had strongly suggested – confirmed really – that Morse's analysis of the case (to which Lewis, and Lewis alone, was hitherto privy) was substantially correct in most respects. Often in the past Morse had similarly been six or so furlongs ahead of the field only later to find himself running on the wrong racecourse. This time, though, it really did look as if the old boy was right; and from Lewis's point of view it was as if he'd dreamed of the winner the night before and was now just going along to the bookmaker's to stick a few quid on a horse that had already passed the winning post.

Fortunately the pressure was temporarily off the troubles at Broadmoor Lea, and it was no difficulty for Lewis to enlist some extra help. Two DCs were assigned to him for the rest of the day; and this pair were soon off to investigate both the City and the County records of car thefts, car break-ins, car vandalism, etc., in the few days immediately following the last sighting of the Swedish Maiden. Carter and Helpston had seemed to Lewis a pretty competent couple; and so, later that Wednesday, it would prove to be the case.

In mid-morning, Lewis rang *The Oxford Mail* and spoke to the editor. He'd like to fax some copy – copy which Morse had earlier drafted – for that evening's edition. All right? No problem, it appeared.

NEW DEVELOPMENTS IN SWEDISH MAIDEN MYSTERY

DETECTIVE Chief Inspector Morse of the Thames Valley CID is confident that recently unearthed evidence has thrown a completely new light on the baffling case of Karin Eriksson, who disappeared in Oxford more than a year ago, and whose rucksack was discovered soon afterwards in a hedgerow-bottom at Begbroke. A body found after a search of Wytham Woods has proved not to be that of the Swedish student, and the chief inspector told our reporter that further searches of the area there have now been called off. Murder inquiries continue, however, and it is understood that the focus of police activity is now once again centred on the Blenheim Estate in Woodstock – the scene of the first phase of intensive inquiries just over a year ago.

The police are also asking anyone to come forward who has any information concerning Dr Alasdair McBryde, until very recently living at Seckham Villa, Park Town, Oxford. Telephone 0865 846000, or your nearest police station.

Later in the day both Chief Superintendent Strange and Chief Inspector Johnson were to read this article: the former with considerable puzzlement, the latter with apparently justifiable exasperation.

And someone else had read the article.

The slim Selina had been more than a little worried ever since Morse had called at the agency. Not worried about any sin of commission; but about one of omission, since she'd been almost certain, when Morse had asked for anything on McBryde, that there *had* been a photograph somewhere. Each Christmas the agency had given a modest little canapé-and-claret do; and later that afternoon in Abingdon' Road. and temporarily minus the mighty Michelle, she had decided where, if anywhere, the photograph might be. She looked in the files under 'Parties, Promotions etc.', and there it was: a black and white six- by four-inch photograph of about a dozen of them, party hats perched on their heads, wine glasses held high in their hands – a festive, liberally lubricated crew. And there, in the middle, the bearded McBryde, his arms round two female co-revellers.

Morse had bought a copy of *The Times* in Menzies bookstall at Oxford railway station. In the context of the case as a whole, the two Letters to the Editor which he read just after Didcot (the crossword finished all but one clue) were not of any great importance. Yet the first was, for Morse, the most memorable letter of them all, recalling a couplet he'd long been carrying around in his mental baggage.

From Mr Gordon Potter

Sir, My interest in the Swedish Maiden verses is minimal; my conviction is that the whole business is a time-consuming hoax. Yet it is time that someone added a brief gloss to the admirable letter printed in your columns (July 24). If we are to seek a priest of Roman Catholic persuasions as the instigator of the verses, let me suggest that he will also almost certainly be an admirer of the greatest poet-scholar of our own century. I refer to A. E. Housman. How else do we explain line 3 of the printed verses ('Dry the azured sky-lit water')? Let me quote Norman Marlow in his critical

commentary, *A. E. Housman*, page 145:
   'Two of the most beautiful lines in Housman's work are surely these:

*And like a skylit water stood
The bluebells in the azured
   wood.*

Here again is a reflection in water, and this time the magic effect is produced by repeating the syllable "like" inside the word "skylit" but inverted as a reflection in water is inverted.'

Yours faithfully
J. GORDON POTTER,
'Arlington',
Leckhampton Road,
Cheltenham,
Glos.

And the second, the sweetest:

From Miss Sally Monroe

Sir, 'Hunt' (l. 18)? 'kiss' (l. 20)? And
so far I only know one poem by
heart. 'Jenny kissed me when we
met', by Leigh Hunt (1784–1859).

Yours faithfully,
SALLY MONROE (aged 9 years)
22 Kingfisher Road,
Bicester,
Oxon.

CHAPTER FORTY-SEVEN

Yonder, lightening other loads,
The seasons range the country roads,
But here in London streets I ken
No such helpmates, only men
(A. E. Housman, *A Shropshire Lad*)

MORSE'S day was satisfactory – but little more.

He had arrived a quarter of an hour late, with the diesel
limping the last two miles into Paddington at walking-pace,
for reasons (Morse suspected) not wholly known even to the
engine-driver. But he still arrived in good time at the Swedish
Embassy in Montague Place for his meeting with Ingmar Engström, a slim, blond fellow in his forties, who seemed to Morse
to exude a sort of antiseptic cleanliness, yet who proved competent and helpful, and willing to instigate immediate inquiries
into the matter which Morse (with the greatest care) explained to
him.

Lunch was brought into Engström's office, and Morse looked
down unenthusiastically at the thin, pale slice of white-pastried
quiche, the half jacket potato, and the large separate bowl of
undressed salad.

'Very good for the waist-line,' commented the good-humoured

Swede. 'And no sugar in *this* either. Guaranteed genuine!' he added, pouring two glasses of chilled orange juice.

Morse escaped from Montague Place as soon as good manners allowed, professing profuse gratitude but refusing further offers of cottage-cheese, low-fat yoghurt, or fresh fruit, and was quite soon to be heard complimenting the landlord of a Holborn pub on keeping his Ruddles County Bitter in such good nick.

Seldom had tea as a meal, never had tea as a beverage, assumed any great importance in Morse's life. Although relieved therefore not to be faced with the choice of China or Indian, he could well have done without the large plastic cup of weak-looking luke-warm tea which he poured for himself from the communal urn in the virtually deserted canteen of the YWCA premises. For a while they chatted amiably, if aimlessly: Morse discovering that Mrs Audrey Morris had married a Welshman, was still married to the same Welshman, had no children, just the one sister – the one in Oxford – and, well, that was that. She'd been trained as a social worker in the East End, and taken the job of superintendent of the YWCA four years since. She enjoyed the job well enough, but the situation in London was getting desperate. All right, the hostel might be two rungs up from the cardboard-box brigade, but all the old categories were gradually merging now into a sort of communal misery: women whose homes had been repossessed; wives who had been battered; youngish girls who were unem-ployed or improvident or penniless – or usually all three; birds of passage; and druggies, and potential suicides, and of course quite frequently foreign students who'd miscalculated their monies – students like Miss Karin Eriksson.

Morse went through the main points of the statement she had made the previous summer, but there was, it seemed, nothing further she could add. Like her younger sister she was consider-ably overweight, with a plump, attractive face in which her smile, as she spoke, appeared guileless and co-operative. So Morse decided he was wasting his time, and sought answers to some other questions: questions about what Karin was *like*, how she behaved, how she'd got on with the others there.

Was it that Morse had expected a litany of seductive charms – the charms of a young lady with full breasts ever bouncing beneath her low-cut blouse, with an almost indecently short skirt tight-fitting over her bottom, and her long, bronzed legs crossed provocatively as she sat sipping a Diet Coke ... or a Cognac? Only *half* expected though, for his knowledge of Karin Eriksson was slowly growing all the time; was growing now as Mrs Morris rather gently recalled a girl who was always going to catch men's eyes, who was certainly aware of her attraction, and who clearly enjoyed the attention which it always brought. But whether she was the sort of young woman whose legs would swiftly – or even slowly – ease apart upon the application of a little pressure, well, Audrey Morris was much more doubtful. She'd given the impression of being able to keep herself, and others, pretty much under control. Oh yes!

'But she – she might lead men on a bit, perhaps?' asked Morse.

'Yes.'

'But maybe' – Morse was having some difficulty – 'not go much further?'

'Much further than what?'

'What I'm saying is, well, we used to have a word for girls like that – when I was at school, I mean.'

'Yes?'

'Yes.'

'"Prick-teaser"? Is that the word you're looking for?'

'Something like that,' said Morse, smiling in some embarrassment as he stood up and prepared to leave; just as Karin Eriksson must have stood up to take her leave from these very premises, with ten pounds in her purse and the firm resolve (if Mrs Morris could be believed) of hitch-hiking her way not only to Oxford, but very much further out along the A40 – to Llandovery, the home of the red kite.

Audrey Morris saw him out, watching his back as he walked briskly towards the underground station at King's Cross, before returning to her office and phoning her sister in Oxford.

'I've just had your inspector here!'

'No problems, I hope?'

'No! Quite dishy though, isn't he?'

'Is he?'

'Come off it! *You* said he was.'

'Did you give him a glass of that malt?'

'What?'

'You didn't give him a *drink*?'

'It's only just gone four now.'

'A-u-d-r-e-y!'

'How was *I* to know?'

'Didn't you smell his *breath*?'

'Wasn't near enough, was I?'

'You didn't manage things at all well, did you, sis!'

'Don't laugh but – I gave him a cup of *tea*.'

In spite of the injunction, the senior partner of Elite Booking Services laughed long and loud at the other end of the line.

Morse arrived back in Oxford at 6.25 p.m., and as he crossed over the bridge from Platform 2 he found himself quietly humming one of the best-known songs from *The Mikado*:

> *My object all sublime*
> *I shall achieve in time*
> *To let the punishment fit the crime,*
> *The punishment fit the crime . . .*

CHAPTER FORTY-EIGHT

Players, Sir! I look on them as no better than creatures set upon tables and joint stools to make faces and produce laughter, like dancing dogs

(Samuel Johnson, *The Life of Samuel Johnson*)

FOR SEVERAL persons either closely or loosely connected with the case being reported in these pages, the evening of Thursday, 30 July, was of considerable importance, although few of the persons involved were aware at the time that the tide of events was now approaching its flood.

7.25 p.m.

One of the three little maids peered out from one side of the tatty, ill-running stage-curtain and saw that the hall was already packed, 112 of them, the maximum number stipulated by the fire regulations; saw her husband David – bless him! – there on the back row. He had insisted on buying himself a ticket for each of the three performances, and that had made her very happy. Did he look just a little forlorn though, contributing nothing to the animated hum of conversation all around? He'd be fine though; and she – *she* felt shining and excited, as she stepped back from the curtain and rejoined her fellow performers. All right, there were only a few square yards 'backstage'; such a little *stage* too; such an inadequate, amateurish orchestra; such a pathetic apology for lighting and effects. And yet . . . and yet the magic was all around, somehow: some competent singers; excellent make-up, especially for the ladies; lovely costumes; super support from the village and the neighbourhood; and a brilliant young pianist, an undergraduate from Keble, who wore a large earring, who could sing the counter-tenor parts from the Handel operas like an angel, and who spent most of his free time on lonely nocturnal vigils watching badgers in the nearby woods.

Yes, for Cathy Michaels the adrenalin was flowing freely, and any worries her husband might be harbouring for her – or she for *him*! – were wholly forgotten as with a few sharp taps of the conductor's baton there fell a hush upon the hall; and with the first few bars of the overture, *The Mikado* had begun. Quickly she looked again in one of the mirrors there at the white-faced, black-haired, pillar-box-red-lipped Japanese lady who was herself; and knew why David found her so attractive. David . . . a good deal older than she was, of course, and with a past of which she knew so very little. But she loved him, and would do anything for him.

7.50 p.m

The four youths, aged twelve, fourteen, seventeen, and seventeen, were still being held in police custody in St Aldate's. Whereas collectively on the East Oxford estates they had, by all accounts, appeared a most intimidating bunch, individually they now looked unremarkable. Quite quickly after their arrest had the bravado of this particular quartet disintegrated, and as Sergeant Joseph Rawlinson now looked again at one of the seventeen-year-olds, he saw only a nervous, surly, not particularly articulate lad. Gone was the bluster and aggression displayed in the back of the police car when they had picked him up from home – and now they were taking him back.

'These things all you had on you, son?'

'S'pose so, yeah.'

Rawlinson picked them up carefully, one by one, and handed them across. 'Fiver, £1, £1, 50p, 10p, 5p, 5p, 5p, 2p, 2p, 1p, OK? Comb; Marlboro cigarettes; disposable lighter; packet of condoms, Featherlite – only one left; half a packet of Polos; two bus tickets, one blue Biro. OK?'

The youth stared sullenly, but said nothing.

'And *this*!' Rawlinson picked up a red-covered diary and flicked quickly through the narrow-ruled pages before putting it in his own jacket pocket. 'We're going to keep this, son. Now I want you to sign *there*.' He handed over a typed sheet and pointed to the bottom of it.

Ten minutes later Philip Daley was once more in the back of a police car, this time heading out to his home in Begbroke, Oxon.

'Makes you wonder, Sarge!' ventured one of the constables as Rawlinson ordered a coffee in the canteen.

'Mm.' Joe Rawlinson was unhappy about committing himself too strongly on the point: his own lad, aged fifteen, had become so bolshie these last six months that his mum was getting very worried about him.

'Still, with this – what's it? – Aggravated Vehicle-taking Bill. Unlimited fines! Might make 'em think a bit harder.'

'Got sod-all to start with though, some of 'em.'

'You're not going soft, Sarge?'

'Oh no! I think I'm getting harder,' said Rawlinson quietly, as he picked up his coffee, and walked over to an empty table at the far corner of the canteen.

He hadn't recognized the lad. But he'd recognized the *name* immediately – from that time the previous summer when he'd been working under Chief Inspector Johnson out at Blenheim. It could, of course, have just been one of those minor coincidences that were always cropping up in life – had it not been for the diary: a bit disturbing, some of the things written in *that*. In fact he'd almost expected to meet his old chief Johnson out on the estates at the weekend, amid the half-bricks and the broken bottles. But someone had said he was off on holiday – lucky bugger! Still, Rawlinson decided to get in touch if he could; try to ring him up tomorrow.

8.15 p. m.

Anders Fastén, a very junior official at the Swedish Embassy, had at last found what he was looking for. It had been a long search, and he realized that if only the files had been kept in a more systematized fashion he would have saved himself many, many hours. He would mention this fact to his boss; and – who knows? – the next tricky passport query might be answered in minutes. But he was pleased to have found it: it was *important*, he'd been informed. In any case, his boss would be pleased. And he much wanted to please his boss, for she was very beautiful.

9 p.m.

Sergeant Lewis had arrived home from HQ half an hour earlier, had a meal of eggs (two), sausages (six), and chips (legion), and now sat back in his favourite chair, turned on the BBC news, and reviewed his day with considerable satisfaction . . .

Especially, of course, had Morse been delighted with the photograph of Alasdair McBryde; and even more delighted with the fact that, on his own initiative, Lewis had given instructions for police leaflets to be printed, and for adverts to be placed in the following day's *Oxford Mail*, Friday's edition of *The Oxford Times* – and the *Evening Standard*.

'Masterstroke, that is!' Morse had exclaimed. 'What made you think of the *Evening Standard*?'

'You said you were sure he'd gone to London, sir.'

'Ah!'

'Didn't meet him by any chance?' Lewis had asked happily . . .

After the weather forecast – another fine sunny day, with temperatures ranging from 22 degrees Celsius in the south – Lewis put out the regular two milk-tokens, locked and bolted the front door, and decided on an early night. He heard his wife humming some Welsh melody as she washed up the plates and he went through to the kitchen and put his arms round her.

'I'm off to bed – bit weary.'

''appy too, by the sound of you. 'ad a good day?'

'Pretty good.'

'That because bloody Morse beggared off and left you on your own?'

'No! Not really.'

She dried her hands and turned to him. 'You enjoy workin' for 'im, don't you?'

'Sometimes,' agreed her husband. 'It's just that he sort of – *lifts* me a bit, if you know what I mean.'

Mrs Lewis nodded, and draped the dish-cloth over the tap. 'Yes, I do,' she replied.

10.30 p.m.

It was half an hour since Dr Alan Hardinge had decided it was time to walk along to St Giles' and take a taxi out to his home on Cumnor Hill. But still he sat sipping Scotch in the White Horse, the narrow pub separating the two wings of Blackwell's bookshop in the Broad. The second of his two lectures had not been an unqualified success, and he was aware that his subject-matter had been somewhat under-rehearsed, his delivery little more than perfunctory. And only one glass of wine to accompany a mediocre menu!

Still, £100 was £100 . . .

He was finding that however hard he tried, it was becoming progressively more difficult for him to get drunk. He hadn't read any decent literature for months, yet Kipling had been a hero in his youth and vaguely he recalled some words in one of the short stories: something about knowing the truth of being in hell 'where the liquor no longer takes hold, and the soul of a man is rotten within him'. He knew though that he was becoming increasingly maudlin, and he opened his wallet to look again at the young girl . . . He remembered the agonies of anxiety they had both experienced, he and his wife, the first time she was *really* late back home; and then that terrible night when she had not come back at all; and now the almost unbearable emptiness ahead of him when she would never come home again, never again . . .

He took out too the photograph of Claire Osborne from amongst his membership and credit cards: a small passport photograph, she staring po-faced at the wall of a kiosk somewhere – not a good photograph, but not a bad likeness. He put it away and drained his glass; it was ridiculous going on with the affair really. But how could he help himself? He was in love with the woman, and he was lately re-acquainted with all the symptoms of love; could so easily spot it in *others* too – or rather the lack of it. He knew perfectly well, for example, that his wife was no longer in love with him, but that she would never let him go; knew too that Claire had never been in love with him, and would end their relationship tomorrow if it suited her.

One other thing was worrying him that night – had been worrying him increasingly since the visit of Chief Inspector

Morse. He wouldn't do anything immediately, but he was fairly sure that before long he would be compelled to disclose the truth about what had occurred a year ago . . .

10.30 p.m.

After watching the weather forecast, Claire Osborne turned off the ITN *News at Ten* – another half-hour of death, destruction, disease, and disaster. She was almost getting anaesthetized to it, she felt, as she poured herself a gin and dry Martini, and studied one of the typed sheets that Morse had sent her:

> MOZART: Requiem (K626)
>
> ---
>
> Helmuth Rilling (Master Works)
> H. von Karajan (Deutsche Grammophon)
> Schmidt-Gaden (Pro Arte)
> Victor de Sabata (Everest)
> Karl Richter (Telefunken)

In two days' time she would have her fortieth birthday and she was going to buy a tape or a record of the *Requiem*. All Morse's versions, he'd said, were records: 'But they're not going to be pressing any more records soon, and some of these are museum-pieces anyway.' Yet for some reason she wanted to buy one of the ones *he'd* got, although she realized it would probably be far more sensible to invest in a CD player. Herbert von Karajan was the only one of the five conductors she'd heard of, and 'Deutsche Grammophon' looked and sounded so impressive . . . Yes, she'd try to get that one. Again she looked down at the sheet, trying to get the correct spelling of that awkward word 'Deutsche' into her head, with its tricky 't', 's', 'c', 'h', 'e' sequence.

Ten minutes later she had finished her drink, and put down the empty glass. She felt very lonely. And thought of Morse. And poured herself another drink, this time putting a little more ice in it.

'*God Almighty!*' she whispered to herself.

4.30 a.m.

Morse woke in the soundless dark. From his youth he had been no stranger to a few semi-erotic daydreams, yet seldom at night did he find himself actually dreaming of beautiful women.

But just now – oddly! – he dreamed a very vivid dream. It had not been of any of the beautiful women he'd so far met in the case – not of Claire Osborne, nor of the curly-headed dietitian, nor of Laura Hobson – but of Margaret Daley, the woman with those blondish-grey streaks in her hair; hair which had prompted Lewis to ask his cardinal question: 'Why do you think people want to make themselves look older than they are, sir? Seems all the wrong way round to me.' But Margaret Daley had appeared quite young in Morse's dream. And there had been a letter somewhere in that dream: 'I thought of you so much after you were gone. I think of you still and ask you to think of me occasionally – perhaps even come to visit me again. In the hope that I don't upset you, I send you my love . . .' But there *was* no letter of course; just the words that someone had spoken in his mind. He got up and made himself a cup of instant coffee, noting on the kitchen calendar that the sun would be rising at 05.19. So he went back to bed and lay on his back, his hands behind his head, and waited patiently for the dawn.

CHAPTER FORTY-NINE

An association of men who will not quarrel with one another is a thing which never yet existed, from the greatest confeder-acy of nations down to a town-meeting or a vestry

(Thomas Jefferson, *Letters*)

DR LAURA HOBSON, one of those who had not been invited across the threshold of Morse's dreams, entered his office the following morning just before nine o'clock, where after being introduced to Sergeant Lewis she took a seat and said her say.

It didn't, she admitted, boil down to very much really, and it was all in the report in any case. But her guess was that the man whose bones were found in Pasticks was about thirty years of age, of medium height, had been dead for at least nine or ten months, might well have been murdered – with a knife-wound to the heart, and that perhaps delivered by a right-handed assailant. The traces of blood found beside and beneath the body were of group O; and although the blood could have been the result of other injuries, or of other agencies, well, she thought it rather doubtful. So that was it. The body had most probably 'exited' (Morse winced) on the spot where the bones were found; not likely to have been carried or dragged there after death. There *were* other tests that could be carried out, but (in Dr Hobson's view at least) there remained little more to be discovered.

Morse had been watching her carefully as she spoke. At their first meeting he'd found her north-country accent (Newcastle, was it? Durham City?) just slightly off-putting; but he was beginning to wonder if after a little while it wasn't just a little *on*-putting. He noticed again, too, the high cheek-bones, and the rather breathless manner of her speaking. Was she *nervous* of him?

Morse was not the only one who looked at the new pathologist with some quiet admiration; and when she handed him the four typed sheets of her report, Lewis asked the question he'd wanted to put for the last ten minutes.

'You from Newcastle?'

'Good to hear it pronounced correctly! Just outside, actually.'

Morse listened none too patiently as the two of them swapped a few local reminiscences before standing up and moving to the door.

'Anyway,' said Lewis, 'good to meet you.' Then, waving the report: 'And thanks for this, luv!'

Suddenly her shoulders tightened, and she sighed audibly. 'Look! I'm not your "luv", Sergeant. You mustn't mind me being so blunt, but I'm no one's "luv" or—'

But suddenly she stopped, as she saw Morse grinning hugely beside the door, and Lewis standing somewhat discomfited beside the desk.

'I'm sorry, it's just that—'

'Please forgive my sergeant, Dr Hobson. He means well – don't you, Lewis?'

Morse watched the slim curves of her legs as she left the office, the colour still risen in her cheeks.

'What was all that about?' began Lewis.

'Bit touchy about what people call her, that's all.'

'Bit like *you*, sir?'

'She's nice, don't you think?' asked Morse, ignoring the gentle gibe.

'To be truthful, sir, I think she's a smasher.'

Somehow this plain statement of fact, made by an honest and honourable man, caught Morse somewhat off his guard. It was as if the simple enunciation of something extremely obvious had made him appreciate, for the first time, its *truth*. And for a few seconds he found himself hoping that Dr Laura Hobson would return to collect something she'd forgotten. But she was a neatly organized young woman, and had forgotten nothing.

Just before Morse and Lewis were leaving for a cup of coffee in the canteen, a call came through from PC Pollard. This rather less-than-dedicated vigilante of Pasticks had been one of four uniformed constables detailed to the compass-point entrances of Blenheim Park; and he was now ringing, with some excitement in his voice, to report that the Wytham Woods Land Rover, driven by David Michaels (whom he'd immediately recognized), had just gone down to the garden centre there. Should he try to see what was happening? Should he – *investigate*?

Morse took the portable phone from Lewis. 'Good man! Yes, try to see what's going on. But don't make it too obvious, all right?'

'How the hell's he going to do that?' asked Lewis when Morse had finished. 'He's in *uniform*.'

'Is he? Oh.' Morse appeared to have no real interest in the matter. 'Make him feel important though, don't you think?'

Chief Inspector Johnson was on his second cup of coffee when Morse and Lewis walked into the canteen. Raising a hand he beckoned Morse over: he'd welcome a brief word, if that was all right? Just the two of them though, just himself and Morse.

Ten minutes later, in Johnson's small office on the second floor, Morse learned of the red diary found the previous day on the person of Philip Daley. But before the two detectives discussed this matter, it was Johnson who'd proffered the olive-branch.

'Look. If there's been a bit of bad feeling – well, let's forget it, shall we? What do you say?'

'No bad feeling on my side,' claimed Morse.

'Well, there was on mine,' said Johnson quietly.

'Yeah! Mine, too,' admitted Morse.

'OK then?'

'OK.'

The two men shook hands firmly, if unsmilingly, and Johnson now stated his case. There'd been a flood of information over the past few days, and one thing was now pretty certain: Daley Junior had been one of the four youths – though not the driver – in the stolen BMW that had killed Marion Bridewell. From all accounts, the back wheels had slewed round in an uncontrollable skid and knocked the poor little lass through a shop window.

'Bit of an odd coincidence, certainly – the boy being involved in both cases,' commented Morse.

'But coincidences never worried you much, did they?'

Morse shrugged. 'I don't reckon he had much to do with the Eriksson case, though.'

'Except he had the camera,' said Johnson slowly.

'Ye-es.' Morse nodded, and frowned. Something was troubling him a little; like a speck of grit in a smoothly oiled mechanism; like a small piece of shell in a soft-boiled egg.

Since the tragedy, Mrs Lynne Hardinge, a slim, well-groomed, grey-haired woman of fifty, had thrown herself with almost frenetic energy into her voluntary activities: Meals on Wheels, Cruse, Help the Aged, Victim Support . . . Everyone was saying what a wonderful woman she was; everyone commented on how well she was coping.

At the time that Morse and Johnson were talking together, she got out of the passenger seat in the eight-windowed Volvo, and taking with her two tin-foiled cartons, main course and sweet, knocked firmly on a door in the Osney Mead estate.

Most of those who received their Meals on Wheels four times a week were grateful and gracious enough. But not quite all.

'It's open!'

'Here we are then, Mrs Gruby.'

'Hope it's not that fish again!'

'Lamb casserole, and lemon pudding.'

'Tuesday's was cold – did you know that?'

'Oh dear!'

The wonderfully well-coping voluntary worker said no more, but her lips moved fiercely as she closed the door behind her. Why didn't you stick it in the fucking oven then, you miserable old bitch? Sometimes she felt she could go quite, *quite* mad. Just recently too she'd felt she could easily *shoot* somebody – certainly that pathetic two-timing husband of hers.

CHAPTER FIFTY

There is but one truly serious philosophical problem, and that is suicide. Judging whether life is or is not worth living amounts to answering the fundamental question of philosophy
(Albert Camus, *The Myth of Sisyphus*)

IT WAS immediately following Morse's almost unprecedentedly alcohol-free lunch (cheese sandwich and coffee) that the crucial break in the case occurred. And it was Lewis's good fortune to convey the tidings to the canteen, where Morse sat reading the *Daily Mirror*.

When earlier in the week Morse had argued that a car would have been required, that a car would have been essential, that a car would have to be disposed of – when earlier Morse had argued these points, the firing plugs in Lewis's practical mind had sputtered into life: cars lost, cars stolen, cars vandalized, cars burned, cars abandoned, cars found on the streets, cars towed away – Lewis had straightway gauged the possibilities; and drawing a vaguely twenty-mile radius round Oxford, after consultation with the Traffic Unit, he had been able to set in motion a programme of fairly simple checks, with attention focused on the few days following the very last sighting of Karin Eriksson.

The key evidence would have been difficult to *miss*, really, once the dates were specified, since Lt. Col. Basil Villiers, MC, had rung the police on no less than twelve occasions during the period concerned, complaining that the car found abandoned and vandalized, and thereafter further vandalized and finally fired, was a blot on the beautiful landscape – a disgrace, an eyesore, and an ugliness; that he (the aforesaid Colonel) had not fought against despotism, dictatorship, totalitarianism, and tyranny to be fobbed off with petty excuses concerning insurance, liability, obligation, and availability of personnel. But it had only been after considerable difficulty (number plates now gone, though registration markings still on the windows) that the owner of the vehicle had been traced, and the offending 'eyesore' towed away from the neighbourhood of the Colonel's bungalow to some vehicular Valhalla – with a coloured photograph the only memento now of what once had been a newborn, sleek, and shining offspring of some Japanese assembly line.

The keying-in of the registration number now (as presumably a year earlier?) had produced, within a few seconds, the name and address of the owner: James Myton, of 24 Hickson Drive, Ealing; or rather *formerly* of 24 Hickson Drive, Ealing, since immediate inquiries at this address had confirmed only that James Myton had not lived there for more than a year. Swansea DVLC had sent three letters to the said address, but without reply. LMJ 594E was a lapsed registration, though still not deleted, it appeared, from the official records kept in South Wales.

As for Myton himself, his name had appeared on Scotland Yard's missing-persons list for the second half of 1991. But in that year over 30,000 persons were registered as 'missing' in London alone; and a recent report, wholly backed by Sir Peter Imbert himself, suggested that the index was becoming so inaccurate that it should be restarted from scratch, with a completely fresh re-check on each of the legion names listed. As Morse saw things though, it was going to take considerably more than a 're-check' to revive any hopes of the missing Mr James Myton ever being found alive again.

By mid-afternoon there was firm corroboration from Ealing that the body found in Pasticks was that of James William Myton, who as a boy had first been taken 'into care' by the local authority; later looked after by an ageing couple (now deceased) in Brighton; and thereafter supervised for a time by HM Borstal Service on the Isle of Wight. But the young man had always shown a bit of practical talent; and in 1989, aged twenty-six, he had emerged into the outside world with a reputation for adequate competence in carpentry, interior design, and photography. For eighteen months he had worked in the TV studios at Bristol. A physical description from a woman living two doors away from him in Ealing suggested 'a weakish sort of mouth in which the lower teeth were set small and evenly spaced, like the crenellations of a young boy's toy fort'.

'She should have been a novelist!' said Morse.

'She *is* a novelist,' said Lewis.

At all events Myton was not now to be found; and unlikely to be found. Frequently in the past he had been a man of no permanent address; but in the present Morse was sure that he was a permanent dweller in the abode of the dead – as the lady novelist might have phrased it in one of her purplier passages.

Yet things were going very well on the whole – going very much as Morse had predicted. And for the rest of the afternoon the case developed quietly: no surprises; no setbacks. At 5.45 p.m. Morse called it a day and drove down to his flat in North Oxford.

For about two hours that afternoon, as on every weekday afternoon, the grossly overweight wife of Luigi Bertolese sat at the receipt of custom in the Prince William Hotel, whilst her husband conducted his daily dealings with Mr Ladbroke, Turf Accountant. The early edition of the *Evening Standard* lay beside her, and she fixed her pair of half-lenses on to her small nose as she began reading through. At such times she might have reminded some of her paying guests of an owl seated quietly on a branch after a substantial meal – half dopey as the eyelids slowly descended, and then more than commonly wise as they rose . . . as they rose again *now* when number 8 came in, after his lunch. And after his drink – by the smell of him.

The photograph was on the front page, bottom left: just a smallish photograph and taken when he'd had a beard, the beard he'd shaved off the day after his arrival at the hotel. Although Maria Bertolese's English was fairly poor, she could easily follow the copy beneath: 'The police are anxious to interview this man, Alasdair McBryde . . .'

She gave him the room-key, handed over two twenty-pound notes, and nodded briefly to the newspaper.

'I doan wanna no trouble for Luigi. His heart is not good – is bad.'

The man nodded, put one of the twenties in his wallet, and gave her back the other: 'For the breakfast girl, please.'

When Luigi Bertolese returned from the betting shop at four o'clock, number 8, cum luggage, had disappeared.

At the ticket office in the main-line Paddington terminus, McBryde asked for a single to Oxford. The 16.20, calling at Reading, Didcot Parkway, and Oxford, was already standing at Platform 9; but there was ten minutes to spare, and from a British Telecom booth just outside the Menzies bookshop there he rang a number (direct line) in Lonsdale College, Oxford.

Dr Alan Hardinge put the phone down slowly. A fluke he'd been in his rooms really. But he supposed McBryde would have caught up with him somewhere, sometime; there would have been a morning or an afternoon or an evening when there had to come a rendering of accounts, a payment of the bill, *eine Rechnung,* as the Germans said. He'd agreed to meet the man of course. What option had he? And he *would* see him; and they would have a distanced drink together, and talk of many things: of what was to be done, and what was not to be done.

And then?

Oh God! What then?

He put his head in his hands and jerked despairingly at the roots of his thick hair. It was the *cumulative* nature of all these bloody things that was so terrible. Several times over the last few days he'd thought of ending it all. But, strangely perhaps, it had not been any fear concerning death itself that had deterred him; rather his own inability to cope with the *practical* aspects of any suicide. He was one of those people against whom all machinery, all gadgetry, would ever wage perpetual war, and never in his life had he managed to come to terms with wires and switches and fuses and screws. There was that way of ending things in the garage, for example – with closed doors and exhaust fumes; but Hardinge suspected he'd cock that up completely. Yet he'd have to do something, for life was becoming intolerable: the failure of his marriage; his rejection by the only woman he'd really grown to love; the futility of academic preferment; his pathetic addiction to pornography; the death of his daughter; and now, just a few minutes ago, the reminder of perhaps the most terrible thing of all . . .

The second performance of *The Mikado,* as Morse recalled, was scheduled, like the first, for 7.30 p.m. Still plenty of time to get ready and go, really. But that evening too he decided against it.

*

The first night had been all right, yes – but all a bit nervy, a bit 'collywobbly', as the other girls had said. They'd be in really good form that second night, though. David had said she'd been fine the first night – *fine!* But she'd be better now; she'd show him!

With five minutes to go, she peeped round the curtain again and scanned the packed audience. David's ticket for each of the three nights had been on the back row, and she could see one empty seat there now, next to the narrow gangway. But she could see no David. He must, she thought, be standing just outside the hall, talking to somebody before the show began. But seat K5 was destined to remain unoccupied that evening until, during the last forty minutes, one of the programme-sellers decided she might as well give her aching feet a welcome rest.

CHAPTER FIFTY-ONE

He that is down needs fear no fall,
He that is low, no pride
(John Bunyan, *The Pilgrim's Progress*)

WHETHER Morse had been expecting something of the kind, Lewis wasn't at all sure. But certain it was that the Chief Inspector appeared less than surprised when the telephone call came through from Dr Alan Hardinge the following morning. Could he see Morse, please? It wasn't desperately urgent – but well, yes it *was* desperately urgent really, at least for him.

Morse was apparently perfectly content for Lewis to interject one or two obvious questions, just to keep things flowing – the meanwhile himself listening carefully, though with a hint of cynicism around his lips. Perhaps, as Lewis saw things, it had been the preliminary niceties that had soured his chief a little:

MORSE: I was very sorry to learn of your daughter's accident, Dr Hardinge. Must have been a – a terrible—

HARDINGE: How would you know? You've no children of
  your own.
MORSE: How did you know that?
HARDINGE: I thought we had a mutual friend, Inspector.

No, it hadn't been a very happy start, though it had finished
far more amicably. Hardinge had readily agreed to have his
statement recorded on tape; and the admirably qualified WPC
Wright was later to make a very crisp and clean transcription,
pleasingly free from the multi-Tipp-Exed alterations that usually
characterized Lewis's struggles with the typewriter:

On Sunday, 7 July 1991, I joined four other men in Seckham Villa,
Park Town, Oxford. I am more embarrassed than ashamed about
the shared interest that brought us together. Those present were:
Alasdair McBryde, George Daley, David Michaels, James Myton,
and myself. McBryde informed us that we might be in for an
interesting afternoon since a young Swedish student would be
coming to sit for what was euphemistically termed a photographic session. We learned she was a beautiful girl, and desperately in need of money. If we wished to watch, that would be an
extra £50: £100 in toto. I agreed. So did Daley. So did Michaels. I
myself had arrived first. Daley and Michaels arrived together a
little later, and I had the impression that the one had probably
picked the other up. I knew next to nothing about these two men
except that they were both in the same line of business – forestry,
that sort of thing. I had met each of them two or three times
before, I had never met them together before.

The fifth man was Myton, whom I'd known earlier, I'm
ashamed to say, as the editor of a series of sex magazines whose
particular slants ranged from bestiality to paedophilia. He was a
smallish, slimly built man, with a weasel-like look about him –
sharp nose and fierce little eyes. He often boasted about his time
with the ITV Zodiac Production team; and however he may have
exaggerated, one thing was perfectly clear: whatever he filmed
for videotapes, whatever he photographed for 'stills', Myton had
the magical touch of the born artist.

The first part of the afternoon I can remember only vaguely.
The room in which we were seated, the basement room, had a
largish, erectile screen, and we were there (all except Myton)
watching some imported hard-porn Danish videos when we were

aware that the eagerly awaited Swedish star had arrived. The doorbell had been rung; McBryde had left us; and soon we were to hear voices just above us, in the garden outside – the voices of Myton and the young woman I now know to have been Karin Eriksson. I remember at that point feeling very excited. But things didn't work out. It soon transpired that the girl had misunderstood the nature of her engagement; that she was happy enough to do a series of nude stills – but only behind a closed door, with a camera, and with one cameraman. No argument.

It was about half an hour later that we heard the awful commotion in the room immediately above us, and we followed McBryde up the stairs. The young woman (we never knew her name until days later) lay on the bed. She lay motionless there, with blood all over the white sheets – vividly red blood. fresh blood. Yet it was not *her* blood – but Myton's! He sat there crumpled up on the floor, clutching his left side and gasping desperately, his eyes widely dilated with pain – and fear. But for the moment it was the naked girl who compelled our attention. There were horridly bright red marks around her throat, and her mouth seemed oddly swollen, with a trickle of blood slowly seeping down her cheek. Yes, her cheek. For it was the angle of her head that was so startling – craned back, as though she were trying so hard to peer over her forehead to the headboard of the bed behind her. Then, not immediately perhaps but so very soon, we knew that she was dead.

If ever my heart sank in fear and froze in panic – it was then! Often in the past I had been in some sex cinema somewhere, and wondered what would happen if there were a sudden fire and the exits were blocked with panic-stricken men. The same sort of thoughts engulfed me now; and then, behind me – terrifying noise! – I heard a sound like a kitchen sink clearing itself, and I turned to see the vomit of dark red blood suddenly spurting from Myton's mouth and spilling in a great gush over the carpet. Six or seven times his body heaved in mighty spasms – before he too, like the girl on the bed, lay still.

Of the sequence of events which had led up to this double tragedy, it is impossible to be certain. I can't know what the others there thought; I don't really know what I thought. I suppose I envisaged Myton filming her as she took up her various poses; then lusting after her and trying to assault her there. But she'd fought him off, with some partial success. More than partial success.

What was clear to us all was that she'd stabbed him with a knife, the sort of multi-purpose knife scouts and guides carry around with them, for she still clutched the knife even then in her right hand as if she'd thought he might make for her again. How she came to have such a weapon beside her – as I say, she was completely naked – I can't explain.

My next clear recollection is of sitting with the other three in the downstairs room drinking neat whisky and wondering what on earth to do, trying to devise some plan! Something! Anything! All of us – certainly three of us – had the same dread fear in mind, I'm sure of it: of being exposed to society, to our friends, families, children, everyone – exposed for what we really were – cheap, dirty-minded perverts. Scandal, shame, ruin – never had I known such panic and despair.

I now come to the most difficult part of my statement, and I can't vouch for the precise motives of all of us, or indeed for some specific details. But the main points of that day are fairly clear to me still – albeit they seem in retrospect to have taken place in a sort of blur of unreality. Let me put it simply. We decided to cover up the whole ghastly tragedy. It must seem almost incredible that we took such enormous trouble to cover ourselves, yet that is what we did. McBryde told us that the only others who knew of the Swedish girl's visit were the model agency, and he said he would see to it that there was no trouble from that quarter. That left – how terrible it all now sounds! – two bodies, two dead bodies. There could be no thought of their being disposed of before the hours of darkness, and so it was agreed that the four of us should reassemble at Seckham Villa at 9.45 p.m.

For the last few months Myton had been living out of suitcases – out of two large, battered-looking brown suitcases. And in fact had been staying with McBryde, on and off, for several of the previous weeks. But McBryde was still cursing himself for letting the two of them, Myton and the girl, go out into the back garden, since if any of the neighbours had seen Karin Eriksson they would quite certainly have remembered her clearly. His fears on this score however seem to have been groundless. As far as Myton's suitcases and personal effects were concerned, McBryde himself would be putting them into the back of his van and carting them off to the Redbridge Waste Reception Centre early the following morning. Myton's car was a much bigger headache but the enormous rise in the number of car-related crimes in Oxford that year suggested a reasonably simple solution. It was decided that I should drive the Honda out to the edge of Otmoor at 10.45 p.m. that same night, kick in all the panels, smash all the windows, and take a hammer to the engine. And this was done. McBryde had followed me in his van – and indeed assisted me in my vandalism before driving me back to Oxford.

That was my rôle. But there was the other huge problem – the disposal of two bodies, also the ditching somewhere of the girl's rucksack. Why we didn't decide to dump the rucksack with Myton's suitcases, I just don't know. And what a tragic mistake that proved! The bodies were eventually loaded into the back of McBryde's van which drove off under the darkness of that night – this is what I understand – first to Wytham, where after Michaels had unlocked the gate leading to the woods the two foresters had transferred Myton's body to the Land Rover, and then driven out to dispose of the body in the heart of the woods somewhere – I never knew where.

Then the same men drove out to Blenheim where Daley, naturally, had easy access to any part of the Great Park, and where Karin Eriksson's body, wrapped in a blanket and weighed down with stones, was pushed into the lake there – again I never knew where.

Looking back, the whole thing seems so very crude and cruel. But some people act strangely when they are under stress – and we were all under tremendous stress that terrible day. Whether the others involved will be willing to corroborate this sequence of events, I don't know. What is to be believed is that this statement has been made of my own free will with no coercion or promptings, and that it is true.

The statement was dated 1.viii.1992, and signed by Dr Alan Hardinge, Fellow of Lonsdale College, Oxford, in the presence of Detective Chief Inspector Morse, Detective Sergeant Lewis, and WPC Wright – no solicitor being present, at Dr Hardinge's request.

*

Whilst Hardinge was still only about halfway through his statement, George Daley, eager as ever to take advantage of overtime,
was boxing some petunias in the walled garden at Blenheim
Garden Centre. He had not heard the footsteps; but he felt the
touch of a hand on his shoulder, and jerked nervously.

'Christ! You got 'ere quick.'

'You said it was urgent.'

'It *is* bloody urgent.'

'What is?'

'Now look—!'

'No, *you* look! The police'll have that statement some time this
morning – probably got it already. And we've agreed – you've
agreed – remember that!'

Daley took off the ever-present hat, and wiped the back of his
right wrist across his sweaty forehead.

'Not any longer I haven't bloody agreed, mate. Look at this!'
Daley took a letter from his pocket. 'Came in the post this
morning, dinnit? That's why I rang. See what I could get done
for? Me! Just for that fuckin' twerp o' mine. No, mate! What we
agreed's no good no longer. We double it – or else no deal. Four,
that's what I want. Not two. Four!'

'*Four?* Where the hell do you reckon that's coming from?'

'Your problem, innit?'

'If I could find it,' said the other slowly, 'how do I know you're
not going—'

'You don't. Trust, innit? I shan't ask nothin' more never though
– not if we make it four.'

'I can't get anything, you know that – not till the bank opens
Monday.'

There was a silence between them.

'You won't regret it, mate,' said Daley finally.

'*You* will, though, if you ever come this sort of thing again.'

'Don't you threaten me!'

'I'm not just threatening you, Daley – I'll bloody *kill* you if you
try it on again.' There was a menace and a power now in his
quiet voice, and he turned to go. 'Better if you come to me –
fewer people about.'

'Don't mind.'

'About ten – no good any earlier. In my office, OK?'

'Make it *outside* your office.'

The other shrugged. 'Makes no difference to me.'

CHAPTER FIFTY-TWO

Everything comes if a man will only wait
(Benjamin Disraeli, *Tancred*)

AN HOUR after Hardinge had left – had been allowed to leave – Lewis came back into Morse's office with three photocopies of the document.

Morse picked up one set of the sheets and looked fairly cursorily, it appeared, at the transcript of Hardinge's statement. 'What did you make of things?'

'One or two things a bit odd, sir.'

'Only one or two?'

'Well, there's two things, really. I mean, there's this fellow Daley, isn't there? He's at Park Town that afternoon and that night he shoves the girl's body into the lake at Blenheim.'

'Yes?'

'Well, then he leaves the girl's rucksack in a hedge-bottom at Begbroke. I mean—'

'I wish you'd stop saying "I mean", Lewis.'

'Well, you'd think he'd have left it miles away, wouldn't you? He could easily have dumped it out at Burford or Bicester or somewhere. I me—'

'Why not put it in the blanket? With the body?'

'Well, yes. Anywhere – except where he left it.'

'I think you're right.'

'Why don't we ask him then?'

'All in good time, Lewis! You just said *two* things, didn't you?'

'Ah, well. It's the same sort of thing, really. They decided to put Myton's body in Wytham Woods, agreed? And they *did* put it there, because we've found it. What I can't understand is why Michaels told you where it *was*. I mean— Sorry, sir!'

'But he didn't, did he? He didn't exactly give us a six-figure grid-reference.'

'He told you about Pasticks, though.'

'Among other places, yes.' For a while Morse looked out across the tarmac yard, unseeing it seemed, though nodding gravely. 'Ye-es! Very good, Lewis! You've put your finger – two fingers –

on the parts of that statement that would worry anyone; anyone even *half* as intelligent as you are.'

Lewis was unsure whether this was exactly the compliment that Morse had intended; but the master was beginning his own analysis:

'You see – ask yourself this. Why did Daley have to dump the rucksack, and then find it *himself*? As you rightly say, why so close to the place they'd just dumped her body? What's the reason? What *could* be the reason? Any reason? Then, again just as you say, why was Michaels prepared to be so helpful to us? Crackers, isn't it – if he didn't want anyone to find the body? So why? Why give us *any* chance of finding it? Why not give us a duff list of utterly improbable sites? God! Wytham's as big as . . .' (Morse had difficulty with the simile) 'as the pond out at Blenheim.'

'"Lake", sir – about two hundred acres of it. Take a bit of dragging, that.'

'Take a *lot* of dragging.'

'Forget it, then?'

'Yes, forget it! I think so. As I told you yesterday, Lewis . . .'

'You still think you were right about that?'

'Oh, yes! No doubt about it. All we've got to do is to sit back and wait. We're going to have people come to *us*, Lewis. We're losing nothing. You can take it from me there'll be no more casualties in this case unless . . . unless it's that silly young sod, Philip Daley.'

'We might as well take a bit of a breather then, sir.'

'Why not? Just one thing you can do on your way home, though. Look in at Lonsdale, will you? See who was on duty at the Porters' Lodge last night, and try to find out if our friend Hardinge had any visitors in his rooms. And if so, how many, and who they were.'

For the moment, however, Lewis seemed reluctant to leave.

'You sure you don't want me to go and pick up Daley and Michaels?'

'I just told you. They'll be coming to *us*. One of 'em will, anyway, unless I'm very much mistaken.'

'Which you seldom are.'

'Which I seldom am.'

'You don't want to tell me which one?'

'Why *shouldn't* I want to tell you which one?'

'Well?'

'All right. I'll bet you a fiver to a cracked piss-pot that the Head Warden, the Lone Ranger, or whatever his name is, will call here – in person or on the phone – before you sit watching the six o'clock news on the telly.'

'Earlier than that, sir – on a Saturday – the TV news.'

'Oh, and before you go, leave these on Johnson's desk, will you? He won't be in till Monday, I shouldn't think, but I promised to keep him fully informed.' He handed over the third set of photocopied pages, and Lewis rose to depart.

'Do you want me to ring you if I find anything?'

'If it's interesting, yes,' said Morse, with apparent indifference.

Earlier that day, Lewis thought he'd had a pretty clear idea of what the case was all about; or what Morse had told him the case was all about. But now on leaving Kidlington HQ his mind was far more confused, as if whatever else had been the purpose of Hardinge's statement it had certainly muddied the waters of *his*, Lewis's, mind, though apparently not that of his chief's.

As it happened (had he remembered it) Morse would have lost any bet that might have been made, for no one, either in person or on the telephone, was to call on him that afternoon. In fact he did nothing after Lewis left. At one point he almost decided to attend the last night of *The Mikado* at Wytham. But he hadn't got a ticket, and it would probably be a sell-out; and in any case he'd bought a CD of Mozart's *Requiem*.

Cathy saw him there that final evening, ten minutes before the curtain was scheduled to rise: the bearded, thick-set, independent soul she'd been so happy to marry in spite of the difference in their ages. He was talking quite animatedly to an attractive woman on the row in front of him, doubtless flirting with her just a little, with that dry, easy, confidential tone he could so easily assume. Yet Cathy felt not the slightest spasm of jealousy – for she knew that it was she who meant almost everything to him.

She let the drape fall back across her line of vision, and went back to the ladies' dressing room where, over her left shoulder, she surveyed herself in the full-length mirror. The simple, short black dresses, with their white collars and red belts, and the suspender-held black stockings, had proved one of the greatest attractions of the show; and each of the three perhaps not-so-little maids, if truth were known, was enjoying the slightly titillating exhibitionism of it all. Cathy had omitted to ask David if he really approved; or if he might be just a teeny bit jealous. She hoped he *was*, of course; but, no, he needn't be. Oh no, he needn't ever be.

Like most amateur and indeed professional productions, *The Mikado* had been put together in disparate bits, with almost all chronological sequencing impossible until the dress rehearsal. Thus it was that David Michaels, though attending a good many practices during the previous month, had little idea of what, perhaps rather grandly, was sometimes called the opera's 'plot'. Nor had his understanding been much forwarded as a result of the first night's performance, for his mind was dwelling then on more important matters. And now, on this final night, his mind was even further distanced, while he watched the on-stage action as if through some semi-opaque gauze; while he listened to the squeaky orchestra as if his ears were stuffed with cotton wool . . .

He recalled that phone call the previous evening, after which he'd driven down to Oxford, had luckily found a parking place just beside Blackwell's bookshop in the Broad, and then walked through Radcliffe Square and across the cobbles into Lonsdale College, where he'd followed his instructions, walked straight past the Porters' Lodge as if on some high behest, and then into Hardinge's rooms in the front quad, where McBryde had already arrived, and where Daley was to appear within minutes.

Over a year it had been since they'd last met – a year in which virtually nothing had occurred; a year during which the police files had been kept open (he assumed); but a year in which he and the others, the quartet of them, would have assumed with ever-growing relief and confidence that no one would, or ever could, now discover the truth about that hot and distant sunny day.

It was that bloody letter in the paper that had stirred it all up again – as well as that man Morse. What a shock it had been when they'd found the body – since he, Michaels, had no idea whatsoever it had been *there* at all. Bad luck, certainly. What a slice of *good* luck though that he'd found the antler-handled knife, because no one was ever going to find *that* again, lying deep as it was in the lake at Blenheim Park. Yes, the last vestige of evidence was at last obliterated, and the situation was beginning to right itself again; or rather *had* been so beginning . . . until he'd taken the second phone call, early that very morning; the call from that cesspit of a specimen out at Begbroke. But Daley could wait for a while; Daley would play along with them for a little longer yet. The one thing Michaels was quite unable to understand was why *Morse* was waiting. And that made him very uneasy. Perhaps everybody was waiting . . .

Suddenly he was conscious of the applause all around him, as the curtain moved jerkily across to mark the end of Act 1 of *The Mikado*.

CHAPTER FIFTY-THREE

As we passed through the entrance archway, Randolph said
with pardonable pride, 'This is the finest view in England'
(Lady Randolph Churchill, on her first visit to Blenheim)

ON MONDAY, 3 August, Chief Inspector Harold Johnson had spent much of the morning with his City colleagues in St Aldate's, and it was not until just gone 11 a.m. that he was in his own office back at Kidlington HQ – where he immediately read the transcript of Hardinge's evidence. Then reread it. It was all new to him, except the bits about the rucksack, of course. Naturally he had to admit that since Morse had been on the case the whole complexion of things had changed dramatically: clues, cars, corpses – why hadn't *he* found any of them? Odd really, though: Morse's obsession had been with Wytham; and his, Johnson's, with Blenheim. And according to the statement Hardinge had made, *both* of them had been right all along. He rang through on the internal extension to Morse's office, but learned that he had just left, with Lewis – destination undisclosed.

Blenheim! He found the glossy brochure on Blenheim Palace still on his shelves, and he turned to the map of the House and Grounds. There it was – the lake! The River Glyme flowed into the estate from the east, first into the Queen Pool, then under Vanbrugh's Grand Bridge into the lake beyond: some two hundred-odd acres in extent, so they'd told him, when first he'd mooted the suggestion of dragging the waters. Too vast an undertaking, though; still was. The Queen Pool was fairly shallow, certainly, and there had been a very thorough search of the ground at its periphery. But nothing had been found, and Johnson had always suspected (rightly, it seemed!) that if Karin Eriksson's body had been disposed of in any stretch of Blenheim there, it had to be in the far deeper, far more extensive waters of the lake; had to be well weighted down too, so the locals had told him, since otherwise it would pretty certainly have surfaced soon after immersion, and floated down to the Grand Cascade, at the southern end of the lake, where the waters resume their narrow flow within the banks of the Glyme.

Johnson flicked through the brochure's lavish illustrations and promised himself he would soon take his new wife to visit the splendid house and grounds built by Queen Anne and her grateful parliament for the mighty Duke. What was that mnemonic they'd learned at school? BROM – yes, that was it: Blenheim, Ramilles, Oudenarde, Malplaquet – that musical quartet of victories. Then, quite suddenly, he had the urge to go and look again at that wonderful sight which bursts upon the visitor after passing through the Triumphal Gate.

He drove out to Woodstock, past the Bear and the church on his left, then across a quadrangle and up to the gate where a keeper sat in his box, and where Johnson (to his delight) was recognized.

'You going through, sir?'

Johnson nodded. 'I thought we had one of our lads at each of the gates?'

'Right. You did, sir. But you took 'em off.'

'When was that?'

'Saturday. The fellow who was on duty here just said he wouldn't be back – that's all I know. Reckon as he thought the case was finished, like.'

'Really?'

Johnson drove on through, and there it was again, bringing back so many memories: in the middle distance the towers and finials of the Palace itself; and there, immediately to his right, the lake with the Grand Bridge and Capability Brown's beechwood landscape beyond it. Breathtaking!

Johnson accepted the fact that he was a man of somewhat limited sensitivity; yet he thought he was a competent police officer, and he was far from happy about the statement he'd just read. If this Hardinge fellow could be believed, the evidence Daley had given a year earlier had been decidedly economical with the truth; and that, to Johnson, was irksome – very irksome. At the time, he'd spent a good while with Daley, going over that wretched rucksack business; and he wanted to have another word with Daley. Now!

He drove down past the Palace to the garden centre; but no one there had seen Daley that morning. He might be out at the mill, perhaps? So Johnson drove out of the estate, through Eagle Lodge, and out on to the A4095, where he turned right through Bladon and Long Hanborough, then right again and in towards the western boundary of the estate, parking beside the piles of newly cut stakes in the yard of the Blenheim Estate Saw-Mill. Only once had he been there when earlier he'd been the big white chief, and he was suddenly aware that it would have been considerably quicker for him to have driven across the park instead of round the villages. Not that it much mattered, though.

No one recognized him here. But he soon learned that Daley's van wasn't there; hadn't been there since Friday afternoon in fact, when he'd been looking after some new plantation, by the lake, and when he'd called at the saw-mill for some stakes for supporting saplings. One of the workers suggested that Daley would probably have taken the van home with him for the weekend – certainly so if he'd been working overtime that weekend; and the odds were that Daley was back planting trees that morning.

Johnson thanked the man and drove to the edge of the estate, only just along the road really; then right along a lane that proclaimed 'No Thoroughfare', till he reached Combe Lodge where, Johnson had been told, the gate would probably be locked. But, well, he *was* a policeman, he'd said.

Johnson read the notice on the tall, wooden, green-painted gate:

ACCESS FOR KEYHOLDERS ONLY.
ALL OTHER VEHICLES MUST USE THE GATE IN WOODSTOCK.
DO NOT DISTURB THE RESIDENTS IN THE LODGE.

But there was no need for him to disturb the (single) resident, since a tractor-cum-trailer was just being admitted, and in its wake the police car was waved through without challenge. A little lax perhaps, as Johnson wondered. Immediately in front of him the road divided sharply; and as a lone, overweight lady, jogging at roughly walking pace, took the fork to the right, Johnson took the fork to the left, past tall oak trees towards the northern tip of the lake. Very soon, some two or three hundred yards ahead on his left, he saw the clump of trees, and immediately realized his luck – for a Blenheim Estate van stood there, pulled in beside an old, felt-roofed hut, its wooden slats green with mildew. He drew in alongside and got out of the car to look through a small side-window of glass.

Nothing. Well, virtually nothing: only a wooden shelf on which rested two unopened bags of food for the pheasants. Walking round to the front of the hut, he tried the top and bottom of the stable-type door: both locked. Then, as he stepped further round, something caught the right-hand edge of his vision, and he looked down at the ground just beyond and behind the hut – his mouth suddenly opening in horror, his body held momentarily in the freezing grip of fear.

CHAPTER FIFTY-FOUR

Michael Stich (W. Germany) beat Boris Becker (W. Germany) 6–4, 7–6, 6–4
(Result of the Men's Singles Championship at Wimbledon, 1991)

AT THE time that Chief Inspector Johnson had set out for Woodstock, Lewis was driving, at slightly above the national speed limit, along the A40 to Cheltenham. It appeared to have been a late, impulsive decision on Morse's part:

'You realize, Lewis, that the only person we've not bothered about in this case so far is auntie whatever-her-name-is from Llandovery.'

'Not an "auntie" exactly, sir. You know, it's like when little girls sometimes call women their aunties—'

'No. I don't know, Lewis.'

'Well, it seems Karin called her Auntie Dot or Doss – this

Mrs Evans. "Dorothy", I seem to remember her Christian name
was.'

'You've profited from your weekend's rest, Lewis!'

'Don't you think we ought to get Daley and Michaels in first
though, sir? I mean, if they're prepared to back up what Dr
Hardinge says—'

'No! If I'm right about this case – which I am! – we'll be in a
far better position to deal with those two gentlemen once we've
seen the Lady of Llandovery. Remember that sign at the Woodstock Road roundabout? Left to Wytham; right to Woodstock;
straight over for the A40 to West Wales, right? So we can be there
in . . .? How far is it?'

'Hundred and thirty? Hundred and forty miles? But don't you
think we should give her a ring just in case—'

'Get the car out, Lewis. The way you drive we'll be there in
three hours.'

'Try for two and a half, if you say so,' replied Lewis with a
radiant smile.

It had been after Cheltenham, after Gloucester and Ross-on-Wye,
after Monmouth and the stretch of beautiful countryside between
Brecon and Llandovery, that Morse had come to life again. Never,
in Lewis's experience, had he been any sort of conversationalist
in a car; but that day's silence had broken all records. And when
finally he did speak, Lewis was once again conscious of the
unsuspected processes of Morse's mind. For the great man,
almost always so ignorant of routes and directions and distances,
suddenly jerked up in his passenger seat:

'The right turn in a couple of miles, Lewis – the A483 towards
Builth Wells.'

'You don't want to stop for a quick pint, sir?'

'I most certainly *do*. But if you don't mind, we'll skip it, all
right?'

'I still think it would've been sensible to ring her, sir. You
know, she might be off for a fortnight in Tenerife or something.'

Morse sighed deeply. 'Aren't you enjoying the journey?' Then,
after a pause: 'I rang her yesterday afternoon, anyway. She'll be
there, Lewis. She'll be there.'

Lewis remained silent, and it was Morse who resumed the
conversation:

'That statement – that statement Hardinge made. They

obviously got together, the four of them – Hardinge, Daley, Michaels, and McBryde – got together and cooked up a story between them. Your porter couldn't give us any names, you say; but he was pretty sure there were at least three, probably four, of 'em in Hardinge's rooms on Friday night. And if they all stick to saying the same – well, we shall have little option but to believe them.'

'Not that *you* will, sir.'

'Certainly not. *Some* of it might be true, though; some of it might be absolutely crucial. And the best way of finding that out is seeing Auntie Gladys here.'

'Dorothy.'

'You see, there was only *one* really important clue in this case: the fact that the Swedish girl's rucksack was found so quickly – *had* to be found – left beside the road-side – *sure* to be found.'

'I think I'm beginning to see that,' said Lewis, unseeing, as he turned left now at Llanwrtyd Wells, and headed out across the Cambrian Hills.

But not for long. After only a couple of miles, on the left, they came to a granite-built guest-house, 'B & B: Birdwatchers Welcome'. Perhaps it was destined to do a fairly decent trade. Was *certainly* so destined, if there were any birdwatchers around, since there was not another house to be espied anywhere in the deeply wooded landscape.

Mrs Evans, a smallish, dark, sprightly woman in her late forties, showed them into the 'parlour'; and was soon telling them something of herself. She and her husband had lived in East Anglia for the first fifteen years of their (childless) marriage; it was there that she'd met Karin for the first time eight or nine years ago. She, Mrs Evans, was no blood relation at all, but had become friendly with the Eriksson family when they had stayed in the guest-house in Aldeburgh. The family had stayed the next year too, though minus Daddy that time; and thereafter the two women had corresponded off and on fairly regularly: birthday cards, Christmas cards, holiday postcards, and so on. And to the three young Eriksson girls she had become 'Auntie Doss'. When Karin had decided to come to England in 1991, Mrs Evans had known about it; and not having seen the girl for six years or so, had suggested to her mother that if Karin was going to get over towards Wales at all there would always be a welcome for her – and a bed. *And* some wonderful birdwatching, since the beautiful red kites were becoming an increasingly common sight there. What *sort* of girl was Karin? Of course, she'd only been thirteen or fourteen when she'd seen her last but, well – lovely, really. Lovely girl. Attractive – very *proper*, though.

As the conversation between them developed, Lewis found himself looking idly round the room: armchairs, horse-hair settee, mahogany furniture, a coffee table piled high with country magazines, and on the wall above the fireplace a large map of Dyffed and the Cambrian Mountains. It seemed to him a rather bleak and sunless room, and he thought that had she reached this far, the young Karin Eriksson would not have felt too happy there . . .

Morse had now got the good lady talking more rapidly and easily, her voice rising and falling in her native Welsh lilt; talking about why they'd moved back to Wales, how the recession was hitting them, how they advertised for guests – in which magazines and newspapers. On and on. And in the middle of it:

'Oh! Would you both like a cup of tea?'

'Very kind – but no,' said Morse, even as Lewis's lips were framing a grateful 'yes'.

'Tell me more about Karin,' continued Morse. '"Proper" you said. Do you mean "prim and proper" – that sort of thing? You know, a bit prudish; a bit . . . straitlaced?'

'Nor, I dorn't mean *that*. As I say it's five or six years back, isn't it? But she was . . . well, her mother said she'd always got plenty of boyfriends, like, but she knew, well . . . she knew where to draw the line – let's put it like that.'

'She didn't keep a packet of condoms under her pillow?'

'I dorn't think so.' Mrs Evans seemed far from shocked by the blunt enquiry.

'Was she a virgin, do you think?'

'Things change, dorn't they? Not *many* gels these days who ought to walk up the aisle in white, if you ask me.'

Morse nodded slowly as if assimilating the woman's wisdom, before switching direction again. What was Karin like at school – had Mrs Evans ever learned that? Had she been in the – what was it? – Flikscouten, the Swedish Girl Guides? Interested in sport, was she? Skiing, skating, tennis, basketball?

Mrs Evans was visibly more relaxed again as she replied: 'She was always good at sport, yes. Irma – Mrs Eriksson – she used to write and tell me when her daughters had won things; you know, cups and medals, certificates and all that.'

'What was Karin best at, would you say?'

'Dorn't know really. As I say it's a few years since—'

'I do realize that, Mrs Evans. It's just that you've been so helpful so far – and if you could just cast your mind back and try – try to remember.'

'Well, morst games, as I say, but—'

'Skiing?'

'I dorn't think so.'

'Tennis?'

'Oh, she loved tennis. Yes, I think tennis was her favourite game, really.'

'Amazing, aren't they – these Swedes! They've only got about seven million people there, is that right? But they tell me about four or five in the world's top-twenty come from Sweden.'

Lewis blinked. Neither tennis nor any other sport, he knew, was of the slightest interest to Morse who didn't know the difference between side-lines and touch-lines. Yet he understood exactly the trap that Morse was digging; the trap that Mrs Evans tumbled into straightaway.

'Edberg!' she said. 'Stefan Edberg. He's her great hero.'

'She must have been very disappointed about Wimbledon last year, I should think, then?'

'She was, yes. She told me she—'

Suddenly Mrs Evans's left hand shot up to her mouth, and for many seconds she sat immobile in her chair as if she'd caught a glimpse of the Gorgon.

'Don't worry,' said Morse quietly. 'Sergeant Lewis will take it all down. Don't talk too fast for him, though: he failed his forty words per minute shorthand test, didn't you, Sergeant?'

Lewis was wholly prepared. 'Don't worry about what he says, Mrs Evans. You can talk just how you like. It's not as if' – turning to Morse – 'she's done much wrong, is it, sir?'

'Not very much,' said Morse gently; 'not very much at all, have you, Mrs Evans?'

'How on earth did you guess *that* one?' asked Lewis an hour later as the car accelerated down the A483 to Llandovery.

'She'd've slipped up sooner or later. Just a matter of time.'

'But all that tennis stuff. You don't follow tennis.'

'In my youth, I'll have you know, I had quite a reliable backhand.'

'But how did you—'

'Prayer and fasting, Lewis. Prayer and fasting.'

Lewis gave it up. 'Talking of fasting, sir, aren't you getting a bit peckish?'

'Yes, I am. Hungry *and* thirsty. So perhaps if we can find one of those open-all-day places . . .'

But they got little further. The car-telephone rang and Morse himself picked it up. Lewis could make out none of the words at the other end of the line – just Morse's syncopated rôle:

'*What?*'

'You *sure*?'

'Bloody 'ell!'

'*Who?*'

'*Bloody* 'ell!'

'Yes.'

'Yes!'

'Two and a half hours, I should think.'

'No! Leave things exactly as they are.'

Morse put down the phone and stared ahead of him like some despondent zombie.

'Something to do with the case?' ventured an apprehensively hesitant Lewis.

'They've found a body.'

'Who?'

'George Daley. Shot. Shot through the heart.'

'Where?'

'Blenheim. Blenheim Park.'

'Whew! That's where Johnson—'

'It was Johnson who found him.'

Suddenly Lewis felt the need for a pint of beer almost as much as Morse; but as the car sped nearer and nearer to Oxford, Morse himself said nothing more at all.

CHAPTER FIFTY-FIVE

Thanatophobia (n): a morbid dread of death, or (sometimes) of the sight of death: a poignant sense of human mortality, almost universal except amongst those living on Olympus
(Small's English Dictionary)

DR LAURA HOBSON knelt again beside the body, this time her bright hazel eyes looking up at a different chief inspector: not at Johnson – but at Morse.

'You reckon he was killed instantly?' asked the latter.

She nodded. 'I'm no expert on ballistics but it was possibly one of those seven-millimetre bullets – the sort that expand on contact.'

'The sort they kill deer with,' added Morse quietly.

'It's' – she fingered the corpse – 'er, sometimes difficult to find the entry-hole. Not in this case, though. Look!'

She pointed a slim finger to a small, blood-encrusted hole, of little more than the diameter of a pencil, just below the left shoulder blade of the man who lay prone on the ground between them. 'But you'll see there's never much of a problem with the *exit* hole.' Gently she eased the body over and away from her, pushing it on to its right side, and pointing to a larger hole that had been blasted just below the heart, a hole almost the size of a mandarin orange.

This time, however, Morse was not looking. He was used to death of course; but accident, and terrible injury, and the sight of much blood – such things he could never stomach. So he turned his eyes away, and for a few moments stood staring around him in that quiet woodland glade, where so very recently someone had shot George Daley in the back, and no doubt watched him fall and lie quite still beneath the giant oak tree there. And the owners of seven-millimetre rifles? Morse knew two of them: David Michaels and George Daley. And whatever else might be in doubt, George Daley would have found it utterly impossible to have shot himself with the rifle that was his.

'Any ideas how long?' asked Morse.

Dr Hobson smiled. 'That's the very first question you always asked Max.'

'He told you?'

'Yes.'

'Well, he never told me the answer – never told me how long, I mean.'

'Shall I tell you?'

'Please do!' Morse smiled back at her, and for a moment or two he found her very attractive.

'Ten, twelve hours. No longer than twelve, I don't think. I'll plump for ten.'

Morse, oblivious of the time for most of the day, now looked at his wrist-watch: 8.25 p.m. That would put the murder at about 10 a.m., say? 10.30 a.m.? Yes . . . that sort of time would figure reasonably well if Morse's thinking was correct. Perhaps he *wasn't* right, though! He'd been so bloody certain in his own mind that the case was drawing gently if sombrely towards a conclusion: no more murder, no more deaths. Huh! That's exactly what he'd told Lewis, wasn't it? Just wait! – that's what he'd said. Things'll work out if only we're prepared to wait. Why, only that day he'd waited, before driving off to Wales, without the slightest premonition of impending tragedy.

And he'd been wrong.

There would be greater tragedies in life, of course, than the murder of the mean and unattractive Daley. No one was going to miss the man dramatically much . . . except of course for Mrs Daley, Margaret Daley – of whom for some reason Morse had so recently dreamed. But perhaps even she might not miss him all that much, as time gradually cured her heart of any residual tenderness. After a decent burial. After a few months. After a few years.

Yet there was always the possibility that Morse was wrong again.

Lewis was suddenly at his side, bending down and picking up the khaki-green pork-pie hat Daley invariably wore on freezing winter mornings and sweltering summer days alike.

'There's not *much* shooting here, it seems, sir – not like Wytham – not at this time of year, anyway. Some of the tenants have got shot-gun rights – for a bit of pigeon-shooting, or rabbits, and pheasants a bit later on. Not much, though. That's why Mr Williams, the keeper there' – Lewis pointed back in the direction of Combe Lodge – 'says he *thinks* he may remember a bit of a pop some time this morning. He can't pin it down much closer than that.'

'Bloody marvellous!' said Morse.

'He says there were quite a lot he let through the gate – there's always quite a lot on Mondays. He *thinks* he remembers Daley going through, some time in the morning, but there's always quite a few estate vans.'

'He thinks a lot, your keeper, doesn't he?'

'And one or two joggers, he says.'

'*Literally* one or two?'

'Dunno.'

'Promise me you'll never take up jogging, Lewis!'

'Can we move him?' asked Dr Hobson.

'As far as I'm concerned,' said Morse.

'Anything else, Inspector?'

'Yes. I'd like to ask you along to the Bear and have a few quiet drinks together – a few *noisy* drinks, if you'd prefer it. But we shall have to go and look round Daley's house, I'm afraid. Shan't we, Lewis?'

Behind the spectacles her eyes twinkled with humour and potential interest: 'Anuther tame, mebby?'

She left.

'Anuther tame, please, Dr Hobson!' said Chief Inspector Morse, but to himself.

CHAPTER FIFTY-SIX

The west yet glimmers with some streaks of day:
Now spurs the lated traveller apace
To gain the timely inn

(Shakespeare, *Macbeth*)

THE HOUSE in which the Daleys had lived for the past eighteen years was deserted. Margaret Daley, so the neighbours said, had been away since the previous Thursday, visiting her sister in Beaconsfield; whilst the boy, Philip, had scarcely been seen since being brought back home by the St Aldate's police. But no forcible entry was needed, for the immediate neighbour held a spare front-door key, and a preliminary search of the murdered man's house was begun at 9.15 p.m.

Two important pieces of evidence were found immediately,

both on the red formica-topped kitchen table. The first was a letter from the Oxford Magistrates' Court dated 31 July – most probably received on Saturday, 1 August? – informing Mr G. Daley of the charges to be preferred against his son, Philip, and of the various legal liabilities which he, the father, would now incur under the new Aggravated Vehicle Theft Act. The letter went on to specify the provisions of legal aid, and to request Daley senior's attendance at the Oxford Crown Court on the following Thursday when the hearing of his son's case would be held. The second piece of evidence was half a page of writing from a temporarily departed son (as it appeared) to a now permanently departed father, conveying only the simple message that he was 'off to try and sort something out': a curiously flat, impersonal note, except for the one *post-scriptum* plea: 'Tell Mum she needn't wurry'.

A copy of *The Oxford Mail* for Friday, 31 July, lay on top of the microwave, and a preoccupied Morse scanned its front page briefly:

JOY-RIDERS GET NEW WARNING

THE DRIVER and co-passenger of a stolen car which had rammed a news-agent's shop on the Broadmoor Lea estate were both jailed for six months and each fined £1,500 at Oxford Crown Court yesterday. Sentencing father-of-three Paul Curtis, 25, and John Terence Bowden, 19, Judge Geoffrey Stephens warned: 'Those who drive recklessly and dangerously and criminally around estates in Oxford can now normally expect custodial sentences – and not short ones. Heavier fines too will be imposed as everything in our power is done to end this spate of crim-inal vandalism.'

(**continued: page 3**)

But Morse read no further, now wandering rather aimlessly around the ground-floor rooms. In the lounge, Lewis pointed to the row of black video-cassettes.

'I should think we know what's on some of *them*, sir.'

Morse nodded. 'Yes. I'd pinch one or two for the night if I had a video.' But his voice lacked any enthusiasm.

'Upstairs, sir? The boy's room . . .?'

'No. I think we've done enough for one night. And I'd like a warrant really for the boy's room. I think Mrs Daley would appreciate that.'

'But we don't really need—'

'C'mon, Lewis! We'll leave a couple of PCs here overnight.' Morse had reached another of his impulsive decisions, and Lewis made no further comment. As they left the house, both detectives noticed again – for it was the first thing they'd noticed as they'd entered – that the seven-millimetre rifle which had earlier stood on its butt by the entrance had now disappeared.

'I reckon it's about time we had a quick word with Michaels,' said Morse as in the thickening light they got into the car.

Lewis refrained from any recrimination. So easily could he have said he'd regularly been advocating exactly such a procedure that day, but he didn't.

At 10.30 p.m., with only half an hour's drinking time remaining, the police car drove up to the White Hart, where Morse's face beamed happily: 'My lucky night. Look!' But Lewis had already spotted the forester's Land Rover parked outside the front of the pub.

David Michaels, seated on a stool in the downstairs bar, with Bobbie curled up happily at his feet, was just finishing a pint of beer as Lewis put a hand on his shoulder.

'Could we have a word with you, sir?'

Michaels turned on his stool and eyed them both without apparent surprise. 'Only if you join me in a drink, all right?'

'Very kind of you,' said Morse. 'The Best Bitter in decent shape?'

'Excellent.'

'Pint for me then, and, er – orange juice is it for you, Sergeant?'

'What do you want a word about?' asked Michaels.

The three of them moved over to the far corner of the flagstoned bar, with Bobbie padding along behind.

'Just one thing, really,' replied Morse. 'You've heard about Daley's murder?'

'Yes.'

'Well . . . I want to take a look in your rifle-cabinet, that's all.'

'When we've finished the drinks?'

'No! Er, I'd like Sergeant Lewis to go up and—'

'Fine! I'd better just give Cathy a ring, though. She'll have the place bolted.'

Morse saw little objection, it seemed, and he and Lewis listened as Michaels used the phone by the side of the bar-counter and quickly told his wife that the police would be coming up – please let them in – they wanted to look in the rifle-cabinet – she knew where the key was – let them take what they wanted – he'd be home in half an hour – see her soon – nothing to worry about – ciao!

'Am I a suspect?' asked Michaels with a wan smile, after Lewis had left.

'Yes,' said Morse simply, draining his beer. 'Another?'

'Why not? I'd better make the most of things.'

'And I want you to come up to Kidlington HQ in the morning. About – about ten o'clock, if that's all right.'

'I'm not dreaming, am I?' asked Michaels, as Morse picked up the two empty glasses.

'I'm afraid not,' said Morse. 'And, er, I think it'll be better if we send a car for you, Mr Michaels . . .'

A very clean and shining Mrs Michaels, smelling of shampoo and bath-salts, a crimson bath-robe round her body, a white towel round her head, let Sergeant Lewis in immediately, handed him the cabinet key, and stood aside as very carefully he lifted the rifle from its stand – one finger on the end of the barrel and one finger under the butt – and placed it in a transparent plastic container. On the shelf above the stand were two gunsmiths' catalogues; but no sign whatever of any cartridges.

Holding the rifle now by the middle of the barrel, Lewis thanked Mrs Michaels, and left – hearing the rattle of the chain and the thud of the bolts behind him as the head forester's wife awaited the return of her husband. For a while he wondered what she must be thinking at that moment. Puzzlement, perhaps? Or panic? It had been difficult to gauge anything from the eyes behind those black-rimmed spectacles. Not much of a communicator at all, in fact, for Lewis suddenly realized that whilst he was there she had spoken not a single word.

It was completely dark now, and the sergeant found himself feeling slightly nervous as he flicked the headlights to full beam along the silent lane.

CHAPTER FIFTY-SEVEN

FALSTAFF: We have heard the chimes at midnight, Master Shallow.

SHALLOW: That we have, that we have, that we have; in faith, Sir John, we have

(Shakespeare, *Henry IV, Part 2*)

OF THE four men who had agreed to concoct (as Morse now believed) a joint statement about the murder of Karin Eriksson, only McBryde had ranged free in the city of Oxford that night. At 6.30 p.m. he had called in at the Eagle and Child, carrying his few overnight possessions in a canvas hold-all, eaten a cheese sandwich, drunk two pints of splendidly conditioned Burton Ale, and begun thinking about a bed for the night. At 7.45 p.m. he had caught a number 20 Kidlington bus outside St Giles' Church and gone up the Banbury Road as far as Squitchey Lane, where he tried the Cotswold House (recommended to him by Hardinge) but found the oblong, white notice fixed across the front door's leaded glass: NO VACANCIES. Just across the way however was the Casa Villa, and here one double room was still available (the last); which McBryde took, considering as many men had done before him that the purchase of an extra two square yards of bed space was something of a waste – and something of a sadness.

At about the time that McBryde was unpacking his pyjamas and sticking his toothbrush into one of the two glasses in his *en suite* bathroom, Philip Daley stood up and counted the coins.

He had caught the coach from Gloucester Green at 2.30 p.m. Good value, the coach – only £4 return for adults. Disappointing though to learn that a single fare was virtually the same price as a return, and sickening that the driver refused to accept his only marginally dishonest assertion that he was still at school. At 6.30 p.m. he had been seated against the wall of an office building next to the Bonnington Hotel in Southampton Row, with a grey and orange scarf arranged in front of him to receive the coins of a stream (as he trusted) of compassionate passers-by; and with a notice, black Biro on cardboard, beside him: UNEMPLOYED HOME-LESS HUNGRY. One of the Oxford boys had told him that COLD AND HUNGRY was best, but the early summer evening was balmy and warm, and anyway it didn't matter much, not that first night. He had £45 in his pocket, and certainly had no intention of letting himself get too hungry. It was just that he wanted to see how things would work out – that was all.

Not very well, though, seemed the answer to that experiment: for he was stiff and even (yes!) a little cold; and the coins amounted to only 83p. He must look too well dressed still, too well fed, too little in need. At nine o'clock he walked down to a pub in Holborn and ordered a pint of beer and two packets of crisps: £2.70. Bloody robbery! Nor were things made easier when a shaven-headed youth with multi-tattooed arms and multi-ringed ears moved in beside him, and asked him if he was the prick who'd been staking out his pitch in the Row; because if so he'd be well advised to fuck off smartish – if he knew what was best for him.

Cathy Michaels repeatedly bent forwards, sideways, backwards, as the heat from the dryer penetrated her thick, raven-black hair, specially cut for *The Mikado* in a horizontal bob, the original blonde just beginning to show again, even if only a few milli-metres or so at the roots. For a moment she felt sure she'd heard the Land Rover just outside, and she turned off the dryer. False alarm, though. Usually she experienced little or no nervousness when left alone in the cottage, even at night; and never when Bobbie was with her. But Bobbie was not with her: he was down at the pub with his master . . . and with the policemen. Suddenly she felt fear almost palpably creeping across her skin, like some soft-footed, menacing insect.

Midnight was chiming, and Morse was pouring himself a night-cap from the green, triangular-columned bottle of Glenfiddich – when the phone went: Dr Hobson. She had agreed to ring him if she discovered anything further before the end of that long, long day. Not that there *was* anything startlingly new, and she realized it could easily wait till morning. But no, it couldn't wait till morning, Morse had insisted.

The bullet that had killed Daley had fairly certainly been fired from a seven-millimetre or a .243 rifle, or something very similar; the bullet had entered the back about 2 inches below the left scapula, had exited (no wince this time from Morse) about 1 inch above the heart, and (this certain now) had been instantly fatal. Time? Between 10 a.m. and 11 a.m. – with just a little leeway either side? – 9.30 a.m. and 11.30 a.m., say? Most probably Daley had been shot from a distance of about 50–80 yards: ballistics might just amend this last finding, but she doubted it.

He'd seemed pleased, and she knew she wanted to please him. There was some music playing in the background, but she failed to recognize it.

'You're not in bed yet?' she ventured.

'Soon shall be.'

'What are you doing?'

'Drinking Scotch.'

'And listening to music.'

'Yes, that too.'

'You're a very civilized copper, aren't you?'

'Only half the time.'

'Well, I'd better gor.'

'Yes.'

'Goodnate, then.'

'Goodnight, and thank you,' said Morse quietly.

After putting down the phone Laura Hobson sat perfectly still and wondered what was happening to her. Why, he was twenty-five years older than she was!

At least.

Blast him!

She acknowledged to herself the ludicrous truth of the matter, but she could barely bring herself to smile.

CHAPTER FIFTY-EIGHT

He who asks the questions cannot avoid the answers
(Cameroonian proverb)

THERE WAS little evidence of strain or undue apprehension on David Michaels' face the following morning when he was shown into Interview Room 2, where Sergeant Lewis was already seated at a trestle table, a tape recorder at his right elbow. He was being held for questioning (Lewis informed him) about two matters: first, about the statement made to the police by Dr Alan Hardinge, a copy of which was now handed to him; second, about the murder of George Daley.

Lewis pointed to the tape recorder. 'Just to make sure we don't misrepresent anything, Mr Michaels. We've been getting a bit of stick recently, haven't we, about the way some interviews have been conducted?'

Michaels shrugged indifferently.

'And you're aware of your legal rights? Should you want to be legally represented—'

But Michaels shook his head; and began reading Hardinge's statement . . .

He had little legal knowledge, but had assumed in this instance that he could be guilty only of some small-scale conspiracy to pervert the strict course of truth – certainly not of justice. It was the criminal 'intention', the *mens rea*, that really mattered (so he'd read), and no one could ever maintain that his own intention had been criminal that afternoon a year ago . . .

'Well?' asked Lewis when Michaels put the last sheet down.

'That's about the size of it, yes.'

'You're quite happy to corroborate it?'

'Why not? One or two little things I wouldn't have remembered but – yes, I'll sign it.'

'We're not asking for a signature. We'll have to ask you to make your *own* statement.'

'Can't I just copy this one out?'

Lewis grinned weakly, but shook his head. He thought he liked Michaels. 'Now, last time you pretended – *pretended* – you'd not got the faintest idea where any body might be found, right?'

'Yes,' lied Michaels.

'And then, this time round, you *still* pretended you didn't really know?'

'Yes,' lied Michaels.

'So why did you nudge Chief Inspector Morse in the right direction?'

'Double bluff, wasn't it? If I was vague enough, and they *found* it, well, no one was going to think I'd had anything to do with the murder.'

'Who told you it was *murder*?'

'The chap standing there on guard in Pasticks: big chap, in a dark blue uniform and checked cap – policeman, I think he was.'

The constable standing wide-legged across the door of the interview room took advantage of the fact that Lewis had his back towards him, and smiled serenely.

'Why didn't you dump the rucksack in the lake as well?' continued Lewis.

For the first time Michaels hesitated: 'Should've done, I agree.'

'Was it because Daley had his eye on the camera – and the binoculars?'

'Well, one thing's for sure: *he* won't be able to tell you, will he?'

'You don't sound as if you liked him much.'

'He was a filthy, mean-minded little swine!'

'But you didn't know him very well, surely?'

'No. I hardly knew him at all.'

'What about last Friday night?'

'What *about* last Friday night?'

Lewis let it go. 'You'd never met him previously – at your little rendezvous in Park Town?'

'No! I'd only just joined,' lied Michaels. 'Look, Sergeant, I'm not proud of that. But haven't you ever wanted to watch a sex film?'

'I've seen plenty. We pick up quite a few of 'em here and there. But I'd rather have a plate of egg and chips, myself. What about you, Constable Watson?' asked Lewis, turning in his chair.

'Me?' said the man by the door. 'I'd much rather watch a sex film.'

'You wouldn't want your wife to know, though?'

'No, Sarge.'

'Nor would you, would you, Mr Michaels?'

'No. I wouldn't want her to know about anything like that,' said Michaels quietly.

'I wonder if Mrs Daley knew – about her husband, I mean?'

'I dunno. As I say, I knew nothing about the man, really.'

'Last night you knew he'd been murdered.'

'A lot of people knew.'

'And a lot of people *didn't* know.'

Michaels remained silent.

'He was killed from a seven-millimetre gun, like as not.'

'Rifle, you mean.'

'Sorry. I'm not an expert on guns and things – not like you, Mr Michaels.'

'And that's why you took my rifle last night?'

'We'd've taken *anyone*'s rifle. That's our job, isn't it?'

'Every forester's got a rifle that sort of calibre – very effective they are too.'

'So where were you between, say, ten o'clock and eleven o'clock yesterday morning?'

'Not much of a problem there. About ten – no – just *after* ten it must have been – I was with a couple of fellows from the RSPB. We – they – were checking on the nesting boxes along the Singing Way. You know, keeping records on first or second broods, weighing 'em, taking samples of droppings – that sort of thing. They do it all the time.'

'You were helping them?'

'Carrying the bloody ladder most of the time.'

'What about *after* that?'

'Well, we all nipped down to the White Hart – about twelve, quarter-past? – and had a couple of pints. Warm work, it was! Hot day, too!'

'You've got the addresses of these fellows?'

'Not on me, no. I can get 'em for you easy enough.'

'And the barman there at the pub? He knows you?'

'Rather too well, Sergeant!'

Lewis looked at his wrist-watch, feeling puzzled and, yes, a little bit lost.

'Can I go now?' asked Michaels.

'Not yet, sir, no. As I say we need some sort of statement from you about what happened last July . . . then we shall just have to get this little lot typed up' – Lewis nodded to the tape recorder – 'then we shall have to get you to read it and sign it . . . and, er, I should think we're not going to get through all that till . . .' Again

Lewis looked at his watch, still wondering exactly where things stood. Then, turning round: 'We'd better see Mr Michaels has some lunch with us, Watson. What's on the menu today?'

'Always mince on Tuesdays, Sarge.'

'Most people'd prefer a sex film,' said Michaels, almost cheerfully.

Lewis rose to his feet, nodded to Watson, and made to leave. 'One other thing, sir. I can't let you go before the chief inspector gets back, I'm afraid. He said he particularly wanted to see you again.'

'And where's he supposed to be this morning?'

'To tell you the truth, I'm not at all sure.'

As he walked back to his office, Lewis reflected on what he had just learned. Morse had been correct on virtually everything so far – right up until this last point. For now surely Morse must be dramatically wrong in his belief that Michaels had murdered Daley? In due course they would have to check up on his alibi; but it was wholly inconceivable that a pair of dedicated ornithologists had conspired with a barman from the local pub in seeking to pervert the course of natural justice. Surely so!

At 12.30 p.m., Dr Hobson rang through from South Parks Road to say that, whilst she was an amateur in the byways of ballistics, she would be astounded if Michaels' gun had been fired at any time within the previous few weeks.

'"Rifle",' muttered Lewis, *sotto voce*.

'Is he, er, there?' the pathologist had asked tentatively.

'Back this afternoon some time.'

'Oh.'

It was beginning to look as if everyone wanted to see Morse. Especially Lewis.

CHAPTER FIFTY-NINE

This is the reason why mothers are more devoted to their
children than fathers: it is that they suffer more in giving them
birth and are more certain that they are their own
(Aristotle, *Nicomachean Ethics*)

THE NOON-DAY sun shone on the pale cinnamon stone of the
colleges, and the spires of Oxford looked down on a scene of
apparent tranquillity as the marked police car drove down
Headington Hill towards the Plain, then over Magdalen Bridge
and into the High. In the back sat Morse, sombre, and now silent,
for he had talked sufficiently to the rather faded woman in her
mid-forties who sat beside him, her eyes red from recent weeping,
her mouth still tremulous, but her small chin firm and somehow
courageous in the face of the terrible events she had only learned
about two hours before – when the front doorbell had rung in her
sister's council house in Beaconsfield. Yet the news that her
husband had been murdered and that her only son had run away
from home had left her not so much devastated as dumbfounded,
as though a separate layer of emotions and reactions had formed
itself between what she knew to be herself, and the external
reality of what had occurred.

It had helped a bit too – talking with the chief inspector, who
seemed to understand a good deal of what she was suffering. Not
that she'd bared her soul *too* much to him about the increasing
repugnance she'd felt for the man she'd married; the man who
had slowly yet inevitably revealed over the years of their lives
together the shallow, devious, occasionally cruel, nature of his
character. There had been Philip, though; and for so long the little
lad had compensated in manifold ways for the declining love and
respect she was feeling for her husband. In nursery school, in
primary school, even at the beginning of secondary school,
certainly until he was about twelve, Philip had almost always
turned to her, his mother; confided in her; had (so preciously!)
hugged her when he was grateful or happy. She had been very
proud that she was the loved and favoured parent.

Whether it was of deliberate, vindictive intent or not, she
couldn't honestly say, but soon after Philip had started at second-

ary school, George had begun to assert his influence over the boy and in some ways to steal his affection away from her; and this by the simple expedient of encouraging in him the idea of growing up, of becoming 'a man', and doing mannish things. At weekends he would take the boy fishing; often he would return from the Royal Sun in the evening bringing a few cans of light ale with him, regularly offering one to his young son. Then the air-gun! For Philip's thirteenth birthday George had bought him an air-gun; and very soon afterwards Philip had shot a sparrow at the bottom of the garden as it was pecking at some bird-seed she herself had thrown down. What a terrible evening that had been between them, husband and wife, when she had accused him of turning their son into a philistine! Progressively too there had been the coarsening of Philip's speech, and of his attitudes; the brittle laughter between father and son about jokes to which she was never privy; reports from school which grew worse and worse; and the friendship with some of the odious classmates he occasionally brought home to listen to pop music in the locked bedroom.

Then, over a year ago, that almighty row between father and son about the rucksack, which had resulted in an atmosphere of twisted bitterness. Exactly what had happened then, she was still uncertain; but she knew that her husband had lied about the time and place he had found the rucksack. How? Because neither George nor Philip had taken the dog for its walk along the dual-carriageway that morning: *she* had. Philip had gone off to Oxford very early to join a coach party the school had organized; and, on waking, her husband had been so crippled with lumbago that he couldn't even make it to the loo, let alone any lay-by on the dual-carriageway. But she knew George *had* found the rucksack, somewhere – or that someone had given it to him – on that very Sunday when the Swedish girl had gone missing; that Sunday when George had been out all afternoon; and then out again later in the evening, drinking heavily, as she recalled. It must have been that Sunday evening too when Philip had found the ruck-sack, probably at the back of the garage where, as she knew, he'd been looking for his climbing boots for the school trip to the Peak District – and where, as she suspected, he'd found the camera and the binoculars. Oh yes! She was on very firm ground there – because *she too had found them*, in Philip's room. Only later did she learn that Philip had removed the spool of film from the camera and almost certainly developed it himself at school, where there was a flourishing photographic society (of which Philip was a member) with dark-room facilities readily available.

A good deal of this information Morse had known already, she sensed that. But appearances were that she'd held his attention as tearfully and fitfully she'd covered most of the ground again. He'd not asked her how she knew about the photographs; yet he surely must have guessed. But he would never know about those other photographs, the pornographic ones, the ones of the Swedish girl whom she had recognized from the passport picture printed, albeit so badly, in *The Oxford Times*. No! She would tell Morse nothing about that. Nor about the joy-riding – and her mental turmoil when first she'd read those words in Philip's diary; words which conjured up for her the confused images of squealing tyres and the anguished shrieks of a small girl lying in a pool of her own blood ... No, it would belittle her son even further if she spoke of things like that, and she would never do it. Wherever he was and whatever he'd done, *Philip would always be her son*.

As the car turned left at Carfax, down towards St Aldate's police station, she saw a dozen or more head-jerking pigeons pecking at the pavement; and then fluttering with sudden loud clapping of wings up to the tower above them. Taking flight. Free! And Margaret Daley, her head now throbbing wildly, wondered if she would ever herself feel free again ...

'Milk and sugar?'

Margaret Daley had been miles away, but she'd heard his words, and now looked up into the chief inspector's face, his eyes piercingly blue, but kindly, and almost vulnerable themselves, she thought.

'No sugar. Just milk, please.'

Morse laid his hand lightly on her shoulder. 'You're a brave woman,' he said quietly.

Suddenly the flood-gates were totally swept away, and she turned from him and wept quite uncontrollably.

'You heard what the lady said,' snarled Morse, as the constable at the door watched the two of them, hesitantly. 'No bloody sugar!'

CHAPTER SIXTY

Music and women I cannot but give way to, whatever my
business is

(Samuel Pepys, *Diary*)

JUST AFTER lunch-time Morse was back in his office at HQ
listening to the tape of Michaels' interview.

'What do you think, sir?'

'I suppose some of it's true,' admitted Morse.

'About not killing Daley, you mean?'

'I don't see how he could have done it – no time, was there?'

'Who did kill him, do you think?'

'Well, there are three things missing from his house, aren't
there? Daley himself, the rifle – and the boy.'

'The son? Philip? You think *he* killed him? Killed his father?
Like Oedipus?'

'The things I've taught you, Lewis, since you've been my
sergeant!'

'Did he love his mum as well?'

'Very much so, I think. Anyway you'll be interested in hearing
what she's got to say.'

'But – but you can't just walk into Blenheim Park with a rifle
on your shoulder—'

'His mum says he used to go fishing there; says his dad bought
him all the gear.'

'Ah. See what you mean. Those long canvas things, you know
– for your rods and things.'

'Something like that. Ten minutes on a bike—'

'Has he *got* a bike?'

'Dunno.'

'But *why*? Why do you think—?'

'Must have been that letter, I suppose – from the Crown
Court . . .'

'And his dad refused to help?'

'Probably. Told his son to clear off, like as not; told him to
bugger off and leave his parents out of it. Anyway, I've got a
feeling the lad's not going to last long in the big city. The Met'll
bring him in soon, you see.'

'You said it was *Michaels*, though. You said you were pretty sure it must have been Michaels.'

'Did I?'

'Yes, you did! But you didn't seem *too* surprised when you just heard the tape?'

'Didn't I?'

Lewis let it go. 'Where do we go from here, then?'

'Nowhere, for a bit. I've got a meeting with Strange first. Three o'clock.'

'What about Michaels? Let him go?'

'Why should we do that?'

'Well, like you say – he just couldn't have done it in the time. Impossible! Even with a helicopter.'

'So?'

Suddenly Lewis was feeling more than a little irritated. 'So what do I tell him?'

'You tell him,' said Morse slowly, 'that we're keeping him here overnight – for further questioning.'

'On what charge? We just can't—'

'I don't think he'll argue too loudly,' said Morse.

Just before Morse was to knock on Chief Superintendent Strange's door that Tuesday afternoon, two men were preparing to leave the Trout Inn at Wolvercote. Most of the customers who had spent their lunch-time out of doors, seated on the paved terrace alongside the river there, were now gone; it was almost closing time.

'You promise to write it down?'

'I promise,' replied Alasdair McBryde.

'Where are you going now?'

'Back to London.'

'Can I give you a lift to the station?'

'I'd be glad of that.'

The two walked up the shallow steps and out across the narrow road to the car park: PATRONS ONLY. NO PARKING FOR FISHERMEN.

'What about you, Alan?' asked McBryde, as Hardinge drove the Sierra left towards Wolvercote.

'I don't know. And I don't really care.'

'Don't say that!' McBryde laid his right hand lightly on the driver's arm. But Hardinge dismissed the gesture with his own right hand as if he were flicking a fly from his sleeve, and the journey down to Oxford station was made in embarrassed silence.

Back in Radcliffe Square, Hardinge parked on double yellow lines in Catte Street, and went straight up to his rooms in Lonsdale. He knew her number off by heart. Of course he did.

'Claire? It's me, Alan.'

'I know it's you. Nothing wrong with my ears.'

'I was just wondering . . . just hoping . . .'

'No! And we're not going to go over all *that* again.'

'You mean you're not even going to *see* me again?'

'That's it!'

'Not *ever*?' His throat was suddenly very dry.

'You know, for a university don, you don't pick some things up very quickly, do you?'

For a while Hardinge said nothing. He could hear music playing in the background; he knew the piece well.

'If you'd told me you enjoyed Mozart—'

'Look – for the last time! – it's finished. Please accept that! *Finished*!'

'Have you got someone else?'

'What?' He heard her bitter laughter. 'My life's been full of "someone elses". You always knew that.'

'But what if I divorced—'

'For Christ's *sake*! Won't you *ever* understand? It's *over*!'

The line was dead, and Hardinge found himself looking down at the receiver as if someone had given him a frozen fillet of fish for which for the moment he could find no convenient receptacle.

Claire Osborne sat by the phone for several minutes after she had rung off, the wonderful trombone passage from the *Tuba Mirum Spargens Sonum* registering only vaguely in her mind. Had she been too cruel to Alan? But sometimes it was necessary to be cruel to be kind – wasn't that what they said? Or was that just a meaningless cliché like the rest of them? 'Someone else?' Alan had asked.

Huh!

The poorly typed letter (no salutation, no subscription) she had received with the cassette that morning was lying on the coffee table, and already she'd read it twenty-odd times:

I enjoyed so much our foreshortened time together, you and the music. One day of the great lost days, one face of all the faces (Ernest Dowson – not me!). A memento herewith. The *Recordare* is my favourite bit – if I'm pushed to a choice. 'Recordare' by the way is the 2nd person singular of the present imperative of the verb 'recordor': it means 'Remember!'

CHAPTER SIXTY-ONE

A reasonable probability is the only certainty
(Edgar Watson Howe, *Country Town Sayings*)

'YOU'RE *sure* about all this, Morse?' Strange's voice was sharp, with an edge of scepticism to it.

'Completely sure.'

'You said that about Michaels.'

'No! I only said I was ninety per cent sure on that.'

'OK.' Strange shrugged his shoulders, tilted his head, and opened his palms in a gesture of acquiescence. 'There are just one or two little things—'

But the phone went on Strange's desk: 'Ah! Ah! Yes! Want to speak to him?'

He handed the phone over to Morse: Dr Hobson. Quite certainly, she said, Michaels' rifle hadn't been fired for weeks. That was all.

Strange had heard the pathologist, just. 'Looks as if you're right about *that*, anyway. We'll give the Met a call. Certain to have scarpered to the capital, don't you reckon, the lad?'

'Ninety per cent sure, sir – and we've already given the Met his description.'

'Oh!'

Morse rose to go, but Strange was not quite finished: 'What first put you on to it?'

For a few moments Morse paused dubiously. 'Several things, I suppose. For example, I once heard someone claim that all three types of British woodpeckers could be found in Wytham Woods. I think I heard it in a pub. Or perhaps I just read it on a beer mat.'

'Useful things, pubs!'

'Then' – Morse ignored the sarcasm – 'I thought if Johnson had opted for Blenheim, it'd pretty certainly turn out to be Wytham.'

'That's grossly unfair.'

'I agree.' Morse got up and walked to the door. 'You know, it's a bit surprising no one ever noticed her accent, isn't it? She must *have* a bit of an accent. I bet you I'll notice it!'

'You're a lucky bugger to hear as well as you do. The wife says I'm getting deafer all the time.'

'Get a hearing aid, sir. They probably wouldn't let you stay in the force, and they'd have to give you a few years' enhancement on the pension.'

'You *think* so? Really?'

'Ninety per cent sure,' said Morse, closing the door behind him and walking thoughtfully back through the maze of corridors to his office.

He'd omitted to acquaint Strange with the biggest clue of all, but it would have taken a little while to explain and it was all a bit nebulous – especially for a man of such matter-of-fact hard-headedness as Strange. But it *had* formed for him, Morse, the focal point of all the mystery. The normal murderer (if such a person may be posited) would seek to cover up all traces of his victim. And if his victim were someone like Karin Eriksson, he would burn the clothes, chuck her jewellery and trinkets into the canal, dispose of the body – sink it in some bottomless ocean or cut it up in little bits and take it to the nearest waste-disposal site; even pack it up in those black plastic bags for the dustmen to cart off, since in Morse's experience the only things they *wouldn't* take were bags containing garden waste. So! So if our murderer wanted to rid the earth of every trace of his victim, why, *why*, had he been so anxious for the rucksack and associated possessions to be found? All right, it hadn't worked out all that well, with accidental factors, as almost always, playing their part. But the rucksack *was* found, very soon; the police *were* informed, very soon; the hunt for Karin's murderer *was* under way, very soon. Now if a young Swedish student goes missing *sans everything*, then there is always *less* than certitude that she is dead: thousands of young persons from all parts of Europe, all parts of the world, disappear regularly; get listed as 'missing persons'. But if a young girl goes missing, and at the same time her possessions are discovered in a hedgerow somewhere nearby, then the implications are all too painfully obvious, the conclusions all too readily drawn: the conclusions that Johnson and almost every other policeman in the Thames Valley had drawn a year ago.

Though not Morse.

Perhaps he could, on reflection, have explained his thinking to Strange without too much difficulty? After all, the key question could be posed very simply, really: why was the murderer so anxious for the police to pursue a murder inquiry? To that strange question Morse now knew the answer; of that he was quite sure. Well, ninety-nine per cent sure: because the police would be looking for a body, *not for someone who was still alive.*

Ten minutes later, Lewis was ready for him, and together the two detectives drove out to Wytham Woods once more.

CHAPTER SIXTY-TWO

The one charm of marriage is that it makes a life of deception absolutely necessary for both parties
(Oscar Wilde, *The Picture of Dorian Gray*)

THERE WERE four of them in the living room of the low-ceilinged cottage: Morse and Lewis seated side by side on the leather settee, Mrs Michaels opposite them in an armchair, and the small attractive figure of the uniformed WPC Wright standing by the door.

'Why haven't you brought David?' asked Mrs Michaels.

'Isn't he still making a statement, Sergeant?' Morse's eyebrows rose quizzically as if the matter were of minor import.

'What are you here for then?' She lifted her eyes and cocked her head slightly to Morse as if she were owed some immediate and convincing explanation.

'We're here about your marriage. There's something slightly, ah, irregular about it.'

'Really? You'll have to check that up with the Registry Office, not me.'

'Regis*ter* Office, Mrs Michaels. It's important to be accurate about things. So let *me* be accurate. David Michaels discovered that the District Office for anyone living in Wytham was at Abingdon, and he went there and answered all the usual questions about when and where you wanted to marry, how old you both were, where you were both born, whether either of you had been married before, whether you were related. And that was that. Two days later you were married.'

'So?'

'Well, everything is really based on *trust* in things like that. If you want to, you can tell a pack of lies. There's one Registrar in Oxford who married the same fellow three times in the same year – one in Reading who managed to marry a couple of sailors!'

Morse looked across at her as if expecting a dutiful smile, but Mrs Michaels sat perfectly still, her mouth tight, her hair framing the clear-skinned features in a semi-circle of the darkest black, the blonde roots so very recently re-dyed.

'Take any reasonably fluent liar – even a fairly clumsy liar,' continued Morse, 'and he'll get away with murder – if you see what I mean, Mrs Michaels. For example, some proof of age is required for anyone under twenty-three, did you know that? But if your fiancé says you're twenty-*four*? Well, he'll almost certainly get away with it. And if you've been married before? Well, if you say you *haven't*, it's going to be virtually impossible to prove, then and there, that you have. Oh yes! It's easy to get married by licence if you're willing to abuse the system.'

'You are saying that I – that we, David and I – we abused the system?'

'You know most English people would have settled for "me and David", Mrs Michaels.' (WPC Wright was aware of that nuance of stress on the word 'English'.)

'I asked you—'

But Morse interrupted her brusquely: 'There was only one thing that couldn't be fiddled in your case: date of birth. You see, some documentation is statutory in that respect – *if the person concerned is a foreign national.*'

A silence now hung over the small room; a palpably tense silence, during which a strange, indefinable look flitted across Mrs Michaels' features as she crossed one leg over the other and clasped her hands round her left knee.

'What's that got to do with me?' she asked.

'You're a foreign national,' said Morse simply, looking across unblinkingly at the lovely girl seated opposite him.

'Do you realize how absurd all this is, Inspector?'

'Did you have to show your passport to the Registrar at Abingdon?'

'There was no *need* for that: I'm *not* a foreign national!'

'No?'

'*No!* My name is – *was* Catharine Adams. I was born in Uppingham, in Rutland – what *used* to be Rutland; I'm twenty-four years old—'

'Can *I* see your passport?' asked Morse quietly.

'As a matter of fact you can't. It's in the post to Swansea – it needs renewing. We are going – me and David! – to Italy in September.' (Lewis could pick up the hint of the accent now, in that word 'Eetaly'.)

'Don't worry! We've already got a copy, you see. The Swedish Embassy sent us one.'

For several moments she looked down at the carpet, the one expensive item in the rather mundane living room in which she'd spent so many hours of her days: a small, rectangular oriental carpet, woven perhaps in some obscure tent in Turkestan. Then, rising, she took a few steps over to a desk, took out her passport, and handed it to Morse.

But Morse knew it all anyway; had already studied the details carefully: the headings, printed in both Swedish and English; the details required, handwritten in Swedish. Underneath the photograph, he read again:

Surname	....
Christian name(s)	....
Height in cms (without shoes)	....
Sex	....
Date of birth	....
Place of birth	....
Civic Reg. No.	....
Date issued	....
How long valid	....
Signature	....
Remarks	....

Katarina Adams (it appeared), height 168 cms in her stock-inged feet, of the female sex, had been born on the 29 September 1968, in Uppsala, Sweden.

'Clever touch that, Uppingham for Uppsala,' commented Morse.

'Uppsála – if we must be accurate, Inspector.'

'"Adams" was your married name – your first married name. And when your husband was killed in a car crash, you kept it. Why not? So . . .'

'So, what else do you want from me?' she asked quietly.

'Just tell me the truth, please! We shall get there in the end, you know.'

She took a deep breath, and spoke quickly and briefly. 'When my sister Karin was murdered, I was in Spain – in Barcelona, as it happened. I got here as soon as I could – my mother had rung me from Sweden. But I could do nothing, I soon realized that. I met David. We fell in love. We were married. I was frightened about work permits and visas and that sort of thing, and David said it would be better if I lied – if *he* lied – about my earlier marriage. Easier and quicker. So? For a start I only went out of the house here a very few times. I wore glasses and I had my hair cut fairly short and dyed black. That's why they asked me to sing in the opera, yes? I looked like the part before they started the auditions.'

Lewis glanced briefly sideways, and thought he saw a look of slight puzzlement on Morse's face.

'Didn't the Registrar *tell* you – tell your husband – that it was all above board anyway?'

'No, I'm sure he didn't. You see we said nothing about this . . . you know. Can't you understand? It was all very strange – all very unsettling and sort of, sort of nervy, somehow. David understood, though—'

'Did you enjoy your holiday in Spain?'

'Very much. Why—?'

'Which airport did you fly from to England?'

'Barcelona.'

'Lots of muggings, they tell me, at Barcelona airport.'

'What's that got to do—?'

'Ever lost *your* handbag? You know, with your keys and passport and credit cards?'

'No. I'm glad to say I haven't.'

'What would you *do* if you lost your passport, say?'

She shrugged. 'I don't know. I'd apply to the Swedish Embassy, I suppose. They'd probably give me a temporary document . . . or something . . .'

'But do you think it would be possible to *fiddle* things, Mrs Michaels? Like it's possible to fiddle a marriage licence?'

'I wish you'd tell me exactly what you're getting at.'

'All right. Let me ask you a simple question. Would it be possible for anyone to apply for someone *else's* passport?'

'Almost impossible, surely? There are all sorts of checks in Sweden: Civic Registration Number – that's what we use in Sweden instead of a birth certificate – details of all the information on the passport that would have to be checked – photograph? No! I don't think it would.'

'I agree with you, I think. *Almost* impossible – though not quite; not for a very clever woman.'

'But I'm *not* a very clever woman, Inspector.'

'No! Again I agree with you.' (Lewis wondered if he'd spotted the slightest trace of disappointment in her eyes.) 'But let's agree it is impossible, right. There *is* another way, though, a very much easier way of acquiring a passport. A childishly easy way. Someone *gives* you one, Mrs Michaels. Someone *sends* you one through the post.'

'You are leaving me many miles behind, Inspector.'

'No, I'm not,' replied Morse, with a quiet factuality that brooked no argument. 'No one – *no one* – lost any passport at Barcelona, or anywhere else. But you and your elder sister are very much alike, aren't you? My sergeant here brought me a photograph of the three of you from Stockholm. You're all blonde and blue-eyed and high-cheekboned and long-legged and everything else people here expect from the Nordic type. Even your younger sister – the shortest of the three of you – she looks very much like Karin too, at least from her photograph.'

Forcibly she interrupted him: 'Listen! Just *one* moment, please! Have *you* ever felt completely confused – like I feel now?'

'Oh, yes! Quite frequently, believe me. But not now. Not now, Mrs Michaels. And you're not confused either. Because that passport there isn't yours. It belongs to your sister Katarina – Katarina Adams. Your sister who still lives in Uppsala. Your sister who told the Swedish authorities that she'd had her passport stolen, and then applied for another. Simple! You see, your name isn't Katarina Adams at all, is it, Mrs Michaels? It's *Karin Eriksson.*'

Her shoulders suddenly sagged, as if she felt that, in spite of any innocent protestations she might make, she was not going to be believed by anyone; as if on that score at least she would perhaps be well advised to leave her case to the testimony of others.

But Morse was pressing home his advantage; and WPC Wright (though not Lewis) found his further questioning embarrassing and tasteless.

'You've got beautiful legs – would you agree?'

'What?' Instinctively she sought to pull the hem of her knee-length skirt an inch or two lower over her elegant legs; but with little effect.

'You know,' continued Morse, 'when I was talking just now about the Nordic type, I was thinking of the films we used to see of all those sexy Swedish starlets. I used to go to the pictures a lot in those days—'

'Do you want me to do a streep-tease for you?'

'You see, my sergeant here and me – and I – we've got quite a big advantage really, because we've had a chance to study your passport – if it *is* yours—'

She was almost at the end of her tether. 'What *is* it?' she shrieked. 'Please! Please *tell* me! What are you *accusing* me of? All of you?'

Resignedly Morse gestured with his right hand to Lewis; and Lewis, in a flat and melancholy voice, intoned the charge:

'Mrs Karin Michaels – Miss Karin Eriksson – I have to inform you that you are under police arrest on suspicion of murdering one James Myton, on the afternoon of Sunday, July seventh, 1991. It is my duty to warn you that anything you may now say in the presence of the three police officers here may be used in evidence in any future proceedings.'

Morse got up, and now stood above her.

'There's no need for you to say anything, not for the time being.'

'You mean you are accusing me – *me* – of being Karin, my sister? The sister who was *murdered*?'

'You're still denying it?' queried Morse quietly.

'Of course! Of *course*, I am!'

'You can prove it, you know. The Swedish authorities tell us they don't use that "Remarks" section very much at all on the passport – only really if there's some obvious distinguishing mark that can help in establishing identity. On the passport though – the one you say is yours – that section's filled in, in

Swedish. And it says, so they tell me, "Pronounced diagonal scar, inner thigh above left knee-cap, eight and a half centimetres in length, result of motoring accident".'

'Yes?' She looked up at the chief inspector as if she almost willed him, dared him, *wanted* him, to prove his accusation.

'So if you *do* have a scar there, it won't necessarily prove *who* you are, will it? But if you haven't . . . if you *haven't*, then you're not now, and never were, the woman described on that passport.'

Karin Eriksson, the murderer of James Myton, now sat completely still for many agonizing seconds. Then slowly, tantalizingly, as if she were some upper-class artiste in a strip-tease parlour, centimetre by centimetre her left hand lifted the hem of the beige velvet skirt above her left knee to reveal the naked flesh upon her inner thigh.

Did she rejoice in the gaze of the two detectives there? Had she secretly always thrilled to the admiration of the young boys in her high school class at Uppsala – of the tutors on her course? Even perhaps, for a short while, to the lust of the crude and ratty-faced Myton, who had sought to rape her out in Wytham Woods, and whom she had then so deliberately murdered?

And as Morse looked down at the smooth and unscarred flesh above her knee, he found himself wondering for a little while whether he too, like Myton, might not at some point on a hot and sultry summer afternoon have found this girl so very beautiful and necessary.

Lewis drove carefully down the road that led along the edge of the woods towards Wytham village. Beside him was WPC Wright; and in the back sat Karin Eriksson and Chief Inspector Morse.

Almost always, at such a stage in any case, Morse felt himself saddened – with the thrill of the chase now over, with the guilty left to face the appropriate retribution. Often had he pondered on the eternal problem of justice; and he knew as did most men of civilized values that the function of law was to provide that framework of order within which men and women could be protected as they went about their legitimate business. Yes, the criminal must be punished for his misdeeds, for that was the law. And Morse was an upholder of the law. Yet he debated now again, as he felt the body of Karin Eriksson close beside him, that fine distinction between the law and justice. Justice was one of those big words that was so often spelled with a capital 'J'; but really it was so much harder to define than Law. Karin would have to face the law; and he turned to look at her – to look at those beautiful blue eyes of hers, moistened now with the quiet film of tears. For a few seconds, at that moment, there seemed almost a bond between them – between Morse and the young woman who had murdered James Myton.

Suddenly, unexpectedly, she whispered something in his right ear.

'Did you ever have sex with a girl in the back of a car?'

'Not in the back,' whispered Morse. 'In the front, of course. Often!'

'Are you telling me the truth?'

'No,' said Morse.

He was conscious of a brimming reservoir of tears somewhere behind his own eyes as the police car came up to the main road and turned left, down past Wytham towards the police HQ. And for a second or two he thought he felt Karin's left leg pressing gently against him, and so very much he hoped that this was so.

CHAPTER SIXTY-THREE

All that's left to happen
Is some deaths (my own included).
Their order, and their manner,
Remain to be learnt
                (Philip Larkin, *Collected Poems*)

THE STATEMENT made by Karin Eriksson added little to Lewis's knowledge of the case. Unprecedentedly, Morse had kept him informed, in key respects, from fairly early on of his suspicions surrounding the Swedish Maiden and, eventually, of his virtual certainties. There were one or two significant discrepancies – particularly concerning the amount of money Karin had with her on her arrival in Oxford, and concerning the number of voyeurs who witnessed her photographic session in Seckham Villa. But from the combined statements of Karin herself and of her (wholly legitimate) husband David, it was a straightforward matter to stitch together the sequence of events that occurred on Sunday, 7 July 1991.

Out on the M40 Karin had almost immediately been picked up by a van en route for the Rover Car Plant at Cowley, in Oxford. Dropped off at the Headington roundabout, she had been picked up, again almost immediately, by a BMW and dropped at the Banbury Road roundabout on the Northern Ring Road. Walking a few hundred yards down the Banbury Road (buses on Sunday seemed infrequent) she had noticed the Cotswold House, and on impulse felt how wonderful it would be to spend at least one night in such attractive-looking B & B accommodation. She had knocked and enquired the rates; had been told that there was one single-room vacancy; but on learning the tariff had decided to find something a little cheaper, a little later. From a phone-box in Wentworth Road, just opposite the Cotswold House, she had phoned the model agency, and fairly soon been collected and driven down to Abingdon Road, where a telephone arrangement was made with McBryde for Karin to present herself at Seckham Villa, at about 2 p.m., for an hour or so's photographic session – the fee suggested, £80–£120, causing her eyebrows to lift in pleasurable surprise. She had declined further help from the agency, and walked up to St Giles', where she had a ham sandwich and half a glass of lager in the Eagle and Child.

At Seckham Villa she had been admitted by McBryde, and soon introduced to Myton. No hard pornography! – she'd immediately made her position clear on that; but, yes, she was willing to pose for a series of nude and semi-nude studies. And for an extra £20 she'd agreed that two other men there could sit in the 'studio' and watch her. Myton, she learned, was a freelance cinematographer in the sex-video world, and almost straightaway she had felt his eyes stripping off her skimpy summer clothing. But he'd seemed all right. Whilst he was preparing his parapher- nalia of tripods, umbrellas, backcloths, reflectors, light-meters, and the rest, she had wandered out briefly into the back garden; and when he had come out a little while later she had found him amusing and good fun. He was a smallish, slim man, with a day's growth of darkish beard, but with much lighter-coloured hair, worn quite long with an absurd short pony-tail held in an elastic band. She had teased him a little about this, and indeed asked him to stand by the wall there while *she* could take a couple of snaps. Soon though McBryde had hurriedly ushered them inside, where she was introduced, perfunctorily, to a man in a light-weight summer suit, and another man in grey slacks and sports jacket, incongruously (as she remembered on that hot day) holding a green pork-pie hat.

Then the 'session'. She had, she confessed, experienced some flush of excitement as the two silent men (McBryde had only come in later) ogled her as she stripped and posed and donned the see-through lingerie provided, and lay there on the bed in gaping gowns and skimpy negligées. Myton had punctuated her posturings with crude encouragements as gradually she'd felt herself relaxing: 'Christ, that's marvellous! Yeah! Ye-eah! Just hold it there, baby! Keep that hand under your tits and sort of, yes, sort of push 'em at me!' Such manner of talk had excited her and, if she were honest with herself, she'd felt a sort of orgasm of sexual vanity.

Afterwards, when she and Myton were alone, she had asked him to take one or two snaps of her with her own camera – just as a reminder really – and he'd readily done so. He'd still not so much as touched her physically, not yet; but he'd asked her where she was going and said he had his car outside if she wanted a lift anywhere. Before leaving McBryde had given her £100, all in ten-pound notes, which she had placed in her money-wallet; and then Myton had driven her back up to the top of the Banbury Road. She told him that she was thinking of going to the charity pop concert at Blenheim the next evening, 8 July, and then – suddenly – as they were passing the Cotswold House she asked him to stop: she *would* stay there now. But a white notice – NO VACANCIES – was across the door, and the lady of the house confirmed sadly that the remaining room had just been taken. As she was getting back into the car, she thought she saw a sparrow-hawk flying over towards the huge trees behind her, and she stopped and sought to focus her binoculars upon it. Fatal moment! Myton asked her if she was interested in birdwatching; and she had shown him her list of hoped-for spottings. Well, *he* knew exactly where she could see the woodpecker – probably see *all* the woodpeckers. In Wytham! He was interested himself in birds: was a member of the RSPB (this later proving untrue) and had a permit for walking in Wytham Woods (also proving to be untrue).

That was the beginning of all her woe.

Setting off from the semi-circular parking area just before the Great Wood, they had walked diagonally across a field and then along some leafy woodland pathway into a thickly forested area, where she remembered the brittle crackling of dead twigs and branches beneath her feet; and then Myton's hands upon her body. At first perhaps she might have been prepared for some limited petting; but very soon he had grown rough and insistent, and told her that he needed her – urgently. Would *have* her! He'd stripped off her thin blouse and pulled her to the floor; but she was herself strong and determined in fighting him off. The pocket of the rucksack in which she kept her binoculars – and her knife – was still open; and she managed to struggle away from him and open the blade of the knife – and plunge it into him . . . It had entered his flesh so easily, like pushing a knife through soft cheese, she said; but a fountain of blood had spurted across the top of her semi-naked body. Unlike the blood though, *he* lay still, utterly still – his eyes wide open and glaring up at her.

She hurled the knife into the trees, picked up her scarlet rucksack, and dressed only in a blood-bespattered skirt she fled the spot in panic – emerging finally into a clearing where, panting and jabbering and whimpering, she ran and ran – she could have no idea how long, how far – before collapsing, and remembering nothing more until she looked up to see a dog, a black and white Welsh Border Collie, and a thickset, bearded man behind the dog, his face anxious and kindly, looking down at her. A Land Rover was parked a few yards away.

In his cottage David Michaels at first had found it scarcely possible to believe the young woman's extraordinary account of what had occurred. It all seemed like some terrible *nightmare*, she'd pleaded: of a frenetic struggle and of a sudden death, if death it were; or of a man lying in the *agony* of death somewhere out there, somewhere in the woods. Indeed were it not for the blood all over her body, it *must* have been a nightmare surely! The mention of the word 'police' had driven her to hysterical tears; and clearly distressing too was the thought of the *car*, the car that from his cottage window Michaels could see even then across the lane. But *he* would deal with things, he'd promised her that – not knowing what he promised. He learned from her of Seckham Villa, and he made his decision. He got her to bath herself, to swallow half a dozen Disprin; and very soon, so suddenly, so miraculously almost, she had fallen deeply asleep, quite naked between the white sheets of his own double bed.

And he realized at that moment that he was just as bad as the rest of them, for he lusted after her, just as other men had lusted after her that afternoon.

At Seckham Villa, Michaels had met the three of them – still there: McBryde, Daley, and Hardinge; and he had begun then to appreciate the complexity of the situation in which they all – including Michaels himself – now found themselves. A plan was conceived. And later executed. Just one detail that was new. Karin's intended visit to the pop concert at Blenheim could be used to their ready advantage, since the discovery of the rucksack and other personal possessions somewhere *near* Blenheim, the day *after* the concert, would throw everyone on to the wrong scent, and would promote dark suspicions of a young lady missing, presumed dead somewhere, doubtless murdered by some drug-crazed, sex-hyped youth whom she'd met at the jamboree. Fear of exposure and financial ruin was more than sufficient motivation for McBryde; fear of exposure and scandal more than sufficient for Hardinge; and a cheque (neither Karin nor David Michaels knew for how much) sufficient to ensure the co-operation of the mercenary Daley.

That night, back in the cottage on the edge of the woods, Karin had become terrifyingly distraught; he had slept with her, for she wished it so; she had sought throughout that night the reassurance of his embrace, and of his love; and gladly, gloriously, he had met her needs.

It had been *her* plan, *her* plea, to go to Wales – away, away somewhere, away anywhere; and the next morning, setting out from Wytham just after 6 o'clock, he had driven there, leaving her in the hands of a kindly woman who must fairly soon (surely, he'd felt) have been in possession of most of the facts herself. The only thing from her rucksack she had taken was £60 – leaving the rest inside her money-wallet: it seemed to them all a convincing detail. From Wales, she had phoned David frequently – sometimes several times each evening. She it was, Karin, who had phoned her mother, together with whom, and with her sisters, the next phase of the plan was conceived: the simple substitution of Katarina's passport, sent to Karin in a plain brown envelope from Barcelona.

Finally, there had been the return to Oxford – and to David Michaels, the man she was learning increasingly to love, and whose solicitude for her, in turn, seemed now to know no bounds. With her hair cut and dyed black, with a pair of black-framed spectacles, she had lived in the cottage in an idyllic state of happiness with David and Bobbie – until a gradual integration into life again: a drink at the village pub, badminton at the village hall, membership of the local operatic society. And marriage! Strange, really, that she could live so happily so near the murder. Yet she could. The nightmare had passed. It was as if a partition existed, a sort of mesh between her and the whole of her life before she'd met David – a mesh like the network of twigs and branches in the spot where the blood had spurted over her.

For the first six months or so David had daily expected to discover the body, especially so as the trees grew bare in that late autumn; or expected others to discover it, as they roamed the ridings and observed the birds, badgers, foxes, squirrels, deer . . . But no. And when Morse had asked him where he himself might think of hiding a body, it had never occurred to him that Karin could have run so far, so very far from Pasticks out along by the Singing Way.

Just one more thing. Uncommonly for Swedish people, the Eriksson family were all Roman Catholic (something Lewis had suspected when he had seen the two crucifixes but, sadly, something he hadn't mentioned to Morse) and Karin had discovered the little church in the Woodstock Road. She had passed her driving test earlier that year, and was in the habit of going to Mass on Sunday mornings when David didn't require the Land Rover; and sometimes, when he did, waiting for him to pick her up after the service. Twice a month or so. Then to confession, about which she hadn't told her husband quite everything – certainly holding back from him her slowly formulating fear that her lack of contrition at having killed Myton was almost a greater sin than the killing itself had been; her fear that she might kill again, kill wildly and regardlessly if anyone came to threaten her own and David's happiness. Yet at the same time, an oddly contradictory wish was gradually growing too: the wish that someone would discover the truth of what she'd done; even that someone would *divulge* that truth . . .

But Father Richards could never do that, he'd said, as he'd comforted her, and prayed with her, and forgiven her in the name of the Almighty Father.

CHAPTER SIXTY-FOUR

The lips frequently parted with a murmur of words.
She seemed to belong rightly to a madrigal
(Thomas Hardy, *The Return of the Native*)

ON THE evening of the day following these events, Wednesday 5 August, Morse, Lewis, and Dr Laura Hobson had enjoyed a little celebration in Morse's office; and at 8.30 p.m. a sober Lewis had driven the other two down to Morse's flat in North Oxford.

'You won't want another drink?' Morse had asked of Lewis, as if the question were introduced by *num*, the Latin interrogative particle expecting the answer 'no'.

'What elegant equipment!' enthused Laura Hobson as she admired Morse's new CD player.

Ten minutes later the pair of them were sitting together, drinking in a diet of Glenfiddich and the finale of *Götterdämmerung*.

'Nothing quite like it in the whole history of music,' announced Morse magisterially, after Brünnhilde had ridden into the flames and the waves of the Rhine had finally rippled into silence.

'You think so?'

'Don't *you*?'

'I prefer Elizabethan madrigals, really.'

For a few moments Morse said nothing, saddened by her lack of sensitivity, it seemed.

'Oh.'

'I *loved* it. Don't be silly!' she said. 'But I've got to be on my way.'

'Can I walk you home?'

'I live too far away. I'm in a temporary flat – in Jericho.'

'I'll drive you home, then.'

'You've had far too much to drink.'

'You can stay here, if you like? I've got a spare pair of pyjamas.'

'I don't usually *wear* pyjamas.'

'No?'

'How many bedrooms do you have?'

'Two.'

'And bedroom number two is free?'

'Just like bedroom number one.'

'No secret passage between them?'

'I could get the builders in.'

She smiled happily, and rose to her feet. 'If there ever *is* going to be anything between us, Chief Inspector, it'll have to be when we're both a bit more sorber. Better that way. I think *you'd* prefer it that way too, if you're honest.' She laid a hand on his shoulder. 'C'mon. Ring for a taxi.'

Ten minutes later she kissed him lightly on the lips, her own lips dry and soft and slightly opened.

Then she was gone.

An hour later Morse lay awake on his back. It was still hot in the bedroom and he had only a light cotton sheet over him. Many varied thoughts were crowding in upon his mind, his eyes ever darting around in the darkness. First it had been the lovely woman who had been there with him that evening; then the case of the Swedish Maiden, with only those last few lines of the complex equation to be completed now; then his failure thus far to locate the bullet that had killed George Daley – this last problem gradually assuming a dominance in his brain . . .

The bullet had been fired from about sixty or so yards – that seemed a firm assumption. So . . . So why hadn't it been found? And why could no one in Blenheim be far more definite about *hearing* it being fired: shooting in Blenheim was not the common occurrence it was in other areas . . . in Wytham, for example. The rifle itself concerned him to a lesser extent: after all, it was far easier to get rid of a rifle than to get rid of a bullet that could have landed up anywhere . . . Morse got out of bed and went to find the Blenheim Park brochure – just as Johnson had done so recently before him. The place where Daley's body had been found could be only – what? – four hundred yards or so from that narrow north-westerly tip of the lake, shaped like the head of one of those cormorants he'd seen in Lyme Regis not all that long ago . . . Yes! He would double the men on the search – on *both* searches, rather. There could be little doubt that Philip Daley must have dumped his father's rifle there somewhere – in the lake itself, like as not. And once they'd found either of them, either the rifle or the bullet—

The phone rang, and Morse grabbed at it.

'That was quick, sir.'

'What do *you* want?'

'The Met, sir. They rang HQ, and Sergeant Dixon thought he ought to let me know—'

'Let *you* know, Lewis? Who the hell's in charge of this bloody case? Just wait till I see Dixon!'

'They thought you'd be asleep, sir.'

'Well, I wasn't, was I?'

'And, well—'

'Well, what?'

'Doesn't matter, sir.'

'It bloody *does* matter! They thought I was in bed with a woman! That's what they thought.'

'I don't know,' admitted the honest and honourable Lewis.

'Or pretty much the worse for booze!'

'Perhaps they thought both,' said Lewis simply.

'Well?'

'Young Philip Daley, sir. Just over an hour ago. Threw himself under a westbound train on the Central Line, it seems – train coming into Marble Arch from Bond Street – driver had no chance, just as he came out of the tunnel.'

Morse said nothing.

'Police knew a bit about the boy. He'd been picked up for shoplifting from a wine store in the Edgware Road and taken in; but the manager decided not to prosecute – he got away with a right dressing-down—'

'That's not *all* you've got to tell me, is it?' said Morse quietly.

'No, sir. You've guessed, I suppose. That was Monday morning, half an hour after the store opened.'

'You're telling me he couldn't have shot his dad, is that it?'

'Not even if he'd been the one to hire that helicopter, sir.'

'Does Mrs Daley know?'

'Not yet.'

'Leave her, Lewis. Leave her. Let her sleep.'

An hour later Morse still lay awake, though now his mind was far more relaxed. It had been like puzzling over a crossword clue and finding a possible answer, but being dissatisfied with that answer, lacking as it did any satisfying inevitability; and then being given an erratum slip, telling him that the *clue* had been wrong in the first place; then being given the *correct* clue; and then . . .

Oh yes!

All along he'd been aware of his dissatisfaction with the *motivation* of Philip Daley for the death of his father. It *could* have happened that way, of course – far odder things in life occurred than that. But the sequence of sudden hatred and carefully plotted murder rang far from true; and Morse considered once more the original facts: the scene of George Daley's murder, beside the little coppice in Blenheim Park, still cordoned off, with nothing but the corpse removed, and even now some weary PC standing guard, or sitting guard . . . Odd really, that! Morse had asked for an almost unprecedentedly large number of men in this case; what's more he'd given them all a quite specific task. Yet no one had come up with anything.

And suddenly he knew why!

He jerked up in the bed, as though crudely galvanized, and considered the erratum slip, smiling now serenely to himself. It could be. It *had* to be! And the new answer to the clue was shining and wholly fitting; an answer that 'filled the eye', as the judges said of the champion dogs at Crufts.

It was 2.40 a.m., and Morse knew that he would have to do something if he were ever to get to sleep. So he made himself a rare cup of Ovaltine, and sat for a while at the kitchen table: impatient, as ever, yet content. What exactly made him remember Heisenberg's Uncertainty Principle, he was by no means sure. Physics had long been a closed science to him, ever since at school he had once tried, without success, to take some readings from an incomprehensible piece of equipment called the Wheatstone Bridge. But Heisenberg was a splendid name and Morse looked him up in his encyclopaedia: 'There is always an uncertainty in the values obtained if simultaneous observation is made of *position* . . .' Morse nodded to himself. *Time* too, as doubtless old Heisenberg had known.

Morse was soon asleep.

When he awoke, at 7 a.m., he thought he might perhaps have dreamed of a choir of beautiful women singing Elizabethan madrigals. But it was all a bit vague in his mind; about as vague as exactly what, as a principle, 'Werner Karl Heisenberg (1901–76)' had had in mind.

CHAPTER SIXTY-FIVE

How strange are the tricks of memory, which, often hazy as a dream about the most important events, religiously preserve the merest trifles

(Sir Richard Burton, *Sind Revisited*)

'YOU APPRECIATE therefore, Lewis' – the two of them stood on the scene of Daley's murder the following morning – 'the paramount importance of leaving everything exactly as it was here.'

'But we've had everybody trampling all over the place.'

Morse beamed. 'Ah, but we've got this, haven't we?' He patted the roof of the Blenheim Estate van affectionately.

'Unless one of the lads's been sitting in there having a smoke.'

'If he has, I'll sever his scrotum!'

'By the way, did you have a word with Dixon this morning?'

'Dixon? What the 'ell's Dixon got to do with anything?'

'Nothing,' murmured Lewis, as he turned away to have a final word with the two men standing by the recovery truck.

'Without getting inside at all, you say?' asked the elder of the two.

'That's what the chief inspector wants, yes.'

'We can't do it without *touching* the bloody thing though, can we, Charlie?'

Morse himself was standing beside the van, deep in thought, it seemed. Then he walked slowly round it, peering with apparently earnest attention at the ground. But the soil was rock-hard there, after weeks of cloudless weather, and after a little while he lost interest and walked back to the police car.

'That's enough here, Lewis. Let's get over to the lodge: it's time we had another word with Mr Williams.'

As before, Williams' evidence, in specific terms, was perhaps unsatisfactory; but, in general outline, it did serve to establish a working framework for the murder – the only one really the police had. Certainly the crucial point – that Daley had driven through Combe Lodge Gate on the morning of his murder – could be pretty confidently reaffirmed. There had been a good deal of to-ing and fro-ing of two blue tractors, with their trailers, that morning, each of them making three trips from the saw-mill down to the area near the Grand Bridge to load up with recently felled timber. Williams had checked up (he said) with the drivers, and the ferrying had not begun until about 9.45 a.m., or a little later perhaps; and if there was one thing he could feel reasonably confident about it was the fact that Daley had come through the gate at the same time as one of the tractors – because although the gate was opened quite frequently that morning, it had not been *specifically* opened (Williams was *almost* sure) for the estate van. He did remember the van though – quite definite he was about that. He hadn't known Daley well; spoken to him a few times of course, and Daley had often come through the lodge, to and from the saw-mill. Usually, between those working at Blenheim, there would be a hand raised in acknowledgement or greeting. And there was another thing: Daley almost always wore his hat, even in the summer; and, yes, Daley had been wearing his hat that Monday morning.

Morse had pressed him on the point. 'You're *sure* about that?'

Williams breathed out noisily. He felt he was sure, yes. But it was a frightening business, this being questioned and giving evidence, and he was now far less sure than he had been about one or two of the things he'd said earlier. That shot he thought he'd heard, for example: he was less and less sure now that he'd heard it at *all*. So it was better, fairer too, to play it a bit more on the cautious side . . . that's what he thought.

'Well, I think so. Trouble is really about the time. You see, it might have been a bit *later*, I think.'

But Morse appeared no longer interested in the time – or in the shot, for that matter.

'Mr Williams! I'm sorry to keep on about this but it's very important. I know that Mr Daley always wore his hat around the park, and I believe you when you say you *saw* his hat. But let's put it another way: are you sure it was *Mr Daley* who was wearing the hat on Monday morning?'

'You mean,' said Williams slowly, 'you mean it mightn't have been him – driving the van?'

'Exactly.'

Oh dear! Williams didn't know . . . hadn't even considered . . . Two women joggers appeared at the lodge, twisted through the kissing-gate and continued their way into the park itself, their breasts bouncing, their legs (as viewed from the rear) betraying the slightly splay-footed run of the fairer sex. Morse followed them briefly with his eyes, and asked his last question:

'Did you notice any jogger coming *this* way, *out* of the park, on Monday morning? About, let's say, half-past ten? Eleven?'

Williams pondered the question. While everything else seemed to be getting more and more muddled in his mind, the chief inspector had just sparked off a fairly vivid recollection. He thought he *had* noticed someone, yes – a woman. There were always lots of joggers at weekends, but not many in the week; not many at all; and certainly not in the middle of the morning. He thought he *could* remember the woman though; could almost see her now, with the nipples of her breasts erect and pushing through the thin material of her T-shirt. Was that Monday *morning*, though? The simple truth was that he just couldn't be certain and again he was unwilling to commit himself too positively.

'I may have done, yes.'

'Thank you very much, sir.'

What exactly he was being thanked for, Mr Williams was not quite clear, and he was aware that he must have appeared a less-than-satisfactory witness. Yet the chief inspector had looked mightily pleased with himself as he'd left; and he'd said 'very much', hadn't he? It was all a bit beyond the gate-keeper of Combe Lodge in Blenheim Park.

CHAPTER SIXTY-SIX

As when that divelish yron engin, wrought
In deepest hell, and framd by furies skill,
With windy nitre and quick sulphur fraught,
And ramd with bollett rowed, ordaind to kill,
Conceivcth fyre
(Edmund Spenser, *The Faerie Queene*)

THE SEMI-CIRCULAR area where birdwatchers and the occasional loving couple were wont to park was packed with police cars and vans when, half an hour after leaving Blenheim, Lewis drove through the perimeter gate ('The woods are closed to Permit Holders until 10.00 a.m. every day except Sunday') and into the compound, on his left, marked off with its horizontal four-barred, black-creosoted fencing. Here, under the direction of

Chief Inspector Johnson, some fifty or so policemen – some
uniformed, some not – were systematically conducting their
search.

'No luck yet?' asked Morse.

'Give us a chance!' said Johnson. 'Lot of ground to cover, isn't
there?'

The large wooden sheds, the stacks of logs and fencing-posts,
the occasional clump of trees, the rank growth of untended
bushes – all precluded any wholly scientific search-pattern. But
there was plenty of time; there were plenty of men; they would
find it, Johnson was confident of that.

Morse led the way up the curving track towards the furthest
point from the compound entrance, towards the hut where David
Michaels had his office, right up against the recently erected deer-
fence. To the left of this track was a line of forty or so fir trees,
about thirty feet high; and to the right, the hut itself, the main
door standing padlocked now. On the wooden sides of this
extensive hut, at the top, were six large bird-boxes, numbered
9–14; and at the bottom there grew rank clumps of nettles. Morse
looked back down the sloping track; retraced his steps, counting
as he went; then stopped at a smaller open-sided shed in which
stood a large red tractor with a timber-lifting device fixed to it.
For a minute or two he stood beside the tractor, behind the shed
wall, and then, as if he were a young boy with an imaginary rifle,
lifted both his arms, curled his right index-finger round an
imaginary trigger, closed his left eye, and slowly turned the rifle
in an arc from right to left, as if some imaginary vehicle were
being driven past – the rifle finally remaining stationary as the
vehicle's imaginary driver dismounted, in front of the head
forester's hut.

'You reckon?' asked Lewis quietly.

Morse nodded.

'That means we probably ought to be concentrating the search
up there, sir.' Lewis pointed back towards Michaels' office.

'Give him a chance! He's not so bright as you,' whispered
Morse.

'About fifty, fifty-five yards. I paced it too, sir.'

Again Morse nodded, and the two of them rejoined Johnson.

'Know much about rifles?' asked Morse.

'Enough.'

'Could you use a silencer on a seven-millimetre?'

'"Sound-moderator" – that's the word these days. No, not

much good. It'd suppress the noise of the explosion, but it couldn't stop the noise of the bullet going through the sound-barrier. And incidentally, Morse, it might be a .243 – don't forget that!'

'Oh!'

'You were thinking it might be around here, weren't you?' Johnson kicked aside a few nettles along the bottom of the shed, and looked at Morse shrewdly, if a little sadly.

Morse shrugged. 'I'd be guessing, of course.'

Johnson looked down at the flattened nettles. 'You never did have much faith in me, did you?'

Morse didn't know what to say, and as Johnson walked away, he too looked down at the flattened nettles.

'You're quite wrong, you know, sir. He's a whole lot brighter than me, is Johnson.'

But again Morse made no reply, and the pair of them walked down to the low, stone-built cottage where until very lately Michaels and his Swedish wife had lived so happily together.

Just as they were entering, they heard a shot from fairly far off. But they paid little attention to it. As Michaels had informed them, no one was ever going to be too disturbed about hearing a gun-shot in Wytham: game-keepers shooting squirrels or rabbits, perhaps; farmworkers taking a pot at the pestilential pigeons.

Inside the cottage, just beside the main entrance, stood the steel security cabinet from which Michaels' rifle had been taken for forensic examination. But there was no longer any legal requirement for the cabinet to be locked, and it now stood open – and empty. Lewis bent down and looked carefully at the groove in which the rifle had stood, noting the scratches where the butt had rested; and beside it a second groove – with equally tell-tale signs.

'I'm sure you're right,' said Lewis.

'If you remember,' said Morse, 'he told us *himself*, Michaels did. When you told him you'd seen no rifles in the hut he said ... he said "Oh, I couldn't keep 'em *there*" – those were his exact words, I think.'

'You're still certain he did it, sir?'

'Yes.'

'What about that "Uncertainty Principle" you were on about this morning?'

'What about it?' asked Morse. Infuriatingly.

'Forget it.'

'What's the time?'

'Nearly twelve.'

'Ah, the prick of noon!'

'Pardon?'

'Forget it.'

'We can walk down if you like, sir. A nice little ten-minute walk – do us good. We can work up a thirst.'

'Nonsense!'

'Don't you enjoy walking – occasionally?'

'Occasionally, yes.'

'So?'

'So drive me down to the White Hart, Lewis! What's the problem?'

CHAPTER SIXTY-SEVEN

Scire volunt secreta domus, atque inde timeri
(They watch for household secrets hour by hour
And feed therefrom their appetite for power)
(Juvenal, *Satire III*)

'WHAT PUT you on it this time?' asked Lewis as they sat opposite each other in the small upstairs bar, Morse with a pint of real ale, Lewis himself with a much-iced orangeade.

'I think it wasn't so much finding Daley like he was – out at Blenheim. It was the photographs they took of him there. I don't think it hit me at the time; but when I looked at the photographs I got the idea somehow that he'd just been dumped there – that he hadn't been shot there at all.'

'You mean you just – well, sort of had a *feeling* about it?'

'No. I don't mean that. You may think I work that way, Lewis, but I don't. I don't believe in some unaccountable intuition that just happens occasionally to turn out right. There's got to be *something* there, however vague. And here we had the hat, didn't we? The hat Daley wore wherever he was, whatever the weather. Same bloody hat! He never took it *off*, Lewis!'

'Probably took it off in bed?'

We don't even know that, do we?' Morse drained his beer. 'Plenty of time for another.'

Lewis nodded. 'Plenty of time! Your round though, sir. I'll have another orange. Lovely. Lots of ice, please!'

'You see,' resumed Morse, a couple of minutes later, 'he was almost certainly wearing his hat when he was shot, and I very much doubt myself that it would have fallen *off*. I'd seen the tight sweat-mark round his forehead when we met him earlier. And even if it *had* fallen off—when he dropped dead – I just had the feeling . . .'

Lewis lifted his eyebrows.

'. . . it wouldn't have fallen *far*.'

'So?'

'So, I reckon it was put down there deliberately, just beside his head – *after* he was shot. Remember where it was? Three or four feet *away* from his head. So the conclusion's firm and satisfactory, as I see it. He was wearing his hat when he was shot, and like as not it stayed on his head. Then when he was moved, and finally dumped, it had come off; and it was placed there beside him.'

'What a palaver!'

Morse nodded. 'But they had to do it. They had to establish an alibi—'

'For David Michaels, you mean?'

'Yes. It was Michaels who shot Daley – I've no doubts on that score. There was the agreement Hardinge told us about, wasn't there, the agreement the four of them made – a statement by the way that contains quite as much truth as falsehood, Lewis. Then something comes along and buggers it all up. Daley got a letter spelling out his financial responsibilities for his boy, and Daley knew that he was the one who had a hold over – well, over *all* the others, really. But particularly over David Michaels! I reckon Daley probably rang him and said he couldn't afford to stick by the agreement; said he was sorry – but he needed more money. And if he didn't get more money pretty soon . . .'

'Blackmail!'

'Exactly. And there may well have been a bit more of *that* than we think.'

'Quite a hold over Michaels, though, when you think of it: knowing he was married to . . . a murderess.'

'Quite a hold. So Michaels agrees – *pretends* he agrees – to go along with it. They'll meet at Wytham earlyish on Monday – quarter to ten, say. No one around much at that time. No birdwatchers allowed in the woods till ten – remember the notice?'

'The RSPB people were there.'

'They turned out to be a blessing in disguise, though.'

'Take it a bit slower, please!'

'Right. Let's just go back a minute. The rendezvous's settled. Daley drives up to Wytham. Michaels has said he'll have some money ready – in notes, no doubt – just after the bank's opened. He's ready. He waits for Daley to drive up to his office. He waits for a clear view of him as he gets out of his estate van. I don't know *exactly* where he was waiting, of course; what I *do* know is that someone as experienced as Michaels, with a telescopic sight, could hit *this*' – Morse picked up his empty glass – 'no problem! – from a hundred, let alone from fifty yards.'

But any further reconstruction of Daley's murder was temporarily curtailed, since Johnson had walked in, and now sat down beside them.

'What'll you have?' asked Morse. 'Lewis here is in the chair.'

'Nothing for me, thank you, er, Lewis. Look! There's this call for you from forensics about the van. I told 'em I wasn't *quite* sure where you were—'

'What'd they say?'

'They found prints all over the shop – mostly Daley's, of course. But like you said, they found other prints – on the tailboard, on the steering wheel.'

'And I was right about them?'

Johnson nodded. 'Yes. They're Karin Eriksson's.'

At lunch-time that same day, Alasdair McBryde came out of the tube station at Manor House and walked briskly down the Seven Sisters Road – finally turning into one of the parking-and-garage areas of a high-rise block of flats that flanks the Bethune Road. He had spotted the unmarked car immediately: the two men seated in the front, one of them reading the *Sun*. It was quite customary for him to spot danger a mile or so off; and he did so now. Number 14 was the garage he was interested in; but softly whistling the Prelude to Act Three of *Lohengrin*, he walked boldly into the nearest open garage (number 9), picked up a half-filled can of Mobiloil, before nonchalantly retracing his steps to the main road; where, still clutching the dirty can, he walked quietly and confidently away in the direction of Stamford Hill.

'False alarm!' said the policeman with the *Sun*, as he resumed his reading of various illicit liaisons among the glitterati.

*

At 3.25 p.m., no more than four or five yards from the spot where Chief Inspector Johnson had earlier stood, there amongst the nettles and the cow-parsley and other less readily recognizable plants and weeds, Constable Roy Wilks made his discovery: a .243 bullet – the bullet (surely!) for which the party had been searching. Never, in his life hitherto, had Wilks been the focus of such attention; and never again (as he duly recognized) would he be likely to experience such felicitous congratulations.

Most particularly from Morse.

CHAPTER SIXTY-EIGHT

The Light of Lights
Looks always on the motive, not the deed,
The Shadow of Shadows on the deed alone
(W. B. Yeats, *The Countess Cathleen*)

'JUST simply, Morse! Just simply! I don't want to know what a clever sod you are. Just a straightforward – brief! – account. If you can manage it.'

Following the final discoveries, new statements had been taken from both David Michaels and Karin Eriksson; and now, the following morning, as he sat in Strange's office, Morse was able to confirm in nearly every respect the pattern of events he'd outlined to Lewis in the White Hart.

Daley had been to the office in Wytham Woods on more than one occasion before, and a meeting had been arranged for 9.45 a.m. on Monday, 3 August. At that time there would, with any luck, be virtually no one around; but only if no one *was* around, would the deed take place. And the deed *did* take place. When Daley got out of the van, Michaels shot him dead with his .243 rifle – the latter buried later out on the Singing Way. To Michaels himself the report had sounded terrifyingly loud; but following it a strangely eerie silence had reasserted itself, and no one had come rushing into the compound there demanding explanation, seeking causes. Nothing. A newly still, clear morning in early August. And a body – which Michaels had swiftly wrapped in black plastic sheeting and lifted into the back of Daley's own van. Only two or three minutes after the murder, this same van was being driven out through Wolvercote, over to the A44 towards Woodstock, left at Bladon, and then into Long Hanborough – and finally up to Combe Lodge, on the western side of the Blenheim Estate. The keys to the lodge gate would doubtless have been somewhere on the body, but the van-driver waited a while and was very quickly rewarded when the gate was opened for a tractor and trailer; and when the van driver, pulling Daley's khaki-green hat down over her short, black hair, moved into the trailer's wake, raising a hand in acknowledgement to any anonymous observer as she drove gratefully through. A few hundred yards along she had spotted an ideal location in which to leave a van, and a body, and a hat. Daley had not been a heavy man, and she herself was a strong young woman; yet she had been unable to lift the corpse – just to pull it over the tail-board, whence it fell with a thud to the hard soil. The plastic sheet was messily sticky with blood, and she had taken it with her as she ran off, across the road, to the tip of the lake, where she washed the blood from her hands and wedged the sheet beneath some reeds. Then, following the arranged plan, she'd jogged her way back – though not, she claimed, through Combe Lodge, as Morse had suggested (and Williams could have sworn) – but down by the western side of the lake, across the small bridge that spans the River Glyme below the Grand Cascade, and out of the park via Eagle Lodge.

'Helluva long way, whichever route she took,' mumbled Strange.

'Some people are fitter than others, sir.'

'Not thinking of *yourself*, are you?'

'No!'

'Bit lucky, though – the fellow at the lodge remembering the van going through.'

'With all respect, sir, I don't think that's true. In fact, it led us all to believe that Daley was alive until after ten o'clock – when David Michaels was miles away with his RSPB pals round the bird-boxes. But Michaels could *never* have done it himself – not by himself – that morning. There was no way at all that *he* could have got out to Blenheim and somehow – somehow – got back to Wytham.'

'But his wife could. That's what you're saying.'

'His wife did.'

'She was a brave girl.'

'She *is* a brave girl, sir.'

'You know, if they'd only have played it straight up and down the wicket from the start – either of them – they'd probably have got away with justifiable homicide, self-defence, take your pick.'

'Perhaps.'

'You don't sound very convinced.'

'I think she's a rather more complex woman than that. Perhaps . . . perhaps she couldn't quite persuade herself that killing Myton had been purely in self-defence.'

'You mean – you mean she might have enjoyed it?'

'I didn't say that, sir.'

Strange shook his head. 'I see what you're getting at, though. Prepared – wasn't she? – to drive Daley's body out to Blenheim and . . .'

'She's a complex woman, as I say, sir. I'm not sure I understand her at all really.'

'Perhaps she's a bit of a mystery even to herself.'

Morse got up to leave. 'Same thing in most cases, isn't it? We never really understand people's motives. In all these things it's as if there's a manifestation – but there's always a bit of a mystery too.'

'Now don't you start going all religious on *me*, Morse!'

'No chance of that.'

'I don't suppose anyone'll miss Daley all that much.'

'No. He was a *small* man—'

'Was he? How tall was he?'

'No. I didn't mean small in that sense. But he *was* physically small, yes. Only weighed eight stone, four pounds.'

'How do you know that?'

'They weighed him, sir – *post mortem*.'

CHAPTER SIXTY-NINE

Just as every person has his idiosyncrasies, so has every typewriter

(*Handbook of Office Maintenance*, 9th edition)

THE FOLLOWING day, Friday, 8 August, Morse's attention was early drawn to the correspondence columns of *The Times*.

From Lt. Colonel Reginald Postill

Sir, Over these past years we have all become aware of the increasing influence of trial (and retrial) by TV. We have seen, for example, the collapse of cases brought against the Birmingham Six and the Guildford Four; and doubtless in the years ahead we may confidently anticipate the acquittal of the Towcester Two and the Winchester One.

Are we now to become similarly conditioned to police inquiries conducted in the nation's quality daily newspapers (including, of course, your own, sir)? I learn that the Thames Valley Police has now been able to prefer charges against persons in the 'Swedish Maiden' case – and this in considerable measure thanks to the original verses published in your correspondence columns. Clearly we should be grateful for such an outcome. But am I alone in being troubled by such a precedent? Am I alone in believing that such affairs, both judicial and investigative, are better left in the hands of those men and women suitably trained in their respective specialisms?

Yours faithfully,
REGINALD POSTILL,
6 Baker Lane,
Shanklin,
Isle of Wight.

Lewis had come into his office as Morse was reading this; and duly read it himself.

'Bit hard that, isn't it? I'd have thought it all helped us quite a bit. I can't myself really see what's wrong with getting a bit of public co-operation and interest.'

'Oh, I agree,' said Morse.

'Perhaps we shouldn't be too much worried about some retired old colonel from the Isle of Wight, sir.'

Morse smiled knowingly across at his old friend. 'What makes you think he's retired?' he asked very quietly.

That same evening, Morse's celebratory mood was undiminished; and he had walked down to Summertown immediately after *The Archers* and carried back up to his flat four bottles of champagne: not the dearest, it must be admitted – yet not the cheapest either. Strange, Johnson, Lewis – and himself. Four of them. Just for a congratulatory glass or two. Dr Laura Hobson

had been invited too (how otherwise?); but she had phoned
earlier in the evening to make her apologies – an emergency;
sorry, she'd love to have been there; but these things couldn't be
helped, could they?

Harold Johnson was the first to leave, at 9.15 p.m. One glass of
bubbly, and the plea that the wife would be awaiting him. Yet of
all of them it was probably Johnson who was the most grateful
soul there that evening: the procedures surrounding the prosecutions of two suspected murderers – David Michaels and Mrs
Michaels – would be entrusted now to him, to Johnson and his
team, since Morse had announced his intention of resuming
immediately his truncated furlough which had begun (so long
ago it seemed) in the Bay Hotel at Lyme Regis.

Three glasses of bubbly and ten minutes later, Strange had
struggled to his feet and announced his imminent departure.

'Thanks! And enjoy your holiday!'

'If you'll let me.'

'Where are you going this time?'

'I was thinking of Salisbury, sir.'

'Why Salisbury?'

Morse hesitated. 'They've just tarted up the cathedral there,
and I thought—'

'You *sure* you're not going religious on me, Morse?'

Two of the champagne bottles were finished, and Morse picked
up a third, starting to twist open the wire round its neck.

'No more for me,' said Lewis.

Morse put the bottle back on the sideboard. 'Would you prefer
a Newcastle Brown?'

'I think I would, to be honest, sir.'

'C'mon, then!'

Morse led the way through to the cluttered kitchen.

'You trying for *my* job, sir?' Lewis pointed to the ancient
portable typewriter that stood at one end of the kitchen table.

'Ah! That! I was just writing a brief line to *The Times*.' He
handed Lewis his effort, a messy, ill-typed, xxxx-infested missive.

'Would you like me to re-type it for you, sir? It's a bit . . .'

'Yes, please. I'd be grateful for that.'

So Lewis sat there, at the kitchen table, and retyped the brief
letter. That it took him rather longer than it should have done
was occasioned by two factors: first, that Lewis himself could

boast only semi-competence in the keyboard-skills; second, that he had found himself looking, with increasingly puzzled interest, at the very first line he'd typed. And then at the second. And then at the third . . . Especially did he find himself examining the worn top segment of the lower-case 'e', and the slight curtailment of the cross-bar in the lower-case 't' . . . For the moment, however, he said nothing. Then, when his reasonably clean copy was completed, he wound it from the ancient machine and handed it to Morse.

'Much better! Good man!'

'You remember, sir, that original article in *The Times*? When they said the typewriter could pretty easily be identified if it was ever found? From the "e"s and the "t"s . . .?'

'Yes?'

'You wrote those verses about the girl yourself, didn't you, sir?'

Morse nodded slowly.

'Bloody hell!' Lewis shook his head incredulously.

Morse poured himself a can of beer. 'Champagne's a lovely drink, but it makes you thirsty, doesn't it?'

'Think anyone *else* suspected?' asked Lewis, grinning down at the typewriter.

'Just the one person. Someone from Salisbury.'

'Didn't you say you would be going there, though? To Salisbury?'

'*Might* be, Lewis. Depends.'

Half an hour after Lewis had left, Morse was listening to Lipatti playing the slow movement of the Mozart piano concerto No. 21, when the doorbell rang.

'It's a bit late I know but . . .'

What had been a semi-scowl on Morse's face now suddenly burgeoned into a wholly ecstatic smile.

'Nonsense! It just so happens I've got a couple of bottles of bubbly . . .'

'Will that be enough, do you think?'

'Come in! I'll just turn this off—'

'Please not! I love it. K 467? Right?'

'Where've you parked?'

'I didn't come by car. I thought you'd probably try to get me drunk.'

Morse closed the door behind them. 'I *will* turn it off, if you don't mind. I've never been able to cope with two beautiful things at the same time.'

She followed Morse into the lounge where once more he picked up bottle number three.

'What time will you have to go, my love?'

'Who said anything about going, Chief Inspector?'

Morse put down the bottle and swiftly retraced his steps to the front door, where he turned the key, and shot the bolts, both top and bottom.

EPILOGUE

Life never presents us with anything which may not be looked upon as a fresh starting point, no less than as a termination

(André Gide, *The Counterfeiters*)

THE CORRESPONDENCE columns of *The Times* carried the following letter on Monday, 10 August 1992:

From Detective Chief Inspector E. Morse

Sir, On behalf of the Thames Valley Police, I wish to record the gratitude of myself and of my fellow officers for the co-operation and assistance of *The Times* newspaper. As a direct result of lines of investigation suggested by some of its correspondents about the 'Swedish Maiden' verses, persons now being held in custody will be duly brought to face trial in accordance with the law's demands.

I am, sir,

Yours,

E. MORSE,
Thames Valley Police HQ,
Kidlington,
Oxon.
[This correspondence is now closed. Ed.]

Like the rest of his staff, the editor had been fascinated by the crop of ideas that sprang from the Swedish Maiden verses; and although the case was now finished he felt he should reply briefly to Morse's letter. In mid-afternoon therefore he dictated a few lines of reciprocal gratitude.

'Do we have a private address for him?' asked his personal secretary.

'No. Just address it to Kidlington HQ – that'll be fine.'

'What about the initial – do we know what that stands for?'

'The "E"?' The editor considered the question for a second or two. 'Er, no. No, I don't think we do.'

The Daughters
of Cain

For the staff of the Pitt Rivers Museum,
Oxford, with my gratitude to them for
their patient help.

Acknowledgements

The author and publishers wish to thank the following who have kindly given permission for use of copyright materials:

Extract from *A Cornishman at Oxford* © A. L. Rowse;

Extract from *The Lesson* by Roger McGough, reprinted by permission of Peters Fraser & Dunlop Group Ltd;

Extracts by Cyril Connolly reproduced by kind permission of the Estate of Cyril Connolly c/o Rogers, Coleridge & White Ltd, 20 Powis Mews, London W11 1JN, © 1944 Cyril Connolly;

Extract from *The Observer* © by Oliver Sacks, 9 January 1994;

Faber & Faber Ltd for the extract from *New Year Letter* by W. H. Auden;

Extract from *Oxford* by Jan Morris, published by permission of Oxford University Press;

Extract from *Back to Methuselah* granted by The Society of Authors on behalf of the Bernard Shaw Estate;

Extract from *The Pitt Rivers Museum, A Souvenir Guide to the Collections* © Pitt Rivers Museum 1993;

Extract from *The Pitt Rivers Museum* taken from *The Memory of War and Children in Exile: Poems 1968–1983*, James Fenton, published by Penguin © 1982;

Kate Champkin for the extracts from *The Sleeping Life of Aspern Williams* by Peter Champkin;

N. F. Simpson for the extract from *One-Way Pendulum*;

Extract from *Berlioz, Romantic and Classic* by Ernest Newman published by Dover Publications;

Extract from *The Times* by Matthew Parris, published 7 March 1994;

Extract from *Marriage and Morals* by Bertrand Russell, published by permission of Routledge (Unwin Hyman);

Extracts from *The New Shorter Oxford English Dictionary*, published by permission of Oxford University Press;

Faber & Faber Ltd for the extract from 'La Figlia Che Piange' in *Collected Poems 1909–1962* by T. S. Eliot.

Oxford is the Latin quarter of Cowley
(Anon)

PROLEGOMENA
Wednesday, 25 May 1994

(i)

Natales grate numeras?
(Do you count your birthdays with gratitude?)
(HORACE, *Epistles II*)

ON MONDAYS to Fridays it was fifty-fifty whether the postman called before Julia Stevens left for school.

So, at 8.15 a.m. on 25 May she lingered awhile at the dark blue front door of her two-bedroomed terraced house in East Oxford. No sign of her postman yet; but he'd be bringing something a bit later.

Occasionally she wondered whether she still felt just a little love for the ex-husband she'd sued for divorce eight years previously for reasons of manifold infidelity. Especially had she so wondered when, exactly a year ago now, he'd sent her that card – a large, tasteless, red-rosed affair – which in a sad sort of way had pleased her more than she'd wanted to admit. Particularly those few words he'd written inside: 'Don't forget we had some good times too!'

If anyone, perhaps, shouldn't she tell *him*?

Then there was Brenda: dear, precious, indispensable Brenda. So there would certainly be *one* envelope lying on the 'Welcome' doormat when she returned from school that afternoon.

Aged forty-six (today) the Titian-haired Julia Stevens would have been happier with life (though only a little) had she been able to tell herself that after nearly twenty-three years she was still enjoying her chosen profession. But she wasn't; and she knew that she would soon have packed it all in anyway, even if . . .

Even if . . .

But she put that thought to the back of her mind.

It wasn't so much the *pupils* – her thirteen- to eighteen-year-olds – though some of them would surely have ruffled the calm of a Mother Teresa. No. It wasn't that. It was the way the *system* was going: curriculum development, aims and objectives (whatever the difference between those was supposed to be!), assessment criteria, pastoral care, parent consultation, profiling, testing . . . God! When was there any time for *teaching* these days? She'd made her own views clear, quite bravely so, at one of the staff meetings earlier that year. But the Head had paid little attention. Why should he? After all, he'd been appointed precisely *because* of his cocky conversance with curriculum development, aims and objectives and the rest . . . A young, shining ideas-man, who during his brief spell of teaching (as rumour had it) would have experienced considerable difficulty in maintaining discipline even amongst the glorious company of the angels.

There was a sad little smile on Julia's pale face as she fished her Freedom Ticket from her handbag and stepped on to the red Oxford City double-decker.

Still, there was one good thing. No one at school knew of her birthday. Certainly, she trusted, none of the pupils did, although she sensed a slight reddening under her high cheekbones as just for a few seconds she contemplated her embarrassment if one of her classes broke out into 'Happy Birthday, Mrs Stevens!' She no longer had much confidence in the powers of the Almighty; but she almost felt herself praying.

But if she were going to target any prayer, she could surely so easily find a better aim (or was it an 'objective'?) than averting a cacophonic chorus from 5C, for example. And in any case, 5C weren't all that bad, really; and she, Julia Stevens, *mirabile dictu*, was one of the few members of staff who could handle that motley and unruly crowd. No. If she were going to pray for anything, it would be for something that was of far greater importance.

Of far greater importance for herself . . .

As things turned out, her anxieties proved wholly groundless. She received no birthday greetings from a single soul, either in the staff-room or in any of the six classes she taught that day.

Yet there was, in 5C, just the one pupil who knew Mrs Stevens' birthday. Knew it well, for it was the same as his own: the twenty-fifth of May. Was it that strange coincidence that had caused them all the trouble?

Trouble? Oh, yes!

In the previous *Sunday Mirror*'s horoscope column, Kevin Costyn had scanned his personal 'Key to Destiny' with considerable interest:

> GEMINI
> Now that the lone planet voyages across
> your next romance chart, you swap false
> hope for thrilling fact. Maximum mental
> energy helps you through to a hard-to-reach
> person who is always close to your heart.
> Play it cool.

'Maximum mental energy' had never been Kevin's strong point. But if such mighty exertion were required to win his way through to such a person, well, for once he'd put his mind to things. At the very least, it would be an improvement on the 'brute-force-and-ignorance' approach he'd employed on that earlier occasion – when he'd tried to make amorous advances to one of his school-mistresses.

When he'd tried to rape Mrs Julia Stevens.

(ii)

> Chaos ruled OK in the classroom
> as bravely the teacher walked in
> the havocwreakers ignored him
> his voice was lost in the din
> (ROGER MCGOUGH, *The Lesson*)

AT THE AGE of seventeen (today) Kevin Costyn was the dominant personality amongst the twenty-four pupils, of both sexes, comprising Form 5C at the Proctor Memorial School in East Oxford. He was fourteen months or so above the average age of his class because he was significantly below the average Intelligence Quotient for his year, as measured by orthodox psychometric criteria.

In earlier years, Kevin's end-of-term reports had semi-optimistically suggested a possible capacity for improvement, should he ever begin to activate his dormant brain. But any realistic hopes of academic achievement had been abandoned many terms ago.

In spite of – or was it because of? – such intellectual shortcomings, Kevin was an individual of considerable menace and power; and if any pupil was likely to drive his teacher to retirement, to resignation, even to suicide, that pupil was Kevin Costyn. Both inside and outside school, this young man could be described only as crude and vicious; and during the current summer term his sole interest in class activities had focused upon his candidature for the British National Party in the school's annual mock-elections.

Teachers were fearful of his presence in the classroom, and blessed their good fortune whenever he was (allegedly) ill or playing hookey or appearing before the courts or cautioned (again!) by the police or being interviewed by probation officers, social workers, or psychiatrists. Only rarely was his conduct less than positively disruptive; and that when some overnight dissipation had sapped his wonted enthusiasm for selective subversion.

Always he sat in the front row, immediately to the right of the central gangway. This for three reasons. First, because he was thus enabled to turn round and thereby the more easily to orchestrate whatever disruption he had in mind. Second, because (without ever admitting it) he was slightly deaf; and although he had little wish to listen to his teachers' lessons, his talent for verbal repartee was always going to be diminished by any slight mis-hearing. Third, because Eloise Dring, the sexiest girl in the Fifth Year, was so very short-sighted that she was compelled (refusing spectacles) to take a ring-side view of each day's proceedings. And Kevin wanted to sit next to Eloise Dring.

So there he sat, his long legs sticking way out beneath his undersized desk; his feet shod in a scuffed, cracked, decrepit pair of winkle-pickers, two pairs of which had been bequeathed by some erstwhile lover to his mother – the latter a blowsy, frowsy single parent who had casually conceived her only son (as far as she could recall the occasion) in a lay-by just off the Cowley Ring Road, and who now lived in one of a string of council properties known to the largely unsympathetic locals as Prostitutes Row.

Kevin was a lankily built, gangly-boned youth, with long, dark, unwashed hair, and a less than virile sprouting on upper lip and chin, dressed that day in a gaudily floral T-shirt and tattered jeans. His sullen, dolichocephalic face could have been designed by some dyspeptic El Greco, and on his left forearm – covered this slightly chilly day by the sleeve of an off-white sweatshirt – was a tattoo. This tattoo was known to everyone of any status in the school, including the Head; and indeed the latter, in a rare moment of comparative courage, had called

Costyn into his study the previous term and demanded to know exactly what the epidermal epigram might signify. And Kevin had been happy to tell him: to tell him how the fairly unequivocal slogan ('Fuck 'em All') would normally be interpreted by anyone; even by someone with the benefit of a university education.

Anyway, that was how Kevin reported the interview.

Whatever the truth of the matter though, his reputation was now approaching its apogee. And with two sentences in a young offenders' unit behind him, how could it have been otherwise? At the same time, his influence, both within the circle of his immediate contemporaries and within the wider confines of the whole school, was significantly increased by two further factors. First, he even managed in some curious manner to exude a crude yet apparently irresistible sexuality, which drew many a girl into his magnetic field. Second, he was – had been since the age of twelve – a devotee of the Martial Arts; and under the tutelage of a diminutive Chinaman who (rumour had it) had once single-handedly left a gang of street-muggers lying pleading for mercy on the pavement, Kevin could appear, often *did* appear, an intimidating figure.

'KC.' That was what was written in red capital letters in the girls' loo: Kevin Costyn; Karate Champion; King of the Condoms; or whatever.

Tradition at the Proctor Memorial School was for pupils to rise to their feet whenever any teacher entered the classroom. And this tradition perpetuated itself still, albeit in a dishonoured, desultory sort of way. Yet when Mrs Stevens walked into 5C, for the first period on the afternoon of her birthday, the whole class, following a cue from Kevin Costyn, rose to its feet in synchronized smartness, the hum of conversation cut immediately ... as if some maestro had tapped his baton on the podium.

And there was a great calm.

(iii)

As I heard the tread of pupils coming up my ancient
creaking stairs, I felt like a tired tart awaiting her clients
(A. L. ROWSE, *On Life as an Oxford Don*)

'IT'S ONLY ME,' he'd spoken into the rusted, serrated Entryphone beside the front door.

He'd heard a brief, distant whirring; then a click; then her voice: 'It's open.'

He walked up the three flights of shabbily carpeted stairs, his mind wholly on the young woman who lived on the top floor. The bone structure of her face looked gaunt below the pallid cheeks; her eyes (for all McClure knew) might once have sparkled like those of glaucopis Athene, but now were dull – a sludgy shade of green, like the waters of the Oxford canal; her nose – tip-tilted in slightly concave fashion, like the contour of a nursery ski-slope – was disfigured (as he saw things) by two cheap-looking silver rings, one drilled through either nostril; her lips, marginally on the thin side of the Aristotelian mean, were ever thickly daubed with a shade of bright orange – a shade that would have been permanently banned from her mouth by any mildly competent beautician, a shade which clashed horribly with the amateurishly applied deep scarlet dye that streaked her longish, dark-brown hair.

But why such details of her face? Her hair? The mind of this young woman's second client that day, Wednesday, May 25, was firmly fixed on other things as a little breathlessly he ascended the last few narrow, squeaking stairs that led to the top of the Victorian property.

The young woman turned back the grubby top-sheet on the narrow bed, kicked a pair of knickers out of sight behind the shabby settee, poured out two glasses of red wine (£2.99 from Oddbins), and was sitting on the bed, swallowing the last mouthful of a Mars bar, when the first knock sounded softly on the door.

She was wearing a creased lime-green blouse, buttoned up completely down the front, black nylon stockings – whose tops came only to mid-thigh, held by a white suspender-belt – and red high-heeled shoes. Nothing more. That's how he wanted her; that's how she was. Beggars were proverbially precluded from overmuch choice and (perforce) 'beggar' she had become, with a triple burden of liabilities: negative equity on her 'studio flat', bought five years earlier at the height of the property boom; redundancy (*in*voluntary) from the sales office of a local engineering firm; and a steadily increasing consumption of alcohol. So she had soon taken on a . . . well, a new 'job' really.

To say that in the course of her new employment she was experiencing any degree of what her previous employer called 'job satisfaction' would be an exaggeration. On the other hand, it was certainly the easiest work she'd ever undertaken, as well as being by far the best paid – and (as she knew) she was quite good at it. As soon as she'd settled her bigger debts, though, she'd pack it all in. She was quite definite about that. The sooner the quicker.

The only thing that sometimes worried her was the possibility of her mother finding out that she was earning her living as a cheap tart. Well, no, that wasn't true. An expensive tart, as her current client would soon be discovering yet again. Yes, fairly expensive; but that didn't stop her feeling very cheap.

At the second knock, she rose from the bed, straightened her left stocking, and was now opening the door. Within only a couple of minutes opening her legs, too, as she lay back on the constricted width of the bed, her mascara'ed eyes focusing on a discoloured patch of damp almost immediately above her head.

Almost immediately above *his* head, too.

It was all pretty simple, really. The trouble was it had never been satisfying, for she had rarely felt more than a minimal physical attraction towards any of her clients. In a curious way she wished she *could* so feel. But no. Not so far. There was occasionally a sort of wayward fondness, yes. And in fact she was fonder of this particular fellow than any of the others. Indeed, she had once surprised herself by wondering if when he died – well, he *was* nearly sixty-seven – she might manage to squeeze out a dutiful tear.

It had not occurred to her at the time that there are other ways of departing this earthly life; had not occurred to her, for example, that her present client, Dr Felix McClure, former Ancient History don of Wolsey College, Oxford, might fairly soon be murdered.

(iv)

A highly geological home-made cake
(CHARLES DICKENS, *Martin Chuzzlewit*)

ONLY ONE communication, it appeared, was awaiting Julia Stevens that same day when she returned home just after 5 p.m.: a brown envelope (containing a gas bill) propped up against the table-lamp just inside her small entrance-hall.

The *white* envelope, unsealed, lay on the table in the living-room; and beside it was a glacé-iced cake, the legend 'Happy Birthday, Mrs Stevens' piped in purple on a white background, with an iced floral arrangement in violet and green, the leaves intricately, painstakingly crafted, and clearly the work of an expert in the skill.

Although Brenda Brooks had been Julia's cleaning-lady for almost four years now, she had never addressed her employer as anything but 'Mrs Stevens'; addressed her so again now, just as on the cake, in the letter folded inside the (NSPCC) birthday card.

Dear Mrs S,
Just a short note to wish you a very happy birthday & I hope you will enjoy your surprise. Don't look at it too closely as I had a little 'accident' & the icing isn't perfect. When I'd made the flowers & when they were drying a basin fell out of the cupboard & smashed the lot. After saying something like 'oh bother' I had to start again. Never mind I got there in the end.
Regarding my 'accident' I will tell you what really happened. My husband decided to pick a fight a few weeks ago & my doctor thinks he could have broken a bone in my hand & so I can't squeeze the bag very well. I was due to start another icing course next week but he has saved me £38.00!
Have a lovely day & I will see you in the morning – can't wait.
Love & best wishes,
Brenda (Brooks)

After rereading the letter, Julia looked down lovingly at the cake again, and suddenly felt very moved – and very angry.

Brenda (she knew) had hugely enjoyed the cake-decorating classes at the Tech. and had become proudly proficient in the icer's art. All right, the injury was hardly of cosmic proportions, Julia realized that; yet in its own little-world way the whole thing was so terribly sad. And as she looked at the cake again, Julia could now see what Brenda had meant. On closer inspection, the 'Mrs' was really a bit of a mess; and the loops in each of the 'y's in 'Happy Birthday' were rather uncertain – decidedly wobbly, in fact – as if formulated with tremulous fingers. 'Lacks her usual Daedalian deftness' was Julia the Pedagogue's cool appraisal; yet something warmer, something deeper inside herself, prompted her to immediate action. She fetched her broadest, sharpest kitchen knife and carefully cut a substantial segment of the cake, in such a way as to include most of the mis-handled 'Mrs'; and ate it all, straightaway.

The sponge-cake was in four layers, striated with cream, strawberry jam, and lemon butter icing. Absolutely delicious; and she found herself wishing she could share it with someone.

Ten minutes later, the phone rang.

'I didn't say nuffin' in class, Miss, but I want to say 'appy birfday.'

'Where are you phoning from, Kevin?'

'Jus' down the road – near the bus-shelter.'

'Would you like to come along and have a piece of birthday cake with me? I mean, it's *your* birthday too, isn't it?'

'Jus' try stoppin' me, Miss!'

The phone went dead. And thoughtfully, a slight smile around her full lips, Julia retraced her steps to the living-room, where she cut two more segments of cake, the second of which sliced through the middle of the more obviously malformed 'y'; cut them with the same knife – the broadest, sharpest knife she had in all her kitchen armoury.

(v)

After working for two weeks on a hard crossword puzzle, Lumberjack Hafey, a teacher in Mandan, became a raving maniac when unable to fill in the last word. When found, he was in the alcove of the old homestead sitting on the floor, pulling his hair and shrieking unintelligible things

(*Illinois Chronicle*, 3 October 1993)

MUCH EARLIER that same day, Detective Sergeant Lewis had found his chief sitting well forward in the black leather chair, shaking his head sadly over *The Times* crossword puzzle.

'Not finished it yet, sir?'

Morse looked up briefly with ill-disguised disdain. 'There is, as doubtless you observe, Lewis, one clue and one clue only remaining to be entered in the grid. The rest I finished in six minutes flat; and, if you must know, without your untimely interruption—'

'Sorry!'

Morse shook his head slowly. 'No. I've been sitting here looking at the bloody thing for ten minutes.'

'Can I help?'

'Extremely improbable!'

'Don't you want to try me?'

Reluctantly Morse handed over the crossword, and Lewis contemplated the troublesome clue: 'Kick in the pants?' (3–5). Three of the eight letters were entered: – I– – L– S –.

A short while later Lewis handed the crossword back across the desk. He'd tried so hard, so very hard, to make some intelligent suggestion; to score some Brownie points. But nothing had come to mind.

'If it's OK with you, sir, I'd like to spend some time down at St Aldate's this morning – see if we can find some link between all these burglaries in North Oxford.'

'Why not? And good luck. Don't give 'em *my* address though, will you?'

After Lewis had gone, Morse stared down at the crossword again. Seldom was it that he failed to finish things off, and that within a pretty smartish time, too. All he needed was a large Scotch . . . and the answer (he knew) would hit him straight between the eyes. But it was only 8.35 a.m. and—

It hit him.

Scotch!

As he swiftly filled in the five remaining blank squares, he was smiling beatifically, wishing only that Lewis had been there to appreciate the *coup de grâce*.

But Lewis wasn't.

And it was only many months later that Lewis was to learn – and then purely by accident – the answer to that clue in *The Times* crossword for 25 May 1994, a day (as would appear in retrospect) on which so many things of fateful consequence were destined to occur.

PART ONE

CHAPTER ONE

Pension: generally understood to mean monies grudgingly bestowed on aging hirelings after a lifetime of occasional devotion to duty
(*Small's Enlarged English Dictionary*, 12th Edition)

JUST AFTER noon on Wednesday, 31 August 1994, Chief Inspector Morse was seated at his desk in the Thames Valley Police HQ building at Kidlington, Oxon – when the phone rang.

'Morse? You're there, are you? I thought you'd probably be in the pub by now.'

Morse forbore the sarcasm, and assured Chief Superintendent Strange – he had recognized the voice – that indeed he was there.

'Two things, Morse – but I'll come along to your office.'

'You wouldn't prefer me—?'

'I need the exercise, so the wife says.'

Not only the wife, mumbled Morse, as he cradled the phone, beginning now to clear the cluttered papers from the immediate desk-space in front of him.

Strange lumbered in five minutes later and sat down heavily on the chair opposite the desk.

'You may have to get that name-plate changed.'

Strange and Morse had never really been friends, but never really been enemies either; and some good-natured bantering had been the order of the day following the recommendation of the Sheehy Report six months earlier that the rank of Chief Inspector should be abolished. *Mutual* bantering, since Chief Superintendents too were also likely to descend a rung on the ladder.

It was a disgruntled Strange who now sat wheezing methodically and shaking his head slowly. 'It's like losing your stripes in the Army, isn't it? It's . . . it's . . .'

'Belittling,' suggested Morse.

Strange looked up keenly. '"Demeaning" – that's what I was

going to say. Much better word, eh? So don't start trying to teach *me* the bloody English language.'

Fair point, thought Morse, as he reminded himself (as he'd often done before) that he and his fellow police-officers should never underestimate the formidable Chief Superintendent Strange.

'How can I help, sir? Two things, you said.'

'Ah! Well, yes. That's *one*, isn't it? What we've just been talking about. You see, I'm jacking the job in next year, as you've probably heard?'

Morse nodded cautiously.

'Well, that's it. It's the, er, pension I'm thinking about.'

'It won't affect the pension.'

'You think not?'

'Sure it won't. It's just a question of getting all the paperwork right. That's why they're sending all these forms around—'

'How do you know?' Strange's eyes shot up again, sharply focused, and it was Morse's turn to hesitate.

'I – I'm thinking of, er, jacking in the job myself, sir.'

'Don't be so bloody stupid, man! This place can't afford to lose me *and* you.'

'I shall only be going on for a couple of years, whatever happens.'

'And . . . and you've had the forms, you say?'

Morse nodded.

'And . . . and you've actually filled 'em *in*?' Strange's voice sounded incredulous.

'Not yet, no. Forms always give me a terrible headache. I've got a phobia about form-filling.'

No words from Morse could have been more pleasing, and Strange's moon-face positively beamed. 'You know, that's exactly what I said to the wife – about headaches and all that.'

'Why doesn't *she* help you?'

'Says it gives her a headache, too.'

The two men chuckled amiably.

'You'd like me to help?' asked Morse tentatively.

'Would you? Be a huge relief all round, I can tell you. We could go for a pint together next week, couldn't we? And if I go and buy a bottle of aspirin—'

'Make it *two* pints.'

'I'll make it two bottles, then.'

'You're on, sir.'

'Good. That's settled then.'

THE DAUGHTERS OF CAIN

Strange was silent awhile, as if considering some matter of great moment. Then he spoke.

'Now, let's come to the second thing I want to talk about – far more important.'

Morse raised his eyebrows. 'Far more important than *pensions*?'

'Well, a bit more important perhaps.'

'Murder?'

'Murder.'

'Not *another* one?'

'Same one. The one near you. The McClure murder.'

'Phillotson's on it.'

'Phillotson's *off* it.'

'But—'

'His wife's ill. Very ill. I want you to take over.'

'But—'

'You see, you haven't got a wife who's very ill, have you? You haven't got a wife at all.'

'No,' replied Morse quietly. No good arguing with that.

'Happy to take over?'

'Is Lewis—?'

'I've just had a quick word with him in the canteen. Once he's finished his egg and chips . . .'

'Oh!'

'*And*' – Strange lifted his large frame laboriously from the chair – 'I've got this gut-feeling that Phillotson wouldn't have got very far with it anyway.'

'*Gut*-feeling?'

'What's wrong with that?' snapped Strange. 'Don't *you* ever get a gut-feeling?'

'Occasionally . . .'

'After too much booze!'

'Or mixing things, sir. You know what I mean: few pints of beer and a bottle of wine.'

'Yes . . .' Strange nodded. 'We'll probably both have a gut-feeling soon, eh? After a few pints of beer and a bottle of aspirin.'

He opened the door and looked at the name-plate again. 'Perhaps we shan't need to change them after all, Morse.'

CHAPTER TWO

Like the sweet apple which reddens upon the topmost bough,
A-top on the topmost twig – which the pluckers forgot
    somehow –
Forgot it not, nay, but got it not, for none could get it till now
            (D. G. ROSSETTI, *Translations from Sappho*)

IT WAS to be only the second time that Morse had ever taken
over a murder inquiry after the preliminary – invariably dramatic
– trappings were done with: the discovery of the deed, the
importunate attention of the media, the immediate scene-of-crime
investigation, and the final removal of the body.

Lewis, perceptively, had commented that it was all a bit
like getting into a football match twenty-five minutes late,
and asking a fellow spectator what the score was. But Morse
had been unimpressed by the simile, since his life would not
have been significantly impoverished had the game of football
never been invented.

Indeed, there was a sense in which Morse was happier to have
avoided any *in situ* inspection of the corpse, since the liquid
contents of his stomach almost inevitably curdled at the sight of
violent death. And he knew that the death there *had* been violent
– very violent indeed. Much blood had been spilt, albeit now
caked and dirty-brown – blood that would still (he supposed) be
much in evidence around the chalk-lined contours of the spot on
the saturated beige carpet where a man had been found with an
horrific knife-wound in his lower belly.

'What's wrong with Phillotson?' Lewis had asked as they'd
driven down to North Oxford.

'Nothing wrong with him – except incompetence. It's his wife.
She's had something go wrong with an operation, so they say.
Some, you know, some internal trouble . . . woman's trouble.'

'The womb, you mean, sir?'

'I don't *know*, do I, Lewis? I didn't ask. I'm not even quite sure
exactly where the womb is. And, come to think of it, I don't even
like the word.'

'I only asked.'

'And I only answered! His wife'll be fine, you'll see. It's him. He's just chickening out.'

'And the Super . . . didn't think he could cope with the case?'

'Well, he couldn't, could he? He's not exactly perched on the topmost twig of the Thames Valley intelligentsia, now is he?'

Lewis had glanced across at the man seated beside him in the passenger seat, noting the supercilious, almost arrogant, cast of the harsh blue eyes, and the complacent-looking smile about the lips. It was the sort of conceit which Lewis found the least endearing quality of his chief: worse even than his meanness with money and his almost total lack of gratitude. And suddenly he felt a shudder of distaste.

Yet only briefly. For Morse's face had become serious again as he'd pointed to the right; pointed to Daventry Avenue; and amplified his answer as the car braked to a halt outside a block of flats:

'You see, we take a bit of beating, don't we, Lewis? Don't you reckon? Me and you? Morse and Lewis? Not *too* many twigs up there above us, are there?'

But as Morse unfastened his safety-belt, there now appeared a hint of diffidence upon his face.

'*Nous vieillissons, n'est-ce pas?*'

'Pardon, sir?'

'We're all getting older – that's what I said. And that's the only thing that's worrying me about this case, old friend.'

But then the smile again.

And Lewis saw the smile, and smiled himself; for at that moment he felt quite preternaturally content with life.

The constable designated to oversee the murder premises volunteered to lead the way upstairs; but Morse shook his head, his response needlessly brusque:

'Just give me the key, lad.'

Only two short flights, of eight steps each, led up to the first floor; yet Morse was a little out of breath as Lewis opened the main door of the maisonette.

'Yes' – Morse's mind was still on Phillotson – 'I reckon he'd've been about as competent in this case as a dyslexic proofreader.'

'I like that, sir. That's good. Original, is it?'

Morse grunted. In fact it had been Strange's own appraisal of

Phillotson's potential; but, as ever, Morse was perfectly happy to take full credit for the *bons mots* of others. Anyway, Strange himself had probably read it somewhere, hadn't he? Shrewd enough, was Strange: but hardly perched up there on the roof of Canary Wharf.

Smoothly the door swung open ... The door swung open on another case.

And as Lewis stepped through the small entrance-hall, and thence into the murder room, he found himself wondering how things would turn out here.

Certainly it hadn't sounded all that extraordinary a case when, two hours earlier, Detective Chief Inspector Phillotson had given them an hour-long briefing on the murder of Dr Felix McClure, former Student – late Student – of Wolsey College, Oxford ...

Bizarre and bewildering – that's what so many cases in the past had proved to be; and despite Phillotson's briefing the present case would probably be no different.

In this respect, at least, Lewis was correct in his thinking. What he could not have known – what, in fact, he never really came to know – was what unprecedented anguish the present case would cause to Morse's soul.

CHAPTER THREE

Myself when young did eagerly frequent
  Doctor and Saint, and heard great Argument
  About it and about: but evermore
Came out by the same Door as in I went
              (EDWARD FITZGERALD,
              The Rubaiyat of Omar Khayyam)

DAVENTRY COURT (Phillotson had begun), comprising eight 'luxurious apartments' built in Daventry Avenue in 1989, had been difficult to sell. House prices had tumbled during the ever-deepening recession of the early nineties, and McClure had bought in the spring of 1993 when he'd convinced himself (rightly) that even in the continuing buyers' market Flat 6 was a bit of a snip at £99,500.

McClure himself was almost sixty-seven years old at the time of his murder, knifed (as Morse would be able to see for himself) in quite horrendous fashion. The knife, according to pathological findings, was unusually broad-bladed, and at least five inches in length. Of such a weapon, however, no trace whatsoever had been found. Blood, though? Oh, yes. Blood almost everywhere. Blood on almost everything. Blood on the murderer too? Surely so.

Blood certainly on his shoes (trainers?), with footprints – especially of the right foot – clearly traceable from the murder scene to the staircase, to the main entrance; but thence virtually lost, soon completely lost, on the gravelled forecourt outside. Successive scufflings by other residents had obviously obliterated all further traces of blood. Or had the murderer left by a car parked close to the main door? Or left on a bicycle chained to the nearest drainpipe? (Or taken his shoes off, Lewis thought.) But intensive search of the forecourt area had revealed nothing. No clues from the sides of the block either. No clues from the rear. No clues at all outside. (Or perhaps just the one clue, Morse had thought: the clue that there *were* no clues at all?)

Inside? Well, again, Morse would be able to see for himself. Evidence of extraneous fingerprints? Virtually none. Hopeless. And certainly no indication that the assailant – murderer – had entered the premises through any first-floor window.

'Very rare means of ingress, Morse, as you know. Pretty certainly came in the same way as he went out.'

'Reminds me a bit of Omar Khayyam,' Morse had muttered.

But Phillotson had merely looked puzzled, his own words clearly not reminding himself of anyone. Or anything.

No. Entry from the main door, surely, via the Entryphone system, with McClure himself admitting whomsoever (not Phillotson's word) – be it man or woman. Someone known to McClure then? Most likely.

Time? Well, certainly after 8.30 a.m. on the Sunday he was murdered, since McClure had purchased two newspapers at about 8 a.m. that morning from the newsagent's in Summertown, where he was at least a well-known face if not a well-known name; and where he (like Morse, as it happened) usually catered for both the coarse and the cultured sides of his nature with the

News of the World and *The Sunday Times*. No doubts here. No hypothesis required. Each of the two news-sheets was found, unbloodied, on the work-top in the 'all-mod-con kitchen'.

After 8.30 a.m. then. But before when? Preliminary findings – well, *not* so preliminary – from the pathologist firmly suggested that McClure had been dead for about twenty hours or so before being found, at 7.45 a.m. the following morning, by his cleaning-lady.

Hypothesis here, then, for the time of the murder? Between 10 a.m., say, and noon the previous day. Roughly. But then every-thing was 'roughly' with these wretched pathologists, wasn't it? (And Morse had smiled sadly, and thought of Max; and nodded slowly, for Phillotson was preaching to the converted.)

One other circumstance most probably corroborating a pre-noon time for the murder was the readily observable, and duly observed, fact that there was no apparent sign, such as the preparation of meat and vegetables, for any potential Sunday lunch in Flat 6. Not that that was conclusive in itself, since it had already become clear, from sensibly orientated inquiries, that it had not been unusual for McClure to walk down the Banbury Road and order a Sunday lunch – 8oz Steak, French Fries, Salad – only £3.99 – at the King's Arms, washed down with a couple of pints of Best Bitter; no sweet; no coffee. But there had been no sign of steak or chips or lettuce or anything much else when the pathologist had split open the white-skinned belly of Dr Felix McClure. No sign of any lunchtime sustenance at all.

The body had been found in a hunched-up, foetal posture, with both hands clutching the lower abdomen and the eyes screwed tightly closed as if McClure had died in the throes of some excruciating pain. He was dressed in a short-sleeved shirt, vertically striped in maroon and blue, a black Jaeger cardigan, and a pair of dark grey flannels – the lower part of the shirt and the upper regions of the trousers stiff and steeped in the blood that had oozed so abundantly.

McClure had been one of those 'perpetual students in life' (Phillotson's words). After winning a Major Scholarship to Oxford in 1946, he had gained a First in Mods, a First in Greats – thereafter spending forty-plus years of his life as Ancient History Tutor in Wolsey College. In 1956 he had married one of his own pupils, an undergraduette from Somerville – the latter, after attaining exactly similar distinction, duly appointed to a Junior Fellowship in Merton, and in 1966 (life jumping forward in decades) running off with one of her own pupils, a bearded undergraduate from Trinity. No children, though; no legal problems. Just a whole lot of heartache, perhaps.

Few major publications to his name – mostly a series of articles written over the years for various classical journals. But at least he had lived long enough to see the publication of his *magnum opus*: *The Great Plague at Athens: Its Effect on the Course and Conduct of the Peloponnesian War*. A long title. A long work.

Witnesses?

Of the eight 'luxurious apartments' only four had been sold, with two of the others being let, and the other two still empty, the 'For Sale' notices standing outside the respective properties – one of them the apartment immediately below McClure's, Number 5; the other Number 2. Questioning of the tenants had produced no information of any value: the newly-weds in Number 1 had spent most of the Sunday morning a-bed – sans breakfast, sans newspapers, sans everything except themselves; the blue-rinsed old lady in Number 3, extremely deaf, had insisted on making a very full statement to the effect that she had heard nothing on that fateful morn; the couple in Number 4 had been out all morning on a Charity 'Save the Whales' Walk in Wytham Woods; the temporary tenants of Number 7 were away in Tunisia; and the affectionate couple who had bought Number 8 had been uninterruptedly employed in redecorating their bathroom, with the radio on most of the morning as they caught up with *The Archers* omnibus. (For the first time in several minutes, Morse's interest had been activated.)

'Not *all* that much to go on,' Phillotson had admitted; yet all the same, not without some degree of pride, laying a hand on two green box-files filled with reports and statements and notes and documents and a plan showing the full specification of McClure's apartment, with arcs and rulings and arrows and dotted lines and measurements. Morse himself had never been able to follow such house-plans; and now glanced only cursorily through the stapled sheets supplied by Adkinsons, Surveyors, Valuers, and Estate Agents – as Phillotson came to the end of his briefing.

'By the way,' asked Morse, rising to his feet, 'how's the wife? I meant to ask earlier . . .'

'Very poorly, I'm afraid,' said Phillotson, miserably.

*

'Cheerful sod, isn't he, Lewis?'

The two men had been back in Morse's office then, Lewis seeking to find a place on the desk for the bulging box-files.

'Well, he must be pretty worried about his wife if—'

'Pah! He just didn't know where to go next – that was his trouble.'

'And we *do*?'

'Well, for a start, I wouldn't mind knowing which of those newspapers McClure read first.'

'If either.'

Morse nodded. 'And I wouldn't mind finding out if he made any phone-calls that morning.'

'Can't we get British Telecom to itemize things?'

'Can we?' asked Morse vaguely.

'You'll want to see the body?'

'Why on earth should I want to do that?'

'I just thought—'

'I wouldn't mind seeing that shirt, though. Maroon and blue vertical stripes, didn't Phillotson say?' Morse passed the index finger of his left hand round the inside of his slightly tight, slightly frayed shirt-collar. 'I'm thinking of, er, expanding my wardrobe a bit.'

But the intended humour was lost on Lewis, to whom it seemed exceeding strange that Morse should at the same time apparently show more interest in the dead man's shirt than in his colleague's wife. 'Apparently' though . . . that was always the thing about Morse: no one could ever really plot a graph of the thoughts that ran through that extraordinary mind.

'Did we learn anything – from Phillotson, sir?'

'You may have done: I didn't. I knew just as much about things when I went into his office as when I came out.'

'Reminds you a bit of Omar Khayyam, doesn't it?' suggested Lewis, innocently.

CHAPTER FOUR

Krook chalked the letter upon the wall – in a very curious
manner, beginning with the end of the letter, and shaping it
backward. It was a capital letter, not a printed one.
'Can you read it?' he asked me with a keen glance
(CHARLES DICKENS, *Bleak House*)

THE sitting-cum-dining-room – the murder room – 12' × 17'2" as
stated in Adkinsons' (doubtless accurate) specifications, was very
much the kind of room one might expect as the main living-area
of a retired Oxford don: an oak table with four chairs around it; a
brown leather settee; a matching armchair; TV; CD and cassette
player; books almost everywhere on floor-to-ceiling shelves; busts
of Homer, Thucydides, Milton, and Beethoven; not enough space
really for the many pictures – including the head, in the Pittura
Pompeiana series, of Theseus, Slayer of the Minotaur. Those were
the main things. Morse recognized three of the busts readily and
easily, though he had to guess at the bronze head of Thucydides.
As for Lewis, he recognized all four immediately, since his
eyesight was now keener than Morse's, and the name of each of
those immortals was inscribed in tiny capitals upon its plinth.

For a while Morse stood by the armchair, looking all round
him, saying nothing. Through the open door of the kitchen – 6'10"
× 9'6" – he could see the Oxford Almanack hanging from the
wall facing him, and finally went through to admire 'St Hilda's
College' from a watercolour by Sir Hugh Casson, RA. Pity,
perhaps, it was the previous year's, for Morse now read its date,
'MDCCCCLXXXXIII'; and for a few moments he found himself
considering whether any other year in the twentieth century – in
any century – could command any lengthier designation. Fourteen characters required for '1993'.

Still, the Romans never knew much about numbers.

'Do you know how many walking-sticks plus umbrellas we've
got in the hall-stand here?' shouted Lewis from the tiny entrance
area.

'Fourteen!' shouted Morse in return.

'How the – how on earth—?'

'For me, Lewis, coincidence in life is wholly unexceptional;

the readily predictable norm in life. You know that by now, surely?'

Lewis said nothing. He knew well where his duties lay in circumstances such as these: to do the donkey-work; to look through everything, without much purpose, and often without much hope. But Morse was a stickler for sifting the evidence; always had been. The only trouble was that he never wanted to waste his own time in helping to sift it, for such work was excessively tedious; and frequently fruitless, to boot.

So Lewis did it all. And as Morse sat back in the settee and looked through McClure's *magnum opus*, Lewis started to go through all the drawers and all the letters and all the piles of papers and the detritus of the litter-bins – just as earlier Phillotson and his team had done. Lewis didn't mind, though. Occasionally in the past he'd found some item unusual enough (well, unusual enough to Morse) that had set the great mind scurrying off into some subtly signposted avenue, or cul-de-sac; that had set the keenest-nosed hound in the pack on to some previously unsuspected scent.

Two things only of interest here, Lewis finally informed Morse. And Phillotson himself had pointed out the potential importance of the first of these, anyway: a black plastic W. H. Smith Telephone Index, with eighteen alphabetical divisions, the collocation of the less common letters, such as 'WX' and 'YZ', counting as one. The brief introductory instructions (under 'A') suggested that the user might find it valuable to record therein, for speed of reference, the telephone numbers of such indispensable personages as Decorator, Dentist, Doctor, Electrician, Plumber, Police . . .

Lewis opened the index at random: at the letter 'M'. Six names on the card there. Three of the telephone numbers were prefixed with the Inner London code, '071'; the other three were Oxford numbers, five digits each, all beginning with '5'.

Lewis sighed audibly. Eighteen times six? That was a hundred and eight . . . Still it might be worthwhile ringing round (had Phillotson thought the same?) provided there were no more than half a dozen or so per page. He pressed the index to a couple of other letters. 'P': eight names and numbers. 'C': just four. What about the twinned letters? He pressed 'KL': seven, with six of them 'L'; and just the one 'K' – and that (interestingly enough?) entered as the single capital letter 'K'. Who was K when he was at home?

Or she?

'What does "K" stand for, sir?'

Morse, a crossword fanatic from his early teens, knew some of the answers immediately: '"King"; "Kelvin" – unit of temperature, Lewis; er, "thousand"; "kilometre", of course; "Köchel", the man who catalogued Mozart, as you know; er . . .'

'Not much help.'

'Initial of someone's name?'

'Why just the initial?'

'Girl's name? Perhaps he's trying to disguise his simmering passion for a married woman – what about that? Or perhaps all the girls at the local knocking-shop are known by a letter of the alphabet?'

'Didn't know you had one up here, sir.'

'Lewis, we have everything in North Oxford. It's just a question of knowing where it is, that's the secret.'

Lewis mused aloud. 'Karen . . . or Kirsty . . .'

'Kylie?'

'You've heard of *her*, sir?'

'Only just.'

'Kathy . . .'

'Well, there's one pretty simple way of finding out, isn't there? Can't you just ring the number? Isn't that what you're supposed to be doing? That sort of thing?'

Lewis picked up the phone and dialled the five-digit number – and was answered immediately.

'Yeah? Wha' d'ya wan'?' a woman's voice bawled at him.

'Hullo. Er – have I got the right number for "K"?'

'Yeah. You 'ave. Bu' she's no' 'ere, is she?'

'No, obviously not. I'll try again later.'

'You a dur'y ol' man, or sump'n?'

Lewis quickly replaced the receiver, the colour rising in his pale cheeks.

Morse, who had heard the brief exchange clearly, grinned at his discomfited sergeant. 'You can't win 'em all.'

'Waste of time, if that's anything to go by.'

'You think so?'

'Don't *you*?'

'Lewis! You were only on the phone for about ten seconds but you learned she was a "she", probably a she with the name of "Kay".'

'I didn't!'

'A she of easy virtue who old Felix here spent a few happy hours with. Or, as you'd prefer it, with whom old Felix regularly spent a few felicitous hours.'

'You can't just say that—'

'Furthermore she's a local lass, judging by her curly Oxfordshire accent and her typical habit of omitting all her "t"s.'

'But I didn't even *get* the woman!'

Morse was silent for a few seconds; then he looked up, his face more serious. 'Are you sure, Lewis? Are you quite sure you haven't just been speaking to the cryptic "K" herself?'

Lewis shook his head, grinned ruefully, and said nothing. He knew – knew again now – why he'd never rise to any great heights in life himself. Morse had got it wrong, of course. Morse nearly always got things hopelessly, ridiculously wrong at the start of every case. But he always seemed to have thoughts that no one else was capable of thinking. Like now.

'Anyway, what's this other thing you've found?'

But before Lewis could answer, there was a quiet tap on the door and PC Roberts stuck a reverential, unhelmeted head into the room.

'There's a Mrs Wynne-Wilson here, sir, from one of the other flats. Says she wants a word, like.'

Morse looked up from his Thucydides. 'Haven't we already got a statement from her, Lewis?'

But it was Roberts who answered. 'She says she made a statement, sir, but when she heard someone else was in charge – well, she said Inspector Phillotson didn't really want to know, like.'

'Really?'

'And she's, well, she's a bit deaf, like.'

'Like what?' asked Morse.

'Pardon?'

'Forget it.'

'Shall I show her in, sir?'

'What? In here? You know what happened here, don't you? She'd probably faint, man.'

'Doubt it, sir. She says she was sort of in charge of nurses at some London hospital.'

'Ah, a matron,' said Morse.

'They don't call them "matrons" any longer,' interposed Lewis.

'Thank you very much, Lewis! Send her in.'

CHAPTER FIVE

O quid solutis est beatius curis,
Cum mens onus reponit, ac peregrino
Labore fessi venimus larem ad nostrum,
Desideratoque acquiescimus lecto?

(What bliss! First spot the house – and then
Flop down – on one's old bed again)

(CATULLUS, 31)

JULIA STEVENS had returned home that same afternoon.

The flight had been on time (early, in fact); Customs had been swift and uncomplicated; the Gatwick–Heathrow–Oxford coach had been standing there, just waiting for her it seemed, welcoming her back to England. From the bus station at Gloucester Green she had taken a taxi (no queue) out to East Oxford, the driver duly helping her with two heavyweight cases right up to the front door of her house – a house which, as the taxi turned into the street, she'd immediately observed to be still standing there, unburned, unvandalized; and, as she could see as she stood inside her own living-room – at long last! – blessedly unburgled.

How glad she was to be back. Almost always, on the first two nights of any holiday away from home, she experienced a weepy nostalgia. But usually this proved to be only a readjustment. Usually, too, at least for the last two days of her statutory annual fortnight abroad, she felt a similar wrench on leaving her summer surroundings; on bidding farewell to her newly made holiday friends. One or two friends in particular.

One or two men, as often as not.

But such had not been the case this time on her package tour round the Swiss and Italian lakes. She couldn't explain why: the coach-driver had been very competent; the guide good; the scenery spectacular; the fellow-tourists pleasantly friendly. But she'd not enjoyed it at all. My god! What was happening to her?

(But she knew exactly what was happening to her.)

Not that she'd said anything, of course. And Brenda Brooks had received a cheerful postcard from a multi-starred hotel on Lake Lucerne:

> Wed.
> Having a splendid time here with a nice lot
> of people. My room looks right across the
> lake. Tomorrow we go over to Triebschen
> (hope I've spelt that right) where Richard
> Wagner spent some of his life. There was a
> firework display last night – tho' nobody
> told us why. Off to Lugano Friday.
>   Love Julia
> PS Give St Giles a big hug for me.

As Julia walked through her front door that afternoon, her house smelt clean and fragrant; smelt of pine and polish and Windolene. Bless her – bless Brenda Brooks!

Then, on the kitchen table, there was a note – the sort of note that she, Julia, had ever come to expect:

> Dear Mrs S,
> I got your card thankyou & I'm glad you
> had a good time. St Giles has been fine,
> there are two more tins of Whiskas in the
> fridge. See you Monday. There's something
> I want to tell you about & perhaps you can
> help – I hope so. Welcome home!!
>   Brenda (Brooks)

Julia smiled to herself. Brenda invariably appended her (bracketed) surname as though the household boasted a whole bevy of charladies. And always that deferential 'Mrs S'. Brenda had worked for her for four years now, and at fifty-two was nearly seven years her senior. Again Julia smiled to herself. Then, as she re-read the penultimate sentence, for a moment she found herself frowning slightly.

It was a pleasant sunny day, with September heralding a golden finale to what had been a hot and humid summer. Indeed, the temperature was well above the average for an autumn day. Yet Julia felt herself shivering slightly as she unlocked and unbolted the rear door. And if a few moments earlier she may have looked a little sad, a little strained – behold now a metamorphosis! A ginger cat parted the ground-cover greenery at the bottom of the small garden and peered up at his mistress; and suddenly Julia Stevens looked very happy once again.

And very beautiful.

CHAPTER SIX

Envy and idleness married together beget curiosity
(THOMAS FULLER, *Gnomologia*)

MORSE DECIDED to interview Laura Wynne-Wilson, should that good lady allow it, in her own ground-floor apartment. And the good lady did so allow.

She was, she admitted, very doubtful about whether that previous policeman had attended to her evidence with sufficient seriousness. Indeed, she had formed the distinct impression that he had listened, albeit politely, in a wholly perfunctory way to what she had to say. Which was? Which was to do with Dr McClure – a nice gentleman; and a *very* good neighbour, who had acted as Secretary of the Residents' Action Committee and written such a *splendid* letter to that cowboy outfit supposedly responsible for the upkeep of the exterior of the properties.

She spoke primly and quietly, a thin smile upon thin lips.

'And what exactly have you got to tell us?' bawled Morse.

'Please don't *shout* at me, Inspector! Deaf people do *not* require excessive volume – they require only clarity of speech and appropriate lip-movement.'

Lewis smiled sweetly to himself as the small, white-haired octogenarian continued:

'What I have to tell you is this. Dr McClure had a fairly regular visitor here. A . . . a lady-friend.'

'Not all that unusual, is it?' suggested Morse, with what he hoped was adequate clarity and appropriate lip-movement.

'Oh, no. After all, it might well have been some female relative.'

Morse nodded. Already he knew that McClure had no living relatives apart from a niece in New Zealand; but still he nodded.

'And then again, Inspector, it might *not*. You see, he had no living relatives in the United Kingdom.'

'Oh.' Morse decided that, unlike Phillotson, he at least would treat the old girl with a modicum of respect.

'No. It was his "fancy woman", as we used to call it. By the way, I quite like that term myself, don't you?'

'Plenty of worse words, madam,' interposed Lewis, though apparently with less than adequate clarity.

'Pardon?' Laura W-W turned herself in the approximate direction of the man taking notes, as if he were merely some supernumerary presence.

And now it was Morse's turn to smile sweetly to himself.

'As I was saying, this . . . this woman came to see him several times – certainly three or four times during the last month.'

'What time of day was that?'

'Always at about half-past seven.'

'And you, er, you actually saw her?'

'"Actually" is a ridiculous word, isn't it? It's a weasel word, Inspector. It means nothing whatsoever. It's a space-filler. Whether I *actually* saw her, I don't know. What I *do* know is that I *saw* her. All right?'

Touché.

Morse's eyes wandered over to the wooden-frame casement, where the thin white lace curtains were pulled back in tight arcs at each side, with potted geraniums at either end of the window ledge, and three tasteful pieces of dark blue and white porcelain positioned between them. But nothing there to clutter the clear view, from where Morse was sitting, over the whole front area of the apartments, especially of the two square, yellow-brick pillars which stood at either side of the entrance drive; and through which, perforce, everyone coming into Daventry Court must surely pass. Everyone except a burglar, perhaps. Or a murderer . . . And this nosey old woman would delight in observing the visitors who called upon her fellow residents, Morse felt confident of that.

'This could be very helpful to our inquiries, you realize that, don't you? If you saw her clearly . . . ?'

'My eyesight is not what it was, Inspector. But I had a good view of her, yes.' She glanced keenly at Morse. 'You see, I'm a nosey old woman with very little else to do – that's what you're thinking, anyway.'

'Well, I – we all like to know what's going on. It's only human nature.'

'Oh, no. I know several people who aren't in the *slightest* bit interested in "what's going on", as you put it. But I'm glad *you're* nosey, like me. That's good.'

Lewis was enjoying the interview immensely.

'Can you tell us something about this woman? Anything?'

'Let's say I found her interesting.'

'Why was that?'

'Well, for a start, I envied her. She was less than half his age, you see – good deal less, I shouldn't doubt.'

'And he,' mused Morse, 'was sixty-six . . .'

'Sixty-seven, Inspector, if he'd lived to the end of the month.'

'How—?'

'I looked him up in *Distinguished People of Today*. He's a Libra.'

Like me, thought Morse. And I wonder how old you are, you old biddy.

'And I'm eighty-three in December,' she continued, 'just in case you're wondering.'

'I was, yes,' said Morse, smiling at her, and himself now beginning to enjoy the interview.

'The other thing that struck me was that she wasn't at *all* nice-looking. Quite the opposite, in fact. Very shabbily dressed – darkish sort of clothes. Sloppy loose blouse, mini-skirt right up to . . .'

'The top of her tibia,' supplied Morse, enunciating the 't' of the last word with exaggerated exactitude.

'Absolutely! And she had a big old shoulder-bag, too.'

I wonder what was in that, thought Morse.

'Anything else you can remember?'

'Long – longish – dark hair. Earrings – great brassy-looking things about the size of hula-hoops. And she had a ring in her nose. I could see that. For all I know, she could have had *two* rings in her nose.'

God helps us all, thought Morse.

'But I'm not sure about that. As I say, my eyesight isn't what it used to be.'

I wonder what it used to be like, thought Lewis.

'Did she come by car?' asked Morse.

'No. If she did, she left it somewhere else.'

'Did she come in from . . . ?' Morse gestured vaguely to his left, towards the Banbury Road.

'Yes. She came from the Banbury Road – not the Woodstock Road.'

'Would you recognize her again?'

For the first time the old lady hesitated, rubbing the thin ringless fingers of her left hand with her right.

'Oh dear. Do you think she may have *murdered* him? I only—'

'No, no. I'm sure she didn't.' Morse spoke with the bogus confidence of a man who was beginning to wonder if she had.

'I only wanted to help. And I'm not at *all* sure if I would recognize her. Perhaps if she dolled herself up in some decent outfit and . . .'

Took that bull-ring out of her nose, thought Morse.

'. . . and took that ring out of her nose.'

Phew!

But some of the bounce had gone out of the old girl, Morse could see that. It was time to wind things up.

'Do you think they went to bed when she came?'

'I expect so, don't you?'

'Things must have changed a good deal since your day, Miss Wynne-Wilson.'

'Don't be silly, Inspector! I could teach some of these young flibbertigibbets a few things about going to bed with men. After all, I spent most of my life looking after men in bed, now didn't I? And, by the way, it's *Mrs* Wynne-Wilson. I don't wear a wedding ring any longer . . .'

Phew!

Morse got to his feet. He had only one more question: 'Were you looking out of the window on Sunday morning – you know, about the time perhaps when Dr McClure was murdered?'

'No. On Sunday mornings I always hear the omnibus edition of *The Archers* on the wireless, that's from ten to eleven. Lovely. I have a really good long soak – and hear everything again.'

Dangerous thing that – having a radio in the bathroom, thought Lewis.

'It's dangerous they tell me – having a wireless propped up on the bath-rail. But I do so enjoy doing silly things, now that I'm so old.'

Phew!

It had not been much of a contest, Lewis appreciated that; but from his scorecard he had little hesitation in declaring Mrs W-W the winner, way ahead of Morse on points.

Quite mistakenly, of course.

CHAPTER SEVEN

For 'tis in vain to think or guess
At women by appearances
(SAMUEL BUTLER, *Hudibras*)

'WHAT DID you make of that, then?' asked Lewis, when the two detectives had returned to McClure's apartment.

Morse appeared disappointed. 'I'd begun to think he was a civilized sort of fellow – you know . . .' Morse gestured vaguely around the bookshelves.

'But he wasn't?'

'We-ell.'

'You mean . . . this woman he was seeing?'

Morse's features reflected disapproval. 'Rings in her *nose*, Lewis? Pretty tasteless, isn't it? Like drinking lager with roast beef.'

'For all you know she may be a lovely girl, sir. You shouldn't really judge people just by appearances.'

'Oh?' Morse's eyes shot up swiftly. 'And why the hell not?'

'Well . . .' But Lewis wasn't sure why. He did have a point, though; he knew he did. Morse was always making snap judgements. All right, one or two would occasionally turn out to be accurate; but most of them were woefully wide of the mark – as, to be fair, Morse himself readily acknowledged.

Lewis thought of events earlier in the day; thought of Phillotson's withdrawal from the present case; thought of Morse's almost contemptuous dismissal of the man's excuses. Almost automatically, it seemed, Morse had assumed him to be parading a few phoney pretexts about his wife's hospitalization in order to avoid the humiliation of failure in a murder case. Agreed, Phillotson wasn't exactly Sherlock Holmes, Lewis knew that. Yet Morse could be needlessly cruel about some of his colleagues. And why did he have to be so *sharp*? As he had been just now?

Still, Lewis knew exactly what to do about his own temporary irritation. Count to ten! – that's what Morse had once told him – before getting on to any high horse; and then, if necessary, count to twenty. Not that there was much sign that Morse ever heeded his own advice. *He* usually only counted to two or three. If that.

Deciding, therefore, the time to be as yet inopportune for any consideration of the old lady's testimony, Lewis reverted to his earlier task. There was still a great deal of material to look through, and he was glad to get down to something whose purpose he could readily grasp. The papers there, all the papers in the drawers and those stacked along the shelves, had already been examined – clearly that was the case. Not radically disturbed, though; not taken away to be documented in some dubious filing-system until sooner or later, as with almost everything in life, being duly labelled 'OBE'.

Overtaken By Events.

Glancing across at Morse, Lewis saw the chief abstracting another book from a set of volumes beautifully bound in golden leather; a slim volume this time; a volume of verse by the look of it. And even as he watched, he saw Morse turning the book through ninety degrees and apparently reading some marginalia beside one of the poems there. For the present, however, the Do Not Disturb sign was prominently displayed, and with his usual competence Lewis resumed his own considerable task.

Thus it was that for the next half-hour or so the two men sat reading their different texts; preparing (as it were) for their different examinations; each conscious of the other's presence; yet each, for the moment, and for different reasons, unwilling to speak his own immediate thoughts.

Especially Morse.

Yet it was the latter who finally broke the silence.

'What did you make of her, then? Our Mrs Wynne-Wilson?'

'"Mrs", sir?' asked Lewis slowly.

Morse threw an interested, inquisitive look at his sergeant. 'Go on!'

'Well, I'd noticed from the start she wasn't wearing a wedding ring. As you did, of course.'

'Of course.'

'But I couldn't see any, you know, any mark of any ring like you'd normally have, wouldn't you? A sort of, you know, pale ring of skin, sort of thing, where the ring had been – before she took it off.'

'Not a particularly fluent sentence that, Lewis, if I may say so.'

'But you noticed that too?'

'Me? Your eyesight's far better than mine.'

'Makes you wonder, though.'

'You reckon she was making it up – about her marriage?'

'Wouldn't surprise me, sir.'

'And apart from that?'

'She seemed a pretty good witness. Her mind's pretty sharp. She got you weighed up all right.'

'Ye-es ... So you don't think she was making anything else up?'

'No. Do you?'

'Lew-is! When will you learn. She's a phoney. She's a phoney from A to Z.'

Lewis's look now was one of semi-exasperation. 'There you go again! I think you're far too quick—'

'Let me tell you something. She just about takes the biscuit, that woman – give or take one or two congenitally compulsive liars we've had in the past.'

Lewis shook his head sadly as Morse continued:

'Wedding ring? You're right. Odds strongly against her having worn one recently. Not necessarily the same as *not* being married though, is it? Suggestive, though, yes. Suggestive that she might be telling a few other fibs as well.'

'Such as?'

'Well, it was obvious she wasn't deaf at all. She heard everything I said. Easy. *Kein Problem.*'

'She didn't hear *me*.'

'She didn't want to hear you, Lewis.'

'If you say so, sir.'

'What about her eyesight? Kept telling us, didn't she, that she couldn't see half as well as she used to? But that didn't stop her giving us a detailed description of the woman who came to visit McClure. She knew she'd got a ring in one of her nostrils – at twenty-odd yards, Lewis! And the only reason she couldn't tell us if she'd got *two* rings in her nose was because she saw her in profile – like she sees everyone in profile coming in through that entrance.'

'Why don't you think she was making all *that* up too, sir – that description she gave?'

'Good point.' Morse looked down at the carpet briefly. 'But I don't think so; that bit rang true to me. In fact, I reckon it was the only thing of any value she did come up with.'

'What about—?'

'Lewis! She's a phoney. She's not even been a *nurse* – let alone a matron or whatever you call 'em.'

'How can you say that?'

'You heard her – we both heard her. Mini-skirt up to mid-tibia – remember me saying that? Mid-*tibia*? Your tibia's *below* your knee, Lewis. You know that. But *she* doesn't.'

'Unless she's deaf, and misheard—'

'She's not deaf, I told you that. She just doesn't know her tibia from her fibula, that's all. Never been near a nursing manual in her life.'

'And you deliberately tricked her about that?'

'*And*, Lewis – most important of all – she claims she's an *Archers* addict, but she doesn't even know when the omnibus edition comes on on a Sunday morning. Huh!'

'I wouldn't know—'

'She's a Walter Mitty sort of woman. She lives in a world of fantasy. She tells herself things so many times – tells other people things so many times – that she thinks they're true. And for her they *are* true.'

'But not for us.'

'Not for us, no.'

'Not even the time she was in the bath?'

'If she was in the bath.'

'Oh.'

'Anyway, I don't somehow think it's going to be of much importance to us, what time the murderer made his entrance . . .'

Morse was whining on a little wearily now; and like Miss (or Mrs) W-W he seemed to be running out of steam.

Both men became silent again.

And soon Lewis was feeling pleased with himself, for he was beginning to realize that the 'second thing' he'd found for Morse was looking far more promising.

And Morse himself, with melancholy mien, sat ever motionless, his eyes staring intently at the page before him: that selfsame page in the book of Latin poetry.

CHAPTER EIGHT

Caeli, Lesbia nostra, Lesbia illa,
Illa Lesbia, quam Catullus unam
Plus quam se atque suos amavit omnes,
Nunc in quadriviis et angiportis
Glubit magnanimi Remi nepotes
(CATULLUS, *Poems LVIII*)

WHEN HE was a boy – well, when he was fifteen – Morse had fallen deeply in love with a girl, a year his junior, who like him had won a scholarship to one of the two local grammar schools: one for boys, one for girls. The long relationship between the pair of them had been so formative, so crucial, so wonderful overall, that when, three years later, he had been called up for National Service in the Army, he had written (for the first twelve weeks) a daily letter to his girl; only to learn on his first weekend furlough, to learn quite accidentally, that one of his friends (friends!) had been openly boasting about the sensually responsive lips of his beloved.

Morse told himself that he had finally grown up that weekend: and that was good. But he'd realized too, at the same time, that his capacity for jealousy was pretty nearly boundless.

It was only many years later that he'd seen those deeply wise words, embroidered in multi-coloured silks, in a B&B establishment in Maidstone:

– *If you love her, set her free*
– *If she loves you, she will gladly return to you*
– *If she doesn't she never really loved you anyway*

Such thoughts monopolized Morse's mind now as he looked again at Poem LVIII – a poem which his Classics master at school had exhorted the class to ignore, as being totally devoid of artistic merit. Such condemnation was almost invariably in direct proportion to the sexual content of the poem in question; and immediately after the lesson was over, Morse and his classmates had sought to find the meaning of that extraordinary word which Catullus had stuck at the beginning of the last line.

Glubit.

In the smaller Latin dictionary, *glubo, -ere* was given only as 'libidinously to excite emotions'. But in the larger dictionary there was a more cryptic, potentially more interesting definition ... And here, in the margin of the book he was holding, McClure had translated the same poem.

> *To totters and toffs – in a levelish ratio –*
> *My darling K offers her five-quid fellatio.*
> *Near Carfax, perhaps, or at Cowley-Road Palais,*
> *Or just by the Turf, up any old alley:*
> *Preferring (just slightly) some kerb-crawling gent*
> *High in the ranks of Her Majesty's Government.*

Morse gave a mental tick to 'Carfax' for *quadriviis*; but thought 'Palais' a bit adolescent perhaps. Had his own translation been as good? Better? He couldn't remember. He doubted it. And it didn't matter anyway.

Or did it?

In the actual text of the poem, McClure had underlined in red Biro the words *Lesbia nostra, Lesbia illa, Illa Lesbia*: my Lesbia, that Lesbia of mine, that selfsame Lesbia.

Jealousy.

That most corrosive of all the emotions, gnawing away at the heart with a greater pain than failure or hatred – or even despair. But it seemed that McClure, like Catullus, had known his full share of it, with an ever-flirting, ever-hurting woman with whom he'd fallen in love; a woman who appeared willing to prostitute, at the appropriate price, whatever she possessed.

And suddenly, unexpectedly, Morse found himself thinking he'd rather like to meet the mysterious 'K'. Then, just as suddenly, he knew he wouldn't; unless, of course, that ambivalent lady held the key to the murder of Felix McClure – a circumstance which (at the time) he suspected was extremely improbable.

CHAPTER NINE

And like a skylit water stood
The bluebells in the azured wood
(A. E. HOUSMAN, *A Shropshire Lad, XLI*)

MORSE SNAPPED Catullus to.

'You didn't hear what I just said, did you, sir?'

'Pardon? Sorry. Just pondering – just pondering.'

'Is it leading us anywhere, this, er, pondering?'

'We're learning quite a bit about this girl of his, aren't we? Building up quite an interesting—'

'The answer's "no" then, is it?'

Morse smiled weakly. 'Probably.'

'Not like you, that, sir – giving up so quickly.'

'No. You're right. We shall have to check up on her.'

'Find out where she lives.'

'What? Not much of a problem there,' said Morse.

'Really?'

'She came on foot, we know that. From the Banbury Road side.'

'I thought you said Mrs Thingummy was making everything up?'

But Morse ignored the interjection. 'Where do *you* think she lives?'

'Just round the corner, perhaps?'

'Doubt it. Doubt he'd meet any local girl locally, if you see what I mean.'

'Well, if she did have a car, she couldn't park it in the Banbury Road, that's for certain.'

'So she hasn't got a car?'

'Well, if she has, she doesn't use it.'

'She probably came by bus then.'

'If you say so, sir.'

'Number twenty-something: down the Cowley Road, through the High to Carfax, along Cornmarket and St Giles', then up the Banbury Road.'

'Has she got a season-ticket, sir?'

'Such flippancy ill becomes you, Lewis.'

'I'm not being flippant. I'm just confused. You'll be telling me next what colour her eyes are.'

'Give me a chance.'

'Which street she lives in . . .'

'Oh, I think I know that.'

Lewis grinned and shook his head. 'Come on, sir, tell me!'

'Pater Street, Lewis – that's where she lives. Named after Walter Pater, you know, the fellow who described the Mona Lisa as a woman who'd learned the secrets of the grave.'

'Pater Street? That's out in Cowley, isn't it?'

Morse nodded. 'McClure mentions Cowley in something he wrote here.' Morse tapped Catullus. 'And then there's this.'

He handed across the postcard he'd found marking the relevant page of notes at the back of the volume – notes including a chicken-hearted comment on *Glubit*: '*sensus obscenus*'.

Lewis took the card; and after glancing at the coloured photograph, 'Bluebells in Wytham Woods', turned to the back where, to the left of McClure's address, he read the brief message, written boldly in black Biro:

P St out this Sat –
either DC or wherever   **K**

The unsmudged postmark gave the date as 10 August 1994.

'Ye-es. I see what you mean, sir. They'd arranged to meet at her place, perhaps, P-something Street, on the Saturday; then on the Wednesday something cropped up . . .'

'She may have had the decorators in.'

'. . . so it had to be "DC", Daventry Court, or "wherever".'

'Probably some hotel room.'

'Cost him, though. Double room'd be – what? – £70, £80, £90?'

'Or a B&B.'

'Even so. Still about £40, £50.'

'Then he's got to pay her for her services, don't forget that.'

'How much do you think, sir?'

'How the hell should *I* know?'

'Maybe she was worth every penny of it,' Lewis suggested quietly.

'Do you know, I very much doubt that,' asserted Morse with

surprising vehemence, now walking over to the phone, consulting the black index, and dialling a number.

'Could be *Princess* Street, sir? That's just off the Cowley Road.'

Morse put his palm over the receiver and shook his head. 'No, Lewis. It's *Pater* Street. Hullo?'

'Yeah? Wha' d'ya wan'?'

'Have I got the right number for "K", please?'

'You 'ave. Bu' she ain't 'ere, is she?'

'That's what I hoped you'd be able to tell me.'

'You another dur'y ol' man or somethin'?'

'If I am, I'm a dirty old police inspector,' replied Morse, in what he trusted was a cultured, authoritative tone.

'Oh, sorry.'

'You say she's not there?'

'She's bin away for a week in Spain. Sent me a topless photo of 'erself from Torremolinos, didn't she? Only this mornin'.'

'A week, you say?'

'Yeah. Went las' Sa'dy – back this Sa'dy.'

'Does she have a . . . a client in North Oxford?'

'An' if she does?'

'You know his name?'

'Nah.'

'What about *her* name?'

'She in some sort of trouble?' Suddenly the voice sounded anxious, softer now – with a final 't' voiced upon that 'sort'.

'I could get all this information from Kidlington Police HQ – you know that, surely? I just thought it would save a bit of time and trouble if you answered me over the phone. Then when we've finished I can thank you for your kind co-operation with the police in their inquiries.'

Hesitation now at the other end of the line.

Then an answer: 'Kay Blaxendale. That's "Kay", K-A-Y. She jus' signs herself "K" – the letter "K".'

'Is that her real name? It sounds a bit posh?'

'It's her professional name. Her real name's Ellie Smith.'

'What about your name?'

'Do you have to know?'

'Yes.'

'Friday Banks – that's me.'

'Have *you* got another name?'

'No.'

'You've got another accent though, haven't you?'

'Pardon?'

'When you want to, you can speak very nicely. You've got a pleasant voice. I just wonder why you try to sound so cheap and common, that's all.'

'Heh! Come off it. I may be common, mista, but I ain't cheap – I can tell yer tha'.'

'All right.'

'Tha' all?'

'Er, do you like bluebells, Miss Banks?'

'Bluebells, you say? Bloody *blue*bells?' She snorted her derision. 'She does, though – Kay does. But me, I'm a red-rose girl, Inspector – if you're thinkin' of sendin' me a bunch of flowers.'

'You never know,' said Morse, as he winked across at Lewis.

'Tha' all?' she repeated.

'Just your address, please.'

'Do you have to know?' (An aspirated 'have'.)

'Yes.'

'It's 35 Princess Street.'

And now it was Lewis's turn, as he winked across at Morse.

CHAPTER TEN

A long time passed – minutes or years – while the two of us sat there in silence. Then I said something, asked something, but he didn't respond. I looked up and I saw the moisture running down his face

(EDUARDO GALEANO, *The Book of Embraces*)

MORSE'S FACE, after he had cradled the phone, betrayed a suggestion of satisfaction; but after a short while a stronger suggestion of *dis*satisfaction.

'Ever heard of a girl called Friday, Lewis?'

'I've heard of that story – *The Man Who Was Thursday*.'

'It's a diminutive of Frideswide.'

'Right. Yes. We learnt about her at school – St Frideswide. Patron saint of Oxford. She cured somebody who was blind, I think.'

'Somebody, Lewis, she'd already herself struck blind in the first place.'

'Not a very nice girl, then.'

'Just like our girl.'

'Anyway, you can cross her off the list of suspects.'

'How do you make that out, Lewis?'

'Unless you still think that girl on the phone's a phoney too.'

'No. I don't think that. Not now.'

'Well, she said McClure's girlfriend was in Spain when he was murdered, didn't she?'

'It's impolite to eavesdrop on telephone conversations.'

Lewis nodded. 'Interesting, too. I felt sure you were going to ask her to send you the photo – you know, the topless photo from Torremolinos.'

'Do you know,' said Morse quietly, 'I think, looking back on it, I should have done exactly that. I must be getting senile.'

'You can still cross her off your list,' maintained an unsympathetic Lewis.

'Perhaps she was never on it in the first place. You see, I don't think it was a woman who murdered McClure.'

'We shall still have to see her, though.'

'Oh yes. But the big thing we've got to do is learn more about McClure. The more we learn about the murdered man, the more we learn about the murderer.'

Music to Lewis's ears. 'But no firm ideas yet, sir?'

'What?' Morse walked over to the front window, but his eyes seemed not so much to be looking out as looking in. 'I once went to hear a panel of writers, Lewis, and I remember they had to answer an interesting question about titles – you know, how important a title is for a book.'

'*The Wind in the Willows* – that's my favourite.'

'Anyway, the other panellists said it was the most difficult thing of the lot, finding a good title. Then this last woman, she said it was no problem for her at all. Said she'd got half a dozen absolutely dazzling titles – but she just hadn't got any books to go with them. And it's the same with me, Lewis, that's all. I've got plenty of ideas already, but nothing to pin 'em to.'

'Not yet.'

'Not yet,' echoed Morse.

'Do you think Phillotson had any ideas – ideas he didn't tell us about?'

'For Christ's sake, forget Phillotson! He wouldn't know what to do if some fellow walked into his nearest nick with a knife dripping with blood and said he'd just murdered his missus.'

At least that's something you're never likely to do, thought Lewis. But the thought was not translated into words.

'Now,' continued Morse, 'just tell me about this second great discovery of yours.'

'Just give me ten more minutes – nearly ready.'

Morse ambled somewhat aimlessly around the rooms so splendidly cited by Messrs Adkinson: Sitting/Dining-Room; Fully Fitted Modern Kitchen; Cloaks/Shower Room; Guest Bedroom; Master Bedroom Suite; Luxury Bathroom. But nothing, it appeared, was able to hold his attention for long; and soon he returned to the murder room.

For Lewis, this brief period of time was profitable. His little dossier – well, three items held together by a paper-clip – was now, he thought, complete. Interesting. He was pleased with himself; trusted that Morse would be pleased with him, too.

Not that Morse had looked particularly pleased with anything these last few minutes; and Lewis watched him taking a few more books from the shelves, seemingly in random manner, opening each briefly at the title page, then shaking it quite vigorously from the spine as if expecting something to fall out. And even as Lewis watched, something did fall out from one of them – nothing less than the whole of its pages. But Lewis's cautious amusement was immediately stifled by a vicious scowl from Morse; and nothing was said.

In fact, over only one of the title pages had Morse lingered for more than a few moments:

THE GREAT PLAGUE AT ATHENS

*Its Effect on the Course and Conduct
of the Peloponnesian War*

BY

FELIX FULLERTON McCLURE M.A., D.PHIL.
Student of Wolsey College, Oxford

Correction.
Late Student of Wolsey College, Oxford . . .

At 5.45 p.m. PC Roberts knocked, and entered in response to Morse's gruff behest.

'Super just rung through, sir—'

'"Rang" through,' muttered Morse.

'—and wanted me to tell you straightaway. It's Mrs Phillotson, sir. She died earlier this afternoon. Seems she had another emergency op . . . and well, she didn't pull through. He didn't tell me any more. He just wanted you to know, he said.'

Roberts left, and Lewis looked on as Morse slowly sat down in the brown leather armchair, staring, it seemed, at the design on the carpet – the eyes, usually so fierce and piercing, now dull and defeated; a look of such self-loathing on his face as Lewis had never seen before.

It was five minutes later that Lewis made an offer which (as he knew) could hardly be refused.

'Fancy a beer, sir? The King's Arms down the road's open – Open All Day, it says outside.'

But Morse shook his head, and sat there in continued silence.

So for a while Lewis pretended to complete an already completed task. Perhaps he should have felt puzzled? But no. He wasn't puzzled at all.

Tomorrow was Thursday . . .

And the next day was Friday . . .

Strange how they'd both cropped up already that day: the Man Who Was Thursday and the Girl Who Was Friday. Yet at this stage of the case, as they sat together in Daventry Court, neither Morse nor Lewis had the vaguest notion of how crucial one of the two was soon to become.

CHAPTER ELEVEN

You; my Lady, certainly don't dye your hair to deceive the others, nor even yourself; but only to cheat your own image a little before the looking-glass

(LUIGI PIRANDELLO, *Henry IV*)

WHEN FOR a second time she had put down the phone, Eleanor Smith stared at her own carpet, in this case a threadbare, tastelessly floral affair that stopped, at each wall, about eighteen inches short of the chipped skirting-boards.

The calls hadn't been unexpected. No. Ever since she'd read of

McClure's murder in the *Oxford Mail* she'd half expected, half feared that the police would be in touch. Twice, at least twice, she remembered sending him a postcard; and once a letter – a rambling, adolescent letter written just after they'd first met when she'd felt particularly lonely on a dark and cloudy day. And knowing Felix, even a bit, she thought he'd probably have kept anything she might have sent him.

Their first meeting for a drink together had been in the Chapters Bar of The Randolph. Good, that had been. No pretences then, on either side. But he'd gently refused to consider her a 'courtesan' if only for the reason (as he'd smilingly informed her) that anagrammatically, and appropriately, the word gave rise to 'a sore——'.

Yes, quite good really, that first evening – that first night, in fact – together. Above all perhaps, from her point of view, it had marked a nascent interest in crossword puzzles, which Felix had later encouraged and patiently fostered . . .

They'd found her telephone number in his flat – of course they had. Not that it was any great secret. Not exactly an ex-directory, exclusive series of digits. A number, rather, that in the early days had been slipped into half the BT phone-boxes in East Oxford, on a card with an amateurishly drawn outline of a curvaceous brunette with bouncy boobs. Her! But it was there; there in that telephone-thing of his on the desk. She knew that, for she'd seen it there. Odd, really. She'd have expected someone with such a fine brain as Felix to have committed her five-figure number to a permanent place in his memory. Seemingly not, though.

Poor old Felix.

She'd never loved anyone in life really – except her mum. But amongst her clients, that rather endearing, kindly, caring sort of idiot, Felix, had perhaps come nearer than anyone.

He'd never mentioned any enemies. But he must have had at least one – that much was certain. Not that she could help. She knew nothing. If she *had* known something, she'd have volunteered the information before now.

Or would she?

The very last thing she wanted was to get involved with the police. With *her* job? Come off it! And in any case there was no point in it. The last time she'd been round to Felix's apartment had been three weeks ago, when he'd cooked steak for the two of them, with a bottle of vintage claret to wash it down; *and* two bottles of expensive champagne, one before ... things; and one after.

Poor old Felix.

A very nice person in the very nasty world in which she'd lived these last few years.

Easy enough fooling the fuzz! Just said she wasn't there, hadn't she? Just said she was in Spain. Just said there'd been this photo of a bare-breasted tourist in Torremolinos. Been a bit of a problem if that second copper'd asked for the photo, though. But he'd sounded all right – they'd both sounded all right. Just not very bright, that's all. Would they check up on her? But what if they did? They'd soon understand why she'd told a few fibs. It was a joke. Bit of fun. No one wanted to get involved in a murder inquiry.

And whatever happened she *couldn't* be a suspect. Felix had been murdered on Sunday 28th August, hadn't he? And on that same Sunday she'd left Oxford at 6.30 a.m. (yes!) on a coach-trip to Bournemouth. Hadn't got back, either, until 9.45 p.m. So there! And thirty-four witnesses could testify to that. Thirty-five, if you included the driver.

Nothing to worry about, then – nothing at all.

And yet she couldn't *help* worrying: worrying about who, in his senses, would want to murder such an inoffensive fellow as Felix.

Or in *her* senses ...

Was there some history, some incident, some background in Felix's life about which she knew nothing? Sure to be, really. Not that he'd ever hinted—

Then it struck her.

There *was* that one thing. Just over a year ago, late May (or was it early June?) when that undergraduate living on Felix's staircase had jumped out of his third-floor window – and broken his neck.

'That undergraduate'? Who was she fooling?

Poor Matthew!

Not that she'd had anything to do with that, either. Well, she'd fervently prayed that she hadn't. After all, she'd only met him once, when Felix had become so furiously jealous.

Jealousy!

At *his* age – forty-one years older than she was. A grandfather, almost. A father, certainly. Yet one of the very few clients who meant anything to her in that continuum of carnality which passed for some sort of purpose in her present life.

Yes, a father-figure.

A foster-father, perhaps.

Not a bloody *step*-father, though! Christ, no.

She looked at herself in the mirror of the old-fashioned dressing-table. The pallor of her skin looked ghastly; and her dark hair, streaked with a reddish-orange henna dye, looked lustreless – and cheap. But she felt cheap all over. And as she rested her oval face on her palms, the index finger of each hand stroking the silver rings at either side of her nostrils, her sludgy-green eyes stared back at her with an expression of dullness and dishonesty.

Dishonesty?

Yes. The truth was that she probably hadn't given a sod for McClure, not really. Come to think of it, he'd been getting something of a nuisance: wanting to monopolize her; pressurizing her; phoning at inconvenient moments – once at a *very* inconvenient moment. He'd become far too obsessive, far too possessive. And what was worse, he'd lost much of his former gaiety and humour in the process. Some men were like that.

Well, hard luck!

Yes, if she were honest with herself, she was glad it was all over. And as she continued to stare at herself, she was suddenly aware that the streaks of crimson in her hair were only perhaps a physical manifestation of the incipient streaks of cruelty in her heart.

CHAPTER TWELVE

To run away from trouble is a form of cowardice and, while it is true that the suicide braves death, he does it not for some noble object but to escape some ill

(ARISTOTLE, *Nicomachean Ethics*)

MORSE HAD finished the previous evening with four pints of Best Bitter (under an ever-tightening waist-belt) at the King's Arms in Banbury Road; and had followed this with half a bottle of his dearly beloved Glenfiddich (in his pyjamas) at his bachelor flat in the same North Oxford.

Unsurprisingly, therefore, he had not exactly felt as fit as a Stradivarius when Lewis had called the following morning; and it was Lewis who now drove out to Leicester.

It was Lewis who *had* to drive out to Leicester.

As the Jaguar reached the outskirts of that city, Morse was looking again through the items (four of them now, not three) which Lewis had seen fit to salvage from McClure's apartment, and which – glory be! – Morse had instantly agreed could well be of importance to the case. Certainly they threw light upon that murky drink-drugs-sex scene which had established itself in some few parts of Oxford University. First was a cutting from the *Oxford Mail* dated Tuesday, 8 June 1993 (fourteen months earlier):

DRUG LINK WITH
DREAM SON'S SUICIDE

At an inquest held yesterday, the Coroner, Mr Arnold Hoskins, recorded a verdict of suicide on the death of Mr Matthew Rodway, a third-year undergraduate reading English at Oxford.

Rodway's body had been discovered by one of the college scouts in the early hours of Friday, 21 May, at the foot of his third-floor window in the Drinkwater Quad of Wolsey College.

There was some discrepancy in the statements read out at the inquest, with suggestions made that Mr Rodway may perhaps have fallen accidentally after a fairly heavy drinking-party in his rooms on Staircase G.

There was also clear evidence, however, that Mr Rodway had been deeply depressed during the previous weeks, apparently about his prospects in his forthcoming Finals examination.

What was not disputed was that Rodway had taken refuge amongst one or two groups where drugs were regularly taken in various forms.

Dr Felix McClure, one of Rodway's former tutors, was questioned about an obviously genuine but unfinished letter found in Rodway's rooms, containing the sentence 'I've had enough of all this.'

Whilst he stoutly maintained that the words themselves were ambivalent in their implication, Dr McClure agreed with the Coroner that the most likely explanation of events was that Rodway had been driven to take his own life.

Pathological evidence substantiated the fact that Rodway had taken drugs, on a regular basis, yet there appeared no evidence to suggest that he was a suicidal type with some obsessive death-wish.

In his summing up, the Coroner stressed the evil nature of trafficking in drugs, and pointed to the ready availability of such drugs as a major contributory factor in Rodway's death.

Taken in the first place to alleviate anxiety, they had in all probability merely served to aggravate it, with the tragic consequences of which the court had heard.

Matthew's mother is reluctant to accept the Coroner's verdict. Speaking from her home in Leicester, Mrs Mary Rodway wished only to recall a bright, caring son who had every prospect of success before him.

'He was so talented in many ways. He was very good at hockey and tennis. He had a great love of music, and played the viola in the National Youth Orchestra.

'I know I'm making him sound like a dream son. Well, that's what he was.' (See Leader, p.8.)

Morse turned to the second cutting, taken from the same issue:

A DEGREE TOO FAR

A recently commissioned study highlights the increasing percentage of Oxford graduates who fail to find suitable employment. Dr Clive Hornsby, Senior Reader in Social Sciences at Lonsdale College, has endorsed the implications of these findings, and suggests that many students, fully aware of employment prospects, strive for higher-class degrees than they are competent to achieve. Others, as yet mercifully few, adopt the alternative course of abandoning hope, of seeking consolation in drink and drugs, and sometimes of concluding that life is not worth the living of it. It may well be that Oxford University, through its various advisory agencies and helplines, is fully aware of these and related problems, although we are not wholly convinced of this. The latest suicide in an Oxford college (see p.1) prompts renewed concern about the pressures on our undergraduate community here, and the ways in which additional advice and help can be provided.

Morse now turned again to the third cutting, taken from the *Oxford Times* of Friday, 18 June 1993: a shorter article, flanked by a photograph of 'Dr F. F. Maclure', a clean-shaven, rather mournful-looking man, pictured in full academic dress.

PASTORAL CARE DEFENDED

Following the latest in a disturbing sequence of suicides, considerable criticism has been levelled against the University's counselling arrangements. But Dr Felix McLure, former Senior Lecturer in Ancient History at Wolsey College, has expressed his disappointment that so many have rushed into the arena with allegations of indifference and neglect. In fact, according to Dr MacClure, the University has been instrumental over the past year in promoting several initiatives, including the formation of Oxford University Counselling and Help (OUCH) of which he was a founder-member. 'More should be done,' he told our reporter. 'We all agree on that score. But there should also be some recognition of the University's present concern and commitment.'

'You'll soon know those things off by heart,' ventured a well-pleased Lewis as he stopped in a leafy lane on the eastern side of the London Road and briefly consulted his street-map, before setting off again.

'It's not that. It's just that I'm a slow reader.'

'What if you'd been a quick reader, sir? Where would you be now?'

'Probably been a proofreader in a newspaper office. They could certainly do with one,' mumbled Morse as he considered 'Maclure' and 'McLure' and 'MacClure' in the last cutting, with still no sign of the genuine article, 'former Senior Lecturer . . .'

Interesting, that extra little piece of the jigsaw – that 'former' . . .

Lewis braked gently outside Number 14 Evington Road South; then decided to continue into the drive, where the low-profile tyres of the Jaguar crunched into the deep gravel.

CHAPTER THIRTEEN

Whatever crazy sorrow saith,
No life that breathes with human breath
Has ever truly longed for death
(ALFRED, LORD TENNYSON, *The Two Voices*)

MRS MARY RODWAY, a smartly dressed, slim-figured, pleasantly featured woman in her late forties, seemed quite willing to talk about herself – at least for a start.

Four years previously (she told the detectives) her husband, a highly salaried constructional engineer, had run off with his Personal Assistant. The only contact between herself and her former marriage-partner was now effected via the agency of solicitors and banks. She lived on her own happily enough, she supposed – if anyone could ever live happily again after the death of an only child, especially a child who had died in such dubious circumstances.

She had seen McClure's murder reported in *The Independent*; and Morse wasted no time in telling her of the specific reason for his visit: the cuttings discovered among the murdered man's papers which appeared firmly to underline his keen interest in her son, Matthew, and perhaps in the reasons for his suicide.

'He was quite wrong – the Coroner. You do realize that?' Mary Rodway lit another cigarette and inhaled deeply.

'You don't believe it was suicide?'

'I didn't say that. What I do say is that the Coroner was wrong in making such a big thing about those hard drugs. That's what they call them: "hard" as opposed to "soft". It's just the same with pornography, I believe, Inspector.'

Whilst Morse nodded his head innocently, Mrs Rodway shook her own in vague exasperation. 'Life's a far more *complicated* thing than that – Matthew's was – and that Coroner, he made it all sound so . . . *un*complicated.'

'Don't be too, er, hard on him, Mrs Rodway. A Coroner's main job isn't dealing with right and wrong, and making moral judgements, and all that sort of thing. He's just there to put the bits and pieces into some sort of pattern, and then to stick some verdict, as best he can, in one of the few slots he's got available to him.'

If Mrs Rodway was at all impressed by this amalgam of metaphors, she gave no indication of it. Perhaps she hadn't even been listening, for she continued in her former vein: 'There were two things – two quite separate things – and they ought to have been *considered* separately. It's difficult to put it into words, Inspector, but you see there are causes of things, and symptoms of things. And in Matthew's case this drugs business was a symptom of something – it wasn't a cause. I *knew* Matthew – I knew him better than anyone.'

'So you think . . . ?'

'I've stopped thinking. What on earth's the good of churning things over and over again in your mind for the umpteenth time?'

She stubbed out a half-smoked cigarette savagely, and immediately lit another.

'You don't mind me smoking?'

'No, no.'

'Can I offer you gentlemen one?' She held out a packet of King-Size Dunhill International, first to Lewis who shook his head with a smile; then to Morse who shook his head with stoical resolve, since only that same morning, when he'd woken up just before six with parched mouth and pounding head, he had decided to forgo – for evermore – the spurious gratification not only of alcohol but of nicotine also.

Perhaps his decision could wait until tomorrow for its full implementation, though; and he relented. 'Most kind, Mrs Rodway. Thank you . . . And it's very valuable, what you're saying. Please do go on.'

'There's nothing more to say.'

'But if you felt – feel – so strongly, why didn't you agree to give evidence at the Inquest?'

'How could I? I couldn't even bear to switch on the TV or the radio in case there might be something about it. *You* couldn't bear that, could you, Inspector? If it had been your child?'

'I – I take your point,' admitted Morse awkwardly.

'You know usually, when things like that happen, you get all the rumour and all the gossip as well. But we didn't have any of that – at the Inquest.'

Three times now Mary Rodway inhaled on her cigarette with such ferocity that she seemed to Lewis hell-bent on inflicting some irreparable damage to her respiratory tract.

But Morse's mind for a few seconds was far away, a glimmer of light at last appearing at the far end of a long, black tunnel.

'So . . .' he picked his slow words carefully, 'you'd hoped that there might be some other evidence given at the Inquest, but you didn't want to provide any of it yourself?'

'Perhaps it wasn't all that important anyway.'

'Please tell me.'

'No.'

Morse looked around the large lounge. The day was warm already, yet he suspected (rightly) that the two long radiators were turned up to full capacity. Much space on the walls was devoted to pictures: prints of still-life paintings by Braque, Matisse, Picasso; photographs and watercolours of great buildings and palaces, including Versailles and Blenheim – and Wolsey College, Oxford. But virtually no people were photographed or represented there. It was as if those 'things' so frequently resorted to by Mrs Rodway in her conversation were now figuring more prominently than people.

'You knew Dr McClure, I think,' said Morse.

'I met him first when Matthew went up to Oxford. He was Matthew's tutor.'

'Didn't he have rooms on the same staircase as Matthew?' (Lewis had spent most of the previous evening doing his homework; *and* Morse's homework.)

'The first year, and the third year, yes. He was out of college his second year.'

'Where was that, do you remember?'

Did Lewis observe a flicker of unease in Mary Rodway's eyes? Did Morse?

'I'm not sure.'

'Oh, it doesn't matter. Sergeant Lewis here can check up on that easily enough.'

But she had her answer now. 'It was in East Oxford somewhere. Cowley Road, was it?'

Morse continued his questioning, poker-faced, as if he had failed to hear the tintinnabulation of a bell: 'What did you think of Dr McClure?'

'Very nice man. Kindly – genuine sort of person. And, as you say, he took a real interest in Matthew.'

Morse produced a letter, and passed it across to Mrs Rodway: a single handwritten sheet, on the pre-printed stationery of 14

Evington Road South, Leicester, dated 2 June, the day after the Coroner's verdict on Matthew Rodway's death.

> Dear Felix
> I was glad to talk to you on the phone however briefly. I was so choked I could hardly speak to you. Please do as we agreed. If you find anything else among M's things which would be upsetting please get rid of them. This includes any of my letters he may have kept. He had two family photos in his room, one a framed one of the two of us. I'd like both of them back. But all clothes and personal effects and papers – get rid of them all for me.
> I must thank you for all you tried to do for Matthew. He often spoke of your kindness, as you know. I'm so sorry, I can't go on with this letter any more.
> Sincerely yours
> Mary

Morse now accepted a second cigarette; and as Mrs Rodway read through the letter Lewis turned his head away from the exhalation of smoke. He was not overmuch concerned about the health risks supposedly linked with passive smoking, but it must have some effect; had already *had* its effect on the room here, where a thin patina of nicotine could be seen on the emulsioned walls. In fact the whole room could surely do with a good wash-down and redecoration? The corners of the high ceiling were deeply stained, and just above one of the radiators an oblong of pristinely bright magnolia served to emphasize a slight neglect of household renovation.

'Did you write that?' asked Morse.

'Yes.'

'Is there anything you want to tell us about it?'

'Pretty clear, isn't it?'

'Did Dr McClure find anything in Matthew's rooms?'

'I don't know.'

'Would he have told you if, let's say, he'd found some drugs?'

'I doubt it.'

'Did he think Matthew was taking drugs?'

It was hard for her to say it. But she said it: 'Yes.'

'Did you ever find out where he got his drugs from?'

'No.'

'Did he ever say anything about his friends being on drugs?'

'No.'

'Do you think they may have been?'

'I only met one or two of them – on the same staircase.'

'Do you think drugs were available inside the college?'

'I don't know.'

'Would Dr McClure have known, if they were?'

'I suppose he would, yes.'

'Was Matthew fairly easily influenced by his friends, would you say?'

'No, I wouldn't.'

The answers elicited from Mrs Rodway hardly appeared to Lewis exciting; or even informative, for that matter. But Morse appeared content to keep his interlocution at low key.

'Do you blame anyone? About the drugs?'

'I'm in no position to blame anyone.'

'Do you blame yourself?'

'Don't we all blame ourselves?'

'What about Dr McClure – where did he put the blame?'

'He did say once . . . I remember . . .' But the voice trailed off as she lit another cigarette. 'It was very odd really. He was talking about all the pressures on young people these days – you know, about youth culture and all that sort of thing, about whether standards were declining in . . . well, in everything, I suppose.'

'What exactly did he say?' prompted Morse gently.

But Mary Rodway was not listening. 'You know, if only Matthew hadn't . . . killed himself that night, whatever the reason was – reason or reasons – he'd probably have been perfectly happy with life a few days later, a week later . . . That's what I can't . . . I can't get over.'

Tears were dropping now.

And Lewis looked away.

But not Morse.

'What exactly did he say?' he repeated.

Mrs Rodway wiped her tears and blew her nose noisily. 'He said it was always difficult to apportion blame in life. But he said . . . he said if he had to blame anybody it would be the students.'

'Is that all?'

'Yes.'

'Why was that an "odd" thing to say, though?'

'Because, you see, he was always on the students' side. Always. So it was a bit like hearing a trade-union boss suddenly siding with the Conservative Party.'

'Thank you. You've been very kind, Mrs Rodway.'

Clearly (as Lewis could see) it was time to depart; and he closed his notebook with what might have passed for a slight flourish – had anyone been interested enough to observe the gesture.

But equally clearly (as Lewis could also see) Morse was momentarily transfixed, the blue eyes gleaming with that strangely distanced, almost ethereal gaze, which Lewis had observed so often before – a gaze which usually betokened a breakthrough in a major case.

As now?

The three of them rose to their feet.

'Did you get to university yourself?' asked Morse.

'No. I left school at sixteen – went to a posh secretarial college – did well – got a good job – met a nice boss – became his PA – and he married me ... As I told you, Inspector, he's got a weakness for his PAs.'

Morse nodded. 'Just one last question. *When* did your husband leave you?'

'I told you, don't you remember? Four years ago.' Suddenly her voice sounded sharp.

'When *exactly*, Mrs Rodway?' Suddenly Morse's voice, too, sounded sharp.

'November the fifth – Bonfire Night. Not likely to forget the date, am I?'

'Not *quite* four years ago then?'

Mrs Rodway made no further reply.

CHAPTER FOURTEEN

Everyone can master a grief but he that has it
(SHAKESPEARE, *Much Ado About Nothing*)

'BIG THING you've got to remember is that it's a great healer –
time. Just give it a while, you'll see.'

It was just before lunchtime that same day, in his office at
Kidlington Police HQ, that Chief Superintendent Strange thus
sought to convey his commiserations to Detective Chief Inspector
Phillotson – going on to suggest that an extended period of
furlough might well be a good thing after . . . well, after things
were over. And if anyone could help in any way, Phillotson only
had to mention it.

'Trouble with things like this,' continued Strange, as he rose
from behind his desk and walked round to place a kindly hand
on his colleague's shoulder, 'is that nothing really helps much at
all, does it?'

'I don't know about that, sir. People are being very kind.'

'I know, yes. I know.' And Strange resumed his seat, contemplating his own kindliness with some gratification.

'You know, sir, I've heard from people I never expected to
show much sympathy.'

'You have?'

'People like Morse, for instance.'

'Morse? When did you see Morse? He told me he was off to
Leicester this morning.'

'No. He put a note through the letter-box, that's all. Must have
been latish last night – it wasn't there when I put the milk-tokens
out . . .'

'I'd say he probably wrote it in a pub, knowing Morse.'

'Does it matter where he wrote it, sir?'

'Course not. But I can't imagine *him* being much comfort to
anybody. He's a pagan, you know that. Got no time for the
Church and . . . Hope and Faith and all that stuff. Doesn't even
believe in God, let alone in any sort of life after death.'

'Bit like some of our Bishops,' said Phillotson sadly.

'Like some Theology dons in Oxford, too.'

'I was still glad to get his letter.'

'What did he say?'

'Said what you just said really, sir; said he'd got no faith in the Almighty; said I just ought to forget all this mumbo-jumbo about meeting . . . meeting up again in some future life; told me just to accept the truth of it all – that she's gone for good and I'll never see her again; told me I'd probably never get over it, and not to take any notice of people who gave you all this stuff about time healing—' Phillotson suddenly checked himself, realizing what he'd just said.

'Doesn't sound much help to me.'

'Do you know, though, in an odd sort of way it was. It was sort of *honest*. He just said that he was sad, when he heard, and he was thinking of me . . . At the end, he said it was always a jolly sight easier in life to face up to the truths than the half-truths. I'm not quite sure what he meant . . . but, well, somehow it helps, when I remember what he said.'

Phillotson could trust himself to say no more, and he rose to leave.

At the door he turned back. 'Did you say Morse went to Leicester this morning?'

'That's where he said he was going.'

'Funny! Odds are I'd have been in Leicester myself. I bet he's gone to see the parents of that lad who killed himself in Wolsey a year or so ago.'

'What's that got to do with things?'

'There were a few newspaper articles, that's all, about the lad, among McClure's papers. *And* a letter from the mother. She started it off "Dear Felix" – as if they'd known each other pretty well, if you see what I mean.'

Strange grunted.

'Do you think I should mention it to Morse, sir?'

'No. For Christ's sake don't do that. He's got far too many ideas already, you can be sure of that.'

CHAPTER FIFTEEN

> Say, for what were hop-yards meant
> Or why was Burton built on Trent?
> Oh many a peer of England brews
> Livelier liquor than the Muse,
> And malt does more than Milton can
> To justify God's ways to man
> (A. E. HOUSMAN, *A Shropshire Lad, LXII*)

THE TURF TAVERN, nestling beneath the old walls of New College, Oxford, may be approached from Holywell Street, immediately opposite Holywell Music Room, via a narrow, irregularly cobbled lane of mediaeval aspect.

A notice above the entrance advises all patrons (although Morse is not a particularly tall man) to mind their heads (DUCK OR GROUSE) and inside the rough-stoned, black-beamed rooms the true connoisseur of beers can seat himself at one of the small wooden tables and enjoy a finely cask-conditioned pint; and it is in order to drink and to talk and to think that patrons frequent this elusively situated tavern in a blessedly music – Muzak – free environment.

The landlord of this splendid hostelry, a stoutly compact, middle-aged ex-Royal Navy man, with a grizzled beard and a gold ring in his left ear, was anticipatorily pulling a pint of real ale on seeing Morse enter, followed by the dutiful Lewis, at 1.50 p.m.

The latter, in fact, was feeling quite pleased with himself. Only sixty-five minutes from Leicester. A bit over the speed-limit all the way along (agreed); but fast driving was one of his very few vices, and the jazzy-looking maroon Jaguar had been in a wonderfully slick and silky mood as it sped down the M40 on the last stretch of the journey from Banbury to Oxford.

Morse had resisted several pubs which, *en route*, had paraded their credentials – at Lutterworth, Rugby, Banbury. But, as Lewis knew, the time of drinking, and of thinking, was surely soon at hand.

In North Oxford, Morse had asked to be dropped off briefly at his flat: 'I ought to call in at the bank, Lewis.' And this news had further cheered Lewis, since (on half the salary) it was invariably *he* who bought about three-quarters of the drinks consumed between the pair of them. Only temporarily cheered, however, since he had wholly misunderstood the mission: five minutes later it was he himself who was pushing a variety of old soldiers through their appropriate holes (White, Green, Brown) in the Summertown Bottle Bank.

Thence, straight down the Banbury Road to the Martyrs' Memorial, where turning left (as instructed) he had driven to the far end of Broad Street. Here, as ever, there appeared no immediate prospect of leaving a car legitimately, and Morse had insisted that he parked the Jaguar on the cobblestone area outside the Old Clarendon building, just opposite Blackwell's.

'Don't worry, Lewis. All the traffic wardens know my car. They'll think I'm on duty.'

'Which you are, sir.'

'Which I am.'

'How are we, Chief Inspector?'

'Less of the "Chief". Sheehy's going to demote me. I'll soon be just an insignificant Inspector.'

'The usual?'

Morse nodded.

'And you, Sergeant?'

'An orange juice,' said Morse.

'Where've you parked?' asked Biff. It was a question which had become of paramount importance in Central Oxford over the past decade. 'I only ask because they're having a blitz this week, so Pam says.'

'Ah! How *is* that beautiful lady of yours?'

'I'll tell her you're here. She should be down soon anyway.'

Morse stood at the bar searching through his pockets in unconvincing manner. 'And a packet of – do you still sell cigarettes?'

Biff pointed to the machine. 'You'll need the right change.'

'Ah! Have you got any change on you by any chance, Lewis . . . ?'

When, at a table in the inner bar, Morse was finally settled behind his pint, his second pint, he took from his inside jacket-pocket the used envelope on which Lewis had seen him scribbling certain headings on their return to Oxford.

'Did you know that Wolsey College is frequently referred to, especially by those who are in it, as "The House"?'

'Can't say I did, no.'

'Do you know why?'

'Let me concentrate on the orange juice, sir.'

'It's because of its Latin name, *Aedes Archiepiscopi*, the House of the Bishop.'

'Well, that explains it, doesn't it?'

'Another peculiarity is that in all the other colleges they call the dons and the readers and the tutors and so on – they call them "Fellows". You with me? But at Wolsey they call them "Students".'

'What do they call the students then?'

'Doesn't *matter* what they call 'em, does it? Look! Let's just consider where we are. We've discovered a couple of possible links in this case so far: McClure's fancy woman; and the Rodway woman, the mother of one of his former pupils. Now neither of 'em comes within a million miles of being a murderer, I know that; but they're both adding to what we know of McClure himself, agreed? He's a respected scholar; a conscientious don—'

'"Student", sir.'

'A conscientious Student; a man who's got every sympathy with his stu—'

Lewis looked across.

'—with the young people he comes into contact with; a founder-member of a society to help dedicated druggies; a man who met Matthew's mum, and probably slipped in between the sheets with her—'

Lewis shook his head vigorously. 'You *can't* just say that sort of thing.'

'And why not? How the hell do you think we're going to get to the bottom of this case unless we make the odd hypothesis here and there? You don't know? Well, let me tell you. We think of anything that's unlikely. That's how. Any bloody idiot can tell you what's *likely*.'

'If you say so, sir.'

'I *do* say so,' snapped Morse. 'Except that what I say is *not* particularly unlikely, is it? They obviously got on pretty well, didn't they? Take that salutation and valediction, for instance.'

Lewis lifted his eyebrows.

'All Christian-name, palsy-walsy stuff, wasn't it? Then there's this business of her husband leaving her – you'll recall I pressed her on that point? And for a very good reason. It was November, a month or so after her precious Matthew had first gone up to Oxford. And it occurred to me, Lewis – and I'm surprised it didn't occur to you – that things may well have been the other way round, eh? She may have left *him*, and it was only then that he started playing around with his new PA.'

'We could always look at a copy of the divorce proceedings.'

'What makes you think they're divorced?'

Lewis surrendered, sipped his orange juice, and was silent.

'But it doesn't matter, does it? It's got bugger-all to do with McClure's murder. You can make a heap of all the money you've got and wager it on *that*. No risk there!'

Lewis fingered the only money he had left in his pockets – three pound coins – and decided that he was hardly going to become a rich man, however long the odds that Morse was offering. But it was time to mention something. Had Morse, he wondered, seen that oblong patch of pristine magnolia . . . ?

'There was,' Lewis began slowly, 'a light-coloured patch on the wall in Mrs Rodway's lounge, sir—'

'Ah! Glad you noticed that. Fiver to a cracked piss-pot that was a picture of *him*, Lewis – of McClure! That's why she took it down. She didn't want us to see it, but something like that's always going to leave its mark, agreed?'

'Unless she put something else up there to cover it.'

Morse scorned the objection. 'She wouldn't have taken a photo of her *son* down, would she? Where's the point of that? Very unlikely.'

'You just said that's exactly what we're looking for, sir – something "unlikely".'

Morse was spared any possible answer to this astute question by the arrival of the landlady, a slimly attractive brunette, with small, neat features, and an extra sparkle in her eyes as she greeted Morse with a kiss on his cheek.

'Not seen you for a little while, Inspector.'

'How's things, beautiful?'

'Another beer?'

'Well, if you insist.'

'I'm not really insisting—'

'Pint of the best bitter for me.'

'You, Sergeant?'

'He's driving,' said Morse.

Biff, the landlord, came over to join them, and the four sat together for the next ten minutes. Morse, after explaining that the word 'Turf' had appeared in the margin of one of McClure's books, asked whether they, either landlord or landlady, would have known the murdered man if they had seen him in the pub ('No'); whether they'd ever seen the young man from Wolsey who'd committed suicide ('Don't think so'); whether they'd ever seen a young woman with rings in her nose and red streaks in her hair ('Hundreds of 'em').

Yet the landlady had one piece of information.

'There's one of the chaps comes in here sometimes who was a scout on that staircase . . . when, you know . . . I heard him talking to somebody about it.'

'That's right.' The landlord was remembering too. 'Said he used to go to the Bulldog – or was it the Old Tom, Pam?'

'Can't remember.'

'He was a scout, you say?' asked Morse.

'Yeah. Only started coming in here after he moved – moved to the Pitt Rivers, I think it was. Well, only just up the road, isn't it?'

'He still comes?'

Biff considered. 'Haven't seen him for a little while now you come to mention it. Have you, love?'

Pam shook her pretty head.

'Know his name?' asked Lewis.

'Brooks – Ted Brooks.'

'Just let me get this clear,' said Lewis, as he and Morse left the Turf Tavern, this time via St Helen's Passage, just off New College Lane. 'You're saying that Mrs Rodway misunderstood what McClure said to her – about the "students"?'

'You've got it. What he meant was that he blamed the dons, the set-up there, the authorities. He wasn't saying they were a load of crooks – just that they should have known what was going on there, and should have done something about it.'

'*If* anything was going on, sir.'

'Which'll be one of our next jobs, Lewis – to find out exactly that.'

*

It was Lewis who spotted it first: the traffic-warden's notice stuck beneath the near-side windscreen-wiper of the unmarked Jaguar.

By three o'clock that afternoon, Mary Rodway had assembled the new passe-partout for the picture-frame. Like most things in the room (she agreed) it had been getting very dingy. But it looked splendid now, as she carefully replaced the remounted photograph, standing back repeatedly and adjusting it, to the millimetre – that photograph of herself and her son which Felix had sent to her as she'd requested.

Nothing further of any great moment occurred that day, except for one thing – something which for Lewis was the most extraordinary, the most 'unlikely' event of the past six months.

'Come in a minute and let me pay you for those cigarettes,' Morse had said, as the Jaguar came to a stop outside the bachelor flat in North Oxford.

CHAPTER SIXTEEN

And sidelong glanced, as to explore,
In meditated flight, the door
(SIR WALTER SCOTT, *Rokeby*)

WHAT MORSE had vaguely referred to as the 'authorities' at Wolsey were immediately co-operative; and at 10 a.m. the following day he and Lewis were soon learning many things about the place: specifically, in due course, about Staircase G in Drinkwater Quad, on which Dr McClure had spent nine years of his university life, from 1984 until his retirement from academe at the end of the Trinity Term, 1993.

From his rooms overlooking the expansive quad ('Largest in Oxford, gentlemen – 264 by 261 feet') the Deputy Bursar had explained, rather too slowly and too pedantically for Morse's taste, the way things, er, worked in the, er, House, it clearly seeming to this former Air-Vice Marshal ('Often mis-spelt, you know – and more often mis-hyphenated') that these non-University people needed some elementary explanations.

Scouts?

Interested in *scouts*, were they?

Well, each scout ('Interesting word – origin obscure') looked after one staircase, and one staircase only – with that area guarded as jealously as any blackbird's territory in a garden, and considered almost as a sort of mediaeval fiefdom ('If you know what I mean?'). Several of the scouts had been with them, what, twenty, thirty years? Forty-nine years, one of them! What exactly did they do? Well, it would be sensible to go and hear things from the horse's mouth, as it were. What?

Escorted therefore through Great Quad, and away to the left of it into what seemed to Morse the unhappily named 'Drinkwater Quad', the policemen thanked their cicerone, the Air-hyphen-Vice Marshal ('One "l" ') and made their way to Staircase G.

Where a surprise was in store for them.

Not really a scout at all – more a girl-guide.

Susan Ewers, too, was friendly and helpful – a married woman (no children yet) who was very happy to have the opportunity of supplementing the family income; very happy, too, with the work itself. The majority of scouts were women now, she explained: only three or four men still doing the job at Wolsey. In fact, she'd taken over from a man – a man who'd left to work at the Pitt Rivers Museum.

'Mr Brooks, was that?' asked Morse.

'Yes. Do you know him?'

'Heard of him, er . . . please go on.'

Her duties? Well, everything really. The immediate area outside; the entrance; the porchway; the stairs; the eight sets of rooms, all of them occupied during term-time, of course; and some of them during the vacs, like now, by delegates and visitors to various do's and conferences. Her first job each morning was to empty all the rubbish-baskets into black bags; then to clean the three WCs, one on each floor (no *en suite* facilities as yet); same with the wash-basins. Then, only twice a week, though, to Hoover all the floors, and generally to dust around, polish any brasswork, that sort of thing; and in general to see that the living quarters of her charges were kept as neat and tidy as could be expected with young men and young women who would (she felt) probably prefer to live in – well, to live in a bit of a mess, really. No bed-making, though. Thank goodness!

Willingly she showed the detectives the rooms at G4, on the second floor of her staircase, where until fourteen months previously the name 'Dr F. F. McClure' had been printed in black Gothic capitals beside the Oxford-blue double doors.

But if Morse had expected to find anything of significance in these rooms, he was disappointed. All fixtures befitting the status of a respected scholar had been replaced by the furniture of standard undergraduate accommodation: a three-seater settee; two armchairs; two desks; two bookcases . . . It reminded Morse of his own unhappy, unsuccessful days at Oxford; but made no other impact.

It might have been helpful to move quietly around the lounge and the spacious bedroom there, and seek to detect any vibrations, any reverberations, left behind by a cultured and (it seemed) a fairly kindly soul.

But clearly Morse could see little point in such divination.

'Is G8 free?' he asked.

'There *is* a gentleman there. But he's not in at the minute. If you want just a quick look inside?'

'It's where Matthew Rodway, the man who . . .'

'I know,' said Susan Ewers quietly.

But G8 proved to be equally disappointing: a three-seater settee, two (faded fabric) armchairs . . . cloned and cleaned of every reminder of the young man who had thrown himself down on to the paved area below the window there – the window at which Morse and Lewis now stood for a little while. Silently.

'You didn't know Mr Rodway, either?' asked Morse.

'No. As I say, I didn't come till September last year.'

'Do people on the staircase still take drugs?'

Mrs Ewers was taken aback by the abruptness of Morse's question.

'Well, they still have parties, like, you know. Drink and . . . and so on.'

'But you've never seen any evidence of drugs – any packets of drugs? Crack? Speed? Ecstasy? Anything? Anything at all?'

Had she?

'No,' she said. Almost truthfully.

'You've never smelt anything suspicious?'

'I wouldn't know what they smell like, drugs,' she said. Truthfully.

As they walked down the stairs, Lewis pointed to a door marked with a little floral plaque: 'Susan's Pantry'.

'That where you keep all your things, madam?'

She nodded. 'Every scout has a pantry.'

'Can we take a look inside?'

She unlocked the door and led the way into a fairly small, high-ceilinged room, cluttered – yet so neatly cluttered – with buckets, mops, bin-liners, black plastic bags, transparent poly-thene bags, light bulbs, toilet rolls, towels, sheets, two Hoovers. And inside the white-painted cupboards rows of cleaners and detergents: Jif, Flash, Ajax, Windolene ... And everything so clean – so meticulously, antiseptically clean.

Morse had little doubt that Susan Ewers was the sort of housewife to polish her bath-taps daily; the sort to feel aggrieved at finding a stray trace of toothpaste in the wash-basin. If cleanliness were next to saintliness, then this lady was probably on the verge of beatification.

So what?

Apart from mentally extending his lively sympathies to *Mr* Ewers, Morse was aware that his thought-processes were hardly operating *vivamente* that morning; and he stood in the slightly claustrophobic pantry, feeling somewhat feckless.

It was Lewis who, as so frequently, was the catalyst.

'What's your husband do, Mrs Ewers?'

'He's – well, at the minute he's unemployed, actually. He did work at the old RAC offices in Summertown, but they made him redundant.'

'When was that?'

'Last year.'

'When exactly?' (If Morse could ask such questions, why not Lewis?)

'Last, er, August.'

'Good thing you getting the job then. Help tide things over a bit, like.'

Lewis smiled sympathetically.

And Morse smiled gratefully.

Bless you, Lewis – bless you!

*

Gestalt – that's what the Germans call it. That flash of unified perception, that synoptic totality which is more than the sum of the parts into which it may be logically analysable; parts, in this case, like drugs and scouts and a suicide and a murder and a staircase and changing jobs and not having a job and retirement and money and times and dates ... Yes, especially times and dates ...

Most probably, in the circumstances, Matthew Rodway's rooms would not have been reoccupied for the few remaining weeks at the end of Trinity Term the previous year; and if (as now) only *some* of the rooms were in use during the Long Vac, it might well be that Mrs Ewers had been the very first person to look closely around the suicide's chambers. But no; that was wrong. McClure had already gone through things, hadn't he? Mrs Rodway had asked him to. But would he have been half as thorough as this newly appointed woman?

He'd questioned her on the point already, he knew that. But he hadn't asked the right questions, perhaps? Not quite.

'Just going back a minute, Mrs Ewers ... When you got Mr Rodway's old rooms ready for the beginning of the Michaelmas Term, had anyone else been in there – during the summer?'

'I don't think so, no.'

'But you still didn't find anything?'

'No, like I just said—'

'Oh, I believe you. If there'd been anything to find, you'd have found it.'

She looked relieved.

'In his rooms, that is,' added Morse slowly.

'Pardon?'

'All I'm saying is that you've got a very tidy mind, haven't you? Let's put it this way. I bet I know the first thing you did when you took over here. I bet you gave this room the best spring-clean – best autumn-clean – it's ever had – last September – when *you* moved in – and the previous scout moved out.'

Susan Ewers looked puzzled. 'Well, I scrubbed and cleaned the place from top to bottom, yes – filthy, it was. Two whole days it took me. But I never found anything – any drugs – honest to God, I didn't!'

Morse, who had been seated on the only chair the room could offer, got to his feet, moved over to the door, and put his penultimate question:

'Do you have a mortgage?'

'Yes.'

'Big one?'

She nodded miserably.

As they stood there, the three of them, outside Susan's Pantry, Morse's eyes glanced back at the door, now closed again, fitting flush enough with the jambs on either side, but with a two-centimetre gap of parallel regularity showing between the bottom of the turquoise-blue door and the linoed floor of the landing.

Morse asked his last question simply and quietly: 'When did the envelopes first start coming, Susan?'

And Susan's eyes jumped up to his, suddenly flashing the unmistakable sign of fear.

CHAPTER SEVENTEEN

Examination: trial; test of knowledge and, as also may be hoped, capacity; close inspection (especially med.)

(*Small's Enlarged English Dictionary*, 1812 Edition)

ON FRIDAY, 2 September, two days after Julia Stevens' return to Oxford, there were already three items of importance on her day's agenda.

First, school.

Not as yet the dreaded restart (three whole days away, praise be!) but a visit to the Secretary's Office to look through the GCSE and A-level results, both lists having been published during her fortnight's absence abroad. Like every self-respecting teacher, she wanted to discover the relative success of the pupils she herself had taught.

In former days it had often been difficult enough for some pupils to *sit* examinations, let alone pass them. And even in the comparatively recent years of Julia's girlhood several of her own classmates had been deemed not to possess the requisite acumen even to attempt the 11 Plus. It was a question of the sheep and the goats – just like the division between those who were lost and those who were saved in the New Testament – a work with which the young Julia had become increasingly familiar, through the crusading fervour of a local curate with whom (aged ten and a half) she had fallen passionately in love.

How things had changed.

Now, in 1994, it was an occasion for considerable surprise if anyone somehow managed to *fail* an examination. Indeed, to be recorded in the Unclassified ranks of the GCSE was, in Julia's view, a feat of quite astonishing incompetence, which carried with it a sort of bravura badge of monumental under-achievement. And as far as Christian doctrine was concerned, it was becoming far easier to cope with sin, now that Hell was (semi-officially) abolished.

She looked through 5C's English results. Very much as she'd expected. Then looked a little more closely at the results of the only pupil in the class whose name had begun with 'C'. Costyn, K: Religious Education, 'Unclassified'; English, 'D'; Maths, 'Unclassified'; Geography, 'Unclassified'; Metalwork, 'Unclassified'. Well, at least he'd got something – after twelve years of schooling . . . thirty-six terms. But it was difficult to imagine him getting much further than the Job Centre. Nowhere else for him to go, was there – except to jail, perhaps?

How she wished that 'D' had been a 'C', though.

At 10.30 a.m. she hurried fairly quickly away from the school premises and made her way on foot to the Churchill Hospital where her appointment at the clinic was for 11 a.m.; and where a few minutes ahead of schedule she was seated in the upstairs waiting-room, no longer thinking of Kevin Costyn and his former classmates – but of herself.

'How are you feeling?' asked Basil Shepstone, a large, balding, slightly stooping South African.

'You want me to undress?'

'I'd love you to undrress,' he said with that characteristic rolling of the 'r'. 'No need today, though. Next time, I'll insist.'

His friendly brown eyes were suddenly sad, and he reached across to place his right hand on her shoulder.

'You want the good news first? Or the bad news?' he asked quietly.

'The good news.'

'Well, your condition's fairly stable. And that's good – that's very good news.'

Julia found herself swallowing hard. 'And the bad news?'

'Well, it's not exactly bad news. Shall I read it?'

Julia could see the Oxfordshire Health Authority heading on the letter, but no more. She closed her eyes.

'It says ... blah, blah, blah ... "In the event of any deterioration, however, we regret to have to inform Mrs Stevens that her condition is inoperable."'

'They can't operate if it gets worse, they mean?'

Shepstone put down the letter. 'I prrefer your English to theirs.'

She sighed deeply; then opened her eyes and looked at him, knowing that she loved him for everything he'd tried to do for her. He had always been so gentle, so kindly, so professional; and now, watching him, she could understand why his eyes remained downcast as his Biro hatched the 'O' of 'Oxfordshire'.

'How long?' she asked simply.

He shook his head. 'Anyone who prredicts something like that – he's a fool.'

'A year?'

'Could be.'

'Six months?'

He looked defeated as he shrugged his broad shoulders.

'Less?'

'As I say—'

'Would you give up work if you were me?'

'Fairly soon, I think, yes.'

'Would you tell anyone?'

He hesitated. 'Only if it were someone you loved.'

She smiled, and got to her feet. 'There are not many people I love. You, of course – and my cleaning-lady – with whom incidentally' – she consulted her wrist-watch – 'in exactly one hour's time, I have a slap-up lunch engagement at the Old Parsonage.'

'You're not inviting me?'

She shook her head. 'We've got some very private things to discuss, I'm afraid.'

After Mrs Stevens had left, the consultant took a handkerchief from his pocket and quickly wiped his eyes. What the dickens was he supposed to say? Because it never really did much good to lie. Or so he believed. He blamed himself, for example, for lying so blatantly to the woman who'd died only two days previously – lying to Mrs Phillotson.

Not much difference in the case-histories.

No hope in either.

CHAPTER EIGHTEEN

Dead flies cause the ointment of the apothecary to send forth a stinking savour: so doth a little folly him that is in reputation for wisdom and honour

(*Ecclesiastes*, ch. 10, v. 1)

MORSE NOW realized that he would have few, if any, further cases of murder to solve during his career with Thames Valley CID. All right, orchestral conductors and High Court judges could pursue their professions into their twilight years, regardless – indeed sometimes completely oblivious – of their inevitably deteriorating talents. But more often than not policemen finished long before any incipient senility; and Morse himself was now within a couple of years of normal retirement.

For many persons it was difficult to tell where the dividing line came between latish middle age and advisable pensionability. Perhaps it had something to do with the point at which nostalgia took over from hope; or perhaps with a sad realization that it was no longer possible to fall in love again; or, certainly in Morse's case, the time when, as now, he had to sit down on the side of the bed in order to pull his trousers on.

Such and similar thoughts were circulating in Morse's mind as on Saturday, 3 September, the morning after his visit with Lewis to Wolsey (and the statement made, immediately thereafter, by Mrs Ewers), he sat in the Summertown Health Centre.

A mild cold had, as usual with Morse, developed into a fit of intermittently barking bronchitis; but he comforted himself with the thought that very shortly, after a sermon on the stupidity of cigarette-smoking, he would emerge from the Centre with a slip of paper happily prescribing a dose of powerful antibiotics.

Clutching his prescription, Morse was about to leave when he remembered *The Times*, left in his erstwhile seat in the waiting-room. Returning, he found that his earlier companions – the anorexic girl and the spotty-faced, overweight youth – had now been joined by a slatternly-looking, slackly dressed young woman, with rings in her nostrils; a woman to whom Morse took an immediate and intense dislike.

Predictably so.

From the chair next to the newcomer he picked up his newspaper, without a word; though not without a hurried glance into the woman's dull green eyes, the colour of the Oxford Canal along by Wolvercote. And if Morse had waited there only a few seconds longer, he would have heard someone call her name: 'Eleanor Smith?'

But Morse had gone.

She'd already got the address of an abortion clinic; but one of her friends, an authority in the field, had informed her that it was now closed. So! So she'd have to find some other place. And the quack ought to be able to point her somewhere not too far away, surely? That's exactly the sort of thing quacks were there for.

In a marked police car, standing on a Strictly Doctors Only lot in the Centre's very restricted parking-area, Lewis sat thinking and waiting; waiting in fact, quite patiently, since the case appeared to be developing in a reasonably satisfactory way.

When, the previous afternoon, Susan Ewers had made (and signed) her statement, many things already adumbrated by Morse had dawned at last on Lewis's understanding.

Suspicion, prima facie, could and should now be levelled against Mr Edward Brooks, the man who had been Mrs Ewers' immediate predecessor as scout on Staircase G in Drinkwater Quad. Why? Morse's unusually simple and unspectacular hypothesis had been stated as follows:

It should be assumed, in all probability, that Brooks had played a key rôle, albeit an intermediary one, in supplying a substantial quantity of drugs to the young people living on his staircase – including Matthew Rodway; that Rodway's suicide had necessarily resulted in some thorough investigation by the college authorities into the goings-on on the staircase; that McClure, already living on the same staircase anyway, had become deeply involved – indeed had probably been the prime mover in seeing that Brooks was 'removed' from his post (coincidentally at the same time as McClure's retirement); that, as Mrs Ewers had now testified, the former scout had continued his trafficking in drugs, and that this information had somehow reached McClure's ears; that McClure had threatened Brooks with exposure, disgrace, criminal prosecution, and almost certain imprisonment; that finally, at a showdown in Daventry Court, Brooks had murdered McClure.

Such a hypothesis had the merit of fitting all the known facts; and if it could be corroborated by the new facts which would doubtless emerge from the meeting arranged for that afternoon at the Pitt Rivers Museum . . .

Yes.

But there was the 'one potential fly in the ointment', as Lewis had expressed himself half an hour earlier.

And Morse had winced at the phrase. 'The cliché's bad enough in itself, Lewis – but what's a "potential fly" look like when it's on the window-pane?'

'Dunno, sir. But if Brooks *was* ambulanced off that Sunday with a heart attack—'

'Wouldn't *you* be likely to have a heart attack if you'd just killed somebody?'

'We can check up straightaway at the hospital.'

'All in good time,' Morse had said. 'You'll have *me* in hospital if you don't get me down to the Health Centre . . .'

Still thinking and still waiting, Lewis looked again at the brief supplementary report from the police pathologist, which had been left on Morse's desk that morning.

Attn. Det. C.I. Morse.

No more re time of McClure's death – but confirmation re probable 'within which': 8 a.m.–12 a.m. 28 Aug. Little more on knife/knife-thrust: blade unusually (?) broad, 4–5 cms and about 14–15 cms in length/penetration. Straight through everything with massive internal and external bleeding (as reported). Blade not really sharp, judging by ugly lacerations round immediate entry-area. Forceful thrust. Man rather than woman? Perhaps woman with

good wrist/arm (or angry heart?). Certainly one or two of our weaker (!) sex I met a year ago on a martial arts course. Full details available if required.
All very technical – but possibly helpful?
                                    Laura Hobson

'At least she understands the full-stop,' Morse had said.

Never having really mastered the full-stop himself, Lewis had refrained from any comment.

Yet they both realized the importance of finding the knife. Few murder prosecutions were likely to get off on the right foot without the finding of a weapon. But they hadn't found a weapon. A fairly perfunctory search had earlier been made by Phillotson and his team; and Lewis himself had instigated a very detailed search of the area surrounding Daventry Court and the gardens of the adjacent properties. But still without success.

Anyway, Morse was never the man to hunt through a haystack for a needle. Much rather he'd always seek to intensify (as he saw it) the magnetic field of his mind and trust that the missing needle would suddenly appear under his nose. Not much intensification as yet, though; the only thing under Morse's nose lately – and that under a towel – had been a bowl of steaming Friar's Balsam.

But here came Morse at last (10.40 a.m.), cum prescription. And Lewis could predict the imminent conversation:

'Chemist just around the corner, Lewis. If you'd just nip along and . . . I'd be grateful. Only problem' – searching pockets – 'I seem . . .'

Lewis was half right anyway.

'There's a chemist's just round the corner. If you'd be so good? I don't know how much these wretched Tories charge these days but' – searching pockets – 'here's a tenner.'

Lewis left him there on the reserved parking lot, just starting *The Times* crossword; and walked happily up to Boots in Lower Summertown.

What was happening to Morse?

The third item appearing on Julia Stevens' agenda the previous day had been postponed. On her arrival at the Old Parsonage

Hotel, a telephone message was handed to her: Mrs Brooks would not be able to make the lunch; she was sorry; she would ring later if she could, and explain; please not to ring her.

Understandably, perhaps, Julia had not felt unduly disappointed, for her mind was full of other thoughts, especially of herself. And she enjoyed the solitude of her glass of Bruno Paillard Brut Premier Cru (daring!) seated on a high stool at the Parsonage Bar, before walking down to the taxi-rank by the Martyrs' Memorial and thence being driven home in style and in a taxi gaudily advertising the Old Orleans Restaurant and Cocktail Bar.

It was not until later that evening that her brain began to weave its curious fancies about what exactly could have caused the problem . . .

Brenda Brooks rang (in a hurry, she'd said) just before the *Nine O'Clock News* on BBC1. Could they make it the next day, Saturday? A bit earlier? Twelve – twelve noon, say?

After she had put down the phone, Julia sat silently for a while, staring at nothing. A little bit odd, that – Brenda ringing (almost certainly) from a telephone-box when she had a phone of her own in the house. It would be something – everything – to do with that utterly despicable husband of hers. For from the very earliest days of their marriage, Ted Brooks had been a repulsive fly in the nuptial ointment; an ointment which had, over the thirteen increasingly unhappy and sometimes desperate years (as Julia had learned), regularly sent forth its stinking savour.

CHAPTER NINETEEN

The true index of a man's character is the health of his wife
(CYRIL CONNOLLY)

AS BRENDA BROOKS waited at the bus-stop that Saturday morning, then again as she made her bus journey down to Carfax, a series of videos, as it were, flashed in a nightmare of repeats across her mind; and her mood was an amalgam of anticipation and anxiety.

It had been three days earlier, Wednesday, 31 August, that she'd been seen at the Orthopaedic Clinic . . .

*

'At least it's not made your fracture.'

'Pardon, doctor?' So nervous had she been that many of his words made little or no sense to her.

'I said, it's not a major fracture, Mrs Brooks. But it *is* a fracture.'

'Oh deary me.'

But she'd finally realized it was something more than a sprain – that's why she'd eventually gone to her GP, who in turn had referred her to a specialist. And now she was hearing all about it: about the meta-something between the wrist and the fingers. She'd try to look it up in that big dark blue *Gray's Anatomy* she'd often dusted on one of Mrs Stevens' bookshelves. Not too difficult to remember: she'd just have to think of 'met a couple' – that's what it sounded like.

'And you'll be very sensible, if you can, to stop using your right hand completely. No housework. Rest! That's what it needs. The big thing for the time being is to give it a bit of support. So before you leave, the nurse here'll let you have one of those "Tubigrips" – fits over your hand like a glove. And, as I say, we'll get you in just as soon as, er . . . are you a member of BUPA, by the way?'

'Pardon?'

'Doesn't matter. We'll get you in just as soon as we can. Only twenty-four hours, with a bit of luck. Just a little op to set the bone and plaster you up for a week or two.'

'It's not quite so easy as that, Doctor. My husband's been in hospital for a few days. He's had a bit of a heart attack, and he's only just home this morning, so . . .'

'We can put you in touch with a home-help.'

'I can do a *little* bit of housework, can't I?'

'Not if you're sensible. Can't you get a cleaning-lady in for a couple of days a week?'

'I *am* a cleaning-lady,' she replied, at last feeling that she'd rediscovered her bearings; re-established her identity in life.

She'd hurried home that morning, inserting and turning the Yale key with her left hand, since it was becoming too painful to perform such an operation with her right.

'I'm back, Ted!'

Walking straight through into the living-room, she found her husband, fully dressed, lounging in front of the TV, his fingers on the black control-panel.

'Christ! Where the 'ell a' you bin, woman?'

Brenda bit her lip. 'There was an emergency – just before my turn. It held everything up.'

'I thought *you* were the bloody emergency from all the fuss you've bin making.'

'Baked beans all right for lunch?'

'*Baked beans?*'

'I've got something nice in for tea.'

A few minutes later she took a tin of baked beans from a pantry shelf; and holding it in her right hand beneath a tin-opener fixed beside the kitchen door, she slowly turned the handle with her left. Slowly – yes, very slowly, like the worm that was finally turning . . .

And why?

If ever Brenda Brooks could begin to contemplate the murder of her husband, she would surely acknowledge as her primary, her abiding motive, the ways in which mentally and verbally he had so cruelly abused her for so long.

But no!

Belittlement had been her regular lot in life; and on that score he was, in reality, robbing her at most of a dignity that she had never known.

Would the underlying motive then be found in the knowledge of her husband's sexual abuse of an adolescent and increasingly attractive step-daughter?

Perhaps.

But it was all so much simpler than that. One thing there had been in her life – just the one thing – in which she could rejoice, in which until so very recently she *had* rejoiced: the skills she had acquired with her hands. And Edward Brooks had robbed her of them; had robbed her even of the little that she had, which was her all.

And for that she could never forgive him.

Brenda decided she needn't replay *all* that last bit to Mrs Stevens; but she did need to explain what had gone wrong the day before. Not that there was much to say, really. What was it *he*'d said when she'd told him she'd been invited out to lunch with Mrs S?

'Well if you think you're going to leave me this lunchtime, you bloody ain't, see? Not while I'm feeling groggy like this.'

Why had she ever married the man?

She'd known it was a mistake even before that ghastly wedding – as she'd prayed for God to boom down some unanswerable objection from the hammer-beam roof when the vicar had invited any just cause or impediment. But the Voice had been silent; and the invited guests were seated quietly on each side of the nave; and the son of Brenda's only sister (a sub-postmistress in Inverness), a spotty but mellifluous young soprano, was all rehearsed to render the 'Pie Jesu' from the Fauré *Requiem*.

Often in life it was difficult enough to gird up one's loins and go through with one's commitments. On this occasion, though, it had been far more difficult *not* to do so . . .

But at least Ted Brooks had relented somewhat, that previous evening – *and she knew why.* He'd decided he was feeling a whole lot better. He thought he might venture out – *would* venture out – into the big wide world again: the big wide world in this case being the East Oxford Conservative Club, well within gentle walking distance, where (he said) he'd be glad to meet the lads again, have a pint – even try a frame of snooker, perhaps. *And* he'd have a bite to eat in the club there; so she needn't bother 'erself about any more bloody baked beans.

Brenda had almost been smiling to herself that evening, when on the pretext of getting another pint of milk from the corner-shop she'd given Mrs S a quick ring from the nearby BT kiosk, just before nine o'clock.

But what . . . what about those other two things?

She was a good ten minutes early; and in leisurely, but tremulous, fashion, she crossed the Broad and walked up St Giles'; past Balliol College; past St John's College; past the Lamb and Flag; and then, waiting for the traffic lights just before Keble Road, she'd quickly checked (yet again) that the letter was there in her handbag.

For a few moments this letter almost assumed as much importance as that second thing – the event which had caught her up in such distress, such fear, since the previous Sunday, when her husband had returned home, the stains on the lower front of his shirt and the top of his grey flannel trousers *almost* adequately concealed by a beige summer cardigan (new from M&S); but only by the *back* of this cardigan, since the front of it was saturated with much blood. And it was only later that she'd noticed the soles of his trainers . . .

Opposite her, the Green Man flashed, and the bleeper bleeped; and Mrs Brenda Brooks walked quickly over to the Old Parsonage Hotel, at Number 1, Banbury Road.

CHAPTER TWENTY

When you live next to the cemetery, you cannot weep for everyone

(Russian proverb)

THE OLD PARSONAGE HOTEL, dating back to 1660, and situated between Keble College to the east and Somerville College to the west, stands just north of the point where the broad plane-tree'd avenue of St Giles' forks into the Woodstock Road to the left and the Banbury Road to the right. Completely refurbished a few years since, and now incorporating such splendid twentieth-century features as *en suite*, centrally heated bedrooms, the stone-built hotel has sought to preserve the intimacy and charm of former times.

With success, in Julia Stevens' judgement.

In the judgement, too, of Brenda Brooks, as she seated herself in a wall-settee, in front of a small, highly polished mahogany table in the Parsonage Bar, lushly carpeted in avocado green with a tiny pink-and-peach motif.

'Lordy me!' Brenda managed to say in her soft Oxfordshire burr, gently shaking her tightly curled grey hair.

Whether, etymologically speaking, such an expression of obvious approval was a conflation of 'Lord' and 'Lumme', Julia could not know. But she was gratified with the reaction, and watched as Brenda's eyes surveyed the walls around her, the lower half painted in gentle gardenia; the upper half in pale magnolia, almost totally covered with paintings, prints, cartoons.

'Lordy me!' repeated Brenda in a hushed voice, her vocabulary clearly inadequate to elaborate upon her earlier expression of delight.

'What would you like to drink?'

'Oh, coffee, please – that'll be fine.'

'No, it won't. I insist on something stronger than coffee. Please!'

Minutes later, as they sipped their gin and slimline tonics, they read through the menu: Julia with the conviction that this was an imaginative selection of goodies; Brenda with more than a little puzzlement, since many of the imported words therein – Bagel, Couscous, Hummus, Linguini, Mozzarella – had never figured in her own cuisine. Indeed, the sight of such exotic fare might well, a decade or so back, have prompted within her a stab of some sympathy with a husband constantly complaining about baked beans, about sardines, about spaghetti . . .

In the past, yes.

But no longer.

'What's it to be, then?'

Brenda shook her head. 'I'm sorry, but I just can't eat anything. I'm all – I'm all full up, Mrs Stevens, if you know what I mean.'

Julia was too sensible to argue; and in any case she understood only too well, for she'd experienced exactly the same the day before when she'd sat on a bar-stool there, alone, feeling . . . well, feeling 'all full up', as Brenda had so economically phrased it.

Half an hour later, as she was finishing her Poached Salmon with Lemon Butter, Salad, and New Potatoes, Julia Stevens had been put in the (latest) picture about Ted Brooks. She'd known all about the verbal abuse which had led to a broken heart; and now she learned of the physical abuse which had led to a broken hand.

'I'm so wicked – did you know that? You know why? I wished' (she whispered closely in Julia's ear) 'I wished him dead! Can you believe that?'

Most people in your position would have *murdered* him, you dear old thing, said Julia, but only to herself. And suddenly the realization that such a viciously cruel man should have ruined the life of such a sweet and lovable woman made her so very angry. Yet, at the same time, so very much in control.

Was it perhaps that the simultaneous keeping of her *own* secret with the hearing of *another's* was an unsuspected source of strength? But Julia had no opportunity of pursuing this interesting line of thought, for Brenda now opened her handbag and passed over the letter she'd received the previous Tuesday – not through the post, but pushed by hand through her letter-box.

'Just read it, please! No need to say anything.'

As Julia put on her school-ma'amish spectacles, she was aware that the woman seated beside her was now in tears.

The silent weeping had subsided into intermittent snuffling as Julia finished reading the agonized and agonizing pages.

'My God,' she whispered.

'But that's not all. There's something else – something even worse. I shall just have to tell somebody, Mrs Stevens – if you can bear it.'

CHAPTER TWENTY-ONE

Hate is the consequence of fear; we fear something before we hate it. A child who fears becomes an adult who hates
(CYRIL CONNOLLY, *The Unquiet Grave*)

Dear mum – dearest mum!

Its been a long time hasn't it and I didn't really want to write but I can't talk about it, I just can't. I was never much good with words but I'm going to try. Its about why I left home and how I couldn't really ever tell you about it. I'm writing now because my friend at the hospital told me about <u>him</u> and she said he's a lot better and going home soon – and all I want you to do is let him get very much worse again and don't look after him – just let him die that's what I want because he bloody deserves it! You thought I left because I hated school and dreamt of boys and sex and got mixed up with drugs and all the punk scene and all that, and you were right in a way because I did. But you got upset about the wrong things, that's what I'm saying. Why did I leave <u>you</u> mum – tell me that. You can't think it was much fun for me with sod all to pay for anything and nowhere to bloody go, I'd just got one thing going for me and that was what you and dear old dad gave me, a good pair of thighs and a good pair of tits all the randy buggers wanted to get their hands on and believe me they paid good money for it. All I'm saying mum is I never really had to slum it after those first few weeks in London anyway. I never had the guts to tell you why but I've got to tell you now so here goes. Don't get too upset about it all, well not about me anyway, just about that horny bastard you married thirteen years ago.

I was thirteen when it started and we had the flu together him and me and so you remember we were both in bed when you went off cleaning one Thursday morning, you see I even remember the day of the week, and he came into my bedroom about eleven and brought me a cup of bovril and he said how nice looking I was getting and what a nice little figure I was getting and all that bullshit and how proud he was to have a daughter like me, well a step-daughter. Then he put his arm round me and started rubbing my neck and back a bit through my pajamas and told me to relax because that would do me good and soon I was lying down again with my back to him, and then I'm not sure how it happened but he was lying down and I could feel his hand inside my pajama top and he was feeling me, and I didn't know what to do because for a start I just thought he was being affectionate and I didn't want to upset him because we'd both be embarassed if I tried to push him away. Please mum try to understand! Perhaps its difficult to know where the line comes between affection and sex but I knew because I felt something hard against me and I knew what it was. I just felt scared then like that first day in school when I was in a room I shouldn't have been in and when I just got kept in for what wasn't my fault at all, but I thought it was my fault. Oh mum I'm not explaining things very well. And then he grabbed my hand and pulled it back behind him and pushed it inside his pajamas and told me to rub him, and I just didn't know what I was doing. It was the first time I'd ever felt a man like that and he was sort of silky and warm and I felt afraid and fascinated at the same time. All I know is I'd done what he wanted before I had the chance of thinking about what I was doing and suddenly there was all that sticky stuff all over my pajama bottoms, and you won't remember but when you came home I told you I'd put them in the washing machine because I'd been sweating. Afterwards he kept on saying that it was me who'd agreed to do it, me who'd started it all not him.

Mum! He was a wicked liar, but even if it was just one per cent me you've got to forgive me. He made the most of everything, my God he did. He said if I told you about what he'd done he'd tell you about what I done, and I got scared stiff you'd find out, and it was like blackmail all the time those next three awful years when he made me do everything he wanted. You could never believe how I loathed him, even the sight of him, I hated him more than I've ever hated anybody since. Well that's it mum, I wonder what your thinking. He's a shit and I never never never want to see him again unless its to stick a bloody great big knife in his great fat gut and watch him squirm and hear him squeal like the great fat pig he is. And if you want any help with sticking the fucking pig you just let me know because I'll only be too glad to help. There's only one other thing to tell you and perhaps its why I've written to you now. I've always kept in touch with Auntie Beryl, its been a secret but she's always let me know how you are and she wrote a fortnight ago and told me how he's been treating you mum – you must have let her know. Your mad to stick it, your a matyr that's what you are. I've just read through all this and I know one thing I said you can do but you can't – not yet – and that's get in touch with me, but its better that way though don't be surprised if you see me. Not just yet though, its been such a long long time and I can't quite face it, not yet. I love you mum, I shall always love you better than anybody.
One last thing and its odd really but I read in the Oxford—

Julia turned over the page but that was the finish: the last part of the letter was missing.

CHAPTER TWENTY-TWO

We all wish to be of importance in one way or another
(RALPH WALDO EMERSON, *Journals*)

LEWIS, on his way for an appointment with the House Matron of Wolsey, had dropped Morse in the Broad, where the Chief Inspector had swilled down a double dosage of penicillin pills with a pint of Hook Norton in the White Horse, before making his way to the Pitt Rivers Museum of Ethnology and Pre-History – for his own appointment.

Sooner or later, inevitably, a golden afternoon will captivate the visitor to Oxford; and as he walked leisurely up Parks Road, past the front of Wadham on his right, past the blue wrought-iron gates at the back of Trinity on his left, Morse felt deeply grateful that he had been privileged to spend so much of his lifetime there.

And one of those captivated visitors might have noticed a smile of quiet satisfaction around Morse's lips that early afternoon as he turned right, just opposite Keble, into the grounds of the Oxford University Museum – that monument to the nineteenth-century Gothic Revival, and the home of the Dodo and the Dinosaur. Some clouds there were in the pale blue sky that September day: some white, some grey; but not many.

No, not many, Morse.

Oddly, he'd enjoyed the short walk, although he believed that the delights of walking were often ludicrously exaggerated. *Solvitur ambulando*, though, as the Romans used to say; and even if the 'ambulando' was meant to be a figurative rather than a physical bit of 'walking' – well, so much the better. Not that there was anything intrinsically wrong with the occasional bit of physical walking; after all, Housman had composed some of his loveliest lyrics while walking around the Backs at Cambridge, after a couple of lunchtime beers.

Solvitur ambulando, yes.

Walk along then, Morse, since perhaps you are now walking towards the solution.

On the stone steps leading up to the entrance porch, he read the notice:

> ## THIS MUSEUM IS OPEN
> ## TO THE PUBLIC
> 12 a.m.–4.30 p.m. Mon–Sat.

It was already past noon, and on the grass a large party of visiting schoolchildren were unharnessing rucksacks and extracting packed lunches as Morse walked hurriedly by. It wasn't that he positively disliked schoolchildren; just that he didn't want to meet any of them.

Inside the glass-roofed, galleried building, Morse continued on his course, quickly past a huge reconstruction of a dinosaur ('Bipedal, but capable of quadripedal locomotion'); quickly past some assembled skeletons of African and Asian elephants. Nor was he long (if at all) detained by the tall show-cases displaying their specimens of the birds and insects of Australasia. Finally, after making his way between a statue of the Prince Consort and a well-stuffed ostrich, Morse emerged from the University Museum into the Pitt Rivers Museum; where he turned right, and knocked on the door of the Administrator.

Capital 'A'.

'Coffee?' she invited.

'No thanks. I've just had some.'

'Some beer, you mean.'

'Is it that obvious?'

'Yes.'

She was a tall, slim woman in her mid-forties, with prematurely white hair, and an attractively diffident smile about her lips.

'Some women,' began Morse, 'have an extraordinarily well-developed sense of smell—' But then he stopped. For a second or two he'd anticipated a little mild flirtation with Jane Cotterell. Clearly it was not to be, though, for he felt her clear, intelligent eyes upon him, and the tone of her voice was unambiguously no-nonsense:

'How can I help you?'

For the next ten minutes she answered his questions.

Brooks had joined the eight-strong team of attendants at the Pitt Rivers Museum – quite separate from the University Museum

– almost exactly a year ago. He worked a fairly regular thirty-five-hour week, 8.30 a.m. to 4.30 p.m., with an hour off for lunch. The attendants had the job of cleaning and maintaining the premises; of keeping a watchful eye on all visitors, in particular on the many school-parties regularly arriving by coach from near and far; sometimes of performing specific tasks, like manning the museum shop; of being helpful and courteous to the public at all times – 'more friendly than fierce'; and above all, of course, of safeguarding the unrivalled collection of anthropological and ethnographic items housed in the museum . . .

'A unique museum, Inspector.'

'Do you ever get anybody trying to steal things?'

'*Very* rarely. Last summer we had someone trying to get into the case with the shrunken heads in it, but—'

'Hope you caught him.'

'*Her*, actually.'

'I'd rather rob a bank, myself.'

'I'd rather not rob at all.'

Morse was losing out, he realized that; and reverted to his questioning about Brooks.

The man was, in the Administrator's view, competent in his job, not frightened of work, punctual, reasonably pleasant with the public; private sort of person, though, something of a loner. There were certainly some of his colleagues with slightly more endearing qualities.

'If you'd known what you know now, would you have appointed him?'

'No.'

'Mind if I smoke?' asked Morse.

'I'd rather you didn't.'

'Did *he* smoke?'

'Not in the museum. No one smokes in the museum.'

'In the Common Room, or whatever you have?'

'I don't know.'

'You don't associate him with drugs at all?'

She glanced at him keenly before replying. 'There are no drugs here – not on my staff.'

'You'd know – if there were?'

'As you say, some women have a particularly well-developed sense of smell, Inspector.'

Morse let it go. 'Have you still got his references?'

The Administrator unlocked a filing-cabinet beside her and

produced a green folder marked 'BROOKS, E.'; and Morse looked
through the half-dozen sheets it contained: Brooks's CV; a carbon
of the letter appointing him w.e.f. 1 September 1993; a photocopied page giving details of Salary, National Insurance, Job
Specification, Shift-Patterns; two open, blandly worded testimonials; and one hand-written reference, equally bland.

Morse read this last item a second time, slowly.

> To the Administrator, Pitt Rivers Museum
> Dear Madam,
>   I understand that Mr Edward Brooks
> has applied to you for the post (as
> advertised in the University Gazette, June
> '93) of Assistant Attendant at the Museum.
>   Brooks has worked as a scout at Wolsey
> College for almost ten years and I
> recommend to you his experience and
> diligence.
>   Yours sincerely,
>   Felix McClure (Dr)

Well, well.

'Did you know Dr McClure?' asked Morse.

'No. And I shan't have a chance of knowing him now, shall I?'

'You heard . . . ?'

'I read it in the *Oxford Mail*. I know all about Mr Brooks's
illness too: his wife rang through early on Monday morning. But
from what they say he's on the mend.'

Morse changed tack once more. 'I know a lot of the exhibits
here are invaluable; but . . . but are there things here that are just
plain *valuable*, if you know what I mean? Commercially valuable,
saleable . . . ?'

'My goodness, yes. I wouldn't mind getting my fingers on
some of the precious stones and rings here. Or do I mean *in* some
of them?'

But Morse appeared to miss the Administrator's gentle
humour.

'Does Mr Brooks have access to, well, to almost everything
here really?'

'Yes, he does. Each of the attendants has a key to the wall-safe where we keep the keys to all the cabinets and drawers and so on.'

'So, if he took a fancy to one of your shrunken heads?'

'No problem. He wouldn't have to use a crowbar.'

'I see.'

Jane Cotterell smiled, and thereby melted a little more of Morse's heart.

'Do I gather you want me to show you a bit about the security system here?'

'Not really,' protested Morse.

She rose to her feet. 'I'd better show you then.'

Twenty minutes later they returned to her office.

'Thank you,' said Morse. 'Thank you for your patience and your time. You're a very important person, I can see that.'

'Really? How—?'

'Well, you've got a capital "A" for a start; then you've got a wall-to-wall carpet; and for all I know you've not only got a parking space, you've probably got one with your name on it.'

'No name on it, I'm afraid.'

'Still . . .'

'What about you?'

'I've got my name on the door, at least for the present. But I've only got a little carpet, with a great big threadbare patch where my megapodic sergeant stands.'

'Is there such a word – "megapodic"?'

'I'll look it up when I get home. I've just treated myself to the *Shorter Oxford*.'

'Where is your home?'

'Top of the Banbury Road . . . Anywhere near you?'

'No. That's quite a way from where I live.' For a few seconds her eyes looked down at the carpet – that old carpet of hers, whose virtues had so suddenly, so unexpectedly expanded.

Only semi-reluctantly, a few minutes earlier, had Brenda Brooks been persuaded to hand over the last sheet of her daughter's letter. Its content, as Julia saw things, was very much as before. But, yes, it *was* a bit self-incriminating; especially that rather fine passage just before the end:

He's undermined everything for me mum, including sex!
But the very worst thing he ever did was to make me feel it
could all have been my fault. Mum! Mum! He's bloody
fucked up my life, and if he ever turns up murdered
somewhere you'll know it was *me*, alright?

Strangely, however, Julia had experienced little sense of shock.
A hardening of heart, rather; and a growing conviction that if
Brooks *were* to turn up murdered somewhere his step-daughter
would not be figuring alone on any list of possible suspects.

CHAPTER TWENTY-THREE

One night I contrived to stay in the Natural History Museum,
hiding myself at closing time in the Fossil Invertebrate Gallery,
and spending an enchanted night alone in the museum, wandering from gallery to gallery with a flashlight
(OLIVER SACKS, *The Observer*, 9 January 1994)

MORSE SPENT a while wandering vaguely around the galleries.
On the ground floor he gave as much of his attention as he could
muster to the tall, glass show-cases illustrating the evolution
of fire-arms, Japanese Noh masks, the history of Looms and
Weaving, old musical instruments, shields, pots, models of boats,
bull-roarers, North American dress, and a myriad precious and
semi-precious stones . . .

Then, feeling like a man who in some great picture gallery has
had his fill of fourteenth-century crucifixions, he walked up a
flight of stone steps to see what the Upper Gallery had to offer;
and duly experienced a similar sense of satiety as he ambled
aimlessly along a series of black-wood, glass-topped display-
cases, severally containing scores of axes, adzes, tongs, scissors,
keys, coins, animal-traps, specialized tools . . . Burmese, Siamese,
Japanese, Indonesian . . .

In one display-case he counted sixty-four Early Medical Instruments, each item labelled in a neat manuscript, in black ink on a
white card, with documentation of provenance and purpose
(where known). Among these many items, all laid out flat on

biscuit-coloured backing-material (clearly recently renovated), his attention was drawn to a pair of primitive tooth-extractors from Tonga; and not for the first time he thanked the gods that he had been born after the general availability of anaesthetics.

But he had seen quite enough, he thought, wholly unaware, at this point, that he had made one extraordinarily interesting observation. So he decided it was time to leave. Very soon Lewis would be at the front waiting for him. Lewis would be on time. Lewis was always on time.

For the moment, however, he was conscious that there was no one else around in the Upper Gallery. And suddenly the place had grown a little forbidding, a little uncanny; and he felt a quick shiver down his spine as he made his way back into the main University Museum.

But even here it was quieter now, more sombre, beneath the glass-roofed atrium, as if perhaps a cloud had passed across the sun outside. And Morse found himself wondering what it would be like to be in this place, be locked in this place, when everyone else had gone; when the schoolchildren were back on their coaches; when the rest of the public, when the attendants, when the Administrator had all left . . . Then perhaps, in the silent, eerie atmosphere, might not the spirits of the Dodo and the Dinosaur, never suspecting their curious extinction, be calling for their mates again on some primeval shore?

Jane Cotterell sat at her desk for several minutes after the door had closed behind Morse. She shouldn't really have said that about the beer. Silly of her! Why, she could just do with a drink herself, and it would have been nice if he'd asked her out for a lunchtime gin. She felt herself wishing that he'd forgotten something: a folding umbrella or a notebook or something. But as she'd observed, the Inspector had taken no notes at all; and outside, the sun now seemed to be shining gloriously once more.

CHAPTER TWENTY-FOUR

Cruelty is, perhaps, the worst kind of sin. Intellectual cruelty is certainly the worst kind of cruelty

(G. K. CHESTERTON, *All Things Considered*)

AFTER READING the (now complete) letter, Julia Stevens re-arranged the pages and read them again; whilst beside her, in a semi-distraught state, sat the original addressee; for whom, strangely enough, one of the most disturbing aspects of the letter was the revelation that her sister Beryl had told her niece the events of that terrible night. Had she (Brenda) made too much of everything when Ted had handled her so roughly? Had it been as much an accident as an incident? But no. No, it hadn't. And whether her account of it had been exaggerated or whether it had been understated – either to her sister over the phone or to her employer in person – certain it was that the recollection of that night in May would remain ever vivid in Brenda's memory . . .

'You're ever so late, Ted. What time is it?'

'Twelve, is it?'

'It's far later than that.'

'If you know what the bloody time is, why the 'ell do you ask me in the first place?'

'It's just that I can't get off to sleep when I know you're still out. I feel worried—'

'Christ! You want to worry when I start gettin' in 'alf-past bloody three, woman.'

'Come to bed now, anyway.'

'I bloody shan't – no!'

'Well, go and sleep in the spare room, then – I've got to get some sleep.'

'All the bloody same to me, innit – if I go in there, or if I stay in 'ere. Might just as well a' bin in different rooms all the bloody time, you know that. Frigid as a fuckin' ice-box! That's what you are. Always 'ave bin.'

'That's just not fair – that's not fair, what you just said!'

'If the bloody cap fits—'

'It can't go on like this, Ted – it just *can't*. I can't stick it any more.'

'Well, bloody *don't* then! Sling your 'ook and go, if you can't stick it! But just stop moanin' at me, d'you hear? Stop fuckin' *moanin'*! All right?'

She was folding her candlewick dressing-gown round her small figure and edging past him at the foot of the double bed, when he stopped her, grabbing hold of her fiercely by the shoulders and glaring furiously into her face before pushing her back.

'You stay where you are!'

Twice previously he had physically maltreated her in a similar way, but on neither occasion had she suffered physical hurt. That night, though, she had stumbled – *had* to stumble – against the iron fireplace in the bedroom; and as she'd put out her right hand to cushion the fall, something had happened; something had snapped. Not that it had been too painful. Not then.

As a young girl Brenda had been alongside when her mother had slipped in the snow one February morning and landed on her wrist; broken her wrist. And passers-by had been so concerned, so helpful, that as she'd sat in the Casualty Department at the old Radcliffe Infirmary, she'd told her daughter that it had almost been worthwhile, the accident – to discover such unsuspected kindness.

But that night Ted had just told her to get up; told her not to be such a bloody ninny. And she'd started to weep then – to weep not so much from pain or shock but from the humiliation of being treated in such a way by the man she had married ...

Julia handed back the letter.

'I think she hates him even more than you do.'

Brenda nodded miserably. 'I must have loved him once, though, mustn't I? I suppose he was – well, after Sid died – he was just *there* really. I suppose I needed something – somebody – and Ted was there, and he made a bit of a fuss of me – and I was lonely. After that ... but it doesn't matter any more.'

For a while there was a silence between the two women.

'Mrs Stevens?'

'Yes?'

'What about this other thing? What am I going to do about it? Please help me! Please!'

It was with anger that Julia had listened to Brenda's earlier confidences; with anger, too, that she had read the letter. The man was an animal – she might have known it; had known it. But the possibility that he was a *murderer*? Could Brenda have got it all wrong? Ridiculously wrong?

Julia had never really got to know Ted Brooks. In the early days of Brenda working for her, she'd met him a few times – three or four, no more. And once, only once, had she gone round to the Brooks's house, when Brenda had been stricken with some stomach bug; and when, as she had left, Ted Brooks's hand had moved, non-accidentally, against her breasts as he was supposedly helping her on with her mackintosh.

Take your horny hands off me, you lecherous sod, she'd thought then; and she had never seen him since that day. Never would, if she could help it. Yet he was not an ill-looking fellow, she conceded that.

The contents of the letter, therefore, had come as something less of a shock than may have been expected, since she had long known that Brenda had fairly regularly been on the receiving end of her husband's tongue and temper, and had suspected other things, perhaps . . .

But Brooks a *murderer*?

She looked across with a sort of loving distress at the busy, faithful little lady who had been such a godsend to her; a little lady dressed now in a navy-blue, two-piece suit; an oldish suit certainly, yet beautifully clean, with the pleats in the skirt most meticulously pressed for this special occasion. She felt an overwhelming surge of compassion for her, and she was going to do everything she could to help. Of course she was.

What about 'this other thing', though? My God, what could she do about that?

'Brenda? Brenda? You know what you said about . . . about the blood? Are you sure? Are you *sure*?'

'Mrs Stevens?' Brenda whispered. 'I wasn't going to tell you – I wasn't even going to tell *you*. But yes, I *am* sure. And shall I tell you why I'm sure?'

It was twenty-past two when Julia's taxi dropped Brenda – not immediately outside her house, but very close, just beside the Pakistani grocer's shop on the corner.

'Don't forget, Brenda! Make sure you run out of milk again

370 THE FOURTH INSPECTOR MORSE OMNIBUS

tonight. Just before nine. And don't say or do anything before then. Agreed? Bye.'

On her way home, Julia spotted the *Oxford Mail* placard outside a newsagent's in the Cowley Road:

> POLICE
> HUNT
> MURDER
> WEAPON

and she asked the taxi-driver to stop.

Just before 3 p.m., Ted Brooks was lining up the shot, his eyes coolly assessing the angle between the white cue-ball and the last colour. Smoothly his cue drove through the line of his aim, and the black swiftly disappeared into the bottom right-hand pocket.

His opponent, an older man, slapped a pound coin down on the side of the table.

'Not done your snooker much harm, Ted.'

'No. Back at work in a fortnight, so the doc says. With a bit o' luck.'

CHAPTER TWENTY-FIVE

The older I grow, the more I distrust the familiar doctrine that age brings wisdom

(H. L. MENCKEN)

As MORSE had expected, Lewis was already sitting waiting for him outside the museum.

'How did things go, sir?'

'All right.'

'Learn anything new?'

'Wouldn't go quite so far as that. What about you?'

'Interesting. That woman, well – she's a sort of major-domo – Amazonian type, sir. I wouldn't like her as Chief Constable.'

'Give it five years, Lewis.'

'Anyway, it's about Matthew Rodway. In the autumn term—'

'We call it the Michaelmas Term here, Lewis.'

'In the Michaelmas Term, in his third year, when he was back in college again—'

'In the House.'

'In the House again, he was sharing rooms with another fellow—'

'Another undergraduate.'

'Another undergraduate called Ashley Davies. But not for long, it seems. Davies got himself temporarily booted out of college—'

'Rusticated.'

'Rusticated that term. Some sort of personal trouble, she said, but didn't want to go into it. Said we should see Davies for ourselves, really.'

'Like me, then, you didn't learn very much.'

'Ah! Just a minute, sir,' smiled Lewis. 'Mr Ashley Davies, our undergraduate, in the Michaelmas Term 1993, was rusticated from the House on the say-so of one Dr Felix McClure, former Student – capital "S", sir – of Wolsey College.'

'The plot thickens.'

'Bad blood, perhaps, sir? Ruined his chances, certainly – Davies was expected to get a First, she'd heard. And he didn't return this year, either. Murky circumstances ... Drugs, do you think?'

'Or booze.'

'Or love.'

'Well?'

'I've got his address. Living with his parents in Bedford.'

'Did any good thing ever come out of Bedford?'

'John Bunyan, sir?'

'You go and see him, then. I can't do everything myself.'

'What's wrong?' asked Lewis quietly.

'I dunno. My chest's sore. My legs ache. My head's throbbing. I feel sick. I feel sweaty. It's the wrong question, isn't it? You mean, what's *right*?'

'Have you had your pills?'

'Course I have. Somebody's got to keep fit.'

'When were you last fit, sir?'

Morse pulled the safety-belt across him and fumbled for a few seconds to fix the tongue into the buckle.

'I don't ever remember feeling really fit.'

'I'm sure you'll blast my head off, sir, but—'

'I ought not to drink so much.'

'I wouldn't be surprised if you'd just washed your pills down with a pint.'

'Would you be surprised if you were quite wrong about that?'

'Washed 'em down with *two* pints, you mean?'

Morse smiled and wiped his forehead with a once-white handkerchief.

'You know the difference between us, sir – between you and me?'

'Tell me.'

'I got married, and so I've got a missus who's always tried to look after me.'

'You're lucky, though. Most people your age are divorced by now.'

'You never – never met a woman – you know, the right woman?'

Morse's eyes seemed focused far away. 'Nearly. Nearly, once.'

'Plenty of time.'

'Nonsense! You don't start things at my age. You pack 'em up. Like the job, Lewis.' Morse hesitated. 'Look, I've not told anybody yet – well, only Strange. I'm packing in the job next autumn.'

Lewis smiled sadly. 'Next Michaelmas, isn't it?'

'I could stay on another couple of years after that but . . .'

'Won't you miss things?'

'Course I bloody won't. I've been very lucky – at least in that respect. But I don't want to push the luck too far. I mean, we might get put on to a case we can't crack.'

'Not this one, I hope?'

'Oh no, Lewis, not this one.'

'What's the programme—?'

But Morse interrupted him: 'You just asked me if I'll miss things and I shan't, no. Only one thing, I suppose. I shall miss you, old friend, that's all.'

He had spoken simply, almost awkwardly, and for a little while Lewis hardly trusted himself to look up. Somewhere behind his eyes he felt a slight prickling; and somewhere – in his heart, perhaps – he felt a sadness he could barely comprehend.

'Not getting very far sitting here, Lewis, are we? What's the programme?'

'That's what I just asked you.'

'Well, there's this fellow from Bedford, you say?'

'Former undergraduate, sir.'

'Yes, well – is he at home?'

'Dunno. I can soon find out.'

'Do that, then. See him.'

'When—?'

'What's wrong with now? The way you drive you'll be back by teatime.'

'Don't *you* want to see him?'

Morse hesitated. 'No. There's something much more important for me to do this afternoon.'

'Go to bed, you mean?'

Slowly, resignedly, Morse nodded. 'And try to fix something up with Brooks. Time we paid him a little visit, isn't it?'

'Monday?'

'What's wrong with tomorrow? That'll be exactly a week after he murdered McClure, won't it?'

CHAPTER TWENTY-SIX

Three may keep a secret if two of them are dead
(BENJAMIN FRANKLIN)

BRENDA BROOKS was in a state of considerable agitation when she went through into the kitchen to put the kettle on. But at least she was relieved to be home before *him*; to have time for a cup of tea; to try to stop shaking. The anguish, the sheer misery of it all, were as strong as ever; with only her growing fear a new element in the tragedy . . .

After the first inevitable bewilderment – after the uncompre-hending questions and the incomprehensible answers – her immediate reaction had been to wash the bloodstained clothing – shirt, trousers, cardigan; but instead, she had followed the fierce instructions given from the invalid's bed that the clothes be carted off to the rubbish dump, and that the affair never be referred to again.

Yet there the event stood – whatever had happened, whatever it all meant – forming that terrible and terrifying secret between them, between husband and wife. No longer a proper secret, though, for she had shared that secret . . . those secrets; or would it not be more honest to say that she had betrayed them? Particularly, therefore, did her fear centre on his return now: the fear that when he came in he would only have to look at her – *to know*. And as she squeezed the tea-bag with the tongs, she could do nothing to stop the constant trembling in her hands.

Automatically almost, between sips of tea, she wiped the tongs clean of any tannin stain and replaced them in the drawer to the right of the sink, in the compartment next to the set of beautifully crafted knives which her sister Beryl had given her for her first wedding – knives of many shapes and sizes, some small and slim, some with much longer and broader blades, which lay there before her in shining and sharpened array.

The phone rang at 2.45 p.m.: the Pitt Rivers Museum.

The phone rang again just before 3 p.m.: Mrs Stevens.
    'Is he home yet?'
    'No.'
    'Good. Now listen!'

The front door slammed at 3.20 p.m., when, miraculously as it seemed to Brenda, the shaking in her hands had ceased.

Almost invariably, whenever he came in, she would use those same three words: 'That you, Ted?' That afternoon, however, there was a change, subconscious perhaps, yet still significant.

'That you?' she asked in a firm voice. Just the two words now – as if the query had become depersonalized, as if she could be asking the information of anyone; dehumanized, as if she could be speaking to a dog.

As yet, still holding out on the battlefield, was a small fortress. It was likely to collapse very soon, of course; but there was the possibility that it might hold out for some little time, since it had been recently reinforced. And when the door had slammed shut she had been suddenly conscious – yes! – of just a little power.

'That you?' she repeated.
    'Who do you think it is?'
    'Cup o' tea?'

'You can get me a can o' beer.'

'The museum just rang. The lady wanted to know how you were. Kind of her, wasn't it?'

'Kind? Was it fuck! Only wanted to know when I'd be back, that's all. Must be short-staffed – that's the only reason she rung.'

'You'd have thought people would be glad of a job like that, with all this unemployment—'

'Would be, wouldn't they, if they paid you decent bloody rates?'

'They pay you reasonably well, surely?'

He glared at her viciously. 'How do you know that? You bin lookin' at my things when I was in 'ospital? Christ, you better not 'a bin, woman!'

'I don't know what they pay you. You've never told me.'

'Exackly! So you know fuck-all about it, right? Look at *you*! You go out for that bloody teacher and what's 'er rates, eh? Bloody slave-labour, that's what you are. Four quid an hour? Less? Christ, if you add up what *she* gets an hour – all those 'olidays and everything.'

Brenda made no answer, but the flag was still flying on the small fortress. And, oddly enough, he was right. Mrs Stevens *did* pay her less than £4 an hour: £10 for three hours – two mornings a week. But Brenda knew why that was, for unlike her husband her employer had told her exactly where she stood on the financial ladder: one rung from the bottom. In fact, Mrs Stevens had even been talking that lunchtime of having to get rid of her B-registration Volvo, which stood in one of the rundown garages at the end of her road, rented at £15 per calendar month.

As Brenda knew, the protection which that rusting, corrugated shack could afford to any vehicle was minimal; but it did mean that the car had a space – which was more than could be said for the length of road immediately outside Julia's own front door, where so often some other car or van was parked, with just as much right to do so as she had (so the Council had informed her). It wasn't that the sale of the old Volvo ('£340, madam – no, let's make it £350') would materially boost her current account at Lloyds; but it would mean a huge saving on all those other wretched expenses: insurance, road tax, servicing, repairs, MOT, garaging . . . what, about £800 a year?

'So why keep it?' that's what Julia had asked Brenda.

She would have been more honest if she had told Brenda why

she was going to sell it. But that lunchtime, at least, the telling of secrets had been all one-way traffic.

After dropping off the drooping Morse, Lewis returned to Kidlington HQ, where before doing anything else he looked at the copy of the *Oxford Mail* that had been left on Morse's desk. He was glad they'd managed to get the item in – at the bottom of page 1:

MURDERED DON

The police are appealing for help in their inquiries into the brutal murder of Dr Felix McClure, discovered knifed to death in his apartment in Daventry Court, North Oxford, last Sunday.

Det. Sergeant Lewis, of Thames Valley C.I.D., informed our reporter that in spite of an extensive search the murder weapon has not been discovered.

Police are asking residents in Daventry Avenue to help by searching their own properties, since it is believed the murderer may have thrown the knife away as he left the scene.

The knife may be of the sort used in the kitchen for cutting meat, probably with a blade about 2″ broad and 5–6″ in length. If found it should be left untouched, and the police informed immediately.

CHAPTER TWENTY-SEVEN

Men will pay large sums to whores
For telling them they are not bores
(W. H. AUDEN, *New Year Letter*)

LATER THAT afternoon it was to be the B–B–B route: Bicester–Buckingham–Bedford. Fortunately for Lewis the detached Davies' residence was on the western outskirts of Bedford; and the door of 248 Northampton Road was answered immediately – by Ashley Davies himself.

After only a little skirmishing Davies had come up with his

own version of the events which had preceded the showdown between himself and Matthew Rodway . . . and Dr Felix McClure: an old carcass whose bones Lewis had been commissioned to pick over yet again.

Davies had known Matthew Rodway in their first year together. They'd met in the University Conservative Association (Lewis felt glad that Morse was abed); but apart from such political sympathy, the two young men had also found themselves fellow members of the East Oxford Martial Arts Club.

'Judo, karate – that sort of thing?' Lewis, himself a former boxer, was interested.

'Not so much the physical side of things – that was part of it, of course. But it's a sort of two-way process, physical and mental; mind and body. Both of us were more interested in the yoga side than anything. You know, "union" – that's what yoga means, isn't it?'

Lewis nodded sagely.

'Then you get into TM, of course.'

'TM, sir?'

'Transcendental Meditation. You know, towards spiritual well-being. You sit and repeat this word to yourself – this "mantra" – and you find yourself feeling good, content . . . happy. Everything was OK, between Matthew and me, until this girl, this woman, joined. I just couldn't take my eyes off her. I just couldn't think of anything else.'

'The TM wasn't working properly?' suggested Lewis helpfully.

'Huh! It wasn't even as if she was attractive, really. Well, no. She *was* attractive, that's the whole point. Not beautiful or good-looking, or anything like that. But, well, she just had to look at you really, just look into your eyes, and your heart started melting away.'

'Sounds a bit of a dangerous woman.'

'You can say that again. I took her out twice – once to the Mitre, once to The Randolph – and she was quite open about things. Said she'd be willing to have sex and so on: fifty quid a time; hundred quid for a night together. No emotional involvement, though – she was very definite about that.'

'You agreed?'

'Well, I couldn't afford that sort of money. Hundred? Plus a B&B somewhere? But I did ask her about coming up to my room one evening – that was just after I'd started sharing with Matthew – when he had to go home for a family funeral. But it was a

Tuesday, I remember, and she said she had to be very careful which day of the week it was. She could only do Saturday or perhaps Sunday because she knew somebody on the staircase and she wasn't prepared to take any risks.'

'What risks?'

'I don't know.'

'One of the other students – undergraduates there?'

For the first time the casually dressed, easy-mannered Davies hesitated. 'She didn't say.'

'Who else could it have been?'

Davies shrugged, but made no reply.

'There were two dons on the staircase, I understand – "Students" don't you call them?'

'Only a bloody pedant would call 'em Students these days.'

'I see. And, er, Dr McClure was one of those dons.'

'You've done your homework.'

'Go on please, sir.'

'Well, I had to go up for a Civil Service Selection thing on November the fifth, Bonfire Night, in Whitehall. Whole weekend of it – Friday, Saturday, Sunday. Anyway, I got so pissed off with all the palaver that I didn't stay for the Sunday session. I caught the ten-something from Paddington back to Oxford on Saturday night and when I got back to the staircase – well, there they were. We had two single beds in the one room, you see; and she was in his bed, and he was in mine. I don't quite know why, but it just made me see red and . . .'

'You'd tried to do the same yourself, though, so you said?'

'I know, yes.'

'You were just jealous, I suppose?'

'It was more than that. It's difficult to explain.'

'You mean, perhaps, if she'd been in *your* bed . . . ?'

'I don't know. You'd have to ask Freud. Anyway, I went berserk. I just went for him, that's all. He'd got nothing on – neither of 'em had – and soon we were wrestling and punching each other and knocking everything all over the bloody place, and there must have been one helluva racket because there was this great banging on the door and, well, we quietened down and I opened the door and there – there he was: that stuffed prick McClure. Well, that's about it, really. Matthew'd got a cut on his mouth and one of his eyes was badly bruised; I'd got a gash on my left arm but . . . no great damage, not considering. McClure wanted to know all about it, of course: who the girl was—'

'Who was she?'

'She called herself Ellie – Ellie Smith.'

'Then?'

'Well, they put me in one of the guest rooms in Great Quad, and Ellie went off – I think McClure put her in a taxi – and that was that. The Senior Tutor sent for me the next morning, and you know the rest.'

'Why didn't Mr Rodway get rusticated too?'

'Well, I'd started it. My fault, wasn't it?'

'Wasn't he disciplined at all?'

'Warned, yes. You get a warning in things like that. Then, if it happens again . . .'

Lewis thought he was beginning to get the picture. 'And perhaps you'd already had a warning yourself, sir?' he asked quietly.

Unblinking, the thickset Davies looked for several seconds into Lewis's eyes before nodding. 'I'd had a fight in a pub in my first year.'

'Much damage done then?'

'He broke his jaw.'

'Don't you mean *you* broke his jaw, sir?'

It was a pleasant little rejoinder, and perhaps Davies should have smiled. But Lewis saw no humour, only what he thought may have been a hint of cruelty, in the young man's eyes.

'You've got it, Sergeant.'

'Was that over a woman as well?'

'Yeah, 'fraid so. There was this other guy and he kept, you know, messing around a bit with this girl of mine.'

'Which pub was that?'

'The Grapes – in George Street. I think this guy thought it was called The Gropes.'

'And you hit him.'

'Yeah. I'd told him to fuck off.'

'And he hadn't.'

'Not straightaway, no.'

'But later he wished he had.'

'You could say that.'

'How did it get reported?'

'The landlord called the police. Bit unlucky, really. Wasn't all that much of a fight at all.'

Lewis consulted his notes. 'You wouldn't say you "went berserk" on that occasion?'

'No.'

'Why do you reckon you got so violent with Mr Rodway, then?'

Davies stared awhile at the carpet, then answered, though without looking up. 'It's simple, really. I was in love with her.'

'And so was Mr Rodway?'

Davies nodded. 'Yeah.'

'Have you seen her since?'

'A few times.'

'Recently?'

'No.'

'Can you tell me why you didn't go back to Oxford – to finish your degree? You were only rusticated for a term, weren't you?'

'Rest of the Michaelmas *and* all the Hilary. And by the time I was back, what with Finals and everything . . . I just couldn't face it.'

'How did your parents feel about that?'

'Disappointed, naturally.'

'Have you told them why I'm here today?'

'They're on a cruise in the Aegean.'

'I see.' Lewis stood up and closed his notebook and walked over to the window, enviously admiring the white Porsche that stood in the drive. 'They've left you the car, I see?'

'No, that's mine.'

Lewis turned. 'I thought you – well, you gave me the impression, sir, that fifty pounds might be a bit on the expensive side . . .'

'I came into some money. That's perhaps another reason I didn't go back to Oxford. Rich aunt, bless her! She left me . . . well, more than enough, let's say.'

Lewis asked a final question as the two men stood in the front porch: 'Where were you last Sunday, sir?'

'Last *Sunday*?'

'Yes. The day Dr McClure was murdered.'

'Oh dear! You're not going to tell me . . . ? What possible reason could I have—'

'I suppose you could say it was because of Dr McClure that . . .'

'That they kicked me out? Yes.'

'You must have hated him for that.'

'No. You couldn't really hate him. He was just an officious bloody bore, that's all.'

'Did you know that he fell in love with Ellie Smith too?'

Davies sighed deeply. 'Yes.'

'Last Sunday, then?' repeated Lewis.

'I went bird-watching.'

'On your own?'

'Yes. I went out – must've been about nine, half-nine? Got back about three.'

'Whereabouts did you go?'

Davies mentioned a few names – woods or lakes, as Lewis assumed.

'Meet anyone you knew?'

'No.'

'Pub? Did you call at a pub? Hotel? Snackbar? Shop? Garage?'

'No, don't think so.'

'Must have been quite a lot of other bird-watchers around?'

'No. It's not the best time of year for bird-watching. Too many leaves still on the trees in late summer. Unless you know a bit about flight, song, habitat – well, you're not going to spot much, are you? Do you know anything about bird-watching, Sergeant?'

'No.'

As Lewis left, he noticed the RSPB sticker on the rear window of a car he would have given quite a lot to drive. Perhaps not so much as fifty pounds, though.

CHAPTER TWENTY-EIGHT

> I do not love thee, Doctor Fell,
> The reason why I cannot tell,
> But this one thing I know full well:
> I do not love thee, Doctor Fell
> (THOMAS BROWN, *I Do Not Love Thee, Doctor Fell*)

STANDING QUITE still behind the curtained window of the first-floor front bedroom, she looked down across the drive at the departing policeman. She had a very good idea of what the interview had been about. Of course she had.

She was completely naked except for the dressing-gown (his) draped around a figure which was beginning to wobble dangerously between the voluptuous and the overblown – the beginnings of a pot-belly quite certainly calling for some fairly regular visits to the Temple Cowley pool in East Oxford, to plough through some thirty or forty lengths a time (for she was an excellent swimmer).

The smell of her was seductive though, she knew that. How else, with that posh eau-de-toilette just squirted everywhere about her person? 'Mimosa Pour Moi' – the last thing Felix had bought her.

Felix . . .

Always (above all perhaps?) he'd adored the sight and the smell of her when she'd just finished drying herself after one of her frequent baths. And how she treasured that letter – well, sort of letter – he'd written that morning in a posh London hotel as he'd sat waiting (and waiting and waiting) to go down to breakfast whilst she reclined luxuriously, reluctant to make any decisive move from the bath-tub.

How she loved a long, hot bath.

Yummy!

And how she loved what he'd written – one of the very few things she carried around in that scuffed shoulder-bag of hers:

> I ask my darling if she is ready for breakfast; and she
> stands in front of me; and with a synchronized circular
> swish of her deodorant-can, she sprays first her left armpit,
> then her right.
>   But she gives no answer.
> I ask my darling if she has been thinking of me during our
> night together; and she forms her lips into a moue and
> rocks her right hand to and fro, as if she was stretching it
> forward to steady a rickety table on the stone-flagged floor
> at The Trout.
>   But she gives no answer.
> I ask my darling why she can't occasionally be more
> punctual for any rendezvous with me; and I would be so
> glad if she could speak and dip into a pool of unconvincing
> excuses.
>   But she gives no answer.
> I ask my darling what she loves most of all in her life; and
> she smiles (at last, a smile!) and she points behind her to
> the deep, scented water in which she has just been soaking

and poaching, her full breasts seemingly floating on the
surface.

It is, I must suppose, the nearest I shall ever come to an
answer.

She'd read it many, many times. Above all she enjoyed reading
about herself in the third person. It was as if she were a key
character in some *roman-à-clef* (Felix had told her about that sort
of book – told her how to pronounce it): a character far more
important on the page than in reality. Oh, yes. Because in real life
she wasn't important at all; nor ever would be. After all, she
wouldn't exactly be riding up to the abortion clinic that Wednesday in a Roller, now would she? God, no. Just standing on that
perishing Platform Number 2, waiting for the early bloody train
up to bloody Birmingham.

Ashley Davies opened the bedroom door and walked up behind
her, unloosening the belt of her (his) dressing-gown.

'God, am I ready—'

But she slipped away from him – and slipped out of the
dressing-gown, fixing first her black suspender-belt, then her
black bra; then pulling a thin dark blue dress over her ridiculously colourful head before hooking a pair of laddered black
stockings up her legs.

Davies had watched her, silently. He felt almost as sexually
aroused by watching her dress as watching her undress.

At last he spoke:

'What's the matter? What have I done wrong?'

She made no reply, but stood tip-tilting her chin towards the
dressing-table mirror as she applied some transparent substance
to her pouting lips.

'Ellie!'

'I'm off.'

'What d'you mean, you're off? I'm taking you out to lunch,
remember?'

'I'm off.'

'You can't do this to me!'

'Just watch me!'

'Is it the police?'

'Could be.'

'But he's gone – it's over – it's all right.'

She picked up a small, overnight grip of faded pink canvas, inscribed with the names of pop groups and punk stars.

'I'm off.'

'When do I see you again?'

'You don't.'

'Ellie!'

'I don't want to see you any more.' (It seemed a long sentence.)

Davies sat down miserably on the side of the double bed in which he and Ellie had slept – half slept – the previous night.

'You don't love me at all, do you?'

'No.'

'Have you ever loved me?'

'No.'

'Did you love Matthew?'

'No.'

'Don't tell me you loved McClure? Don't tell me you loved *that* prick?'

'About the only thing about him I did love.'

'Christ! You shouldn't *say* things like that.'

'Why ask, then?'

'Have you ever loved anybody?'

'Me mum, yeah.'

'Nobody else?'

'Me dad – me real dad, I suppose. Can't remember.'

With a series of upward brushes she applied some black colouration to her eyelashes.

'Where d'you think you're going now?'

'Oxford.'

Davies sighed miserably, stood up, and reached inside his trouser-pocket for his car-keys.

'Come on, then.'

'I'm not going with *you*.'

'What's that supposed to mean?'

'I'll hitch a lift.'

'You can't do that.'

'Course I bloody can. That's all they're lookin' for, most of these lecherous sods. All I gotta do—'

'*Ellie!*'

'First car, like as not. You see.'

*

In fact, Ellie Smith's prediction was unduly optimistic, since the first car drove past her with little observable sign of interest, no detectable sign of deceleration.

The second car did exactly the same.

But not the third.

CHAPTER TWENTY-NINE

My predestinated lot in life, alas, has amounted to this: a mens not particularly sana in a corpore not particularly sano
(VISCOUNT MUMBLES, *Reflections on My Life*)

ON THE following day, Sunday 4 September, Ted Brooks was sitting up in bed, two pillows behind his back, reading the more salacious offerings in the *News of the World*. It was exactly 11.30 a.m., he knew that, since he had been looking at his wrist-watch every minute or so since 11.15.

Now, for some reason, he began to feel slightly less agitated as the minute-hand moved slowly up in the climb towards the twelve – the 'prick of noon', as Shakespeare has it. His mind, similarly, was moving slowly; perhaps it had never moved all that quickly anyway.

Whatever happened, though, he was going to make the most of his heart attack – his 'mild' heart attack, as they'd assured him in the Coronary Care Unit. Well, he hoped it was mild. He didn't want to die. Course he bloody didn't. Paradoxically, however, he found himself wishing it wasn't *all that* mild. A heart attack – whatever its measurement on the Richter Scale – was still a heart attack; and the maximum sympathy and attention should be extracted from such an affliction, so Brenda'd better bloody understand *that*.

He shouted downstairs for a cup of Bovril. But before the beverage could arrive, he heard the double-burred ring of the telephone: an unusual occurrence in the Brooks's household at any time; and virtually unprecedented on a Sunday.

He got out of bed, and stood listening beside the bedroom door as Brenda answered the call in the narrow entrance-hall at the bottom of the stairs.

'Oh, I see . . .'

'I do understand, yes . . .'

'Look, let me try to put him on . . .'

She found him sitting on the side of the bed, pulling on his socks.

'Thames Valley Police, Ted. They want to come and talk to you.'

'Christ!' he hissed. 'Don't they know I've only just got out of 'ospital?'

Brenda's upper lip was trembling slightly, but her voice sounded strangely calm. 'Would you like to speak to him yourself? Or tell me what to say? I don't care – but don't let's keep him waiting.'

'What's 'is name, this feller?'

'Lewis. Detective Sergeant Lewis.'

Lewis put down the phone.

Like Brooks a few minutes earlier, he was sitting on the side of the bed – Morse's bed.

'That's fixed that up, then, sir. I still feel you'd be better off staying in bed, though.'

'Nonsense!'

Lewis looked with some concern across at his chief, lying back against three pillows, in pyjamas striped in maroon, pale blue, and white, with an array of bottles and medicaments on the bedside table: aspirin, Alka Seltzer, indigestion tablets, penicillin, paracetamol – and a bottle of The Macallan, almost empty.

He looked blotchy.

He looked ghastly.

'No rush, is there, sir?' Lewis asked in a kindly manner.

'Not much danger of me rushing today.' Morse put down the book he'd been reading, and Lewis saw its title: *The Anatomy of Melancholy*.

'Trying to cheer yourself up, sir?'

'Oddly enough, I am. Listen to this: "There is no greater cause of melancholy than idleness; no better cure than busyness" – that's what old Burton says. So tell me all about Bedford.'

So Lewis told him, trying so very hard to miss nothing out; and conscious, as always, that Morse would probably consider of vital importance those things he himself had assumed to be obviously trivial.

And vice versa, of course.

Morse listened, with only the occasional interruption.

'So you can see, sir, he's not got much of an alibi, has he?'

'Lew-is! We won't *want* another suspect. We know who killed McClure: the fellow we're off to see this afternoon. All we're looking for is a bit more background, a slightly different angle on things. We can't take Brooks in yet – well, we *can*; but he's not going to run away. We ought to wait for a bit more evidence to accumulate.'

'We certainly haven't got much, to be truthful, have we?'

'You've still got people looking for the knife?'

Lewis nodded. 'Eight men on that, sir. Doing the houses Phillotson's lads didn't – along most of the road, both sides.'

Morse grunted. 'I don't like this fellow Brooks.'

'You've not even *seen* him yet.'

'I just don't like this drugs business.'

'I doubt if Davies had any part in that. Didn't seem the type at all.'

'Just in on the sex.'

'He fell for that woman in a pretty big way, no doubt about that.'

'Mm. And you say there may have been somebody in the house while you were there?'

'As I say, I heard the loo flushing.'

'Well, a trained detective like you would, wouldn't he?'

'When the cat's away . . .'

'Looks like it.'

'I think he's the sort of fellow who just welcomes all the floozies with open arms—'

'And open flies.'

'You don't think . . .' The thought struck Lewis for the first time. 'You don't think . . . ?'

'The loo-flusher was one and the same as our staircase Lulu? No. Not a chance. Forget it! The really interesting thing is what Davies told you about her – about Ellie Smith, or whatever her name is.'

Morse broke off, wearily, wiping the glistening perspiration from his forehead with a grubby white handkerchief taken from his pyjama top – top number three, in fact, for he had already sweated his way through two pairs of pyjamas since taking to his bed the previous afternoon.

'Did you take your dose this morning, sir?'

Morse nodded. 'Double dose, Lewis. That's always been the secret for me.'

'I meant the medicine, not the Malt.'

Morse grinned weakly, his forehead immediately prickling with moisture once more, like a windscreen in persistent drizzle.

He lit a cigarette; and coughed revoltingly, his chest feeling like a chunk of excoriated flesh. Then spoke:

'She said she couldn't see him on a weekday, right? Saturday OK, though, and perhaps Sunday. Why? Pretty clearly because she knew somebody there on the staircase; and you thought – be honest, now! – you thought it must be somebody who buggered off to his cottage in the Cotswolds somewhere every weekend, and left the coast clear. You thought it was one of the two Students, didn't you? You thought it was McClure.'

'To be honest with you, I didn't, no. I thought it was somebody who didn't work after Saturday lunchtime until starting up again on Monday morning. I thought it was the scout. I thought it was Brooks.'

'Oh!'

'Wasn't I supposed to think that?'

Morse wiped his brow yet again. 'I'm not really up to things at the minute, am I?'

'No, I don't think you are.'

'Oh!'

'I think Brooks wasn't just a pusher; I think he was a pimp as well. And it was probably too risky for him to let any of his girls get into the college – into the *House*, sir. So, if this particular girl *was* going to get in, it was going to be at weekends, when he wasn't there, when she could make her own arrangements, take her own risks, and set her own fee – without cutting him in at all.'

Morse was coughing again. 'Why don't I put you in charge of this case, Lewis?'

'Because I couldn't handle it.'

'Don't you think you can handle Brooks?'

'No.'

'You think we ought to wait a couple of days, don't you – before we see him?'

'Yes.'

'And you think I'll agree to that?'

'No.'

Morse closed Burton's immortal work, and folded the duvet aside.

'Will you do me a quick favour, Lewis, while I get dressed?'

'Course.'

'Just nip out and get me the *News of the World*, will you?'

CHAPTER THIRTY

Randolph, you're not going to like this, but I was in bed with your wife

(*Murder Ink: Alibis we never want to hear again*)

AT 1.15 P.M., on the way to the Brooks's residence in East Oxford, they had called briefly at Daventry Avenue. Still no sign of any murder weapon.

'Give 'em a chance,' Lewis had said.

Morse had insisted on taking the Jaguar, with Lewis driving: he thought the finale of *Die Walküre* might well refresh his drooping spirits, and the tape (he said) was already in position there. But strangely enough he hadn't turned it on; even more strangely he appeared ready to engage in conversation in a car.

Most unusual.

'You ought to invest in a bit of Wagner, Lewis. Do you far more good than all that rubbish you play.'

'Not when you're there, I don't.'

'Thank God!'

'I don't get on to you, for what you like.'

'What do *you* like best?'

Lewis came up to the roundabout at the Plain, and took the second exit, the one after St Clements, into the Cowley Road.

'I'll tell you what I can't stand, sir – the bagpipes.'

Morse smiled. 'Somebody once said that was his favourite music – the sound of bagpipes slowly fading away into the distance.'

It was a quarter to two when Ted and Brenda Brooks, side by side on the living-room settee, sat facing the two detectives:

Morse in the only armchair there, Lewis on an upright chair imported for the occasion from the kitchen.

Brooks himself, in his late forties, dressed in a white, short-sleeved shirt and well-pressed grey slacks, looked pale and strained. But soon he appeared to relax a little, and was confirming, with an occasional nod of his greying head, the background details which Morse now briefly rehearsed: his years as a scout at Wolsey, where he had got to know Matthew Rodway ('Yup'); and Dr McClure ('Yup'); his present employment at the Pitt Rivers Museum ('Yup').

The skirmishing had been very civilized, and Mrs Brooks asked them all if they'd like a cup of tea.

But Morse declined, speaking, as it appeared, for all three of them, and turning back to Brooks and to the trickier part of the examination paper.

'Do you want your wife to be here, sir, while I ask you – I'm sorry – some rather awkward questions?'

'She stays. You stay, don't you, Bren? Nothing she shouldn't know about, Inspector.'

Lewis watched the man carefully, but could see no greater signs of nervousness than was normal among witnesses being interviewed by the police. Wasn't *she*, Mrs Brooks, the more obviously nervous of the two?

'Mr Brooks,' Morse began. 'I know you've been in hospital, but please bear with me. We have evidence that there was some trading in drugs on your old staircase over the last three or four years.'

'Nothin' to do wi' me if there was.'

'You knew nothing of it?'

'No.'

'It's difficult for us, you see, because we have a statement to the effect that you did know something about it.'

'Christ! I'd like to know who it was as told you that. Load o' bloody lies!'

'You'd have no objections to coming along to HQ and going through that statement with us?'

'I can't – not just now, I can't – but I will – I'll be 'appy to – when I'm better. You don't want to give me another bloody 'eart attack, do you?'

Brooks's manner of speaking, which had begun in a gentle Oxfordshire burr, had suddenly switched into the coarse articulation with which he was wont to address his wife.

'Would you have known, Mr Brooks, if there had been drugs?'

'No job o' mine to interfere. Everybody's got their own lives to live.'

'There were parties there, on the staircase?'

'You try an' stop 'em!'

'Did *you* try?'

'If you talk to people they'll all tell you I were a good scout. That's all that worried me.'

'I'm afraid we shan't be able to talk to Dr McClure, shall we?'

'There's others.'

'Did you like Dr McClure?'

'OK, yeah.'

'You both left at the same time, I believe.'

'So wha'?'

'I just wondered if you had a farewell drink together, that's all.'

'Don't know much about Town and Gown, do you?'

Morse turned to Lewis. 'Sergeant?'

'We've obviously got to interview anyone, sir, who had a link with Dr McClure. That's why we're here, as I told you on the phone. So I shall have to ask you where you were last Sunday – Sunday the twenty-eighth of August.'

'Huh! Last Sunday?' He turned to his wife. 'Hear that, Bren? Not bloody difficult, that one, is it? You tell 'em. You remember better 'an I do. Bloody 'ell! If you reckon I 'ad anything to do wi' *that* – last *Sunday*? Christ!'

Brenda Brooks folded her hands nervously in her lap, and for the first time Morse noticed that the right hand, beneath an elastic support, might be slightly deformed. Perhaps she held them to stop them shaking? But there was nothing she could do about her trembling upper lip.

'Well ... Ted woke me about three o'clock that Sunday morning—'

'More like 'alf-two.'

'—with this awful pain in his chest, and I got up to find the indigestion tablets and I made a cup o' tea and you seemed better, didn't you, Ted? Well, a bit better anyway and I slept a bit and he did, just a bit, but it was a bad night.'

'Terrible!'

'I got up at six and made some more tea and asked Ted if he wanted any breakfast but he didn't and the pain was still there, and I said we ought to ring the doctor but Ted said not yet, well, you know, it was Sunday and he'd have to come out special, like. Anyway he got up about ten because I remember we sat in the kitchen listening to *The Archers* at quarter-past while I got the meat ready – lamb and mint sauce – but Ted couldn't face it. Then about half-past one, quarter to two, it got so bad, well, it was no good hanging on any longer and I rang the ambulance and they came in about . . . well, it was only about ten minutes – ever so quick. He was on a machine at half-past two – about then, weren't you, Ted?'

'Intensive Care,' said the ex-scout, not without a touch of pride. 'The pain 'ad got t'rific – I knew it were summat serious. Told you so at the time, didn't I, Bren?'

Brenda nodded dutifully.

It had immediately become clear to Morse that there was now a very considerable obstacle between him and any decision to arrest Edward Brooks on suspicion of murder; a considerable objection even to leaving his name on the list of suspects – which indeed would be a dramatic setback for the whole case, since Brooks's name was the *only* one appearing on Morse's list.

He looked across now at the faithful little lady sitting there in her skirt and summer blouse next to her husband. If she persisted in her present lies (for Morse was convinced that such they were) it was going to be extremely difficult to discredit her testimony, appearing, as she did, to possess that formidable combination of nervousness and innocence. Any jury would strongly sympathize.

Morse changed tack completely.

'Do you know, I'm beginning to feel a bit thirsty, Mrs Brooks. Does that offer of a cuppa still stand?'

After Mrs Brooks had put the kettle on and taken the china cups from the dresser, she stood close to the kitchen door. Her hearing was still good. It was the white-haired one who was speaking . . .

'Have you got a car, sir?'

'Not 'ad one for ten year or more.'

'How do you get to work?'

'Still go on the bus, mostly.'

'You don't bike?'

'Why d'you ask that?'

'I saw your cycling helmet in the hall, that's all.'

'So?'

'Didn't mind me asking, did you?'

'Why the 'ell should I?'

'Well, Dr McClure was knifed to death, as you know, and there was an awful lot of blood all over the place – and all over the murderer, like as not. So if he'd driven off in a car, well . . . these clever lads in the labs, they can trace the tiniest speck of blood . . .'

'As I said, though, I 'aven't got a car.'

'I still think we'd quite like to have a look at your bike. What do you think, Sergeant Lewis?'

'Not a question of "liking", sir. I'm afraid we shall *have* to take it away.'

'Well, that's where you're wrong, 'cos I 'aven't got no bike no longer, 'ave I? Bloody stolen, wasn't it? Sat'day lunchtime, that were – week yesterday. Just went to the Club for a pint and when I got out – there it was, gone! Lock 'n' all on the back wheel. Ten bloody quid, that fancy lock cost me.'

'Did you report the theft, sir?'

'Wha'? Report a stolen bike? In Oxford? You must be jokin'.'

Mrs Brooks came in with a tray.

'I must ask you to report the theft of your bike, sir,' said Lewis quietly. 'To St Aldate's.'

'Milk and sugar, Inspector?'

For the first time her eyes looked unflinchingly straight into his, and suddenly Morse knew that behind the nervousness, behind the fear, there lay a look of good companionship. He smiled at her; and she, fleetingly, smiled back at him.

And he felt touched.

And he felt poorly again.

And he felt convinced that he was sitting opposite the man who had murdered Felix McClure; felt it in his bones and in his brains; would have felt it in his soul, had he known what such a thing was and where it was located.

When ten minutes later Mrs Brooks was about to show them out, Morse asked about the two photographs hanging on the wall of the entrance-hall.

'Well, that one' – she pointed to a dark, broody-looking girl in her mid-teens or so – 'that's my daughter. That's Ellie. Her first name was Kay, really, but she likes to be called Ellie.'

Phew!

With an effort, Lewis managed not to exchange glances with Morse.

'That one' – she pointed to a photograph of herself arm-in-arm, in front of a coach, with a younger, taller, strikingly attractive woman – 'that's me and Mrs Stevens, when we went on a school-party to Stratford last year. Lovely, it was. And with a bit of luck I'll be going with her again this next week. She teaches at the Proctor Memorial School. I clean for her . . . Well, as I say . . . I clean for her.'

It seemed for a few seconds that she was going to add a gloss to that last repeated statement. But her husband had shouted from within, and Morse managed not to look down at that disfigured palm again as Brenda Brooks's hands indulged in a further spasm of floccillation.

CHAPTER THIRTY-ONE

There is nothing which has yet been contrived by man by which so much happiness is produced as by a good tavern
(SAMUEL JOHNSON, *Obiter Dictum*,
21 March 1776)

'WELL, *well*! What do you make of all that?'

The Jaguar was gently negotiating half a dozen traffic-calming humps, before reaching the T-junction at the Cowley Road.

'Not now, Lewis!'

'How're you feeling, sir?'

'Just change the first letter of my name from "M" to "W".'

'You should be in bed.'

Morse looked at his wrist-watch. 'Nearest pub, Lewis. We need to think a little.'

Morse was comparatively unfamiliar with the part of Oxford in which he now found himself. In his own undergraduate days, it had seemed a long way out, being dubbed a 'Bridge Too Far' – on the farther side, the eastern side, the *wrong* side, of Magdalen Bridge – beyond the pale, as it were. Yet even then, three decades earlier, it had been (as it still was) a cosmopolitan, commercial area of fascinating contrasts: of the drab and the delightful; of boarded-up premises and thriving small businesses; of decay and regeneration – a Private Sex Shop at the city-centre end, and a police station at the far Ring Road end, with almost everything between, including (and particularly) a string of highly starred Indian restaurants. Including too (as Morse now trusted) a local pub selling real ale.

Lewis himself knew the area well; and after turning right at the T-junction, he almost immediately turned left into Marsh Road, pulling up there beside the Marsh Harrier.

Ashley Davies, he thought, would almost certainly have approved.

The *Good Pubs of Oxford* guide always reserved its highest praise for those hostelries where conversation was not impeded (let alone wholly precluded) by stentorian juke-boxes. And certainly Morse was gratified to find no music here. Yet he appeared to Lewis clearly ill-at-ease as he started – well, almost finished really – his first swift pint of Fuller's 'London Pride'.

'What's worrying you, sir?'

'I dunno. I've just got a sort of premonition—'

'Didn't know you believed in them.'

'—about this copy-cat-crime business. You know, you get a crime reported in the press – somebody pinching a baby from outside a supermarket, say – and before you can say "Ann Robinson" somebody else's having a go at the same thing.'

Lewis followed the drift of Morse's thought. 'The article we placed in the *Oxford Mail*?'

'Perhaps.'

'You mean, we shouldn't perhaps . . . ?'

'Oh, no! It was our duty to print that. And for all we know it could still produce something. Though I doubt it.'

Morse drained his beer before continuing: 'You know, that knife's somewhere, isn't it? The knife that someone stuck into McClure. The knife that *Brooks* stuck into McClure. That's the infuriating thing for me. Knowing that the bloody thing's *somewhere*, even if it's at the bottom of the canal.'

'Or the Cherwell.'

'Or the Isis.'

'Or the gravel-pits . . .'

But the conversation was briefly interrupted whilst Lewis, on the landlord's announcement of Last Orders, was now despatched to the bar for the second round.

Perhaps it was Morse's bronchial affliction which was affecting his short-term memory, since he appeared to be suffering under the misapprehension that it was he who had purchased the first.

Whatever the case, however, Morse quite certainly looked happier as he picked up his second pint, and picked up the earlier conversation.

'Brooks wouldn't have been too near any water, would he?'

'Not that far off, surely. And he'd have to go over Magdalen Bridge on his way home, anyway.'

'On his blood-saddled bike . . .'

'All he'd need to do was drop his knife over the bridge there – probably be safe till Kingdom Come.'

Morse shook his head. 'He'd have been worried about being seen.'

Lewis shrugged. 'He could have waited till it was dark.'

'It was bloody *morning*, Lewis!'

'He could've ditched it earlier. In a garden or somewhere.'

'No! We'd have found it by now, surely.'

'We're still trying,' said Lewis, quietly.

'You know' – Morse sounded weary – 'it's not quite so easy as you think – getting rid of things. You get a guilt-complex about being seen. I remember a few weeks ago trying to get rid of an old soldier in a rubbish-bin in Banbury Road. And just after I'd dropped it in, somebody I knew drove past in a car, and waved . . .'

'He'd seen you?'

'What makes you think it was a "he"?'

'You felt a bit guilty?'

Morse nodded. 'So it's vitally important that we find the knife. I just can't see how we're going to make a case out against Brooks unless we can find the murder weapon.'

'Have you thought of the other possibility, sir?'

'What's that?' Morse looked up with the air of a Professor of Mathematics being challenged by an innumerate pupil.

'He took the knife home with him.'

'No chance. We're talking about instinctive behaviour here. You don't stab somebody – and then just go back home and wash your knife up in Co-op detergent with the rest of the cutlery – and put it back in the kitchen drawer.'

'There'd be a knife missing, though – from a set, perhaps.'

'So what? Knives get lost, broken . . .'

'So *Mrs* Brooks would probably know?'

'But she's not going to tell us, is she?'

Morse seemed to relax as he leaned back against the wall-seat, and looked around him.

'You sure it *was* Brooks?' asked Lewis quietly.

'Too many coincidences, Lewis. All right, they play a far bigger part in life than most of us are prepared to admit. But not in this case. Just think! Brooks left Wolsey, for good, on exactly the same day as the man who was murdered – McClure. Not only that, the pair of them had been on the same staircase together – exactly the same staircase – for several years. Then, a year later, Brooks has a heart attack on exactly the same day as McClure gets murdered. Just add all that up – go on, Lewis!'

'Like I say, though, you've always believed in coincidences.'

'Look! I could stomach two, perhaps – but not *three*.'

Lewis, who'd believed that Morse could easily stomach at least four, was not particularly impressed; and now, looking around him, he saw that he and Morse were the only clients left in the Marsh Harrier.

It was 3.10 p.m.

'We'd better be off, sir.'

'Nonsense! My turn, isn't it?'

'It's way past closing time.'

'Nonsense!'

But the landlord, after explaining that serving further drinks after 3 p.m. on Sundays was wholly against the law, was distinctly unimpressed by Morse's assertion that he, the latter, *was* the law. And a minute or so later it was a slightly embarrassed Lewis who was unlocking the passenger door of the Jaguar – before making his way back to North Oxford.

CHAPTER THIRTY-TWO

These are, as I began, cumbersome ways
to kill a man. Simpler, direct and much more neat
is to see he is living somewhere in the middle
of the twentieth century, and leave him there
(EDWIN BROCK, *Five Ways to Kill a Man*)

PERPETUALLY, on the drive back to North Oxford, Morse had been wiping the perspiration from his forehead; and Lewis was growing increasingly worried, especially when, once back home, Morse immediately poured himself a can of beer.

'Just to replace the moisture,' Morse had averred.

'You ought to get the doc in, you know that. And you ought not to be drinking any more, with all those pills.'

'Lewis!' Morse's voice was vicious. 'I appreciate your concern for my health. But never again – never! – lecture me about what I drink. Or if I drink. Or when I drink. *Is – that – clear?*'

In a flush of anger, Lewis rose to his feet. 'I'll be getting back—'

'Siddown!'

Morse took out a cigarette, and then looked up at the still-standing Lewis. 'You don't think I ought to smoke, either?'

'It's your life, sir. If you're determined to dig yourself an early grave . . .'

'I don't want to die, not just yet,' said Morse quietly.

And suddenly, as if by some strange alchemy, Lewis felt his anger evaporating; and, as bidden, he sat down.

Morse put the cigarette back in its packet. 'I'm sorry – sorry I got so cross. Forgive me. It's just that I've always valued my independence so much – too much, perhaps. I just don't like being told what to do, all right?'

'All right.'

'Well, talk to me. Tell me what you thought about Brooks.'

'No, sir. You're the thinker – that's why you get a bigger pay-packet than me. You tell *me*.'

'Well, I think exactly the same as I did before. After young Rodway's suicide, McClure found out about the availability of drugs on the staircase there – cannabis, amphetamines, cocaine, crack, ecstasy, LSD, heroin, whatever – and he also found out that it was Brooks who was supplying them, and making a pretty penny for himself in the process. Then, at some point, McClure told Brooks he'd got two options: either he packed up his job as a scout and left; or else he'd be reported to the University authorities – and probably the police – and faced with criminal proceedings. So Brooks had just about enough nous to read the writing on the wall: he resigned, and got another job, with a reluctant McClure providing a lukewarm testimonial to the Pitt Rivers Museum. But there were too many links with his former clients – and not just on the old staircase; and he kept up his lucrative little sideline *after* he'd left Wolsey – until McClure somehow got wind of the situation – and confronted him – and told him that this time it wasn't just an empty threat. I suspect Brooks must have had some sort of hold on McClure, I don't know. But Brooks said he was ready to step into line, and do whatever McClure wanted. *And he arranged a meeting with McClure* – at McClure's place in Daventry Court, a week ago today. That's the way I see it.'

'So you don't believe a word of his alibi?'

'No. And it isn't *his* alibi at all – it's hers. Mrs Brooks's alibi for him.'

'And you think he biked up to see McClure?'

'He biked, yes. Whether he'd already decided to murder McClure then, I don't know. But he took a murder weapon with him, a knife from his wife's kitchen drawer; and I've not the slightest doubt he took as many precautions as he could to keep himself from being recognized – probably wrapped a scarf round his face as if he'd got the toothache. And with his cycling helmet—'

'You're making it all up, sir.'

Morse wiped his brow once more. 'Of *course* I am! In a case like this you've got to put up some . . . some scaffolding. You've got to sort of take a few leaps in the dark, Lewis. You've got to hypothesize . . .'

'Hypothesize about the knife then, sir.'

'He threw it in the canal.'

'So we're not going to find it?'

'I'm sure we're not. We'd have found it by now.'

'Unless, as I say, he took it home with him – and washed it up and wiped it dry and then put it back in the kitchen drawer.'

'Ye-es.'

'Probably he *did* mean to throw it in the canal, or somewhere. But something could have stopped him, couldn't it?'

'Such as?'

'Such as a heart attack,' suggested Lewis gently.

Morse nodded. 'If he suddenly realized he hadn't got any time to . . . if he suddenly felt a terrible pain . . .'

' "T'rific", that's what he said.'

'Mm.'

'What about the bike, though? He must have ridden it up to Daventry Court, mustn't he? So if he'd felt the pain starting, you'd have thought he'd get back home as fast as he could.'

Morse shook his head. 'It doesn't add up, does it? He must have ditched his bike somewhere on the way back.'

'Where, though?'

Morse pondered the problem awhile. Then, remembering Brooks's contempt for anyone taking the trouble to report a bicycle-theft in Oxford, he suddenly saw that it had ceased to be a problem at all.

'Do you know a poem called "Five Ways to Kill a Man"?'

'No.'

Wearily Morse rose to his feet, fetched an anthology of modern verse from his shelves, looked up Brock in the index, turned to the poem – and read the last stanza aloud.

But Lewis, though not unaccustomed to hearing Morse make some apposite quotation from the poets between draughts of real ale, could see no possible connection in logic here.

'I'm not with you.'

Morse looked down at the stanza again; then slowly recited his own parody of the lines:

> 'There are several cumbersome ways
> of losing a bike – like pushing it in the canal.
> Neater and simpler, though, is to take it somewhere
> like Cornmarket in Oxford – and just leave it there.'

'You ought to have been a poet, sir.'

'I am a poet, Lewis.'

Morse now coughed violently, expectorating into a tissue a disgusting gobbet of yellowish-green phlegm streaked with bright blood.

Lewis, although he saw it, said nothing.

And Morse continued:

'First thing is to get Brooks in, and go through Susan Ewers' statement with him. She's a good witness, that one – and he'll have to come up with something better than he gave us this afternoon.'

'When shall we bring him in, though? He's got a point, hasn't he? We don't want to give him another heart attack.'

'Don't we?'

'Day or two?'

'Day or three.'

Morse finished his beer. It had taken that swift drinker an inordinately long time to do so; and if Morse had experienced a premonition earlier, Lewis himself now sensed that his chief was seriously ill.

'What about the photograph, sir? Mrs Brooks's daughter?'

'Interesting question. I wonder. I wonder where that young lady fits into the picture.'

'Pretty well everywhere, wouldn't you say?'

'Ye-es. "Kay" – "K" – "Eleanor" – "Ellie" – we've got to assume she's the same girl, I suppose: Mrs B's daughter – Mr B's step-daughter – staircase-tart for Messrs Rodway and Davies – mistress for Dr McClure . . .'

'She must be quite a girl.'

'But what about that other photograph, Lewis? The school-mistress? D'you know, I've got a feeling she might be able to shed a little light—'

But Morse was coughing uncontrollably now, finally disappearing into the bathroom, whence was heard a series of revolting retches.

Lewis walked out into the entrance-hall, where he flicked open Morse's black plastic telephone-index to the letter 'S'. He was lucky. Under 'Summertown Health Centre' he found an 'Appointments' number; and an 'Emergency' number.

He rang the latter.

That same afternoon, just after four o'clock, Dr Richard Rayson, Chaucerian scholar, and fellow of Trinity College, Oxford, strolled round his garden in Daventry Avenue. For almost three weeks he had been away with his family in the Dolomites. Gardening, in truth, had never been the greatest passion of his life; and as he stood surveying the state of his neglected front lawn, the epithet which sprang most readily to his literate mind was 'agrestal':

somewhat overgrown; run to seed; wild, as the *Shorter Oxford* might define it.

Yet strangely, for such an unobservant man, he'd spotted the knife almost immediately – a couple of feet or so inside the property, between an untrimmed laurel bush and the vertical slats of a front fence sorely in need of some re-creosoting. There it was, lying next to a semi-squashed tin of Coca Cola.

Nina Rayson, a compensatingly practical sort of partner, had welcomed her husband's discovery, promptly washing it in Sainsbury's 'Economy' washing-up liquid, and forthwith adding it to her own canteen of cutlery. A good knife, it was: a fairly new, sturdy, unusually broad-bladed instrument, in no immediate need of any further sharpening.

That same evening, at nine-thirty, Brenda Brooks was aware that her jangled nerves could stand very little more that day. Paradoxically, though, she felt almost competent about coping with the loathsome man she'd just seen to bed, with a cup of tea, two digestive biscuits, and one sleeping tablet. At least she knew him: knew the *worst* about him – for there was nothing but the worst to know. It was now the *unknown* that was worrying her the more deeply: that strange technical jargon of the doctors and nurses at the hospital; the brusque yet not wholly unsympathetic questions of the two policemen who had earlier called there.

She found herself neurotically dreading any phone-call; any ringing of the doorbell. Anything.

What was that?

What was *that*?

Was she imagining things – imagining noises?

There it was again: a muffled, insistent, insidious, tapping . . .

Fearfully, she edged towards the front door.

And there, behind the frosted glass, she saw a vaguely human silhouette; and she turned the Yale lock, and opened the door, her heart fluttering nervously.

'You!' she whispered.

CHAPTER THIRTY-THREE

It is an inexorable sort of festivity – in September 1914 they tried to cancel it, but the Home Secretary himself admitted that he was powerless to do so

(JAN MORRIS, *Oxford*)

OXFORD's St Giles' Fair is held annually on the first Monday and Tuesday after the first Sunday every September, with the whole area of St Giles' brought into use, from the Martyrs' Memorial up to (and beyond) St Giles' Church at the northern end, where the broad, tree-lined avenue bifurcates to form the Woodstock Road to the left and the Banbury Road to the right.

In mid-afternoon on Tuesday, 6 September (two days after Lewis had telephoned the Summertown Health Centre), Kevin Costyn was sauntering under the plane trees there, along the various rides and amusements and candy-floss stalls. Nothing could really kindle his imagination or interest, for the Naked Lady of earlier years, in her rat-infested cage, no longer figured in the fair's attractions. And as Kevin considered the jazzy, jolty, vertiginous cars and carriages, he felt no real wish to part with any of his limited money.

That day the children in the state schools in Oxfordshire had returned to their classrooms; and for the first time in twelve years Costyn himself was not one of them. No more school. But no job yet, either. He'd signed on at the Job Centre. Even taken away some literature on *Youth Employment Schemes and Opportunities*. Not that he was going to read that bumf. He wasn't interested in jobs. Just money. Well, not *just* money, no.

Smugly he grinned to himself as he stood outside the Bird and Baby and watched the gigantic, gyrating structure of the Big Wheel.

The previous month he'd been part of a three-man ram-raid at a Summertown supermarket, but it hadn't proved the windfall they'd expected. Shop windows – *replaced* shop windows – were being made of tougher glass; and several regular, and formerly profitable, targets were now protected by concrete frontal pillars. That wasn't the real trouble, though. It was getting rid of the stuff that was getting trickier all the time. Cigarettes had usually been the best bet: lightweight, handy to stack, easy to sell. But booze was becoming one helluva job to sell; and the cases of whisky, gin, and vodka they'd got away with then had changed hands for a miserly £850, though according to Costyn's (admittedly less than competent) calculation their street-value would have been four times that amount. It was the police – becoming far cannier at tracking down the wholesale-market contacts – they were the real trouble.

There must be easier ways of being able to afford the life of Riley, surely?

Yes, occasionally there were ...

It had been Kevin Costyn himself who had answered the door the previous afternoon, to find Mrs Stevens standing there – a subtly scented Mrs Stevens, with a moist, red beauty at herlips.

Could she come in? She'd come in.

Would he listen to what she had to say? He'd listened.

Would he be willing to do as she asked? He'd be willing.

Would he be able to do what she wanted? He'd be able.

Payment? What about payment? Did he understand she had very little money? He'd understood.

How would he like her to pay him, then?

Well ...

'What time's your mother back?' she'd asked.

No one over the past few years had deemed it necessary, or deemed it wise, to challenge Costyn's minority; nor did the young barmaid now, as she pulled him a pint of Burton Ale in the Bird and Baby ('Open All Day').

Ten minutes later he made his way to the Gents, where he spat a globule of phlegm on to the tiled floor, and where his left hand was directing his urination whilst his right hand was seeking, wholly ineffectually, to spell out FUCK in red Biro on the corrugated surface of the wall in front of him.

'Fuck' was a key word in Costyn's limited vocabulary. Had already been so for many years, ever since, night after night, his mum and dad (*perhaps*, his dad) had bawled their mutual 'fuck-off's at each other. Until the day when his dad had apparently interpreted the injunction rather too literally – and just, well, 'fucked off'. Indeed, so significant had the word become to the sole son of that hapless, unhappy union, that he regularly inserted it, in its present-participial form, into any lengthy-ish word which seemed to invite some internal profanation. Such a process is known, in the Homeric epics, as 'tmesis' – although, in truth, Costyn knew of 'Homer' only as a breed of pigeon; for his father had once kept such a pigeon, trained (once released) to find its way home from the most improbable distances. Which is more than its owner had done, once he had left his home, and his wife, and his son . . . and his pigeon.

Before leaving the Gents, Costyn made a purchase. The condom machine looked, even to him, pretty theft-proof; and he decided for once to pay for his potential pleasures. For a few seconds he mentally debated the respective merits of 'lubrication', 'sensitivity', and 'silkiness'; finally plumping for the latter as he thought – yet again! – of the blouse that he'd slowly eased down over the suntanned shoulders of Mrs Julia Stevens.

At 4 p.m., standing waiting for a Cowley Road bus outside Marks and Spencer in Queen's Street, Costyn recognized an ex-pupil of the Proctor Memorial immediately in front of him; and he put a hand on her untanned shoulder.

'Bin 'avin' a ride, darlin'?'

She turned round. 'Wha' d'you want?'

'What about a little ride with *me*, darlin'? I got the necessaries.'

'Fuck off!'

Few girls ever spoke to him in such a fashion. But Costyn felt little resentment as he fingered the two packets of Silken Dalliance in his pocket . . .

Payment for his services?

'Half now; half later,' that's what Mrs Stevens had promised. And as he sat upstairs on the Cowley Road bus, Costyn savoured yet again that intoxicating cocktail of excitement and sensuality.

Half later . . . when the job was done; when the jobs (plural, perhaps), were done.

Was it terribly risky, what he'd so willingly agreed to do? Especially since she wasn't exactly sure of when she'd be calling on him. So what? Much riskier for her than for him. Not that she'd ever need to worry about *him*: he'd never breathe a word of it to any living soul.

Never.

And anyone who thought he would was suffering under a misapprefuckinhension.

CHAPTER THIRTY-FOUR

The gaudy, blabbing, and remorseful day
Is crept into the bosom of the sea
(SHAKESPEARE, *Henry IV, Part II*)

(i)

ON WEDNESDAY, 7 September 1994, at 11.20 a.m., Ms Ellie Smith sat in a taxi, every half-minute or so nervously consulting her wrist-watch and cursing herself for not having taken up Ashley Davies's offer.

Rightly or wrongly, before walking out on him the previous weekend, she'd informed him of her situation: she was twelve weeks' pregnant; she was determined to have another abortion; she had an appointment at a South Birmingham clinic for preliminary consultation and advice. But when Davies had rung her the previous afternoon, she'd turned down his offer of a lift – once again. He'd been quite insistent really, saying that he'd got to be in Oxford later the next day, anyway; and it was so quick to Brum now – M40, M42 – and in *his* car, well, they'd do it in an hour almost; save her no end of time and trouble – and the rail fare into the bargain.

But she'd refused.

She was going by train, catching the 9.11 a.m. from Oxford, due to arrive at Birmingham New Street at 10.30 a.m., which would give her a whole hour to get to the clinic, only five miles distant from the railway station.

That was the plan.

But with the combination of a 'signalling failure' just before Leamington Spa and a security scare at Coventry, the train had finally rumbled into New Street forty-eight minutes late – and she'd had no option but to take a taxi. Not that she need have bothered too much, for it was 11.55 a.m. before she was called into the consulting-room.

Looking back on things, Ms Smith knew that she had been strangely impressed by the small, white-coated Pakistani doctor – a kindly, compassionate man, with Spaniel eyes – who had gently encouraged her at least to consider the alternative: that of keeping the child she had conceived.

She felt glad that she had tried to present herself in rather more conventional guise, putting on bra and pants (both!) beneath her only presentable summer dress – *and* removing the rings from her nostrils. Admittedly that left her hair, still streaked with crimson like the horizon in an angry sunset; but she felt (dare she admit it to herself?) somehow . . . expiated!

She couldn't really think why.

No, she *could* think why.

It was something to do with being with her mum once more . . .

The 15.09 train from New Street, timetabled to arrive in Oxford at 16.31 p.m., arrived virtually on time. And half an hour later Ellie Smith was back at her flat, reading the brief note contained in the white envelope ('By Hand') which she'd found propped up at the foot of her white-painted door on the third floor:

> Hope things went OK. Any chance of you thinking again?
> If there's even a remote chance of its being mine, I'll marry you and make an honest woman of you yet. Don't be cross with me for badgering you.
>> Ashley, with lots and lots of kisses.

As she put her key into the lock, Ellie Smith wondered whether she'd sadly misjudged Mr Ashley Davies.

(ii)

'THANKS for coming,' said a sombre Phillotson.

In vain Lewis sought to find some suitable rejoinder.

'Morse on the mend?'

'Out tomorrow, so they say.'

'Will he be fit enough to carry on – with the case?'

'Dunno, sir. I suppose he'll please himself whatever happens.'

'I suppose he will, yes.'

Lewis moved away, and briefly surveyed the wreaths laid out there, including a splendid display of white lilies from the Thames Valley Police HQ.

Phillotson's wife had lived a gently unspectacular life, and died at the age of forty-six. Not much of an innings, really; and not too much of a memorial either, although her husband, her next of kin, and all of her friends, would hope that the little rose-bush (*Rosa rubrifolia*), already happily stuck into a wodge of blackly-rich compost in the Garden of Remembrance, would thrive and prosper – and, metempsychotically, as it were, take over.

If Chief Inspector Morse had been present at the short service, he would have been impatient with what he saw as the pretentious prayers; and yet, almost certainly, he would have welcomed the hymn that was played there – 'O Love that wilt not let me go' – and his quiet unmusical baritone would probably have mingled with the singing.

But Morse was not one of the thirty-seven mourners Lewis counted at the Oxford Crematorium that Wednesday lunchtime.

(iii)

'WHAT EXACTLY'S *wrong* with you, Morse?'

'I'm only here for observation.'

'Yes, I know that. But what exactly is it they're *observing*?'

Morse drew a deep breath. 'I'm suffering from bronchi-something beginning with "e"; my liver and kidneys are disintegrating; my blood pressure isn't quite off the top of the scale – not yet; I'm nursing another stomach ulcer; and as if that wasn't enough I'm on the verge of diabetes, because my pancreas, they tell me, isn't producing sufficient insulin to counteract my occasional intake of alcohol. Oh yes, and my cholesterol's dangerously high.'

'I see. Perhaps I should have asked what exactly's *right* with you, Morse.'

Strange shifted his great bulk awkwardly on the small wooden chair beside Morse's bed in Ward 7 of the John Radcliffe Two Hospital out at Headington, whither, in spite of his every protestation of being in excellent health, Morse had been conveyed by ambulance, half an hour after the doctor had been summoned the previous Sunday afternoon.

'I had an endoscopy yesterday,' continued Morse.

'Sounds painful. Where do they stick that?'

'In the *mouth*, sir.'

'Ah. No more dramatic finds?'

'No more corpses under the floorboards.'

'Well, the wife'll be very pleased if you can last out till – fairly soon, isn't it? – when you've got a speaking engagement, I understand.'

'I *have*?'

'You know – the WI group-meeting in Kidlington. Likely to be a good crowd there, she says. So try to make it, old man. She's, er . . . you know, she's the President this year. Means a lot to her.'

'Tell her I'll be there, even if they have to wheel me in.'

'Good. Good. "The Grislier Aspects of Murder." Nice little title, that.'

With which Morse's mind reverted to the investigation. 'If you see Lewis, sir, tell him to call in tonight, will you? I'd like to know how things are going.'

'He was going to Mrs Phillotson's funeral this lunchtime.'

'What? Nobody told me about that.'

'No, well . . . we didn't want to, er . . . Not a nice subject, death, is it?'

The clock showed 2.45 p.m. when Strange made his way out of Ward 7; and for several minutes Morse lay back on his pillows and pondered. Perhaps a hospital was an appropriate place to meditate on death, for there was plenty of it going on all around. But most men or women preferred not to think or talk about it. Morse had known only one person who positively relished discussing the topic – Max the police pathologist, who in a macabre kind of way had almost made a friend of Death. But Death had made no reciprocal arrangement; and Max was police pathologist no longer.

(iv)

ALTHOUGH THE autumn term had only begun the day before, clearly one or two of the local schools had been planning, well in advance, to despatch their pupils on some of the dreaded GCSE 'projects' at the earliest possible opportunity. Certainly, until about 4.05 p.m., twenty or so schoolchildren had still been studying a range of anthropological exhibits in the Upper Gallery of the Pitt Rivers Museum.

Which was rather worrying.

But by 4.15 p.m., the galleries were virtually – by 4.20 p.m., totally – deserted. And from where he stood, beside the collection made in the South Pacific by Captain Cook on his second visit there in 1772, the young man observed most carefully whilst a suntanned, balding attendant walked briskly round the Upper Gallery, doubtless checking that no bags or satchels or writing-pads had inadvertently been left behind; and in so doing, as was immediately apparent, giving a quick, upward 'lift' to each of the glass covers of the locked cabinets there, like a potential car-thief swiftly moving along a line of vehicles in a Park and Ride and testing the doors.

Two minutes later, the young man was following in the attendant's same pre-closure tracks; but stopping now, at a particular spot, where he looked down at a collection of knives – knives of all shapes and sizes, knives from many parts of the world – displayed in Cabinet Number 52.

Quickly, his heart pounding, he took a chisel from his summer sweatshirt and inserted its recently sharpened edge between the metal rim of the display-case top and the darkly stained wooden slat below it, into which the cabinet's lock was set.

Easy!

No great splintering of wood or moaning of metal. Just a single, quick 'click'. Yet it had been a bad moment; and the young man checked anxiously to his left, then to his right, before lifting the glass lid and putting a hand inside.

It was 4.29 p.m. when he walked through the museum shop. He might have bought a postcard of the forty-foot-high Haida Totem Pole (British Columbia), but an assistant was already totting up the takings, and he wished to cause no trouble. As the prominent notice had advised him as he'd entered, the Pitt Rivers Museum of Ethnology and Pre-History closed at 4.30 p.m. each day.

(v)

AT THE Proctor Memorial School, the take-up for the *Twelfth Night* trip to the Shakespeare Theatre had been encouraging. Before the end of the summer term, Julia Stevens had made her usual block-booking of thirty-one seats; and with twenty-three pupils (mostly fifth- and sixth-formers), two other members of staff, plus two parents, only three tickets had been going begging.

Only *two*, in fact – and those soon to be snapped up with alacrity at the box office – because Julia Stevens had invited Brenda Brooks (as she had done the previous year) to join the school-party.

At the Stratford Coach Park, the three teachers had distributed the brown-paper-wrapped rations: two rolls, one with mayon-naised-curried-chicken, the other with a soft-cheese filling; one packet of crisps; and one banana – with a plastic cup of orangeade.

On the way back, though not on the way out, Mrs Stevens and Mrs Brooks sat side by side in the front seats: the former semi-listening (with some gratification) to her pupils' pronouncements on the performances of Sirs Toby Belch and Andrew Aguecheek; the latter, until Woodstock, trying to read the latest instalment of a romantic serial in *Woman's Weekly*, before apparently falling into a deep slumber, and not awakening therefrom until, two minutes before midnight on Wednesday, 7 September, the coach made its first stop at Carfax Tower, from where the streets of Oxford looked strangely beautiful; and slightly sinister.

PART TWO

CHAPTER THIRTY-FIVE

In me there dwells
No greatness, save it be some far-off touch
Of greatness to know well I am not great
(ALFRED, LORD TENNYSON, *Lancelot and Elaine*)

AFTER RINGING the emergency number the previous Sunday, it
had been a sad sight that confronted Lewis in the bathroom:
Morse standing creased over the pedestal basin, his cheeks wholly
drained of colour, his vomit streaked with blood forming a
chrysanthemum pattern, scarlet on white, across the porcelain.

Dr Paul Roblin had been adamant.

Ambulance!

Lewis had woken up to the truth an hour or so later: for a
while at least, he was going to be left alone with a murder
investigation.

Such a prospect would normally have daunted him; yet the
present case was unusual in that it had already established itself
into a pattern. In the past, the more spectacular cases on which
he and Morse had worked together had often involved some
bizarre, occasionally some almost incredible, twists of fate. But
the murder of Dr Felix McClure appeared – surely *was* – a
comparatively straightforward affair. There could be little doubt
– none in Morse's mind – about the identity of the murderer. It
was just a question of timing now, and patience: of the accumulation, the aggregation of evidence, against a man who'd had the
means, the motive, and the opportunity, to murder McClure.
Only concerning the actual commission of the crime was there
lack of positive evidence. Lack of any evidence. And what a
feather in his cap it would be if he, Lewis, could come up with
something on *that*, during Morse's reluctant, yet enforced,
immobility.

For the present, then, it was he who was sole arbiter of the
course of further inquiries; of the most productive deployment of
police resources. He had not been born great, Lewis was aware of

that; nor did the rank of Detective Sergeant mark him out as a man who had achieved any significant greatness. Yet for a few days now, some measure of vicarious greatness was being thrust upon him; and he would have been encouraged by the Latin proverb (had he known it) that 'Greatness is but many small littles', since it was upon a series of 'small littles' that he embarked over the following three days – Monday, Tuesday, Wednesday, 5, 6, 7 September.

Over these few days many statements were taken from people, both Town and Gown, some fairly closely, some only peripherally, connected with the murdered man and with his putative murderer. And it was Lewis himself who had visited the JR2 on Tuesday afternoon for it to be confirmed, quite unequivocally, that Mr Edward Brooks had been admitted, via Casualty, to the Coronary Care Unit at 2.32 p.m. on Sunday, 28 August; that Brooks had spent twenty-four hours in Intensive Care before being transferred to Level 7, whence he had been discharged three days later.

Whilst in the hospital, Lewis had called in to see Morse (his second visit), but had refused to be drawn into any discussion of new developments in the inquiry. This for two reasons: first, that there were no new developments; and, second, that Superintendent Strange had strongly urged against such a course of action – 'Start talking about it, and he'll start thinking about it. And once he starts thinking, he'll start thinking about drinking, whatever the state of his innards . . .' So Lewis stayed only a few minutes that afternoon, taking a 'Get Well' card from Mrs Lewis, and a small bunch of seedless white grapes from himself, the latter immediately confiscated by the hawk-eyed ward-sister.

From the JR2, Lewis had gone on to interview the Brooks's family GP, Dr Philip Gregson, at the Cowley Road Health Centre.

The brief medical report on Edward Brooks which Lewis read there was quite optimistic: 'Mild heart attack – condition now stable – surprisingly swift recovery. GP appt 1 wk; JR2 out/p appt 2 wk.'

About Brenda Brooks, however, Gregson was more circumspect. She had, yes, suffered a very nasty little injury to her right hand; and, yes, he had referred her to a specialist. But he couldn't comment in any way upon his colleague's findings. If further information were considered necessary . . .

In such fashion was it that Lewis's queries were concluded late that Tuesday afternoon – with the telephone number of an orthopaedic surgeon, and with the knowledge that he was getting nowhere fairly slowly.

Yet only twenty-four hours were to elapse before the first major breakthrough in the case was destined to occur.

CHAPTER THIRTY-SIX

Is this a dagger which I see before me,
The handle towards my hand?
(SHAKESPEARE, *Macbeth*)

IT TOOK a long time, an inordinately long time, for the penny to drop.

Dr Richard Rayson had been wholly unaware of the great excitement which had been witnessed by the residents of Daventry Avenue over the previous week. Yet his inability to establish any connection between the discovery of a knife and the death of a neighbour is readily explicable. In the first place, the physical police presence around Daventry Court had been withdrawn on the day prior to his return from abroad. Then, too, Rayson had not as yet reinstated his standing order with the Summertown newsagent for the daily delivery of the *Oxford Mail*; he had therefore missed the brief item tucked away at the bottom of page 3 on Monday (would probably have missed it anyway). And finally, and most significantly, his communications with his neighbours, on either side, had been almost completely severed of late – this breakdown occasioned by a series of increasingly bitter differences of view over the maintenance of boundary fences, the planting of inter-property trees, an application for planning permission, and (most recently) the dangerous precedent of a teenage party.

Thus, after spending the whole of the Monday and Tuesday with his wife in regrooming their garden, it was only at lunchtime on Wednesday, 7 September, that Rayson was reintroduced into the mainstream of Oxford life and gossip – at a cocktail reception in Trinity College to meet a group of librarians from Oklahoma.

'Fine drop of claret, what, Richard?' one of his colleagues had affirmed.

'Beautifully balanced little wine, George.'

'By the way, you must have known old McClure, I suppose? Lives only a few doors from you, what? *Lived*, rather.'

Rayson had frowned. 'McClure?'

'You know, the poor sod who got himself knifed?'

McClure. Felix McClure. Knifed.

The knife.

Just after five o'clock that afternoon, Detective Sergeant Lewis stood looking down at the prime exhibit, laid out on the Formica-topped surface of the kitchen in Rayson's elegant detached house in Daventry Avenue – seven properties distant, on the Woodstock Road side, from the scene of McClure's murder. As Rayson had explained over the phone, the knife had been found just inside the front fence, had been picked up, washed, dried, put away, picked up again, used to cut a roll of boiled ham, rewashed, re-dried, put away again – and picked up yet again when Rayson had returned from Trinity in the late afternoon, and examined it with a sort of ghoulish fascination.

With no prospects, therefore, of the exhibit retaining any incriminating fingerprints or bloodstains, Lewis in turn now picked up the black-handled knife, its blade unusually broad at the base, but tapering to a sharp-looking point at the end. And concurrently several thoughts coursed through his mind – exciting thoughts. There was the description, for a start, of the murder weapon – so very similar to this knife – which had appeared in the *Oxford Mail*, the description which was perhaps worrying Morse somewhat when he'd mentioned his premonition about the possibility of a copy-cat killing. Then there was the firm likelihood that the second of Morse's necessary prerequisites had now been met – not only a body, but also a weapon; and this one surely seemed to fit the bill so very nicely. And then – by far the most exciting thought of all – the strong possibility that the knife had come from a set of such knives, *one of which Lewis had seen so very recently*: that slim, elegant, black-handled little knife with which Mrs Brenda Brooks had sliced the Madeira cake the previous Sunday afternoon.

CHAPTER THIRTY-SEVEN

I enjoy convalescence; it is the part that makes the illness worth while

(GEORGE BERNARD SHAW)

ON THURSDAY, 8 September, as on the previous day, so many things were happening in close sequence that it is difficult for the chronicler to decide upon the most comprehensible way in which to record events, events which were to some degree contemporaneous but which also overlapped and which in their full implications stretched both before and beyond their strict temporal occurrence.

Let the account begin at Morse's flat in North Oxford.

Morse was due to be discharged at ten o'clock that morning. Lewis had rung through to the ward-sister half an hour earlier to save Morse any wait for an ambulance and to chauffeur him home in style – only to discover that his chief had already discharged himself, getting a lift from one of the consultants there who was on his way out to Bicester.

Lewis rang the doorbell at 9.45 a.m., experiencing a customary qualm of semi-apprehension as he waited outside that lonely flat – until a fully dressed Morse, his cheeks rosy-red, suddenly appeared on the threshold, panting like a breathless bulldog.

'I'm just starting a new regimen, Lewis. No more nicotine, limited – very limited – alcohol, plenty of fresh fruit and salad, and regular exercise. What about that? I've' – he paused awhile to get his breath – 'I've just done a dozen press-ups. You'd never have thought that possible a week ago, now, would you?'

'You must be feeling quite, er, elated, sir.'

'"Knackered" is the word I think you're looking for, Lewis. But come in! Good to see you. Have a drink.'

Almost as if he were trespassing, Lewis entered the lounge and sat down.

'Nothing for me, thanks.'

'I'll just . . .' Morse quickly drained a tumbler of some pale amber liquid that stood on one of the shelves of the book-lined room beside the Deutsche Grammophon cassettes of *Tristan und Isolde*. 'A small, celebratory libation, that, Lewis – in gratitude to whatever gods there be that temporarily I have survived the perils and dangers of this mortal life.'

Lewis managed a grin, half sad, half happy – and immediately told Morse about the knife.

'I don't believe it! We'd had those gardens searched.'

'Only up to six either side, sir. If only we'd gone a couple further.'

'But why didn't this fellow Rayson find it earlier? Is he blind or something?'

'He was in Italy.'

'Oh.'

'You don't sound all that pleased about it.'

'What? Course I am. Well done!'

'I know you were a bit worried about that *Oxford Mail* article . . .'

'I was?'

'You know, the premonition you had—'

'Nonsense! I don't even know what a premonition is.'

'Well, if that description's anywhere near accurate, sir, I think we've got the knife that was used to kill McClure. And I think I know where it came from. And I think you do, too.'

The small round-faced clock on the mantelpiece showed two minutes after ten, and for a while Morse sat in silence. Then, of a sudden, he jumped to his feet and, against all the medical advice he'd so meekly accepted over the previous few days, insisted on being driven immediately to police HQ, stopping (as it happened) only briefly along the journey, in a slip-road on the left, just opposite the Sainsbury supermarket in Kidlington, to buy a packet of Dunhill King-Size cigarettes.

Brenda Brooks had spent the previous night not in her own house in Addison Road but in the spare bedroom, the only other bedroom, of Julia Stevens' house in Baldwin Road. After Mrs Stevens had left for school at 8.15 a.m., Brenda had eaten a bowl of Corn Flakes and a round of toast and marmalade. Her appointment at the hairdresser's was for 9.15 a.m.; and fairly soon after her breakfast she was closing the Oxford-blue front door behind her, testing (as always) that the lock was firmly engaged, and walking down towards the Cowley Road for her Special Offer Wash-and-Perm.

On her way home, well over an hour and a half later, she bought two salmon fillets, a pack of butter, and a carton of ecologically friendly washing-up liquid.

The sun was shining.

As she turned into Addison Road she immediately spotted the marked police car, parked on the double yellow lines across the road from her house; spotted a second car, too, the elegant-looking lovingly polished maroon-coloured Jaguar she'd seen the previous Sunday afternoon.

Even as she put her key into the Yale lock, she felt the hand on her shoulder, heard the man's voice, and heard, too, the ringing of the telephone just inside the hall.

'Get a move on,' said Morse quickly. 'You may just catch it.'

But the ringing stopped just before she could reach the phone; and taking off her lightweight summer coat, and gently patting the back of her blue-rinsed curls, she turned to the two men who stood just outside, the two men she'd seen the previous Sunday afternoon.

'If it's Ted you want, you'll have to come back later, I'm afraid. He's up at the JR2 – he's got an Outpatient appointment.'

'When do you expect him back?' asked Lewis.

'I don't know really. He'll be back for lunch, I should think, unless he calls in at the Club for a game of snooker.'

'How did he get to the hospital?'

Mrs Brooks hesitated. 'I . . . I don't know.' The fingers of her left hand were plucking their way along the invisible rosary she held in her right. 'You'd better come in, hadn't you?'

Haltingly, nervously, as they sat again in the lounge, in the same sedentary formation as before, Mrs Brooks sought to explain the situation. She had been to Stratford the previous evening with a friend and hadn't returned until late – about midnight – as she'd known she would, anyway. And she'd stayed with this person, this friend, at her house – overnight. Ted knew all about the arrangement. He was due at Outpatients the next morning, and she hadn't wanted to disturb his night's sleep – *hadn't* disturbed his night's sleep. He was getting along quite nicely and the doctors said how important it was to rest – to have regular rest and sleep. He hadn't shown her the little blue appointments card from the Oxfordshire Health Authority, but she thought he was due at the hospital somewhere between nine and ten.

'You haven't been here, in this house, since – since when?' asked Morse, rather brusquely.

'Four o'clock, yesterday afternoon. Or just before. The coach left at five.'

'You don't seem to have been too worried about Mr Brooks coping . . . with meals, that sort of thing?'

'Don't you think so, Inspector?' Her eyes, rather sad and weary now, looked into Morse's; and it was Morse who was the first to look away.

Lewis sounded a kindlier note. 'You've just come back from the hairdresser's?'

She nodded the tightly permed hair. 'The Golden Scissors, in Cowley Road.'

'Er . . . what was the play, by the way?'

'*Twelfth Night.*'

'Did you enjoy it?'

She half-smiled. 'Well, I couldn't quite follow all the – you know, what they were saying. But I loved it, yes, and I'd love to see it again.'

'And you went with . . . with a friend, you say?'

'Yes, with a school-party.'

'And this friend . . . ?'

Lewis was noting her name and address when the telephone rang once more; and this time Mrs Brooks reached the hall swiftly. As she did so, Morse immediately pointed in the opposite direction, and Lewis, equally swiftly, stepped quietly into the kitchen where he opened a drawer by the side of the sink.

Morse meanwhile listened keenly to one side of a telephone conversation.

'Yes?'

'Is he all right?'

'I don't understand.'

'What's happened, do you think?'

'No. I wasn't here, you see.'

'Of course I will.'

'Can you just give me the number again?'

'All right.'

Brenda Brooks put down the phone slowly, her face anxious as she walked back into the lounge – only a few seconds after Lewis, with a silent thumbs-up sign, had reappeared from the kitchen and quickly resumed his seat.

'Anything important?' asked Morse.

'It was the hospital. Ted's not been there. Not yet. So the lady at Appointments says. He was due there at twenty-past nine, it seems.'

'What do you think's happened to him?' asked Morse quietly.

'That's what she asked me. I don't know.'

'I'm sure everything's fine,' continued Morse. 'He's probably just got the time wrong.'

'That's exactly what she said,' whispered Brenda Brooks.

'She'll ring you back – when he gets there.'

'That's . . . that's exactly . . .'

But the tears had started now.

She opened her handbag and took out a handkerchief, and said, 'Sorry'; said 'Sorry' five times. And then, 'Oh dear! Where's my purse? I must have . . .' She got up and went to the hall where she patted the pockets of her summer coat, and came back and looked rather fecklessly around. 'I must have . . .'

'You did some shopping, didn't you? You may have left it . . . ?' suggested Lewis.

A few minutes later, Mrs Brooks was seated in the back of the police car, impatient and worried; but so glad to be away from the two detectives – who now stood in her kitchen.

'What do you reckon, sir?'

'About Brooks? Buggered off, hasn't he – sensible chap! He must have guessed we were on his tail.'

'What about her? She seemed glad to get away.'

'She's worried about her purse – money, cards, keys . . .'

'More than that, I think.'

'Well, *you* made her feel a bit guilty, didn't you, checking up on her hairdresser – and Stratford.'

'What?'

'Quite right too, Lewis. She was telling us a load of lies, wasn't she? She knows exactly where he is! He may treat her like a skivvy, but she's still his missus.'

Lewis opened the drawer again, this time selecting four knives, of different sizes, but of the same basic pattern, of the same make – each with a black handle, one side of which, the side of the cutting-edge, was slightly sinuous, with an indented curve at the top to fit the joint of the index finger, and a similar curve at the lower end for the little finger.

Four knives.

Four from a set of five?

But if so, the fifth was missing . . . yet not really all that far away, neatly docketed and safely stored as it was in an Exhibits Locker at Thames Valley Police HQ.

Oh, yes!

Lewis nodded to himself, and to Morse.

And Morse nodded to himself, and to Lewis.

It seemed to Morse no great surprise that Mr Edward Brooks, ex-scout of Wolsey, and current assistant custodian of the Pitt Rivers Collection, had decided to make a bolt for it – once news of the discovery of that fatal fifth knife had leaked out.

Which it hadn't . . .

Lewis had seen to that.

CHAPTER THIRTY-EIGHT

The museum has retained much of its Victorian character. Painstakingly hand-written labels can still be found attached to some of the artefacts in the crammed black cases there
(*The Pitt Rivers Museum, A Souvenir Guide*)

THE DETAILS of what was to prove the key discovery in the case – or, to be more accurate, the 'lack-of-key' discovery in the case – were not communicated by the City Police to Kidlington HQ until just after 1 p.m. that same day, although the discovery had in fact been made as early as 8.45 a.m.

Janis Lawrence, an unmarried young woman, lived with her mother, an unmarried middle-aged woman, on the Cutteslowe Estate in North Oxford. The household was completed by Janis's four-year-old son, Jason – a name chosen not to commemorate the intrepid leader of the Argonauts but the lead guitarist of a long-forgotten pop group. Jason found it impossible to pass by any stone or small brick without picking it up and hurling it at anything which moved across his vision – dogs, prams, pedestrians, motor-vehicles, and similar obstructions. Thus it was that Janis Lawrence was ever longing for the time when she could transfer complete responsibility for the child to the hapless teachers of the local Cutteslowe Primary School. And when she had learned of a temporary (August to September) cleaning job at the Pitt Rivers Museum, she had applied for it. And got it.

The Cutteslowe Estate in North Oxford, built in the 1930s, had achieved national notoriety because of the Cutteslowe Wall, a seven-foot high, spiked-topped, brick-built wall, which segregated the upper-middle-class residents of the Banbury Road from the working-class tenants of the Council Estate. But the wall had been demolished in 1959; and on the bright morning of Thursday, 8 September 1994, as on each weekday for the past month, Janis walked without hindrance up to the Banbury Road, where she caught a bus down to Keble Road, thence walking across to Parks Road, and into the museum itself, where from Mondays to Saturdays she began work at 8.30 a.m.

Her first job as always was to clear up any litter, such as the rings of zig-zag shavings often left behind by pupils who had sharpened their pencils the previous afternoon. And for a short while that morning, as she cleaned the floor and dusted the cabinets in the Upper Gallery, she paid little attention to the bright yellow splinter of wood on the floor below one of the cabinets there – until she noticed that the glass-topped lid was not resting flush upon its base. Then, too, she became aware of the slight disarray of the cabinet's contents, since there appeared one unfilled space in the ranks of the exhibits there, with both the artefact to the left of this gap, and the artefact to the right of it, knocked somewhat askew on the light beige hessian material which formed the backing for the display: 'Knives from Africa and South-East Asia'.

Janis reported her discovery immediately. And just after 9 a.m. Mr Herbert Godwin, attendant with responsibility for the Upper Gallery, was staring down at Cabinet 52.

'Oh dear!'

'Somebody's pinched somethin', Bert?'

'I reckon you could say that again.'

'What's gone?'

'Good question.'

'When could it have been, though?'

'Dunno. *After* I checked last night. Must have been. I allus check on these cabinets.'

'Well, it couldn't have been this morning. Nobody else's been here, 'cept me.'

'Have you got summat hidden in your knicker-pocket, Janis?'

'I've told you *before*, Bert. I only wear knickers on a Sunday.'

Gently Herbert Godwin patted the not-unattractive Janis on her ample bottom: 'We'd better go and inform our superiors, my love.'

Paradoxically Jane Cotterell, Administrator of the Museum, was attending a meeting that morning at the Ashmolean on 'Museum Security'. But straightway she was summoned to the telephone and was soon issuing her orders: the University Marshal was to be informed immediately, as were the police; the lower steps to the Upper Gallery were to be roped across, with the 'Temporarily Closed' sign positioned there; Dr Cooper, the Assistant Curator (Documentation) – and *only* Dr Cooper – should go along and, without touching anything, seek to ascertain, from his inventory lists, which object(s) had been stolen. She herself would be back in the Pitt Rivers as soon as she could possibly manage it.

Which was three-quarters of an hour later, her return coinciding with the arrival of the police from St Aldate's; *and* with the production of a sheet of paper on which she found the following sketch:

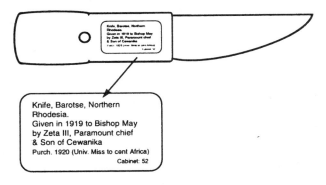

Knife, Barotse, Northern
Rhodesia.
Given in 1919 to Bishop May
by Zeta III, Paramount chief
& Son of Cewanika
Purch. 1920 (Univ. Miss to cent Africa)
Cabinet: 52

'That's it!' exclaimed a jubilant-looking Dr Cooper, as if the museum had suddenly acquired a valuable new exhibit, instead of losing one. 'Forty-seven knives – forty-seven! – there were in that cabinet. And you know how many there are now, Jane?'

'Forty-*six*, perhaps?' suggested the Administrator innocently.

CHAPTER THIRTY-NINE

Yes
You have come upon the fabled lands where myths
Go when they die
(JAMES FENTON, 'The Pitt Rivers Museum')

AT FIVE minutes to two, parked in front of the Radcliffe Science Library, Morse switched off *The Archers* (repeat).
'Well, we'd better go and have a look at things, I suppose.'

In retrospect, the linkage (if there were one) appeared so very obvious. Yet someone had to make it first, that someone being Jane Cotterell: the linkage between the earlier visit of the police; the museum's employment of Edward Brooks; the murder by knifing of Dr McClure; and now the theft of another knife, from one of the museum's cabinets.

Thus, it was Jane Cotterell herself who had argued that the City Police should link their inquiry into the theft with the Kidlington HQ inquiry into the murder of McClure; and Jane Cotterell herself who greeted Morse and Lewis, in the Pitt Rivers' Upper Gallery, at 2 p.m.

'It's what I was afraid of, though God knows why,' mumbled Morse to himself as he looked down at Cabinet 52, now dusted liberally with fine aluminium fingerprint-powder.

Ten minutes later, whilst Lewis was taking statements from Janis Lawrence and Herbert Godwin, Morse was seated opposite the Administrator, quickly realizing that he was unlikely to learn (at least from her) more than two fairly simple facts: first, that almost certainly the cabinet had been forced between 4.15 and 4.30 p.m. the previous afternoon; second, since the contents of the cabinet had been fully documented only six months earlier – when exhibits had been rearranged and cabinets relined – it could be stated quite authoritatively that one artefact, *and one only*, the Northern Rhodesian Knife, had been abstracted.

Yet Morse seemed uneasy.

'Could one of your own staff have pinched it?'

'Good Lord, no. Why should any of them want to do that? Most of them have access to the key-cupboard anyway.'

'I see.' Morse nodded vaguely; and stood up. 'By the way, what do you line your cabinets with? What material?'

'It's some sort of new-style hessian – supposed to keep its colour for yonks, so the advert said.'

Morse smiled, suddenly feeling close to her. 'Can I say something? I'd never have expected you to say "yonks".'

She smiled back at him, shyly. 'You wouldn't?'

It seemed a good moment for one of them to say something more, to elaborate on this intimate turn of the conversation. But neither did so. And Morse reverted to his earlier line of inquiry.

'You don't think anyone could have hidden himself, after closing time, and spent the night here in the museum?'

'Or herself? No. No, I don't. Unless they stood pretty motionless all through the night. You see, the place is positively bristling with burglar alarms. And anyway, it would be far too spooky, surely? I couldn't do it. Could *you*?'

'No. I've always been frightened of the dark myself,' admitted Morse. 'It's a bit eerie, this place, even in broad daylight.'

'Yes,' she said softly. 'When you come in here you enter a place where all the lovely myths go when they die.'

Suddenly Morse felt very moved.

After he had left her office, Jane felt guilty about not telling Morse that the 'myths' bit was far from original. And indeed she'd looked around to try to find him, to tell him so.

But he had left.

CHAPTER FORTY

Thursday is a bad day. Wednesday is quite a good day. Friday is an even better one. But Thursday, whatever the reason, is a day on which my spirit and my resolution, are at their lowest ebb. Yet even worse is any day of the week upon which, after a period of blessed idleness, I come face to face with the prospect of a premature return to my labours

(DIOGENES SMALL, *Autobiography*)

AN HOUR later, Morse was seated in the black leather chair in his office, still considering the sketch of the knife – when Lewis came back from the canteen carrying two polystyrene cups of steaming coffee.

'Northern Rhodesia, Lewis. Know where that is? Trouble is they keep changing all these place-names in Africa.'

'Zambia, sir. You know that.'

Morse looked up with genuine pain in his eyes. 'I never did any Geography at school.'

'You get a newspaper every day, though.'

'Yes, but I never look at the international news. Just the Crossword – and the Letters.'

'That's not true. I've often seen you reading the Obituaries.'

'Only to look at the years when they were born.'

Morse unwrapped the cellophane from his cigarettes, took one from the packet, and lit it, inhaling deeply.

'*You'll* be in the obituary columns if you don't soon pack up smoking. Anyway, you said you *had* packed it up.'

'I have, Lewis. It's just that I need to make a sort of gesture – some sort of sacrifice. That's it! A sacrifice. All right? You see, I'm only going to smoke this one cigarette. Only one. And the rest of them?'

Morse appeared to have reached a fateful decision. He picked up the packet and flicked it, with surprising accuracy, into the metal waste-bin.

'Satisfied?'

Lewis reached for the phone and rang the JR2 Outpatients department: no news. Then he rang Brenda Brooks: no news.

Edward Brooks was still missing.

'You don't think somebody's murdered *him*, sir?'

But Morse, as he studied yet again the details of the stolen knife, appeared not to hear. 'Would you rather be a bishop – or a paramount chief?'

'I don't want to be either, really.'

'Mm. I wouldn't have minded if they'd made me a paramount chief.'

'I thought they had, sir.'

'Where would a paramount chief go from here, Lewis?'

'I just asked you, sir, whether—'

'I heard you. The answer's "no". Brooks is alive and well. No. He may not be well, of course – but he's alive. You can bet your Granny Bonds on that.'

'Where *do* we go from here, then?'

'Well, I'm going to spend the rest of the afternoon in bed. I want to feel fresh for this evening. I've got a date with a beautiful lady.'

'Who's she?'

'Mrs Stevens – Julia Stevens.'

'When did you fix that up?'

'While you were getting the coffee.'

'You want me to come along?'

'Lew-is! I just told you. It's a *date*.'

'Didn't you believe Mrs Brooks? About where she spent last night?'

'I believed *that* all right. It's just that I reckon she knows where her husband is, that's all. And it's on the cards that if she does know, she probably told her friend, Mrs Stevens.'

'What would you like me to do, sir?'

'I'd like you to go and see Mrs Brooks's daughter – Ellie Smith, or whatever she calls herself. She's a key character in this case, don't you reckon? McClure's mistress – and Brooks's step-daughter.'

'Shouldn't *you* be seeing her then?'

'All in good time. I'm only just out of hospital, remember?'

'You mean she's not so attractive as Mrs Stevens.'

'Purely incidental, that is.'

'Anything else?'

'Yes. You'd better get back to the museum for a while. I don't think we're going to get very far on the fingerprint front – but you never know.'

Lewis was frowning. 'I just don't see the link myself – between the McClure murder, and now this Pitt Rivers business.'

'*She* saw a link, though, didn't she? Jane Cotterell? Clever lass, that one.'

'But she said whoever else it was, it couldn't have been Brooks who took the knife.'

'Exactly.'

'So?'

'So what?'

'So where's the link?'

Morse's eyes remained unblinking for several seconds, staring at nothing it seemed, and yet perhaps staring at everything. 'I'm not at all sure now that there is a link,' he said quietly. 'To find some connection between one event and another ensuing event is often difficult; and especially difficult perhaps when they *appear* to have a connection . . .'

Morse was aware of feeling worried at the prospect – the actuality, really – of his return to work. For, in truth, he had little real idea of the correct answers to the questions Lewis had just asked. He needed some assistance from somewhere; and as he drove down to North Oxford he patted his jacket-pocket where he felt the reassurance of the square packet he had retrieved from the waste-bin immediately after Lewis had left for the Pitt Rivers Museum.

CHAPTER FORTY-ONE

His failing powers disconcerted him, for what he would do with women he was unsure to perform, and he could rarely accept the appearance of females who thought of topics other than *coitus*

(PETER CHAMPKIN, *The Sleeping Life of Aspern Williams*)

NOW JULIA STEVENS was very fair to behold, for there was a gentle beauty in the pallor of the skin beneath that Titian hair, and the softest invitation in the redness of her lips. And as he sat opposite her that evening, Morse was immediately made aware of an animal magnetism.

'Care for a drink, Inspector?'

'No – er, no thank you.'

'Does that mean "yes"?'

'Yes.'

'Scotch?'

'Why not?'

'Say when.'

'When.'

'Cheers!'

'Mind if I smoke?'

'Yes, I do.'

She left the room, and reappeared with an ashtray. Perhaps they were beginning to understand each other.

'Mrs Brooks stayed the night here?' began Morse.

'Yes.'

'You see, her husband's missing – he failed to keep an appointment at the hospital this morning.'

'I know. Brenda rang me.'

'You'd both been to Stratford, I understand.'

'Yes.'

'Enjoy the play?'

'No.'

'Why?'

'My life will not be significantly impoverished if I never see another Shakespearian comedy.'

'Mrs Brooks enjoyed it though, I believe?'

Julia nodded, with a slow reminiscence. 'Bless her! Yes. She's not had much to smile about recently.'

'Have *you*?'

'Not much, really, no. Why do you ask that?'

But Morse made no direct answer. 'Isn't it just a bit odd, perhaps, that Mrs Brooks didn't call in to see if her husband was all right?'

'Odd? It's the most natural thing in the world.'

'Is it?'

'She hates him.'

'And why's that?'

'He treats her in such a cruel way – that's why.'

'How do you know that?'

'Brenda's told me.'

'You've no first-hand evidence?'

'I've always tried to avoid him.'

'Aren't you being a bit unfair, then?'

'I don't think so.'

'Have you any idea where he might be?'

'No. But I hope somebody's stuck a knife into him somewhere.'

As he looked across at the school-mistress, Morse found himself wondering whether her pale complexion was due not so much to that inherited colouration so common with the auburn type, as to some illness, possibly; for he had observed, in a face almost completely devoid of any other cosmetic device, some skin-tinted application to the darkened rings beneath her eyes.

'Did Mrs Brooks go out last night, after you'd got back?'

Julia smiled tolerantly. 'You mean, did she just nip out for a few minutes and bump him off?'

'*Could* she have gone out? That's all I'm asking.'

'Technically, I suppose – yes. She'd have a key to get back in here with. I just wonder what you think she did with the body, that's all.'

'She *didn't* go out – is that what you're telling me?'

'Look! The only thing I know for certain is that she was fast asleep when I took her a cup of tea just before seven this morning.'

'So she'd been with you the whole time since yesterday afternoon?'

'Since about a quarter to four, yes. I would have picked her up in the car, but the wretched thing wanted to stay at home in the garage. Suffering from electrical trouble.'

Morse, who didn't know the difference between brake fluid and anti-freeze, nodded wisely. 'You should get a car like mine. I've got a *pre*-electrics model.'

Julia smiled politely. 'We took a bus up to school and, well, that's about it, really.'

'Did you actually go into the Brooks's house?'

'Well, I suppose I did, yes – only into the hallway, though.'

'Was Mr Brooks there?'

'Only just. He was getting ready to go out, but he was still there when we left.'

'Did you speak to him?'

'You mean ... ask him politely if he was feeling better? You must be joking.'

'Did his wife speak to him?'

'Yes. She said "goodbye".'

'She didn't say "cheerio" or "see you soon"?'

'No. She said "goodbye".'

'What about you? Did *you* go out last night?'

'Do you suspect me as well?'

'Suspect you of what, Mrs Stevens?'

Julia's clear, grey eyes sparkled almost gleefully. 'Well, if somebody's bumped off old Brooks—'

'You look as if you hope someone has.'

'Didn't I make that clear from the start, Inspector?'

'Have you actually *seen* Mrs Brooks since you left home this morning?'

'No. I've been in school all day. Bad day, Thursday! No free periods. Then we had a staff meeting after school to try to decide whether we're all satisfying the criteria for the National Curriculum.'

'Oh.'

It was a dampener; and for a little while each was silent, with Morse looking around the neatly cluttered room. He saw, on the settee beside Julia, a copy of Ernest Dowson's *Poems*. He pointed to it:

'You enjoy Dowson?'

'You've *heard* of him?'

> *'They are not long, the weeping and the laughter,*
> *Love and desire and hate . . .'*

'I'm impressed. Can you go on?'

'Oh, yes,' said Morse quietly.

For some reason, and for the first time that evening, Julia Stevens betrayed some sign of discomfiture, and Morse saw, or perhaps he saw, a film of tears across her eyes.

'Anything else I can do for you, Inspector?'

Yes, you can take me to bed with you. I may feel no love for you, perhaps, but I perceive the beauty and the readiness of this moment, and soon there will be no beauty and no readiness.

'No, I think that's all,' he said.

The phone rang as they walked into the narrow hallway, and Julia quickly picked up the receiver.

'Hullo? Oh, hullo! Look, I'll ring you back in five minutes, all right? Just give me the number, will you?' She wrote down five digits on a small yellow pad beside the phone, and said 'Bye' – as did a male voice at the other end of the line (if Morse had heard aright).

As they took leave of each other at the doorway, it seemed for a moment that they might have embraced, however perfunctorily.

But they did not do so.

It might have been possible, too, for Morse to have spotted the true importance of what Julia Stevens had told him.

But he did not do so.

CHAPTER FORTY-TWO

You can lead a whore to culture
but you can't make her think
(Attributed to Dorothy Parker)

'HAVEN'T YOU got any *decent* music in this car?' she asked, as Lewis drove down the Iffley Road towards Magdalen Bridge.

'Don't you like it? That's your Mozart, that is. That's your slow movement of the Clarinet Concerto. I keep getting told I ought to educate my musical tastes a bit.'

'Bit miserable, innit?'

'Don't you go and say that to my boss.'

'Who's he when he's at home?'

'Chief Inspector Morse. Chap you're going to see. You're getting the VIP treatment this morning.'

'Don't you think I'm used to that, Sergeant?'

Lewis glanced across briefly at the young woman beside him in the front seat; but he made no reply.

'Don't believe me, do you?' she asked, a curious smile on her lips.

'Shall I . . . ?' Lewis's left hand hovered over the cassette 'on-off' switch.

'Nah! Leave it.'

She leaned back languorously; and even to the staid Lewis, as he made his way up to Kidlington, she seemed to exude a powerful sexuality.

When he had rung her late the previous afternoon, Lewis had been unable to get an answer; also been unable to get an answer in the early evening, when he had called at the house in Princess Street, off the Iffley Road, where she had her bed-sitter-cum-bathroom, and where he had left a note for her to call him back as soon as possible. Which was not very soon at all, in fact, since it had been only at 9.45 that morning when she'd rung, expressing the preference to be interviewed at Kidlington, and when Morse (sounding, from his home, in adequate fettle) had stated his intention to be present at the interview.

After Lewis had parked outside the HQ building, his passenger eased herself out of the car; and then, standing on the tarmac in full view of a good many interested eyes, stretched out her arms horizontally, slowly pressing them back behind her as far as the trapezius muscles would allow, her breasts straining forward against her thin blouse. Lewis, too, observed the brazen gesture with a gentle smile – and wondered what Morse would make of Ms Eleanor Smith.

In fact the answer would appear to be not very much, for the interview was strangely low-key, with Morse himself clearly deciding to leave everything to Lewis. First, Ms Smith gave what (as both detectives knew) was a heavily censored account of her lifestyle, appearing in no way surprised that for a variety of reasons she should be worthy of police attention – even police suspicion, perhaps. She'd had nothing to do with the murder of poor Dr McClure, of course; and she was confident that she could produce, if it proved necessary, some corroborative witnesses to account for most of her activities on that Sunday, 28 August: thirty-five of them, in fact, including the coach-driver. Yes, she'd known Matthew Rodway – and liked him. Yes, she'd known, still knew, Ashley Davies – and liked him as well; in fact it was with Davies she had been out the previous evening when the police had tried to contact her.

'You must have been with him a long time?' suggested Lewis.

Ms Smith made no reply, merely fingering her right (re-ringed) nostril with her right forefinger.

She was dismissive with the series of questions Lewis proceeded to put about drugs, and her knowledge of drugs. Surely the police didn't need *her* to tell them about what was going on? The easy availability of drugs. Their widespread use? What century were the police living in, for God's sake? And Morse found himself quietly amused as Lewis, just a little disconcerted now, persisted with this line of inquiry like some sheltered middle-aged father learning all about sex-parties and the like from some cruelly knowing little daughter of ten.

Last Wednesday? Where had she been then? Well, if they must know, she'd been in Birmingham for most of that day, on . . . well, on a personal matter. She'd got back to Oxford, back to Oxford station, at about half-past four. The train – surprise, surprise! – had been on time. And then? (Lewis had persisted.) Then she'd invited one of her friends – one of her girlfriends – up to her flat – her bed-sit! – where they'd drunk a bottle of far-from-vintage champers; and this muted celebration (the occasion for which Eleanor failed to specify) was followed by a somewhat louder merry-making at the local pub; whence she had gone home, whence she'd been *escorted* home, at closing-time. And if they wanted to know whether she'd woken up with a bad head, the answer was 'yes' – a bloody *dreadful* head.

Why all this interest in Wednesday, though? Why Wednesday afternoon? Why Wednesday evening? That's what she wanted to know.

Morse and Lewis had exchanged glances then. If she were telling the truth, it was not this woman, not McClure's former mistress, not Brooks's step-daughter, who had stolen the knife from Cabinet 52 – or done anything with it afterwards. Not, at least, on the Wednesday evening, for Lewis had been making a careful note of times and places and names; and if Eleanor Smith had been fabricating so much detail, she was doing it at some considerable peril. And after another glance from Morse, and a nod, Lewis told her of the theft from the Pitt Rivers, which had now pretty certainly been pinpointed to between 4.20 p.m. and 4.30 p.m. on Wednesday, the seventh; told her, too, of the disappearance of her step-father.

Ah, her step-father! Well, she could tell them something about him, all right. He was a pig. She'd buggered off from home because of him; and the miracle was that her mother hadn't buggered off from home because of him, too. She'd no idea (she claimed) that he was missing. But that wasn't going to cause her too much grief, was it? She just hoped that he'd remain missing, that's all; hoped they'd find him lying in a gutter somewhere with a knife – *that* knife – stuck firmly in his bloody guts.

The Chief Inspector had not spoken a single word to the woman he'd so recently heralded as his key witness in the case; and the truth was that, like some maverick magnet, he had felt half repelled, half attracted by the strange creature seated there, with her off-hand (*deliberately* common, perhaps?) manner of speech; with her lack of any respect for the dignity of police procedure; with her contempt concerning the well-being of her step-father, Mr Edward Brooks.

A note had been brought into the room a few minutes earlier and handed to Morse. And now, with the interview apparently nearing its end, Morse jerked his head towards the door and led the way into the corridor. The press, he told Lewis, had got wind of the Pitt Rivers business, and questions were being asked about a possible linkage with the murder inquiry. Clearly some of the brighter news editors were putting two and two together and coming up with an aggregate considerably higher than the sum of the component parts. Lewis had better go and mollify the media, and not worry too much about concealing any confidential information – which shouldn't be terribly difficult since there *was* no confidential information. He himself, Morse, would see that Ms Smith was escorted safely home.

CHAPTER FORTY-THREE

The scenery in the play was beautiful, but the actors got in front of it

(ALEXANDER WOOLLCOTT)

SHE SPOKE as Morse came up to the first roundabout on his way towards Oxford:

'Have you got *any* decent music in this car?'

'Such as what?'

'Well, your nice sergeant played me some Mozart. Fellah playin' the clarinet.'

'Jack Brymer, was it?'

'Dunno. He was great, though. It'd pay him to join a jazz group.'

'You think so?'

'If he's lookin' to the future.'

'He's about eighty.'

'Really? Ah well, you're no chicken yourself, are you?'

Morse, unsmiling, kept his eyes on the road.

'Your sergeant said you was tryin' to educate his musical tastes.'

'Did he?'

'You don't think *I* need a bit of educatin'?'

'I doubt it. I'd guess you're a whole lot better educated than you pretend to be. For all I know, you're probably quite a sensitive and appreciative lass – underneath.'

'Yeah? Christ! What the 'ell's *that* s'posed to mean?'

Morse hesitated before answering her. 'I'll tell you what your trouble is, shall I? You're suffering from a form of inverted snobbery, that's all. Not unusual, you know, in girls – in young ladies of . . . in young ladies like you.'

'If that's supposed to be a bloody insult, mister, you couldn't a' done much bleedin' better, could you?'

'I'm only guessing – don't be cross. I don't know you at all, do I? We've never even spoken—'

'Except on the phone. Remember?'

Morse almost managed a weak smile as he waited at the busy Cutteslowe roundabout.

'I remember.'

'Great, that was. You know, pretendin' to be somebody else. I sometimes think I should a' been an actress.'

'I think you are an actress – that's exactly what I was saying.'

'Well, I'll tell you somethin'. Right at this minute there's one thing I'd swap even for an Oscar.'

'What's that?'

'Plate of steak and chips. I'm starvin'.'

'Do you know how much steak costs these days?'

'Yeah. £3.99 at the King's Arms just down the road here: salad and chips chucked in. I saw it on the way up.'

'It says "French Fries", though, on the sign outside. You see, that's exactly what I meant about—'

'Yeah, you told me. I'm sufferin' summat chronic from inverted snobbery.'

'Don't *you* ever eat?' demanded Ellie, wiping her mouth on the sleeve of her blouse, and draining her third glass of red wine.

'Not very often at meal-times, no.'

'A fellah needs his calories, though. Got to keep his strength up – if you know what I mean.'

'I usually take most of my calories in liquid form at lunchtimes.'

'Funny, isn't it? You bein' a copper and all that – and then drinkin' all the beer you do.'

'Don't worry. I'm the only person in Oxford who gets more sober the more he drinks.'

'How do you manage that?'

'Years of practice. I don't recommend it though.'

'Wouldn't help you much with a bleedin' breathalyser, would it?'

'No,' admitted Morse quietly.

'Do you know when you've had enough?'

'Not always.'

'You had enough now?'

'Nearly.'

'Can I buy *you* something?'

'You know, nineteen times out of twenty ... But I've got to drive you home and then get back to give Sergeant Lewis his next music lesson.'

'What's all them weasel words s'posed to mean?'

'Pint of Best Bitter,' said Morse. 'If you insist.'

'Would you ever think of giving *me* a music lesson?' she asked, as after a wait at the lights in Longwall Street the Jaguar made its way over Magdalen Bridge.

'No.'

'Why not?'

'You want me to be honest?'

'Why not?'

'I just couldn't stick looking at those rings in your nose.'

She felt the insult like a slap across the face; and had the car still been queuing at the Longwall lights she would have jumped out of the Jaguar and left him. But they were travelling now quite quickly up the Iffley Road, and by the time they reached Princess Street she was feeling fractionally less furious.

'Look! Just tell your sergeant somethin' from me, will you?'

'*I'm* in charge of the case,' said Morse defensively, 'not Sergeant Lewis.'

'Well, you could a' fooled me. You never asked me nothin' – not at the station, did you? You hadn't said a single word till we got in the car.'

'Except on the phone. Remember?' said Morse quietly.

'Yeah, well, like I said, that was good fun ...' But the wind had been taken from her sails, and she glanced across at Morse in a slightly new light. In the pub, as she'd noticed, he'd averted his gaze from her for much of the time. And now she knew why ... He was a bit different – a lot different, really – from the rest of them; the rest of the men *his* age, anyway. Felix had once told her that she looked at people with eyes that were 'interested and interesting', and she would never forget that: it was the most wonderful compliment anyone had ever paid her. But this man,

Morse, hadn't even looked at her eyes; just looked at his beer for most of the time.

What the hell, though.

Bloody police!

'Look, somethin' for you or your sergeant, OK? If he wants to check up about Wednesday, when I went to Brum, I went to an abortion clinic there. Sort o' consultation. But I decided I wasn't goin' to go through with it – not this time, OK? Then, about last night, I went out with Ashley – Ashley Davies – and he asked me to marry him. With or without me bloody nose-rings, mister, OK?'

With that she opened the near-side door and jumped out.

She slammed it so hard that for a moment Morse was worried that some damage might have been incurred by the Jaguar's (pre-electrics) locking mechanism.

'And you can stuff your fuckin' Mozart, OK?'

CHAPTER FORTY-FOUR

No small art is it to sleep: it is necessary to keep awake all day for that purpose

(FRIEDRICH NIETZSCHE)

IT IS sometimes maintained, and with some cause, that insomnia does not exist. The argument, put most briefly, is that anyone unable to fall asleep has no real *need* to fall asleep. But there were several key players in the present drama who would have readily challenged such an argument that night – the night of Friday, 9 September.

Morse himself, who only infrequently had the slightest trouble in falling asleep, often had the contrary problem of 'falling awake' during the small hours, either to visit the loo, or to drink some water – the latter liquid figuring quite prominently with him during the night, though virtually never during the day. Yet sleep was as important to Morse as to any other soul; and specifically on the subject of sleep, the Greek poets and the Greek prose-writers had left behind several pieces of their literary baggage in the lumber-room of Morse's mind. And if, for him, the whole of the classical corpus had to be jettisoned except for one single passage, he would probably have opted for the scene depicting the death of Sarpedon, from Book XVI of the *Iliad*, where those swift companions, the twin brothers Sleep and Death, bear the dead hero to the broad and pleasant land of Lycia. And so very close behind Homer's words would have been those of Socrates, as he prepared to drink the hemlock, that if death were just one long and dreamless sleep then mortals could have nought to fear.

That night, though, Morse had a vivid dream – a dream that he was playing the saxophone in a jazz ensemble, yet (even in his dream) ever wondering whence he had acquired such dazzling virtuosity, and ever worried that his skill would at any second desert him in front of his adulatory audience – amongst whom he had spotted a girl with two rings in her nose; a girl who could never be Eleanor Smith, though, since the girl in the dream was disfigured and ugly; and Eleanor Smith could never be that . . .

Julia Stevens tossed back and forth in her bed that night, repeatedly turning over the upper of her two pillows as she sought to cool her hot and aching head. At half-past midnight, she got up and made herself another cup of Ovaltine, swallowing with it two further Nurofen. A great block of pain had settled this last week at the back of her head, and there was a ceaseless surge of something (blood?) that broke in rhythmic waves inside her ears.

During the daytime, she had so little fear of dying; but recently, in the hours of darkness, Fear had been stalking her bedroom, reporting to her its terrifying tales, and bullying her into confessing (Oh, God!) that, no, she didn't want to die. In her dream that night, when finally she drifted off into a fitful sleep, she beheld an image of the Pale Horse; and knew that the name of the one who rode thereon was Death . . .

Covering the space over and alongside the single bed pushed up against the inside wall of the small bedroom, were three large posters featuring Jimi Hendrix, Jim Morrison, and Kurt Cobain – rock idols who during their comparatively short lives had regularly diced with drugs and death. At 1 a.m., still dressed, Kevin

Costyn was sitting on the bed, his back against the creaking headboard, listening on his Walkman to some ear-blasting fury of punk music. In a perverse sort of way, he found it quite soothing. *Eroticon IV*, a crudely pornographic paperback, lay open on the bed beside him; but for the moment Kevin's mind was not beset with sexual fantasies.

Surprisingly, in a week of virtually unparalleled excitement, his thoughts were now centred more soberly on the nature of his surroundings: the litter-strewn front gardens along the road, with derelict, disembowelled cars propped up in drives; the shoddy, undusted, threadbare house in which he lived with his feckless mother; above all the sordid state of his own bedroom, and particularly of the dingy, soiled, creased sheets in which he'd slept for the past seven weeks or more. It was the contrast that had caught his imagination – the contrast between all this and the tidy if unpretentious terrace in which Mrs Julia Stevens lived; the polished, clean, sweet-smelling rooms in her house; above all, the snow-white, crisply laundered sheets on her inviting bed.

He thought he'd always known what makes the difference in life.

Money.

And as he took off his socks and trousers and got into bed, he found himself wondering how much money Mrs Stevens might have saved in life.

In the past few weeks Mrs Rodway was beginning to sleep more soundly. Sleeping pills, therapy, exercise, holidays, diet – none of them had been all that much help. But she had discovered something very simple which did help: she *counted*. One thousand and one; one thousand and two . . . and after a little while she would stop her counting, and whisper some few words aloud to herself: 'And – there – was – a – great – calm' . . . Then she would begin counting again, backwards this time: one thousand and five; one thousand and four . . .

Sometimes, as she counted, she almost managed not to think of Matthew. On a few nights recently, she didn't have to count at all. But this particular night was not one of them . . .

The previous evening, Ashley Davies had taken Ellie Smith to a motel near Buckingham where he, flushed with the success of his marriage proposal, and she, much flushed with much champagne, had slept between pale green sheets – an idyllic introit, one might have thought, to their newly plighted state.

And perhaps it was.

But as Davies lay awake, alone, this following night, he began to doubt that it was so.

His own sexual enjoyment had been intense, for *in medio coitu* she had surrendered her body to his with a wondrous abandon. Yet before and after their love-making – both! – he had sensed a disturbing degree of reserve in her, of holding back. Twice had she turned her mouth away from him when his lips had craved some full commitment, some deeper tenderness. And in retrospect he knew that there must be some tiny corner in her heart which she'd not unlocked as yet to any man.

In the early hours, she had turned fully away from him, seeming to grow colder and colder, as if sleep and the night were best; as if, too, somewhere within her was a secret passion committed already to someone else . . .

Restless, too, that night was the scout now given responsibility for Staircase G in the Drinkwater Quad at Wolsey. At 2 a.m. she went downstairs to the kitchen to make herself a cup of tea, looking in the mirror there at a neatly featured face, with its auburn hair cut in a fringe across the forehead: getting just a little long now, and almost covering a pair of worried eyes.

Susan had agreed to check and sign (at 10 o'clock the following morning, Saturday) the statement earlier made to Sergeant Lewis. And the prospect worried her. It was like reporting some local vandals to the police, when there was always the fear that those same vandals would return to wreak even greater havoc, precisely for having been reported. In her own case, though – as Susan was too intelligent not to appreciate – the risk was considerably greater. This was not a case of vandalism; but of murder. As such, she'd had little option but to make a full (if guarded) statement; yet she feared she would now be open to some sort of retaliation – to threats of physical violence, perhaps, from a man who, by an almost unanimous verdict, was seen as a very nasty piece of work indeed.

Back in bed, Susan tried a cure she'd once been told: to close one's eyes gently (yes, *gently*) and then to look (yes, *look*) at a point about four or five inches in front of one's nose. Such a strategy, it was claimed, would ensure that the eyeballs remained fairly still, being focused as they were upon some specific point, however notional that point might be; and since it had been demonstrated that the rapid revolving of the eyeballs in their sockets was a major cause of sleeplessness, insomniacs most certainly should experiment along such lines.

That night, therefore, Mrs Susan Ewers had so experimented, though with only limited success. As it happened, however, her apprehension was wholly groundless, since Edward Brooks was never destined to become a threat to Susan or to any other living person. One of those twins from Morse's schooldays, the one whose name was Death, had already claimed him for his own; and together with his brother, Sleep, had borne him off, though not perhaps to the broad and pleasant land of Lycia, wherein Sarpedon lies.

CHAPTER FORTY-FIVE

Keep careful watch too on the moral faults of your patients, which may cause them to tell untruths about things prescribed – and things proscribed

(*Corpus Hippocraticum*)

A WEEK in a murder inquiry, especially one in which there is virtually no development, can be a wearisome time. And so it was for Sergeant Lewis in the days between Friday 9 and Friday 16 September.

The whereabouts and movements of key characters in the Pitt Rivers inquiry, most particularly on the evening and night of Wednesday the seventh, immediately after the knife had been stolen, had been checked and in every case confirmed, with appropriate statements made and (with the more obvious misspellings corrected) duly signed and filed. Nothing else, though.

Nothing else, either, on the murder scene. House-to-house inquiries in Daventry Avenue had come to an end; and come to nothing. Three former undergraduates from Staircase G on Drinkwater Quad had been traced with no difficulty; but with no real consequence either, since apart from confirming the general availability of drugs during their years in Oxford they had each denied any specific knowledge of drug-trafficking on their own staircase.

What worried Lewis slightly was that Morse appeared just as interested in the disappearance of a knife as in the death of a don, as though the connection between the two events (Morse had yet again reversed his views) was both logically necessary and self-evidently true.

But *was* it?

And on the morning of Thursday, 15 September, he had voiced his growing doubt.

'Brooks, sir – Brooks is the only real connection, isn't he? Brooks who's top of your murder-suspects; and Brooks who's got a job at the Pitt Rivers.'

'Have you ever thought, Lewis, that it could have been Brooks who stole the knife?'

'You can't be serious?'

'No. Brooks didn't steal the knife. Sorry. Go on!'

'Well, you said so yourself early on: we often get people who do copy-cat things, don't we? And whoever stole the knife – well, it might not have anything to do with the murder at all. Somebody just read that bit in the *Oxford Mail* and . . .'

'Ye-es. To tell you the truth, I've been thinking the same.'

'It could just be a coincidence.'

'Yes, it could. Perhaps it was.'

'I mean, you've often said coincidences happen all the time; just that some of us don't spot 'em.'

'Yes, I've often thought that.'

'So there may be no causal connection after all—?'

'Stop sounding like a philosopher, Lewis, and go and get us some coffee.'

Morse, too, was finding this period of inactivity frustrating. *And* a time of considerable stress, since for three whole days now he had not smoked a single cigarette, and had arrived at that crucial point where his self-mastery had already been demonstrated, his victory over nicotine finally won. So? So it was no longer a question of relapsing, of reindulging. If he wished to re-*start*, though . . . for, in truth, the fourth day was proving even harder than the third.

The earlier wave of euphoria was ebbing still further on the fifth day, when it was his own turn to have a medical check-up, and when ten minutes before his appointment time he checked in at the Outpatients reception at the JR2 and sat down in the appropriate area to await his call, scheduled for 9.20 a.m. By some minor coincidence (yes!) this was the same time that Mr Edward Brooks had been expected for his own designated brand of Outpatient care – an appointment which had not been kept eight days earlier . . . and which was unkept still.

After undergoing a fairly thorough examination; after skilfully parrying the questions put to him about avoirdupois and alcohol; after politely declining a suggested consultation with a dietitian; after going along the corridor to have three further blood-samples taken – Morse was out again; out into the morning sunshine, with a new date (six whole weeks away!) written into his little blue card, and with the look of a man who feels fresh confidence in life. What was it that the doc had said?

'You know, I'm not quite sure why, but you're over things pretty well. You don't deserve to be, Mr Morse; but, well, you seem surprisingly fit to me.'

Walking along to the southern car park and savouring still the happy tidings, Morse caught sight of a young woman standing at the bus-stop there. By some minor coincidence (yes!) they had earlier been present together in the same waiting-room at the Summertown Health Centre, where neither had known the other. And now, here they were together again, on the same morning, at the same time, at the same hospital, both of them (as it appeared) on their way back home.

'Good morning, Miss Smith!' said the cheerful Chief Inspector, taking care to articulate a clear 'Miss', and not (as he always saw it) the ugly, pretentious, fuzzy 'Ms'.

Little that morning could have dampened Morse's spirits, for the gods were surely smiling on him. Even had she ignored his greeting, he would have walked serenely past, with little sense of personal slight. Yet perhaps he would have felt a touch of disappointment too; for he had seen the sadness in her face, and knew that for a little while he wanted to be with her.

CHAPTER FORTY-SIX

I once knew a person who spoke in dialect with an accent
(IRVIN COBB)

'THERE'S NO need really,' she said, manoeuvring herself into the passenger seat. 'I'm not short o' money, you know.'

'How long have you been waiting?'

'Long enough! Mind if I smoke?' she asked, as Morse turned left into Headley Way.

'Go ahead.'

'You want one?'

'Er, no thanks – not for me.'

'You *do* smoke, though. Else your wife does. Ashtray's full, innit? Think I'd make a good detective?'

'Which way's best?' asked Morse.

'Left at the White Horse.'

'Or *in* the White Horse, perhaps?'

'Er, no thanks – not for me,' she mimicked.

'Why's that?'

'They're not bloody open yet, that's why.' It was meant to be humorous, no doubt, but her voice was strained; and glancing sideways, Morse guessed that something was sorely wrong with her.

'Want to tell me about it?'

'Why the 'ell should I tell *you*?'

Morse breathed in deeply as she stubbed out her cigarette with venom. 'I think you've been in hospital overnight. I could see a bit of a white nightie peeping out of the hold-all. The last time we met you told me you were expecting a baby, and the JR1 is where they look after babies, isn't it? They wouldn't normally take a mum who's had a miscarriage, though – that'd be the Churchill. But if you had a *threatened* miscarriage, with some internal bleeding, perhaps, then they might well get you into the JR1 for observation. That's the sort of thing a policeman gets to know, over the years. And please remember,' he added gently, 'I only asked if you wanted to tell me about it.'

Tears coursed down cheeks that were themselves wholly

devoid of make-up; washing down with them, though, some of the heavy eye-shadow from around her dull-green eyes.

'I lost it,' she said, finally.

For a moment or two Morse considered placing his hand very gently, very lightly on hers, but he feared that his action would be misconstrued.

'I'm sorry,' he said simply, not speaking again until he reached Princess Street.

She got out of the car and picked up her hold-all from the back. 'Thank you.'

'I wasn't much help, I'm afraid. But if I *can* ever be of any help, you've only got to give me a ring.' He wrote down his ex-directory telephone number.

'Well, you could help now, actually. It's a lousy little place I live in – but I'd be quite glad if you'd come in and have a drink with me.'

'Not this morning.'

'Why the 'ell *not*, for Christ's sake? You just said to give you a ring if I needed any help – and I bloody *do*, OK? *Now*.'

'All right. I'll come in and have one quick drink. On one condition, though.'

'What's that?'

'You don't slam the car door. Agreed?'

'Doesn't seem *too* lousy a little place?' suggested Morse as, whisky in hand, he leaned back in the only armchair in the only room – the fairly large room, though – which was Eleanor Smith's bed-sitter-cum-bathroom.

'I can assure you it *is*. Crawling with all those microscopic creatures – you've seen photographs of them?'

Morse looked at her. Was he imagining things? Hadn't she just spoken to him with a degree of verbal and grammatical fluency that was puzzlingly at odds with her habitual mode of speech. 'Crawlin' wiv all them little bugs an' things' – wasn't *that* how she'd normally have expressed herself?

'I think I know why you're lookin' at me like that,' she said.

'Pardon?'

In answer, she placed an index finger on each nostril. On each ringless nostril.

And Morse nodded. 'Yes, I prefer you as you are now.'

'So you said.'

'You know that your step-father's still missing?'

'So what? You want me to break out into goose-pimples or something?'

'Why do you hate him so much?'

'Next question.'

'All right. You said you were going to get married. Does all this – the loss of your baby – does it make any difference?'

'Gettin' deep, ain't we? Cigarette?'

Ellie held out the packet; and stupidly, inevitably, Morse capitulated.

'You're still going ahead with getting married?'

'Why not? It's about time I settled down, don't you think?'

'I suppose so.'

'What else can I tell you?'

Well, if she was inviting questions (Morse decided) it was a good opportunity to probe a little more deeply into the heart of the mystery, since he was convinced that the key to the case – the key to *both* cases – lay somewhere in those late afternoon hours of Wednesday, 7 September, when someone had stolen the knife from the Pitt Rivers Museum.

'After your trip to Birmingham, you *could* have caught an earlier train back?'

She shrugged. 'Dunno. I didn't, though.'

'Do you remember exactly what time you asked your friend up here – when you got back that afternoon?'

'Exactly? Course I can't. *She* might. Doubt it, though. We were both tight as ticks later that night.'

Was she lying? And if so, why?

'On that Wednesday—'

But she let him get no further. 'Christ! Give it a rest about Wednesday, will you? What's wrong with Tuesday? Or Monday? I 'aven't a bleedin' clue what I was doin' them days. So why *Wednesday*? Like I say, I know where I was all the bloody time that day.'

'It's just that there may be a connection between Dr McClure's murder and the theft of the knife.'

She seemed unimpressed, but mollified again. 'Drop more?'

'No, I must be off.'

'Please yourself.' She poured herself another Scotch, and lit another cigarette. 'Beginnin' to taste better. I hadn't smoked a fag for three days – three days! – before that one in your car. Tasted terrible, that first one.'

Morse rose to his feet and put his empty glass down on the cluttered mantelpiece, above which, on the white chimney-breast, four six-inch squares in different shades of yellow had been painted – with the name of each shade written in thick pencil inside each square: Wild Primrose, Sunbeam, Buttermilk, Daffodil White.

'Which d'you like best?' she asked. 'I'm considering some redecoration.'

There it was again, in that last sentence – the gear-shift from casual slang to elegance of speech. Interesting . . .

'But won't you be leaving here – after you're married?'

'Christ! You can't leave it alone, can you? All these bloody questions!'

Morse turned towards her now, looking down at her as she sat on the side of the bed.

'Why did you invite me here? I only ask because you're making me feel I'm unwelcome – an intruder – a Nosey Parker. Do you realize that?'

She looked down into her glass. 'I felt lonely, that's all. I wanted a bit of company.'

'Haven't you told Mr Davies – about your miscarriage?'

'No.'

'Don't you think—'

'Augh, shut up! You wouldn't know what it feels like, would you? To be on your own in life . . .'

'I'm on my own all the time,' said Morse.

'That's what they all say, did you know that? All them middle-aged fellows like you.'

Morse nodded and half-smiled; and as he walked to the door he looked at the chimney-breast again.

'Yellow's a difficult colour to live with; but I'd go for the Daffodil White, if I were you.'

Leaving her still seated on the bed, he trod down the narrow, squeaking stairs to the Jaguar, where for a few minutes he sat motionless, with the old familiar sensation tingling across his shoulders.

Why hadn't he thought of it before?

CHAPTER FORTY-SEVEN

Given a number which is a square, when can we write it as the sum of two other squares?

(DIOPHANTUS, *Arithmetic*)

LEWIS WAS eager to pass on his news. Appeals on Radio Oxford and Fox FM, an article in the *Oxford Mail*, local enquiries into the purchase, description, and condition of Brooks's comparatively new bicycle, had proved, it appeared, successful. An anonymous phone-call (woman's voice) had hurriedly informed St Aldate's City Police that if they were interested there was a 'green bike' chained to the railings outside St Mary Mags in Cornmarket. No other details.

'Phone plonked down pronto,' the duty sergeant had said.

'Sure it wasn't a "Green dyke" chained to the railings?' Lewis had asked, in a rare excursion into humour.

Quite sure, since the City Police were now in possession of one bicycle, bright green – awaiting instructions.

The call had come through just after midday, and Lewis felt excitement, and gratification. Somebody – some mother or wife or girlfriend – had clearly decided to push the hot property back into public circulation. Once in a while procedure and patience paid dividends. Like now.

If it was Brooks's bike, of course.

Morse, however, on his rather late return from lunch, was to give Lewis no immediate opportunity of reporting his potentially glad tidings.

'Get on all right at the hospital, sir?'

'Fine. No problem.'

'I've got some news—'

'Just a minute. I saw Miss Smith this morning. She'd been in the JR1 overnight.'

'All right, is she?'

'Don't know about that. But she's a mixed-up young girl, is our Eleanor,' confided Morse.

'Not really a *girl*, sir.'

'Yes, she is. Half my age, Lewis. Makes me feel old.'

'Well, perhaps . . .'

'She gave me an idea, though. A beautiful idea.' Morse stripped the cellophane from a packet of cigarettes, took one out, and lit it from a box of matches, on which his eyes lingered as he inhaled deeply. 'You know the problem we're faced with in this case? We've got to square the first case – the murder of McClure.'

'No argument there.'

'Then we've got to square the second case – the theft of a Northern Rhodesian knife. And the connection between these two—'

'But you said perhaps there wasn't any connection.'

'Well, there is and now *I know what it is.*'

'I see,' said Lewis, unseeing.

'As I say, if we square the first case, and then we square the second case ... all we've got to do is to work out the sum of the two squares.'

Lewis looked puzzled. 'I'm not quite following you, sir.'

'Have you heard of "Pythagorean Triplets"?'

'We did Pythagoras' Theorem at school.'

'Exactly. The most famous of all the triplets, that is – "3, 4, 5": $3^2 + 4^2 = 5^2$. Agreed?'

'Agreed.'

'But there are more spectacular examples than that. The Egyptians, for example, knew all about "5961, 6480, 8161".'

'That's good news, sir. I didn't realize you were up on things like that.'

Morse looked down at the desk. 'I'm not. I was just reading from the back of this matchbox here.'

Lewis grinned as Morse continued.

'There was this fellow called Fermat, it seems – I called in at home and looked him up. He knew all about "things like that", as you put it: square-roots, and cube-roots, and all that sort of stuff.'

'Has he got much to do with *us*, though – this fellow?'

'Dunno, Lewis. But he was a marvellous man. In one of the books on arithmetic he was studying he wrote something like: "I've got a truly marvellous demonstration of this proposition which this margin is too narrow to contain." Isn't that a wonderful sentence?'

'If you say so, sir.'

'Well, I've worked out the square of three and the square of four and I've added them together and I've come up with – guess what, Lewis!'

'Twenty-five?'

'Much more! You see, this morning I suddenly realized where we've been going wrong in this case. We've been assuming what we were *meant* to assume ... No. Let me start again. As you know, I felt pretty certain almost from the beginning that McClure was murdered by Brooks. And I think now, though I can't be certain of course, that Brooks himself was murdered last week. And I know – listen, Lewis! – I now know what Brooks's murderer *wanted* us to think.'

Lewis looked at the Chief Inspector, and saw that not uncommon, strangely distanced, almost mystical look in the gentian-blue eyes.

'You see, Brooks's body is somewhere where we'll never find it – I feel oddly sure about that. Pushed in a furnace, perhaps, or buried under concrete, or left in a rubbish-dump—'

'Waste Reception Area, sir.'

'Wherever, yes. But consider the *consequences* of the body never being found. We all jump to the same conclusion – the conclusion our very intelligent Administrator at the Pitt Rivers jumped to: that there was a direct link between the murder of Brooks and the theft of the knife. Now, there was a grand deception here. The person who murdered Brooks wanted us to take one fact for granted, and almost – almost! – he succeeded.'

'Or she.'

'Oh, yes. Or she ... But as I say the key question is this: why was the knife stolen? So let me tell you. That theft was a great big bluff! For what purpose? To convince us that Brooks was murdered after 4.30 p.m. on that Wednesday the seventh. But he wasn't,' asserted Morse slowly. '*He was murdered the day before –* he was murdered on Tuesday the sixth.'

'But he was seen alive on the Wednesday, sir. His wife saw him – Mrs Stevens saw him—'

'Liars!'

'Both of 'em?'

'Both of them.'

'You mean ... you mean *they* murdered Brooks?'

'That's exactly what I do mean, yes. As I see things, it must have been Julia Stevens who supplied the brains, who somehow arranged the business with the knife. But what – *what*, Lewis – if Brooks was murdered by *another* knife – a household knife, let's say – a knife just like the one McClure was murdered with, the knife that was found in Daventry Avenue, the knife that was missing from the Brooks's kitchen.'

Lewis shook his head slowly. 'Why all this palaver, though?'

'Good question. So I'll give you a good answer. To give the murderer – murderers – watertight alibis for that *Wednesday*. I sensed something of the sort when I interviewed Julia Stevens; and I suddenly *knew* it this morning when I was interviewing our punk-wonder.'

'She's in it, too, you reckon?'

Morse nodded. 'All three of them have been telling us the same thing, really. In effect they've been saying: "Look! I don't mind being suspected of doing something on Tuesday – but *not on the Wednesday*." They're happy about not having an alibi for the day Brooks was murdered. It was for the day afterwards – the Wednesday – that for some reason they figured an alibi was vital. And – surprise, surprise! – they've each of 'em got a beautiful alibi for then. It's been very clever of them – this sort of casual indifference they've shown for the *actual* day of the murder, the Tuesday. You see, they all knew they'd be the likely suspects, and they've been very gently, very cleverly, pushing us all along in the direction they wanted.'

'All three of them, you think?'

'Yes. They'd *all* have gladly murdered Brooks, even if they hadn't known he was a murderer himself: the wife he'd treated so cruelly; the step-daughter he'd probably abused; and Julia Stevens, who could see how her little cleaner was being knocked about by the man she'd married. So they hatch a plot. They arrange for the knife to be stolen, having made sure that none of *them* could have stolen it—'

'Ellie Smith could have stolen it,' interposed Lewis quietly.

'Yes . . . perhaps she could, yes. But I don't think so. Didn't the attendant think it was more likely to have been a man? No. My guess is that they bribed someone to steal it – someone they could trust . . . someone *one* of them could trust.'

'Ashley Davies?'

'Why not? He's got his reward, hasn't he?'

'You think that's a reward, sir, marrying *her*?'

Morse was silent awhile. 'Do you know, Lewis, it might be. It might be . . .'

'What did they do with the knife?'

'That's the whole point. That's what I'm telling you. *They didn't use the stolen knife at all*. They just got rid of it.'

'But you can't just get rid of things like that.'

'Why not? Stick it in a black bag and leave it for the dustmen. You could leave a dismembered corpse in one of those and get away with it. *Kein Problem*. The only thing the dustmen won't take is garden-refuse – that's a well-known fact, isn't it?'

'You seem to be assuming an awful lot of brains somewhere.'

'Look, Lewis! There seems to be a myth going round these days that criminals are a load of morons and that CID personnel are all members of Mensa.'

'Perhaps I should apply then,' said Lewis slowly.

'Pardon?'

'Well, I've been very clever, sir, while you were away. I think I've found Brooks's bike.'

'You have? Why the hell didn't you tell me before?'

CHAPTER FORTY-EIGHT

It'll do him good to lie there unconscious for a bit. Give his brain a rest

(N. F. SIMPSON, *One-Way Pendulum*)

AT THE Proctor Memorial School that Friday afternoon the talk was predominantly of a ram-raid made on an off-licence in the Blackbird Leys Estate the previous evening, when by some happy chance a routine police patrol-car had been cruising round the neighbourhood just as three youths were looting the smashed shop in Verbena Avenue; when, too, a little later, the same police car had been only fifty or so yards behind when the stolen getaway car had crashed at full speed into a juggernaut lorry near the Horspath roundabout on the Eastern Ring Road . . .

When the chase was over one of the three was seated dead in the driving seat, his chest crushed by the collapsed steering-wheel; another, the one in the front passenger seat, had his right foot mangled and trapped beneath the engine-mounting; the third, the one seated in the back, had severe lacerations and contusions around the head and face and was still unconscious after the firemen had finally cut free his colleagues in crime from the concertina'ed Escort.

The considerable interest in this incident – accident – is readily explicable, since two of the youths, the two who survived the crash, had spent five years at the Proctor Memorial School; had spent fifteen terms mocking the attempts of their teachers to instil a little knowledge and a few of the more civilized values into their lives. Had they received their education at one of the nation's more prestigious establishments – an Eton, say, or a Harrow, or a Winchester – the youths would probably have been designated 'Old Boys' instead of the 'former pupils' printed in the late afternoon edition of the *Oxford Mail*. And the former pupil who had been seated in the back of the car had left his Alma Mater only the previous term.

His name was Kevin Costyn.

Julia Stevens walked round to her former pupil's house during the lunch-break that Friday, wishing, if she could, to speak to Kevin's mother. But the doorbell, like most of the other fixtures there by the look of things, was out of order; and no one answered her repeated knockings. As she slowly turned and walked back through the neglected, litter-strewn front garden, a young woman, with two small children in a push-chair, stopped for a moment by the broken gate, and spoke to her.

'The people in there are usually out.'

That was all.

Perhaps, thought Julia Stevens, as she made her way thoughtfully back to school – perhaps that brief, somewhat enigmatic utterance could explain more about her former pupil than she herself had ever learned.

In the Major Trauma Ward, on Level 5 of the JR2 in Headington, she explained to the ward-sister that she had rung an hour earlier, at 6 p.m., and been told that it would be all right for her to visit Mr Kevin Costyn.

'How is he?'

'Probably not quite so bad as he looks. He's had a CT test – Computerized Tomography – and there doesn't *seem* to be any damage but we're a little bit worried about his brain, yes. And he looks an awful mess, I'm afraid. Please prepare yourself, Mrs Stevens.'

He was awake, and recognized her immediately.

'I'm sorry,' he whispered, speaking through a dreadfully

lopsided mouth, like one who has just received half a dozen injections of local anaesthetic into one half of the jaw.

'Sh! I've just come to see how you're getting on, that's all.'

'I'm sorry.'

'Listen! I'm the teacher, remember? Just let *me* do the talking.'

'That were the worst thing I ever done in my life.'

'Don't talk about it now! *You* weren't driving.'

He turned his face towards her, revealing the left cheek, so terribly bloodied and stitched and torn.

'It's not that, Mrs Stevens. It's when I asked you for the money.' His eyes pleaded with her. 'I should never a' done that. You're the only person that was ever good to me, really – and then I go and . . .'

His words were faltering further, and there was a film of tears across his eyes.

'Don't worry about that, Kevin!'

'Will you promise me something? *Please?*'

'If I can, of course I will.'

'*You* won't worry if I don't worry.'

'I promise.'

'There's no need, you see. I won't ever tell anybody what I done for you – honest to God, I won't.'

A few minutes later, Julia was aware of movement behind her, and she turned to see the nurse standing there with a uniformed policeman, the latter clutching his flat hat rather awkwardly to his rib-cage.

It was time to go; and laying her hand for a few seconds on Kevin's right arm, an arm swathed in bandages and ribbed with tubes, she took her leave.

As she waited for the lift down to the ground floor, she smiled sadly to herself as she recalled the nurse's words: 'But we're a little bit worried about his brain' . . . just like almost all the staff at the Proctor Memorial School had been, for five years . . . for fifteen terms.

And then, as she tried to remember exactly where she'd parked the Volvo, she found herself, for some reason, thinking of Chief Inspector Morse.

CHAPTER FORTY-NINE

I sometimes wonder which would be nicer – an opera without an interval, or an interval without an opera
(ERNEST NEWMAN, *Berlioz, Romantic and Classic*)

OF THE four separate operas which comprise *Der Ring des Nibelungen* (an achievement which in his view ranked as one of the seven great wonders of the modern world), *Siegfried* had always been Morse's least favourite. And on the evening of Saturday, 17 September, he decided he would seek again to discover whether the fault lay with himself or with Wagner. But the evening was destined not to pass without its interruptions.

At 7.35 p.m. Lewis had rung through with the dramatic news that the handle-bars and the saddle on the bicycle recovered from the railings outside the parish church of St Mary Magdalene still bore traces of blood, and that preliminary tests pointed strongly to its being McClure's blood. Such findings, if confirmed, would provide the police with their first physical link between Felix McClure and Edward Brooks, since the latter's wife, Brenda, had now identified the bike as her husband's; as had one of the assistants at Halford Cycles on the Cowley Road, where Brooks had purchased the bike four months previously. A warrant, therefore, should be made out asap for the arrest of Mr Edward Brooks – with Morse's say-so.

And Morse now said so.

The fact that the person against whom the warrant would be issued was nowhere to be found had clearly taken some of the cream from Lewis's éclair. But Morse seemed oddly content: he maintained that Lewis was doing a wonderful job, but forbad him to disturb him again that evening, barring some quite prodigious event – such as the birth of another Richard Wagner.

So Morse sat back again, poured himself another Scotch, lit another cigarette, and turned *Siegfried* back on.

Paradise enow.

Very few people knew Morse's personal (ex-directory) telephone number, and in fact he had changed it yet again a few months earlier. When, therefore, forty minutes further into *Siegfried*, the telephone rang once more, Morse knew that it must be Lewis again; and thumping down his libretto with an ill grace, he answered tetchily.

'What do you want this time?'

'Hullo? Chief Inspector Morse?' It was a woman's voice, and Morse knew whose. Why had he been such a numbskull as to give his private number to the pink-haired punk-wonder?

'Yes?'

'Hi! You told me if ever I wanted any help, all I'd got to do was pick up the phone, remember?'

'How can I help?' asked Morse wearily, a hint of exasperation in his voice.

'You don't sound overjoyed to hear from me.'

'Just a bit tired, that's all.'

'Too tired for me to treat you to a pint?'

Morse wasn't quite sure at that moment whether his spirits were rising or falling. 'Sometime next week, perhaps?' he suggested.

'No. I want to see you tonight. Now. Right *now*.'

'I'm sorry, I can't see you tonight—'

'Why not?'

'Well, to tell you the truth, I'm in the bath.'

'Wiggle the water a bit so I can hear.'

'I can't do that – I'd get the phone wet.'

'So you didn't really mean what you said at all.'

'Yes, I did. I'll be only too glad to help. What's the trouble?'

'It's no good – not over the phone.'

'Why on earth not?'

'You'll see.'

'I don't follow you.'

'I'm just going out to catch a bus to the City Centre. With a bit of luck I'll be there in twenty minutes – outside Marks and Sparks – that's where it stops, and then I'm going to walk up St Giles', and I'm goin' in the Old Parsonage for a drink. I'll stay there half an hour. And if you've not turned up by then, I'll just take a taxi up to your place – OK with you?'

'No, it's not. You don't know where I live anyway—'

'Nice fellah, Sergeant Lewis. I could fall for 'im.'

'He's never told you my address!'

'Why don't you ring and ask 'im?'

Morse looked at his wrist-watch: almost half-past eight.

'Give me half an hour.'

'Won't you need a bit longer?'

'Why's that?'

'Well, you've got to get yourself dried and then get dressed and then make sure you can find your wallet and then catch a bus—'

'Make it three-quarters of an hour, then,' said Morse, wondering, in fact, where his wallet was, for he seldom used it when Lewis was around.

Lewis himself rang again that evening, about ten minutes after Morse had left. The path lab had confirmed that the blood found on the recovered bicycle was McClure's; and on his way home (a little disappointed) he pushed a note to that effect through the front door of Morse's bachelor flat – together with the newspaper cutting from the previous week's *Oxford Times* received from one of his St Aldate's colleagues:

THIEVES PUT SPOKE IN THINGS

An optimistic scheme to provide free bicycles was scrapped yesterday by the Billingdon Rural District Council.

The cycles, painted green, and repaired by young offenders on community service, were put into specially constructed stands outside the church for villagers to use and then return.

However within thirty-six hours of the scheme being launched, all twelve cycles, purchased at a cost of £1100, had disappeared.

The chair of the Council, Mrs Jean Ashton, strongly defended the initiative. 'The bikes are still somewhere on the road,' she maintained.

DC Watson of the Thames Valley Police agreed: 'Most of them probably in Oxford or Banbury, resprayed a bright red.'

Ashley Davies also had repeatedly rung an Oxford number that Saturday evening, but with similar lack of success; and he (like Sergeant Lewis) felt some disappointment. Ellie had told him that she would be out all day, but suggested that he gave her a ring in the evening. His news could wait – well, it wasn't really 'news', at all. He just wanted her to know how efficient he'd been.

He'd visited the plush, recently opened Register Office in New Road, where he'd been treated with courtesy and competence. In the circumstances 'Notice by Certificate' (he'd been informed) would be the best procedure – with Saturday, 15 October a possible, probable, marriage date, giving ample time for the requisite notices to be posted both at Bedford and at Oxford. He'd agreed to ring the Registrar the following Monday with final confirmation.

A few 'family' to witness the ceremony would have been nice. But, as Ashley was sadly aware, his own mother and father had long since distanced themselves from 'that tart'; and although Ellie's mum could definitely be counted upon, no invitation would ever be sent to her step-father – and that not just because he had left no forwarding address, but because Ellie would never allow even the mention of his name.

Only one wedding guest so far then. But it would be easy to find a few others; and anyway the legal requirement (Ellie, oddly enough, had known all about this) was only for two.

Ashley rang her number again at 10 p.m. Still no answer. And for more than a few minutes he felt a surge of jealousy as he wondered where she was, and with whom she was spending the evening.

CHAPTER FIFTY

There is not so variable a thing in nature as a lady's head-dress: within my own memory I have known it rise and fall above thirty degrees

(JOSEPH ADDISON, *The Spectator*)

SHE WAS nowhere to be seen in the area known as the Parsonage Bar, which (as we know) served as a combined bar and restaurant. There were, however, two temporarily unescorted young women there, one blonde, the other brunette. The former, immaculately coiffured, and dressed in a white suit, would attract interest wherever she went; the latter, her hair cut stylishly short, and dressed in a fold-over Oxford-blue creation, would perhaps attract her own fair share of attention too, but her face was turned away from Morse, and it was difficult for him to be certain.

With no real ale on offer, he ordered a glass of claret, and stood at the bar for a couple of minutes watching the main door; then sat on one of the green bar-stools for a further few minutes, still watching the main door.

But Miss Smith made no entrance.

'Are you on your own?'

The exaggeratedly seductive voice had come from directly behind him, and Morse swivelled to find one of the two women, the brunette, climbing somewhat inelegantly on to the adjoining stool.

'For the moment I am, yes. Er, can I buy – ?'

He had been looking at her hair, a rich dark brown, with bottled-auburn highlights. But it was not her hair that had caused the mid-sentence hiatus, for now he was looking into her eyes – eyes that were sludgy-green, like the waters of the Oxford Canal.

'Ye gods!' he exclaimed.

'Didn't recognize me, did you? I've been sittin' waitin'. Good job I've got a bit of initiative.'

'What will you have to drink?'

'Champagne. I fancy some champagne.'

'Oh.' Morse looked down at the selection of 'Wines available by the Glass'.

'Can't we stretch to a bottle?' she asked.

Morse turned over the price-list and surveyed 'A Selection of Vintage Champagnes', noting with at least partial relief that most of them were available in half-bottles. He pointed to the cheapest (cheapest!) of these, a Brut Premier Cru: £18.80.

'That should be all right, perhaps?'

She smiled at him slyly. 'You look a little shell-shocked, Inspector.'

In fact Morse was beginning to feel annoyed at the way she was mocking him, manipulating him. He'd show her!

'Bottle of Number 19, waiter.'

Her eyebrows lifted and the green eyes glowed as if the sun were shining on the waters. She had crossed her legs as she sat on the bar-stool, and Morse now contemplated a long expanse of thigh.

'"Barely Black" they're called – the stockings. Sort of sexy name, isn't it?'

Morse drained his wine, only newly aware of why Eleanor Smith could so easily have captivated (*inter alios*) Dr Felix McClure.

They sat opposite each other at one of the small circular-topped tables.

'Cheers, Inspector.'

'Cheers.'

He noticed how she held the champagne glass by the stem, and mentally awarded her plus-one for so doing; at the same time cancelling it with minus-one for the fingernails chewed down to the quicks.

'It's OK – I'm workin' on it.'

'Pardon?'

'Me fingernails – you were lookin' at 'em, weren't you? Felix used to tell me off about 'em.' She speared first a green, then a black olive.

'You can't blame me for not recognizing you. You look completely different – your hair . . .'

'Yeah. Got one o' me friends to cut it and then I washed it out – four times! – then I put some other stuff on, as near me own colour as I could get. Like it?'

She pushed her hair back from her temples and Morse noticed the amethyst earrings in the small, neat ears.

'Is your birthday in February?'

'I say! What a clever old stick you are.'

'Why this . . . this change of heart, though?'

She shook her head. 'Just change of appearance. You can't change your heart. Didn't you know that?'

'You know what I mean,' said Morse defensively.

'Well, like I told you, I'm gettin' spliced – got to be a respectable girl now – all that sort o' thing.'

Morse watched her as she spoke and recalled from the first time he'd seen her the glossy-lipsticked mouth in the powder-pale face. But everything had changed now. The rings had gone too, at least temporarily, from her nose; and from fingers, too, for previously she had worn a whole panoply of silverish rings. Now she wore just one, a slender, elegant-looking thing, with a single diamond, on the third finger of her left hand.

'How can I help you?' asked Morse.

'Well, I thought you might like to *see* me for starters – that wouldn't 'ave bin no good over the blower, would it?'

'Why do you have to keep talking in that sort of way? You've got a pleasant voice and you can speak very nicely. But sometimes you deliberately seem to try to sound like a . . .'

'A trollop?'

'Yes.'

Neither of them spoke for a while. Then it was Ellie:

'I wanted to ask you two things really.'

'I'm all ears.'

'Actually you've got quite nice ears, for a man. Has anyone ever told you that?'

'Not recently, no.'

'Look. You think my step-father's dead, don't you?'

'I'm not sure what I think.'

'If he is dead, though, *when* do you think . . . ?'

'As I say – I just don't know.'

'Can't you guess?'

'Not to you, Miss Smith, no.'

'Can't you call me "Ellie"?'

'All right.'

'What do I call you?'

'They just call me Morse.'

'Yes – but your Christian name?'

'Begins with "E", like yours.'

'No more information?'

'No more information.'

'OK. Let me tell you what's worrying me. You think Mum's had something to do with all this, don't you?'

'As I say—'

'I agree with you. She may well have had, for all I know – and good luck to her if she did. But *if* she did, it must have been before that Wednesday. You know why? Because – she doesn't know this – but I've been keeping an eye on her since then, and there's no way – *no way* – she could have done it after . . .'

'After what?' asked Morse quietly.

'Look, I've read about the Pitt Rivers business – everybody has. It's just that . . . I just wonder if something has occurred to you, Inspector.'

'Occasionally things occur to me,' said Morse.

'Have you got any cigarettes, by the way?'

'No, I've given up.'

'Well, as I was saying, what if the knife was stolen on the Wednesday afternoon to give everybody the impression that the murder – if there *is* a murder – was committed *after* that Wednesday afternoon? Do you see what I mean? OK, the knife was *stolen* then – but what if it wasn't *used*? What if the murder was committed with a *different* knife?'

'Go on.'

'That's it really. Isn't that enough?'

'You realize what you're saying, don't you? If your step-father *has* been murdered; if he was murdered *before* the theft of the knife, then your mother is under far more suspicion, not less. As you say, quite rightly, she's got a continuous alibi from the time she left for Stratford with Mrs Stevens on that Wednesday, but she hasn't got much of one for the day before. In fact she probably hasn't got one at all.'

Ellie looked down at the avocado-coloured carpet, and sipped the last of her champagne.

'Would you like me to go and get a packet of cigarettes, Inspector?'

Morse drained his own glass.

'Yes.'

Whilst she was gone (for he made no effort to carry out the errand himself) Morse sat back and wondered exactly what it was that Ellie Smith was trying to tell him . . . or what it was that she was trying *not* to tell him. The point she had just made was exactly the one which he himself (rather proudly) had made to Sergeant Lewis, except that she had made it rather better.

'Now, second thing,' she said as each of them sat drinking again and (now) smoking. 'I want to ask you a favour. I said, didn't I, that me and Ashley—'

'Ashley and I.'

'Ashley and I are getting married, at the Registry Office—'

'Register Office,' corrected the pedantic Inspector.

'—and we wondered – *I* wondered – if you'd be willing to come along and be a witness.'

'Why me?'

'Because . . . well, no reason really, perhaps, except I'd like you to be there, with me mum. It'd make me . . . I'd be pleased, that's all.'

'When is it – the wedding?'

'"Wedding"? Sounds a bit posh, doesn't it? We're just getting married: no bridesmaids, no bouquets – and not too much bloody confetti, I hope.'

An avuncular Morse nodded, like an understanding senior citizen.

'Not like all the razzmatazz you probably had at your wedding,' she said.

Morse looked down at the carpet, as she had done earlier; then looked up again. For a second or two it was as though an electric current had shot across his forehead, and for some strange reason he found himself wanting to reach out across the table and just for a moment touch the hand of the young woman seated opposite.

'How are you getting home, Ellie?'

In the taxi ('Iffley Road – then the top of the Banbury Road,' Morse had instructed), Ellie had interlaced her fingers into his; and Morse felt moved and confused and more than a little loving.

'Did you see that watercolour?' she asked. 'The one just by our table? *Our* table?'

'No.'

'It was lovely – with fields and sheep and clouds. And the clouds . . .'

'What about them?' asked Morse quietly.

'Well, they were white at the top and then a sort of middling, muddy grey, and then a darker grey at the bottom. Clouds are like that, aren't they?'

'Are they?' Morse, the non-Nephologist, had never consciously contemplated a cloud in his life, and he felt unable to comment further.

'It's just that – well, all I'm tryin' to say is that I enjoyed bein' with you, that's all. For a little while I felt I was on the top o' one o' them clouds, OK?'

After the taxi had dropped her off, and was making its way from East Oxford to North Oxford, Morse realized that he too had almost been on top of one of 'them clouds' that evening.

Back in his flat, he looked with some care at the only watercolour he had. The clouds there had been painted exactly as Ellie Smith had said. And he nodded to himself, just a little sadly.

CHAPTER FIFTY-ONE

Needles and pins, needles and pins,
When a man marries his trouble begins
(Old nursery rhyme)

IN THE waiting area of the Churchill Hospital, immediately Mrs Stevens had been called in to see her specialist, at 10.35 a.m. on Tuesday, 20 September, Brenda Brooks picked up a surprisingly recent issue of *Good Housekeeping*, and flicked through its glossy pages. But she found it difficult to concentrate on any particular article.

Brenda was a person who took much pleasure in the simple things of life. Others, she knew, had their yearnings for power or wealth or knowledge, but two of her own greatest delights were cleanliness and tidiness. What a joy she felt each week, for example, when she watched the dustmen casually hurl her black bags into the back of the yellow rubbish-cart – then seeing them no more. It seemed like Pilgrim finally ridding himself of his burden of sin.

For her own part, she had seldom made any mess at all in her life. But there was always an accumulation of things to be thrown away: bits of cabbage-leaves, and empty tins, and cigarette stubs from her husband's ashtrays . . . Yes. It was always good to see the black bags, well, *disappear* really. You could put almost anything in them: bloodstained items like shirts, shoes, trousers – anything.

There were the green bags, too – the bags labelled 'Garden Waste', issued by Oxford City Council, at 50p apiece. Householders were permitted to put out two such bags every week; but the Brooks's garden was small, and Brenda seldom made use of more than one a fortnight.

Then there were those strong, transparent bags which Ted had brought home a couple of years ago, a heavy stack of them piled in the garden shed, just to the left of the lawn-mower. Precisely what purpose her husband had envisaged for such receptacles had been unclear, but they had occasionally proved useful for twigs and small branches, because the material from which they were manufactured was stout, heavy-duty stuff, not easily torn.

But the real joy of Brenda's life had ever centred on the manual skills – knitting, needlework, embroidery – for her hands had always worked confidently and easily with needles and crochet-hooks and bodkins and such things. Of late, too, she had begun to extend the area of her manual competence by joining a cake-icing class, although (as we have seen) it had been only with considerable and increasing pain that she had been able to continue the course, before finally being compelled to pack it up altogether.

She was still able, however, to indulge in some of her former skills; had, in fact, so very recently indulged in them when, wearing a leather glove instead of the uncomfortable Tubigrip, she had stitched the 'body-bag' (a word she had heard on the radio) in which her late and unlamented husband was destined to be wrapped. Never could she have imagined, of course, that the disposal of a body would cause a problem in her gently undemanding life. But it had, and she had seen to it. Not that the task had been a labour of love. Far from it. It had been a labour of hate.

She had watched, a few months earlier, some men who had come along and cut down a branch overarching the road there, about twelve feet long and about nine inches across. (Wasn't a human head about nine inches across?) The men had got rid of that pretty easily: just put it in that quite extraordinary machine they had – from which, after a scream of whirring, the thick wood had come out the other end . . . sawdust.

Then there was the furnace up at the Proctor Memorial School – that would have left even less physical trace perhaps. But (as Mrs Stevens had said) there was a pretty big problem of 'logistics' associated with such waste-disposal. And so, although Brenda had not quite understood the objection, this method had been discounted.

The Redbridge Waste Reception Area had seemed to her a rather safer bet. It was close enough, and there was no one there to ask questions about what you'd brought in your bags – not like the time she and Ted had come through Customs and the man with the gold on his hat had discovered all those cigarettes . . . No, they didn't ask you anything at the rubbish dump. You just backed the car up to the skip, opened the boot, and threw the bags down on to the great heap already there, soon to be carted away, and dumped, and bulldozed into a pit, and buried there.

But none of these methods had found favour.

Dis aliter visum.

The stiffish transparent bags measured 28½ inches by 36 inches, and Brenda had taken three. After slitting open the bottoms of two of them, she had stitched the three together cunningly, with a bodkin and some green garden string. She had then repeated the process, and prepared a second envelope. Then a third.

It was later to be recorded that at the time of his murder Mr Edward Brooks was 5 feet 8 inches in height, and 10½ stones in weight. And although the insertion of the body into the first, the second, and the third of the winding-sheets had been a traumatic event, it had not involved too troublesome an effort physically. Not for her, anyway.

Edward Brooks had been almost ready for disposal.

Almost.

By some happy chance, the roll of old brown carpet which had stood for over two years just to the right of the lawn-mower measured 6 feet by 6 feet.

Ideal.

With some difficulty the body had been manipulated into its container, and four lengths of stout cord were knotted – very neatly! – around the bundle. The outer tegument made the whole thing a bit heavier, of course – but neater, too. And neatness, as we have seen, was an important factor in life (and now in death) for Brenda Brooks. The parcel, now complete, was ready for carriage.

It might be expected perhaps – expected certainly? – that such an experience would permanently have traumatized the soul of such a delicate woman as Mrs Brenda Brooks. But, strangely enough, such was not the case; and as she thought back on these things, and flicked through another few pages of *Good Housekeeping*, and waited for Mrs Stevens to re-emerge, she found herself half-smiling – if not with cruelty at least with a grim satisfaction . . .

There was an empty Walkers crisp packet on the floor, just two seats away; and unostentatiously Brenda rose and picked it up, and placed it in the nearest wastepaper basket.

Mrs Stevens did not come out of the consulting-room until 11.20 a.m. that morning; and when she finally did, Brenda saw that her dearest friend in life had been weeping . . .

*

It had been that last little bit really.

'You've got some friends coming over from California, you say?'

'Yes. Just after Christmas. I've not seen them for almost ten years. I went to school with her – with the wife.'

'Can I suggest something? Please?' He spoke quietly.

'Of course.' Julia had looked up into the brown eyes of Basil Shepstone, and seen a deep and helpless sadness there. And she'd known what he was going to say.

'If it's possible ... if it's at all possible, can you get your friends to come over, shall we say, a month earlier? A month or two earlier?'

CHAPTER FIFTY-TWO

I said this was fine utterance and sounded well though it could have been polished and made to mean less
      (PETER CHAMPKIN, *The Sleeping Life of Aspern Williams*)

THE CASE was not progressing speedily.

That, in his own words, is what Lewis felt emboldened to assert the following morning – the morning of Wednesday, 21 September – as he sat in Morse's office at HQ.

'Things are going a bit slow, sir.'

'That,' said Morse, 'is a figure of speech the literati call "hyperbole", a rhetorical term for "exaggeration". What I think you're trying to tell me is that we're grinding to a dead halt. Right?'

Lewis nodded.

And Morse nodded.

They were both right . . .

Considerable activity had centred on the Brooks's household following the finding of the bicycle, with Brenda Brooks herself gladly co-operating. Yet there seemed little about which she was able to co-operate, apart from the retraction of her earlier statement that her husband had been at home throughout the morning of Sunday, 28 August. In a nervous, gentle recantation, she was now willing (she'd said) to tell the police the whole truth. He had gone out on his bike, earlyish that morning; he had returned in a taxi, latish that morning – with a good deal of blood on his clothing. Her first thought, naturally enough, was that he'd been involved in a road accident. Somehow she'd got him into his pyjamas, into bed – and then, fairly soon afterwards, she'd called the ambulance, for she had suddenly realized that he was very ill. The bloodstained clothing she had put into a black bag and taken to the Redbridge Waste Reception Area the following morning, walking across the Iffley Road, then via Donnington Bridge Road to the Abingdon Road.

Not a very heavy load, she said.

Not so heavy as Pilgrim's, she thought.

That was almost all, though. The police could look round the house – of course they could. There was nothing to hide, and they could take away whatever they liked. She fully understood: murder, after all, was a serious business. But no letters, no receipts, no addresses, had been found; few photographs, few mementos, few books; no drugs – certainly no drugs; nothing much at all apart from the pedestrian possessions of an undistinguished, unattractive man, whose only memorable achievement in life had been the murder of an Oxford don.

There had been just that one discovery, though, which had raised a few eyebrows, including (and particularly) the eyebrows of Brenda Brooks. Although only £217 was in Brooks's current account at Lloyds Bank (Carfax branch), a building society book, found in a box beside Brooks's bed, showed a very healthy balance stashed away in the Halifax – a balance of £19,500. The box had been locked, but Brenda Brooks had not demurred when Lewis had asked her permission to force the lid – a task which he had accomplished with far more permanent damage than had been effected by the (still unidentified) thief at the Pitt Rivers Museum . . .

'You think he's dead?' asked Lewis.

'Every day that goes by makes it more likely.'

'We need a body, though.'

'We do. At least – with McClure – we had a body.'

'And a weapon.'

'And a weapon.'

'But with Brooks we've still not got a body.'

'And still not got a weapon,' added Morse rather miserably.

Ten minutes later, without knocking, Strange lumbered into the office. He had been on a week's furlough to the west coast of Scotland and had returned three days earlier. But this was his first day back at HQ, having attended a two-day Superintendents' Conference at Eastbourne.

He looked less than happy with life.

'How're things going, Morse?'

'Progressing, sir,' said Morse uneasily.

Strange looked at him sourly. 'You mean they're *not* progressing, is that it?'

'We're hoping for some developments—'

'Augh, don't give me that bullshit! Just tell me where we are – and don't take all bloody day over it.'

So Morse told him.

He knew (he said) – well, was ninety-nine per cent certain – that Brooks had murdered McClure: they'd got the knife from Brooks's kitchen, *without* any blood on it, agreed – but now they'd got his bike, *with* blood on it – McClure's blood on it. The only thing missing was Brooks himself. No news of him. No trace of him. Not yet. He'd last been seen by his wife, Brenda Brooks, and by Mrs Stevens – by the two of them together – on the afternoon of Wednesday, 7 September, the afternoon that the knife was stolen from the Pitt Rivers.

'Where does that leave us then?' asked Strange. 'Sounds as if you might just as well have taken a week's holiday yourself.'

'For what it's worth, sir, I think the two women are lying to us. I don't think they *did* see him that Wednesday afternoon. I think that one of them – or both of them – murdered Brooks. But not on that Wednesday – and not on the Thursday, either. I think that Brooks was murdered the day *before*, on the Tuesday; and I think that all this Pitt Rivers thingummy is a blind, arranged so that we should think there *was* a link-up between the two things. I think that they got somebody, some accomplice, to pinch the African knife – well, *any* knife from one of the cabinets there—'

'All right. You think – and you seem to be doing one helluva lot of "thinking", Morse – that the knife was stolen *the day after* Brooks was murdered.'

'Yes, sir.'

'Go on.'

Morse was very conscious that he had scarcely thought through his conclusions with any definitive clarity, but he ploughed on:

'It's all to do with their alibis. They couldn't have stolen the knife themselves – they were on a school bus going to Stratford. And so if we all make the obvious link, which we *do*, between the murder of Brooks and the theft, then they're in the clear, pretty well. You see, if Brooks's body is ever found, which I very strongly doubt—'

'What makes you say that?'

'Because if he's found, he won't have the Pitt Rivers knife stuck in him at all. It'll be *another* knife – like as not another kitchen knife. But they're certainly never going to let us find the body. That would mean the alibis they've fixed up for themselves have gone for a Burton.'

'What's the origin of that phrase?'

Morse shook his head. 'Something to do with beer, is it?'

Strange looked at his watch: just after midday. 'You know I was a bit surprised to find you here, Morse. I thought you'd probably gone for a Burton yourself.'

Morse smiled dutifully, and Lewis grinned hugely, as Strange continued: 'It's all too fanciful, mate. Stop thinking so much – and *do* something. Let's have a bit of action.'

'There's one other thing, sir. Lewis here got on to it . . .'

Morse gestured to his sergeant, the latter now taking up the narrative.

'Fellow called Davies, Ashley Davies. He's got quite a few connections with things, sir. He was on Staircase G in Drinkwater Quad when Matthew Rodway was there – had a fight with him, in fact, and got himself kicked out' – he looked at Morse – 'rusticated. The fight was about a girl, a girl called Eleanor Smith; and *she* was the girl who was Dr McClure's mistress. And now, Davies has got himself engaged to be married to her – *and* she's Brooks's step-daughter.'

'That's good, Lewis. That's just the sort of cumulative evidence I like to hear. Did *he* murder Brooks?'

'It's not that so much, sir. It's just that the Chief Inspector here . . .'

Lewis tailed off, and Morse took over.

'It's just that I'd been wondering why Miss Smith had agreed to marry him, that's all. And I thought that perhaps he might have done some favour for her. Lewis here found that he was in Oxford that Wednesday afternoon, and if it *was* Davies who went to the Pitt Rivers—'

'What! You're bringing *her* into it now? The daughter?'

'Step-daughter, sir.'

Strange shook his head. 'That's bad, Morse. You're in Disney-land again.'

Morse sighed, and sat back in the old black leather chair. He knew that his brief résumé of the case had been less than well presented; and, worse than that, realized that even if he'd polished it all up a bit, it still wouldn't have amounted to much. Might even have amounted to less.

Strange struggled to his feet.

'Hope you had a good holiday, sir,' remarked Lewis.

'No, I didn't. If you really want to know it was a bloody awful holiday. I got pissed off with it – rained all the bloody time.'

Strange waddled over to the door and stood there, offering a final piece of advice to his senior chief inspector: 'Just let's get cracking, mate. Find that body – or get Lewis here to find it for you. And when you do – you mark my words, Morse! – you'll find that thingummy knife o' yours stuck right up his rectum.'

After he was gone, Lewis looked across at a subdued and silent Morse.

'You know that "all the bloody time", sir? That's what they call – what the literati call – "hyperbole".'

Morse nodded, grinning weakly.

'And he wasn't just pissed off on his holiday, was he?'

'He wasn't?'

'No, sir. He was pissed *on* as well!'

Morse nodded again, grinning happily now, and looking at his watch.

'What about going for a Burton, Lewis?'

CHAPTER FIFTY-THREE

'Jo, my poor fellow!'

'I hear you, sir, in the dark, but I'm a-gropin – a-gropin – let me catch hold of your hand.'

'Jo, can you say what I say?'

'I'll say anythink as you say, sir, for I knows it's good.'

'OUR FATHER.'

'Our Father! – yes, that's wery good, sir.'
(CHARLES DICKENS, *Bleak House*)

WE MUST now briefly record several apparently disparate events which occurred between 21 and 24 September.

On Wednesday, 21, Julia Stevens was one of four people who rang the JR2 to ask for the latest bulletin on Kevin Costyn, who the previous day had been transferred to the Intensive Care Unit. His doctors had become increasingly concerned about a blood-clot in the brain, and a decision would very shortly be taken about possible surgery. For each of the four (including Kevin's mother) the message, couched in its conventionally cautious terms, was the same: 'Critical but stable'.

Not very promising, Julia realized that. Considerably better, though, than the prognosis on her own condition.

As she lay in bed that night, she would gladly have prayed for herself, as well as for Kevin, had she managed to retain any residual faith in a personal deity. But she had not so managed. And as she lay staring up at the ceiling, knowing that she could never again look forward to any good nights, quite certainly not to any cheerful awakenings, she pondered how very much more easy such things must be for people with some comfortable belief in a future life. And for just a little while her resolution wavered sufficiently for her to find herself kneeling on the Golden Floor and quietly reciting the opening lines of the Lord's Prayer.

Photographs of the three young men involved in the Eastern Ring Road accident had appeared on page 2 of *The Star* (22 September), a free newspaper distributed throughout Oxford each Thursday. Below these photographs, a brief article had made no mention whatsoever of the concomitant circumstances of the 'accident'. But it was the dolichocephalic face of Kevin Costyn, appropriately positioned between his dead partner-in-crime, to the left, and his amputee partner-in-crime, to the right, that had caught the attention of one of the attendants at the Pitt Rivers Museum. In particular it had been the sight of the small crucifix earring that had jerked his jaded memory into sudden overdrive. Earlier the police had questioned all of them about whether they could remember anything unusual, or *anyone* unusual, on that Wednesday afternoon when Cabinet 52 had been forced. Like each of his colleagues, he'd had to admit that he couldn't.

But now he could.

Just before the museum closed, on Thursday, 22 September, he walked along the passage, up the stone steps, and diffidently knocked on the door of the Administrator (capital 'A').

Late that same afternoon Morse asked Lewis an unusual question.

'If you had to get a wedding present, what sort of thing would you have in mind – for the bride?'

'You don't do it that way, sir. You buy a present for both of them. They'll have a list, like as not – you know, dinner-service, saucepans, set of knives—'

'Very funny!'

'Well, if you don't want to lash out too much you can always get her a tin-opener or an orange-squeezer.'

'Not exactly much help in times of trouble, are you?'

'Ellie Smith, is it?'

'Yes.' Morse hesitated. 'It's just that I'd like to buy her something . . . for herself.'

'Well, there's nothing to stop you giving her a personal present – just forget the wedding bit. Perfume, say? Scarf? Gloves? Jewellery, perhaps? Brooch? Pendant?'

'Ye-es. A nice little pendant, perhaps . . .'

'So long as her husband's not going to mind somebody else's present hanging round her neck all the time.'

'Do people still get jealous these days, Lewis?'

'I don't think the world'll get rid of jealousy in a hurry, sir.'

'No. I suppose not,' said Morse slowly.

Five minutes later the phone rang.

It was the Administrator.

In the Vaults Bar at The Randolph at lunchtime on Friday, 23 September, Ellie Smith pushed her half-finished plate of lasagne away from her and lit a cigarette.

'Like I say, though, it's nice of him to agree, isn't it?'

'Oh, give it a rest, Ellie! Don't start talking about *him* again.'

'You jealous or something?'

Ashley Davies smiled sadly.

'Yeah, I suppose I am.'

She leaned towards him, put her hand on his arm, and gently kissed his left cheek.

'You silly noodle!'

'Perhaps everybody feels a bit jealous sometimes.'

'Yeah.'

'You mean *you* do?'

Ellie nodded. 'Awful thing – sort of corrosive. Yuk!'

There was a silence between them.

'What are you thinking about?' he asked.

Ellie stubbed out her cigarette, and pushed her chair back from the table. 'Do you really want to know?'

'Please tell me.'

'I was just wondering what *she*'s like that's all.'

'Who are you talking about?'

'*Mrs* Morse.'

The sun had drifted behind the clouds, and Ashley got up and paid the bill.

A few minutes later, her arm through his, they walked along Cornmarket, over Carfax, and then through St Aldate's to Folly Bridge, where they stood and looked down at the waters of the Thames.

'Would you like to go on a boat trip?' he asked.

'What, this afternoon?'

'Why not? Up to Iffley Lock and back? Won't take long.'

'No. Not for me.'

'What would you like to do?'

She felt a sudden tenderness towards him, and wished to make him happy.

'Would you like to come along to my place?'

The sun had slipped out from behind the clouds, and was shining brightly once more.

CHAPTER FIFTY-FOUR

Cambridge has espoused the river, has opened its arms to the river, has built some of its finest Houses alongside the river. Oxford has turned its back on the river, for only at some points

downstream from Folly Bridge does the Isis glitter so gloriously
as does the Cam

(J. J. SMITHFIELD-WATERSTONE,
Oxford and Cambridge: A Comparison)

THE TWO rivers, the Thames (or Isis) and the Cherwell, making
their confluence just to the south of the City Centre, have long
provided enjoyable amenities for Oxford folk, both Town and
Gown: punting, rowing, sculling, canoeing, and pleasure-boating.
For the less athletic, and for the more arthritic, the river-cruise
down from Folly Bridge via the Iffley and Sandford locks to
Abingdon, has always been a favourite.

For such a trip, Mr Anthony Hughes, a prosperous accountant
now living out on Boar's Hill, had booked two tickets on a fifty-
passenger steamer, the *Iffley Princess*, timetabled to sail from Folly
Bridge at 9.15 a.m. on Sunday, 25 September.

The previous evening he had slowly traced the course of the
river on the Ordnance Survey Map, pointing out to his son such
landmarks as the Green Bank, the Gut, the concrete bridge at
Donnington, Haystacks Corner, and the rest, which they would
pass before arriving at Iffley Lock.

For young James, the morrow's prospects were magical. He
was in several ways an attractive little chap – earnest, bespectacled, bright – with his name down for the Dragon School in
North Oxford, a preparatory school geared (indeed, fifth-geared)
to high academic and athletic excellence. The lad was already
exhibiting an intelligent and apparently insatiable interest both in
his own locality and in the Universe in general. Such Aristotelian
curiosity was quite naturally a great delight to his parents; and
the four-and-a-half-year-old young James was picking up, and
mentally hoarding, bits of knowledge with much the same sort of
regularity that young Jason was picking up, and physically
hurling, bits of brick and stone around the Cutteslowe Estate.

Spanning the fifty-yard-wide Isis, and thus linking the Iffley
Road with Abingdon Road, Donnington Bridge was a flattish
arc of concrete, surmounted by railings painted, slightly
incongruously, a light Cambridge-blue. And as the *Iffley Princess*
rounded the Gut, young James pointed to the large-lettered
SOMERVILLE, followed by two crossed oars, painted in black on
a red background, across the upper part of the bridge, just below
the parapet railings.

'What's that, Dad?'

But before the proud father could respond, this question was followed by another:

'What's *that*, Dad?'

Young James pointed to an in-cut, on the left, where a concrete slipway had been constructed to allow owners of cars to back the boats they were towing directly down into the river. There, trapped at the side of the slipway, was what appeared to be an elongated bundle, a foot or so below the surface of the nacre-green water. And several of the passengers on the port side now spotted the same thing: something potentially sinister; something wrapped up; but something no longer wholly concealed.

Fred Andrews, skipper of the *Iffley Princess*, pulled over into Salters' Boat Yard, only some twenty yards below the bridge. He was an experienced waterman, and decided to dial 999 immediately. It was only after he had briefly explained his purpose to his passengers that an extraordinarily ancient man, seated in the bow of the boat, and dressed in a faded striped blazer, off-white flannels, and a straw boater, produced a mobile telephone from somewhere about his person, and volunteered to dial the three nines himself.

CHAPTER FIFTY-FIVE

It's a strong stomach that has no turning
(OLIVER HERFORD)

FROM Donnington Bridge Road, Lewis turned right into Meadow Lane, then almost immediately left, along a broad track, where wooden structures on the right housed the Sea Cadet Corps and the Riverside Centre. Ahead of him, painted in alternate bands of red and white, was a barrier, open now and upright; and beyond the barrier, four cars, one Land Rover, and one black van; and a group of some fifteen persons standing round something – something covered with greyish canvas.

Forty or fifty other persons were standing on the bridge, just to the left, leaning over the railings and surveying the scene some fifty feet below them, like members of the public watching the Boat Race on one of the bridges between Mortlake and Putney. And seated silently beside Lewis, Morse himself would willingly have allowed any one of these ghoulish gawpers to look in his stead beneath the canvas, at the body just taken from the Thames.

Events had moved swiftly after the first emergency call to St Aldate's. PC Carter had arrived within ten minutes in a white police car and had been more than grateful for the advice of the Warden of the Riverside Centre, a dark, thickset man, who had dealt with many a body during his twenty-five years' service there. The Underwater Search Unit had been summoned from Sulhamstead; and in due course a doctor. The body, that of a man, still sheeted in plastic, but now in danger of slithering out of its wrapping of carpet, had been taken from the water, placed at the top of the slipway – and promptly covered up, untouched. St Aldate's CID had been contacted immediately, and Inspector Morrison had arrived to join a scene-of-crimes officer and a police photographer. With the arrival of a cheerful young undertaker, just before noon, the cast was almost complete.

Apart from Morse and Lewis.

The reasons for such a sequence of events were clear enough to those directly and closely involved; clear even to a few of the twitchers, with their powerful binoculars, who had swelled the ranks of the bridge spectators. For this was clearly not a run-of-the-mill drowning. Even through the triple layers of plastic sheeting in which the body was wrapped, one thing stood out clearly (*literally* stood out clearly): the broad handle of a knife which appeared to be wedged firmly into the dead man's back. And when, under Morrison's careful directions – after many photographic flashings, from many angles – the stitching at the top of the improvised body-bag had been painstakingly unpicked, and one pocket of the corpse had been painstakingly picked (as it were), the identity of the man was quickly established.

On the noticeboard in the foyer of St Aldate's station was pinned a photograph of a 'Missing Person' whom the police were most anxious to trace; and beneath the photograph there appeared a name, together with a few physical details. But it was not the corpse's blackened features which Morrison had recognized; it was the name he found in the sodden wallet.

The name of Edward Brooks.

Thus was a further relay of telephone-calls initiated. Thus was Morse himself now summoned to the scene.

Sometimes procedures worked well; and sometimes (as now) there was every reason for the police to be congratulated on the way situations were handled. On this occasion one thing only (perhaps two?) had marred police professionalism.

PC Carter, newly recruited to the Force, had been reasonably well prepared for the sight of a body, particularly one so comparatively well preserved as this one. What he had been totally unprepared for was the indescribable stench which had emanated from the body even before the Inspector had authorized the opening of the envelope: a stench which was the accumulation, it seemed, of the dank depths of the river, of blocked drains, of incipient decomposition – of death itself. And PC Carter had turned away, and vomited rather noisily into the Thames, trusting that few had observed the incident.

But inevitably almost everyone, including the audience in the gods, had noticed the brief, embarrassing incident.

It was Morse's turn now.

Phobias are common enough. Some persons suffer from arachnophobia, or hypsophobia, or myophobia, or pterophobia ... Well-nigh everyone suffers occasionally from thanatophobia; many from necrophobia – although Morse was not really afraid of dead bodies at all, or so he told himself. What he really suffered from was a completely new phobia, one that was all his own: *the fear of being sick* at the sight of bodies which had met their deaths in strange or terrible circumstances. Even Morse, for all his classical education, was unable to coin an appropriately descriptive, or etymologically accurate, term for such a phobia: and even had he been so able, the word would certainly have been pretentiously polysyllabic.

Yet, for all his weakness, Morse was a far more experienced performer than PC Carter; and hurriedly taking the Warden to one side, he had swiftly sought directions to the nearest loo. It was not, therefore, into the Thames, but into a lone lavatory-pan in the Riverside Centre, that Chief Inspector Morse vomited, late that Sunday morning.

'Been in the river about a fortnight, they reckon,' ventured Lewis when Morse finally emerged.

'Good! That fits nicely,' replied the pale-faced Morse.

'You OK, sir?'

'Course I'm bloody OK, man!' snapped Morse.

But Lewis was not in the least offended, for he and Morse were long acquainted; and Lewis knew all his ways.

CHAPTER FIFTY-SIX

He could not be a lighterman or river-carrier; there was no clue to what he looked for, but he looked for something with a most intent and searching gaze

(CHARLES DICKENS, *Our Mutual Friend*)

IF A few minutes earlier it had been his stomach that was churning over, it was now the turn of Morse's brain; and somehow he managed, at least for a while, to look down again at the semi-sealed body. Heavy condensation between the plastic layers was preventing any close inspection of the knife stuck into the corpse's back. But Morse was determined to be patient: better than most, he knew the value of touching nothing further there; and to be truthful he had been more than a little surprised that Morrison had gone as far as he had.

Nothing further, therefore, was touched until the arrival of the police pathologist, Dr Laura Hobson, whose bright red Metro joined the little convoy of vehicles half an hour later. Briefly she and Morse conversed. After which, with delicate hands, she performed a few delicate tasks; whilst Morse walked slowly from the scene, along a track between a line of trees and the riverbank, up to a building housing the Falcon Rowing Club, some seventy yards upstream to his right. Here he stood looking around him, wondering earnestly what exactly he should be looking for.

After returning to the slipway, he took the Warden to one side and put to him some of the questions that were exercising his mind. Where perhaps might the corpse have been pushed into the river? How could the corpse have been conveyed to such a spot? In which direction, and how far, could the corpse have been conveyed by the prevailing flow of the waters?

The Warden proved to be intelligent and informative. After stressing the importance, in all such considerations, of time of year, weather conditions, river-temperature, volume of water, and frequency of river-traffic; after giving Morse a clear little lesson on buoyancy and flotation, he suggested a few likely answers. As follows.

The strong probability was that the body had not been shifted all that far by the prevailing flow; indeed, if it had been slightly more weighted down, the body might have rested permanently on the bottom; as things were, the body could well have been put into the river at a point just beside the Falcon Rowing Club; certain it was that the body would not have drifted *against* the north–south movement of the tide. The only objection to such a theory was that it would have been an inordinately long way for anyone to carry such a weighty bundle. With the barrier locked down across the approach road to the slipway, no car (unless authorized) could even have reached the river at that point, let alone turned right there and deposited a body sixty, seventy yards upstream.

Unless . . .

Well, there were just over a hundred members of the Riverside Club who possessed boats, who used the slipway fairly regularly, and who were issued with a key to the barrier. Not infrequently (the Warden confessed) a boat-owner neglected to close the barrier behind him; or deliberately left it open for a colleague known to be sailing up behind. And so . . . if the barrier happened to be left open – well, not much of a problem, was there?

'You know what I'd've done, Mr Holmes, if I'd had to dispose of a body here?' Morse's eyes slowly rose to the top of Donnington Bridge, where public interest was, if anything, increasing, in spite of the makeshift screen which had now been erected around the body.

'You tell me.'

'I'd have driven here, about two o'clock in the morning, and pushed it over the bridge.'

'Helluva splash, you'd make,' said the Warden.

'Nobody around to hear it, though.'

'A few people around then, Inspector. You know who they are?'

Morse shook his head.

'Three lots o' people, really: lovers, thieves, police.'

'Oh!' said Morse.

Twenty minutes later the young pathologist got to her feet – the grim, grisly preliminary examination over.

'Mustn't do much more here,' she reported. 'Been in the river between a week and a fortnight, I'd guess. Difficult to say – he's pretty well preserved. Neat little job of packaging somebody did there. But we'll sort him out later. All right?'

Morse nodded. 'We're in your hands.'

'Not much doubt he's been murdered, though – unless he died, then somebody stuck a knife in him, then wrapped him all up and put him in the river here.'

'Seems unlikely,' conceded Morse.

Dr Hobson was packing up her equipment when Morse spoke again:

'You'll be sure not to touch the knife until—?'

'You've not got much faith in some of your colleagues, have you?'

She was an attractive young woman; and when first she had taken over from the sadly missed Max, Morse had felt he could almost have fallen a little in love with her. But now he dreamed of her no longer.

Morse had taken the sensible (almost unprecedented) precaution of refraining from a few pints of beer on a Sunday lunchtime; and at 3.15 p.m. he and Lewis stood in the path lab beside the prone body of Edward Brooks, the plastic bags in which he had been inserted lying folded neatly at his feet, like the linen wraps at the Resurrection. Apart from Dr Hobson herself, two further forensic assistants and a fingerprint expert stood quite cheerfully around the body, in which the handle of a broad knife stood up straight.

Yet it was not the handle itself, so carefully dusted now with fingerprint-powder, which had riveted Morse's attention. It was the label attached to the side of the handle; a label whose lettering, though washed and smudged by the waters of the Thames, was still partially legible on its right-hand side:

```
orthern

to Bishop May
amount chief
anika
v. Miss to cent Africa)
              Cabinet: 52
```

'*I just do not believe this,*' whispered Morse slowly.

'Pardon, sir?'

But Morse was not listening. He touched Laura Hobson lightly on the shoulder of her starched white coat, and for the second time that day asked for the quickest way to the nearest Gents.

CHAPTER FIFTY-SEVEN

Karl Popper teaches that knowledge is advanced by the positing and testing of hypotheses. Countless hypotheses, I believe, are being tested at once in the unconscious mind; only the winning shortlist is handed to our consciousness

(MATTHEW PARRIS, *The Times*, 7 March 1994)

THE FOLLOWING day, Monday, 26 September, both Morse and Lewis arrived fairly early, just after 7 a.m., at Thames Valley HQ.

Morse himself had slept poorly, his eyeballs ceaselessly circling in their sockets throughout the night as the dramatic new development in the case had gradually established itself into the pattern of his thinking; for in truth he had been astonished at the discovery that Brooks had been murdered *after* the theft of the Rhodesian knife; murdered in fact *by* the Rhodesian knife.

As he had hitherto analysed the case, assessing motive and opportunity and means, Morse had succeeded in convincing himself that two or perhaps three persons, acting to some degree in concert, had probably been responsible for Brooks's murder. Each of the three (as Morse saw things) would have regarded the death of Brooks, though for slightly different reasons, as of considerable benefit to the human race.

Three suspects.

Three women: the superficially gentle Brenda Brooks, who had suffered sorely in the rôle of the neglected and maltreated wife; the enigmatic Mrs Stevens, who had developed a strangely strong bond between herself and her cleaning-lady; and the step-daughter, Eleanor Smith, who had left home in her mid-teens, abused (how could Morse know?) mentally, or verbally, or physically, or sexually even . . .

Women set apart from the rest of their kind by the sign of the murderer – by the mark of Cain.

A confusing figuration of 'if's' had permutated itself in Morse's restless brain that previous night, filtering down to exactly the same shortlist as before, since the Final Arbiter had handed to Morse the same three envelopes. In the first, as indeed in the second, the brief verdict was typed out in black letters: 'Not Guilty'; but in the third, Morse had read the even briefer verdict, typed out here in red capitals: 'GUILTY'. And the name on the front of the third envelope was – *Eleanor Smith*.

For almost an hour, Morse and Lewis had spoken together that morning: spoken of thoughts, ideas, hypotheses. And when he returned from the canteen with two cups of coffee at 8 a.m., Lewis stated, starkly and incontrovertibly, the simple truth they both had to face:

'You know, I just don't see – I just *can't* see – how Brenda Brooks, or this Mrs Stevens – how either of them could have done it. We've not exactly had a video-camera on them since the knife was stolen – but not far off. All right, they'd got enough motive. But I just don't see when they had the opportunity.'

'Nor do I,' said Morse quietly. And Lewis was encouraged to continue.

'I know what you mean about Mrs Stevens, sir. And I agree. There's somebody pretty clever behind all this, and she's the only one of the three who's got the brains to have thought it all out. But as I say . . .'

Morse appeared a little pained as Lewis continued:

'. . . she couldn't have done it. And Mrs Brooks couldn't have done it either, could she? She's got the best motive of any of them, and she'd probably have the nerve as well. But she couldn't have *planned* it all, surely, even if somehow she had the opportunity – that night, say, after she got back from Stratford. I just don't see it.'

'Nor do I,' repeated Morse, grimacing as he sipped another mouthful of weak, lukewarm coffee.

'So unless we're looking in completely the wrong direction, sir, that only leaves . . .'

But Morse was only half listening. 'Unless', Lewis had just

said ... the same word the Warden had used the previous day when he'd been talking of the red-and-white striped barrier. In Morse's mind there'd earlier been a *logical* barrier to his hypothesis that Brooks's body must have been taken to the Thames in some sort of vehicle – as well as that *literal* barrier. But the Warden had merely lifted that second barrier, hadn't he? Just physically lifted it out of the way.

So what if he, Morse, were now to lift that earlier barrier too?

'Lewis! Get the car, and nip along and have a word with the headmaster of the Proctor Memorial. Tell him we'd like to see Mrs Stevens again. We can either go round to her house or, if she prefers, she can come here.'

'Important, is it, sir?'

'Oh, yes,' said Morse. 'And while you're at it, you can drop me off at the path lab. I want another quick word with the lovely Laura.'

CHAPTER FIFTY-EIGHT

Now faith is the substance of things hoped for, the evidence of things not seen

(*Hebrews*, ch. 11, v. 1)

COMING OUT of her lab to greet Morse, Dr Laura Hobson appeared incongruously contented with her work. She pointed to the door behind her.

'You'd better not go in there, Chief Inspector. Not for the minute. We've nearly finished, though – the main bits, anyway.'

'Anything interesting?'

'Do you call stomach contents interesting?'

'No.'

'Looks as if they've got some vague prints all right, though – on the knife. I'll keep my fingers crossed for you. We're all hoping, you know that.'

'Thank you.' Morse hesitated. 'It may sound a bit far-fetched I know, but ...'

'Yes?'

'The knife – I'm doing a little bit of hoping myself – the knife used to murder McClure was very similar to' – Morse nodded towards the main lab – 'to the knife that was stolen from the Pitt Rivers.'

'Yes, I knew that.'

'What I was wondering is this. Is there any possibility – any possibility at all – that Brooks was murdered with *another* knife – one of the same type, one with the same sort of blade – *then* for the knife you've got in there – the one with the possible prints on it – to be stuck in him . . . *afterwards*?'

Laura Hobson looked at him curiously.

'Have two knives, you mean? Stick one in him, take it out, then stick the other in?'

Morse looked uneasy, yet there was still some flicker of hope in his face. 'When I said "afterwards", I meant, well, a few *hours* later – a day even?'

With a sad smile, she shook her head. 'No chance. Unless your murderer's got the luck of the devil and the skill of a brain-surgeon—'

'Or a boy with a model-aeroplane kit?'

'—you'd have some clear *external* evidence of the two incisions – and don't forget he was stabbed through his clothes.'

'And there aren't . . . ?'

'No. No signs at all. Besides that, though, you'd have all the *internal* evidence: the two separate termini of the knife-points; two distinct sets of lacerations on either side of—'

'I see, yes,' mumbled Morse.

'I don't know whether you do, though. Look! Let me explain. Whenever you have a knife-wound—'

'Please, not!' said Morse. 'I believe all you say. It's just that I've never been able to follow all these physiological labellings. They didn't teach us any of that stuff at school.'

'I know,' said Laura quietly. 'You did Greek instead. You told me once, remember, in our . . . in our earlier days, Chief Inspector?'

Feeling more than a little embarrassed, Morse avoided her eyes.

'How would it have helped, anyway?' continued Laura, in a more business-like tone.

'Well, I've been assuming all along that the theft of the knife from the Pitt Rivers was a blind: a blind to establish an alibi, or alibis; to try to establish the fact that Brooks wasn't murdered until *after* the knife was stolen.'

She nodded, appreciating the point immediately. 'You mean,

if he'd been murdered on a particular day with one knife, and then, the day after, a second knife was stolen; and if the first knife was subsequently removed from the body, and the second knife inserted into the wound – people like the police, like you, could well have been misled about the time of death.'

'That's a splendidly constructed sentence,' said Morse.

'Waste of breath, though, really. *I* wouldn't have been misled.'

'You're sure?'

'Ninety-nine per cent sure.'

'Could you just rule out the other one per cent – for me? Please?'

'Waste of time. But I will, yes, if that's what you want.'

'I'm very grateful.'

'Don't you want to see the contents of his pockets? His clothes?'

'I suppose I ought to, yes.'

Again she looked at him curiously. 'It's as if you've been putting your . . . well, your *faith* in something, isn't it? And I feel I've let you down.'

'I lost all my faith a long time ago, I'm afraid.'

'Much better to have *evidence*, in our job.'

Morse nodded; and followed Laura Hobson's shapely legs into a side-room, where she gestured to a table by the window.

'I'll leave you to it, Chief Inspector.'

Morse sat down and first looked through the official 'In Possession Property' form, listing the items found on Brooks's person.

The wallet which had been removed at the river-side to establish identity (and which Morse had already looked through, anyway) was among the items, and he quickly examined its few (now dry) contents once more: one £10 note; one £5 note; a Lloyds Bank plastic card; an ID card for the Pitt Rivers Museum; a card showing official membership of the East Oxford Conservative Club. Nothing else. No photographs; no letters.

Nor were the other items listed and laid out there in small transparent bags of any obvious interest: a black comb; a white handkerchief; £2.74 in assorted coinage; what had once been a half-packet of now melted indigestion tablets; and a bunch of seven keys. It was this latter item only which appeared to Morse worthy of some brief consideration.

The biggest key, some 3 inches in length, was grimy dark brown in colour, and looked like a door-key; as perhaps did the two Yale keys, one a khaki colour, the other shinily metallic. The other four keys were (possibly?) for things like a garden shed or a bicycle-lock or a briefcase or a box or . . . But Morse's brain was suddenly engaged now: the fourth small key, a sturdy, silvery key, had the number 'X10' stamped upon it; and Morse gazed through the window, and wondered. Was it one of a set of keys? A key to what? A key to where? Would it help to spend a few hours sorting out these seven keys and matching them to their locks? Probably not. Probably a waste of time. But he ought to do it, he knew that. So he would do it. Or rather he'd get Lewis to do it.

From the dead man's clothing Morse quickly decided that nothing could be gleaned which could further the investigation one whit; and he was standing up now, preparing to leave, when Laura came back into the small room.

Phone-call for Morse. Sergeant Lewis. In her office.

Lewis was ringing from the Head's office of the Proctor Memorial School. Mrs Julia Stevens had been granted temporary leave from her duties. Well, indefinite leave really – but the terminological inexactitude had avoided any difficult embarrassment all round. She would not be returning to school, ever; she had only a few months to live; and a supply teacher had already taken over her classes. Soon everyone would have to know, of course; but not yet. She wasn't at home, though; she'd gone away on a brief holiday, abroad – the Head had known that, too. Gone off with a friend, destination unknown.

'Do we know who the friend is?' asked Morse.

'Well, *you* do, don't you?'

'I could make a guess.'

'Makes you wonder if they're guilty after all, doesn't it?'

'Or innocent,' suggested Morse slowly.

The condition of Kevin Costyn was markedly improved. With no surgery now deemed necessary, he had been removed from the ICU the previous lunchtime; and already the police had been given permission to interview him – at least about the accident.

Very soon he would be interviewed about other matters, too.

But although he was reluctantly willing to talk about ram-raiding and stolen vehicles, he would say nothing whatsoever about the murder of Edward Brooks. He may have lied and cheated his way through life, but there was one promise, now, that he was never going to break.

Seated in the sunshine outside a small but fairly expensive hotel overlooking La Place de la Concorde, Julia reached out and clinked her friend's glass with her own; and both women smiled.

'How would you like to live here, Brenda?'

'Lordy me! Lovely. Lovely, isn't it, Mrs Stevens?'

'Anywhere you'd rather be?'

'Oh no. This is the very best place in the whole world – apart from Oxford, of course.'

Since she'd arrived, Julia had felt so very tired; but so very happy, too.

CHAPTER FIFTY-NINE

St Anthony of Egypt (c. 251–356 AD): hermit and founder of Christian monasticism. An ascetic who freely admitted to being sorely beset by virtually every temptation, and most especially by sexual temptation. Tradition has it that he frequently invited a nightly succession of naked women to parade themselves in front of him as he lay, hands manacled behind his back, in appropriately transparent yet not wholly claustrophobic sacking

(SIMON SMALL, *An Irreverent Survey of the Saints*)

AT 9.30 A.M. on Tuesday, 27 September, Morse walked down the High from Carfax. There were several esteemed jewellers' shops there, he knew that; and he looked in their windows. He was somewhat uncertain, however, of what exactly to purchase – and wholly uncertain about whether his present errand was being made easier, or more difficult, by his strong suspicion now that it had been Eleanor Smith who had murdered her step-father (the same Eleanor who had formally identified the body the previous day). Perhaps in a sense it was going to be easier, though, since in all probability he wasn't looking for a wedding present any longer, the prospect of an imminent marriage now seeming increasingly remote. Yet for some reason he still wanted to buy the girl a present: a personal present.

Something like Lewis had suggested.

'How much is that?' he asked a young female assistant in the shop just across from the Covered Market.

'Nice little pendant, isn't it, sir? Delicate, tasteful, and quite inexpensive, really.'

'How much is it?' repeated Morse.

'Only £35, sir.'

Only!

Morse looked down at the representation on the tiny oval pendant of – of somebody? 'St Christopher, is it?'

'St Anthony, sir. A well-known Christian saint.'

'I thought he was the patron saint of Lost Property.'

'Perhaps you're thinking of a later St Anthony?'

But Morse wasn't. He thought there'd only been one St Anthony.

'If . . . if I bought this, I'd need a chain as well, wouldn't I?'

'It would be difficult to wear without a chain, yes.'

She was laughing at him, Morse knew that; but it hadn't been a very bright question. And very soon he was surveying a large selection of chains: chains with varied silver- or gold-content; chains of slightly larger or slightly smaller links; chains of different lengths; chains of differing prices.

So Morse made his purchase: pendant plus chain (the cheapest).

Then, after only a few steps outside the jeweller's up towards Carfax Tower, he performed a sudden U-turn, returning to the shop and asking if he could please exchange the chain (not the pendant) for something a little more expensive. The assistant (still smiling at him?) was happily co-operative; and five minutes later Morse started walking once again up towards Carfax. With a different chain.

With the most expensive chain there.

He was ready for the interview.

When earlier he had rung Eleanor Smith, she had sounded in no way surprised that the police should wish to take her finger-prints – for 'elimination purposes', as Morse had emphasized. And when he'd explained that it was against the rule-book for anyone who had been at the scene of the riverside discovery (as *he* had been) to go anywhere near the homes of those who might possibly be involved with the, er, the investigation, she'd agreed to go along to Thames Valley HQ. A car would pick her up. At 11.15 a.m.

Morse just had time to call in at Sainsbury's supermarket, on the Kidlington roundabout, where he made his few purchases swiftly, and found himself the only person at the 'small-basket' check-out. Just the four items, in fact: two small tins of baked beans; one small brown loaf; and a bottle of Glenfiddich.

CHAPTER SIXTY

When the Himalayan peasant meets the he-bear in his pride,
He shouts to scare the monster, who will often turn aside.
But the she-bear thus accosted rends the peasant tooth and
    nail.
For the female of the species is more deadly than the male
            (RUDYARD KIPLING, *The Female of the Species*)

'WHAT LINE are you going to take with her, sir?'

'I'm not at all sure. All I know is that if any of our three ladies actually murdered Brooks – and pretty certainly one of them did – we can forget the other two, wherever they're sunning themselves at the minute. It's odds on that one of them, or both of them, had some part to play in the plot; but I'm sure that neither of them could have murdered Brooks. It's a physical impossibility, knowing what we do about dates and times. But *she* could have done. Ellie Smith could have done – if only just. She went to Birmingham that Wednesday – you've checked on that. But we can't be sure when she came back, can we? You see, if she'd come back an hour, even half an hour earlier . . .'

'*She* could have stolen the knife, you mean?'

'Or she could have got someone to steal it for her.'

'Ashley Davies.'

'Yes. Could well have been. Then he gets his reward: he gets the hand of the increasingly desirable Miss Smith – a young woman he's had his lecherous eyes on even when she was a sleep-around-with-anybody girl.'

'What about the attendant at the Pitt Rivers, though? He says he probably saw this young fellow Costyn there.'

'It's always dodgy though – this identification business. We can't rely on that.'

Lewis nodded. 'He doesn't seem to have any real link with the case, anyway.'

'Except with Mrs Stevens. She taught him, remember. And I suppose if he's on drugs or something – got a regular habit to feed – short of cash – and if she was prepared to pay—'

'You mean she got him to steal the knife – for somebody else? For Ellie Smith, say?'

'Who else?'

'But you've always thought—'

'Give it a bloody rest, Lewis, will you?' snarled Morse. 'Do you think I get any pleasure from all this? Do you think I *want* to get Ellie Smith in here this morning and take her prints and tell her that she's a bloody liar and that she knifed her sod of a step-father?'

He got up and walked to the window.

'No, I don't think that,' said the ill-used Lewis quietly. 'It's just that I'm getting confused, that's all.'

'And you think I'm *not*?'

No, Lewis didn't think that. And he wondered whether his next little item of news was likely to clarify or further to befuddle the irascible Chief Inspector's brain.

'While you were shopping, I went down to Wolsey and had another look in Mrs Ewers' pantry.'

'And?'

'Well, something rang a bit of a bell when we found Brooks's body: those plastic bags. Do you remember when we first went to the Staircase?'

'The pile of them there in the pantry, yes.'

Lewis sought to hide his disappointment. 'You never said anything.'

'There's no end of those around.'

'I just thought that if Brooks used to take a few things home occasionally, unofficially – toilet-rolls, cartons of detergent, that sort of thing . . .'

'We could have a look in Brooks's place, yes. Where do you reckon he'd keep them?'

'Garden shed?'

'We'd need a search warrant . . . unless, Lewis—'

'Oh no! I'm not forcing any more locks, sir. Look what a mess I made of the box in his bedroom.'

'Perhaps you won't need to.' Morse opened a drawer of his desk and took out the bunch of keys. 'I'd like to bet one of these fits the garden shed; but I doubt we're going to find any bags there. They'll have been too careful for that.'

'What are you thinking of exactly?'

'Well, you'd have expected a few prints on the plastic bags, don't you think? But there aren't any, it seems. The water wouldn't have washed them off completely, I'm told. So they wore gloves all the time. And then they took good care to make sure the body wouldn't float, agreed? There's a gash in the bags, through all three layers – I don't think that was caused accidentally in the river. I think it was made deliberately, to let the air out, and get the body to sink . . . at least, temporarily. That's what the Warden thought, too.'

Yes, Lewis remembered. Holmes had claimed that unless any body was weighted down it would almost certainly have come up towards the surface sooner or later because of the body's natural gases.

'Why do you think they – somebody – went to all that trouble with the bags, sir? It's almost as if . . .'

'Go on, Lewis!'

'As if somebody *wanted* the body to be found.'

'Ye-es.' Morse was gazing across the yard once more. 'You know what's buggering us up the whole time, don't you? It's simply that we're going to have one helluva job making out a case against *anybody*. If somebody like Helena Kennedy, QC, was hired for the defence, she'd make mincemeat of us: we've got all the motive in the world; and all the means – but we just can't find any bloody *opportunity* . . . except at about teatime on that Wednesday afternoon. They've been too clever for us. But it's not just cleverness: it's ruthlessness too. Not a blatant ruthlessness, but certainly a latent ruthlessness – latent in all three of them. Something that suddenly hardened into a cold-blooded resolve to get rid of Brooks – not just because they knew, *must* have known, that he was a murderer himself, but for an even better reason. Hatred.'

There was a knock at the door, and a WPC announced that Ms Smith was now seated in Reception.

'Bring her up, please,' said Morse, quickly opening a small, square black box, lined with white satin, and passing it across to Lewis.

'What d'you think?'

Lewis, like Dr Hobson the previous day, looked across at Morse most curiously.

'But if what you say's right, sir, she's going to have to postpone the happy day indefinitely – for quite a few years, perhaps.'

'She can still sit in a cell and twiddle it in her fingers. No law against that, is there?'

But before Lewis could remind Morse of the very strict and very sensible prison regulations regarding necklaces and the like, there was another knock at the door, and Morse swiftly took back the pendant of St Anthony – plus his golden chain.

CHAPTER SIXTY-ONE

The total amount of undesired sex endured by women is probably greater in marriage than in prostitution
(BERTRAND RUSSELL, *Marriage and Morals*)

AFTER ROLLING the little finger of her left hand across the pad, after pressing it firmly on to the fingerprint-form, Eleanor Smith had finished; and Lewis now asked her to add her signature to the form.

'That didn't take very long, did it?' said Morse patronizingly.

'Does all this mean you've found some fingerprints on the knife?' she asked.

Morse was slightly hesitant. 'We think so, yes. Unidentified prints – unidentified as yet. As I explained, though, it's just a matter of elimination.'

She looked rather weary; gone was the sparkle that had characterized the latter part of that champagne evening at the Old Parsonage.

'You think they could be mine?'

Rather weary too was Morse's smile.

'We've got to have *some* suspects, haven't we? In fact my sergeant here's got a long list of 'em.'

She turned to Lewis. 'Whereabouts am I on the list?'

'We always try to put the most attractive at the top, don't we, sir?'

Morse nodded his agreement, wishing only that he'd thought of such a splendid rejoinder himself.

'And when exactly am I supposed to have murdered that shithouse?'

She looked from one to the other, and Morse in turn looked to Lewis the Interlocutor.

'Perhaps,' said the latter slowly, 'when you got back from Birmingham that Wednesday?'

'I see . . . And did I pinch the knife as well?'

'I – we don't think you could have done that because, as you told us, you didn't get back into Oxford until after the museum had closed. We checked up on the train time: it got into Oxford Station at 16.35 – just three minutes late.'

'You still don't sound as if you believe me.'

'We don't think you took the knife,' said Morse.

The slight but perceptible stress on the 'you' was clearly not lost on Suspect Number One.

'You suggestin' somebody else pinched it – then slipped it to me on the way home from the railway station? Then I just called in to have a chat with him and decided to murder the old bugger there and then – is that what you're thinking?'

'There are more unlikely scenarios than that,' said Morse quietly.

'Oh, not you! How I hate that bloody word "scenario".'

She had touched a raw spot, for Morse hated the word too. Yet he'd not been able to come up with anything better; and he made no protest as Ellie Smith continued, changing down now into her lower-gear register of speech.

'And what am I s'posed to 'ave done with 'im then?'

'Well, we were hoping you could give us a few ideas yourself.'

'Is this turnin' into a bleedin' interview or something?'

'No,' said Morse simply. 'You're under no obligation to answer anything. But sooner or later we're going to have to ask all sorts of questions. Ask you, ask your mother . . . Where is your mother, by the way?'

'Abroad somewhere.'

'How do you know that?'

'She sent me a postcard.'

'Where from?'

'The postmark was smudged – I couldn't read it.'

'Must have had a stamp on it?'

'Yeah. I'm no good at them names of foreign countries, though.'

'Some of them aren't very difficult, you know. "France", for instance?'

She made no reply.

'Have you still got the postcard?'

'No. Threw it away, didn't I?'

'What was the picture on it?'

'A river, I think.'

'Not the Thames?'

'Not the Thames.'

'You're not being much help, you know.'

'That's where you're wrong, though.'

She produced a small pasteboard business card and handed it to Morse.

'You were asking me about that Wednesday, weren't you? Well, I met a fellow on the train, and he got a bit, you know, a bit friendly and flirty, like; said if I ever wanted any, you know, work or anything . . .'

Morse looked at the white card: 'Mike Williamson, Modelling and Photographic Agency', with a Reading address and telephone number.

'He'll remember me – for sure, Inspector. I can promise you that.'

She smiled, her eyes momentarily recapturing the sparkle that Morse could recall so well.

'Better check, Lewis.'

But as Lewis got up and moved towards the phone, Morse held up his hand: 'Office next door, please.'

'Why did you want him out of the way?'

Morse ignored the question, feeling quite irrationally jealous. 'What did this fellow offer you?'

'Oh, Christ, come off it!' Her eyes flashed angrily now. 'What the 'ell d'you think? He just thought I was an intelligent, ill-educated, expensive prostitute – which I am.'

'Which you *were*.'

'Which I *am*, Morse. By the way, you don't mind me calling you "Morse", do you? I did ask you – remember? – if I could call you something more pally and civilized but . . .'

'What about Mr Davies? When you're married—'

'To Ashley? That's all off. He came last night and we stayed up till God knows when, talking about it – going round and round in the same old circles. But I just can't go through with it. I like him – he's nice. But I just . . . I just don't fancy him, that's all; and I could never love him – never. So it's not fair, is it? Not fair on him. Not fair on me, either, really.'

'So you won't be needing me any more – for the wedding,' said Morse slowly.

"Fraid not, no. There wouldn't have been a wedding anyway, though, would there – not if you're going to arrest me?'

For a brief while the two looked at each other across the desk, their eyes locked together with a curiously disturbing intimacy.

The phone rang.

It was Strange; and Ellie got to her feet.

'Please, stay!' whispered Morse, his hand over the mouthpiece. 'Yes, sir. Yes . . . Can you just give me five minutes . . . ? I'll be straight along.'

'Why d'you want me to stay?' she asked, after Morse had put down the receiver.

He took the little black box from the drawer and handed it to her.

'It's not wrapped up, I'm afraid. I'm not much good at that sort of thing.'

'Wha—?' She held the box in her left hand and opened it with her right, taking hold of the gold chain lovingly and gently, and slowly lifting up St Anthony.

'Wha's this for?'

'I bought it for you.'

'But like I say—'

'I want you to have it, that's all. I've never bought anything like that for anybody – and, as I say, I just want you to have it.'

Ellie had been looking down at the pendant and suddenly the tears began. 'Oh God!' she whispered.

'Do you like it?'

'It's . . . it's the most wonderful . . .' But she could get no further. She stood up and walked round the desk, and kissed Morse fully and softly on the mouth; and Morse felt the wetness of her cheek against his own.

'I must go,' said Morse. 'My boss'll be getting impatient.'

She nodded. 'You know what I just said – about Ashley? That I couldn't marry him because I didn't love him? Well, that wasn't really the reason why I broke it off.'

In his brain Morse had become convinced that Eleanor Smith must be guilty of her step-father's murder; but in his heart he felt grieved as he awaited her words, for he knew exactly what they would be.

Yet he was wrong.

Spectacularly wrong.

'The real reason is I've . . . I've fallen in love with somebody else.'

Morse wondered if he'd heard correctly. 'What?'

'You gettin' deaf or something?'

'Not – not with that charlatan from the modelling agency, surely?'

She shook her head crossly, like some unhappy, exasperated little girl who will stamp her foot until she can get her own way, her own selfish way. *Now.*

'Are you going to listen to me, or not? Can't you guess? Can't you see? Can't you *see*?' She was standing beside the door, her head held high, her sludgy-green eyes closed, trying so hard to hold back the brimming tears. 'I've fallen in love with you, you stupid sod!'

CHAPTER SIXTY-TWO

dactyloscopy (n): the examination of fingerprints (Early Twentieth Century)

(*The New Shorter Oxford English Dictionary*)

ALWAYS HAD Morse been a reluctant dactyloscopist, and throughout his police career all the arches and whorls and loops, all the peaks and the troughs and the ridges, had ever remained a deep mystery to him – like electricity, and the Wheatstone Bridge. He was therefore perfectly happy, on Friday, 30 September, to delegate the fingerprinting of Mesdames Brooks and Stevens to Sergeant Lewis – for the two overseas travellers had returned to Oxford early that afternoon. Immigration officials at

Heathrow, Gatwick, and Stansted airports had been alerted about them; and the phone-call from Heathrow had been received at Thames Valley HQ just after midday: the two had boarded the Oxford City Link coach, scheduled to arrive at its Gloucester Green terminus in Oxford at 2.30 p.m.

Neither had appeared to show any undue surprise or discomfiture when Lewis, accompanied by a fingerprint officer, had taken them into the manager's office there, and trotted out the 'purely for elimination' line.

After his colleague had left for the fingerprint bureau at St Aldate's (where there was now a computerized search facility) Lewis had returned to Kidlington HQ, to find Morse dispiritedly scanning some of the documents in the case.

But the Chief Inspector perked up with the return of his sergeant.

'No problems?'

'No problems, sir.'

'You're a betting man, Lewis?'

'Only very occasionally: Derby, Grand National . . .'

'Will you have a bet with *me*?'

'50p?'

'Can't we be devils, and make it a quid?'

'All right. I've got to be careful with the money, though – we've got the decorators in.'

Morse appeared surprised. 'I thought you did all that sort of stuff yourself?'

'I used to, sir, when I had the time and the energy. Before I started working for you.'

'Well, take your pick!'

'Pardon?'

'The fingerprints. Brenda Brooks or Julia Stevens – who do you go for?'

Lewis frowned. 'I can't really see his wife doing it, you know that. I just don't think she'd have the strength for one thing.'

'Really?' Morse seemed almost to be enjoying himself.

'Mrs Stevens, though . . . Well, she's a much stronger person, a much stronger character, isn't she? And she's got the brains—'

'And she's got nothing to lose,' added Morse more sombrely.

'Not much, no.'

'So your money's on her, is it?'

Lewis hesitated. 'You know, sir, in detective stories there are only two rules really, aren't there? It's never the butler;

and it's never the person you think it is. So – so I'll go for Mrs Brooks.'

'Leaving me with Mrs Stevens.'

'You'd have gone for her anyway, sir.'

'You think so?'

But Lewis didn't know what he was thinking, and changed the subject.

'Did you have any lunch earlier, sir?'

'Not even a pint,' complained Morse, lighting a cigarette.

'You're not hungry?'

'A bit.'

'What about coming back and having a bite with us? The missus'd be only too glad to knock something up for you.'

Morse considered the proposition. 'What do you normally have on Fridays? Fish?'

'No. It's egg and chips on Fridays.'

'I thought that was on Wednesdays.'

Lewis nodded. 'And Mondays.'

'You're on,' decided Morse. 'Give her a ring and tell her to peel another few spuds.'

'Only one thing, sir – as I said. We're in a bit of a pickle at home, I'm afraid – with the decorators in.'

'Have you got the beer in, though? That's more to the point, surely.'

It was Lewis himself who took the call from the fingerprint bureau half an hour later. No match. No match anywhere. Whoever it was who had left some fingerprints on the Rhodesian knife, it had *not* been Mrs Brenda Brooks or Mrs Julia Stevens; nor, as they'd already learned, Ms Eleanor Smith. One other piece of information. Classifying and identifying fingerprints was an immensely complicated job and they couldn't be absolutely sure yet; but it was looking almost certain now that the fingerprints on the knife-handle didn't match those of any known criminals either – well over two million of them – in the Scotland Yard library.

'So you see what it means, Sarge? Whoever murdered your fellow doesn't look as if he had any previous conviction.'

'Or *she*,' added Lewis, after putting down the phone.

There was no need to relay the message, since a glum-looking Morse had heard it all anyway.

In silence.
A silence that persisted.

The report that Lewis had written on the visit to Matthew Rodway's mother was on the top of Morse's pile.

'Hope I didn't make too many spelling mistakes, sir?' ventured Lewis finally.

'What? No, no. You're improving. Slowly.'

'I don't suppose she gives tuppence really – Mrs Rodway, I mean – about who killed Brooks. So long as somebody did.'

Morse grunted inarticulately. His thoughts drifted back to their meeting with Mrs Rodway. It seemed an age ago now; but as his eyes skimmed through the report once again he could clearly visualize that interview, and the room, and the slim and still embittered Mrs Rodway . . .

'I know it's probably nonsense, sir, but you don't think that *she* could have murdered Brooks, do you?'

'She had as good a motive as anybody,' admitted Morse.

'Perhaps we ought to have another little ride out there and take her fingerprints.'

'Not today, Lewis. I'm out for a meal, if you remember.'

'I'll see you there, sir, if you don't mind. About six, is that all right?'

'What are *you* going to do?'

'Lots of little things. Make a bit more progress with the keys, for a start. I'm expected at the Pitt Rivers in twenty minutes.'

After Lewis had left, Morse lit yet another cigarette and leaned back in the black leather chair, looking purposelessly around his office. He noticed the thin patina of nicotine on the emulsioned walls. Yes, the place could do with a good wash-down and redecoration: the corners of the ceiling especially were deeply stained . . .

Suddenly, he felt a brief frisson of excitement as if there were something of vital importance in what he'd just read, or what he'd just thought, or what he'd just seen. But try as he might, he was unable to isolate the elusive clue; and soon he knew it was of no use trying any more.

It had gone.

CHAPTER SIXTY-THREE

Fingerprints *do* get left at crime scenes. Even the craftiest of
perpetrators sometimes forget to wipe up everywhere
(*Murder Ink, Incriminating Evidence*)

HER FIRST sentence, spoken with an attractive Welsh lilt, was a
perfect anapaestic pentameter:
'We shall have to eat here in the kitchen, Inspector, all
right?'
'Wherever, Mrs Lewis. Have no fears.'
'We've got the decorators in, see? But just go and sit down in
the lounge – where I've put out some beer and a glass.' (Anapaestic hexameter.)
As he passed the dining-room, Morse stopped to look inside.
The decorators had finished for the day; almost finished
altogether, it seemed, for only around the main window were
some paint-stained white sheets still lying across the salmon-pink
carpet, with all of the furniture now pushed back into place
except for a bookcase, which stood awkwardly in mid-room, a
wooden step-ladder propped up against it. Clearly, though, there
would be no problem about its own relocation, either, for the site
of its former habitation was marked by an oblong of strawberry-
red carpet to the left of the window.
Mrs Lewis was suddenly behind him.
'You like the colour?'
'Very professionally painted,' said Morse, a man with no
knowledge whatsoever of professionalism in painting and
decorating.
'You were looking at the carpet, though, weren't you now?'
she said shrewdly. 'Only had it five years – and they told us the
colours in all of their carpets would last till eternity.' (Anapaests
everywhere.)
'I suppose everything fades,' said Morse. It hardly seemed a
profound observation – not at the time.
'It's the sun really, see. That's why you get most of your
discolouration. In the cupboards – on the lining for the cupboards
– you hardly get fading at all.'
Morse moved on into the lounge where he opened a can of

Cask Flow Beamish, sat contentedly back in an armchair, and was watching the *Six O'Clock News* when Lewis came in.

'You look pleased with yourself,' said Morse.

'Well, that's two more of the keys accounted for: that second Yale opens the staff entrance door at the back of the Pitt Rivers, just off South Parks Road; and that little "X 10" key – remember? – that's a Pitt Rivers key, too: it's a key to a wall-safe there that's got rows and rows of little hooks in it, with a key on each of 'em – keys to all the display cabinets.'

Morse grunted a perfunctory 'Well done!' as he reverted his attention to the news.

Mrs Lewis produced a slightly unladylike whistle a few minutes later: 'On the table, boys!'

Morse himself had acquired one culinary skill only – that of boiling an egg; and he was not infrequently heard to boast that such a skill was not nearly so common as was generally assumed. But granted that Morse (in his own estimation) was an exemplary *boiler* of eggs, Mrs Lewis (*omnium consensu*) was a first-class *frier*; and the milkily opaque eggs, two on each plate, set beside their mountains of thick golden chips, were a wonderful sight to behold.

As Morse jolted out some tomato sauce, Lewis picked up his knife and fork. 'You know, sir, if they ever find a body with an empty plate of eggs and chips beside it—'

'I think you mean a plate empty of eggs and chips, Lewis.'

'Well, I reckon if the fingerprints on the knife don't match any of those in our criminal library, the odds are they'll probably be mine.'

Morse nodded, picked up his own knife and fork, found (blessedly!) that the plate itself was hot – and then he froze, as if a frame on the family video had suddenly been switched to 'Pause'.

'Everything all right, sir?'

Morse made no reply.

'You – you're feeling all right, sir?' persisted a slightly anxious Lewis.

'Bloody 'ell!' whispered Morse tremulously to himself in a voice just below audial range. Then, louder: 'Bloody 'ell! You've done it again, Lewis. You've done it *again!*'

Unprecedentedly Lewis was moved to lay down both knife and fork.

'You know we had a little bet ...' Morse's voice was vibrant now.

'When we both lost.'

'No. When to be more accurate neither of us won. Well, I'd like to bet you something else, Lewis. I'd like to bet you that I know whose fingerprints are on that knife in Brooks's back!'

'That's more than the fingerprint-boys do.'

Morse snorted. 'I'm very tempted to report *them* for professional incompetence.' Then his voice softened. 'But I can forgive them. Yes, I can understand them.'

'I'm lost, sir, I'm afraid.'

'Shall I tell you,' asked Morse, 'whose fingerprints we found on that knife?'

His blue eyes looked so fiercely across the kitchen table that for a few moments Lewis wondered whether he was suffering from some slight stroke or seizure.

'Shall I tell you?' repeated Morse. 'You see, there's a regular procedure which you know all about; which *every* CID man knows all about. A procedure that wasn't – couldn't have been – followed in this case: that when you take fingerprints from the scene of any murder you take everybody's – including the corpse's.'

Lewis felt the blood in his veins growing cold – like the plate in front of him.

'You can't mean ...?'

'But I do, Lewis. That's exactly what I do mean. *The prints are those of Edward Brooks himself.*'

CHAPTER SIXTY-FOUR

Gestalt (n): chiefly *Psychol.* An integrated perceptual structure or unity conceived as functionally more than the sum of its parts

(*The New Shorter Oxford Dictionary*)

As Morse well knew, it was difficult enough to describe to someone else such a comparatively simple physical action as walking, say – let alone something considerably more complicated such as serving a ball in a game of tennis. How much more difficult then, later that same evening, for him to answer Lewis's direct question about the cerebral equivalent of such a process.

'What put you on to it, sir?'

What indeed?

It was perhaps perfectly possible to describe the mental gymnastics involved in the solving of a cryptic crossword clue. But how did one explain those virtually inexplicable convolutions of the mind which occasionally led to some dramatic, some penny-dropping moment, when the answers to a whole *series* of cryptic clues – and those not of the cruciverbalist but of the criminological variety – combined to cast some completely new illumination on the scene? How did one begin to explain such a sudden, almost irrational, psychological process?

'With difficulty,' was the obvious answer; but Morse was trying much harder than that, as he now sought to identify the main constituents which had led him to his quite extraordinary conclusion.

It was all to do with the fortuitous collocation of several memories, several recollections, which although occurring at disparate points in the case – and before – had suddenly come together in his mind, and coalesced.

There had been the report (Lewis's own) on the interview with Mrs Rodway, when he had so easily been able to revisualize some of the smallest details of the room in which they had spoken with her, and particularly that oblong patch above the radiator where a picture had been hanging.

Then there had been (only that very evening) a second oblong, prompting memory further, when he had looked down at the pristine strawberry-red in the lounge there, and when Mrs Lewis had spoken of the unfading linings in her cupboards.

And then, working backwards (or was it forwards?) there had been the visit to the Pitt Rivers Museum, when the Administrator had pointed with pride to the fine quality of the hessian lining for her cabinet-exhibits, with its optimistic guarantee of Tithonian immortality.

Then again, a much more distant memory from his childhood of a case of cutlery, a family heirloom, where over the years each knife, each fork, each spoon, had left its own imprint, its own silhouette, on the blue plush lining of the case. Things always left their impressions, did they not?

Or did they?

Perhaps in the Pitt Rivers cabinets, in those slightly sombre, sunless galleries, the objects displayed there – the artefacts, the relics from the past – were leaving only very faint impressions, like the utensils in Mrs Lewis's kitchen cupboards.

No impressions at all, possibly . . .

Then, and above all, the discrepancy between the pathologist's report on the knife used to murder McClure, and the statement given by the Raysons about the knife found in their own front garden: the 'blade not really sharp', in the former; the 'blade in no immediate need of sharpening', in the latter. Not a big discrepancy, perhaps; but a hugely significant one – and one which should never, never have passed unnoticed.

Yes, all the constituents were there: separate, though, and unsynthesized – waiting for a catalyst.

Lewis!

Lewis the Catalyst.

For it was Lewis who had returned from his p.m. investigations with the information that one of the small keys found in Brooks's pocket fitted a wall-safe in the museum; in which, in turn, were to be found row upon row of other keys, including the key to Cabinet 52. It was Lewis, too, who so innocently had asserted, as he picked up a knife with which to eat his meal, that his own fingerprints would soon be found thereon . . .

And whither had such ratiocination finally led the Chief Inspector, as, like Abraham, he had made his way forth from his tent in the desert knowing not whither he went? To that strangest of all conclusions: that on Wednesday, 7 September, from Cabinet 52 in the Pitt Rivers Museum in Oxford – *nothing whatsoever had been stolen.*

CHAPTER SIXTY-FIVE

Behold, I shew you a mystery
(St Paul, I *Corinthians*, ch. 15, v. 51)

A council of war was called in Caesar's tent two days later, on Sunday, 2 October, with three other officers joining Chief Superintendent Strange in the latter's Kidlington HQ office at 10 a.m.: Chief Inspector Morse, Chief Inspector Phillotson, and Sergeant Lewis. Morse, invited to put a case for a dramatic intensification of inquiries, for a series of warrants, and for a small cohort of forensic specialists, did so with complete conviction.

He knew now (or so he claimed) what had been the circumstances of each of the murders, those of McClure and Brooks; and he would, with his colleagues' permission, give an account of those circumstances, not seeking to dwell on motives (not for the present) but on methods – on *modi operandi*.

Strange now listened, occasionally nodding, occasionally lifting his eyebrows in apparent incredulity, to the burden of Morse's reconstructions.

McClure lived on a staircase where Brooks was the scout. The latter had gained access to drugs and became a supplier to several undergraduates, one of whom, Matthew Rodway, had become very friendly with McClure – probably not a homosexual relationship, though – before committing suicide in tragic and semi-suspicious circumstances. As a result of this, McClure had insisted that Brooks resign from his job; but agreed that he, McClure, would not report the matter to the Dean, and would even provide a job-testimonial, provided that Brooks forswore his dealings in drugs.

Feelings between the two men were bitter.

Things settled down, though.

Then it came to McClure's notice that Brooks had *not* finished with his drug-dealing after all; that some of the junkies were still in touch with him. A furious McClure threatened disclosure to Brooks's new employers and to the police, and a meeting between the two was arranged (or not arranged – how could one know?). Certain it was, however, that Brooks went to visit McClure. And murdered him.

On the way home, on his bicycle, Brooks suddenly became aware that he was seriously ill. He managed to get as far as St Giles', but could get no further. He left his bicycle outside St Mary Mags, without even bothering to lock it, perhaps, and covering himself as best he could, got a taxi from the rank there up to East Oxford – and very soon got an ambulance up to the JR2, minus the bloodstained clothing which his wife disposed of.

One thing above all must have haunted Brooks's mind once he knew he would recover from his heart attack: he was still in possession of the knife he'd used to murder McClure, because whatever happened *he couldn't throw it away*. He ordered his wife

THE DAUGHTERS OF CAIN

to lock it up somewhere, probably in the box in his bedroom, and she did as he asked, surely having enough common sense to handle the knife – both then and later – with the greatest delicacy, pretty certainly wearing the glove she'd taken to using to protect her injured right hand. She was terrified – certainly at that point – of incurring the anger of a fearsomely cruel man who had physically maltreated her on several occasions, and who in earlier years had probably abused his step-daughter – the latter now putting in an appearance after many moons away from home, no doubt after somehow learning of Brooks's illness.

Brenda Brooks had an ally.

Two allies, in fact: because we now become increasingly aware of the unusually strong bond of friendship and affection between her and the woman for whom she cleaned, Mrs Julia Stevens, a schoolma'am who, although this fact has only recently become known to us, was suffering from an inoperable brain-tumour.

A plot was hatched, an extraordinarily clever plot, designed to throw the police on to the wrong track; a plot which succeeded in so doing.

'Let me explain.'

'At last,' mumbled Strange.

Brenda Brooks took Mrs Stevens wholly into her confidence, with both now knowing perfectly well not only who had murdered McClure but also exactly where the knife had come from – and why Brooks was unable to get rid of it.

On the Saturday before McClure's murder, the very last thing in the afternoon, Brooks had taken the knife from Cabinet 52 in the Pitt Rivers Museum, fully intending to replace it the very first thing on the following Monday morning, when he planned to turn up for work half an hour or so early and to restore it to its position amongst the fifty-odd other knives there. Nobody would have missed it; nobody *could* have missed it, since the museum was closed on Sundays.

'Why—?' Strange had begun. But Morse had anticipated the question.

Why Brooks should have acted in such a devious way, or whether he had taken the knife with the deliberate intention of committing murder, it was now only possible to guess. The only slight clue (thus far) was that one of the few books found in the Brooks's virtually illiterate household was a library copy of *The Innocence of Father Brown*, in which Chesterton suggested a battlefield as the safest place to conceal a corpse ... with the possible implication that a cabinet of weapons might be the safest place to conceal a knife.

But Brooks couldn't restore the knife. Not yet.

His great hope was that no one would notice its absence. *And no one did.* Apart from the attendant circumstance of so many other knives, one further factor was greatly in his favour: the cabinet had been recently relined, and there was no outwardly physical sign that any object could be missing. The normal routine, when anything was taken out, was for a printed white card – 'Temporarily Removed' – to be inserted over the space left vacant. But there *was* no space left vacant, since Brooks had only to move two or three other knives along a little to effect a balanced row of exhibits. And as day followed day, no one in fact noticed that anything at all was missing.

But, apart from Brooks, two other persons now knew of all this.

One of whom was Julia Stevens.

And the beautifully clever idea was born: if . . . if Brooks were to be murdered with the very same knife which he himself had stolen . . .

Ah, yes!

Two things only were required.

First, a knife, a different but *wholly* similar knife, *would have to be planted* – somewhere in, or near, Daventry Avenue. For when it was found – as surely sooner or later it would be – the police, with a little luck, would discover that it had been taken from one of the Brooks's kitchen drawers.

Second, the cabinet from which the actual murder weapon had been taken ('Cabinet 52' was clearly marked on the tag) *would have to be broken into* so that its contents would inevitably be checked. For then, and then only, would the pedigree of the missing knife become known.

Someone was therefore delegated to break open that cabinet, to ruffle around a few of the knives there – exactly the *opposite* of what Brooks had done earlier – and the deception was launched. The 'theft' was duly spotted, and reported; the missing knife was fairly quickly identified; and, above all, the crucial alibis were established.

How so?

Because of the wholly incontestable fact that any person found murdered by means of that stolen knife must have been murdered *after that knife was stolen.*

But the truth was that Brooks was murdered *before* the knife was stolen – probably murdered the day before, since the two women lied about seeing him alive on the afternoon when they set off with the school-party for Stratford.

The only thing now calling for some sort of explanation was the curious circumstance of Brooks's body being so elaborately wrapped up in plastic, then wrapped up again in a brown carpet, before being dumped into the Isis, just upstream from Donnington Bridge, almost certainly driven there in the boot of a car. Mrs Stevens' car? Most probably, since she was the only one of them to own such a means of transport.

Well (as Morse saw it) the reason was fairly obvious: if and when (and *when* rather than if) the body was found, such wrapping would ensure one vital thing: that the knife would still be found with the body – still be found *in* the body, it could be hoped. There would be no danger of it being lost; and thereby no danger that the alibis so cunningly, so painstakingly, devised would be discounted or destroyed.

'So you see,' finished Detective Chief Inspector Morse, 'the two women we assumed could never have murdered Brooks have overnight moved up to the top of the list.' He looked up with a fairly self-satisfied smile to Chief Superintendent Strange. 'And with your permission, sir, we shall go ahead immediately, apply for a couple of search warrants—'

'Why only two warrants?' asked Detective Chief Inspector Phillotson.

CHAPTER SIXTY-SIX

The mind is its own place, and in itself
Can make a heaven of hell, a hell of heaven
(JOHN MILTON, *Paradise Lost*, Book 1)

THE FOLLOWING day, a call was put through to Morse ('Must be Morse') from Mr Basil Shepstone, Senior Neurologist at Oxford's Churchill Hospital; and twenty minutes later the two men were seated together in Shepstone's consulting-room.

Mrs Julia Stevens (Morse learned) had been admitted at midday, having earlier been discovered unconscious at the side of her bed by her cleaning-lady. Some speedy deterioration in her mental condition had been expected; but the dramatic (the literal) collapse in her physical condition had come as some surprise. A recent biopsy (Morse learned) had confirmed *glioblastoma multiforma*, a fast-growing tumour of the neuroglia in the brain: wholly malignant, sadly inoperable, rapidly fatal.

When Julia had been admitted, it was immediately apparent that, somewhere on the brain, pressure had become intolerably severe: she had been painfully sick again in the ambulance; clearly she was experiencing some considerable difficulty with both sight and speech; showing signs too of spatial disorientation. Yet somehow she had managed to make it clear that she wished to speak to the policeman Morse.

Twice during the early afternoon (Shepstone reported), her behaviour had grown disturbingly aggressive, especially towards one of the young nurses trying to administer medication. But that sort of behaviour – often involving some fairly fundamental personality change – was almost inevitable with such a tumour.

'Had you noticed any "personality change" before?' asked Morse.

Shepstone hesitated. 'Yes, perhaps so. I think . . . well, let's put it this way. The commonest symptom would be a general loss of inhibition, if you know what I mean.'

'I don't think I do.'

'Well, I mean one obvious thing is she probably wouldn't be over-worried about the reactions and opinions of other people – other professional colleagues, in her case. Let's say she'd be more willing than usual to speak her mind in a staff-meeting, perhaps. I don't think she was ever *too* shy a person; but like most of us she'd probably always felt a bit diffident – a bit insecure – about life and . . . and things.'

'She's an attractive woman, isn't she?'

Shepstone looked across at Morse keenly.

'I know what you're thinking. And the answer's probably "yes". I rather think that if over these past few months someone had asked . . . to go to bed with her . . .'

'When you say "someone" – you mean some *man*?'

'I think I do, yes.'

'And you say she's been a bit violent today.'

'Aggressive, certainly.'

Morse nodded.

'It's really,' continued Shepstone, 'the unexpectedness rather than the nature of behaviour that always sticks out in these cases. I remember at the Radcliffe Infirmary, for example, a very strait-laced old dear with a similar tumour getting out of her bed one night and dancing naked in the fountain out the front there.'

'But *she* isn't a strait-laced old dear,' said Morse slowly.

'Oh, no,' replied the sad-eyed Consultant. 'Oh, no.'

For a while, when Julia had regained some measure of her senses in the hospital, she knew that she was still at home in her own bed, really. It was just that someone was trying to confuse her, because the walls of her bedroom were no longer that soothing shade of green, but this harsher, crueller white.

Everything was white.

Everyone was wearing white . . .

But Julia felt more relaxed now.

The worry at the beginning had been her complete disorientation: about the time of day, the day, the month – the year, even. And then, just as the white-coated girl was trying to talk to her, she'd felt a terrible sense of panic as she realized that she was unaware of *who she was*.

Things were better now, though; one by one, things were clicking into place; and some knowledge of herself, of her life, was slowly surfacing, with the wonderful bonus that the dull, debilitating headache she'd lived with for so many months was gone. Completely gone.

She knew the words she wanted to say – about seeing Morse; or at least her *mind* knew. Yet she was aware that those words had homodyned little, if at all, with the words she'd actually used:

'One thousand and one, one thousand and two . . .'

But she could write.

How could that be?

If she couldn't speak?

No matter.

She could write.

As he looked down at her, Morse realized that even in her terminal illness Julia Stevens would ever be an attractive woman; and he placed a hand lightly on her right arm as she lay in her short-sleeved nightdress, and smiled at her. And she smiled back, but tightly, for she was willing herself to make him understand what so desperately she wished to tell him.

At the scene of the terrible murder that had taken place in Brenda's front room, when she, Julia, had stood there, helpless at first, a spectator of a deed already done, she had vowed, if ever need arose, to take all guilt upon herself. And the words were in her mind: words that were all untrue, but words that were ready to be spoken. She had only to repeat repeat *repeat* them to herself: 'I murdered him I murdered him *I* murdered him . . .' And now she looked up at Morse and forced her mouth to speak those self-same words:

'One thousand and three, one thousand and four, one thousand and five . . .'

Aware, it seemed, even as she spoke, of her calamitous shortcomings, she looked around her with frenzied exasperation as she sought to find the pencil with which earlier she'd managed to write down 'MORSE'. Her right arm flailed about her wildly, knocking over a glass of orange juice on the bedside table, and tears of frustration sprang in her eyes.

Suddenly three nurses, all in white, were at her side, two of them seeking to hold her still as the third administered a further sedative. And Morse, who had intended to plant a tender kiss upon the Titian hair, was hurriedly ushered away.

CHAPTER SIXTY-SEVEN

We can prove whatever we want to; the only real difficulty is to know what we want to prove

(EMILE CHARTIER, *Système des beaux arts*)

EVENTS WERE now moving quickly towards their close. There was much that was wanting to be found – was found – although Lewis was not alone in wondering exactly what Morse himself wanted to be found. Certainly one or two minor surprises were still in store; but in essence it was only the corroborative, substantiating detail that remained to be gleaned – was gleaned – by the inquiry team from their painstaking forensic investigations, and from one or two further painful encounters.

Morse was reading a story when just after 3 p.m. on Tuesday, 4 October, Lewis returned from the JR2 where he had interviewed a rapidly improving Costyn – to whom, as it happened, he had taken an instant dislike, just as earlier in the case Morse had felt an instinctive antipathy towards Ms Smith.

Lewis had learned nothing of any substance. About the ram-raid, Costyn had been perkily co-operative, partly no doubt because he had little option in the matter. But about any (surely most probable?) visit to the Pitt Rivers Museum; about his relations (relationship?) with Mrs Stevens; about any (possible?) knowledge of, implication in, co-operation with, the murder of Edward Brooks, Costyn had been cockily dismissive.

He had nothing to say.

How could he have anything to say?

He knew nothing.

If Lewis was ninety-five per cent convinced that Costyn was lying, he had been one hundred per cent convinced that Ashley Davies, whom he'd interviewed the day before, could never have been responsible for the prising open of Cabinet 52. In fact Davies *had* been in Oxford that afternoon; and for some considerable while, since between 3.45 p.m. and 4.45 p.m. he had been sitting in the chair of Mr J. Balaguer-Morris, a distinguished and unimpeachable dental-surgeon practising in Summertown.

Quod erat demonstrandum.

Lewis sensed therefore (as he knew Morse did) that the two young men had probably always been peripheral to the crime in any case. But *someone* had gone along to the Pitt Rivers; *someone's* services could well have been needed for the disposal of the body in the Isis. For although Brooks had not been a heavy man, it would have been quite extraordinarily difficult for one woman to have coped alone; rather easier for two, certainly; and perhaps not all that difficult for three of them. Yet the help of a strong young man would have been a godsend, surely?

With the Magistrates finding no objections, the three search warrants had been immediately authorized, and the spotlight was now refocusing, ever more closely, on the three women in the case:

Brenda Brooks
Julia Stevens
Eleanor Smith . . .

The previous afternoon, great activity at the Brooks's residence had proved dramatically productive. At the back of the house, one of the small keys from Lewis's bunch had provided immedi- ate, unforced access to the garden shed. No transparent plastic bags were found there; nor any damning snippet of dark green garden-twine like that which had secured the bundle of the corpse. Yet something *had* been found there: fibres of a brown material which looked most suspiciously similar – which later proved to be identical – to the carpeting that had covered the body of Edward Brooks.

Brenda Brooks, therefore, had been taken in for questioning the previous evening, on two separate occasions being politely reminded that anything she said might be taken down in writing and used as evidence. But there seemed hardly any valid reason for even one such caution, since from the very start she had appeared too shocked to say anything at all. Later in the evening she had been released on police bail, having been formally charged with conspiracy to murder. As Morse saw things the decision to grant bail had been wholly correct. There was surely little merit in pressing for custody, since it was difficult to envisage that gentle little lady, once freed, indulging in any orgy of murder in the area of the Thames Valley Police Authority.

In any case, Morse liked Mrs Brooks.

Just as he liked Mrs Stevens – in whose garage earlier that same day a forensic team had made an equally dramatic finding, when they had examined the ancient Volvo, *in situ*, and dis- covered, in the boot, fibres of a brown material which looked most suspiciously similar – which later proved to be identical – to the carpeting that had covered the body of Edward Brooks . . .

Morse had nodded to himself with satisfaction on receiving each of these reports. So careful, so clever, they'd been – the two women! Yet even the cleverest of criminals couldn't think of everything: they all made that one little mistake, sooner or later; and he should be glad of that.

He *was* glad.

He himself had taken temporary possession of the long- overdue library book found in the Brooks's bedroom, noticing with some self-congratulation that the tops of two pages in the story entitled 'The Broken Sword' had been dog-eared. By Brooks? Were the pages worth testing for fingerprints? No. Far too fanciful a notion. But Morse told himself that he would re- read the story once he got the chance; and indeed his eye had already caught some of the lines he remembered so vividly from his youth:

Where does a man kick a pebble? On the beach.
Where does a wise man hide a leaf? In the forest . . .

Yes. Things were progressing well – and quickly.

There was that third search warrant, of course: one that had been granted, though not yet served.

The one to be served on Ms Smith . . .

Of whom, as it happened, Morse had dreamed the previous night – most disturbingly. He had watched her closely (how on earth?) as semi-dressed in a plunging Versace creation she had exhibited herself erotically to some lecherous Yuppie in the back of a BMW. And when Morse had awoken, he had felt bitterly angry with her; and sick; and heartachingly jealous.

He had known better nights; known better dreams.

Yet life is a strange affair; and only ten minutes after Lewis had returned that Tuesday afternoon Morse received a call from Reception which quickened his heartbeat considerably.

CHAPTER SIXTY-EIGHT

She turned away, but with the autumn weather
Compelled my imagination many days,
Many days and many hours
(T. S. ELIOT, *La Figlia Che Piange*)

SHE CLOSED the passenger-seat door, asking the man to wait there, in the slip-road, for ten minutes – no longer; then to drive in and pick her up.

She walked quite briskly past the blue sign, with its white lettering, 'Thames Valley Police HQ'; then up the longish gradient to the brick-and-concrete building.

At Reception she quickly made her errand clear.

'Is he expecting you, Miss?' asked the man seated there.

'No.'

'Can I ask what it's in connection with?'

'A murder.'

The grey-haired man looked up at her with some curiosity. He

thought he might have seen her before; then decided that he
hadn't. And rang Morse.

'Let her in, Bill. I'll be down to collect her in a couple of
minutes.'

After entering her name neatly in the Visitors' Log, Bill pressed
the mechanism that opened the door to the main building. She
was carrying a small package, some 5 inches by 3 inches, and he
decided to keep a precautionary eye on her. Normally he would
not have let her through without some sort of check. But he'd
always been encouraged to use his discretion, and in truth she
looked more like a potential traveller than a potential terrorist.
And Chief Inspector Morse had sounded happy enough.

He pointed the way. 'If you just go and sit and wait there,
Miss . . . ?'

So Ellie Smith walked over the darkly marbled floor to a small,
square waiting-area, carpeted in blue, with matching chairs set
against the walls. She sat down and looked around her. Many
notices were displayed there, of the 'Watch Out', 'Burglars
Beware' variety; and photographs of a police car splashing
through floods, and a friendly bobby talking to a farmer's wife in
a local village; and just opposite her a large map . . .

But her observations ceased there.

To her left was a flight of white-marbled stairs, down which
the white-haired Morse was coming towards her.

'Good to see you. Come along up.'

'No, I can't stay. I've got a car waiting.'

'But we can take you home. *I* can take you home.'

'No. I'm . . . I'm sorry.'

'Why have you come?' asked Morse quietly, seating himself
beside her.

'You've had Mum in. She told me all about it. She's on bail,
isn't she? And I just wondered where it all leaves her – and me,
for that matter?'

Morse spoke gently. 'Your mother has been charged in connection with the murder of your step-father. Please understand that
for the present—'

'She told me you might be bringing *me* in – is that right?'

'Look! We can't really talk here. Please come up—'

She shook her head. 'Not unless you're arresting me. Anyway,
I don't trust myself in that office of yours. Remember?'

'Look, about your mother. You'll have to face the fact – just like we have to – that . . . that it seems very likely at the minute that your mother was involved in some way in the murder of your step-father.' Morse had chosen his hesitant words carefully.

'All right. If you're not going to tell me, never mind.'

She stood up; and Morse stood up beside her. She held out the small parcel she had been carrying in her right hand and offered it to him.

'For you,' she said simply.

'What is it?'

'Promise me one thing?'

'If I can.'

'You won't open it till you get home tonight.'

'If you say so.'

Morse suddenly felt very moved; felt very lost, very helpless, very upset.

'Well – that's it then. That's all I came for . . . really.'

'I'll ring you when I've opened it, I promise.'

'Only when you get home.'

'Only when I get home.'

'You've got a note of my number, haven't you?'

'I have it by heart.'

'I have to go. Hope you'll like it.' She managed to speak the words; but only just as she picked up St Anthony and fondled him between the thumb and forefinger of her left hand. And almost, for a moment or two, as they stood there, it was as if they might embrace; but the Assistant Chief Constable suddenly came through Reception, raising his hand to Morse in friendly greeting.

She turned away; and left.

As she stepped out of the building, a red BMW was beside her immediately; and she got in, casting one lingering look behind her as she locked her safety-belt.

'I was rather hoping you'd bring her up, sir. She's getting a bit of a smasher, that one, don't you think?'

But Morse, reclosing the door quietly behind him, made no reply. Suddenly his life seemed joyless and desolate.

'Coffee, sir?' asked Lewis in a low voice, perhaps understanding many things.

Morse nodded.

After Lewis was gone, he didn't wait.

He couldn't wait.

Inside the bluebell-patterned wrapping-paper was a small, silver, delicately curving hip-flask.

Oh God!

The letter enclosed with it bore no salutation:

> My mum rung me up and told me everything, but she never killed him. I know that better than anybody because I killed him.
>
>   I'm not much cop at writing but I wish we could have gone out for shampers together again. That was the happiest night of my life, because for some cockeyed reason I loved you with all the love I've got. I hope you like the little present. I wish I could finish this letter in the way I'd like to but I can't quite think of the right words, you know I'm trying though. If only you'd known how much I wanted you to kiss me in the taxi so some few kisses now from me
>
> xxxx Ellie xxxx

Unmanned with anguish, Morse turned away as Lewis came back with the coffee, folded the letter carefully, and put it in a drawer of his desk.

Neither man spoke.

Then Morse opened the drawer, took out the letter, and passed it over to Lewis.

The silence persisted long after Lewis had read it.

Finally Morse got to his feet. 'If I ever see her again, Lewis, I shall have to tell her that "rang" is the more correct form of the past tense of the verb "to ring", when used transitively.'

'I don't think she'd mind very much what you told her,' said Lewis very quietly.

Morse said nothing.

'Mind if I have a look at the present, sir?'

Morse passed over the hip-flask.

'Remember that crossword clue, Lewis? "Kick in the pants?" – three-hyphen-five?'

Lewis nodded and smiled sadly.

Hip-flask.

CHAPTER SIXTY-NINE

Amongst the tribes of Central Australia, every person has, besides a personal name which is in common use, a secret name which was bestowed upon him or her soon after birth, and which is known to none but the fully initiated

(JAMES FRAZER, *The Golden Bough*)

'You MUST admit what a trusting, stupid brain I've got, Lewis. "Don't open it till you get home," she said, and I just thought that . . .'

'*Numquam animus*, sir, as you tell me the ancient Romans used to say.'

'We'd better get along there.'

'You think she's done a bunk?'

'Sure she has.'

'With Davies?'

'Has Davies got a red BMW?'

'Not unless he's changed his car.'

'I wonder if it's that randy sod from Reading. Where's his card?'

'The traffic boys'll be able to tell us in a couple of ticks.'

'Can't wait that long.'

He found the card, the number – and dialled, informing the woman who answered that he was ringing from police HQ about a stolen car, a red BMW, and he was just checking to make sure . . .

Mr Williamson was out, Morse learned. But there was no need to worry. He *did* have a red BMW all right, but it hadn't been stolen. In fact, she'd seen him get into it earlier that afternoon. Going to Oxford, he'd said.

Half an hour later, in Princess Street, it became clear that Ellie Smith had decamped in considerable haste. In her bed-sit-cum-bathroom there had been little enough accommodation for many possessions anyway; yet much had been left behind: the bigger items (perforce) – fridge, TV, record player, microwave; a selection of clothing and shoes, ranging from the sedate to the sensational; pictures and posters by the score, including a life-sized Technicolor photograph of Marilyn Monroe, a framed painting by Paul Klee, and (also framed) a fading Diploma from East Oxford Senior School, Prize for Art, awarded to Kay Eleanor Brooks, signed by C. P. Taylor (Head), and dated July 1983.

'Not much here in the drawers, sir. An Appointments' Book, though, stuck at the back.'

'Which I am not particularly anxious to see,' said Morse, sitting himself down on the bed.

'You know – if you don't mind me saying so, sir – it was a bit cruel, wasn't it? Her leaving her mum for all those years and not really getting in touch with her again until—'

He broke off.

'Sir!'

Morse looked up.

'There's a telephone number here for that Tuesday the sixth, with something written after it: "GL" – and what looks like the figure "1".'

Morse got up, and went to look over Lewis's shoulder. 'It could be a lower-case letter "l".'

'Shall I give the number a go?'

Morse shrugged his shoulders disinterestedly. 'Please yourself.'

Lewis dialled the number, and a pleasing, clear Welsh voice answered, with an obviously well-practised formula:

'Gareth Llewellyn-Jones. Can I 'elp you?'

'Sergeant Lewis, Thames Valley Police, sir. We're investigating a murder, and think you might be able to help us confirm one or two things.'

'My goodness me! Well, I can't really, not for the moment, like. I'm in the middle of a tutorial, see?'

'Can you give me a time when you will be free, sir?'

'Could be important,' said Lewis, after putting down the phone. 'If she was . . . out all night—'

'Don't you mean "in" all night?' said Morse bitterly. 'In bed with some cock-happy client of hers – that's what you mean, isn't it? So stop being so bloody mealy-mouthed, man.'

Lewis counted up to seven. 'Well, if she was, she couldn't have had too much of a hand in things with Brooks.'

'Of course she did!' snapped Morse. 'I don't believe her though when she says she murdered him – she's just trying to shield her mother, that's all – because it was her mother who murdered him.'

'Isn't it usually the other way round, though?'

'What do you mean?'

'Isn't it usually mums who try to shield their kids?'

The word 'kid' did to Morse what 'scenario' did to Ellie Smith; and he was about to remonstrate – when suddenly he clapped a cupped right hand hard over his forehead.

'What year did the Brooks marry?'

'Can't remember exactly. Twelve years ago, was it? We can soon check.'

'What time are you seeing Armstrong-Jones?'

'Llewellyn-Jones, sir. Half-past eight. After he's had dinner in Hall.'

'Good. I'm glad you're not letting our own inquiries interfere with his college routine.'

'It wasn't like that—'

'Come on, Lewis!' Morse pointed to the Diploma. 'When you said Ellie Smith must have been a bit cruel to run away from her mother, you were right, in a way. But she didn't run away from her mother at all, Lewis. She ran away from her *father*, her natural father.'

'But she could just have changed her name, surely?'

'Nonsense!'

Morse consulted the directory lying beside the phone: only one C. P. Taylor, with an Abingdon Road address. He rang the number, and learned, yes indeed, that he was speaking to the former Head of East Oxford Senior School, who would willingly help if he could. That same evening? Why not?

After Lewis had dropped Morse ('I'll find my own way home') at a rather elegant semi-detached property in the Abingdon Road, he himself proceeded to Lonsdale College, where his mission was quietly and quickly productive.

Llewellyn-Jones freely admitted that he'd met the young woman he'd always known as 'Kay' fairly regularly for sexual purposes: never in his college rooms; more often than not in a hotel; and twice in her own little place – as was the case on Tuesday, 6 September, when he'd spent the evening with her, and would have spent longer but for a phone-call – half-past nine? quarter to ten? – which had galvanized her into panicky activity. *She'd* have to leave: *he'd* have to leave. Obviously some sort of emergency; but he knew no more, except perhaps that he thought the voice on the phone was that of a woman.

Lewis thanked the dark, dapper little Welshman, and assured him that the information given would of course be treated with the utmost confidentiality.

But Gareth Llewellyn-Jones appeared little troubled:

'I'm a bachelor, Sergeant, see? And I just loved being with her, that's all. In fact, I could've . . . But I don't think she's the sort of woman who could ever really fall arse-orver-tit for any man – certainly not for me.'

He smiled, shook his head, and bade farewell to Lewis from the Porters' Lodge.

As Lewis drove up to his home in Headington, he realized that Morse had almost certainly been right about Ellie Smith's involvement in the murder.

With a tumbler of most welcome Scotch beside him, Morse sat back to listen.

'Kay Brooks? Oh yes, I remember *her*,' said the ex-headmaster, a thin, mildly drooping man in his early seventies. 'Who wouldn't . . . ?'

Aged eleven, she'd started at his school as a lively, slightly devil-may-care lass, with long dark hair and a sweet if somewhat cheeky sort of smile. Bright – well above average; and very good at sketching, painting, design, that type of thing. But . . . well, something must have gone a bit sour somewhere. By her mid-teens, she'd become a real handful: playing hookey, surly, inattentive, idle, a bit cruel, perhaps. Trouble at home, like as not? But no one knew. Kay's mother had come along to see him a couple of times but—

Morse interrupted:

'That's really what I've come about, sir. It may not be important, but I rather think you probably mean her *step*-mother, don't you?'

'Pardon?' Taylor looked as if he had mis-heard.

'You see, I think Brooks, Edward Brooks, the man fished out of the Isis, could well have been her real father, not her *step*-father.'

'Nonsense!' (The second time the word had been used in the past half-hour.) 'I can understand what you're thinking, Inspector; but you're wrong. She *changed* her name when her mother got remarried; changed it to her mother's new name. You see, I knew her, knew her mother, well before then.'

Morse looked puzzled. 'Is that sort of thing usual?'

Taylor smiled. 'Depends, doesn't it? Some people would give an arm and a leg to change their names. Take me, for instance. My old mum and dad – bless their hearts but . . . you know what they christened me? "Cecil Paul". Would you credit it? I was "Cess-pool" before I'd been at school a fortnight. You know the sort of thing I mean?'

Oh, yes, Morse knew exactly the sort of thing he meant.

'And I'm afraid,' continued Taylor, 'that Kay got teased pretty mercilessly about her name – about her surname, that is. So it was only natural, really, that when the opportunity arose to change it . . .'

'What *was* her surname?' asked Morse.

Taylor told him.

Oh dear!

Poor Ellie!

After gladly becoming Eleanor 'Brooks' on her mother's remarriage, so very soon, it seemed, had she come to detest her newly adopted name. And when she had left home, she had plumped for 'Smith' – a good, common-stock, unexceptionable sort of name that could cause her pain no more.

Yes, Morse knew all about being teased because of a name – in his own case a Christian name. And he felt so close to Ellie Smith at that moment, so very caring towards her, that he would have sacrificed almost anything in the world to find her there, waiting for him, when he got back home.

'Ellie Morse'?

'*Eleanor* Morse'?

Difficult to decide.

But gladly would Morse have settled for either as he walked slowly up into Cornmarket, where he stood waiting twenty-five minutes for a bus to take him up to his bachelor flat in North Oxford.

CHAPTER SEVENTY

Then grief forever after; because forever after nothing less
would ever do
                    (J. G. F. POTTER, *Anything to Declare?*)

THE SUBJECT of each of these last two inquiries, the young
woman who has been known (principally) in these pages as Ellie
Smith, had hurriedly wiped her eyes and for a considerable time
said nothing after getting into Mike Williamson's car. Her
thoughts were temporarily concentrated not so much on Morse
himself as on what she could have told him; or rather on what
she could never have told him . . .

It had been that terrible Tuesday night, when her mother had
phoned, pleading in such deep anguish for her daughter's help;
when she'd got rid of that quite likable cock-happy little Welshman; and finally reached the house – a full five minutes before
that other woman had arrived in a car – to find her mother
standing like a zombie in the entrance hall, continuously massag-
ing a gloved right hand with her left, as if she had inflicted upon
it some recent and agonizing injury; and when, after going into
the kitchen, she'd looked down on her step-father lying prone on
the lino there, a strange-looking, wooden-handled knife stuck –
so accurately it had seemed to her – halfway between the
shoulder-blades. Strangely enough, there hadn't been too much
blood. Perhaps he'd never had all that much blood in him. Not
warm blood, anyway.

Then the red-headed woman had arrived, and taken over – so
coolly competent she'd been, so organized. It was as if the plot of
the drama had already been written, for clearly the appropriate
props had been duly prepared, waiting only to be fetched from
the back-garden shed. Just the *timing*, it appeared, had gone
wrong, as if a final rehearsal had suddenly turned into a first-
night performance. And it was her mother surely who'd been
responsible for that: jumping the starting-gate and seizing the
reins in her own hands – her own hand, rather (singular).

Then, ten minutes later, following a rapidly spoken telephone
conversation, the young man had appeared, to whom the red-
headed woman had spoken in hushed tones in the hallway; a

young man whom, oddly enough, she knew by sight, since the two of them had attended the same Martial Arts classes together. But she said nothing to him. Nor he to her. Indeed he seemed hardly aware of her presence as he began to manoeuvre the awkward corpse into its polythene winding sheet – sheets, rather (plural).

She'd even found herself remembering his name.

Kevin something . . .

As the car turned right from Park End Street into the railway station, Ellie's mind jerked back to the present, aware that Williamson's left hand had crept above the top of her suspendered right stocking. But she would always be able to handle people like Williamson, who now reminded her of their proposed agreement as he humped the two large suitcases from the boot.

'You ring me, like you said, OK?'

Ellie nodded, adding a verbal gloss to her unspoken promise as she took his business card from her handbag and mechanically recited the telephone number.

'Right, then. And don't forget we can do real business with a body like yours, kid.'

It would have been a nice gesture if he had offered to carry her cases up the steps to the automatic doors; or even as far as the ticket window. But he didn't; and of that she was glad. Had he done so she would probably have felt obliged to buy a ticket for Paddington, for she had spoken to him vaguely of 'friends in London'. As it was, once he had driven off, she bought a single ticket to Liverpool, and with aching arms crossed over the footbridge to Platform Two – where she stood for twenty-five minutes, forgetting for a while the future plight of her mother; forgetting the minor role she herself had played in the murder of a man she had learned to hate; yet remembering again now, as she fingered the gold pendant, the man who had given it to her, the man for whom she would have sacrificed anything. If only he could have loved her.

EPILOGUE

Life is a progress from want to want, not from enjoyment to enjoyment
(SAMUEL JOHNSON, in Boswell's *The Life of Samuel Johnson*)

IT IS now Friday, 28 October 1994, the Feast of St Simon and St Jude, and this chronicle has to be concluded, with brief space only remaining to record a few marginal notes on some of the characters who played their roles in these pages.

On Thursday, 20 October, Mrs Brenda Brooks was rearrested, additionally charged with the murder of her husband, Mr Edward Brooks, and remanded in custody at Holloway Prison. From which institution, four days later, she was granted temporary leave of (escorted) absence to attend a midday funeral service at the Oxford Crematorium, where many teachers from the Proctor Memorial School were squeezed into the small chapel there, together with a few relatives, and a few friends – though the couple from California were unable to make the journey at such short notice.

Two others completed (almost completed) the saddened congregation: the facially scarred Kevin Costyn and a pale-looking Chief Inspector Morse, neither of whom participated in (what seemed to the latter) the banal revision of Archbishop Cranmer's noble words for the solemn service of the dead.

And one other mourner: a dark-suited, prosperous-looking, middle-aged man, who went last of all into the chapel; and sat down, as it happened, next to Morse, on the back row of the left-hand side of the aisle. A minute earlier, wholly unobserved, he had added his own floral tribute to the many others laid out in the Garden of Remembrance there: a wreath of white lilies. The card attached bore no salutation, no valediction – just the same words that Julia Stevens had read on a birthday card some eighteen months before:

'Don't forget we had some good times too!'

St Giles's (enforced) new home is some little way from Oxford. Yet that aristocratic cat is not displeased with his environment – particularly with the wildlife opportunities offered in the open field just behind Number 22, Kingfisher Way, Bicester; and with the soft, beige leather settee on which he now sleeps for long stretches of the day until his attractive young mistress returns from her duties at the Oxford University Press.

Janis Lawrence, only temporarily she trusts, is now unemployed once more; and her familiar, exasperated 'Stop frownin' them bricks, Jason!' is still often to be heard in the streets of the Cutteslowe Estate.

On the whole, Mrs Lewis is well pleased with the work of the decorators; and extremely pleased with her husband's present to her of a new set of five black-handled knives, including one (Number 4) whose blade, unusually broad at its base, curves to a dangerous-looking point.

The former dwelling of Dr Felix McClure has now been on the market for two weeks, its lounge completely recarpeted. But Mrs (Miss?) Laura Wynne-Wilson, though maintaining a dedicated vigil behind her carefully parted lace curtains, has yet to spot any prospective client arriving to view the property. And Messrs Adkinson, renowned for their meticulous room-measurements, are a little worried that the vicious murder enacted in Number 6 has, quite understandably, postponed the prospect of any immediate purchase.

And what of Morse?

His proposed lunchtime meeting with Strange, with a view to launching a twin assault on the complexities of form-filling, has not yet been arranged; and Morse is not pursuing the matter with any sense of great urgency, since he is undecided about the 'sooner or later' of his own eventual retirement, and curiously unsettled about the immediate months ahead of him . . .

He knew, of course, that it would be utterly hopeless to ring Ellie Smith, and therefore he rang her number only three times in the week following her disappearance; only twice in the second week. After all, as Morse recalled from his believing days, Hope is one of the greatest of all the Christian virtues.

In the third week, his normal routine in life appeared to reassert itself; and at about 9.30 p.m. he was again regularly to be observed walking fairly purposefully down the Banbury Road to one of the local hostelries. He has promised himself most faithfully that he will dramatically curtail his consumption of alcohol wef 1 November; which same day will also mark his permanent renunciation of nicotine.

In the meantime there is much work still to be done in the aftermath of the case – the aftermath of both cases, rather. And above all else in Morse's life there remains the searching out of Ellie Smith, since as a police officer that is his professional duty and, as a man, his necessary purpose.

Death is Now
My Neighbour

For
Joan Templeton
with gratitude

Acknowledgements

The author and publishers wish to thank the following who have kindly given permission for use of copyright materials:

Extract from *The Dance* by Philip Larkin reproduced by permission of Faber & Faber Ltd;

Extract from the *News of the World* reproduced by permission of the *News of the World*;

Extract from Fowler's *Modern English Usage* reproduced by permission of Oxford University Press;

Ace Reporter by Helen Peacocke reproduced by kind permission of the author;

Extract from *Major Barbara* by Bernard Shaw reproduced by permission of The Society of Authors on behalf of the Bernard Shaw Estate;

Extract from *The Brontës* by Juliet Barker reproduced by permission of Weidenfeld and Nicolson;

Extract from *The Dry Salvages* by T. S. Eliot reproduced by permission of Faber & Faber Ltd;

Extract from *Summoned by Bells* by John Betjeman reproduced by permission of John Murray (Publishers) Ltd;

Extract from *Aubade* by Philip Larkin reproduced by permission of Faber & Faber Ltd;

Extract from *May-Day Song for North Oxford* by John Betjeman, from *Collected Poems of John Betjeman*, reproduced by permission of John Murray (Publishers) Ltd;

Extract from *This Be the Verse* by Philip Larkin reproduced by permission of Faber & Faber Ltd;

Every effort has been made to trace all copyright holders but if any has been inadvertently overlooked, the author and publishers will be pleased to make the necessary arrangement at the first opportunity.

Quickly, bring me a beaker of wine,
so that I may wet my mind and say
something clever

(ARISTOPHANES)

PROLEGOMENON
January, 1996

A decided boon, therefore, are any multiple-choice items for those pupils in our classrooms who are either inured to idleness, or guilty of wilful ignorance. Such pupils, if simply and appropriately instructed, have only to plump for the same answer on each occasion – let us say, choice (a) from choices (a) (b) (c) (d) – in order to achieve a reasonably regular score of some 25% of the total marks available. This is a wholly satisfactory return for academic incompetence

(*Crosscurrents in Assessment Criteria: Theory and Practice*, HMSO, 1983)

'WHAT TIME DO you call this, Lewis?'

'The missus's fault. Not like her to be late with the breakfast.'

Morse made no answer as he stared down at the one remaining unsolved clue:

'Stand for soldiers? (5–4)'

Lewis took the chair opposite his chief and sat waiting for some considerable while, leafing through a magazine.

'Stuck, sir?' he asked finally.

'If I was – if I *were* – I doubt I'd get much help from you.'

'You never know,' suggested Lewis good-naturedly. 'Perhaps—'

'Ah!' burst out Morse triumphantly – as he wrote in TOAST-RACK. He folded *The Times* away and beamed across at his sergeant.

'You – are – a – genius, Lewis.'

'So you've often told me, sir.'

'*And* I bet you had a boiled egg for breakfast – with *soldiers*. Am I right?'

'What's that got—?'

'What are you reading there?'

Lewis held up the title page of his magazine.

'Lew-is! There are more important things in life than the *Thames Valley Police Gazette*.'

'Just thought you might be interested in one of the articles here . . .'

Morse rose to the bait. 'Such as?'

'There's a sort of test – you know, see how many points you can score: ARE YOU REALLY WISE AND CULTURED?'

'Very doubtful in your case, I should think.'

'You reckon you could do better than I did?'

'Quite certain of it.'

Lewis grinned. '*Quite* certain, sir?'

'Absolutely.'

'Want to have a go, then?' Lewis's mouth betrayed gentle amusement as Morse shrugged his indifference.

'Multiple-choice questions – you know all about—?'

'Get *on* with it!'

'All you've got to do is imagine the world's going to end in exactly one week's time, OK? Then you've got to answer five questions, as honestly as you can.'

'And you've already answered these questions yourself?'

Lewis nodded.

'Well, if *you* can answer them . . . Fire away!'

Lewis read aloud from the article:

Question One
Given the choice of only four CDs or cassettes, which one of the following would you be likely to play at least once?

   (a) A Beatles album

   (b) Fauré's *Requiem*

   (c) *An Evening with Victor Borge*

   (d) The complete overtures to Wagner's operas

With a swift flourish, Morse wrote down a letter.

Question Two
Which of these videos would you want to watch?

   (a) *Casablanca* (the film)

   (b) England's World Cup victory (1966)

   (c) *Copenhagen Red-Hot Sex* (2 hours)

   (d) *The Habitat of the Kingfisher* (RSPB)

A second swift flourish from Morse.

Question Three
With which of the following women would you wish to spend some, if not all, of your surviving hours?

   (a) Lady Thatcher
   (b) Kim Basinger
   (c) Mother Teresa
   (d) Princess Diana

A third swift flourish.

Question Four

If you could gladden your final days with one of the following, which would it be?

   (a) Two dozen bottles of vintage champagne
   (b) Five hundred cigarettes
   (c) A large bottle of tranquillizers
   (d) A barrel of real ale

Flourish number four, and the candidate (confident of imminent success, it appeared) sat back in the black leather armchair.

Question Five

Which of the following would you read during this period?

   (a) Cervantes' *Don Quixote*
   (b) Dante's *The Divine Comedy*
   (c) A bound volume of *Private Eye* (1995)
   (d) Homer's *Iliad*

This time Morse hesitated some while before writing on the pad in front of him. 'You did the test yourself, you say?'

Lewis nodded. 'Victor Borge; the football; Princess Diana; the champagne; and *Private Eye*. Just hope Princess Di likes Champers, that's all.'

'There must be worse ways of spending your last week on earth,' admitted Morse.

'I didn't do so well, though – not on the marking. I'm not up there among the cultured and the wise, I'm afraid.'

'Did you expect to be?'

'Wouldn't you?'

'Of course.'

'Let's hear what you picked, then.'

'My preferences, Lewis' (Morse articulated his words with precision) 'were as follows: (b); (c); (b); (c); none of them.'

Turning to the back page, Lewis reminded himself of the answers putatively adjudged to be correct.

'I don't believe it,' he whispered to himself. Then, to Morse: 'You scored the maximum!'

'Are you surprised?'

Lewis shook his head in mild bewilderment.

'You chose, what, the *Requiem*?'

'Well?'

'But you've never believed in all that religious stuff.'

'It's important if it's *true*, though, isn't it? Let's just say it's a bit like an insurance policy. A beautiful work, anyway.'

'Says here: "Score four marks for (b). Sufficient recommendation that it was chosen by three of the last four Popes for their funerals."'

Morse lifted his eyebrows. 'You didn't know that?'

Lewis ignored the question and continued:

'Then you chose the sex video!'

'Well, it was either that or the kingfisher. I've already seen *Casablanca* a couple of times – and no one's ever going to make me watch a football match again.'

'But I mean, a sex video . . .'

Morse, however, was clearly unimpressed by such obvious disapprobation. 'It'd be the choice of those three Popes as well, like as not.'

'But it all gets – well, it gets so plain *boring* after a while.'

'So you keep telling me, Lewis. And all I'm asking is the chance to get as bored as everybody else. I've only got a *week*, remember.'

'I like your next choice, though. Beautiful girl, Kim Basinger. *Beautiful*.'

'Something of a toss-up, that – between her and Mother Teresa. But I'd already played the God-card.'

'Then' (Lewis considered the next answer) 'Arrghh, come off it, sir! You didn't even go for the beer! You're supposed to answer these questions *honestly*.'

'I've already got plenty of booze in,' said Morse. 'Certainly enough to see me through to Judgement Day. And I don't fancy facing the Great Beyond with a blinding hangover. It'll be a new experience for me – tranquillizers . . .'

Lewis looked down again, and proceeded to read out the reasons for Morse's greatest triumph. 'It says here, on Question Five, "Those choosing any of the suggested titles are clearly unfit for high honours. If any choice whatsoever is made, four marks will therefore be deducted from the final score. If the answer is a timid dash – or similar – no marks will be awarded, but no marks will be deducted. A more positively negative answer – e.g. 'Come off it!' – will be rewarded with a bonus of four marks."' Again Lewis shook his head. 'Nonsense, isn't it? "Positively negative", I mean.'

'Rather nicely put, I'd've thought,' said Morse.

'Anyway,' conceded Lewis, 'you score twenty out of twenty according to this fellow who seems to have all the answers.' Lewis looked again at the name printed below the article. '"Rhadamanthus" – whoever he is.'

'Lord Chief Justice of Appeal in the Underworld.'

Lewis frowned, then grinned. 'You've been cheating! You've got a copy—'

'No!' Morse's blue eyes gazed fiercely across at his sergeant. 'The first I saw of that *Gazette* was when you brought it in just now.'

'If you say so.' But Lewis sounded less than convinced.

'Not surprised, are you, to find me perched up there on the topmost twig amongst the intelligentsia?'

'"The wise and the cultured", actually.'

'And that's another thing. I think I shall go crackers if I hear three things in my life much more: "Hark the Herald Angels Sing"; *Eine Kleine Nachtmusik*; and that wretched bloody word "actually".'

'Sorry, sir.'

Suddenly Morse grinned. 'No need to be, old friend. And at least you're right about one thing. I did cheat – in a way.'

'You don't mean *you* . . . ?'

Morse nodded.

It had been a playful, pleasant interlude. Yet it would have warranted no inclusion in this chronicle had it not been that one or two of the details recorded herein were to linger significantly in the memory of Chief Inspector E. Morse, of the Thames Valley Police HQ.

PART ONE

CHAPTER ONE

> In hypothetical sentences introduced by 'if' and referring to past time, where conditions are deemed to be 'unfulfilled', the verb will regularly be found in the pluperfect subjunctive, in both protasis and apodosis
>
> (Donet, *Principles of Elementary Latin Syntax*)

IT IS PERHAPS unusual to begin a tale of murder with a reminder to the reader of the rules governing conditional sentences in a language that is incontrovertibly dead. In the present case, however, such a course appears not wholly inappropriate.

If (*if*) Chief Inspector Morse had been on hand to observe the receptionist's dress – an irregularly triangled affair in blues, greys, and reds – he might have been reminded of the uniform issued to a British Airways stewardess. More probably, though, he might not, since he had never flown on British Airways. His only flight during the previous decade had occasioned so many fears concerning his personal survival that he had determined to restrict all future travel to those (statistically) far more precarious means of conveyance – the car, the coach, the train, and the steamer.

Yet almost certainly the Chief Inspector would have noted, with approval, the receptionist herself, for in Yorkshire she would have been reckoned a bonny lass: a vivacious, dark-eyed woman, long-legged and well figured; a woman – judging from her ringless, well-manicured fingers – not overtly advertising any marital commitment, and not averse, perhaps, to the occasional overture from the occasional man.

Pinned at the top-left of her colourful dress was a name-tag: 'Dawn Charles'.

Unlike several of her friends (certainly unlike Morse) she was quite content with her Christian name. Sometimes she'd felt *slightly* dubious about it; but no longer. Out with some friends in the Bird and Baby the previous month, she'd been introduced to a rather dashing, rather dishy undergraduate from Pembroke

College. And when, a little later, she'd found herself doodling inconsequentially on a Burton beer-mat, the young man, on observing her sinistrality, had initiated a wholly memorable conversation.

'Dawn? That *is* your name?'

She'd nodded.

'Left-handed?'

She'd nodded.

'Do you know that line from Omar Khayyam? "Dreaming when Dawn's left hand was in the sky . . ." Lovely, isn't it?'

Yes, it was. Lovely.

She'd peeled the top off the beer-mat and made him write it down for her.

Then, very quietly, he'd asked her if he could see her again. At the start of the new term, perhaps?

She'd known it was silly, for there must have been at least twenty years difference in their ages. If only . . . if only he'd been ten, a dozen years older . . .

But people *did* do silly things, and hoped their silly hopes. And that very day, 15 January, was the first full day of the new Hilary Term in the University of Oxford.

Her Monday–Friday job, 6–10 p.m., at the clinic on the Banbury Road (just north of St Giles') was really quite enjoyable. Over three years of it now, and she was becoming a fixture there. Most of the consultants greeted her with a genuine smile; several of them, these days, with her Christian name.

Nice.

She'd once stayed at a four-star hotel which offered a glass of sherry to incoming guests; and although the private Harvey Clinic was unwilling (perhaps on medical grounds?) to provide such laudable hospitality, Dawn ever kept two jugs of genuine coffee piping hot for her clients, most of them soberly suited and well-heeled gentlemen. A number of whom, as she well knew, were most seriously ill.

Yes, there had been several occasions when she had heard a few brief passages of conversation between consultant and client which she *shouldn't* have heard; or which, having heard, she should have forgotten; and which she should never have been willing to report to anyone.

Not even to the police.

Quite certainly not to the Press . . .

As it happened, 15 January was to prove a day unusually easy for her to recall, since it marked the twenty-fifth anniversary of the clinic's opening in 1971. By prior negotiation and arrangement, the clinic was visited that evening, between 7 p.m. and 8.30 p.m., by Radio Oxford, by the local press, and by Mr Wesley Smith and his crew from the Central TV studios out at Abingdon. And particularly memorable for Dawn had been those precious moments when the camera had focused upon her: first, when (as instructed) she had poured a cup of genuine coffee for a wholly bogus 'client'; second, when the cameraman had moved behind her left shoulder as she ran a felt-tipped pen through a name on the appointments list in front of her – but only, of course, after a full assurance that no viewer would be able to read the name itself when the feature was shown the following evening.

Yet Dawn Charles was always to remember the name:

Mr J. C. Storrs.

It had been a fairly new name to her – another of those patients, as Dawn suspected (correctly), whose influence and affluence afforded the necessary leverage and £ s d to jump the queues awaiting their calls to the hospitals up in Headington.

There was something else she would always remember, too . . .

By one of those minor coincidences (so commonplace in Morse's life) it had been just as most of the personnel from the media were preparing to leave, at almost exactly 8.30 p.m., that Mr Robert Turnbull, the Senior Cancer Consultant, had passed her desk, nodded a greeting, and walked slowly to the exit, his right hand resting on the shoulder of Mr J. C. Storrs. The two men were talking quietly together for some while – Dawn was certain of that. But certain of little else. The look on the consultant's face, as far as she could recall, had been neither that of a judge who has just condemned a man to death, nor that of one just granting a prisoner his freedom.

No obvious grimness.

No obvious joy.

And indeed there was adequate cause for such uncertainty on Dawn's part, since the scene had been partially masked from her by the continued presence of several persons: a pony-tailed reporter scribbling a furious shorthand as he interviewed a nurse; the TV crew packing away its camera and tripods; the Lord Mayor speaking some congratulatory words into a Radio Oxford microphone – all of them standing between her and the top of the three blue-carpeted stairs which led down to the double-doored exit, outside which were affixed the vertical banks of well-polished brass plates, ten on each side, the fourth from the top on the left reading:

> ### ROBERT H. TURNBULL

If only Dawn Charles could have recalled a little more.

'If' – that little conjunction introducing those unfulfilled conditions in past time which, as Donet reminds us, demand the pluperfect subjunctive in both clauses – a syntactical rule which Morse himself had mastered early on in an education which had been far more fortunate than that enjoyed by the receptionist at the Harvey Clinic.

Indeed, over the next two weeks, most people in Oxford were destined to be considerably more fortunate than Dawn Charles: she received no communication from the poetry-lover of Pembroke; her mother was admitted to a psychiatric ward out at Littlemore; she was (twice) reminded by her bank manager of the increasing problems arising from the large margin of negative equity on her small flat; and finally, on Monday morning, 29 January, she was to hear on Fox FM Radio that her favourite consultant, Mr Robert H. Turnbull, MB, ChB, FRCS, had been fatally injured in a car accident on Cumnor Hill.

CHAPTER TWO

The Master shall not continue in his post beyond the age of sixty-seven. As a simple rule, therefore, the incumbent Master will be requested to give notice of impending retirement during the University term immediately prior to that birthday. Where, however, such an accommodation does not present itself, the Master is required to propose a particular date not later than the end of the first week of the second full term after the statutory termination (*vide supra*)

(Paragraph 2 (a), translated from the Latin, from the
Founders' Statutes of Lonsdale College, Oxford)

SIR CLIXBY BREAM would be almost sixty-nine years old when he retired as Master of Lonsdale. A committee of Senior Fellows, including two eminent Latin scholars, had found itself unable to interpret the gobbledegook of the Founders' Statutes (*vide supra*); and since no 'accommodation' (whatever that was) had presented itself, Sir Clixby had first been persuaded to stay on for a short while – then for a longer while.

Yet this involved no hardship.

He was subject to none of the normal pressures about moving to somewhere nearer the children or the grandchildren, since his marriage to Lady Muriel had been *sine prole*. Moreover, he was blessedly free from the usual uxorial bleatings about a nice little thatched cottage in Dorset or Devon, since Lady Muriel had been in her grave these past three years.

The position of Head of House at any of the Oxbridge Colleges was just about the acme of academic ambition; and since three of the last four Masters had been knighted within eighteen months of their appointments, it had been natural for him to be attracted by the opportunity of such pleasing preferment. And he *had* been so attracted; as, even more strongly, had the late Lady Muriel.

Indeed, the incumbent Master, a distinguished mathematician in his earlier days, had never enjoyed living anywhere as much as in Oxford – ten years of it now. He'd learned to love the old city more and more the longer he was there: it was as simple as that. Of course he was somewhat saddened by the thought of his imminent retirement: he would miss the College – miss the challenges of running the place – and he knew that the sight of the furniture van outside the wisteria-clad front of the Master's Lodge would occasion some aching regret. But there were a few unexpected consolations, perhaps. In particular, he would be able (he supposed) to sit back and survey with a degree of detachment and sardonic amusement the in-fighting that would doubtless arise among his potential successors.

It was the duty of the Fellows' Appointments Committee (its legality long established by one of the more readily comprehensible of the College Statutes) to stipulate three conditions for those seeking election as Master: first, that any candidate should be 'of sound mind and in good health'; second, that the candidate should 'not have taken Holy Orders'; third, that the candidate should have no criminal record within 'the territories administered under the governance of His (or Her) Most Glorious Majesty'.

Such stipulations had often amused the present Master.

If one judged by the longevity of almost all the Masters appointed during the twentieth century, physical well-being had seldom posed much of a problem; yet mental stability had never been a particularly prominent feature of his immediate predecessor, nor (by all accounts) of his predecessor's predecessor. And occasionally Sir Clixby wondered what the College would say of himself once he was gone . . . With regard to the exclusion of the clergy, he assumed that the Founders (like Edward Gibbon three centuries later) had managed to trace the source of all human wickedness back to the Popes and the Prelates, and had rallied to the cause of anticlericalism . . . But it was the possibility of the candidate's criminality which was the most amusing. Presumably any convictions for murder, rape, sodomy, treason, or similar misdemeanours, were to be discounted if shown to have taken place *outside* the jurisdiction of His (or Her) Most Glorious Majesty. Very strange.

Strangest of all, however, was the absence of any mention in the original Statute of academic pedigree; and, at least theoretically, there could be no bar to a candidate presenting himself with only a Grade E in GCSE Media Studies. Nor was there any stipulation that the successful candidate should be a senior (or, for that matter, a junior) member of the College, and on several occasions 'outsiders' had been appointed. Indeed, he himself, Sir Clixby, had been imported into Oxford from 'the other place', and then (chiefly) in recognition of his reputation as a resourceful fundraiser.

On this occasion, however, outsiders seemed out of favour. The College itself could offer at least two candidates, each of whom would be an admirable choice; or so it was thought. In the Senior Common Room the consensus was most decidedly in favour of such 'internal' preferment, and the betting had hardened accordingly.

By some curious omission no entry had hitherto been granted to either of these ante-post favourites in the pages of *Who's Who*. From which one may be forgiven for concluding that the aforesaid work is rather more concerned with the third cousins of secondary aristocrats than with eminent academics. Happily, however, both of these personages had been considered worthy of mention in Debrett's *People of Today 1995*:

STORRS, Julian Charles; *b* 9 July 1935; *Educ* Christ's Hosp, Services S Dartmouth, Emmanuel Coll Cambridge (BA, MA);

m Angela Miriam Martin 31 March 1974; *Career* Capt RA (Indian Army Secondment); Pitt Rivers Reader in Social Anthropology and Senior Fellow Lonsdale Coll Oxford; *Recreations* taking taxis, playing bridge.

CORNFORD, Denis Jack; *b* 23 April 1942; *Educ* Wyggeston GS Leicester, Magdalen Coll Oxford (MA, DPhil); *m* Shelly Ann Benson 28 May 1994; *Career* University Reader in Mediaeval History and Fellow Lonsdale Coll Oxford; *Recreations* kite-flying, cultivation of orchids.

Each of these entries may appear comparatively uninformative. Yet perhaps in the more perceptive reader they may provoke one or two interesting considerations.

Was, for example, the Senior Fellow of Lonsdale so affluent that he could afford to take a taxi everywhere? Did he never travel by car, coach, or train? Well, quite certainly on special occasions he would travel by train.

Oh, yes.

As we shall see.

And why was Dr Cornford, soon to be fifty-four years old, so recently converted to the advantages of latter-day matrimony? Had he met some worthy woman of comparable age?

Oh, no.

As we shall see.

CHAPTER THREE

> How right
> I should have been to keep away, and let
> You have your innocent–guilty–innocent night
> Of switching partners in your own sad set:
> How useless to invite
> The sickening breathlessness of being young
> Into my life again
>
> (Philip Larkin, *The Dance*)

DENIS CORNFORD, *omnium consensu*, was a fine historian. Allied with a mind both sharp and rigorously honest was a capacity for the assemblage and interpretation of evidence that was the envy of the History Faculty at Oxford. Yet in spite of such qualities, he was best known for a brief monograph on the Battle of Hastings, in which he maintained that the momentous conflict between Harold of England and William of Normandy had taken place one year earlier than universally acknowledged. In 1065.

In the Trinity Term of 1994, Cornford – a slimly built, smallish, pleasantly featured man – had taken sabbatical leave at Harvard; and there – somehow and somewhere, in Cambridge, Massachusetts – something quite extraordinary had occurred. For six months later, to the amazement and amusement of his colleagues, the confirmed bachelor of Lonsdale had returned to Oxford with a woman who had agreed to change her name from Shelly Benson to Shelly Cornford: a student from Harvard who had just gained her Master's degree in American History, twenty-six years old – exactly half the age of her new husband (for this was her second marriage).

It is perhaps not likely that Shelly would have reached the semi-final heats of any Miss Massachusetts beauty competition: her jawline was slightly too square, her shoulders rather too strong, her legs perhaps a little on the sturdy side. Yet there were a good many in Lonsdale College – both dons and undergraduates – who were to experience a curious attraction to the woman now putting in fairly regular appearances in Chapel, at Guest Nights, and at College functions during the Michaelmas Term of 1994. Her wavy, shoulder-length brown hair framed a face in which the widely set dark brown eyes seemed sometimes to convey the half-promise of a potential intimacy, whilst her quietly voiced New England accent could occasionally sound as sweetly sensual as some enchantress's.

Many were the comments made about the former Shelly Benson during those first few terms. But no one could ever doubt what Denis Cornford had seen in her, for it was simply what others could now so clearly see for themselves. So from the start Shelly Cornford was regularly lusted after; her husband secretly envied. But the couple themselves appeared perfectly happy: no hint of infidelity on her part; no cause for jealousy on his.

Not yet.

Frequently during those days they were to be seen walking hand-in-hand the short distances from their rooms in Holywell Street to the King's Arms, or the Turf Tavern ('Find Us If You Can!'), where in bars blessedly free from juke-box and fruit-machine Shelly had quickly acquired a taste for real ale and a love for the ambience of the English public house.

Occasionally the two of them ventured further afield in and around Oxford; and one evening, just before Christmas 1994, they had taken the No. 2 bus from Cornmarket up to another King's Arms, the one in the Banbury Road, where amid many unashamedly festive young revellers Cornford watched as his (equally young) wife, with eyes half-closed, had rocked her shoulders sensuously to the thudding rhythm of some pop music, her black-stockinged thighs alternately lifted and lowered as though she were mentally disco-dancing. And at that point he was conscious of being the oldest person in the bar, by about twenty years; inhabiting alien territory there; wholly excluded from the magic circle of the night; and suddenly sadly aware that he could never even begin to share the girlish animality of the woman he had married.

Cornford had said nothing that evening.

Nor had he said anything when, three months later, at the end-of-term Gaudy, he had noticed, beneath the table, the left hand of Julian Storrs pressed briefly against Shelly's right thigh as she sat drinking rather a lot of Madeira, after drinking rather a lot of red wine at dinner, after drinking rather a lot of gin at the earlier reception ... her chair perhaps unnecessarily close to the Senior Fellow seated on her right, the laughing pair leaning together in some whispered, mutual, mouth-to-ear exchange. Perhaps it was all perfectly harmless; and Cornford sought to make little of it. Yet he ought (he knew it!) to have said a few words on that occasion – lightly, with a heavy heart.

It was only late in the Michaelmas Term 1995 that Cornford finally did say something to his wife ...

They had been seated one Tuesday lunchtime in the Turf Tavern, he immediately opposite his wife as she sat in one of the wooden wall-seats in the main bar, each of them enjoying a pint of London Pride. He was eagerly expounding to her his growing conviction that the statistical evidence concerning the number of deaths resultant from the Black Death in 1348 had been wildly misinterpreted, and that the supposed demographic effects consequent upon that plague were – most decidedly! – extremely suspect. It should all have been of some interest, surely? And yet Cornford was conscious of a semi-preoccupied gaze in Shelly's eyes as she stared over his left shoulder into some more fascinating area.

All right. She *ought* to have been interested – but she wasn't. Not everyone, not even a trained historian like his wife, was going to be automatically enthralled by any re-evaluation of some abstruse mediaeval evidence.

He'd thought little of it.

And had drunk his ale.

They were about to leave when a man, in his early thirties or so, walked over to them – a tall, dark, slimly built Arab with a bushy moustache. Looking directly into Shelly's eyes, he spoke softly to her:

'Madame! You are the most beautiful lady I see!'

Then, turning to Cornford: 'Please excuse, sir!' With which, picking up Shelly's right hand, he imprinted his full-lipped mouth most earnestly upon the back of her wrist.

After the pair of them had emerged into the cobbled lane that led up again into Holywell Street, Cornford stopped and so roughly pushed his wife's shoulder that she had no choice but to stand there facing him.

'You – are – a – bloody – flirt! Did you know that? All the time we were in there – all the time I was telling you—'

But he got no further.

The tall figure of Sir Clixby Bream was striding down towards them.

'Hell-*o*! You're both just off, I can see that. But what about another little snifter? Just to please me?'

'Not for me, Master.' Cornford trusted that he'd masked the bitterness of his earlier tone. 'But if . . . ?' He turned to his wife.

'No. Not now. Another time. Thank you, Master.'

With Shelly still beside him, Cornford walked rather blindly on, suspecting (how otherwise?) that the Master had witnessed the awkward, angry scene. And then, a few steps later – almost miraculously – he felt his wife's arm link with his own; heard the wonderful words spoken in her quiet voice: 'Denis, I'm so very sorry. Do please forgive me, my darling.'

As the Master stooped slightly to pass beneath the entrance of the Turf Tavern, an observer skilled in the art of labiomancy would have read the two words on his smoothly smiling mouth:

'Well! Well!'

CHAPTER FOUR
Wednesday, 7 February

DISCIPLE (weeping): O Master, I disturb thy meditations.

MASTER: Thy tears are plural; the Divine Will is one.

DISCIPLE: I seek wisdom and truth, yet my thoughts are ever of lust and the necessary pleasures of a woman.

MASTER: Seek not wisdom and truth, my son; seek rather forgiveness. Now go in peace, for verily hast thou disturbed my meditations – of lust and of the necessary pleasures of a woman

(K'ung-Fu-Tsu, from *Analects XXIII*)

'WELL, AT LEAST it's *left* on time.'

'Not surprising, is it? The bloody thing *starts* from Oxford. Give it a chance, though. We'll probably run into signalling failure somewhere along the line.'

She smiled, attractively. 'Funny, really. They've been signalling on the railways for – what? – a hundred and fifty years, and with all these computers and things . . .'

'Over one hundred and seventy years, if we want to be accurate – and why shouldn't we? Eighteen twenty-five when the Stockton to Darlington line was opened.'

'Yeah. We learned about that in school. You know, Stephenson's *Rocket* and all that.'

'No, my dear girl. A few years later, that was. Stephenson's first locomotive was called *The Locomotion* – not very difficult to remember, is it?'

'No.'

The monosyllable was quietly spoken, and he knew that he'd made her feel inadequate again.

She turned away from him to look through the carriage window, spotting the great sandstone house in Nuneham Park, up towards the skyline on the left. More than once he'd told her something of its history, and about Capability Brown and Somebody Adams; but she was never able to remember things as accurately as he seemed to expect. He'd told her on their last train journey, for example, about the nationalization of the railways after World War II: 1947 (or was it 1948?).

So what?

Yet there was one year she would *never* forget: the year the network changed its name to 'British Rail'. Her father had told her about that; told her she'd been born on that very same day. In that very same year, too.

In 1965.

'Drinks? Refreshments?'

An overloaded trolley was squeezing a squeaky passage along the aisle; and the man looked at his wrist-watch (10.40 a.m.) as it came alongside, before turning to the elegantly suited woman seated next to him:

'Fancy anything? Coffee? Bit too early for anything stronger, perhaps?'

'Gin and tonic for me. And a packet of plain crisps.'

Sod him! He'd been pretty insufferable so far.

A few minutes later, after pouring half his can of McEwan's Export Ale into a plastic container, he turned towards her again; and she felt his dry, slightly cracked lips pressed upon her right cheek. Then she heard him say the wonderful word that someone else had heard a month or two before; heard him say 'Sorry'.

She opened her white leather handbag and took out a tube of lip-salve. As she passed it to him, she felt his firm, slim fingers move against the back of her wrist; then move along her lower arm, beneath the sleeve of her light mauve Jaeger jacket: the fingers of a pianist. And she knew that very soon – the Turbo Express had just left Reading – the pianist would have been granted the licence to play with her body once more, as though he were rejoicing in a gentle Schubert melody.

She had never known a man so much in control of himself.

Or of her.

The train stopped just before Slough.

When, ten minutes later, it slowly began to move forward again, the Senior Conductor decided to introduce himself over the intercom.

'Ladies and Gentlemen. Due to a signalling failure at Slough, this train will now arrive at Paddington approximately fifteen minutes late. We apologize to customers for this delay.'

The man and the woman, seated now more closely together, turned to each other – and smiled.

'What are you thinking?' she asked.

'You often ask me that, you know. Sometimes I'm not thinking of anything.'

'Well?'

'I was only thinking that our Senior Conductor doesn't seem to know the difference between "due to" and "owing to".'

'Not sure *I* do. Does it matter?'

'Of course it matters.'

'But you won't let it come between us?'

'I won't let anything come between us,' he whispered into her ear.

For a few seconds they looked lovingly at each other. Then he lowered his eyes, removed a splayed left hand from her stockinged thigh, and drank his last mouthful of beer.

'Just before we get into Paddington, Rachel, there's something important I ought to tell you.'

She turned to him – her eyes suddenly alarmed.

He wanted to put a stop to the affair?

He wanted to get rid of her?

He'd found another woman? (Apart from his wife, of course.)

'Tickets, please!'

He looked as if he might be making his maiden voyage, the young ticket-collector, for he was scrutinizing each ticket proffered to him with preternatural concentration.

The man took both his own and the young woman's ticket from his wallet: cheap-day returns.

'This yours, sir?'

'Yes.'

'You an OAP?'

'As a matter of fact I am not, no.' (The tone of his voice was quietly arrogant.) 'To draw a senior-citizen pension in the United Kingdom a man has to be sixty-five years of age. But a Senior Railcard is available to a man who has passed his sixtieth birthday – as doubtless you know.'

'Could I see your Railcard, sir?'

With a sigh of resignation, the man produced his card. And the slightly flustered, spotty-faced youth duly studied the details.

Valid: until 07 MAY 96;
Issued to: Mr J. C. Storrs.

'How the hell does he think I got my ticket at Oxford without showing *that*?' asked the Senior Fellow of Lonsdale.

'He's only doing his duty, poor lad. And he's got awful acne.'

'You're right, yes.'

She took his hand in hers, moving more closely again. And within a few minutes the PADDINGTON sign passed by as the train drew slowly into the long platform. In a rather sad voice, the Senior Conductor now made his second announcement: 'All change, please! All change! This train has now terminated.'

They waited until their fellow-passengers had alighted; and happily, just as at Oxford, there seemed to be no one on the train whom either of them knew.

In the Brunel Bar of the Station Hotel, Storrs ordered a large brandy (two pieces of ice) for his young companion, and half a pint of Smith's bitter for himself. Then, leaving his own drink temporarily untouched, he walked out into Praed Street, thence making his way down to the cluster of small hotels in and around Sussex Gardens, several of them displaying VACANCIES signs. He had 'used' (was that the word?) two of them previously, but this time he decided to explore new territory.

'Double room?'

'One left, yeah. Just the one night, is it?'

'How much?'

'Seventy-five pounds for the two – with breakfast.'

'How much without breakfast?'

Storrs sensed that the middle-aged peroxide blonde was attuned to his intentions, for her eyes hardened knowingly behind the cigarette-stained reception counter.

'Seventy-five pounds.'

One experienced campaigner nodded to another experienced campaigner. 'Well, thank you, madam. I promise I'll call back and take the room – after I've had a look at it – if I can't find anything a little less expensive.'

He turned to go.

'Just a minute! . . . No breakfast, you say?'

'No. We're catching the sleeper to Inverness, and we just want a room for the day – you know? – a sort of habitation and a place.'

She squinted up at him through her cigarette smoke.

'Sixty-five?'

'Sixty.'

'OK.'

He counted out six ten-pound notes as, pushing the register forward, she reached behind her for Key Number 10.

It was, one may say, a satisfactory transaction.

Her glass was empty, and without seating himself he drained his own beer at a draught.

'Same again?'

'Please!' She pushed over the globed glass in which the semi-melted ice-cubes still remained.

Feeling most pleasantly relaxed, she looked around the thinly populated bar, and noticed (again!) the eyes of the middle-aged man seated across the room. But she gave no sign that she was aware of his interest, switching her glance instead to the balding, grey-white head of the man leaning nonchalantly at the bar as he ordered their drinks.

Beside her once more, he clinked their glasses, feeling (just as she did) most pleasantly relaxed.

'Quite a while since we sat here,' he volunteered.

'Couple o' months?'

'Ten weeks, if we wish to be exact.'

'Which, of course, we do, sir.'

Smiling, she sipped her second large brandy. Feeling good; feeling increasingly good.

'Hungry?' he asked.

'What for?'

He grinned. 'An hour in bed, perhaps – before we have a bite to eat?'

'Wine thrown in?'

'I'm trying to bribe you.'

'Well . . . if you *want* to go to bed for a little while first . . .'

'I *think* I'd quite enjoy that.'

'One condition, though.'

'What?'

'You tell me what you were going to tell me – on the train.'

He nodded seriously. 'I'll tell you over the wine.'

It was, one may say, a satisfactory arrangement.

As they got up to leave, Storrs moved ahead of her to push open one of the swing-doors; and Rachel James (for such was she), a freelance physiotherapist practising up in North Oxford, was conscious of the same man's eyes upon her. Almost involuntarily she leaned her body backward, thrusting her breasts against the smooth white silk of her blouse as she lifted both her hands behind her head to tighten the ring which held her light brown hair in its pony-tail.

A pony-tail ten inches long.

CHAPTER FIVE

Then the smiling hookers turned their attention to our shocked reporters.
  'Don't be shy! You paid for a good time, and that's what we want to give you.'
  Our men feigned jet-lag, and declined
                    (Extract from the *News of the World*, 5 February, 1995)

GEOFFREY OWENS had a better knowledge of Soho than most people.

He'd been only nineteen when first he'd gone to London as a junior reporter, when he'd rented a room just off Soho Square, and when during his first few months he'd regularly walked around the area there, experiencing the curiously compulsive attraction of names like Brewer Street, Greek Street, Old Compton Street, Wardour Street . . . a sort of litany of seediness and sleaze.

In those days, the mid-seventies, the striptease parlours, the porno cinemas, the topless bars – all somehow had been more wholesomely sinful, in the best sense of that word (or was it the worst?). Now, Soho had quite definitely changed for the better (or was it the worse?): more furtive and tawdry, more dishonest in its exploitation of the lonely, unloved men who would ever pace the pavements there and occasionally stop like rabbits in the headlights.

Yet Owens appeared far from mesmerized when in the early evening of 7 February he stopped outside Le Club Sexy. The first part of this establishment's name was intended (it must be assumed) to convey that *je-ne-sais-quoi* quality of Gallic eroticism; yet the other two parts perhaps suggested that the range of the proprietor's French was somewhat limited.

'Lookin' for a bit o' fun, love?'

The heavily mascara'd brunette appeared to be in her early twenties – quite a tall girl in her red high heels, wearing black stockings, a minimal black skirt, and a low-cut, heavily sequined blouse stretched tightly over a large bosom – largely exposed – beneath the winking light bulbs.

Déjà vu.

And, ever the voyeur, Owens was momentarily aware of all the old weaknesses.

'Come in! Come down and join the fun!'

She took a step towards him and he felt the long, blood-red fingernails curling pleasingly in his palm.

It was a good routine, and one that worked with many and many a man.

One that seemed to be working with Owens.

'How much?'

'Only three-pound membership, that's all. It's a private club, see – know wha' I mean?' For a few seconds she raised the eyes beneath the empurpled lids towards Elysium.

'Is Gloria still here?'

The earthbound eyes were suddenly suspicious – yet curious, too.

'Who?'

'If Gloria's still here, she'll let me in for nothing.'

'Lots o' names 'ere, mistah: real names – stage names . . .'

'So what's your name, beautiful?'

'Look, you wanna come in? Three pound – OK?'

'You're not being much help, you know.'

'Why don't you just fuck off?'

'You don't know Gloria?'

'What the 'ell do you *want*, mate?' she asked fiercely.

His voice was very quiet as he replied. 'I used to live fairly close by. And she used to work here, then – Gloria did. She was a stripper – one of the best in the business, so everybody said.'

For the second time the eyes in their lurid sockets seemed to betray some interest.

'When was that?'

'Twenty-odd years ago.'

'Christ! She must be a bloody granny by now!'

'Dunno. She had a child, though, I know that – a daughter . . .'

A surprisingly tall, smartly suited Japanese man had been drawn into the magnetic field of Le Club Sexy.

'Come in! Come down and—'

'How much is charge?'

'Only three pound. It's a private club, see – and you gotta be a member.'

With a strangely trusting, wonderfully polite smile, the man took a crisp ten-pound note from his large wallet and handed it to the hostess, bowing graciously as she reached a hand behind her and parted the multicoloured vertical strips which masked from public view the threadbare carpeting on the narrow stairs leading down to the secret delights.

'You give me change, please? I give you ten pound.'

'Just tell 'em downstairs, OK?'

'Why you not give me seven pound?'

'It'll be OK – OK?'

'OK.'

Halfway down the stairs, the newly initiated member made a little note in a little black book, smiling (we may say) scrutably. He was a member of a Home Office Committee licensing all 'entertainment premises' in the district of Soho.

His expenses were generous: needed to be.

Sometimes he enjoyed his job.

'Don't you ever feel bad about that sort of thing?'

'What d'you mean?'

'He'll never get his change, will he?'

'Like I said, why don't you just fuck off!'

'Gloria used to feel bad sometimes – quite a civilized streak in that woman somewhere. You'd have liked her ... Anyway, if you do come across her, just say you met me, Geoff Owens, will you? She'll remember me – certain to. Just tell her I've got a little proposition for her. She may be a bit down on her luck. You never know these days, and I wouldn't want to think she was on her uppers ... or her daughter was, for that matter.'

'What's her daughter got to do with it?' The voice was sharp.

Owens smiled, confidently now, lightly rubbing the back of his right wrist across her blouse.

'Quite a lot, perhaps. You may have quite a lot to do with it, sweetheart!'

She made no attempt to contradict him. 'In the pub' (she pointed across the street) 'half an hour, OK?'

She watched him go, the man with a five o'clock shadow who said his name was Owens. She'd never seen him before; but she'd recognize him again immediately, the dark hair drawn back above his ears, and tied in a pony-tail about eight or nine inches long.

Apart from the midnight 'milk-float', which gave passengers the impression that it called at almost every hamlet along the line, the 11.20 p.m. was the last train from Paddington. And a panting Owens jumped into its rear coach as the Turbo Express suddenly juddered and began to move forward. The train was only half-full, and he found a seat immediately.

He felt pleased with himself. The assignation in the pub had proved to be even more interesting than he'd dared to expect; and he leaned back and closed his eyes contentedly as he pondered the possible implications of what he had just learned . . .

He jolted awake at Didcot, wondering where he was – realizing that he had missed the Reading stop completely. Determined to stay awake for the last twelve minutes of the journey, he picked up an *Evening Standard* someone had left on the seat opposite, and was reading the sports page when over the top of the newspaper he saw a man walking back down the carriage – *almost* to where he himself was sitting – before taking his place next to a woman. And Owens recognized him.

Recognized Mr Julian Storrs of Lonsdale.

Well! Well! Well!

At Oxford, his head still stuck behind the *Evening Standard*, Owens waited until everyone else had left the rear carriage. Then, himself alighting, he observed Storrs arm-in-arm with his companion as they climbed the steps of the footbridge which led over the tracks to Platform One. And suddenly, for the second time that evening, Owens felt a shiver of excitement – for he immediately recognized the woman, too.

How could he fail to recognize her?

She was his next-door neighbour.

CHAPTER SIX
Monday, 19 February

Many is the gracious form that is covered with a veil; but on
withdrawing this thou discoverest a grandmother
(Musharrif-Uddin, *Gulistan*)

PAINSTAKINGLY, in block capitals, the Chief Inspector wrote his
name, E. MORSE; and was beginning to write his address when
Lewis came into the office at 8.35 a.m. on Monday, 19 February.

'What's that, sir?'

Morse looked down at a full page torn from one of the previous
day's colour supplements.

'Special offer: two free CDs when you apply to join the Music
Club Library.'

Lewis looked dubious. 'Don't forget you have to buy a book
every month with that sort of thing. Life's not all freebies, you
know.'

'Well, it is in this case. You've just got to have a look at the
first thing they send you, that's all – then send it back if you don't
like it. I think they even refund the postage.'

Lewis watched as Morse completed and snipped out the
application form.

'Wouldn't it be fairer if you agreed to have *some* of the books?'

'You think so?'

'At least *one* of them.'

Intense blue eyes, slightly pained, looked innocently across the
desk at Sergeant Lewis.

'But I've already got this month's book – I bought it for myself
for Christmas.'

He inserted the form into an envelope, on which he now wrote
the Club's address. Then he took from his wallet a sheaf of plastic
cards: Bodleian Library ticket; Lloyds payment card; RAC Break-
down Service; blood donor card; Blackwell's Bookshops; Oxford
City Library ticket; phonecard ... but there appeared to be no
booklet of first-class stamps there. Or of second-class.

'You don't, by any chance, happen to have a stamp on you,
Lewis?'

'What CDs are you going for?'

'I've ordered Janáček, the *Glagolitic Mass* – you may not know it. Splendid work – beautifully recorded by Simon Rattle. And Richard Strauss, *Four Last Songs* – Jessye Norman. I've got several recordings by other sopranos, of course.'

Of course . . .

Lewis nodded, and looked for a stamp.

It was not infrequent for Lewis to be reminded of what he had lost in life; or rather, what he'd never had in the first place. The one Strauss he knew was the 'Blue Danube' man. And he'd only recently learned there were two of *those*, as well – Senior and Junior; and which was which he'd no idea.

'Perhaps you'll be in for a bit of a let-down, sir. Some of these offers – they're not exactly up to what they promise.'

'You're an expert on these things?'

'No . . . but . . . take Sergeant—' Lewis stopped himself in time. Just as well to leave a colleague's weakness cloaked in anonymity. 'Take this chap I know. He read this advert in one of the tabloids about a free video – sex video – sent in a brown envelope with no address to say where it had come from. You know, in case the wife . . .'

'No, I don't know, Lewis. But please continue.'

'Well, he sent for one of the choices—'

'*Copenhagen Red-Hot Sex*?'

'No. *Housewives on the Job* – that was the title; and he expected, you know . . .'

Morse nodded. 'Housewives "on the job" with the milkman, the postman, the itinerant button-salesmen . . .'

Lewis grinned. 'But it wasn't, no. It just showed all these fully dressed Swedish housewives washing up the plates and peeling the potatoes.'

'Serves Sergeant Dixon right.'

'You won't mention it, sir!'

'Of course I won't. And you're probably right. You never really get something for nothing in this life. I never seem to, anyway.'

'Really, sir?'

Morse licked the flap of the white envelope. Then licked the back of the first-class stamp that Lewis had just given him.

The phone had been ringing for several seconds, and Lewis now took the call, listening briefly but carefully, before putting his hand over the mouthpiece:

'There's been a murder, sir. On the doorstep, really – up in Bloxham Drive.'

PART TWO

CHAPTER SEVEN

In addition to your loyal support on the ballot paper, we shall
be grateful if you can agree to display the enclosed sticker in
one of your windows
(Extract from a 1994 local election leaflet distributed by the
East Oxford Labour Party)

IT REMINDED Morse of something – that rear window of Number
17.

As a young lad he'd been fascinated by a photograph in one of
his junior school textbooks of the apparatus frequently fixed
round the necks of slaves in the southern states of America: an
iron ring from whose circumference, at regular intervals, there
emanated lengthy, fearsome spikes, also of iron. The caption, as
Morse recalled, had maintained that such a device readily pre-
vented any absconding cotton-picker from passing himself off as
an enfranchised citizen.

Morse had never really understood the caption.

Nor indeed, for some considerable while, was he fully
to understand the meaning of the neat bullet-hole in the
centre of the shattered glass, and the cracks that radiated from
it regularly, like a young child's crayoning the rays of the
sun.

Looking around him, Morse surveyed the area from the
wobbly paving-slabs which formed a pathway at the rear of the
row of terraced houses stretching along the northern side of
Bloxham Drive, Kidlington, Oxfordshire. About half of the thirty-
odd young trees originally planted in a staggered design beside
and behind this path had been vandalized to varying degrees:
some of them wholly extirpated; some cruelly snapped in the
middle of their gradually firming stems; others, with many of
their burgeoning branches torn off, standing wounded and forlorn amid the unkempt litter-strewn area, once planned by some
Environmental Officer as a small addendum to England's green
and pleasant land.

Morse felt saddened.

As did Sergeant Lewis, standing beside him.

Yet it is appropriate here to enter one important qualification. Bloxham Drive, in the view of most of its residents, was showing some few signs of unmistakable improvement. The installation of sleeping-policemen had virtually eliminated the possibilities of joy-riding; many denizens were now lying more peacefully in their beds after the eviction of one notoriously anti-social household; and over the previous two or three years the properties had fallen in price to such an extent as to form an attractive proposition to those few of the professional classes who were prepared to give the street the benefit of the doubt. To be more specific, three such persons had taken out mortgages on properties there: the properties standing at Number 1, Number 15, and Number 17.

But – yes, agreed! – Bloxham Drive and the surrounding streets was still an area a league and a league from the peaceful, leafy lanes of Gerrards Cross; and still the scene of some considerable crime.

Crime which now included murder . . .

The call had come through to Lewis at 8.40 a.m.

Just over one hour previously, whilst the sky was still unusually dark, Mrs Queenie Norris, from Number 11, had (as was her wont) taken out her eight-year-old Cavalier King Charles along the rear of the terrace, ignoring (as was her wont) the notices forbidding the fouling of pavements and verges. That was when she'd noticed it: noticed the cracked back window at Number 17 – yet failed to register too much surprise, since (as we have seen) vandalism there had become commonplace, and any missile, be it bottle or brick, would have left some similar traces of damage.

Back from her walk, Mrs Norris, as she was later to explain to the police, had felt increasingly uneasy. And just before the weather forecast on Radio 4, she had stepped out once again, now minus the duly defecated Samson, and seen that the light in the kitchen of Number 17 was still on, the blind still drawn down to the bottom of the casement.

This time she had knocked quietly, then loudly, against the back door.

But there had been no reply to her reiterated raps; and only then had she noticed that behind the hole in the kitchen window – *immediately* behind it – was a corresponding hole in the thin beige-brown material of the blind. It was at that point that she'd felt the horrid crawl of fear across her skin. Her near-neighbour worked in North Oxford, almost invariably leaving home at about a quarter to eight. And now it was coming up to the hour. Had reached the hour.

Something was wrong.

Something, Mrs Norris suspected, was seriously wrong; and she'd rung 999 immediately.

It had been ten minutes later when PCs Graham and Swift had finally forced an entry through the front door of the property to discover the grim truth awaiting them in the back kitchen: the body of a young woman lying dead upon her side, the right cheek resting on the cold red tiles, the light brown hair of her pony-tail soaked and stiffened in a pool of blood. Indeed it was not only the dreams of the two comparatively inexperienced constables, but also those of the hardened Scenes-of-Crime Officers, that would be haunted by the sight of so much blood; such a copious outpouring of blood.

And now it was Morse's turn.

'Oh dear,' said Lewis very quietly.

Morse said nothing, holding back (as ever) from any close inspection of a corpse, noting only the bullet wound, somewhere at the bottom of the neck, which clearly had been the cause of death, the cause of all the blood. Yet (as ever, too) Morse, who had never owned a camera in his life, had already taken several mental flashes of his own.

It seemed logical to assume that the murder had occurred towards the end of a fairly conventional breakfast. On the side of a wooden kitchen table – the side nearest the window – a brown plastic-topped stool had been moved slightly askew. On the table itself was a plate, a small heap of salt sprinkled with pepper at its edge, on which lay a brown eggshell beside a wooden eggcup; and alongside, on a second plate, half a round of toasted brown bread, buttered, and amply spread from a jar of Frank Cooper's

Oxford Marmalade. And one other item: a white mug bearing the legend GREETINGS FROM GUERNSEY; bearing, too, the remains of some breakfast coffee, long since cold and muddily brown.

That was what Morse saw. And for the present that was enough; he wished to be away from the dreadful scene.

Yet before he left, he forced himself to look once more at the woman who lay there. She was wearing a white nightdress, with a faded-pink floral motif, over which was a light blue dressing-gown, reaching about halfway down the shapely, slim, unstockinged legs. It was difficult to be sure about things, of course; but Morse suspected that the twisted features of the face had been – until so very recently – just as comely as the rest of her. And for a few seconds his own face twisted, too, as if in sympathy with the murdered woman lying at his feet.

The SOCOs had now arrived; and after brief, perfunctory greetings, Morse was glad to escape and leave them to it. Bidding Lewis to initiate some immediate house-to-house inquiries, on both sides of the street, he himself stepped out of the front door into Bloxham Drive, now the scene of considerable police activity, with checkered-capped officers, the flashing blue lights of their cars, and a cordon of blue-and-white tape being thrown round the murder-house. A knot of local inhabitants, too, stood whispering there, shivering occasionally in the early morning cold, yet determined to witness the course of events unfolding.

And the media.

Recognizing the Chief Inspector, two press men (how so early there?) pleaded for just the briefest interview – a sentence even; a TV crew from Abingdon had already covered Morse's exit from the house; and a Radio Oxford reporter waved a bulbous microphone in front of his face.

But Morse ignored them all with a look of vacuous incomprehension worthy of some deaf-mute, and proceeded to walk slowly to the end of the street (observing, all the time *observing*), where he turned left down one side of the terraced row, then left again, retracing his earlier steps along the uneven paving slabs behind the houses, stopping briefly where he and Lewis had stopped before; then completing the circuit and again curtly dismissing the converging reporters with a wave of his right hand as he walked back along the front of the terrace.

It would be untrue to say that Morse's mind had been particularly acute on this peripatetic reconnaissance. Indeed, only one single feature of the neighbourhood had made much of an impression upon him.

A political impression.

Very soon (the evidence was all around him) there was to be an election for one of the local council seats – death of an incumbent, perhaps? – and clearly, if unusually, there appeared to be considerable interest in the matter. Stickers were to be observed in all but two of the front windows of the north-side terrace: green stickers with the red lettering of the Labour candidate's name; white stickers with the royal blue lettering of the Conservative's. With little as yet upon which his mind could fix itself, Morse had taken a straw poll of the support shown, from Number 1 to Number 21. And hardly surprisingly, perhaps, in this marginally depressed and predominantly working-class district, the advantage was significantly with the Labour man, with six stickers to the Tory's two.

One of the stickers favouring the latter cause was displayed in the ground-floor window of Number 15. And for some reason Morse had found himself standing and wondering for a while outside the only other window in the Drive parading its confidence in the Conservative Party – and in a candidate with the splendidly patriotic name of Jonathan Bull; standing and wondering outside Number 1, at the main entrance to Bloxham Drive.

CHAPTER EIGHT

Oft have we seen him at the peep of dawn
Brushing with hasty steps the dews away
(Thomas Gray, *Elegy Written
in a Country Churchyard*)

IN HIS EARLIER years Geoffrey Owens had been an owl, preferring to pursue whatever tasks lay before him into the late hours of the night, often through into the still, small hours. But now, in his mid-forties, he had metamorphosed into a lark, his brain seeming perceptibly clearer and fresher in the morning. It had been no hardship, therefore, when he was invited, under the new flexi-time philosophy of his employers, to start work early and finish work early – thereby receiving a small bonus into the bargain. And, since the previous September, Owens had made it his regular practice to leave his home in Bloxham Drive just before 7 a.m., incidentally thus avoiding the traffic jams which began to build up in the upper reaches of the Banbury Road an hour or so later; and, on his return journey, missing the corresponding jams the other way as thousands of motorists left the busy heart of Oxford for the comparative peace of the northern outskirts, and the neighbouring villages – such as Kidlington.

It was, all in all, a happy enough arrangement. And one which had applied on Monday, 19 February.

Owens had left his house at about ten minutes to seven that morning, when he had, of course, passed the house on the corner, Number 1, where a woman had watched him go. But if he in turn had spotted her, this was in no way apparent, for he had passed without a wave of recognition, and driven up to the junction, where he had turned right, on his way down into Oxford. But if he had not seen her, quite definitely she had seen him.

Traffic had been unusually light for a Monday (more often than not the busiest morning of the week) even at such a comparatively early hour; and without any appreciable hold-up Owens soon reached the entrance barrier of the large car park which serves the Oxfordshire Newspapers complex down in Osney Mead, just past the railway station along the Botley Road.

Owens had come to Oxford three years previously with an impressive-looking CV, in which the applicant asserted his 'all-round experience in the fields of reporting, copy-editing, advertising, and personnel management'. And he had been the unanimous choice of the four members of the interviewing panel. Nor had there been the slightest reason since for them to rue their decision. In fact, Owens had proved a profitable investment. With his knowledge of English grammar way above average, his job description had quickly been modified, with an appropriate increase in salary, to include responsibility for recasting the frequently ill-constructed paragraphs of his junior colleagues, and for correcting the heinous errors in orthography which blighted not a few of their offerings; and, in addition to these new tasks, to stand in as required when the Personnel Manager was called away on conferences.

As a result of these changes, Owens himself, nominally the group's senior reporter, had become more and more desk-bound, venturing out only for the big stories. Like now. For as he stood in Bloxham Drive that morning, he was never in doubt that this would be one of those 'big stories' – not just for himself but also for the steadily increasing number of media colleagues who were already joining him.

All of them waiting . . .

Waiting, in fact, until 11.30 a.m. – well before which time, as if by some sort of collective instinct, each was aware that something grotesque and gruesome had occurred in the house there numbered 17.

CHAPTER NINE

Instead of being arrested, as we stated, for kicking his wife down a flight of stairs and hurling a lighted kerosene lamp after her, the Revd James P. Wellman died unmarried four years ago

(Correction in a US journal, quoted by Burne-Jones
in a letter to Lady Horner)

AT 11.15 A.M. LEWIS suggested that someone perhaps ought to say something.

For the past hour and a half a group of police officers had been knocking on neighbourhood doors, speaking to residents, taking brief preliminary statements. But as yet nothing official had been released to the representatives of the media assembled in a street now increasingly crowded with curious onlookers.

'Go ahead!' said Morse.

'Shall I tell them all we know?'

'That won't take you long, will it?'

'No need to keep anything back?'

'For Chrissake, Lewis! You sound as if we've *got* something to hide. If we have, why don't you tell *me*?'

'Just wondered.'

Morse's tone softened. 'It won't matter much what you tell 'em, will it?'

'All right.'

'Just one thing, though. You can remind 'em that we'd all welcome a bit of accuracy for a change. Tell 'em to stick an "h" in the middle of Bloxham Close – that sort of thing.'

'Bloxham *Drive*, sir.'

'Thank you, Lewis.'

With which, a morose-looking Morse eased himself back in the armchair in the front sitting-room, and continued his cursory examination of the papers, letters, documents, photographs, taken from the drawers of a Queen-Anne-style escritoire – a rather tasteful piece, thought Morse. Family heirloom, perhaps.

Family . . .

Oh dear!

That was always one of the worst aspects of suicides and murders: the family. This time with Mum and Dad and younger sister already on their way up from Torquay. Still, Lewis was wonderfully good at that sort of thing. Come to think of it, Lewis was quite good at several things, really – including dealing with the Press. And as Morse flicked his way somewhat fecklessly through a few more papers, he firmly resolved (although in fact he forgot) to tell his faithful sergeant exactly that before the day was through.

Immediately on confronting his interlocutors, Lewis was invited by the TV crew to go some way along the street so that he could be filmed walking before appearing in front of the camera talking. Normal TV routine, it was explained: always see a man striding along somewhere before seeing his face on the screen. So, would Sergeant Lewis please oblige with a short perambulation?

No, Sergeant Lewis wouldn't.

What he would do, though, was try to tell them what they wanted to know. Which, for the next few minutes, he did.

A murder had occurred in the kitchen of Number 17 Bloxham Drive: B-L-O-X-H-A-M –

One of the neighbours (unspecified) had earlier alerted the police to suspicious circumstances at that address –

A patrol car had been on the scene promptly; forced open the front door; discovered the body of a young woman –

The woman had been shot dead through the rear kitchen window –

The body had not as yet been officially identified –

The property appeared to show no sign – no *other* sign – of any break-in –

That was about it, really.

Amid the subsequent chorus of questions, Lewis picked out the raucous notes of the formidable female reporter from the *Oxford Star*:

'What time was all this, Sergeant?'

As it happened, Lewis knew the answer to that question very well. But he decided to be economical with the details of the surprisingly firm evidence already gleaned . . .

The Jacobs family lived immediately opposite Number 17, where the lady of the house, in dressing-gown and curlers, had opened her front door a few minutes after 7 a.m. in order to pick up her two pints of Co-op milk from the doorstep. Contemporaneously, exactly so, her actions had been mirrored across the street where another woman, also in a dressing-gown (though without curlers), had been picking up her own single pint. Each had looked across at the other; each had nodded a matutinal greeting.

'You're quite *sure*?' Lewis had insisted. 'It was still a bit dark, you know.'

'We've got some street-lamps, haven't we, Sergeant?'

'You *are* sure, then.'

'Unless she's got – unless she had a twin sister.'

'Sure about the *time*, too? That's very important.'

She nodded. 'I'd just watched the news headlines on BBC1 – I like to do that. Then I turned the telly off. I might have filled the kettle again . . . but, like I say, it was only a few minutes past seven. Five past, at the outside.'

It therefore seemed virtually certain that there was a time-span of no more than half an hour during which the murder had occurred: between 7.05 a.m., when Mrs Jacobs had seen her neighbour opposite, and 7.35 a.m. or so, when Mrs Norris had first noticed the hole in the window. It was unusual – *very* unusual – for such exactitude to be established at so early a stage in a murder inquiry; and there would be little need in this case for the police to be dependent upon (what Morse always called) those prevaricating pathologists . . .

'About quarter past seven,' answered the prevaricating Lewis.

'You're quite *sure*?' It was exactly the same question Lewis himself had asked.

'No, not sure at all. Next question?'

'Why didn't everybody hear the shot?' (The same young, ginger-headed reporter.)

'Silencer, perhaps?'

'There'd be the sound of breaking glass surely?' (A logically minded man from the *Oxford Star*.)

A series of hand gestures and silent lip-movements from the TV crew urged Lewis not to look directly into the camera.

Lewis nodded. 'Yes. In fact several of the neighbours think they heard something – two of them certainly did. But it could have been lots of things, couldn't it?'

'Such as?' (The importunate ginger-knob again.)

Lewis shrugged. 'Could have been the milkman dropping a bottle—?'

'No broken glass here, though, Sergeant.'

'Car backfiring? We don't know.'

'Does what the neighbours heard fit in with the time all right?' (The TV interviewer with his fluffy cylindrical microphone.)

'Pretty well, yes.'

The senior reporter from the *Oxford Mail* had hitherto held his peace. But now he asked a curious question, if it was a question:

'Not the two *immediate* neighbours, were they?'

Lewis looked at the man with some interest.

'Why do you say that?'

'Well, the woman who lives there' (a finger pointed to Number 19) 'she was probably still asleep at the time, and she's stone-deaf without her hearing-aid.'

'Really?'

'And the man who lives there' (a finger pointed to Number 15) 'he'd already left for work.'

Lewis frowned. 'Can you tell me how you happen to know all this, sir?'

'No problem,' replied Geoffrey Owens. 'You see, Sergeant, *I* live at Number 15.'

CHAPTER TEN

Where lovers lie with ardent glow,
Where fondly each forever hears
The creaking of the bed below –
Above, the music of the spheres
(Viscount Mumbles, 1797–1821)

WHEN LEWIS RETURNED from his encounter with the media,
Morse was almost ready to leave the murder-house. The morning
had moved towards noon, and he knew that he might be thinking
a little more clearly if he were drinking a little – or at least be
starting to think when he started to drink.

'Is there a real-ale pub somewhere near?'

Lewis, pleasantly gratified with his handling of the Press and
TV, was emboldened to sound a note of caution.

'Doesn't do your liver much good – all this drinking.'

Surprisingly Morse appeared to accept the reminder with
modest grace.

'I'm sure you're right; but my medical advisers have warned
me it may well be unwise to give up alcohol at my age.'

Lewis was not impressed, for he had heard the same words –
exactly the same words – on several previous occasions.

'You've had a good look around, sir?'

'Not really. I know I always find the important things. But I
want *you* to have a look around. You usually manage to find the
*un*important things – and often they're the things that really
matter in the end.'

Lewis made little attempt to disguise his pleasure, and
straightway relented.

'We could go up to the Boat at Thrupp?'

'Excellent.'

'You don't want to stay here any longer?'

'No. The SOCOs'll be another couple of hours yet.'

'You don't want to see . . . *her* again?'

Morse shook his head. 'I know what she looks like – *looked*
like.' He picked up two coloured photographs and one postcard,
and made towards the front door, handing over the keys of the

maroon Jaguar to Lewis. 'You'd better drive – if you promise to stick to the orange juice.'

Once on their way, Lewis reported the extraordinarily strange coincidence of the press man, Owens, living next door to the murdered woman. But Morse, who always looked upon any coincidence in life as the norm rather than the exception, was more anxious to set forth the firm details he had himself now gleaned about Ms Rachel James, for there could now be no real doubt of her identity.

'Twenty-nine. Single. No offspring. Worked as a freelance physiotherapist at a place in the Banbury Road. CV says she went to school at Torquay Comprehensive; left there in 1984 with a clutch of competent O-levels, three A-levels – two Bs, in Biology and Geography, and an E in Media Studies.'

'Must have been fairly bright.'

'What do you mean? You need to be a moron to get an E in Media Studies,' asserted Morse, who had never seen so much as a page of any Media Studies syllabus, let alone a question paper.

He continued:

'Parents, as you know, still alive, on their way here—'

'You'll want me to see them?'

'Well, you *are* good at that sort of thing, aren't you? And if the mother's like most women she'll probably smell the beer as soon as I open the door.'

'Good reason for you to join me on the orange juice.'

Morse ignored the suggestion. 'She bought the property there just over four years ago for £65,000 and the value's been falling ever since by the look of things, so the poor lass is one of those figuring in the negative equity statistics; took out a mortgage of £55,000 – probably Mum and Dad gave her the other £10,000; and the saleable value of Number 17 is now £40,000, at the most.'

'Bought at the wrong time, sir. But some people *were* a bit irresponsible, don't you think?'

'I'm not an economist, as you know, Lewis. But I'll tell you what would have helped her. Helped so many in her boots.'

'A win on the National Lottery?'

'Wouldn't help *many*, that, would it? No. What she could have done with is a healthy dose of inflation. It's a good thing – inflation – you know. Especially for people who've got nothing to start with. One of the best things that happened to some of us. One year I remember I had three jumps in salary.'

'Not many would agree with you on that, though, would they? Conservative and Labour both agree about inflation.'

'Ah! Messrs Bull and Thomas, you mean?'

'You noticed the stickers?'

'I notice most things. It's just that some of them don't register – not immediately.'

'What'll you have, sir?'

'Lew-is! We've known each other long enough, surely.'

As Morse tasted the hostelry's Best Bitter, he passed over a photograph of Rachel James.

'Best one of her I could find.'

Lewis looked down at the young woman.

'Real good-looker,' he said softly.

Morse nodded. 'I bet she'd have set a few hearts all a-flutter.'

'Including yours, sir?'

Morse drank deeply on his beer before replying. 'She'd probably have a good few boyfriends, that's all I'm suggesting. As for my own potential susceptibility, that's beside the point.'

'Of course.' Lewis smiled good-naturedly. 'What else have we got?'

'What do you make of this? One of the few interesting things there, as far as I could see.'

Lewis now considered the postcard handed to him. First, the picture on the front: a photograph of a woodland ride, with a sunlit path on the left, and a pool of azured bluebells to the right. Then turning over the card, he read the cramped lines amateurishly typed on the left-hand side:

> Ten Times I beg, dear Heart, let's Wed!
>   (Thereafter long may Cupid reigne)
> Let's tread the Aisle, where thou hast led
>   The fifteen Bridesmaides in thy Traine.
> Then spend our honeyed Moon a-bed,
>   With Springs that creake againe – againe!
>   (John Wilmot, 1672)

That was all.
No salutation.

No valediction.

And on the right-hand side of the postcard – nothing: no address, with the four dotted, parallel lines devoid of any writing, the top right-hand rectangle devoid of any stamp.

Lewis, a man not familiar with seventeenth-century love-lyrics, read the lines, then read them again, with only semi-comprehension.

'Pity she didn't get round to filling in the address, sir. Looks as if she might be proposing to somebody.'

'Aren't you making an assumption?'

'Pardon?'

'Did you see a typewriter in the house?'

'She could have typed it at work.'

'Yes. You must get along there soon.'

'You're the boss.'

'Nice drop o' beer, this. In good nick.' Morse drained the glass and set it down in the middle of the slightly rickety table, whilst Lewis took a gentle sip of his orange juice; and continued to sit firmly fixed to his seat.

Morse continued:

'No! You're making a false assumption – I *think* you are. You're assuming she'd just written this to somebody and then forgotten the fellow's address, right? Pretty unlikely, isn't it? If she was proposing to him.'

'Perhaps she couldn't find a stamp.'

'Perhaps . . .'

Reluctantly Morse got to his feet and pushed his glass across the bar. 'You don't want anything more yourself, do you, Lewis?'

'No thanks.'

'You've nothing less?' asked the landlady, as Morse tendered a twenty-pound note. 'You're the first ones in today and I'm a bit short of change.'

Morse turned round. 'Any change on you, by any chance, Lewis?'

'You see,' continued Morse, 'you're still assuming she wrote it, aren't you?'

'And she didn't?'

'I think someone wrote the card to *her*, put it in an envelope, and then addressed the envelope – not the card.'

'Why not just address the card?'

'Because whoever wrote it didn't want anyone else to read it.'

'Why not just phone her up?'

'Difficult – if he was married and his wife was always around.'

'He could ring her from a phone-box.'

'Risky – if anyone saw him.'

Lewis nodded without any conviction: 'And it's only a bit of poetry.'

'Is it?' asked Morse quietly.

Lewis picked up the card again. 'Perhaps it's this chap called "Wilmot", sir – the date's just there to mislead us.'

'Mislead *you*, perhaps. John Wilmot, Earl of Rochester, was a court poet to Charles II. He wrote some delightfully pornographic lyrics.'

'So it's – it's all genuine?'

'I didn't say that, did I? The name's genuine, but not the poem. Any English scholar would know that's not seventeenth-century verse.'

'I'm sure you're right, sir.'

'And if I'm right about the card coming in an envelope – fairly recently – we might be able to find the envelope, agreed? Find a postmark, perhaps? Even a bit of handwriting?'

Lewis looked dubious. 'I'd better get something organized, then.'

'All taken care of! I've got a couple of the DCs looking through the wastepaper baskets and the dustbin.'

'You reckon this is important, then?'

'Top priority! You can see that. She's been meeting some man – meeting him secretly. Which means he's probably married, probably fairly well known, probably got a prominent job, probably a local man—'

'Probably lives in Peterborough,' mumbled Lewis.

'That's exactly why the postmark's so vital!' countered an unamused Morse. 'But if he's an Oxford man . . .'

'Do you know what the population of Oxford *is*?'

'I know it to the nearest *thousand*!' snapped Morse.

Then, of a sudden, the Chief Inspector's mood completely changed. He tapped the postcard.

'Don't be despondent, Lewis. You see, we know just a little about this fellow already, don't we?'

He smiled benignly after draining his second pint; and since no other customers had as yet entered the lounge, Lewis resignedly got to his feet and stepped over to the bar once more.

Lewis picked up the postcard again.

'Give me a clue, sir.'

'You know the difference between nouns and verbs, of course?'

'How could I forget something like that?'

'Well, at certain periods in English literature, all the nouns were spelt with capital letters. Now, as you can see, there are *eight* nouns in those six lines – each of them spelt with a capital letter. But there are *nine* capitals – forgetting the first word of each line. Now which is the odd one out?'

Lewis pretended to study the lines once more. He'd played this game before, and he trusted he could get away with it again, as his eyes suddenly lit up a little.

'Ah . . . I think – I *think* I see what you mean.'

'Hits you in the eye, doesn't it, that "Wed" in the first line? And that's what it was *intended* to do.'

'Obviously.'

'What's it mean?'

'What, "Wed"? Well, it means "marry" – you know, get hitched, get spliced, tie the knot—'

'What else?'

'Isn't that enough?'

'What *else*?'

'I suppose you're going to tell me it's Anglo-Saxon or something.'

'Not exactly. Not far off, though. Old English, in fact. And what's it short for?'

'"Wednesday"?' suggested Lewis tentatively.

Morse beamed at his sergeant. 'Woden's day – the fourth day of the week. So we've got a *day*, Lewis. And what else do you need, if you're going to arrange a date with a woman?'

Lewis studied the lines yet again. 'Time? Time, yes! I see what you mean, sir. "Ten Times" . . . "fifteen Bridesmaides" . . . Well, well, well! Ten-fifteen!'

Morse nodded. 'With a.m. likelier than p.m. Doesn't say where though, does it?'

Lewis studied the lines for the fifth time.

'"Traine", perhaps?'

'Well done! "Meet me at the station to catch the ten-fifteen a.m. train" – that's what it says. And we know where that train goes, don't we?'

'Paddington.'

'Exactly.'

'If only we knew who he was . . .'

Morse now produced his second photograph – a small passport-sized photograph of two people: the woman, Rachel James (no doubt of that), turning partially round and slightly upward in order to kiss the cheek of a considerably older man with a pair of smiling eyes beneath a distinguished head of greying hair.

'Who's he, sir?'

'Dunno. We could find out pretty quickly, though, if we put his photo in the local papers.'

'*If* he's local.'

'Even if he's not local, I should think.'

'Bit dodgy, sir.'

'Too dodgy at this stage, I agree. But we can try another angle, can't we? Tomorrow's Tuesday, and the day after that's Wednes-day – Woden's day . . .'

'You mean he may turn up at the station?'

'If the card's fairly recent, yes.'

'Unless he's heard she's been murdered.'

'Or unless he murdered her himself.'

'Worth a try, sir. And if he *does* turn up, it'll probably mean he didn't murder her . . .'

Morse made no comment.

'Or, come to think of it, it might be a fairly clever thing to do if he *did* murder her.'

Morse drained his glass and stood up.

'You know something? I reckon orange juice occasionally germinates your brain cells.'

As he drove his chief down to Kidlington, Lewis returned the conversation to where it had begun.

'You haven't told me what you think about this fellow Owens – the dead woman's next-door neighbour.'

'Death is always the next-door neighbour,' said Morse sombrely. 'But don't let it affect your driving, Lewis!'

CHAPTER ELEVEN
Wednesday 21 February

Orandum est ut sit mens sana in corpore sano
(Our aim? Just a brain that's not addled with pox,
And a guaranteed clean bill-of-health from the docs)
(Juvenal, *Satires X*)

THE NEXT MEETING of the Lonsdale Fellows had been convened for 10 a.m.

In the Stamper Room.

William Leslie Stamper, b. 1880, had graduated from Oxford University in 1903 with the highest marks (it is said) ever recorded in Classical Moderations. The bracketed caveat in the previous sentence would be unnecessary were it not that the claim for such distinction was perpetuated, in later years, by one person only – by W. L. Stamper himself. And it is pointless to dwell upon the matter since no independent verification is available: the relevant records had been removed from Oxford to a safe place, thereafter never to be seen again, during the First World War – a war in which Stamper had not been an active participant, owing to an illness which was unlikely to prolong his eminently promising career as a don for more than a couple of years or so. Such non-participation in the great events of 1914–18 was a major sadness (it is said) to Stamper himself, who was frequently heard to lament his own failure to figure among the casualty lists from the fields of Flanders or Passchendaele.

Now, the reader may readily be forgiven for assuming from the preceding paragraph that Stamper had been a time-server; a dissembling self-seeker. Yet such an assumption is highly questionable, though not necessarily untrue. When, for example, in 1925, the Mastership of Lonsdale fell vacant, and nominations were sought amid the groves of Academe, Stamper had refused to let his name go forward, on the grounds that if ten years earlier he had been declared unfit to fight in defence of his country he could hardly be considered fit to undertake the governance of the College; specifically so, since the Statutes stipulated a candidate whose body was no less healthy than his brain.

Thereafter, in his gentle, scholarly, pedantic manner, Stamper had passed his years teaching the esoteric skills of Greek Prose and Verse Composition – until retiring at the age of sixty-five, two years before the statutory limit, on the grounds of ill-health. No one, certainly not Stamper himself (it is said), anticipated any significant continuation of his life, and the College Fellows unanimously backed a proposal that the dear old boy should have the privilege, during the few remaining years of his life, of living in the finest set of rooms that the College had to offer.

Thus it was that the legendary Stamper had stayed on in Lonsdale as an honorary Emeritus Fellow, with full dining rights, from the year of his retirement, 1945, to 1955; and then to 1965 . . . and 1975; and almost indeed until 1985, when he had finally died at the age of 104 – and then not through any dysfunction of the bodily organs, but from a fall beside his rooms in the front quad after a heavy bout of drinking at a Gaudy, his last words (it is said) being a whispered request for the Madeira to be passed round once again.

The agenda which lay before Sir Clixby Bream and his colleagues that morning was short and fairly straightforward:

  (i)   To receive apologies for absence
  (ii) To approve the minutes of the previous meeting (already circulated)
  (iii) To consider the Auditors' statement on College expenditure, Michaelmas 1995
  (iv) To recommend appropriate procedures for the election of a new Master
  (v)   AOB

Items (i)–(iii) took only three minutes, and would have taken only one, had not the Tutor for Admissions sought an explanation of why the 'Stationery etc' bill for the College Office had risen by four times the current rate of inflation. For which increase the Domestic Bursar admitted full responsibility, since instead of ordering 250 Biros he had inadvertently ordered 250 *boxes* of Biros.

This confession put the meeting into good humour, as it passed on to item (iv).

The Master briefly restated the criteria to be met by potential applicants: first, that he be not in Holy Orders; second, that he be mentally competent, and particularly so in the 'Skills of the Arithmetick' (as the original Statute had it); third, that he be free from serious bodily infirmity. On the second criterion, the Master suggested that since it was now virtually impossible (a gentle glance here at the innumerate Professor of Arabic) to fail GCSE Mathematics, there could be little problem for anyone. As far as the third criterion was concerned however (the Master grew more solemn now) there was a sad announcement he had to make. One name previously put forward had been withdrawn – that of Dr Ridgeway, the brilliant micro-biologist from Balliol, who had developed serious heart trouble at the comparatively youthful age of forty-three.

Amid murmurs of commiseration round the table, the Master continued:

'Therefore, gentlemen, we are left with two nominations only . . . unless we . . . unless anyone . . . ? No?'

No.

Well, that was pleasing, the Master declared: he had always wished his successor to be appointed from within the College. And so it would be. Voting would take place in the time-honoured way: a single sheet of paper bearing the handwritten name of the preferred candidate, with the signature of the Voting Fellow beneath it, must be delivered to the Master's Lodge before noon on the nineteenth of March, one month away.

The Master proceeded to wish the two candidates well; and Julian Storrs and Denis Cornford, by chance seated next to each other, shook hands smilingly, like a couple of boxers before the weigh-in for a bruising fight.

That was not quite all.

Under AOB, the Tutor for Admissions was moved to make his second contribution of the morning.

'Perhaps it may be possible, Master, in view of the current plethora of pens in the College Office, for the Domestic Bursar to send us each a free Biro with which we can write down our considered choices for Master?'

It was a nice touch, typical of an Oxford SCR; and when at 10.20 a.m. they left the Stamper Room and moved outside into the front quad, most of the Fellows were grinning happily.

But not the Domestic Bursar.

Nor Julian Storrs.

Nor Denis Cornford.

CHAPTER TWELVE

The virtue of the camera is not the power it has to transform the photographer into an artist, but the impulse it gives him to keep on looking – and looking

(Brooks Atkinson, *Once Around the Sun*)

EARLIER THAT SAME morning Morse and Lewis had been sitting together drinking coffee in the canteen at Kidlington Police HQ.

'Well, that's them!' said an unwontedly ungrammatical Morse as he pointed to the photograph which some darkroom boy had managed to enlarge and enhance. 'Our one big clue, that; one *small* clue, anyway.'

As Lewis saw things, the enlargement appeared to have been reasonably effective as far as the clothing was concerned; yet, to be truthful, the promised 'enhancement' of the two faces, those of the murdered woman and of the man so close beside her, seemed to have blurred rather than focused any physiognomical detail.

'Well?' asked Morse.

'Worse than the original.'

'Nonsense! Look at that.' Morse pointed to the tight triangular knot of the man's tie, which appeared – just – above a high-necked grey sweater.

Yes. Lewis acknowledged that the colour and pattern of the tie were perhaps a little clearer.

'I think I almost recognize that tie,' continued Morse slowly. 'That deepish maroon colour. And that' (he pointed again) 'that narrow white stripe . . .'

'We never had ties at school,' ventured Lewis.

But Morse was too deeply engrossed to bother about his sergeant's former school uniform, or lack of it, as with a magnifying glass he sought further to enhance (?) the texture of the small relevant area of the photograph.

'Bit o' taste there, Lewis. Little bit o' class. I wouldn't be surprised if it's the tie of the Old Wykehamists' Classical Association.'

Lewis said nothing.

And Morse looked at him almost accusingly. 'You don't seem very interested in what I'm telling you.'

'Not too much, perhaps.'

'All right! Perhaps it's not a public-school tie. So what tie do *you* think it is?'

Again Lewis said nothing.

After a while, a semi-mollified Morse picked up the photograph, returned it to its buff-coloured Do-Not-Bend envelope, and sat back in his seat.

He looked tired.

And, as Lewis knew, he was frustrated too, since necessarily the whole of the previous day had been spent on precisely those aspects of detective work that Morse disliked the most: admin, organization, procedures – with as yet little opportunity for him to indulge in the things he told himself he did the best: hypotheses, imaginings, the occasional leap into the semi-darkness.

It was now 9 a.m.

'You'd better get off to the station, Lewis. And good luck!'

'What are *you* planning to do?'

'Going down into Oxford for a haircut.'

'We've got a couple of new barbers' shops opened here. No need to—'

'I – am – going – down – into – Oxford, all right? A bit later, I'm going to meet a fellow who's an expert on ties, all right?'

'I'll give you a lift, if you like.'

'No. It only takes one of those shapely lasses in Shepherd and Woodward's about ten minutes to trim my locks – and I'm not meeting this fellow till eleven.'

'King's Arms, is it?'

'Ah! You're prepared to guess about *that*.'

'Pardon?'

'So why not have a guess about the tie? Come on!'

'I dunno.'

'Nor do *I* bloody know. That's exactly why we've got to guess, man.'

Lewis stood by the door now. It was high time he went.

'I haven't got a clue about all those posh ties you see in the posh shops in the High. For all I know he probably got it off the tie-rack in Marks and Spencer's.'

'No. I don't think so.'

'Couldn't we just cut a few corners? Perhaps we ought to put the photo in the *Oxford Mail*. We'd soon find out who he was then.'

Morse considered the possibility anew.

'Ye-es ... and if we find he's got nothing to do with the murder ...'

'We can eliminate him from inquiries.'

'Ye-es. Eliminate his marriage, too—'

'—if he's married—'

'—and ruin his children—'

'—if he's got any.'

'You just get off to the railway station, Lewis.'

Morse had had enough.

CHAPTER THIRTEEN

It is the very temple of discomfort
(John Ruskin, *The Seven Lamps of Architecture* –
referring to the building of a railway station)

AT 9.45 A.M. LEWIS was seated strategically at one of the small round tables in the refreshment area adjacent to Platform One. Intermittently an echoing loudspeaker announced arrivals or apologies for delays; and, at 9.58, recited a splendid litany of all the stops on the slow train to Reading: Radley, Culham, Appleford, Didcot Parkway, Cholsey, Goring and Streatley ...

Cholsey, yes.

Mrs Lewis was a big fan of Agatha Christie, and he'd often promised to take her to Cholsey churchyard where the great crime novelist was buried. But one way or another he'd never got round to it.

The complex was busy, with passengers constantly leaving the station through the two automatic doors to Lewis's right, to walk down the steps outside to the taxi-rank and buses for the city centre; passengers constantly entering through those same doors, making for the ticket-windows, the telephones, the Rail Information office; passengers turning left, past Lewis, in order to buy newspapers, sweets, paperbacks, from the Menzies shop – or sandwiches, cakes, coffee, from the Quick Snack counter alongside.

From where he sat, Lewis could just read one of the display screens: the 10.15 train to Paddington, it appeared, would be leaving on time – no minutes late. But he had seen no one remotely resembling the man whose photograph he'd tucked inside his copy of the *Daily Mirror*.

At 10.10 a.m. the train drew in to Platform One, and passengers were now getting on. But still there was no one to engage Lewis's attention; no one standing around impatiently as if waiting for a partner; no one sitting anxiously consulting a wrist-watch every few seconds, or walking back and forth to the exit doors and scanning the occupants of incoming taxis.

No one.

Lewis got to his feet and went out on to the platform, walking quickly along the four coaches which comprised the Turbo Express for Paddington, memorizing as best he could the face he'd so earnestly been studying that morning. But, again, he could find no one resembling the man who had once sat beside the murdered woman in a photographic booth.

No one.

It was then, at the last minute (quite literally so), that the idea occurred to him.

A young-looking ticket-collector was leaning out of one of the rear windows whilst a clinking refreshment-trolley was being lifted awkwardly aboard. Lewis showed him his ID; showed him the photograph.

'Have you ever seen either of these two on the Paddington train? Or any other train?'

The acne-faced youth examined the ID card as if suspecting, perchance, that it might be a faulty ticket; then, equally carefully, looked down at the photograph before looking up at Lewis.

Someone blew a whistle.

'Yes, I have. Seen *him*, anyway. Do you want to know his name, Sergeant? I remember it from his Railcard.'

CHAPTER FOURTEEN

A well-tied tie is the first serious step in life
(Oscar Wilde)

MORSE CAUGHT a No. 2A bus into the centre of Oxford, alighting at Carfax, thence walking down the High and entering Shepherd and Woodward's, where he descended the stairs to Gerrard's hairdressing saloon.

'The usual, sir?'

Morse was glad that he was being attended to by Gerrard himself. It was not that the proprietor was gifted with trichological skills significantly superior to those of his attractive female assistants; it was just that Gerrard had always been an ardent admirer of Thomas Hardy, and during his life had acquired an encyclopaedic knowledge of the great man's works.

'Yes, please,' answered Morse, looking morosely into the mirror at hair that had thinly drifted these last few years from ironish-grey to purish-white.

As Morse stood up to wipe the snippets of hair from his face with a hand-towel, he took out the photograph and showed it to Gerrard.

'Has he ever been in here?'

'Don't think so. Shall I ask the girls?'

Morse considered. 'No. Leave it for the present.'

'Remember the Hardy poem, Mr Morse? "The Photograph"?'

Morse did. Yet only vaguely.

'Remind me.'

'I used to have it by heart but . . .'

'We all get older,' admitted Morse.

Gerrard now scanned the pages of his extraordinary memory.

'You remember Hardy'd just burnt a photo of one of his old flames – he didn't know if she was alive or not – she was someone from the back of beyond of his life – but he felt awfully moved – as if he was putting her to death somehow – when he burned the photo . . . Just a minute . . . just a minute, I think I've got it:

Well – she knew nothing thereof did she survive,
And suffered nothing if numbered among the dead;
*   Yet – yet – if on earth alive*
Did she feel a smart, and with vague strange anguish strive?
If in heaven, did she smile at me sadly and shake her head?'

Morse felt saddened as he walked out into the High. Hardy always managed to make him feel sad. And particularly so now, since only a few days earlier he'd consigned a precious photograph to the flames: a photograph hitherto pressed between pages 88–89 of his *Collected Poems of A. E. Housman* – the photograph of a dark-haired young woman seated on a broken classical column somewhere in Crete. A woman named Ellie Smith; a woman whom he'd loved – and lost.

Morse pondered the probabilities. Had other photographs been burned or torn to little pieces since the murder of Rachel James – photographs hitherto kept in books or secret drawers?

Perhaps Lewis was right. Why not publish the photo in the *Oxford Mail*? Assuredly, there'd be hundreds of incoming calls: so many of them wrong, of course – but some few of them probably right . . .

Morse turned left into Alfred Street, and walked down the narrow cobbled lane to the junction with Blue Boar Street, where he tried the saloon-bar door of the Bear Inn.

Locked – with the opening hour displayed disappointingly as midday. It was now 11.20 a.m., and Morse felt thirsty. Perhaps he was always thirsty. That morning, though, he felt preternaturally thirsty. In fact he would gladly have swallowed a pint or two of ice-cold lager – a drink which at almost any other time would have been considered a betrayal by a real-ale addict like Morse.

He tapped lightly on the glass of the door. Tapped again. The door was opened.

A few minutes later, after offering identification, after a brief explanation of his purpose, Morse was seated with the landlord, Steven Lowbridge, at a table in the front bar.

'Would you like a coffee or something?' asked Sonya, his wife.

Morse turned round and looked towards the bar, where a row of beers paraded their pedigrees on the hand-pumps.

'Is the Burton in good nick?'

The landlord (Morse learned) had been at the Bear Inn for five years, greatly enjoying his time there. A drinking-house had been on the site since 1242, and undergraduates and undergraduettes were still coming in to crowd the comparatively small pub: from Oriel and Christ Church mostly; from Lincoln and Univ, too.

And the ties?

The Bear Inn was nationally – internationally – renowned for its ties: about five thousand of them at the last count. Showcases of ties covered the walls, covered the ceilings, in each of the bars: ties from Army regiments, sports clubs, schools and OB associations; ties from anywhere and everywhere. The collection started (Morse learned) in 1954, when the incumbent landlord had invited any customer with an interesting-looking tie to have the last three or four inches of its back-end cut off – in exchange for a couple of pints of beer. Thereafter, the snipped-off portions were put on display in cabinets, with a small square of white card affixed to each giving provenance and description.

Morse nodded encouragingly as the landlord told his well-rehearsed tale, occasionally casting a glance at the cabinet on the wall immediately opposite: Yale University Fencing Club; Kenya Police; Welsh Schoolboys' Hockey Association; Women's Land Army . . .

Ye gods!

What a multitude of ties!

Morse's glass was empty; and the landlady tentatively suggested that the Chief Inspector would perhaps enjoy a further pint?

Morse had no objection; and made his way to the Gents where, as he washed his hands, he wondered whither all the washbasin plugs in the world could have disappeared – plugs from every pub, from every hotel, from every public convenience in the land. Somewhere (Morse mused) there must surely be a prodigious pile of basin-plugs, as high as some Egyptian pyramid.

Back in the bar, Morse produced his photograph and pointed to the little patch of tie.

'Do you think there's anything like that here?'

Lowbridge looked down at the slimly striped maroon tie, shaking his head dubiously.

'Don't *think* so . . . But make yourself at home – please have a look round – for as long as you like.'

Morse experienced disappointment.

If only Lewis were there! Lewis – so wonderfully competent with this sort of thing: checking, checking, checking, the contents of the cabinets.

Help, Lewis!

But Lewis was elsewhere. And for twenty-five minutes or so, Morse moved round the two bars, with increasing fecklessness and irritation.

Nothing was matching . . .

Nothing.

'Find what you're after?' It was the darkly attractive Sonya, just returned from a shopping expedition to the Westgate Centre.

'No, sadly no,' admitted Morse. 'It's a bit like a farmer looking for a lost contact lens in a ploughed field.'

'That what you're looking for?'

Sonya Lowbridge pointed to the tie in the photograph that still lay on the table there.

Morse nodded. 'That's it.'

'But I can tell you where you can find that.'

'You can?' Morse's eyes were suddenly wide, his mouth suddenly dry.

'Yep! I was looking for a tie for Steve's birthday. And you'll find one just like that on the tie-rack in Marks and Spencer's.'

CHAPTER FIFTEEN

A Slave has but one Master; yet ambitious folk have as many masters as there are people who may be useful in bettering their position

(La Bruyère, *Characters*)

'WELL?'

Julian Storrs closed the front door behind him, hung up his dripping plastic mac, and took his wife into his arms.

'No external candidates – just the two of us.'

'That's wonderful news!' Angela Storrs moved away from her husband's brief, perfunctory embrace, and led the way into the lounge of the splendidly furnished property in Polstead Road, a thoroughfare linking the Woodstock Road with Aristotle Lane (the latter, incidentally, Morse's favourite Oxford street-name).

'Certainly not bad news, is it? If the gods just smile on us a little . . .'

'Drink?'

'I think I may have earned a small brandy.'

She poured his drink; poured herself a large Dry Martini; lit a cigarette; and sat beside him on the brown leather settee. She clinked her glass with his, and momentarily her eyes gleamed with potential triumph.

'To *you*, Sir Julian!'

'Just a minute! We've got to win the bloody thing first. No pushover, old Denis, you know: good College man – fine scholar – first-class brain—'

'Married to a second-class tart!'

Storrs shook his head with an uneasy smile.

'You're being a bit cruel, love.'

'Don't call me "love" – as if you come from Rotherham, or somewhere.'

'What's wrong with Rotherham?' He put his left arm around her shoulders, and forced an affectionate smile to his lips as he contemplated the woman he'd married just over twenty years previously – then pencil-slim, fresh-faced, and wrinkle-free.

Truth to tell, she was aging rather more quickly than most women of her years. Networks of varicose veins marred the long, still-shapely legs; and her stomach was a little distended around the waistband of the elegant trouser-suits which recently she almost invariably wore. The neck had grown rather gaunt, and there were lines and creases round her eyes. Yet the face itself was firmly featured still; and to many a man she remained an attractive woman – as she had appeared to Julian Storrs when first he had encountered her . . . in those extraordinary circumstances. And few there were who even now could easily resist the invitation of those almond eyes when after some dinner party or drinks reception she removed the dark glasses she had begun to wear so regularly.

Having swiftly swallowed her Martini, Angela Storrs got to her feet and poured herself another – her husband making no demur. In fact, he was quite happy when she decided to indulge her more than occasional craving for alcohol, since then she would usually go to bed, go to sleep, and reawaken in a far more pleasant frame of mind.

'What are your chances – honestly?'

'Hope is a Christian virtue, you know that.'

'Christ! Can't you think of anything better to say than that?'

He was silent awhile. 'It means a lot to you, Angela, doesn't it?'

'It means a lot to you, too,' she replied, allowing her slow words to take their full effect. 'It *does*, doesn't it?'

'Yes,' he replied softly, 'it means almost everything to me.'

Angela got up and poured herself another Martini.

'I'm glad you said that. You know why? Because it doesn't just mean *almost* everything to me – it means *literally* everything. I want to be the Master's Wife, Julian. I want to be Lady Storrs! Do you understand how much I want that?'

'Yes . . . yes, I think I do.'

'So . . . so if we have to engage in any "dirty-tricks" business . . .'

'What d'you mean?'

'Nothing specific.'

'What d'you mean?' he repeated.

'As I say . . .'

'Come on! Tell me!'

'Well, let's say if it became known in the College that Shelly Cornford was an insatiable nymphomaniac . . . ?'

'That just isn't *fair*!'

Angela Storrs got to her feet and drained the last drop of her third drink.

'Who said it *was*?'

'Where are you going?'

'Upstairs, for a lie-down, if you don't object. I'd had a few before you got back – hadn't you noticed? But I don't suppose so, no. You haven't really noticed me much at all recently, have you?'

'What's that supposed to mean?'

But she was already leaving the room, and seemed not to hear.

Storrs took another small sip of his brandy, and pulled the copy of the previous evening's *Oxford Mail* from the lower shelf of the coffee-table, its front-page headline staring at him again:

MURDER AT KIDLINGTON
Woman Shot Through Kitchen Window

*

'What did you tell Denis?'

'He's got a tutorial, anyway. I just said I'd be out shopping.'

'He told you about the College Meeting?'

She nodded.

'You pleased?'

'Uh, uh!'

'It'll be a bit of a nerve-racking time for you.'

'You should know!'

'Only a month of it, though.'

'What d'you think his chances are?'

'Difficult to say.'

'Will *you* vote for him?'

'I don't have a vote.'

'Unless it's a tie.'

'Agreed. But that's unlikely, they tell me. Arithmetically quite impossible – if all twenty-three Fellows decide to vote.'

'So you won't really have much say in things at all.'

'Oh, I wouldn't say that. I'll be a bit surprised if one or two of the Fellows don't ask me for a little advice about, er, about their choice.'

'And?'

'And I shall try to be helpful.'

'To Denis, you mean?'

'Now I didn't *say* that, did I?'

The great cooling-towers of Didcot power-station loomed into view on the left, and for a while little more was said as the two of them continued the drive south along the A34, before turning off, just before the Ridgeway, towards the charming little village of West Ilsley.

'I feel I'm letting poor old Denis down a bit,' he said, as the dark blue Daimler pulled up in front of the village pub.

'Don't you think *I* do?' she snapped. 'But I don't keep on about it.'

At the bar, he ordered a dry white wine for Shelly Cornford and a pint of Old Speckled Hen for himself; and the pair of them studied the Egon Ronay menu chalked up on a blackboard before making their choices, and sitting down at a window-table over-looking the sodden village green.

'Do you think we should stop meeting?' He asked it quietly.

She appeared to consider the question more as an exercise in logical evaluation than as any emotional dilemma.

'I don't want that to happen.'

She brushed the back of her right wrist down the front of his dark grey suit.

'Pity we've ordered lunch,' he said quietly.

'We can always give it a miss.'

'Where shall we go?'

'Before we go anywhere, I shall want *you* to do something for *me*.'

'You mean something for Denis?'

She nodded decisively.

'I can't really promise you too much, you know that.'

She looked swiftly around the tables there, before moving her lips to his ear. '*I* can, though. I can promise you everything, Clixby,' she whispered.

From his room in College, Denis Cornford had rung Shelly briefly just before 11 a.m. She'd be out later, as she'd mentioned, but he wanted to tell her about the College Meeting as soon as possible.

He told her.

He was pleased – she could sense that.

She was pleased – he could sense that.

Cornford had half an hour to spare before his next tutorial with a very bright first-year undergraduette from Nottingham who possessed one of the most astonishingly retentive memories he had ever encountered, and a pair of the loveliest legs that had ever folded themselves opposite him. Yet he experienced not even the mildest of erotic daydreams as now, briefly, he thought about her.

He walked over to the White Horse, the narrow pub between the two Blackwell's shops just opposite the Sheldonian; and soon he was sipping a large Glenmorangie, and slowly coming to terms with the prospect that in a month's time he might well be the Master of Lonsdale College. By nature a diffident man, he was for some curious reason beginning to feel a little more confident about his chances. Life was a funny business – and the favourite often failed to win the Derby, did it not?

Yes, odd things were likely to happen in life.

Against all the odds, as it were.

His black-stockinged student was sitting cross-legged on the wooden steps outside his room, getting to her feet as soon as she saw him. Being with Cornford, talking with him for an hour every week – that had become the highlight of her time at Oxford. But History was the great fascination in his life – not her.

She knew that.

CHAPTER SIXTEEN

Prosōpagnoia (n.): the failure of any person to recognize the face of any other person, howsoever recently the aforementioned persons may have mingled in each other's company
(*Small's Enlarged English Dictionary*, 13th Edition, 1806)

FROM OXFORD RAILWAY station, at 10.20 a.m., Lewis had tried to ring Morse at HQ. But to no avail. The dramatic news would have to wait awhile, and at least Lewis now had ample time to execute his second order of the day.

There had been just the two of them at the Oxford Physiotherapy Centre – although 'Centre' seemed a rather grandiloquent description of the ground-floor premises of the large, detached red-brick house halfway down the Woodstock Road ('1901' showing on the black drainpipe): the small office, off the spacious foyer; the single treatment room, to the right, its two beds separated by mobile wooden screens; and an inappropriately luxurious loo, to the left.

Rachel James's distressed partner, a plain-featured, muscular divorcée in her mid-forties, could apparently throw little or no light on the recent tragedy. Each of them a fully qualified physiotherapist, they had gone freelance after a difference of opinion with the Hospital Trust, and two years earlier had decided to join forces and form their own private practice: women for the most part, troubled with ankles and knees and elbows and shoulders. The venture had been fairly successful, although they would have welcomed a few more clients – especially Rachel, perhaps, who (as Lewis learned for a second time) had been wading deeper and deeper into negative equity.

Boyfriends? – Lewis had ventured.

Well, she was attractive – face, figure – and doubtless there had been a good many admirers. But no specific beau; no one that Rachel spoke of as anyone special; no incoming calls on the office phone, for example.

'That hers?' Lewis had asked.

'Yes.'

Lewis took down a white coat from its hook behind the door and looked at the oval badge: CHARTERED SOCIETY OF

PHYSIOTHERAPY printed round a yellow crest. He felt inside the stiffly starched pockets.

Nothing.

Not even Morse (Lewis allowed the thought) could have made much of *that*.

Each of the two women had a personal drawer in the office desk, and Lewis looked carefully through the items which Rachel had kept at hand during her own working hours: lipstick; lip-salve; powder-compact; deodorant stick; a small packet of tissues; two Biros, blue and red; a yellow pencil; a pocket English dictionary (OUP); and a library book. Nothing else. No personal diary; no letters.

Again Lewis felt (though wrongly this time) that Morse would have shared his disappointment.

As for Morse, he had called in at his bachelor flat in North Oxford before returning to Police HQ. Always, after a haircut, he went through the ritual of washing his hair – and changing his shirt, upon which even a few stray hairs left clinging seemed able to effect an intense irritation on what, as he told himself (and others), was a particularly sensitive skin.

When he finally returned to HQ he found Lewis already back from his missions.

'You're looking younger, sir.'

'No, you're wrong. I reckon this case has put years on me already.'

'I meant the haircut.'

'Ah, yes. Rather nicely done, isn't it?'

'You had a good morning, sir – apart from the haircut?'

'Well, you know – er – satisfactory. What about you?'

Lewis smiled happily.

'Do you want the good news first or the bad news?'

'The bad news.'

'Well, not "bad" – just not "news" at all, really. I don't think we're going to get many leads from her workplace. In fact I don't think we're going to get any.' And Lewis proceeded to give an account of his visit to the Oxford Physiotherapy Centre.

'What time did she get there every morning?'

Lewis consulted his notes. 'Five past, ten past eight – about then. Bit early. But if she left it much later she'd hit the heavy Kidlington traffic down into Oxford, wouldn't she?'

'Mm ... The first treatments don't begin till quarter to nine, you say.'

'Or nine o'clock.'

'What did she do before the place opened?'

'Dunno.'

'*Read*, Lewis!'

'Well, like I said, there was a library book in her drawer.'

'What was it?'

'I didn't make a note.'

'Can't you remember?'

Ye-es, Lewis thought he could. Yes!

'Book called *The Masters*, sir – by P. C. Snow.'

Morse laughed and shook his head.

'He wasn't a bloody police constable, Lewis! You mean C. P. Snow.'

'Sorry, sir.'

'Interesting, though.'

'In what way?'

But Morse ignored the question.

'*When* did she get it from the library?'

'How do I know?'

'You just,' said Morse slowly, sarcastically, 'take fourteen days from the date printed for the book's return, which you could have found, if you'd looked, by gently opening the front cover.'

'Perhaps they let you have three weeks – at the library she borrowed it from.'

'And which library was that?'

Somehow Lewis managed to maintain his good humour.

'Well, at least I can give you a very straight answer to that: I haven't the faintest idea.'

'And what's the good news?'

This time, it was Lewis's turn to make a slow, impressive pronouncement:

'I know who the fellow is – the fellow in the photo.'

'You do?' Morse looked surprised. 'You mean he turned up at the station?'

'In a way, I suppose he did, yes. There was no one like him standing around waiting for his girlfriend. But I had a word with this ticket-collector – young chap who's only been on the job for a few weeks. And he recognized him straightaway. He'd asked to look at his rail pass and he remembered him because he got a bit shirty with him – and probably because of that he remembered his name as well.'

'A veritable plethora of pronouns, Lewis! Do you know how many *he*'s and *him*'s and *his*'s you've just used?'

'No. But I know *one* thing – he told me his name!' replied Lewis, happily adding a further couple of potentially confusing pronouns to his earlier tally. 'His name's *Julian Storrs*.'

For many seconds Morse sat completely motionless, feeling the familiar tingling across his shoulders. He picked up his silver Parker pen and wrote some letters on the blotting pad in front of him. Then, in a whispered voice, he spoke:

'*I know him, Lewis.*'

'You didn't recognize him, though—?'

'Most people,' interrupted Morse, 'as they get older, can't remember names. For them "A name is troublesome" – anagram – seven letters – what's that?'

'"Amnesia"?'

'Well done! I'm all right on names, usually. But as I get older it's *faces* I can't recall. And there's a splendid word for this business of not being able to recognize familiar faces—'

'"Pro-sop-a-something", isn't it?'

Morse appeared almost shell-shocked as he looked across at his sergeant. 'How in heaven's name . . . ?'

'Well, as you know, sir, I didn't do all that marvellously at school – as I told you, we didn't even have a school tie – but I was ever so good at one thing' (a glance at the blotting pad) 'I was best in the class at reading things upside-down.'

CHAPTER SEVENTEEN

Facing the media is more difficult than bathing a leper
(Mother Teresa of Calcutta)

THERE HAD BEEN little difficulty in finding out information on Julian Charles Storrs – a man to whom Morse (as he now remembered) had been introduced only a few months previously at an exhibition of Thesiger's desert photography in the Pitt Rivers Museum. But Morse said nothing of this to Lewis as the pair of them sat together that same evening in Kidlington HQ;

said nothing either of his discovery that the tie whose provenance he had so earnestly sought was readily available from any Marks & Spencer's store, priced £6.99.

'We shall have to see this fellow Storrs soon, sir.'

'I'm sure we shall, yes. But we've got nothing against him, have we? It's not a criminal offence to get photographed with some attractive woman ... Interesting, though, that she was reading *The Masters*.'

'I've never read it, sir.'

'It's about the internal shenanigans in a Cambridge College when the Master dies. And recently I read in the *University Gazette* that the present Master of Lonsdale is about to hang up his mortar-board – see what I mean?'

'I think I do,' lied Lewis.

'Storrs is a Fellow at Lonsdale – the Senior Fellow, I think. So if he suggested she might be interested in reading that book ...'

'Doesn't add up to much, though, does it? It's *motive* we've got to look for. Bottom of everything – motive is.'

Morse nodded. 'But perhaps it does add up a bit,' he added quietly. 'If he wants the top job badly enough – and if she reminded him she could go and queer his pitch ...'

'Kiss-and-tell sort of thing?'

'Kiss-and-*not*-tell, if the price was right.'

'Blackmail?' suggested Lewis.

'She'd have letters.'

'The postcard.'

'Photographs.'

'*One* photograph.'

'Hotel records. Somebody would use a credit card, and it wouldn't be *her*.'

'He'd probably pay by cash.'

'You're not trying to *help* me by any chance, are you, Lewis?'

'All I'm trying to do is be honest about what we've got – which isn't much. I agree with you, though: it wouldn't have been *her* money. Not exactly rolling in it, that's for sure. Must have been a biggish lay-out – setting up the practice, equipment, rent, and everything. And she'd got a mortgage on her own place, and a car to run.'

Yes, a car. Morse, who never took the slightest interest in any car except his own, visualized again the white Mini which had been parked outside Number 17.

'Perhaps you ought to look a bit more carefully at that car, Lewis.'

'Already have. Log-book in the glove-compartment, road atlas under the passenger seat, fire-extinguisher under the back seat—'

'No drugs or pornography in the boot?'

'No. Just a wheel-brace and a Labour Party poster.'

Lewis looked at his watch: 8.35 p.m. It had been a long day, and he felt very tired. And so, by the look of him, did his chief. He got to his feet.

'Oh, and two cassettes: Ella Fitzgerald and a Mozart thing.'

'*Thing?*'

'Clarinet thing, yes.'

'Concerto or Quintet, was it?'

Blessedly, before Lewis could answer (for he had no answer), the phone rang.

Chief Superintendent Strange.

'Morse? In your office? I almost rang the Red Lion.'

'How can I help, sir?' asked Morse wearily.

'TV – that's how you can help. BBC want you for the *Nine O'Clock News* and ITV for *News at Ten*. One of the crews is here now.'

'I've already told 'em all we know.'

'Well, you'd better think of something else, hadn't you? This isn't just a murder, Morse. This is a *PR exercise.*'

CHAPTER EIGHTEEN
Thursday, 22 February

For example, in such enumerations as 'French, German, Italian and Spanish', the two commas take the place of 'ands'; there is no comma after 'Italian', because, with 'and', it would be otiose. There are, however, some who favour putting one there, arguing that, since it may sometimes be needed to avoid any ambiguity, it may as well be used always for the sake of uniformity

(Fowler, *Modern English Usage*)

JUST AFTER LUNCHTIME on Thursday, Morse found himself once again wandering aimlessly around Number 17 Bloxham

Drive, a vague, niggling instinct suggesting to him that earlier he'd missed something of importance there.

But he was beginning to doubt it.

In the (now-cleared) kitchen, he switched on the wireless, finding it attuned to Radio 4. Had it been *on* when the police had first arrived? Had she been listening to the *Today* programme when just for a second, perhaps, she'd looked down at the gush of blood that had spurted over the front of her nightclothes?

So what if she had been? – Morse asked himself, conscious that he was getting nowhere.

In the front living-room, he looked again along the single shelf of paperbacks. Women novelists, mostly: Jackie Collins, Jilly Cooper, Danielle Steel, Sue Townsend . . . He read four or five of the authors' opening sentences, without once being instantly hooked, and was about to leave when he noticed Craig Raine's *A Choice of Kipling's Prose* – its white spine completely uncreased, as if it had been a very recent purchase. Or a gift? Morse withdrew the book and flicked through some of the short stories that once had meant – still meant – so very much to him. 'They' was there, although Morse confessed to himself that he had never really understood its meaning. But genius? Christ, ah! And 'On Green-how Hill'; and 'Love-o'-Women' – the latter (Morse was adamant about it) the greatest short story in the English language. He looked at the title page: no words *to* anyone; *from* anyone. Then, remembering a book he'd once received from a lovely, lost girl, he turned to the inside of the back cover: and there, in the bottom right-hand corner, he saw the pencilled capitals: FOR R FROM J – RML.

'Remember My Love.'

It could have been anyone though – so many names beginning with 'J': Jack, James, Jason, Jasper, Jeremy, John, Joseph, Julian . . .

So what?

Anyway, these days, Morse, it could have been a woman, could it not?

Upstairs, in the front bedroom, he looked down at the double bed that almost monopolized the room, and noted again the two indented pillows, one atop the other, in their Oxford-blue pillowcases, whereon for the very last time Rachel James had laid her pretty head. The winter duvet, in matching blue, was still turned back as she had left it, the under-sheet only lightly creased.

Nor was it a bed (of this Morse felt certain) wherein the murdered woman had spent the last night of her life in passionate love-making. Better, perhaps, if she had . . .

Standing on the bedside table was a glass of stale-looking water, beside which lay a pair of bluish earrings whose stones (Morse suspected) had never been fashioned from earth's more precious store.

But the Chief Inspector was forming something of a picture, so he thought.

Picture . . . Pictures . . .

Two framed pictures only on the bedroom walls: the statutory Monet; and one of Gustav Klimt's gold-patterned compositions. Plenty of posters and stickers, though: anti deer-hunting; anti export of live animals; anti French nuclear tests; pro the NHS; pro the whales; pro legalized abortion. About par for the course at her age, thought Morse. Or at *his* age, come to think of it.

He pulled the side of the curtains slightly away from the wall, and briefly surveyed the scene below. An almost reverent hush now seemed to have settled upon Rachel's side of the street. One uniformed policeman stood at the front gate – but only the one – talking to a representative of the Press – but only the one: the one who had lived next door to the murdered woman, at Number 15; the one with the pony-tail; the one whom Morse would have to interview so very soon; the one he ought already to have interviewed.

Then, from the window, he saw his colleague, Sergeant Lewis, getting out of a marked police car; and thoughtfully he walked down the stairs. Odd – very odd, really – that with all those stickers around the bedroom, the one for the party the more likely (surely?) to further those advertised causes had been left in the boot of her car, where earlier Lewis had found it. Why hadn't she put it up, as so many other householders in the terrace had done, in one of her upper or lower windows?

Aware that whatever had been worrying him had still not been identified, Morse turned the Yale lock to admit Lewis, the latter carrying the lunchtime edition of the *Oxford Mail*.

'I reckon it's about time we interviewed *him*,' began Lewis, pointing through the closed door.

'All in good time,' agreed Morse, taking the newspaper where, as on the previous two days, the murder still figured on page one, although no longer as the lead story.

POLICE PUZZLED BY KIDLINGTON KILLING

THE BRUTAL murder of the physiotherapist Rachel James, which has caused such a stir in the local community, has left the police baffled, according to Inspector Morse of the Thames Valley CID.

The murdered woman was seen as a quietly unobtrusive member of the community with no obvious enemies, and as yet the police have been unable to find any plausible motive for her murder.

Neighbours have been swift to pay their tributes. Mrs Emily Jacobs, who waved a greeting just before Rachel was murdered, said she was a friendly, pleasant resident who would be sadly missed.

Similar tributes were paid by other local inhabitants who are finding it difficult to come to terms with their neighbourhood being the scene of such a terrible murder and a centre of interest for the national media.

For the present, however, Bloxham Drive has been sealed off to everyone except local residents, official reporters and a team of police officers carefully searching the environs of No. 17.

But it seems inevitable that the street will soon be a magnet for sightseers, drawn by a ghoulish if natural curiosity, once police activity is scaled down and restrictions are lifted.

A grim-faced Sergeant Lewis, after once again examining the white Mini still parked outside the property, would make no comment other than confirming that various leads were being followed.

Rachel's parents, who live in Devon, have identified the body as that of their daughter, and a bouquet of white lilies bearing the simple inscription 'To our darling daughter' lies in cellophaned wrapping beside the front gate of No. 17.

The tragedy has cast a dark cloud over the voting taking place today for the election of a councillor to replace Terry Burgess who died late last year following a heart attack.

'Nicely written,' conceded Morse. 'Bit pretentious, perhaps . . . and I do wish they'd all stop *demoting* me!'

'No mistakes?'

Morse eyed his sergeant sharply. 'Have I missed something?'

Lewis said nothing, smiling inexplicably, as Morse read through the article again.

'Well, I'd've put a comma after "reporters" myself. Incidentally, do you know what such a comma's called?'

'Remind me.'

'The "Oxford Comma".'

'Of course.'

'Why are you grinning?'

'That's just it, sir. It's that "grim-faced". Should be "grin-faced", shouldn't it? You see, the missus rang me up half an hour ago: she's won fifty pounds on the Premium Bonds. Bond, really. She's only got one of 'em.'

'Congratulations!'

'Thank you, sir.'

For a final time Morse looked through the article, wondering whether the seventeenth word from the beginning and the seventeenth word from the end had anything to do with the number of the house in which Rachel James had been murdered. Probably not. (Morse's life was bestrewn with coincidences.)

'Is that pony-tailed ponce still out there?' he asked suddenly.

Lewis looked out of the front window.

'No, sir. He's gone.'

'Let's hope he's gone to one of those new barbers' shops you were telling me about.' (Morse's views were beset with prejudices.)

CHAPTER NINETEEN

She is disturbed
When the phone rings at 5 a.m.
And with such urgency
Aware that one of these calls
Will summon her to witness another death
Commanding more words than she
The outside observer can provide – and yet
Note-pad poised and ready
She picks up the receiver

(Helen Peacocke, *Ace Reporter*)

AT 2.25 P.M. THAT same day, Morse got into the maroon Jaguar and after looking at his wrist-watch drove off. First, down to the Cutteslowe Roundabout, thence straight over and along the Banbury Road to the Martyrs' Memorial, where he turned right into Beaumont Street, along Park End Street, and out under the railway bridge into Botley Road, where just beyond the river bridge he turned left into the Osney Industrial Estate.

There was, in fact, one vacant space in the limited parking-lots beside the main reception area to Oxford City and County Newspapers; but Morse pretended not to notice it. Instead he asked the girl at the reception desk for the open-sesame to the large staff car-park, and was soon watching the black-and-white barrier lift as he inserted a white plastic card into some electronic contraption there. Back in reception, the same young girl retrieved the precious ticket before giving Morse a VISITOR badge, and directing him down a corridor alongside, on his left, a vast open-plan complex, where hundreds of newspaper personnel appeared too preoccupied to notice the 'Visitor'.

Owens (as Morse discovered) was one of the few employees granted some independent square-footage there, his small office hived off by wood-and-glass partitions.

'You live, er, she lived next door, I'm told,' began Morse awkwardly.

Owens nodded.

'Bit of luck, I suppose, in a way – for a reporter, I mean?'

'For me, yes. Not much luck for her, though, was it?'

'How did you first hear about it? You seem to have been on the scene pretty quickly, sir.'

'Della rang me. She lives in the Drive – Number 1. She'd seen me leave for work.'

'What time was that?'

'Must have been . . . ten to seven, five to seven?'

'You usually leave about then?'

'I do now, yes. For the past year or so we've been working a fair amount of flexi-time and, well, the earlier I leave home the quicker I'm here. Especially in term-time when—' Owens looked shrewdly across his desk at Morse. 'But you know as much as I do about the morning traffic from Kidlington to Oxford.'

'Not really. I'm normally going the other way – North Oxford to Kidlington.'

'Much more sensible.'

'Yes . . .'

Clearly Owens was going to be more of a heavyweight than he'd expected, and Morse paused awhile to take his bearings. He'd made a note only a few minutes since of exactly how long the same distance had taken him, from Bloxham Drive to Osney Mead. And even with quite a lot of early afternoon traffic about – even with a couple of lights against him – he'd done the journey in fourteen and a half minutes.

'So you'd get here at about . . . about *when*, Mr Owens?'

The reporter shrugged his shoulders. 'Quarter past? Twenty past? Usually about then.'

A nucleus of suspicion was beginning to form in Morse's brain as he sensed that Owens was perhaps exaggerating the length of time it had taken him to reach work that Monday morning. If he *had* left at, say, ten minutes to seven, he could well have been in the car park at – what? – seven o'clock? With a bit of luck? So why . . . why had Owens suggested quarter past – even twenty past?

'You can't be more precise?'

Again Morse felt the man's shrewd eyes upon him.

'You mean the later I got here the less likely I am to be a suspect?'

'You realize how important times are, Mr Owens – a sequence of times – in any murder inquiry like this?'

'Oh yes, I know it as well as you do, Inspector. I've covered quite a few murders in my time . . . So . . . so why don't you ask Della what time she saw me leave? Della Cecil, that is, at Number 1. She'll probably remember better than me. And as for getting here . . . well, that'll be fairly easy to check. Did you know that?'

Owens took a small white rectangular card from his wallet, with a number printed across the top – 008 14922 – and continued: 'I push that in the thing there and the whatsit goes up and something somewhere records the time I get into the car park.'

Clearly the broad-faced, heavy-jowled reporter had about as much specialist knowledge of voodoo-technology as Morse, and the latter switched the thrust of his questions.

'This woman who saw you leave, I shall have to see her – you realize that?'

'You wouldn't be doing your job if you didn't. Cigarette, Inspector?'

'Er, no, no thanks. Well, er, perhaps I will, yes. Thank you. This woman, as I say, do you know her well?'

'Only twenty houses in the Drive, Inspector. You get to know most people, after a while.'

'You never became, you know, more friendly? Took her out? Drink? Meal?'

'Why do you ask that?'

'I've just got to find out as much as I can about everybody there, that's all. Otherwise, as you say, I wouldn't be doing my job, would I, Mr Owens?'

'We've had a few dates, yes – usually at the local.'

'Which is?'

'The Bull and Swan.'

'Ah, "Brakspear", "Bass", "Bishop's Finger" . . .'

'I wouldn't know. I'm a lager man myself.'

'I see,' said a sour-faced Morse. Then, after a pause, 'What about Rachel James? Did you know her well?'

'She lived next *door*, dammit! Course I knew her fairly well.'

'Did you ever go inside her house?'

Owens appeared to consider the question carefully. 'Just the twice, if I've got it right. Once when I had a few people in for a meal and I couldn't find a corkscrew and I knocked on her back door and she asked me in, because it was pissing the proverbials, while she looked around for hers. The other time was one hot day last summer when I was mowing the grass at the back and she was hanging out her smalls and I asked her if she wanted me to do her patch and she said she'd be grateful, and when I'd done it she asked me if I'd like a glass of something and we had a drink together in the kitchen there.'

'Lager, I suppose.'

'Orangeade.'

Orangeade, like water, had never played any significant rôle in Morse's diet, but he suddenly realized that at that moment he would have willingly drunk a pint of anything, so long as it was ice-cold.

Even lager.

'It was a hot day, you say?'

'Boiling.'

'What was she wearing?'

'Not much.'

'She was an attractive girl, wasn't she?'

'To me? I'm always going to be attracted to a woman with not much on. And, as I remember, most of what she'd got on that day was mostly off, if you follow me.'

'So she'd have a lot of boyfriends?'

'She was the sort of woman men would lust after, yes.'

'Did you?'

'Let's put it this way, Inspector. If she'd invited me to bed that afternoon, I'd've sprinted up the stairs.'

'But she didn't invite you?'

'No.'

'Did she invite other men?'

'I doubt it. Not in Bloxham Drive, anyway. We don't just have Neighbourhood Watch here; we've got a continuous Nosey-Parker Surveillance Scheme.'

'Even in the early morning?'

'As I told you, somebody saw me go to work on Monday morning.'

'You think others may have done?'

'Bloody sure they did!'

Morse switched tack again. 'You wouldn't remember – recognize – any of her occasional boyfriends?'

'No.'

'Have you heard of a man called Julian Storrs?'

'Yes.'

'You know him?'

'Not really, no. But he's from Lonsdale, and I interviewed him for the *Oxford Mail* last year – December, I think it was – when he gave the annual Pitt Rivers Lecture. On Captain Cook, as I recall. I'd never realized how much the natives hated that fellow's guts – you know, in the Sandwich Islands or somewhere.'

'I forget,' said Morse, as if at some point in his life he *had* known . . .

At his local grammar school, the young Morse had been presented with a choice of the 3 Gs: Greek, Geography, or German. And since Morse had joined the Greek option, his knowledge of geography had ever been fatally flawed. Indeed, it was only in his late twenties that he had discovered that the Balkan States and the Baltic States were not synonymous. Yet about Captain Cook's voyages Morse should (as we shall see) have known at least a little – *did* know a little – since his father had adopted that renowned British navigator, explorer, and cartographer as his greatest hero in life – unlike (it seemed) the natives of those 'Sandwich Islands or somewhere'. . .

'You never saw Mr Storrs in Bloxham Drive?'

In their sockets, Owens' eyes shot from bottom left to top right, like those of a deer that has suddenly sniffed a predator.

'Never. Why?'

'Because' (Morse leaned forward a few inches as he summoned up all his powers of creative ingenuity) 'because someone in the Drive – this is absolutely confidential, sir! – says that he was seen, fairly recently, going into, er, another house there.'

'*Which* house?' Owens' voice was suddenly sharp.

Morse held up his right hand and got to his feet. 'Just a piece of gossip, like as not. But we've got to check out every lead, you know that.'

Owens remained silent.

'You've always been a journalist?'

'Yes.'

'Which papers . . . ?'

'I started in London.'

'Whereabouts?'

'Soho – around there.'

'When was that?'

'Mid-seventies.'

'Wasn't that when Soho was full of sex clubs and striptease joints?'

'*And* more. Gets a bit boring, all that stuff though, after a time.'

'Yes. So they tell me.'

'I read your piece today in the *Oxford Mail*,' said Morse as the two men walked towards reception. 'You write well.'

'Thank you.'

'I can't help remembering you said "comparatively" crime-free area.'

'That was in yesterday's.'

'Oh.'

'Well . . . we've only had one burglary this last year, and we've had no joy-riders around since the council put the sleeping-policemen in. We still get a bit of mindless vandalism, of course – you'll have seen the young trees we tried to plant round the back. And litter – litter's always a problem – and graffiti . . . And someone recently unscrewed most of the latches on the back gates – you know, the things that click as the gates shut.'

'I didn't know there was a market for those,' muttered Morse.

'And you're wasting your time if you put up a name for your house, or something like that. I put a little notice on my front gate. Lasted exactly eight days. Know what it was?'

Morse glanced back at the corporate workforce seated in front of VDU screens at desks cluttered with in-trays, out-trays, file-cases, handbooks, and copy being corrected and cosseted before inclusion in forthcoming editions of Oxford's own *Times, Mail, Journal, Star* . . .

'"No Free Newspapers"?' he suggested *sotto voce*.

Morse handed in his Visitor badge at reception.

'You'll need to give me another thing to get out with.'

'No. The barrier lifts automatically when you leave.'

'So once you're in . . .'

She smiled. 'You're in! It's just that we used to get quite a few cars from the Industrial Estate trying it on.'

Morse turned left into the Botley Road and drove along to the Ring-Road junction where he took the northbound A34, coming off at the Pear Tree Roundabout, and thence driving rather too quickly up the last stretch to Kidlington HQ – where he looked at his wrist-watch again.

Nine and a half minutes.

Only nine and a half minutes.

CHAPTER TWENTY

It is a capital mistake to theorize before one has data
(Conan Doyle, *Scandal in Bohemia*)

As MORSE CLIMBED the stairs to Lewis's office he was experiencing a deep ache in each of his calves.

'Hardest work I've done today, that!' he admitted as, panting slightly, he flopped into a chair.

'Interview go OK, sir?'

'Owens? I wouldn't trust that fellow as far as I could kick him.'

'Which wouldn't be too far, in your present state of health.'

'Genuine journalist he may be – but he's a phoney witness, take it from me!'

'Before you go on, sir, we've got the preliminary post-mortem report here.'

'You've read it through?'

'Tried to. Bullet-entry in the left sub-mandibular—'

'Lew-is! Spare me the details! She was shot through the window, through the blind, in the morning twilight. You mustn't expect much accuracy about the thing! You've been watching too many old cowboy films where they mow down the baddies at hundreds of yards.'

'Distance of about eighteen inches to two feet, that's what it says, judging from—'

'What's it say about the *time*?'

'She's not quite so specific there.'

'Why the hell not? We told her *exactly* when the woman was shot!'

'Dr Hobson says the temperature in the kitchen that morning wasn't much above zero.'

'Economizing everywhere, our Rachel,' said Morse rather sadly.

'And it seems you get this sort of "refrigeration factor"—'

'In which we are not particularly interested, Lewis, because we *know*—' Morse suddenly stopped. 'Unless . . . unless our distinguished pathologist is suggesting that Rachel may have been murdered just a *little* earlier than we've been assuming.'

'I don't think she's trying to suggest anything, sir. Just giving us the facts as far as she sees them.'

'I suppose so.'

'Do you want to read the report?'

'I shall have to, shan't I, if *you* can't understand it?'

'I didn't say that—'

But again Morse interrupted him, almost eagerly now recounting his interview with Owens . . .

'. . . So don't you see, Lewis? *He* could have done it. Quarter of an hour it took me, to the newspaper offices via Banbury Road;

ten minutes back via the Ring Road. So if he left home about ten to seven – clocked into the car park at seven, say – hardly anything on the roads – then drove straight *out* of the car park – there's no clocking out there – that's the system they have – drove hell for leather back to Bloxham Close—'

'*Drive*, sir.'

'—parks his car up on the road behind the houses' (Morse switched now to the vivid present tense) ' – goes through the vandalized fence there – down the grass slope – taps on her window – the thin blinds still drawn' (Morse's eyes seemed almost mesmerized) ' – sees her profile more clearly as she gets nearer – for a second or two scrutinizes the dark outline at the gas-lit window—'

'It's electric there.'

'—then he fires through the window into her face – and hits her just below the jaw.'

Lewis nodded this time. 'The sub-mandibular bit, you're right about that.'

'Then he goes up the bank again – gets in his car – back to Osney Mead. But he daren't go into the car park again – of course not! So he leaves his car somewhere near, and goes into the office from the rear of the car park. Nobody much there to observe his comings and goings – most of the people get in there about eightish, so I learn. *Quod erat demonstrandum!* I know you're going to ask me what his motive was, and I don't know. But this time we've found the murderer before we've found the motive. Not grumbling too much about that, are you?'

'Yes! It just won't hold water.'

'And why's that?'

'There's this woman from Number 1, for a start. Miss Cecil—'

'Della – Owens called her Della.'

'She saw him leave, didn't she? About seven o'clock? That's why she knew he'd be at his desk when she rang him as soon as she saw the police arrive – just after eight.'

'One hour – one whole hour! You can do a lot in an hour.'

'You still can't put a quart into a pint pot.'

'We've now gone metric, by the way, Lewis. Look, what if they're in it *together* – have you thought of that? Owens is carrying a torch for that Miss Cecil, believe me! When I happened to mention Julian Storrs—'

'You didn't do that, surely?'

'—and when I said he'd been seen knocking at one of the other doors there—'

'But nobody—'

'—he was jealous, Lewis! And there are only two houses in the Close' (Lewis gave up the struggle) 'occupied by nubile young women: Number 17 and Number 1, Miss James and Miss Cecil, agreed?'

'I thought you just said they were in it *together*.'

'I said they might be, that's all. I'm just thinking aloud, for Christ's sake! One of us has got to think. And I'm a bit weary and I'm much underbeered. So give me a chance!'

Lewis waited a few seconds. Then:

'Is it my turn to speak, sir?'

Morse nodded weakly, contemplating the threadbare state of Lewis's carpet.

'I don't know whether you've been down the Botley Road in the morning recently – even in the fairly early morning – but it's one of the worst bottlenecks in Oxford. You drove there and back in mid-afternoon, didn't you? But you want Owens to do three journeys between Kidlington and Osney Mead. First he drives to work – perhaps fairly quickly, agreed. Twenty minutes, say? He drives back – a bit quicker? Quarter of an hour, say. He parks his car somewhere – it's not going to be in Bloxham Drive, though. He murders his next-door neighbour. Drives back into Oxford after that – another twenty, twenty-five minutes *at least* now. Finds a parking space – and this time it's not going to be in the car park, as you say. Walks or runs to his office, not going in the front door, either – for obvious reasons. Gets into his office and is sitting there at his desk when his girlfriend – if you're right about that – rings him up and tells him he'll be in for a bit of a scoop if he gets out again to Bloxham Drive. It's just about possible, sir, if *all* the lights are with him *every* time, if almost everybody's decided to walk to work that morning. But it's very improbable even then. And remember it's *Monday* morning – the busiest morning of the week in Oxford.'

Morse looked hurt.

'You still think it's just *about* possible?'

Lewis considered the question again.

'No, sir. I know you always like to think that most murders are committed by next-door neighbours or husbands or wives—'

'But what if this woman at Number 1 isn't telling us the truth?'

queried Morse. 'What if she never made that phone-call at all? What if she's in it with him? What if she's more than willing to provide him with a nice little alibi? You see, you're probably right about the time-scale of things. He probably *wouldn't* have had time to get back here to Kidlington, commit the murder, and then return to the office and be sitting quietly at his desk when she rang him.'

'So?'

'So she's lying. Just like *he* is! He got back here – easy! – murdered Rachel James – and *stayed* here, duly putting in an appearance as the very first reporter on the scene!'

'I'm sorry, sir, but she *isn't* lying, not about this. I don't know what you think the rest of us have been doing since Monday morning but we've done quite a bit of checking up already. And she's *not* lying about the phone-call to Owens' office. One of the lads went along to BT and confirmed it. The call was monitored and it'll be listed on the itemized telephone bill of the subscriber – Number 1 Bloxham Drive!'

'Does it give the *time*?'

Lewis appeared slightly uneasy. 'I'm not quite sure about that.'

'And if our ace-reporter Owens is privileged enough to have an answerphone in his office – which he *is* . . .'

Ye-es. Perhaps Morse was on to something after all. Because if the two of them *had*, for some reason, been working together . . . Lewis put his thoughts into words:

'You mean he needn't have gone in to work at all . . . Ye-es. You say that electronic gadget records the number on your card, and the time – but it doesn't record the car itself, right?'

Morse nodded encouragement. And Lewis, duly encouraged, continued:

'So if somebody *else* had taken his card – and if *he* stayed in the Drive all the time . . .'

Morse finished it off for him: 'He's got a key to Number 1 – he's in there when she drives off – he walks along the back of the terrace – shoots Rachel James – goes back to Number 1 – rings up his own office number – waits for the answerphone pips – probably doesn't say anything – just keeps the line open for a minute or two – and Bob's your father's brother.'

Lewis sighed. 'I'd better get on with a bit of fourth-grade clerical checking, sir – this parking business, the phone-call, any of his colleagues who might have seen him—'

'Or her.'

'It's worth checking, I can see that.'

'Tomorrow, Lewis. We're doing nothing more today.'

'And this woman at Number 1?'

'Is she a nice-looking lass?'

'Very much so.'

'You leave that side of things to me, then.'

Morse got to his feet and went to the door. But then returned, and sat down again.

'That "refrigeration factor" you mentioned, Lewis – time of death and all that. Interesting, isn't it? So far, we've been assuming that the bullet went through the window and ended up in the corpse, haven't we? But if – just *if* – Rachel James had been murdered a bit *earlier*, inside Number 17, and then someone had fired through the window *at some later stage* ... You see what I mean? Everybody's alibi is up the pole, isn't it?'

'There'd be another bullet, though, wouldn't there? We've got the one from Rachel's neck; but there'd be another one some-where in the kitchen if someone fired—'

'Not necessarily the murderer, remember!'

'But if *someone* fired just through the window, without aiming at anything ...'

'Did the SOCOs have a good look at the ceiling, the walls – the floorboards?'

'They did, yes.'

'Somebody might have picked it up and pocketed it.'

'Who on earth—'

'I've not the faintest idea.'

'Talking of bullets, sir, we've got another little report – from ballistics. Do you want to read it?'

'Not tonight.'

'Very short, sir.'

He handed Morse the single, neatly typed paragraph:

Ballistics Report: Prelim.
17 Bloxham Drive, Kidlington, Oxon

.577 heavy-calibre revolver. One of the Howdah pistols probably –
perhaps the Lancaster Patent four-barrel. An old firing-piece but if
reasonably well cared for could be in good working nick like as not in
1996.

    Acc. to recent catalogues readily available in USA: $370 to $700.
Tests progressing.

ASH
22.ii.96

Morse handed the report back. 'I'm not at all sure I know what
"calibre" means. Is it the diameter of the bullet or the diameter of the
barrel?'

    'Wouldn't they be the same, sir?'

    Morse got up and walked wearily to the door once more.

    'Perhaps so, Lewis. Perhaps so.'

CHAPTER TWENTY-ONE

A Conservative is one who is enamored of existing evils, as
distinguished from the Liberal, who wishes to replace them
with others

          (Ambrose Bierce, *The Devil's Dictionary*)

MORSE DID NOT go straight home to his North Oxford flat
that evening; nor, *mirabile dictu*, did he make for the nearest
hostelry – at least not immediately. Instead, he drove to Bloxham
Drive, pulling in behind the single police car parked outside
Number 17, in which a uniformed officer sat reading the *Oxford
Mail*.

    'Constable Brogan, sir,' was the reply in answer to Morse's
question.

    'Happen to know if Number 1's at home?'

    'The one with the N-reg Rover, you mean?'

    Morse nodded.

'No. But she keeps coming backwards and forwards all the time. She seems a very busy woman, that one.'

'Anything to report?'

'Not really, sir. We keep getting a few gawpers, but I just ask them to move along.'

'Gently, I trust.'

'Very gently, sir.'

'How long are you on duty for?'

'Finish at midnight.'

Morse pointed to the front window. 'Why don't you nip in and watch the telly?'

'Bit cold in there.'

'You can put the gas-fire on.'

'It's electric, sir.'

'Please yourself!'

'Would that be official, sir?'

'*Anything* I say's official, lad.'

'My lucky night, then.'

Mine, too, thought Morse as he looked over his shoulder to see an ash-blonde alighting from her car outside Number 1.

He hastened along the pavement in what could be described as an arrested jog, or perhaps more accurately as an animated walk.

'Good *evening*.'

She turned towards him as she inserted her latchkey.

'Yes?'

'A brief word – if it's possible . . . er . . .'

Morse fumbled for his ID card. But she forestalled the need.

'Another police sergeant, are you?'

'Police, yes.'

'I can't spare much time – not tonight. I've got a busy few hours ahead.'

'I shan't keep you long.'

She led the way through into a tastefully furbished and furnished front room, taking off her ankle-length white mackintosh, placing it over the back of the red leather settee, and bidding Morse sit opposite her as she smoothed the pale blue dress over her hips and crossed her elegant, nylon-clad legs.

'Do you mind?' she asked, lifting a cigarette in the air.

'No, no,' muttered Morse, wishing only that she'd offered one to him.

'What can I do for you?' She had a slightly husky, upper-class voice, and Morse guessed she'd probably attended one of the nation's more prestigious public schools.

'Just one or two questions.'

She smiled attractively. 'Go ahead.'

'I understand that my colleague, Sergeant Lewis, has spoken to you already.'

'Nice man – in a gentle, shy sort of way.'

'Really? I'd never quite thought of him . . .'

'Well, you're a bit older, aren't you?'

'What job do you do?'

She opened her handbag and gave Morse her card.

'I'm the local agent for the Conservative Party.'

'Oh dear! I *am* sorry,' said Morse, looking down at the small oblong card:

> Adèle Beatrice Cecil
> Conservative Party Agent
> 1 Bloxham Drive
> Kidlington, Oxon, OX5 2NY
> For information please ring
> 01865 794768

'Was that supposed to be a sick joke?' There was an edge to her voice now.

'Not really. It's just that I've never had a friend who's a Tory, that's all.'

'You mean you didn't vote for us today?'

'I don't live in this ward.'

'If you give me your address, I'll make sure you get some literature, Sergeant.'

'Chief Inspector, actually,' corrected Morse, oblivious of the redundant adverb.

She tugged her dress a centimetre down her thighs. 'How can I help?'

'Do you know Mr Owens well?'

'Well enough.'

'Well enough to hand him a newspaper scoop?'

'Yes.'

'Have you ever slept with him?'

'Not much finesse about you, is there?'

'Just a minute,' said Morse softly. 'I've got a terrible job to do – just up the street here. And part of it's to ask some awkward questions about what's going on in the Close—'

'*Drive.*'

'To find out who knows who – *whom*, if you prefer it.'

'They did teach us English grammar at Roedean, yes.'

'You haven't answered my question.'

Adèle breathed deeply, and her grey eyes stared across almost fiercely.

'Once, yes.'

'But you didn't repeat the experience?'

'I said "once" – didn't you hear me?'

'You still see him?'

'Occasionally. He's all right: intelligent, pretty well read, quite good fun, sometimes – and he promised he'd vote Conservative today.'

'He sounds quite compatible.'

'Are you married, Inspector?'

'*Chief* Inspector.'

'Are you?'

'No.'

'Do you wish you were?'

Perhaps Morse didn't hear the question.

'Did you know Rachel James fairly well?'

'We had a heart-to-heart once in a while.'

'You weren't aware of any one particular boyfriend?'

She shook her head.

'Would you say she was attractive to men?'

'Wouldn't you?'

'I only saw her the once.'

'I'm sorry.' She said it quietly. 'Please, forgive me.'

'Do you know a man called Storrs? Julian Storrs?'

'Good gracious, yes! Julian? He's one of our Vice-Presidents. We often meet at do's. In fact, I'm seeing him next week at a fund-raising dinner at The Randolph. Would you like a complimentary ticket?'

'No, perhaps not.'

'Shouldn't have asked, should I? Anyway,' she got to her feet, 'I'll have to be off. They'll be starting the count fairly soon.'

They walked to the front door.

'Er . . . when you rang Mr Owens on Monday morning, just after eight o'clock you say, you did *speak* to him, didn't you?'

'Of course.'

Morse nodded. 'And one final thing, please. My sergeant found some French letters—'

'French letters? How old *are* you, Chief Inspector? Condoms, for heaven's sake.'

'As I say, we found two packets of, er, condoms in one of her bedroom drawers.'

'Big deal!'

'You don't know if she ever invited anyone home to sleep with her?'

'No, I don't.'

'I thought,' said Morse hesitantly, 'most women were on the pill these days?'

'A lot of them *off* it, too – after that thrombosis scare.'

'I suppose so, yes. I'm . . . I'm not really an expert in that sort of thing.'

'And don't forget safe sex.'

'No. I'll . . . I'll try not to.'

'Did she keep them under her nighties?'

Morse nodded sadly, and bade goodnight to Adèle Beatrice Cecil.

ABC.

As he walked slowly along to the Jaguar, he felt a slight tingling behind the eyes at the thought of Rachel James, and the nightdress she'd been wearing when she was murdered; and the condoms so carefully concealed in her lingerie drawer – along with the hopes and fears she'd had, like everyone. And he thought of Auden's immortal line on A. E. Housman:

Kept tears like dirty postcards in a drawer.

As he started the Jaguar, Morse noticed the semi-stroboscopic light inside the lounge; and trusted that PC Brogan had managed to activate the heating system in Number 17 Bloxham Drive.

CHAPTER TWENTY-TWO

O Beer! O Hodgson, Guinness, Allsopp, Bass!
Names that should be on every infant's tongue!
(Charles Stuart Calverly)

MORSE HEADED SOUTH along the Banbury Road, turning left
just after the Cutteslowe Roundabout, and through the adjoining
Carlton and Wolsey Roads (why hadn't the former been christened 'Cardinal'?); then, at the bottom of the Cutteslowe Estate,
down the steeply sloping entry to the Cherwell, a quietly civilized
public house where the quietly civilized landlord kept an ever-
watchful eye on the Brakspear and the Bass. The car-phone rang
as he unfastened his safety-belt.

Lewis.

Speaking from HQ.

'I thought I'd told you to go home! The eggs and chips are
getting cold.'

Lewis, as Morse earlier, showed himself perfectly competent
at ignoring a question.

'I've had a session on the phone with Ox and Cow Newspapers,
sir – still at work there, quite a few of them. Owens' car-park card
is number 14922 and it was registered by the barrier contraption
there at 7.04 on Monday morning. Seems he's been in fairly early
these last couple of months. Last week, for example, Monday to
Friday, 7.37, 7.06, 7.11, 7.00, 7.18.'

'So what? Shows he can't get up that early on Monday
mornings.'

'That's not all, though.'

'It *is*, Lewis! It's still the *card* you're on about – not the *car*!
Can't you see that?'

'Please listen to me for a change, sir. The personnel fellow who
looked out the car-park things for me, he just happened to be in
earlyish last Monday morning himself: 7.22. There weren't many
others around then, but one of the ones who was ... Guess who,
sir?'

'Oh dear!' said Morse for the second time that evening.

'Yep. Owens! Pony-tail 'n' all.'

'Oh.'

In that quiet monosyllable Lewis caught the depth of Morse's disappointment. Yet he felt far from dismayed himself, knowing full well as he did, after so many murder investigations with the pair of them in harness, that Morse's mind was almost invariably at its imaginative peak when one of his ill-considered, top-of-the-head hypotheses had been razed to the ground – in this case by some lumbering bulldozer like himself. And so he understood the silence at the other end of the line: a long silence, like that at the Cenotaph in commemoration of the fallen.

Lewis seldom expected (seldom received) any thanks. And in truth such lack of recognition concerned him little, since only rarely did Morse show the slightest sign of graciousness or gratitude to anyone.

Yet he did so now.

'Thank you, my old friend.'

At the bar Morse ordered a pint of Bass and proceeded to drink it speedily.

At the bar Morse ordered a second pint of Bass and proceeded to drink it even more speedily – before leaving and driving out once more to Bloxham Drive, where no one was abroad and where the evening's TV programmes appeared to be absorbing the majority of the households.

Including Number 17.

The Jaguar door closed behind him with its accustomed aristocratic click, and he walked slowly through the drizzle along the street. Still the same count: six for Labour; two for the Tories; and two apparently unprepared to parade their political allegiances.

Yes! YES!

Almost everything (he saw it now so clearly) had been pushing his mind towards that crucial clue – towards the breakthrough in the case.

It had not been Owens who had murdered Rachel James – almost certainly he *couldn't* have done it, anyway.

And that late evening, as if matching his slow-paced walk, a slow and almost beatific smile had settled round the mouth of Chief Inspector Morse.

CHAPTER TWENTY-THREE
Friday, 23 February

Thirteen Unlucky: The Turks so dislike the number that the word is almost expunged from their vocabulary. The Italians never use it in making up the numbers of their lotteries. In Paris, no house bears that number

(Brewer's Dictionary of Phrase and Fable)

As Lewis pulled into Bloxham Drive, he was faced with an unfamiliar sight: a smiling, expansive-looking Morse was leaning against the front gate of Number 17, engaged in a relaxed, impromptu press conference with one camera crew (ITV), four reporters (two from national, two from local newspapers – but no Owens), and three photographers. Compared with previous mornings, the turn-out was disappointing.

It was 9.05 a.m.

Lewis just caught the tail-end of things. 'So it'll be a waste of time – staying on here much longer. You won't expect me to go into details, of course, but I can tell you that we've finished our investigations in this house.'

If the 'this' were spoken with a hint of some audial semi-italicization, it was of no moment, for no one appeared to notice it.

'Any leads? Any new leads?'

'To the murder of Rachel James, you mean?'

'Who else?'

'No. No new leads at all, really . . . Well, perhaps one.'

On which cryptic note, Morse raised his right hand to forestall the universal pleas for clarification, and with a genial – perhaps genuine? – smile, he turned away.

'Drive me round the block a couple of times, Lewis. I'd rather all these people buggered off, and I don't think they're going to stay much longer if they see us go.'

Nor did they.

Ten minutes later the detectives returned to find the Drive virtually deserted.

'How many houses are there here, Lewis?'

'Not sure.' From Number 17 Lewis looked along to the end of

the row. Two other houses – presumably Numbers 19 and 21, although the figures from the front gate of the latter had been removed. Then he looked across to the other side of the street where the last even-numbered house was 20. The answer, therefore, appeared to be reasonably obvious.

'Twenty-one.'

'That's an *odd* number, isn't it?'

Lewis frowned. 'Did you think I thought it was an *even* number?'

Morse smiled. 'I didn't mean "odd" as opposed to "even"; I meant "odd" as opposed to "normal".'

'Oh!'

'Lew-is! You don't build a street of terraced houses with one side having ten and the other side having eleven, now do you? You get a bit of symmetry into things; a bit of regularity.'

'If you say so.'

'And I *do* say so!' snapped Morse, with the conviction of a fundamentalist preacher asserting the divine authority of Holy Writ.

'No need to be so sharp, sir.'

'I should have spotted it from day one! From those political stickers, Lewis! Let's count, OK?'

The two men walked along the odd-numbered side of Bloxham Drive. And Lewis nodded: six Labour; two Tory; two don't-knows.

Ten.

'You see, Lewis, we've perhaps been a little misled by these minor acts of vandalism here. We've got several houses minus the numbers originally screwed into their front gates – *and their back gates*. So we were understandably confused.'

Lewis agreed. 'I still am, sir.'

'How many odd numbers are there between one and twenty-one – inclusive?'

'I reckon it's ten, sir. So I suppose there must be eleven.'

Morse grinned. 'Write 'em down!'

So Lewis did, in his notebook: 1, 3, 5, 7, 9, 11, 13, 15, 17, 19, 21. Then counted them.

'I was right, sir. Eleven.'

'But only ten houses, Lewis.'

'I don't quite follow.'

'Of course you do. It happens quite often in hotel floors and hotel room numbers ... and street numbers. They miss one of them out.'

Enlightenment dawned on Lewis's honest features.

'Number thirteen!'

'Exactly! Do you know there used to be people in France called "fourteeners" who made a living by going along to dinner parties where the number of guests was thirteen?'

'Where do you find all these bits and pieces?'

'Do you know, I think I saw that on the back of a matchbox in a pub in Grimsby. I've learned quite a lot in life from the back of matchboxes.'

'What's it all got to do with the case, though?'

Morse reached for Lewis's notebook, and put brackets round the seventh number. Then, underneath the first few numbers, he wrote in an arrow, →, pointing from left to right.

'Lewis! If you were walking along the back of the houses, starting from Number 1 – she must be feeling a bit sore about the election, by the way ... Well, let's just go along there.'

The two men walked to the rear of the terrace, where (as we have seen) several of the back gates had been sadly, if not too seriously, vandalized.

'Get your list, Lewis, and as we go along, just put a ring round those gates where we *haven't* got a number, all right?'

At the end of the row, Lewis's original list, with its successive emendations, appeared as follows:

1, 3, 5, ⑦ 9, 11, (13), ⑮⑰ 19, ㉑

——→

'You see,' said Morse, 'the vandalism gets worse the further you get into the Close, doesn't it? As it gets further from the main road.'

'Yes.'

'So just picture things. You've got a revolver and you walk along the back here in the half-light. *You know the number you want.* You know the morning routine, too: breakfast at about seven. All you've got to do is knock on the kitchen window, wait till you see the silhouette behind the thin blind, the silhouette of a face with one distinctive feature – a pony-tail. You walk along the back; you see Number 11; you move along to the next house – Number 13 – *you think*! And so the house after that *must* be Number 15. And to confirm things, there's the pony-tailed silhouette. You press the trigger – and there you have it, Lewis! The Horseman passes by. But you've got it wrong, haven't you? Your intended victim is living at Number 15, not Number 17!'

'So,' said Lewis slowly, 'whoever stood at the kitchen window thought he – or she – was firing . . .'

Morse nodded sombrely. 'Yes. Not at Rachel James, but *Geoffrey Owens*.'

CHAPTER TWENTY-FOUR

Men entitled to bleat BA after their names
(D. S. MacColl)

THE SENIOR COMMON Room at Lonsdale is comparatively small, and for this reason has a rather more intimate air about it than some of the spacious SCRs in the larger Oxford Colleges. Light-coloured, beautifully grained oak panelling encloses the room on all sides, its colouring complemented by the light brown leather sofas and armchairs there. Copies of almost all the national dailies, including the *Sun* and the *Mirror*, are to be found on the glass-topped coffee-tables; and indeed it is usually these tabloids which are flipped through first – sometimes intently studied – by the majority of the dons.

Forgathered here on the evening of Friday, 23 February (7.00 for 7.30) was a rather overcrowded throng of dons, accompanied by wives, partners, friends, to enjoy a Guest Night – an occasion celebrated by the College four times per term. A white-coated scout stood by the door with a silver tray holding thinly fluted glasses of sherry: either the pale amber 'dry' variety or the darker brown 'medium', for it was a basic assumption in such a setting that no one could ever wish for the deeply umbered 'sweet'.

A begowned Jasper Bradley took a glass of dry, drained it at a swallow, put the glass back on to the tray, and took another. He was particularly pleased with himself that day; *and* with the *Classical Quarterly*, whose review of *Greek Moods and Tenses*

(J. J. Bradley, 204 pp, £45.50, Classical Press) contained the wonderful lines which Bradley had now by heart:

> A small volume, but one which plumbs the unfathomed mysteries of the aorist subjunctive with imaginative insights into the very origins of language.

Yes. He felt decidedly chuffed.

'How's tricks?' he asked, looking up at Donald Franks, a very tall astrophysicist, recently head-hunted from Cambridge, whose dark, lugubrious features suggested that for his part he'd managed few imaginative insights that week into the origins of the universe.

'So-so.'

'Who d'you fancy then?'

'What – of the women here?'

'For the Master's job.'

'Dunno.'

'Who'll you vote for?'

'Secret ballot, innit?'

Mr and Mrs Denis Cornford now came in, each taking a glass of the medium sherry. Shelly looked extremely attractive and perhaps a little skimpily dressed for such a chilly evening. She wore a lightweight white two-piece suit; and as she bent down to pick up a cheese nibble her low-cut, bottle-green blouse gaped open to reveal a splendid glimpse of her beautiful breasts.

'Je-sus!' muttered Bradley.

'She certainly flouts her tits a bit,' mumbled the melancholy Franks.

'You mean "flaunts" 'em, I think.'

'If you say so,' said Franks, slightly wounded.

Bradley moved to the far end of the room where Angela Storrs stood talking to a small priest, clothed all in black, with buckled shoes and leggings.

'Ah, Jasper! Come and meet Father Dooley from Sligo.'

Clearly Angela Storrs had decided she had now done her duty; for soon she drifted away – tall, long-legged, wearing a dark grey trouser-suit with a white high-necked jumper. There was about her an almost patrician mien, her face high-cheekboned and pale, with the hair swept back above her ears and fastened in a bun behind. It was obvious to all that she had been a very attractive woman. But she was aging a little too quickly perhaps; and the fact that over the last two or three years she had almost invariably worn trousers did little to discourage the belief that her legs had succumbed to an unsightly cordage of varicose veins. If she were on sale in an Arab wife-market (in the cruel words of one of the younger dons) she would have passed her best-before date several years earlier.

'I knew the Master many years ago – and his poor wife. Yes . . . that was long ago,' mused the little priest.

Bradley was ready with the appropriate response of scholarly compassion.

'Times change, yes. *Tempora mutantur: et nos mutamur in illis.*'

'I think,' said the priest, 'that the line should read: *Tempora mutantur: nos et mutamur in illis.* Otherwise the hexameter won't scan, will it?'

'Of course it won't, sorry.'

The scout now politely requested dons – wives – partners – guests – to proceed to the Hall. And Jasper Bradley, eminent authority on the aorist subjunctive in Classical Greek, walked out of the SCR more than slightly wounded.

Sir Clixby Bream brought up the rear as the room emptied, and lightly touched the bottom of Angela Storrs standing just in front of him.

Sotto voce he lied into her ear: 'You're looking ravishing tonight. And I'll tell you something else – I'd far rather be in bed with you now than face another bloody Guest Night.'

'So would I!' she lied, in a whisper. 'And I've got a big favour to ask of *you*, too.'

'We'll have a word about it after the port.'

'*Before* the port, Clixby! You're usually blotto after it.'

Sir Clixby banged his gavel, mumbled *Benedictus benedicat*, and the assembled company seated themselves, the table-plan having positioned Julian Storrs and Denis Cornford at diagonally opposite ends of the thick oak table, with their wives virtually opposite each other in the middle.

'I love your suit!' lied Shelly Cornford, in a not unpleasing Yankee twang.

'You look very nice, too,' lied Angela Storrs, smiling widely and showing such white and well-aligned teeth that no one could be in much doubt that her upper plate had been disproportionately expensive.

After which preliminary skirmish, each side observed a dignified truce, with neither a further word nor a further glance between them during the rest of the dinner.

At the head of the table, the little priest sat on the Master's right.

'Just the two candidates, I hear?' he said quietly.

'Just the two: Julian Storrs and Denis Cornford.'

'The usual shenanigans, I assume? The usual horse-trading? Clandestine cabals?'

'Oh no, nothing like that. We're all very civilized here.'

'How do you know that?'

'Well, you've only got to hear what people say – the way they say it.'

The little priest pushed away his half-eaten guinea-fowl.

'You know, Clixby, I once read that speech often gets in the way of genuine communication.'

CHAPTER TWENTY-FIVE

Saturday, 24 February

There never was a scandalous tale without some foundation
(Richard Brinsley Sheridan, *The School for Scandal*)

WHILST THE GUEST NIGHT was still in progress, whilst still the port and Madeira were circulating in their time-honoured directions, an over-wearied Morse had decided to retire comparatively early to bed, where almost unprecedentedly he enjoyed a deep, unbroken slumber until 7.15 the following morning, when gladly would he have turned over and gone back to sleep. But he had much to do that day. He drank two cups of instant coffee (which he preferred to the genuine article); then another cup, this time with one slice of brown toast heavily spread with butter and Frank Cooper's Oxford Marmalade.

By 8.45 he was in his office at Kidlington HQ, where he found a note on his desk:

Please see Chief Sup. Strange a s a p

The meeting, almost until the end, was an amiable enough affair, and Morse received a virtually uninterrupted hearing as he explained his latest thinking on the murder of Rachel James.

'Mm!' grunted Strange, resting his great jowls on his palms when Morse had finished. 'So it *could* be a contract-killing that went cockeyed, you think? The victim gets pinpointed a bit too vaguely, and the killer shoots at the wrong pig-tail—'

'Pony-tail, sir.'

'Yes – through the wrong window. Right?'

'Yes.'

'What about the motive? The key to this sort of mess is almost always the *motive*, you know that.'

'You sound just like Sergeant Lewis, sir.'

Strange looked dubiously across the desk, as if a little uncertain as to whether he *wanted* to sound just like Sergeant Lewis.

'Well?'

'I agree with you. That's one of the reasons it could have been a case of misidentity. We couldn't really find any satisfactory motive for Rachel's murder anywhere. But if somebody wanted *Owens* out of the way – well, I can think of a dozen possible motives.'

'Because he's a news-hound, you mean?'

Morse nodded. 'Plenty of people in highish places who've got some sort of skeleton in the sideboard—'

'Cupboard.'

'Who'd go quite a long way to keep the, er, cupboard firmly locked.'

'Observed openly masturbating on the M40, you mean? Weekend away with the PA? By the way, *you've* got a pretty little lass for a secretary, I see. Don't you ever lust after her?'

'I seem to have lost most of my lust recently, sir.'

'We all do. It's called getting old.'

Strange lifted his large head, and eyed Morse over his half-lenses.

'Now about the case. It won't be easy, will it? You've no reason to think he's got a lot of stuff stashed under his mattress?'

'No . . . no, I haven't.'

'You'd no real reason for thinking he'd killed Rachel?'

'No . . . no, I hadn't.'

'So he's definitely out of the frame?'

Morse considered the question awhile. ''Fraid so, yes. I wish he weren't.'

'So?'

'So I'll – *we'll* think of some way of approaching things.'

'Nothing irregular! You promise me that! We're just about getting over one or two unsavoury incidents in the Force, aren't we? And we're not going to start anything here. Is that clear, Morse?'

'To be fair, sir, I usually do go by the book.'

Strange pointed a thick finger.

'Well, *usually*'s not bloody good enough for me! You – go – by – the book, matey! Understood?'

Morse walked heavily back to his office, where a refreshed-looking Lewis awaited him.

'Everything all right with the Super?'

'Oh, yes. I just told him about our latest thinking—'

'*Your* latest thinking.'

'He understands the difficulties. He just doesn't want us to bend the rules of engagement too far, that's all.'

'So what's the plan?'

'Just nip and get me a drink first, will you?'

'Coffee?'

Morse pondered. 'I think I'll have a pint of natural, lead-free orange juice. Iced.'

'So what's the plan?' repeated Lewis, five minutes later.

'Not quite sure, really. But if I'm right, if it *was* something like a contract-killing, it must have been arranged because Owens was threatening to expose somebody. And if he was—'

'Lot of "if's", sir.'

'*If* he was, Lewis, he must have some evidence tucked away somewhere: vital evidence, damning evidence. It could be in the form of newspaper-cuttings or letters or photographs – anything. *And* he must have been pretty sure about his facts if he's been trying to extort some money or some favours or whatever from any disclosures. Now, as I see it, he must have come across most of his evidence in the course of his career as a journalist. Wouldn't you think so? Sex scandals, that sort of thing.'

'Like as not, I suppose.'

'So the plan's this. I want you, once you get the chance, to go and see the big white chief at the newspaper offices and get a look at all the confidential stuff on Owens. They're sure to have it in his appointment-file or somewhere: previous jobs, references, testimonials, CV, internal appraisals, comments—'

'Gossip?'

'Anything!'

'Is that what you mean by not bending the rules too much?'

'We're *not* bending the rules – not too much. We're on a *murder* case, Lewis, remember that! Every member of the public's got a duty to help us in our inquiries.'

'I just hope the editor agrees with you, that's all.'

'He does,' said Morse, a little shamefacedly. 'I rang him while you went to the canteen. He just wants us to do it privately, that's all, and confidentially. Owens only works alternate Saturdays, and this is one of his days off.'

'You don't want to do it yourself?'

'It's not that I don't *want* to. But you're so much better at that sort of thing than I am.'

A semi-mollified Lewis elaborated: 'Then, if anything sticks out as important . . . just follow it up . . . and let you know?'

'Except for one thing, Lewis. Owens told me he worked for quite a while in Soho when he started. And if there's anything suspicious or interesting about that period of his life . . .'

'You'd like to do that bit of research yourself.'

'Exactly. I'm better at that sort of thing than you are.'

'What's your programme for today, then?'

'Quite a few things, really.'

'Such as?' Lewis looked up quizzically.

'Well, there's one helluva lot of paperwork, for a start. *And* filing. So you'd better stay and give me a hand for a while – after you've fetched me another orange juice. And please tell the girl not to dilute it quite so much this time. And just a cube or two more ice perhaps.'

'And then?' persisted Lewis.

'And then I'm repairing to the local in Cutteslowe, where I shall be trying to thread a few further thoughts together over a pint, perhaps. And where I've arranged to meet an old friend of mine who may possibly be able to help us a little.'

'Who's that, sir?'

'It doesn't matter.'

'Not—?'

'Where's my orange juice, Lewis?'

CHAPTER TWENTY-SIX

MARIA: No, I've just got the two O-levels – and the tortoise, of course. But I'm fairly well known for some other accomplishments.
JUDGE: Known to whom, may I ask?
MARIA: Well, to the police for a start.
(Diana Doherty, *The Re-trial of Maria Macmillan*)

AT TEN MINUTES to noon Morse was enjoying his pint of Brakspear's bitter. The Chief Inspector had many faults, but unpunctuality had never been one of them. He was ten minutes early.

JJ, a sparely built, nondescript-looking man in his mid-forties, walked into the Cherwell five minutes later.

When Morse had rung at 8.30 a.m., Malcolm 'JJ' Johnson had been seated on the floor, on a black cushion, only two feet away from the television screen, watching a hard-core porn video and drinking his regular breakfast of two cans of Beamish stout – just after the lady of the household had left for her job (mornings only) in one of the fruiterers' shops in Summertown.

Accepted wisdom has it that in such enlightened times as these most self-respecting burglars pursue their trade by day; but JJ had always been a night-man, relying firmly on local knowledge and reconnaissance. And often in the daylight hours, as now, he wondered why he didn't spend his leisure time in some more purposeful pursuits. But in truth he just couldn't think of any. At the same time, he did realize, yes, that sometimes he was getting a bit bored. Over the past two years or so, the snooker table had lost its former magnetism; infidelities and fornication were posing too many practical problems, as he grew older; and even darts and dominoes were beginning to pall. Only gambling, usually in Ladbrokes' premises in Summertown, had managed to retain his undivided attention over the years: for the one thing that never bored him was acquiring money.

Yet JJ had never been a miser. It was just that the acquisition of money was a necessary prerequisite to the *spending* of money;

and the spending of money had always been, and still was, the greatest purpose of his life.

Educated (if that be the word) in a run-down comprehensive school, he had avoided the three Bs peculiar to many public-school establishments: beating, bullying, and buggery. Instead, he had left school at the age of sixteen with a delight in a different triad: betting, boozing, and bonking – strictly in that order. And to fund such expensive hobbies he had come to rely on one source of income, one line of business only: burglary.

He now lived with his long-suffering, faithful, strangely influential, common-law wife in a council house on the Cutteslowe Estate that was crowded with crates of lager and vodka and gin, with all the latest computer games, and with row upon row of tasteless seaside souvenirs. And home, after two years in jail, was where he wanted to stay.

No! JJ didn't want to go back inside. And that's why Morse's call had worried him so. So much, indeed, that he had turned the video to 'Pause' even as the eager young stud was slipping between the sheets.

What did Morse want?

'Hello, Malcolm!'

Johnson had been 'Malcolm' until the age of ten, when the wayward, ill-disciplined young lad had drunk from a bottle of Jeyes Fluid under the misapprehension that the lavatory cleaner was lemonade. Two stomach-pumpings and a week in hospital later, he had emerged to face the world once more; but now with the sobriquet 'Jeyes' – an embarrassment which he sought to deflect, five years on, by the rather subtle expedient of having the legend 'JJ – all the Js' tattooed longitudinally on each of his lower arms.

Morse drained his glass and pushed it over the table.

'Coke, is it, Mr Morse?'

'Bit early for the hard stuff, Malcolm.'

'Half a pint, was it?'

'Just tell the landlord "same again".'

A Brakspear it was – and a still mineral water for JJ.

'One or two of those gormless idiots you call your pals seem anxious to upset the police,' began Morse.

'Look. I didn't 'ave nothin' to do with that – 'onest! You know me.' Looking deeply unhappy, JJ dragged deeply on a king-sized cigarette.

'I'm not really interested in that. I'm interested in your doing me a favour.'

JJ visibly relaxed, becoming almost his regular, perky self once more. He leaned over the table, and spoke quietly:

'I'll tell you what. I got a red-'ot video on up at the country mansion, if you, er . . .'

'Not this morning,' said Morse reluctantly, conscious of a considerable sacrifice. And it was now *his* turn to lean over the table and speak the quiet words:

'I want you to break into a property for me.'

'Ah!'

The balance of power had shifted, and JJ grinned broadly to reveal two rows of irregular and blackened teeth. He pushed his empty glass across the table.

'Double vodka and lime for me, Mr Morse. I suddenly feel a bit thirsty, like.'

For the next few minutes Morse explained the mission; and JJ listened carefully, nodding occasionally, and once making a pencilled note of an address on the back of a pink betting-slip.

'OK,' he said finally, 'so long as you promise, you know, to see me OK if . . .'

'I can't promise anything.'

'But you will?'

'Yes.'

'OK, then. Gimme a chance to do a bit o' recce, OK? Then gimme another buzz on the ol' blower, like, OK? When had you got in mind?'

'I'm not quite sure.'

'OK – that's it then.'

Morse drained his glass and stood up, wondering whether communication in the English language could ever again cope without the word 'OK'.

'Before you go . . .' JJ looked down at his empty glass.

'Mineral water, was it?' asked Morse.

'Just tell the landlord "same again".'

*

Almost contented with life once more, JJ sat back and relaxed after Morse had gone. Huh! Just the one bleedin' door, by the sound of it. Easy. Piece o' cake!

Morse, too, was pleased with the way the morning had gone. Johnson, as the police were well aware, was one of the finest locksmiths in the Midlands. As a teenager he'd held the reputation of being the quickest car-thief in the county. But his incredible skills had only really begun to burgeon in the eighties, when all manner of house-locks, burglar-alarms, and safety-devices had surrendered meekly to his unparalleled knowledge of locks and keys and electrical circuits.

In fact 'JJ' Johnson knew almost as much about burglary as J. J. Bradley knew about the aorist subjunctive.

Perhaps more.

CHAPTER TWENTY-SEVEN

The faults of the burglar are the qualities of the financier
(Bernard Shaw, *Major Barbara*)

IN FACT, MORSE'S campaign was destined to be launched that very day.

Lewis had called back at HQ at 2 p.m. with a slim folder of photocopied documents – in which Morse seemed little interested; and with the news that Geoffrey Owens had left his home the previous evening to attend a weekend conference on Personnel Management, in Bournemouth, not in all likelihood to be back until late p.m. the following day, Sunday. In this latter news Morse seemed more interested.

'Well done, Lewis! But you've done quite enough for one day. You look weary and I want you to go home. Nobody can keep up the hours you've been setting yourself.'

As it happened, Lewis was feeling wonderfully fresh; but he *had* promised that weekend to accompany his wife (if he could) on her quest for the right sort of dish-washer. They could well afford the luxury now, and Lewis himself would welcome some alleviation of his domestic duties at the sink.

'I'll accept your offer – on one condition, sir. You go off home, too.'

'Agreed. I was just going anyway. I'll take the folder with me. Anything interesting?'

'A few little things, I suppose. For instance—'

'Not now!'

'Aren't you going to tell me how *your* meeting went?'

'*Not now!* Let's call it a day.'

As the two detectives walked out of the HQ block, Morse asked his question casually:

'By the way, did you discover which swish hotel they're at in Bournemouth?'

Back in his flat, Morse made two phone-calls: the first to Bournemouth; the second to the Cutteslowe Estate. Yes, a Mr Geoffrey Owens was present at the conference there. No, Mr Malcolm Johnson had not yet had a chance to make his recce – of course he hadn't! But, yes, he would repair the omission forthwith in view of the providential opportunity now afforded (although Johnson's own words were considerably less pretentious).

'And no more booze today, Malcolm!'

'What me – drink? On business? Never! And you better not drink, neither.'

'Two sober men – that's what the job needs,' agreed Morse.

'What time you pickin' me up then?'

'No. You're picking *me* up. Half past seven at my place.'

'OK. And just remember you got more to lose than I 'ave, Mr Morse.'

Yes, far more to lose, Morse knew that; and he felt a shudder of apprehension about the risky escapade he was undertaking. His nerves needed some steadying.

He poured himself a goodly measure of Glenfiddich; and shortly thereafter fell deeply asleep in the chair for more than two hours.

Bliss.

Johnson parked his filthy F-reg Vauxhall in a fairly convenient lay-by on the Deddington Road, the main thoroughfare which runs at the rear of the odd-numbered houses in Bloxham Drive. As instructed, Morse stayed behind, in the murky shadow of the embankment, as Johnson eased himself through a gap in the perimeter fence, where vandals had smashed and wrenched away several of the vertical slats, and then, with surprising agility, descended the steep stretch of slippery grass that led down to the rear of the terrace.

The coast seemed clear.

Morse looked on nervously as the locksmith stood in his trainers at the back of Number 15, patiently and methodically doing what he did so well. Once, he snapped to taut attention hard beside the wall as a light was switched on in one of the nearby houses, throwing a yellow rectangle over the glistening grass – and then switched off.

Six minutes.

By Morse's watch, six minutes before Johnson turned the knob, carefully eased the door open, and disappeared within – before reappearing and beckoning a tense and jumpy Morse to join him.

'Do you want the lights on?' asked Johnson as he played the thin beam of his large torch around the kitchen.

'What do *you* think?'

'Yes. Let's 'ave 'em on. Lemme just go and pull the curtains through 'ere.' He moved into the front living-room, where Morse heard a twin swish, before the room burst suddenly into light.

An ordinary, somewhat spartan room: settee; two rather tatty armchairs; dining-table and chairs; TV set; electric fire installed in the old fireplace; and above the fireplace, on a mantelshelf patinated deep with dust, the only object perhaps which any self-respecting burglar would have wished to take – a small, beautifully fashioned ormolu clock.

Upstairs, the double bed in the front room was unmade, an orange bath-towel thrown carelessly across the duvet; no sign of pyjamas. On the bedside table two items only: Wilbur Smith's *The Seventh Scroll* in paperback, and a packet of BiSoDoL Extra indigestion tablets. An old-fashioned mahogany wardrobe monopolized much of the remaining space, with coats/suits/trousers on their hangers, and six pairs of shoes neatly laid in parallels at the bottom; and on the shelves, to the left, piles of jumpers, shirts, pants, socks, and handkerchiefs.

The second bedroom was locked.

'Malcolm!' whispered Morse down the stairwell.

Two and a half minutes later, Morse was taking stock of a smaller but clearly more promising room: a large bookcase containing a bestseller selection from over the years; one armchair;

one office chair; the latter set beneath a veneered desk with an imitation leather top, four drawers on either side, and between them a longer drawer with two handles – locked.

'Malcolm!' whispered Morse down the stairwell.

Ninety seconds only this time, and clearly the locksman was running into form.

The eight side-drawers contained few items of interest: stationery, insurance documents, car documents, bank statements, pens and pencils – but in the bottom left-hand drawer a couple of pornographic paperbacks. Morse opened *Topless in Torremolinos* at random and read a short paragraph.

In its openly titillating way, it seemed to him surprisingly well written. And there was that one striking simile where the heroine's bosom was compared to a pair of fairy-cakes – although Morse wasn't at all sure what a fairy-cake looked like. He made a mental note of the author, Ann Berkeley Cox, and read the brief dedication on the title page, 'For Geoff From ABC', before slipping the book into the pocket of his mackintosh.

Johnson was seated in an armchair, in the living-room, in the dark, when Morse came down the stairs holding a manila file.

'Got what you wanted, Mr Morse?'

'Perhaps so. Ready?'

With the house now in total darkness, the two men felt their way to the kitchen, when Morse stopped suddenly.

'The torch! Give me the torch.'

Retracing his steps to the living-room, he shone the beam along an empty mantelpiece.

'Put it back!' he said.

Johnson took the ormolu clock from his overcoat-pocket and replaced it carefully on its little dust-free rectangle.

'I'm glad you made me do that,' confided Johnson quietly. 'I shouldn't 'a done it in the first place. Anyway, me conscience'll be clear now.'

There was a streak of calculating cruelty in the man, Morse knew that. But in several respects he was a lovable rogue; even sometimes, as now perhaps, a reasonably honest one. And oddly it was Morse who was beginning to worry – about his own conscience.

He went quickly up to the second bedroom once more and slipped the book back in its drawer.

At last, as quietly as it had opened, the back door closed behind them and the pair now made their way up the grassy gradient to the gap in the slatted perimeter fence.

'You've not lost your old skills,' volunteered Morse.

'Nah! Know what they say, Mr Morse? Old burglars never die – they simply steal away.'

In the darkened house behind them, on the mantelshelf in the front living-room, a little dust-free rectangle still betrayed the spot where the beautifully fashioned ormolu clock had so recently stood.

CHAPTER TWENTY-EIGHT

When you have assembled what you call your 'facts' in logical order, it is like an oil-lamp you have fashioned, filled, and trimmed; but which will shed no illumination unless first you light it

(Saint-Exupéry, *The Wisdom of the Sands*)

BACK IN HIS flat, Morse closed the door and shot the bolts, both top and bottom. It was an oddly needless precaution, yet an explicable one, perhaps. As a twelve-year-old boy, he remembered so vividly returning from school with a magazine, and locking all the doors in spite of his certain knowledge that no other member of the family would be home for several hours. And then, even then, he had waited awhile, relishing the anticipatory thrill before daring to open the pages.

It was just that sensation he felt now as he switched on the electric fire, poured a glass of Glenfiddich, lit a cigarette, and settled back in his favourite armchair – not this time, however, with the *Naturist Journal* which (all those years ago now) had been doing the rounds in Lower IVA, but with the manila file just burgled from the house in Bloxham Drive.

The cover was well worn, with tears and creases along its edges; and maroon rings where once a wine glass had rested, amid many doodles of quite intricate design. Inside the file was a sheaf of papers and cuttings, several of them clipped or stapled together, though not arranged in any chronological or purposeful sequence.

Nine separate items.

– Two newspaper cuttings, snipped from one of the less inhibited of the Sunday tabloids, concerning a Lord Hardiman, together with a photograph of the aforesaid peer fishing in his wallet (presumably for Deutschmarks) outside a readily identifiable sex establishment in Hamburg's Reeperbahn. Clipped to this material was a further photograph of Lord Hardiman arm-in-arm with Lady Hardiman at a polo match in Great Windsor Park (September 1984).

– A letter (August 1979) addressed to Owens from a firm of solicitors in Cheltenham informing the addressee that it was in possession of letters sent by him (Owens) to one of their clients (unspecified); and that some arrangement beneficial to each of the parties might possibly be considered.

– A glossy, highly defined photograph showing a paunchy elderly man fondling a frightened-looking prepubescent girl, both of them naked. Pencilled on the back was an address in St Albans.

– A stapled sheaf of papers showing the expenses of a director in a Surrey company manufacturing surgical appliances, with double exclamation-marks against several of the mammoth amounts claimed for foreign business trips.

– A brief, no-nonsense letter (from a woman, perhaps?) in large, curly handwriting, leaning italic-fashion to the right: 'If you contact me again I shall take your letters to the police – I've kept them all. You'll get no more money from me. You're a despicable human being. I've got nothing more to lose, not even my money.' No signature but (again) a pencilled address, this time in the margin, in Wimbledon.

– Four sets of initials written on a small page probably torn from the back of a diary:

AM ✓   DC ✓   JS ✓   CB

Nothing more – except a small tick in red Biro against the first three.

– Two further newspaper cuttings, paper-clipped together. The first (*The Times* Diary, 2.2.96) reporting as follows:

> After a nine-year tenure Sir Clixby Bream is retiring as Master of Lonsdale College, Oxford. Sir Clixby would, indeed should, have retired earlier. It is only the inability of anyone in the College (including the classicists) to understand the Latin of the original Statutes that has prolonged Sir Clixby's term. The present Master has refused to speculate whether such an extension of his tenure has been the result of some obscurity in the language of the Statutes themselves; or the incompetence of his classical colleagues, none of whom appears to have been nominated as a possible successor.

The second, a cutting from the *Oxford Mail* (November 1995) of an article written by Geoffrey Owens; with a photograph alongside, the caption reading, 'Mr Julian Storrs and his wife Angela at the opening of the Polynesian Art Exhibition at the Pitt Rivers Museum.'

– A smudgy photocopy of a typed medical report, marked 'Strictly Private and Confidential', on the notepaper of a private health clinic in the Banbury Road:

Ref:	Mr J. C. Storrs
Diagnosis:	Inoperable liver cancer confirmed. For second opn. see letter Dr O. V. Maxim (Churchill)
Prognosis:	Seven/eight months, or less. Possibly(??) a year. No longer.
Patient Notes:	Honesty best in this case. Strong personality.
Next Appt:	See book, but a s a p.
	RHT

Clipped to this was a cutting from the obituary columns of one of the national dailies – *The Independent*, by the look of it –

announcing the death of the distinguished cancer specialist Robert H. Turnbull.

– Finally, three photographs, paper-clipped together:
(i) A newspaper photograph of a strip-club, showing in turn (though indistinguishably) individual photographs of the establishment's principal performers, posted on each side of the narrow entrance; showing also (with complete clarity) the inviting legend: SEXIEST RAUNCHIEST SHOW IN SOHO.
(ii) A full-length, black-and-white photograph of a tallish bottle-blonde in a dark figure-hugging gown, the thigh-slit on the left revealing a length of shapely leg. About the woman there seemed little that was less than genuinely attractive – except the smile perhaps.
(iii) A colour photograph of the same woman seated completely naked, apart from a pair of extraordinarily thin stiletto heels, on a bar-stool somewhere – her overfirm breasts suggesting that the smile in the former photograph was not the only thing about her that might be semi-artificial. The legs, now happily revealed in all their lengthy glory, were those of a young dancer – the legs of a Cyd Charisse or a Betty Grable, much better than those in the *Naturist Journal* . . .

Morse closed the file, and knew what he had read: an agenda for blackmail – and possibly for murder.

CHAPTER TWENTY-NINE
Sunday, 25 February

He was advised by a friend, with whom he afterwards lost touch, to stay at the Wilberforce Temperance Hotel
(Geoffrey Madan, *Notebooks*)
I hate those who intemperately denounce beer – and call it Temperance

(G. K. Chesterton)

SOCRATES, ON HIS last day on earth, avowed that death, if it be but one long and dreamless sleep, was a blessing most devoutly to be wished. Morse, on the morning of Sunday, 25 February –

without going quite so far as Socrates – could certainly look back on his own long and dreamless sleep with a rare gratitude, since the commonest features of his nights were regular visits to the loo, frequent draughts of water, occasional doses of Nurofen and Paracetamol, an intake of indigestion tablets, and finally (after rising once more from his crumpled bed-linen) a tumbler of Alka-Seltzer.

The Observer was already poking thickly through the letterbox as he hurriedly prepared himself a subcontinental breakfast.

10.30 a.m.

It was 11.15 a.m. when he arrived at HQ, where Lewis had already been at work for three hours, and where he was soon regaling the chief about his visit to the newspaper offices.

A complete picture of Owens – built up from testimonials, references, records, impressions, gossip – showed a competent, hard-working, well-respected employee. That was the good news. And the bad? Well, it seemed the man was aloof, humourless, unsympathetic. In view of the latter shortcomings (Lewis had suggested) it was perhaps puzzling to understand why Owens had been sent off on a personnel management course. Yet (as the editor had suggested) some degree of aloofness, humourlessness, lack of sympathy, was perhaps precisely what was required in such a rôle.

Lewis pointed to the cellophane folder in which his carefully paginated photocopies were assembled.

'And one more thing. He's obviously a bit of a hit with some of the girls there – especially the younger ones.'

'In spite of his pony-tail?'

'Because of it, more likely.'

'You're not serious?'

'And you're never going to catch up with the twentieth century, are you?'

'One or two possible leads?'

'Could be.'

'Such as?'

'Well, for a start, the Personnel Manager who saw Owens on Monday. I'll get a statement from him as soon as he gets back from holiday – earlier, if you'd like.'

Morse looked dubious. 'Ye-es. But if somebody intended to

murder Owens, not Rachel James ... well, Owens' alibi is neither here nor there really, is it? You're right, though. Let's stick to official procedure. I've always been in favour of rules and regulations.'

As Lewis eyed his superior officer with scarcely disguised incredulity, he accepted the manila file handed to him across the desk; and began to read.

Morse himself now opened the 'Life' section of *The Observer* and turned to the crossword set by Azed (for Morse, the Kasparov of cruciverbalists) and considered 1 across: 'Elephant-man has a mouth that's deformed (6)'. He immediately wrote in MAHOUT, but then put the crossword aside, trusting that the remaining clues might pose a more demanding challenge, and deciding to postpone his hebdomadal treat until later in the day. Otherwise, he might well have completed the puzzle before Lewis had finished with the file.

'How did you come by this?' asked Lewis finally.

'Yours not to reason how.'

'He's a blackmailer!'

Morse nodded. 'We've found no evidential motive for Rachel's murder, but ...'

'... dozens of 'em for his.'

'About *nine*, Lewis – if we're going to be accurate.'

Morse opened the file, and considered the contents once more. Unlike that of the obscenely fat child-fondler, neither photograph of the leggy blonde stripper was genuinely pornographic – certainly not the wholly nude one, which seemed to Morse strangely unerotic; perhaps the one of her in the white dress, though ... 'Unbuttoning' had always appealed to Morse more than 'unbuttoned'; 'undressing' than 'undressed'; 'almost naked' to completely so. It was something to do with Plato's idea of process; and as a young classical scholar Morse had spent so many hours with that philosopher.

'Quite a bit of leg-work there, sir.'

'Yes. Lovely legs, aren't they?'

'No! I meant there's a lot of work to do there – research, going around.'

'You'll need a bit of help, yes.'

'Sergeant Dixon – couple of his lads, too – that'd help.'

'Is Dixon still eating the canteen out of jam doughnuts?'

Lewis nodded. '*And* he's still got his pet tortoise—'

'—always a step or two in front of him, I know.'

For half an hour the detectives discussed the file's explosive material. Until just after noon, in fact.

'Coffee, sir?'

'Not for me. Let's nip down to the King's Arms in Summertown.'

'Not for me,' echoed Lewis. 'I can't afford the time.'

'As you wish.' Morse got to his feet.

'Do you think you should be going out quite so much – on the booze, I mean, sir?' Lewis took a deep breath and prepared for an approaching gale, force ten. 'You're getting worse, not better.'

Morse sat down again.

'Let me just tell you something, Lewis. I care quite a bit about what you think of me as a boss, as a colleague, as a detective – as a *friend*, yes! But I don't give two bloody monkeys about what you think of me as a boozer, all right?'

'No, it's not all right,' said Lewis quietly. 'As a professional copper, as far as solving murders are concerned—'

'*Is* concerned!'

'—it doesn't matter. Doesn't matter to me at all.' (Lewis's voice grew sharper now.) 'You do your job – you spend all your time sorting things out – I'm not worried about that. And if the Chief Constable told me you *weren't* doing your job, I'd resign myself. But he *wouldn't* say that – never. What he'd say – what others would say – what others *are* saying – is that you're ruining yourself. Not the Force, not the department, not the murder inquiries – nothing! – *except yourself.*'

'Just hold on a second, will you?' Morse's eyes were blazing.

'No! No, I won't. You talked about me as a friend, didn't you, just now? Well, as a friend I'm telling you that you're buggering up your health, your retirement, your life – everything!'

'Listen!' hissed Morse. 'I've never myself tried to tell any other man how to live his life. And I will *not* be told, at my age, how I'm supposed to live mine. Even by you.'

After a prolonged silence, Lewis spoke again.

'Can I say something else?'

Morse shrugged indifferently.

'Perhaps it doesn't matter much to most people whether you

kill yourself or not. You've got no wife, no family, no relatives, except that aunt of yours in Alnwick—'

'She's dead, too.'

'So, what the hell? What's it matter? Who cares? Well, *I* care, sir. And the missus cares. And for all I know that girl Ellie Smith, *she* cares.'

Morse looked down at his desk. 'Not any longer, no.'

'And *you* ought to care – care for yourself – just a bit.'

For some considerable while Morse refrained from making any answer, for he was affected by his sergeant's words more deeply than he would ever be prepared to admit.

Then, finally:

'What about that coffee, Lewis?'

'And a sandwich?'

'And a sandwich.'

By early afternoon Morse had put most of his cards on the table, and he and Lewis had reached an agreed conclusion. No longer could either of them accept that Rachel James had been the intended victim: each of them now looked towards Geoffrey Owens as by far the likelier target. Pursuance of the abundant clues provided by the Owens file would necessarily involve a great deal of extra work; and fairly soon a strategy was devised, with Lewis and Dixon allocated virtually everything except the Soho slot.

'You know, I could probably fit that in fairly easily with the Wimbledon visit,' Lewis had volunteered.

But Morse was clearly unconvinced:

'The Soho angle's the most important of the lot.'

'Do you honestly believe that?'

'Certainly. That's why—'

The phone rang, answered by Morse.

Owens (he learned) had phoned HQ ten minutes earlier, just after 3 p.m., to report that his property had been burgled over the weekend, while he was away.

'And you're dealing with it? ... Good ... Just the one item you say, as far as he knows? ... I see ... Thank you.'

Morse put down the phone; and Lewis picked up the file, looking quizzically across the desk.

But Morse shook his head. 'Not the file, no.'

'What, then?'

'A valuable little ormolu clock from his living-room.'

'Probably a professional, sir – one who knows his clocks.'

'Don't ask me. I know nothing about clocks.'

Lewis grinned. 'We both know somebody who does though, don't we, sir?'

CHAPTER THIRTY

This world and the next – and after that *all* our troubles will be over

> (Attributed to General Gordon's aunt)

NO KNOCK. THE door opened. Strange entered.

'Haven't they mentioned it yet, Morse? The pubs are open all day on Sundays now.'

As Strange carefully balanced his bulk on the chair opposite, Morse lauded his luck that Lewis had taken the Owens material down the corridor for photocopying.

'Just catching up on a bit of routine stuff, sir.'

'Really?'

'Why are *you* here?'

'It's the wife,' confided Strange. 'Sunday afternoons she always goes round the house dusting everything. Including me!'

Morse was smiling dutifully as Strange continued: 'Making progress?'

'Following up a few things, yes.'

'Mm . . . Is your brain as bright as it used to be?'

'I'm sure it's not.'

'Mm . . . You don't *look* quite so bright, either.'

'We're all getting older.'

'Worse luck!'

'Not really, surely? "No wise man ever wished to be younger."'

'Bloody nonsense!'

'Not my nonsense – Jonathan Swift's.'

Elbows on the desk, Strange rested his large head on his large hands.

'I'm probably finishing in September, I suppose you'd heard.'

Morse nodded. 'I'm glad they're letting you go.'

'What the 'ell's *that* supposed to mean?'

'Well, I should think Mrs Strange'll be pleased to have you around, won't she? Retirement, you know . . . Getting up late and watching all the other poor sods go off to work, especially on Monday mornings. That sort of thing. It's what we all work for, I suppose. What we all wait for.'

'You mean,' muttered Strange, '*that's* what I've been flogging me guts out all this time for – thirty-two years of it? I used to do your sort of job, you know. Caught nearly as many murderers as you in me day. It's just that I used to do it a bit different, that's all. Mostly used to wait till they came to *me*. No problem, often as not: jealousy, booze, sex, next-door neighbour between the sheets with the missus. *Motive* – that's what it's all about.'

'Not always quite so easy, though, is it?' ventured Morse, who had heard the sermon several times before.

'Certainly not when *you're* around, matey!'

'This case needs some very careful handling, sir. Lots of sensitive inquiries—'

'Such as?'

'About Owens, for a start.'

'You've got some new evidence?'

'One or two vague rumours, yes.'

'Mm . . . I heard a vague rumour myself this afternoon. I heard Owens' place got burgled. I suppose you've heard that, too?' He peered at Morse over his half-lenses.

'Yes.'

'Only one thing pinched. Hm! A clock, Morse.'

'Yes.'

'We've only got one or two clock specialists on the patch, as far as I remember. Or is it just the one?'

'The one?'

'You've not seen him – since they let him out again?'

'Ah, Johnson! Yes. I shall have to call round to see him pretty soon, I suppose.'

'What about tomorrow? He's probably your man, isn't he?'

'I'm away tomorrow.'

'Oh?'

'London. Soho, as a matter of fact. Few things to check out.'

'I don't know why you don't let Sergeant Lewis do all that sort of tedious leg-work.'

Morse felt the Chief Superintendent's small, shrewd eyes upon him.

'Division of labour. Someone's got to do it.'

'You know,' said Strange, 'if I hadn't got a Supers' meeting in the morning, I'd join you. See the sights . . . and everything.'

'I don't think Mrs Strange'd approve.'

'What makes you think I'd tell her?'

'She's – she's not been all that well, has she?'

Strange slowly shook his head, and looked down at the carpet. 'What about you, sir?'

'Me? I'm fine, apart from going deaf and going bald and haemorrhoids and blood pressure. Bit overweight, too, perhaps. What about you?'

'I'm fine.'

'How's the drinking going?'

'Going? It's going, er . . .'

' "Quickly"? Is that the word you're looking for?'

'That's the word.'

Strange appeared about to leave. And – blessedly! – Lewis (Morse realized) must have been aware of the situation, since he had put in no appearance.

But Strange was not quite finished: 'Do you ever worry how your liver's coping with all this booze?'

'We've all got to die of something, they say.'

'Do you ever think about that – about dying?'

'Occasionally.'

'Do you believe in life after death?'

Morse smiled. 'There was a sign once that Slough Borough Council put up near one of the churches there: NO ROAD BEYOND THE CEMETERY.'

'You don't think there is, then?'

'No,' answered Morse simply.

'Perhaps it's just as well if there isn't – you know, rewards and punishments and all that sort of thing.'

'I don't want much reward, anyway.'

'Depends on your ambition. You never had much o' that, did you?'

'Early on, I did.'

'You could've got to the top, you know that.'

'Not doing a job I enjoyed, I couldn't. I'm not a form-filler, am I? Or a committee-man. Or a clipboard-man.'

'Or a *procedure*-man,' added Strange slowly, as he struggled to his feet.

'Pardon?'

'Bloody piles!'

Morse persisted. 'What did you mean, sir?'

'Extraordinary, you know, the sort of high-tech stuff we've got in the Force these days. We've got a machine here that even copies colour photos. You know, like the one— Oh! Didn't I mention it, Morse? I had a very pleasant little chat with Sergeant Lewis in the photocopying room just before I came in here. By the look of things, you've got quite a few alternatives to go on there.'

'Quite a lot of "choices", sir. Strictly speaking, you only have "alternatives" if you've just got the two options.'

'Fuck off, Morse!'

That evening Morse was in bed by 9.45 p.m., slowly reading but a few more pages of Juliet Barker's *The Brontës*, before stopping at one sentence and reading it again:

Charlotte remarked, 'I am sorry you have changed your residence as I shall now again lose my way in going up and down stairs, and stand in great tribulation, contemplating several doors, and not knowing which to open.'

It seemed as good a place to stop as any; and Morse was soon nodding off, in a semi-upright posture, the thick book dropping on to the duvet, the whisky on his bedside table (unprecedentedly) unfinished.

CHAPTER THIRTY-ONE

A time
Older than the time of chronometers, older
Than time counted by anxious worried women
Lying awake, calculating the future,
Trying to unweave, unwind, unravel
And piece together the past and the future

(T. S. Eliot, *The Dry Salvages*)

THE RESULT OF one election had already been declared, with Mr Ivan Thomas, the Labour candidate, former unsuccessful aspirant to municipal honours, now preparing to assume his duties as councillor for the Gosforth ward at Kidlington, near Oxford.

At Lonsdale College, five miles further south, in the golden heart of Oxford, the likely outcome of another election was still very much in the balance, with the wives of the two nominees very much – and not too discreetly, perhaps – to the fore in the continued canvassing. As it happened, each of them (like Morse) was in bed – or in *a* bed – comparatively early that Sunday evening.

Shelly Cornford was always a long time in the bathroom, manipulating her waxed flossing-ribbon in between and up and down her beautifully healthy teeth. When finally she came into the bedroom, her husband was sitting up against the pillows reading the *Sunday Times* Books Section. He watched her as she took off her purple Jaeger dress, and then unfastened her black bra, her breasts bursting free. So very nearly he said something at that point; but the back of his mouth was suddenly dry, and he decided not to. Anyway, it had been only a small incident, and his wife was probably completely unaware of how she could affect some other men – with a touch, a look, a movement of her body. But he'd never been a jealous man.

Not if he could help it.

She got into bed in her Oxford-blue pyjamas and briefly turned towards him.

'Why wasn't Julian at dinner tonight?'

'Up in Durham – some conference he was speaking at. He's back tonight – Angela's picking him up from the station, so she said.'

'Oh.'

'Why do you ask?'

'No reason, darling. Night-night! Sweet dreams, my sweetie!'

She blew a kiss across the narrow space between their beds, turned her back towards him, and snuggled her head into the green pillows.

'Don't be too long with the light, please.'

A few minutes later she was lying still, breathing quite rhythmically, and he thought she was asleep.

As quietly as he could, he manoeuvred himself down beneath

the bedclothes, and straightway turned off the light. And tried, tried far too hard, to go to sleep himself . . .

. . . After evensong earlier that same evening in the College Chapel, the Fellows and their guests had been invited (as was the custom) to the Master's Lodge, where they partook of a glass of sherry before dining at 7.30 p.m. at the top table in the main hall, the students seated on the long rows of benches below them. It was just before leaving the Master's Lodge that Denis had looked round for his wife and found her by the fireplace speaking to David Mackenzie, one of the younger dons, a brilliant mathematician of considerable corpulence, who hastily folded the letter he had been showing to Shelly and put it away.

Nothing in that, perhaps? Not in itself, no. But he, Denis Cornford, knew what was in the letter. And that, for the simplest of all reasons, since Mackenzie had shown him the same scented purple sheets in the SCR the previous week; and Cornford could recall pretty accurately, though naturally not verbatim, the passage he'd been invited to consider. Clearly the letter had been, thus far, the highlight of Mackenzie's term:

> Remember what you scribbled on my menu that night? Your handwriting was a bit wobbly(!) and I couldn't quite make out just that one word: 'I'd love to take you out and make a f— of you'. I *think* it was 'fuss' and it certainly begins with an 'f'. Could be naughty; could be perfectly innocent. *Please* enlighten me!

Surely it was ridiculous to worry about such a thing. But there was something else. The two of them had been giggling together like a pair of adolescents, and looking at each other, and she had put a hand on his arm. And it was almost as if they had established a curious kind of intimacy from which he, Denis Cornford, was temporarily excluded.

Could be naughty.

Could be perfectly innocent . . .

'Would you still love me if I'd got a spot on my nose?'

'Depends how big it was, my love.'

'But you still want my body, don't you,' she whispered, 'in spite of my varicose veins?'

Metaphorically, as he lay beside her, Sir Clixby side-stepped her full-frontal assault as she turned herself towards him.

'You're a very desirable woman, and what's more you know it!' He moved his hands down her naked shoulders and fondled the curves of her bosom.

'I *hope* I can still do something for you,' she whispered. 'After all, you've promised to do something for me, haven't you?'

Perhaps Sir Clixby should have been a diplomat:

'Do you know something? I thought the Bishop was never going to finish tonight, didn't you? I shall have to have a word with the Chaplain. God knows where he found *him*?'

She moved even closer to the Master. 'Come on! We haven't got all night. Julian's train gets in at ten past ten.'

Two of the College dons stood speaking together on the cobblestones outside Lonsdale as the clock on Saint Mary the Virgin struck ten o'clock; and a sole undergraduate passing through the main gate thought he heard a brief snatch of their conversation:

'Having a woman like *her* in the Lodge? The idea's unthinkable!'

But who the woman was, the passer-by was not to know.

CHAPTER THIRTY-TWO
Monday, 26 February

How shall I give thee up, O Ephraim? How shall I cast thee off, O Israel?

(*Hosea*, ch. II, v. 8)

AT 8.45 A.M. THERE were just the two of them, Morse and Lewis, exchanging somewhat random thoughts about the case, when the young blonde girl (whom Strange had already noticed) came in with the morning post. She was a very recent addition to the typing pool, strongly recommended by the prestigious Marlborough College in the High, her secretarial skills corroborated by considerable evidence, including a Pitman Shorthand Certificate for 120 wpm.

'Your mail, sir. I'm . . .' (she looked frightened) 'I'm terribly sorry about the one on top. I just didn't notice.'

But Morse had already taken the letter from its white envelope, the latter marked, in the top left-hand corner, 'Strictly Private and Personal'.

Hullo Morse

    Tried you on the blower at Christmas but they said you were otherwise engaged probably in the boozer. I'm getting spliced. No, don't worry! I'm not asking you for anything this time!! He's nice and he's got a decent job and he says he loves me and he's okay in bed so what the hell. I don't really love him and you bloody well know why that is, don't you, you miserable stupid sod. Because I fell in love with you and I'm just as stupid as you are. St Anthony told me to tell you something but I'm not going to. I want to put my arms round you and hug you tight. God help me! Why didn't you look for me a bit harder Morse?

Ellie

No address.

Of course, there was no address.

'Did you read this?' Morse spoke in level tones, looking up at his secretary with unblinking eyes.

'Only till . . . you know, I realized . . .'

'You shouldn't have opened it.'

'No, sir,' she whispered.

'You can type all right?'

She nodded.

'And you can take shorthand?'

She nodded, despairingly.

'But you can't read?'

'As I said, sir . . .' The tears were starting.

'I heard what *you* said. Now just you listen to what *I'm* saying. This sort of thing will never happen again!'

'I promise, sir, it'll—'

'Listen!' Morse's eyes suddenly widened with an almost manic gleam, his nostrils flaring with suppressed fury as he repeated in a slow, soft voice: 'It won't happen again – not if you want to work for me any longer. Is that clear? *Never*. Now get out,' he hissed, 'and leave me, before I get angry with you.'

After she had left, Lewis too felt almost afraid to speak.

'What was all that about?' he asked finally.

'Don't you start poking your bloody nose—' But the sentence went no further. Instead, Morse picked up the letter and passed it over, his saddened eyes focused on the wainscoting.

After reading the letter, Lewis said nothing.

'I don't have much luck with the ladies, do I?'

'She's still obviously wearing the pendant.'

'I hope so,' said Morse; who might have said rather more, but there was a knock on the door, and DC Learoyd was invited into the sanctum.

Morse handed over the newspaper cuttings concerning Lord Hardiman, together with the photograph, and explained Learoyd's assignment:

'Your job's to find out all you can. It doesn't look all that promising, I know. Hardly blackmail stuff these days, is it? But Owens thinks it is. And that's the point. We're not really interested in how many times he's been knocking on the doors of the knocking-shops. It's finding the nature of his connection with *Owens*.'

Learoyd nodded his understanding, albeit a little unhappily.

'Off you go, then.'

But Learoyd delayed. 'Whereabouts do you think would be a good place to start, sir?'

Morse's eyeballs turned ceilingward.

'What about looking up His Lordship in *Debrett's Peerage*, mm? It might just tell you where he lives, don't you think?'

'But where can I find a copy?'

'What about that big building in the centre of Oxford – in Bonn Square. You've heard of it? It's called the Central Library.'

Item 2 in the manila file, as Lewis had discovered earlier that morning, was OBE (Overtaken By Events, in Morse's shorthand). The Cheltenham firm of solicitors had been disbanded in 1992, its clientèle dispersed, to all intents and purposes now permanently incommunicado.

*

Item 3 was to be entrusted into the huge hands of DC Elton, who now made his entrance; and almost immediately his exit, since he passed no observations, and asked no questions, as he looked down at the paunchy paedophiliac from St Albans.

'Leave it to me, sir.'

'And while you're at it, see how the land lies *here*.' Morse handed over the documentation on Item 4 – the accounts sheets from the surgical appliances company in Croydon.

'Good man, that,' commented Lewis, as the door closed behind the massive frame of DC Elton.

'Give me Learoyd every time!' confided Morse. 'At least he's got the intelligence to ask a few half-witted questions.'

'I don't quite follow you.'

'Wouldn't *you* need a bit of advice if you called in at some place selling surgical appliances? With Elton's great beer-gut they'll probably think he's called in for a temporary truss.'

Lewis didn't argue.

He knew better.

Also OBE, as Lewis had already discovered, was Item 5. The address Owens had written on the letter was – had been – that of a home for the mentally handicapped in Wimbledon. A Social Services inspection had uncovered gross and negligent malpractices; and the establishment had been closed down two years previously, its management and nursing staff redeployed or declared redundant. Yet no prosecutions had ensued.

'Forlorn hope,' Lewis had ventured.

And Morse had agreed. 'Did you know that "forlorn hope" has got nothing to do with "forlorn" or "hope"? It's all Dutch: "Verloren hoop" – "lost troop".'

'Very useful to know, sir.'

Seemingly oblivious to such sarcasm, Morse contemplated once more the four sets of initials that comprised Item 6:

AM✓   DC✓   JS✓   CB

with those small ticks in red Biro set against the first three of them.

'Any ideas?' asked Lewis.

'"Jonathan Swift", obviously, for "JS". I was only talking about him to the Super yesterday.'

'Julian Storrs?'

Morse grinned. 'Perhaps *all* of 'em are dons at Lonsdale.'

'I'll check.'

'So that leaves Items seven and eight – both of which I leave in your capable hands, Lewis. And lastly my own little assignment in Soho, Item nine.'

'Coffee, sir?'

'Glass of iced orange juice!'

After Lewis had gone, Morse re-read Ellie's letter, deeply hurt, and wondering whether people in the ancient past had found it quite so difficult to cope with disappointments deep as his. But at least things were over; and in the long run that might make things much easier. He tore the letter in two, in four, in eight, in sixteen, and then in thirty-two – would have torn it in sixty-four, had his fingers been strong enough – before dropping the little square pieces into his wastepaper basket.

'No ice in the canteen, sir. Machine's gone kaput.'

Morse shrugged indifferently and Lewis, sensing that the time might be opportune, decided to say something which had been on his mind:

'Just one thing I'd like to ask . . .'

Morse looked up sharply. 'You're not going to ask me where Lonsdale is, I hope!'

'No. I'd just like to ask you not to be too hard on that new secretary of yours, that's all.'

'And what the hell's that got to do with you?'

'Nothing really, sir.'

'I *agree*. And when I want your bloody advice on how to handle my secretarial staff, I'll come and ask for it. Clear?'

Morse's eyes were blazing anew. And Lewis, his own temperature now rising rapidly, left his superior's office without a further word.

*

Just before noon, Jane Edwards was finalizing an angry letter, spelling out her resignation, when she heard the message over the intercom: Morse wanted to see her in his office.

'Si' down!'

She sat down, noticing immediately that he seemed tired, the whites of his eyes lightly veined with blood.

'I'm sorry I got so cross, Jane. That's all I wanted to say.'

She remained where she was, almost mesmerized.

Very quietly he continued: 'You *will* try to forgive me – please?'

She nodded helplessly, for she had no choice.

And Morse smiled at her sadly, almost gratefully, as she left.

Back in the typing pool Ms Jane Edwards surreptitiously dabbed away the last of the slow-dropping tears, tore up her letter (so carefully composed) into sixty-four pieces; and suddenly felt, as if by some miracle of St Anthony, most inexplicably happy.

CHAPTER THIRTY-THREE

A recent survey has revealed that 80.5% of Oxford dons seek out the likely pornographic potential on the Internet before making use of that facility for purposes connected with their own disciplines or research. The figure for students, in the same university, is 2% lower

(Terence Benczik, *A Possible Future for Computer Technology*)

UNTIL THE AGE OF twelve, Morse's reading had comprised little beyond a weekly diet of the *Dandy* comic, and a monthly diet of the *Meccano Magazine* – the legacy of the latter proving considerably the richer, in that Morse had retained a lifelong delight in model train-sets and in the railways themselves. Thus it was that as he stood on Platform One at Oxford Station, he was much looking forward to his journey. Usually, he promised himself a decent read of a decent book on a trip like this. But such potential pleasures seldom materialized; hadn't materialized that afternoon either, when the punctual 2.15 p.m. from Oxford arrived fifty-nine minutes later at Paddington, where Morse immediately took a taxi to New Scotland Yard.

Although matters there had been prearranged, it was purely by chance that Morse happened to meet Paul Condon, the Metropolitan Commissioner, in the main entrance foyer.

'They're ready for you, Morse. Can't stay myself, I'm afraid. Press conference. It's not just the ethnic minorities I've upset this time – it's the ethnic majorities, too. All because I've published a few more official crime-statistics.'

Morse nodded. He wanted to say something to his old friend: something about never climbing in vain when you're going up the Mountain of Truth. But he only recalled the quotation after stepping out of the lift at the fourth floor, where Sergeant Rogers of the Porn Squad was awaiting him.

Once in Rogers' office, Morse produced the photograph of the strip-club. And immediately, with the speed of an experienced ornithologist recognizing a picture of a parrot, Rogers had identified the premises.

'Just off Brewer Street.' He unfolded a detailed map of Soho. 'Here – let me show you.'

The early evening was overcast, drizzly and dank, when like some latter-day Orpheus Morse emerged from the depths of Piccadilly Circus Underground; whence, after briefly consulting his A–Z, he proceeded by a reasonably direct route to a narrow, seedy-looking thoroughfare, where a succession of establishments promised XXXX videos and magazines (imported), sex shows (live), strip-tease (continuous) – and a selection of freshly made sandwiches (various).

And there it was! Le Club Sexy. Unmistakably so, but prosaically and repetitively now rechristened *Girls Girls Girls*. It made the former proprietors appear comparatively imaginative.

Something – some aspiration to the higher things in life, perhaps – prompted Morse to raise his eyes from the ground-floor level of the gaudily lurid fronts there to the architecture, some of it rather splendid, above.

Yet not for long.

'Come in out of the drizzle, sir! Lovely girls here.'

Morse showed his ID card, and moved into the shelter of the tiny entrance foyer.

'Do you know *her*?'

The young woman, black stockings and black mini-skirt meeting at the top of her thighs, barely glanced at the photograph thrust under her eyes.

'No.'

'Who runs this place? I want to see him.'

'*Her*. But she ain't 'ere now, is she? Why don't you call back later, handsome?'

A helmeted policeman was ambling along the opposite pavement, and Morse called him over.

'OK,' the girl said quickly. 'You bin 'ere before, right?'

'Er – one of my officers, yes.'

'Me mum used to know her, like I told the other fellah. Just a minute.'

She disappeared down the dingy stairs.

'How can I help you, sir?'

Morse showed his ID to the constable.

'Just keep your eyes on me for a few minutes.'

But there was no need.

Three minutes later, Morse had an address in Praed Street, no more than a hundred yards from Paddington Station where earlier, at the entrance to the Underground, he had admired the bronze statue of one of his heroes, Isambard Kingdom Brunel.

So Morse now took the Tube back. It had been a roundabout sort of journey.

She was in.

She asked him in.

And Morse, from a moth-eaten settee, agreed to sample a cup of Nescafé.

'Yeah, Angie Martin! Toffee-nosed little tart, if you know wo' I mean.'

'Tell me about her.'

'You're the *second* one, encha?'

'Er – one of my officers, yes.'

'Nah! He wasn't from the fuzz. Couldna bin! Giv me a couple o' twennies 'e did.'

'What did he want to know?'

'Same as you, like as not.'

'She was quite a girl, they say.'

'Lovely on 'er legs, she was, if you know wo' I mean. Most of 'em, these days, couldn't manage the bleedin' Barn Dance.'

'But *she* was good?'

'Yeah. The men used to love 'er. Stick fivers down 'er boobs and up 'er suspenders, if you know wo' I mean.'

'She packed 'em in?'

'Yeah.'

'And then?'

'Then there was this fellah, see, and he got to know 'er and see 'er after the shows, like, and 'e got starry-eyed, the silly sod. Took 'er away. Posh sort o' fellah, if you know wo' I mean. Dresses, money, 'otels – all that sort o' thing.'

'Would you remember *his* name?'

'Yeah. The other fellah – 'e showed me his photo, see?'

'His name?'

'Julius Caesar, I fink it was.'

Morse showed her the photograph of Mr and Mrs Julian Storrs.

'Yeah. That's 'im an' 'er. That's Angie.'

'Do you know why I'm asking about her?'

She looked at him shrewdly, an inch or so of grey roots merging into a yellow mop of wiry hair.

'Yeah, I got a good idea.'

'My, er, colleague told you?'

'Nah! Worked it out for meself, dint I? She was tryin' to forget wo' she was, see? She dint want to say she were a cheap tart who'd open 'er legs for a fiver, if you know wo' I mean. Bi' o' class, tho', Angie. Yeah. Real bi' o' class.'

'Will you be prepared to come up to Oxford – we'll pay your expenses, of course – to sign a statement?'

'Oxford? Yeah. Why not? Bi' o' class, Oxford, innit?'

'I suppose so, yes.'

'Wo' she done? Wo' sort of inquiry you workin' on?'

'Murder,' said Morse softly.

Mission accomplished, Morse walked across Praed Street and into the complex of Paddington Station, where he stood under the high Departures Board and noted the time of the next train: Slough, Maidenhead, Reading, Didcot, Oxford.

Due to leave in forty minutes.

He retraced his steps to the top of the Underground entrance, crushed a cigarette-stub under his heel, and walked slowly down towards the ticket-office, debating the wisdom of purchasing a second Bakerloo Line ticket to Piccadilly Circus – from which station he might take the opportunity of concentrating his attention on the ground-floor attractions of London's Soho.

CHAPTER THIRTY-FOUR

The average, healthy, well-adjusted adult gets up at seven-thirty in the morning feeling just plain terrible
               (Jean Kerr, *Where Did You Put the Aspirin*?)

WITH A LECTURE A.M. and a Faculty Meeting early p.m., Julian Storrs had not been able to give Lewis much time until late p.m.; but he was ready and waiting when, at 4 o'clock precisely, the front doorbell rang at his home, a large red-bricked property in Polstead Road, part of the Victorian suburb that stretches north from St Giles' to Summertown.

Lewis accepted the offer of real coffee, and the two of them were soon seated in armchairs opposite each other in the high-ceilinged living-room, its furniture exuding a polished mahogany elegance, where Lewis immediately explained the purpose of his call.

As a result of police investigations into the murder of Rachel James, Storrs' name had moved into the frame; well, at least his photograph had moved into the frame.

Storrs himself said nothing as he glanced down at the twin passport photograph that Lewis handed to him.

'That *is* you, sir? You and Ms James?'

Storrs took a deep breath, then exhaled. 'Yes.'

'You were having an affair with her?'

'We . . . yes, I suppose we were.'

'Did anybody know about it?'

'I'd hoped not.'

'Do you want to talk about it?'

Storrs talked. Though not for long . . .

He'd first met her just over a year earlier when he'd pulled a muscle in his right calf following an ill-judged decision to take up jogging. She was a physiotherapist, masseuse, manipulator – whatever they called such people now; and after the first two or three sessions they had met together *outside* the treatment room. He'd fallen in love with her a bit – a lot; must have done, when he considered the risks he'd taken. About once a month, six weeks, they'd managed to be together when he had some lecture to give or meeting to attend. Usually in London, where they'd book a double room, latish morning, in one of the hotels behind Paddington, drink a bottle or two of champagne, make love together most of the afternoon and – well, that was it.

'Expensive sort of day, sir? Rail-fares, hotel, champagne, something to eat . . .'

'Not really expensive, no. Off-peak day returns, one of the cheaper hotels, middle-range champagne, and we'd go to a pub for a sandwich at lunchtime. Hundred and twenty, hundred and thirty pounds – that would cover it.'

'You didn't give Ms James anything for her services?'

'It wasn't like that. I think – I hope – she enjoyed being with me. But, yes, I did sometimes give her something. She was pretty short of money – you know, her mortgage, HP commitments, the rent on the clinic.'

'How much, sir?'

'A hundred pounds. Little bit more sometimes, perhaps.'

'Does Mrs Storrs know about this?'

'No – and she mustn't!' For the first time Lewis was aware of the sharp, authoritative tone in the Senior Fellow's voice.

'How did you explain spending so much?'

'We have separate accounts. I give my wife a private allowance each month.'

Lewis grinned diffidently. 'You could always have said they were donations to Oxfam.'

Storrs looked down rather sadly at the olive-green carpet. 'You're right. That's just the sort of depths I would have sunk to.'

'Why didn't you get in touch with us? We made several appeals for anybody who knew Rachel to come forward. We guaranteed every confidence.'

'You must understand, surely? I was desperately anxious not to get drawn into things in any way.'

'Nothing else?'

'What do you mean?'

'Was someone trying to blackmail you, sir, about your affair with her?'

'Good God, no! What on earth makes you think that?'

Lewis drank the rest of his never-hot now-cold real coffee, before continuing quietly:

'I don't believe you, sir.'

And slowly the truth, or some of it, was forthcoming.

Storrs had received a letter about a fortnight earlier from someone – no signature – someone giving a PO Box address; someone claiming to have 'evidence' about him which would be shouted from the rooftops unless a payment was duly made.

'Of?' asked Lewis.

'Five thousand pounds.'

'And you paid it?'

'No. But I was stupid enough to send a thousand, in fifty-pound notes.'

'And did you get this "evidence" back?'

Storrs again looked down at the carpet, and shook his head.

'You didn't act very sensibly, did you, sir?'

'In literary circles, Sergeant, that is what is called "litotes".'

'Did you keep the letter?'

'No,' lied Storrs.

'Did you keep a note of the PO Box number?'

'No,' lied Storrs.

'Was it care of one of the local newspapers?'

'Yes.'

'*Oxford Mail?*'

'*Oxford Times.*'

The living-room door opened, and there entered a darkly elegant woman, incongruously wearing a pair of sunglasses, and dressed in a black trouser-suit – 'Legs right up to the armpits', as Lewis was later to report.

Mrs Angela Storrs briefly introduced herself, and picked up the empty cups.

'Another coffee, Sergeant?'

Her voice was Home Counties, rather deep, rather pleasing.

'No thanks. That was lovely.'

Her eyes smiled behind the sunglasses – or Lewis thought they smiled. And as she closed the living-room door softly behind her, he wondered where she'd been throughout the interview. Outside the door, perhaps, listening? Had she heard what her husband had said? Or had she known it all along?

Then the door quietly opened again.

'You won't forget you're out this evening, darling? You haven't *all* that much time, you know.'

Lewis accepted the cue and hurried on his questioning apace:

'Do you mind telling me exactly what you were doing between seven a.m. and eight a.m. last Monday, sir?'

'Last Monday morning? Ah!' Lewis sensed that Julian Storrs had suddenly relaxed – as if the tricky part of the examination was now over – as if he could safely resume his wonted donnish idiom.

'How I wish every question my students asked were susceptible to such an unequivocal answer! You see, I was in bed with my wife and we were having sex together. And why do I recall this so readily, Sergeant? Because such an occurrence has not been quite so common these past few years; nor, if I'm honest with you, quite so enjoyable as once it was.'

'Between, er, between seven and eight?' Lewis's voice was hesitant.

'Sounds a long time, you mean? Huh! You're right. More like twenty past to twenty-five past seven. What I do remember is Angela – Mrs Storrs – wanting the news on at half past. She's a great *Today* fan, and she likes to know what's going on. We just caught the tail-end of the sports news – then the main headlines on the half-hour.'

'Oh!'

'Do you believe me?'

'Would Mrs Storrs remember . . . as clearly as you, sir?'

Storrs gave a slightly bitter-sounding laugh. 'Why don't you ask her? Shall I tell her to come through? I'll leave you alone.'

'Yes, I think that would be helpful.'

Storrs got to his feet and walked towards the door.

'Just one more question, sir.' Lewis too rose to his feet. 'Don't you think you were awfully naïve to send off that money? I think anyone could have told you you weren't going to get anything back – except another blackmail note.'

Storrs walked back into the room.

'Are you a married man, Sergeant?'

'Yes.'

'How would you explain – well, say a photograph like the one you showed me?'

Lewis took out the passport photo again.

'Not too difficult, surely? You're a well-known man, sir – quite a distinguished-looking man, perhaps? So let's just say one of your admiring undergraduettes sees you at a railway station and says she'd like to have a picture taken with you. You know, one of those "Four colour photos in approximately four minutes" places. Then she could carry the pair of you around with her, like some girls carry pictures of pop stars around.'

Storrs nodded. 'Clever idea! I wish *I'd* thought of it. Er . . . can I ask *you* a question?'

'Yes?'

'Why are you still only a sergeant?'

Lewis made no comment on the matter, but asked a final question:

'You're standing for the Mastership at Lonsdale, I understand, sir?'

'Ye-es. So you can see, can't you, why all this business, you know . . . ?'

'Of course.'

Storrs' face now suddenly cleared.

'There are just the two of us: Dr Cornford – Denis Cornford – and myself. And may the better man win!'

He said it lightly, as if the pair of them were destined to cross swords in a mighty game of Scrabble – and called through to Angela, his wife.

CHAPTER THIRTY-FIVE

Keep your eyes wide open before marriage,
half shut afterwards

(Benjamin Franklin,
Poor Richard's Almanack)

IN OXFORD THAT same early evening the clouds were inkily black, the forecast set for heavy rain, with most of those walking along Broad Street or around Radcliffe Square wearing raincoats and carrying umbrellas. The majority of these people were students making their way to College Halls for their evening meals, much as their predecessors had done in earlier times, passing through the same streets, past the same familiar buildings and later returning to the same sort of accommodation, and in most cases doing some work for the morrow, when they would be listening to the same sort of lectures. Unless, perhaps, they were students of Physics or some similar discipline where breakthroughs ('Breaksthrough, if we are to be accurate, dear boy') were as regular as inaccuracies in the daily weather forecasts.

But that evening the forecast was surprisingly accurate; and at 6.45 p.m. the rains came.

Denis Cornford looked out through the window on to Holywell Street where the rain bounced off the surface of the road like arrowheads. St Peter's (Dinner, 7.00 for 7.30 p.m.) was only ten minutes' walk away but he was going to get soaked in such a downpour.

'What do you think, darling?'

'Give it five minutes. If it keeps on like this, I should get a cab. You've got plenty of time.'

'What'll you be doing?' he asked.

'Well, I don't think I'll be venturing out too far, do you?' She said it in a gentle way, and there seemed no sarcasm in her voice. She came up behind him and placed her hands on his shoulders as he stood indecisively staring out through the sheeted panes.

'Denis?'

'Mm?'

'Do you really want to be Master all *that* much?'

He turned towards her and looked directly into her dazzlingly attractive dark eyes, with that small circular white light in the centre of their irises – eyes which had always held men, and tempted them, and occasioned innumerable capitulations.

'Yes, Shelly. Yes, I do! Not quite so badly as Julian, perhaps. But badly enough.'

'What would you give – to be Master?'

'Most things, I suppose.'

'Give up your work?'

'A good deal of that would go anyway. It would be different work, that's all.'

'Would you give *me* up?'

He took her in his arms. 'Of course, I would!'

'You don't really mean—?'

He kissed her mouth with a strangely passionate tenderness.

A few minutes later they stood arm-in-arm at the window looking out at the ceaselessly teeming rain.

'I'll ring for a cab,' said Shelly Cornford.

*

On Mondays the dons' attendance at Lonsdale Dinner was usually fairly small, but Roy Porter would be there, Angela Storrs knew that: Roy Porter was almost always there. She rang him in his rooms at 6.55 p.m.

'Roy?'

'Angela! Good to hear your beautiful voice.'

'Flattery will get you exactly halfway between nowhere and everywhere.'

'I'll settle for that.'

'You're dining tonight?'

'Yep.'

'Would you like to come along afterwards and cheer up a lonely old lady?'

'Julian away?'

'Some Brains Trust at Reading University.'

'Shall I bring a bottle?'

'Plenty of bottles here.'

'Marvellous.'

'Nine-ish?'

'About then. Er . . . Angela? Is it something you want to talk about or is it just . . . ?'

'Why not both?'

'You want to know how things seem to be going with the election?'

'I'm making no secret of that.'

'You do realize I don't know anything definite at all?'

'I don't expect you to. But I'd like to talk. You can understand how I feel, can't you?'

'Of course.'

'And I've been speaking to Julian. There *are* one or two little preferments perhaps in the offing, if he's elected.'

'Really?'

'But like you, Roy, I don't know anything definite.'

'I understand. But it'll be good to be together again.'

'Oh, yes. Have a drink or two together.'

'Or three?'

'Or four?' suggested Angela Storrs, her voice growing huskier still.

The phone rang at 7.05 p.m.

'Shelly?'

'Yes.'

'You're on your own?'

'You know I am.'

'Denis gone?'

'Left fifteen minutes ago.'

'One or two things to tell you, if we could meet?'

'What sort of things?'

'Nothing definite. But there's talk about a potential benefaction from the States, and one of the trustees met Denis – met *you*, I gather, too – and, well, I can tell you all about it when we meet.'

'*All* about it?'

'It's a biggish thing, and I think we may be slightly more likely to pull it off, perhaps, if Denis . . .'

'And you'll be doing your best?'

'I can't promise anything.'

'I know that.'

'So?'

'So?'

'So you're free and I'm free.'

'On a night like this? Far too dangerous. Me coming to the Master's Lodge? No chance.'

'I agree. But, you see, one of my old colleagues is off to Greece – he's left me his key – just up the Banbury Road – lovely comfy double bed – crisp clean sheets – central heating – *en suite* facilities – mini bar. Tariff? No pounds, no shillings, no pence.'

'You remember pre-decimalization?'

'I'm not *too* old, though, am I? And I'd just love to be with you now, at this minute. More than anything in the world.'

'You ought to find a new variation on the theme, you know! It's getting a bit of a cliché.'

'Cleesháy', she'd said; but however she'd pronounced it, the barb had found its mark; and Sir Clixby's voice was softer, more serious as he answered her.

'I need you, Shelly. Please come out with me. I'll get a taxi round to you in ten minutes' time, if that's all right?'

There was silence on the other end of the line.

'Shelly?'

'Yes?'

'Will that be all right?'

'No,' she replied quietly. 'No it won't. I'm sorry.'

The line was dead.

*

Just before nine o'clock, Cornford rang home from St Peter's:

'Shelly? Denis. Look, darling, I've just noticed in my diary . . . You've not had a call tonight, have you?'

Shelly's heart registered a sudden, sharp stab of panic.

'No, why?'

'It's just that the New York publishers said they might be ringing. So, if they do, please make a note of the number and tell 'em I'll ring them back. All right?'

'Fine. Yes.'

'You having a nice evening?'

'Mm. It's lovely to sit and watch TV for a change. No engagements. No problems.'

'See you soon.'

'I hope so.'

Shelly put down the phone slowly. 'I've just noticed in my diary,' he'd said. But he hadn't, she knew that. She'd looked in his diary earlier that day, to make sure of the time of the St Peter's do. That had been the only entry on the page for 26.2.96.

Or, as she would always think of it, 2/26/96.

Just before ten o'clock, Julian Storrs rang his wife from Reading; rang three times.

The number was engaged.

He rang five minutes later.

The number was still engaged.

He rang again, after a further five minutes.

She answered.

'Angie? I've been trying to get you these last twenty minutes.'

'I've only been talking to Mum, for Christ's sake!'

'It's just that I shan't be home till after midnight, that's all. So I'll get a taxi. Don't worry about meeting me.'

'OK.'

After she had hung up, Angela Storrs took a Thames Trains timetable from her handbag and saw that Julian could easily be catching an earlier train: the 22.40 from Reading, arriving Oxford 23.20. Not that it mattered. Perhaps he was having a few drinks with his hosts? Or perhaps – the chilling thought struck her – he was checking up on her?

Hurriedly she rang her mother in South Kensington. And kept on kept on kept on talking. The call would be duly registered on the itemized BT lists and suddenly she felt considerably easier in her mind.

Morse had caught the 23.48 from Paddington that night, and at 01.00 sat unhearing as the Senior Conductor made his lugubrious pronouncement: 'Oxford, Oxford. This train has now terminated. Please be sure to take all your personal possessions with you. Thank you.'

From a deeply delicious cataleptic state, Morse was finally prodded into consciousness by no less a personage than the Senior Conductor himself.

'All right, sir?'

'Thank you, yes.'

But in truth things were not all right, since Morse had been deeply disappointed by his evening's sojourn in London. And as he walked down the station steps to the taxi-rank, he reminded himself of what he'd always known – that life was full of disappointments: of which the most immediate was that not a single taxi was in sight.

CHAPTER THIRTY-SIX

Tuesday, 27 February

Initium est dimidium facti
(Once you've started, you're halfway there)
(Latin proverb)

AN UNSHAVEN MORSE was still dressed in his mauve and Cambridge-blue pyjamas when Lewis arrived at 10 o'clock the following morning. Over the phone half an hour earlier he had learned that Morse was feeling 'rough as a bear's arse' – whatever that was supposed to mean.

For some time the two detectives exchanged information about their previous day's activities; and fairly soon the obvious truth could be simply stated: Owens was a blackmailer. Specifically, as far as investigations had thus far progressed, with the Storrs' household being the principal victims: he, for his current infidelity; she, for her past as a shop-soiled Soho tart. One thing seemed certain: that *any* disclosure was likely to be damaging, probably fatally damaging, to Julian Storrs' chances of election to the Mastership of Lonsdale.

Morse considered for a while.

'It still gives us a wonderful motive for one of them murdering Owens – not much of a one for murdering Rachel.'

'Unless Mrs Storrs was just plain jealous, sir?'

'Doubt it.'

'Or perhaps Rachel got to know something, and was doing a bit of blackmailing herself? She needed the money all right.'

'Yes.' Morse stroked his bristly jaw and sighed wearily. 'There's such a lot we've still got to check on, isn't there? Perhaps you ought to get round to Rachel's bank manager this morning.'

'Not this morning, sir – or this afternoon. I'm seeing his lordship, Sir Clixby Bream, at a quarter to twelve; then I'm going to find out who's got access to the photocopier and whatever at the Harvey Clinic.'

'Waste o' time,' mumbled Morse.

'I dunno, sir. I've got a feeling it may all tie in together somehow.'

'What with?'

'I'll know more after I've been to Lonsdale. You see, I've already learned one or two things about the situation there. The present Master's going to retire soon, as you know, and the new man's going to be taking up the reins at the start of the summer term—'

'*Trinity* Term.'

'—and they've narrowed it down to two candidates: Julian Storrs and a fellow called Cornford, Denis Cornford – he's a Lonsdale man himself, too. And they say the odds are fairly even.'

'Who's this "they" you keep talking about?'

'One of the porters there. We used to play cricket together.'

'Ridiculous game!'

'What's *your* programme today, sir?'

But Morse appeared not to hear his sergeant's question.

'Cup o' tea, Lewis?'

'Wouldn't say no.'

Morse returned a couple of minutes later, with a cup of tea for Lewis and a pint glass of iced water for himself. He sat down and looked at his wrist-watch: twenty-five past ten.

'What's your programme today?' repeated Lewis.

'I've got a meeting at eleven-thirty this morning. Nothing else much. Perhaps I'll do a bit of thinking – it's high time I caught up with you.'

As Lewis drank his tea, talking of this and that, he was aware that Morse seemed distanced – seemed almost in a world of his own. Was he listening at all?

'Am I boring you, sir?'

'What? No, no! Keep talking! That's always the secret, you know, if you want to start anything – start *thinking*, say. All you've got to do is listen to somebody talking a load of nonsense, and somehow, suddenly, something emerges.'

'I wasn't talking nonsense, sir. And if I was, *you* wouldn't have known. You weren't listening.'

Nor did it appear that Morse was listening even now – as he continued: 'I wonder what time the postman comes to Polstead Road. Storrs usually caught the ten-fifteen train from Oxford, you say . . . So he'd leave the house about a quarter to ten – bit earlier, perhaps? He's got to get to the station, park his car, buy a ticket – buy *two* tickets . . . So if the postman called about then . . . perhaps Storrs met him as he left the house and took his letters with him, and read them as he waited for Rachel, then stuffed 'em in his jacket-pocket.'

'So?'

'So if . . . What do most couples do after they've had sex together?'

'Depends, I suppose.' Lewis looked uneasily at his superior. 'Go to sleep?'

Morse smiled waywardly. 'It's as tiring as that, is it?'

'Well, if they did it more than once.'

'Then she – *she*, Lewis – stays awake and goes quietly through his pockets and finds the blackmail letter. By the way, did you ask him *when* he received it?'

'No, sir.'

'Well, find out! She sees the letter and she knows she can blackmail *him*. Not about the affair they're having, perhaps – they're both in that together – but about something else she discovered from the letter . . . You know, I suspect that our Ms James was getting a bit of a handful for our Mr Storrs. What do *you* think?' (But Lewis was given no time at all to think.) 'What were the last couple of dates they went to London together?'

'That's something else I shall have to check, sir.'

'Well, check it! You see, we've been coming round to the idea that somebody was trying to murder Owens, haven't we? And murdered Rachel by mistake. But perhaps we're wrong, Lewis. Perhaps we're wrong.'

Morse looked flushed and excited as he drained his iced water and got to his feet.

'I'd better have a quick shave.'

'What else have you got on your programme—?'

'As I say, you see what happens when you start talking nonsense! You're indispensable, old friend. Absolutely *indispensable*!'

Lewis, who had begun to feel considerable irritation at Morse's earlier brusque demands, was now completely mollified.

'I'll be off then, sir.'

'No you won't! I shan't be more than a few minutes. You can run me down to Summertown.'

(*Almost* completely mollified.)

'You still haven't told me what—' began Lewis as he waited at the traffic-lights by South Parade.

But a clean-shaven Morse had suddenly stiffened in his safety-belt beside him.

'What did you say the name of that other fellow was, Lewis? The chap who's standing against Storrs?'

'Cornford, Denis Cornford. Married to an American girl.'

'"DC", Lewis! Do you remember in the manila file? Those four sets of initials?'

Lewis nodded, for in his mind's eye he could see that piece of paper as clearly as Morse:

AM✓   DC✓   JS✓   CB

'There they are,' continued Morse, 'side-by-side in the middle – Denis Cornford and Julian Storrs, flanked on either side by Angela Martin – I've little doubt! – and – might it be? – Sir Clixby Bream.'

'So you think Owens might have got something on all—?'

'Slow down!' interrupted Morse. 'Just round the corner here.'

Lewis turned left at the traffic-lights into Marston Ferry Road and stopped immediately outside the Summertown Health Centre.

'Wish me well,' said Morse as he alighted.

PART THREE

CHAPTER THIRTY-SEVEN
Tuesday, 27 February

The land of Idd was a happy one. Well, almost. There was one
teeny problem. The King had sleepless nights about it and the
villagers were very scared. The problem was a dragon called
Diabetes. He lived in a cave on top of a hill. Every day he
would roar loudly. He never came down the hill but everyone
was still very scared just in case he did

(Victoria Lee, *The Dragon of Idd*)

FROM THE WAITING-ROOM on the first floor, Morse heard his
name called.

'How can I help?' asked Dr Paul Roblin, a man Morse had
sought so earnestly to avoid over the years, unless things were
bordering on the desperate.

As they were now.

'I think I've got diabetes.'

'Why do you think that?'

'I've got a book. It mentions some of the symptoms.'

'Which are?'

'Loss of weight, tiredness, a longing for drink.'

'You've had the last one quite a while though, haven't you?'

Morse nodded wearily. 'I've lost weight; I could sleep all the
time; and I drink a gallon of tap-water a day.'

'As *well* as the beer?'

Morse was silent, as Roblin jabbed a lancet into the little finger
of his left hand, squeezed the skin until a domed globule
appeared, then smeared the blood on to a test-strip. After thirty
seconds, he looked down at the reading. And for a while sat
motionless, saying nothing. 'How did you get here, Mr Morse?'

'Car.'

'Is your car here?'

'No, I had a lift. Why?'

'Well, I'm afraid I couldn't let you drive a car now.'

'Why's that?'

'It's serious. Your blood sugar level's completely off the end of the chart. We shall have to get you to the Radcliffe Infirmary as soon as we can.'

'What are you telling me?'

'You should have seen me way before this. Your pancreas has packed in completely. You'll probably be on three or four injections of insulin a day for the rest of your life. You may well have done God-knows-what damage to your eyes and your kidneys – we shall have to find out. The important thing is to get you in hospital immediately.'

He reached for the phone.

'I only live just up the road,' protested Morse.

Roblin put his hand over the mouthpiece. 'They'll have a spare pair of pyjamas and a toothbrush. Don't worry!'

'You don't realize—' began Morse.

'Hello? Hello! Can you get an ambulance here – Summertown Health Centre – straightaway, please . . . The Radcliffe Infirmary . . . Thank you.'

'You don't realize I'm in the middle of a murder inquiry.'

But Roblin had dialled a second number, and was already speaking to someone else.

'David? Ah, glad you're there! Have you got a bed available? . . . Bit of an emergency, yes . . . He'll need an insulin-drip, I should think. But you'll know . . . Yes . . . Er, Mr Morse – initial "E". He's a chief inspector in the Thames Valley CID.'

Half an hour later – weight (almost thirteen stone), blood pressure (alarmingly high), blood sugar level (still off the scale), details of maternal and paternal grandparents' deaths (ill-remembered), all of these duly recorded – Morse found himself lying supine, in a pair of red-striped pyjamas, in the Geoffrey Harris Ward in the Radcliffe Infirmary, just north of St Giles', at the bottom of the Woodstock Road. A tube from the insulin-drip suspended at the side of his bed was attached to his right arm by a Sellotaped needle stuck into him just above the inner wrist, allowing little, if any, lateral movement without the sharpest reminder of physical agony.

It was this tube that Morse was glumly considering when the Senior Consultant from the Diabetes Centre came round: Dr David Matthews, a tall, slim, Mephistophelian figure, with darkly ascetic, angular features.

'As I've told you all, I'm in the middle of a murder inquiry,' reiterated Morse, as Matthews sat on the side of the bed.

'And can I tell *you* something? You're going to forget all about that, unless you want to kill yourself. With a little bit of luck you may be all right, do you understand? So far you don't seem to have done yourself all that much harm. Enough, though! But you're going to have to forget everything about work – *everything* – if you're going to come through this business without too much damage. You do know what I mean, don't you?'

Morse didn't. But he nodded helplessly.

'Only here four or five days, if you do as we tell you.'

'But, as I say—'

'No "buts", I'm afraid. Then you might be home Saturday or Sunday.'

'But there's so much to do!' remonstrated Morse almost desperately.

'Weren't those the words of Cecil Rhodes?'

'Yes, I think they were.'

'The last words, if I recall aright.'

Morse was silent.

And the Senior Consultant continued: 'Look, there are three basic causes of diabetes – well, that's an over-simplification. But you're not a medical man.'

'Thank you,' said Morse.

'Hereditary factors, stress, excessive booze. You'd score five . . . six out of ten on the first. Your father had diabetes, I see.'

'Latish in life.'

'Well, you're not exactly a youngster yourself.'

'Perhaps not.'

'Stress? You're not too much of a worryguts?'

'Well, I worry about the future of the human race – does that count?'

'What about booze? You seem to drink quite a bit, I see?'

So Morse told him the truth; or, to be more accurate, told him between one-half and one-third of the truth.

Matthews got to his feet, peered at the insulin-drip, and marginally readjusted some control thereon.

'Six out of ten on the second; ten out of ten on the third, I'm afraid. And by the way, I'm not allowing you any visitors. None at all – not even close relatives. Just me and the nurses here.'

'I haven't got any close relatives,' said Morse.

Matthews now stood at the foot of his bed. 'You've already had *somebody* wanting to see you, though. Fellow called Lewis.'

After Matthews had gone, Morse lay back and thought of his colleague. And for several minutes he felt very low, unmanned as he was with a strangely poignant gratitude.

CHAPTER THIRTY-EIGHT
Thursday, 29 February

The relations between us were peculiar. He was a man of habits, narrow and concentrated habits, and I had become one of them. But apart from this I had uses. I was a whetstone for his mind, I stimulated him. He liked to think aloud in my presence

(Conan Doyle, *The Adventures of the Creeping Man*)

'AND 'OW IS 'E TODAY, then?' asked Mrs Lewis when her husband finally returned home on Thursday evening, and when soon the fat was set a-sizzling in the chip-pan, with the two eggs standing ready to be broken in the frying pan.

'On the mend.'

'They always say that.'

'No. He's genuinely on the mend.'

'Why can't 'e 'ave visitors then? Not contagious, is it, this diabetes?'

Lewis smiled at her. Brought up as she had been in the Rhondda Valley, the gentle Welsh lilt in her voice was an abiding delight with him – though not, to be quite truthful, with everyone.

'He'll probably be out this weekend.'

'And back to work?'

Lewis put his hands on his wife's shoulders as she stood watching the pale chips gradually turning brown.

'This weekend, I should think.'

'You've always enjoyed working with 'im, 'aven't you?'

'Well . . .'

'I've often wondered why. It's not as if 'e's ever treated you all that well, is it?'

'I'm the only one he's ever treated well,' said Lewis quietly.

She turned towards him, laterally shaking the chips with a practised right hand.

'And 'ow are *you* today, then? The case going OK?'

Lewis sat down at the red Formica-topped kitchen table and surveyed the old familiar scene: lacy white doily, knife and fork, bottle of tomato ketchup, bread and butter on one side, and a glass of milk on the other. He should have felt contented; and as he looked back over another long day, perhaps he did.

Temporarily, Chief Superintendent David Blair from the Oxford City Force had been given overall responsibility for the Rachel James murder inquiry, and he had spent an hour at Kidlington Police HQ earlier that afternoon, where Lewis had brought him up to date with the latest developments.

Not that they had amounted to much . . .

The reports from DCs Learoyd and Elton were not destined significantly to further the course of the investigation. Lord Hardiman, aged eighty-seven, a sad victim of Alzheimer's disease, and now confined to his baronial hall in Bedfordshire, was unlikely, it seemed, to squander any more of his considerable substance in riotous living along the Reeperbahn. Whilst the child-fondler, recognized immediately by his erstwhile neighbours, was likewise unlikely to disturb the peace for the immediate future, confined as he was at Her Majesty's Pleasure in Reading for the illegal publication and propagation of material deemed likely to deprave and corrupt.

More interestingly, Lewis had been able to report on his own inquiries, particularly on his second interview with Julian Storrs, who had been more willing now to divulge details of dates, times, and hotels for his last three visits to Paddington with Rachel James.

And after that, to report on his interview with Sir Clixby Bream, who had informed Lewis of the imminent election of a new Master, and who had given him a copy of the College Statutes (fortunately, rendered *Anglice*) with their emphasis upon the need for any candidate for the Mastership to be in good physical health (*in corpore sano*).

'Nobody can guarantee good health,' Blair had observed.

'No, but sometimes you can almost guarantee *bad* health, perhaps, sir?'

'We're still no nearer to finding how Owens got a copy of that letter?'

'No. I went round to the Harvey Clinic again yesterday. No luck, though. The doc who wrote the letter got himself killed, as you know, and all his records have been distributed around . . . reallocated, sort of thing.'

'They're all in a mess, you mean?'

Lewis nodded. 'Somehow Owens got to know that he hadn't got much time left, didn't he? So he's got three things on him: he knows a good deal about Angela Storrs' past; he knows he was having an affair with Rachel James; and he knows he's pretty certainly hiding his medical reports from his colleagues in College – from everybody, perhaps.'

Quite certainly Morse would have complained about the confusing profusion of third-person pronouns in the previous sentence. But Blair seemed to follow the account with no difficulty.

'From his wife, too?' he asked.

'I wouldn't be surprised.'

'You know, Morse once told me that any quack who tells you when you're going to die is a bloody fool.'

Lewis grinned. 'He's told me the same thing about a dozen times.'

'He's getting better, you say?'

'Out by the weekend, they think.'

'You hope so, don't you?'

Lewis nodded, and Blair continued quietly:

'You're peculiar companions, you know, you and Morse. Don't you think? He can be an ungrateful, ungracious sod at times.'

'Almost always, sir,' admitted Lewis, smiling to himself as if recalling mildly happy memories.

'He'll have to take things more easily now.'

'Would you care to tell him that?'

'No.'

'Just one thing more, sir – about Owens. I really think we ought to consider the possibility that he's in a bit of danger. There must be quite a few people who'd gladly see him join Rachel in the mortuary.'

'What do you suggest, Sergeant?'

'That's the trouble, isn't it? We can't just give him a bodyguard.'

'There's only one way of keeping an eye on him all the time.'

'Bring him in, you mean, sir? But we can't do that – not yet.'

'No. No good bringing him in and then having to let him go. We shall need something to charge him with. I don't suppose . . .' Blair hesitated. 'I don't suppose there's any chance that *he* murdered Rachel James?'

'I don't think so, myself, no.'

'What's Morse think?'

'He *did* think so for a start, but . . . Which reminds me, sir. I'd better make another trip to the newspaper offices tomorrow.'

'Don't go and do everything yourself, Sergeant.'

'Will you promise to tell the Chief Inspector that?'

'No,' replied Blair as he prepared to leave; but hesitantly so, since he was feeling rather worried himself now about what Lewis had said.

'What did Morse think about the possibility of Owens getting himself murdered?'

'Said he could look after himself; said he was a streetwise kid from the start; said he was a survivor.'

'Let's hope he's right.'

'Sometimes he is, sir,' said Lewis.

CHAPTER THIRTY-NINE

We forget ourselves and our destinies in health; and the chief use of temporary sickness is to remind us of these concerns
(Ralph Waldo Emerson, *Journals*)

SISTER JANET MCQUEEN – an amply-bosomed woman now in her early forties, single and darkly attractive to the vast majority of men – had been considerably concerned about her new patient: one E. Morse. Patently, in spite of his superficial patter, the man knew nothing whatsoever of medicine, and appeared unaware, and strangely unconcerned, about his physical well-being; ill-being, rather.

On several occasions during the following days she'd spent

some time with him, apologizing for the two-hourly check on his blood sugar levels (even during the night); explaining the vital rôle of the pancreas in the metabolic processes; acquainting him with the range, colour, purpose, and possible efficacy, of the medication and equipment now prescribed – single-use insulin syringes, Human Ultratard, Human Actrapid, Unilet Lancets, Exactech Reagent Strips, Enalapril Tablets, Frusemide Tablets, Nifedipine Capsules . . .

He'd seemed to understand most of it, she thought. And from their first meeting she'd realized that the prematurely white-haired man was most unusual.

'Glad about the pills,' he'd said.

'You are?'

'Different colours, aren't they? White, pink, brown-and-orange. Good, that is. Gives a man a bit of psychological confidence. In the past, I've always thought that confidence was a bit overrated. Not so sure now, though, Sister.'

She made no answer. But his words were to remain in her mind; and she knew that she would look forward to talking with this man again.

By Tuesday evening, Morse's blood sugar level had fallen dramatically. And at coffee-time on Wednesday morning, Sister McQueen came to his bedside, the fingers of her right hand almost automatically feeling his pulse as she flicked the watch from the starched white lapel of her uniform.

'Shall I survive till the weekend?'

'You hardly deserve to.'

'I'm OK now, you mean?'

She snorted in derision; but winsomely so.

'You know why we didn't want you to have any visitors?'

'You wanted me all to yourself?' suggested Morse.

She shook her head slowly, her sensitive, slim lips widening into a saddened smile.

'No. Dr Matthews thought you were probably far too worried about life – about your work – about other things, perhaps. And he didn't want to take any chances. Visitors are always a bit of a stress.'

'He needn't have worried too much about that.'

'But you're wrong, aren't you?' She got to her feet. 'You've had four people on the phone every day, regular callers – regular as well-adjusted bowels.'

Morse looked up at her.

'Four?'

'Somebody called Lewis – somebody called Strange – somebody called Blair. All from the police, I think.'

'*Four*, you said?'

'Ah yes. Sorry. And somebody called Jane. She works for you, she said. Sounds awfully sweet.'

As he lay back after Sister had gone, and switched on the headphones to Classic FM, Morse was again aware of how low he had sunk, since almost everything – a kindly look, a kindly word, a kindly thought, even the *thought* of a kindly thought – seemed to push him ever nearer to the rim of tears. Forget it, Morse! Forget yourself and forget your health! For a while anyway. He picked up *The ABC Murders* which he'd found in the meagre ward-library. He'd always enjoyed Agatha Christie: a big fat puzzle ready for the reader from page one. Perhaps it might help a little with the big fat puzzle waiting for him in the world outside the Radcliffe Infirmary . . .

ABC.

Alexander Bonaparte Cust.

Adèle Beatrice Cecil.

Ann Berkeley Cox . . .

Within five minutes Morse was asleep.

On Thursday afternoon, a slim, rather prissy young dietitian came to sit beside Morse's bed and to talk quickly, rationally, and at inordinate length, about such things as calories and carrots and carbohydrates.

'And if you ever feel like a pint of beer once a week, well, you just go ahead and have one! It shouldn't do you much harm.'

Morse's spirit groaned within him.

The Senior Consultant himself came round again the following morning. The insulin-drip had long gone; blood-readings were gradually reverting to a manageable level; blood pressure was markedly down.

'You've been very lucky,' said Matthews.

'I don't deserve it,' admitted Morse.

'No. You don't.'

'When are you going to let me go?'

'Home? Tomorrow, perhaps. Work? Up to you. I'd take a fortnight off myself – but then I've got far more sense than you have.'

Well before lunchtime on Saturday, already dressed and now instructed to await an ambulance, Morse was seated in the entrance corridor of the Geoffrey Harris Ward when Sister McQueen came to sit beside him.

'I'm almost sorry to be going,' said Morse.

'You'll miss us?'

'I'll miss *you*.'

'Really?'

'Could I ring you – here?' asked Morse diffidently.

'In those immortal words: "Don't ring us – we'll ring you."'

'You mean you *will* ring me?'

She shook her head. 'Perhaps not. And it doesn't matter, does it? What matters is that you look after yourself. You're a nice man – a very nice man! – and I'm so glad we met.'

'If I did come to see you, would you look after me?'

'Bed and Breakfast, you mean?' She smiled. 'You'd always be welcome in the McQueen Arms.'

She stood up as an ambulance-man came through the flappy doors.

'Mr Morse?' he asked.

'I'd love to be in the McQueen arms,' Morse managed to say, very quietly.

As he was driven past the Neptune fountain in the forecourt of the Radcliffe Infirmary, he wondered if Sister had appreciated that shift in key, from the upper-case Arms to the lower-case arms.

He hoped she had.

CHAPTER FORTY
Sunday, 3 March

Important if true
(Inscription A.W. Kinglake wished
to see on all churches)

Forgive us for loving familiar hymns and religious feelings
more than Thee, O Lord
(From the United Presbyterian Church Litany)

'BUT I'D BETTER not call before the *Archers'* omnibus?' Lewis
had suggested the previous evening.

'Don't worry about that. I've kept up with events in Ambridge
all week. And I don't want to hear 'em again. I just wonder when
these scriptwriters will understand that beautiful babies are about
as boring as happy marriages.'

'About ten then, sir?'

Morse, smartly dressed in clean white shirt and semi-well-
pressed grey flannels, was listening to the last few minutes of the
Morning Service on Radio 4 when Lewis was quickly admitted –
and cautioned.

'Sh! My favourite hymn.'

In the silence that followed, the two men sat listening with
Morse's bleating, uncertain baritone occasionally accompanying
the singing.

'Didn't know you were still interested in that sort of thing,'
volunteered Lewis after it had finished.

'I still love the old hymns – the more sentimental the better,
for my taste. Wonderful words, didn't you think?' And softly,
but with deep intensity, he recited a few lines he'd just sung:

> *'I trace the rainbow through the rain*
> *And feel the promise is not vain*
> *That Morn shall tearless be.'*

But Lewis, who had noted the moisture in Morse's eyes, and
who had sensed that the promise of the last line might soon be

broken, immediately injected a more joyful note into the conversation.

'It's really good to have you back, sir.'

Apparently unaware that any reciprocal words of gratitude were called for, Morse asked about the case; and learned that the police were perhaps 'treading water' for the time being, and that Chief Superintendent Blair was nominally i/c pro tem.

'David Blair. Best copper in the county' (Lewis was about to nod a partial agreement) 'apart from me, of course.'

And suddenly Lewis felt very happy that he was back in harness with this arrogant, ungracious, vulnerable, lovable man with whom he had worked so closely for so many years; a man who looked somewhat slimmer, somewhat paler than when he had last seen him, but who sounded not a whit less brusque as he now asked whether Lewis had checked up on the time when Storrs had left home for his last visit with Rachel to Paddington, and the time when the postman had delivered the mail in Polstead Road that same morning.

And Lewis had.

9.45–9.50 a.m.

9.10–9.20 a.m.

Respectively.

'From which, Lewis, we may draw *what* conclusions?'

'Precious few, as far as I can see.'

'Absolutely! What other new facts have you got for me?'

So Lewis told him.

It was ten minutes short of noon when Morse dropped the mini-bombshell.

'The Cherwell, do you think, Lewis? The landlord there always keeps a decent pint.'

'But beer's full of sugar, isn't it? You can't—'

'Lewis! This diabetes business is all about *balance*, that's all. I've got to take all this insulin because I can't produce any insulin *myself* – to counteract any sugar intake. But if I didn't have any sugar intake to counteract, I'd be in one helluva mess. I'd become *hypoglycaemic*, and you know what that means.'

Not having the least idea, Lewis remained silent as Morse took out a black pen-like object from his pocket, screwed off one end, removed a white plastic cap from the needle there, twisted a calibrator at the other end, unbuttoned his shirt, and plunged the needle deep into his midriff.

Lewis winced involuntarily.

But Morse, looking up like some young child expecting praise after taking a very nasty-tasting medicine, seemed wholly pleased with himself.

'See? That'll take care of things. No problem.'

With great care, Lewis walked back from the bar with a pint of Bass and a glass of orange juice.

'I've been waiting a long time for this,' enthused Morse, burying his nose into the froth, taking a gloriously gratifying draught of real ale, and showing, as he relaxed back, a circle of blood on his white shirt just above the waist.

After a period of silence, during which Morse several times raised his glass against the window to admire the colour of the beer, Lewis asked the key question.

'What have they said about you starting work again?'

'What do you say about us seeing Storrs and Owens this afternoon?'

'You'll have a job with Storrs, sir. Him and his missus are in Bath for the weekend.'

'What about Owens?'

'Dunno. Perhaps he's away, too – on another of his personnel courses.'

'One easy way of finding out, Lewis. There's a telephone just outside the Gents.'

'Look, sir! For heaven's sake! You've been in hospital a week—'

'Five days, to be accurate, and only for observation. They'd never have let me out unless—'

But he got no further.

The double doors of the Cherwell had burst open and there, framed in the doorway, jowls a-quiver, stood Chief Superintendent Strange – looking around, spying Morse, walking across, and sitting down.

'Like a beer, sir?' asked Lewis.

'Large single-malt Scotch – no ice, no water.'

'And it's the same again for me,' prompted Morse, pushing over his empty glass.

'I might have known it,' began Strange, after regaining his breath. 'Straight out of hospital and straight into the nearest boozer.'

'It's *not* the nearest.'

'Don't remind me! Dixon's already carted me round to the Friar Bacon – the King's Arms – the Dew Drop – and now here. And it's about time somebody reminded you that you're in the Force to reduce the crime-level, not the bloody beer-level.'

'We were talking about the case when you came in, sir.'

'*What* case?' snapped Strange.

'The murder case – Rachel James.'

'Ah yes! I remember the case well; I remember the address, too: Number 17 Bloxham Drive, wasn't it? Well, you'd better get off your arse, matey' (at a single swallow, he drained the Scotch which Lewis had just placed in front of him) 'because if you *are* back at work, you can just forget that beer and get over smartish to Bloxham Drive again. Number 15, this time. Another murder. Chap called Owens – Geoffrey Owens. I think you've heard of him?'

PART FOUR

CHAPTER FORTY-ONE

For now we see through a glass darkly; but then face to face
(*I Corinthians*, ch. 13, v. 12)

DÉJÀ VU.

The street, the police cars, the crowd of curious onlookers, the SOCOs – repetition almost everywhere, as if nothing was found only once in the world. Just that single significant shift: the shift from one terraced house to another immediately adjacent.

Morse himself had said virtually nothing since Strange had brought the news of Owens' murder; and said nothing now as he sat in the kitchen of Number 15, Bloxham Drive, elbows resting on the table there, head resting on his hands. For the moment his job was to bide his time, he knew that, during the interregnum between the activities of other professionals and his own assumption of authority: a necessary yet ever frustrating interlude, like that when an in-flight air-stewardess rehearses the safety drill before take-off.

By all rights he should have felt weary and defeated; but this was not the case. Physically, he felt considerably fitter than he had the week before; and mentally, he felt eager for that metaphorical take-off to begin. Some people took little or no mental exercise except that of jumping to conclusions; while Morse was a man who took excessive mental exercise and who *still* jumped to dubious conclusions, as indeed he was to do now. But as some of his close colleagues knew – and most especially as Sergeant Lewis knew – it was at times like this, with preconceptions proved false and hypotheses undone, that Morse's brain was wont to function with astonishing speed, if questionable lucidity.

As it did now.

Lewis walked through just before 2 p.m.

'Anything I can do for the minute, sir?'

'Just nip out and get me the *Independent on Sunday*, will you? And a packet of Dunhill.'

'Do you think—?' But Lewis stopped; and waited as Morse reluctantly took a five-pound note from his wallet.

For the next few minutes Morse was aware that his brain was still frustrated and unproductive. And there was something else, too. For some reason, and for a good while now, he had been conscious that he might well have missed a vital clue in the case (cases!) which so far he couldn't quite catch. It was a bit like going through a town on a high-speed train when the eyes had *almost* caught the name of the station as it flashed so tantalizingly across the carriage-window.

Lewis returned five minutes later with the cigarettes, which Morse put unopened into his jacket-pocket; and with the newspaper, which Morse opened at the Cryptic Crossword ('Quixote'), glanced at 1 across: 'Some show dahlias in the Indian pavilion (6)' and immediately wrote in 'HOWDAH'.

'Excuse me, sir – but how do you get that?'

'Easiest of all the clue-types, that. The letters are all there, in their proper, consecutive order. It's called the "hidden" type.'

'Ah, yes!' Lewis looked and, for once, Lewis saw. 'Shall I leave you for two or three minutes to finish it off, sir?'

'No. It'll take me at least five. And it's time you sat down and gave me the latest news on things here.'

Owens' body Morse had already viewed, howsoever briefly, sitting back, as it had been, against the cushions of the living-room settee, the green covers permeated with many pints of blood. His face unshaven, his long hair loose down to the shoulders, his eyes open and staring, almost (it seemed) as if in permanent disbelief; and two bullet wounds showing raggedly in his chest. Dead four to six hours, that's what Dr Laura Hobson had already suggested – a margin narrower than Morse had expected, though wider than he'd hoped; death, she'd claimed, had fairly certainly been 'instant' (or 'instantaneous', as Morse would have preferred). There were no signs of any forcible entry to the house: the front door had been found still locked and bolted; the tongue of the Yale on the back door still engaged, though not clicked to the locked position from the inside. On the mantelpiece above the electric fire (not switched on) was a small oblong virtually free of the generally pervasive dust.

The body would most probably not have been discovered that

day had not John Benson, a garage mechanic from Hartwell's Motors, agreed to earn himself a little untaxed extra income by fixing a few faults on Owens' car. But Benson had been unable to get any answer when he called just after 11.15 a.m.; had finally peered through the open-curtained front window; had rapped repeatedly, and increasingly loudly, against the pane when he saw Owens lying asleep on the settee there.

But Owens was not asleep. So much had become gradually apparent to Benson, who had dialled 999 at about 11.30 a.m. from the BT phone-box at the entrance to the Drive.

Thus far no one, it appeared, had seen or heard anything untoward that morning between seven and eight o'clock, say. House-to-house inquiries would soon be under way, and might provide a clue or two. But concerning such a possibility Morse was predictably (though, as it happened, mistakenly) pessimistic. Early Sunday morning was not a time when many people were about, except for dog-owners and insomniacs: the former, judging from the warnings on the lamp-posts concerning the fouling of verges and footpaths, not positively encouraged to parade their pets along the street; the latter, if there were any, not as yet coming forward with any sightings of strangers or hearings of gunshots.

No. On the face of it, it had seemed a typical, sleepy Sunday morning, when the denizens of Bloxham Drive had their weekly lie-in, arose late, walked around their homes in dressing-gowns, sometimes boiled an egg, perhaps – and settled down to read in the scandal sheets about the extra-marital exploits of the great and the not-so-good.

But one person had been given no chance to read his Sunday newspaper, for the *News of the World* lay unopened on the mat inside the front door of Number 15; and few of the others in the Drive that morning were able to indulge their delight in adulterous liaisons, stunned as they were by disbelief and, as the shock itself lessened, by a growing sense of fear.

At 2.30 p.m. Morse was informed that few if any of the neighbours were likely to be helpful witnesses – except the old lady in Number 19. Morse should see her himself, perhaps?

'Want me to come along, sir?'

'No, Lewis. You get off and try to find out something about

Storrs – *and* his missus. Bath, you say? He probably left details of where he'd be at the Porters' Lodge – that's the usual drill. And do it from HQ. Better keep the phone here free.'

Mrs Adams was a widow of some eighty summers, a small old lady who had now lost all her own teeth, much of her wispy white hair, and even more of her hearing. But her wits were sharp enough, Morse sensed that immediately; and her brief evidence was of considerable interest. She had slept poorly the previous night; got up early; made herself some tea and toast; listened to the news on the radio at seven o'clock; cleared away; and then gone out the back to empty her waste-bin. *That*'s when she'd seen him!

'Him?'

'Pardon?'

'You're sure it was a *man*?'

'Oh yes. About twenty – twenty-five past seven.'

The case was under way.

'You didn't hear any shots or bangs?'

'Pardon?'

Morse let it go.

But he managed to convey his thanks to her, and to explain that she would be asked to sign a short statement. As he prepared to leave, he gave her his card.

'I'll leave this with you, Mrs Adams. If you remember anything else, please get in touch with me.'

He thought she'd understood; and he left her there in her kitchen, holding his card about three or four inches from her pale, rheumy eyes, squinting obliquely at the wording.

She was not, as Morse had quickly realized, ever destined to be called before an identity parade; for although she might be able to spot that all of them were men, any physiognomical differentiation would surely be wholly beyond the capacity of those tired old eyes.

Poor Mrs Adams!

Sans teeth, sans hair, sans ears, sans eyes – and very soon, alas, sans everything.

Seldom, in any investigation, had Morse so badly mishandled a key witness as now he mishandled Mrs Arabella Adams.

CHAPTER FORTY-TWO

Alibi (*adv.*): in another place, elsewhere
(*Small's Latin-English Dictionary*)

SOME PERSONS IN life eschew all sense of responsibility, and are never wholly at ease unless they are closely instructed as to what to do, and how and when to do it. Sergeant Lewis was not such a person, willing as he was always to shoulder his share of responsibility and, not infrequently, to face some apportionment of blame. Yet, to be truthful, he was ever most at ease when given some specific task, as he had been now; and he experienced a pleasing sense of purpose as he drove up to Police HQ that same afternoon.

One thing only disturbed him more than a little. For almost a week now Morse had forgone, been forced to forgo, both beer and cigarettes. And what foolishness it was to capitulate, as Morse *had* done, to both, within the space of only a couple of hours! But that's what life was all about – personal decisions; and Morse had clearly decided that the long-term disintegration of his liver and his lungs was a price well worth paying, even with diabetes, for the short-term pleasures of alcohol and nicotine.

Yet Morse was still on the ball. As he had guessed, Storrs had left details of his weekend whereabouts at the Porters' Lodge. And very soon Lewis was speaking to the Manager of Bath's Royal Crescent Hotel – an appropriately cautious man, but one who was fully co-operative once Lewis had explained the unusual and delicate nature of his inquiries. The Manager would ring back, he promised, within half an hour.

Lewis picked up the previous day's copy of the *Daily Mirror*, and sat puzzling for a few minutes over whether the answer to 1 across – 'River (3)' – was CAM, DEE, EXE, FAL, and so on through the alphabet; finally deciding on CAM, when he saw that it would fit neatly enough with COD, the fairly obvious answer to 1 down – 'Fish (3)'. He had made a firm start. But thereafter he had proceeded little, since the combination which had found favour with the setter of the crossword (EXE/EEL) had wholly eluded him. His minor hypothesis, like Morse's earlier major one, was sadly undone.

But he had no time to return (quite literally) to square one, since the phone rang. It had taken the Manager only fifteen minutes to assemble his fairly comprehensive information . . .

Mr and Mrs J. Storrs had checked into the hotel at 4 p.m. the previous afternoon, Saturday, 2 March: just the one night, at the special weekend-break tariff of £125 for a double room. The purpose of the Storrs' visit (almost certainly) had been to hear the Bath Festival Choir, since one of the reception staff had ordered a taxi for them at 7 p.m. to go along to the Abbey, where the Fauré *Requiem* was the centrepiece of the evening concert. The couple had been back in the hotel by about half past nine, when they had immediately gone into the restaurant for a late, pre-booked dinner, the only extra being a bottle of the house red wine. If the sergeant would like to see the itemized bill . . . ?

No one, it appeared, had seen the couple after about 11 p.m., when they had been the last to leave the restaurant. Before retiring, however, Mr Storrs had rung through to room service to order breakfast for the two of them, in their room, at 7.45 a.m.: a full English for himself, a Continental one for his wife.

Again, the itemized order was available if the sergeant . . .

Latest check-out from the hotel (as officially specified in the brochure) was noon. But the Storrs had left a good while before then. As with the other details (the Manager explained) some of the times given were just a little vague, since service personnel had changed. But things could very soon be checked. The account had been settled by Mr Storrs himself on a Lloyds Bank Gold Card (the receptionist recalled this clearly), and one of the porters had driven the Storrs' BMW round to the front of the hotel from the rear garage – being tipped (it appeared) quite liberally for his services.

So that was that.

Or *almost* so – since Lewis was very much aware that Morse would hardly be overjoyed with such findings; and he now asked a few further key questions.

'I know it's an odd thing to ask, sir, but are you completely sure that these people *were* Mr and Mrs Storrs?'

'Well, I . . .' The Manager hesitated long enough for Lewis to jam a metaphoric foot inside the door.

'You knew them – know them – *personally*?'

'I've only been Manager here for a couple of years. But, yes – they were here twelve months or so ago.'

'People change, though, don't they? *He* might have changed quite a bit, Mr Storrs, if he'd been ill or . . . or something?'

'Oh, it was *him* all right. I'm sure of that. Well, *almost* sure. And he signed the credit-card bill, didn't he? It should be quite easy to check up on that.'

'And you're quite sure it was *her*, sir? Mrs Storrs? Is there any possibility at all that he was spending the night with someone else?'

The laugh at the other end of the line was full of relief and conviction.

'Not – a – chance! You can be one hundred per cent certain of that. I think everybody here remembers her. She's, you know, she's a bit sharp, if you follow my meaning. Nothing unpleasant – don't get me wrong! But a little bit, well, *severe*. She dressed that way, too: white trouser-suit, hair drawn back high over the ears, beauty-parlour face. Quite the lady, really.'

Lewis drew on his salient reminiscence of Angela Storrs:

'It's not always easy to recognize someone who's wearing sunglasses, though.'

'But she wasn't wearing sunglasses. Not when I saw her, anyway. I just happened to be in reception when she booked in. And it was *she* who recognized *me*! You see, the last time they'd been with us, *she* did the signing in, while Mr Storrs was sorting out the luggage and the parking. And I noticed the registration number of their BMW and I mentioned the coincidence that we were both "188J". She reminded me of it yesterday. She said they'd still got the same car.'

'You can swear to all this?'

'Certainly. We had quite a little chat. She told me they'd spent their honeymoon in the hotel – in the Sarah Siddons suite.'

Oh.

So that was that.

An alibi – for both of them.

Lewis thanked the Manager. 'But please do keep all this to yourself, sir. It's always a tricky business when we're trying to eliminate suspects in a case. Not *suspects*, though, just . . . just people.'

A few minutes later Lewis again rang the Storrs' residence in Polstead Road; again listening to Mrs Storrs on the answerphone:

'If the caller will please speak clearly after the long tone . . .' The voice was a little – what had the Manager said? – a little 'severe', yes. And quite certainly (Lewis thought) it was a voice likely to intimidate a few of the students if she became the new Master's wife. But after waiting for the 'long tone', Lewis put down the phone without leaving any message. He always felt awkward and tongue-tied at such moments; and he suddenly realized that he hadn't got a message to leave in any case.

CHAPTER FORTY-THREE

Horse-sense is something a horse has that prevents him from betting on people

(Father Mathew)

MORSE WAS STILL seated at the kitchen table in Number 15 when Lewis rang through.

'So it looks,' concluded Lewis, 'as if they're in the clear.'

'Ye-es. How far is it from Oxford to Bath?'

'Seventy, seventy-five miles?'

'Sunday morning. No traffic. Do it in an hour and a half – no problem. Three hours there and back.'

'There's a murder to commit in the middle, though.'

Morse conceded the point. 'Three and a half.'

'Well, whatever happened, he didn't use his *own* car. That was in the hotel garage – keys with the porter.'

'Haven't you heard of a *duplicate* set of car-keys, Lewis?'

'What if he was locked in – or blocked in?'

'He *un*locked himself, and *un*blocked himself, all right?'

'He must have left about four o'clock this morning then, because he was back in bed having breakfast with his missus before eight.'

'Ye-es.'

'I just wonder what Owens was doing, sir – up and about and dressed and ready to let the murderer in at half past five or so.'

'Perhaps he couldn't sleep.'

'You're not taking all this seriously, are you?'

'All right. Let's cross 'em both off the list, I agree.'

'Have we *got* a list?'

Morse nodded. 'Not too many on it, I know. But I'd like to see our other runner in the Lonsdale Stakes.'

'Do you want *me* to see him?'

'No. You get back here and look after the shop till the SOCOs have left – they're nearly through.'

With which, Morse put down the phone, got to his feet, and looked cautiously through into the hallway; then walked to the front door, where a uniformed PC stood on guard.

'Has the Super gone?' asked Morse.

'Yes, sir. Five minutes ago.'

Morse walked back to the kitchen and opened the door of the refrigerator. The usual items: two pints of Co-op milk, Flora margarine, a packet of unsmoked bacon rashers, five eggs, a carton of grapefruit juice, two cans of Courage's bitter . . .

Morse found a glass in the cupboard above the draining-board, and poured himself a beer. The liquid was cool and sharp on his dry throat; and very soon he had opened the second can, his fingers almost sensuously feeling the cellophane-wrapped cigarettes in his pocket, still unopened.

By the time the SOCOs were ready to move into the kitchen, the glass had been dried and replaced on its shelf.

'Can we kick you out a little while, sir?' It was Andrews, the senior man.

'You've finished everywhere else?'

'Pretty well.'

Morse got to his feet.

'Ah! Two cans of beer!' observed Andrews. 'Think they may have had a drink together before . . . ?'

'Not at that time of the morning, no.'

'I dunno. I used to have a friend who drank a pint of Guinness for breakfast every morning.'

'Sounds a civilized sort of fellow.'

'Dead. Cirrhosis of the liver.'

Morse nodded morosely.

'Anyway, we'll give the cans a dusting over, just in case.'

'I shouldn't bother,' said Morse.

'Won't do any harm, surely?'

'I said, I shouldn't *bother*,' snapped Morse.

And suddenly Andrews understood.

*

Upstairs there was little to detain Morse. In the front room the bed was still unmade, a pair of pyjamas neatly folded on the top pillow. The wardrobe appeared exactly as he'd viewed it earlier. Only one picture on the walls: Monet's miserable-looking version of a haystack.

The 'study' (Morse's second visit there too!) was in considerable disarray, for the desk-drawers, now liberally dusted with fingerprint powder, had been taken out, their contents strewn across the floor, including the book which had stimulated some interest on Morse's previous visit. The central drawer likewise had been removed, and Morse assumed that after discovering the theft of the manila file Owens had seen no reason to repair the damaged lock.

Nothing much else of interest upstairs, as far as Morse could see; just that one, easy conclusion to be drawn: that the murderer had been looking for something – some documents, some papers, some evidence which could have constituted a basis for blackmail.

Exactly what Morse had been looking for.

Exactly what Morse had found.

He smiled sadly to himself as he looked down at the wreckage of the room. Already he had made a few minor blunders in the investigations; and one major, tragic blunder, of course. But how fortunate that he'd been able to avail himself of JJ's criminal expertise, since otherwise the crucial evidence found in the manila file would have vanished now for ever.

Downstairs, Morse had only the living-room to consider. The kitchen he'd already seen; and the nominal 'dining-room' was clearly a room where Owens had seldom, if ever, dined – an area thick with dust and crowded with the sorts of items most householders regularly relegate to their lofts and garden sheds: an old electric fire, a coal scuttle, a box of plugs and wires, a traffic cone, an ancient Bakelite wireless, a glass case containing a stuffed owl, a black plastic lavatory-seat, six chairs packed together in the soixante-neuf position – and a dog-collar with the name 'Archie' inscribed on its disc.

Perhaps, after all, there had been some little goodness somewhere in the man?

Morse had already given permission for the body to be removed, and now for the second time he ventured into the living-room.

Not quite so dust-bestrewn here, certainly; but manifestly Owens had never been a house-proud man. Surfaces all around were dusted with powder, and chalk-marks outlined the body's former configuration on the settee. But the room was dominated by blood – the stains, the smell of blood; and Morse, as was his wont, turned his back on such things, and viewed the contents of the room.

He stood enviously in front of the black, three-decked Revox CD-cassette player which stood on a broad shelf in the alcove to the left of the front window, with dozens of CDs and cassettes below it, including, Morse noted with appreciation, much Gustav Mahler. And indeed, as he pressed the 'Play' panel, he immediately recognized *Das Lied von der Erde*.

No man is wholly bad, perhaps . . .

On the shelf beneath was an extended row of videos: *Fawlty Towers*, *Morecambe and Wise Christmas Shows*, *Porridge*, and several other TV classics. And two (fairly obviously) pornographic videos: *Grub Screws*, its crudely lurid, technicolor cover-poses hardly promising a course in carpentry with the Open University; and the plain-covered, yet succinctly entitled *Sux and Fux*, which seemed to speak quite unequivocally for itself. Morse himself had no video mechanism on his rented TV set; but he was in the process of thinking about the benefits of such a facility when Lewis came in, the latter immediately instructed to have a look around.

Morse's attention now turned to the single row of books in the opposite alcove. Mostly paperbacks: P. D. James, Jack Higgins, Ruth Rendell, Wilbur Smith, Minette Walters . . . *RAC Handbook*, *World Atlas*, *Chambers Dictionary*, *Pevsner's Oxfordshire* . . .

'See this?' Lewis suddenly raised aloft the *Grub Screws*. 'The statutory porn video, sir. Good one, that! Sergeant Dixon had it on at his stag-night.'

'You'd like to see it again, you mean?'

'*Again?* Not for me, sir. Those things get ever so boring after a while. But don't let me stop you if . . .'

'What? Me? I've got more important things to do than watch that sort of thing. High time I saw Cornford, for a start. Fix something up, Lewis. The sooner the quicker.'

After Lewis had gone, Morse felt unwilling to face the chorus of correspondents and the battery of cameras which awaited those periodically emerging from the front of Number 15. So he sat down, yet again, in the now empty kitchen; and pondered.

Always in his life, he had wanted to know the *answers* to things. In Sunday School he had once asked a question concerning the topographical position of Heaven, only to be admonished by an unimaginative middle-aged spinster for being so very silly. And he had been similarly discouraged when as a young grammar-school boy he had asked his Divinity master who it was, if God had created the Universe, who in turn had created God. And after receiving no satisfactory answer from his Physics master about what sort of thing could possibly exist out there at the end of the world, when space had run out, Morse had been compelled to lower his sights a little, thereafter satisfying his intellectual craving for answers by finding the values of 'x' and 'y' in (ever more complicated) algebraic equations, and by deciphering the meaning of (ever more complicated) chunks of choruses from the Greek tragedies.

Later, from his mid-twenties onwards, his need to *know* had transferred itself to the field of crossword puzzles, where he had so often awaited with almost paranoiac impatience the following day's answer to any clue he'd been unable to solve the day before. And now, as he sat in Bloxham Drive on that overcast, chilly Sunday afternoon in early March, he was aware that there *was* an answer to this present puzzle: probably a fairly simple answer to the question of what exactly had taken place earlier that morning. For a sequence of events *had* taken place, perhaps about 7.30. Someone had knocked on the door; had gained entry; had shot Owens twice; had gone upstairs to try to find something; had left via the kitchen door; had gone away, on foot, on a bike, in a car.

Who?

Who, Morse? For it was *someone* – someone with a human face and with a human motive. If only he could put together all the clues, *he would know.* And even as he sat there some pattern would begin to clarify itself in his mind, presenting a logical sequence of events, a causative chain of reactions. But then that same pattern would begin to blur and fade, since there was destined to be no flash of genuine insight on that afternoon.

Furthermore, Morse was beginning to feel increasingly worried about his present failure – like some hitherto highly acclaimed novelist with a score of bestsellers behind him who is suddenly assailed by a nightmarish doubt about his ability to write that one further winner; by a fear that he has come to the end of his creative output, and must face the possibility of defeat.

Lewis came back into the kitchen once more.

Dr Cornford would be happy to meet Morse whenever it suited. Five o'clock that afternoon? Before Chapel? In his rooms in Lonsdale?

Morse nodded.

'And I rang the Storrs again, sir. They're back in Oxford. Seems they had a bit of lunch in Burford on the way. Do you want me to go round?'

Morse looked up in some puzzlement.

'What the hell for, Lewis?'

CHAPTER FORTY-FOUR

The bells would ring to call her
In valleys miles away:
'Come all to church, good people;
Good people, come and pray.'
But here my love would stay

(A. E. Housman,
A Shropshire Lad XXI)

MORSE ENQUIRED AT the Lodge, then turned left and walked along the side of the quad to the Old Staircase, where on the first floor he saw, above the door to his right, the Gothic-style white lettering on its black background: DR D. J. CORNFORD.

'I suppose it's a bit early to offer you a drink, Chief Inspector?'

Morse looked at his wrist-watch.

'Is it?'

'Scotch? Gin? Vodka?'

'Scotch, please.'

Cornford began to pour an ever increasingly liberal tot of Glenmorangie into a tumbler.

'Say "when"!'

It seemed that the Chief Inspector may have had some difficulty in enunciating the monosyllable, for Cornford paused when the tumbler was half filled with the pale golden malt.

'When!' said Morse.

'No ice here, I'm afraid. But I'm sure you wouldn't want to adulterate it, anyway.'

'Yes, I would, if you don't mind. Same amount of water, please. We've all got to look after our livers.'

Two doors led off the high-ceilinged, oak-panelled, book-lined room; and Cornford opened the one that led to a small kitchen, coming back with a jug of cold water.

'I would have joined you normally – without the water! – but I'm reading the Second Lesson in Chapel tonight' (it was Cornford's turn to consult his wrist-watch) 'so we mustn't be all that long. It's that bit from the Epistle to the Romans, Chapter thirteen – the bit about drunkenness. Do you know it?'

'Er, just remind me, sir.'

Clearly Cornford needed no copy of the text in front of him, for he immediately recited the key verse, with appropriately ecclesiastical intonation:

Let us walk honestly, as in the day; not in rioting and drunkenness, not in chambering and wantonness, not in strife and envying . . .

'You'll be reading from the King James version, then?'

'Absolutely! I'm an agnostic myself; but what a tragedy that so many of our Christian brethren have opted for these new-fangled versions! "Boozing and Bonking", I should think they translate it.'

Morse sat sipping his Scotch contentedly. He could have suggested 'Fux and Sux'; but decided against it.

Cornford smiled. 'What do you want to see me about?'

'Well, in a way it's about that last bit of your text: the "strife and envying" bit. You see, I know you're standing for the Mastership here . . .'

'Yes?'

Morse took a deep breath, took a further deepish draught, and then told Cornford of the murder that morning of Geoffrey Owens; told him that various documents from the Owens household pointed to a systematic campaign of blackmail on Owens' part; informed him that there was reason to believe that he, Cornford, might have been – almost certainly *would* have been – one of the potential victims.

Cornford nodded quietly. 'Are you sure of this?'

'No, not sure at all, sir. But—'

'But you've got your job to do.'

'You haven't received any blackmail letters yourself?'

'No.'

'I'll be quite blunt, if I may, sir. Is there anything you can think of in the recent past, or distant past, that could have been used to compromise you in some way? Compromise your candidature, say?'

Cornford considered the question. 'I've done a few things I'm not very proud of – haven't we all? – but I'm fairly sure I got away with them. That was in another country, anyway ...'

Morse finished the quotation for him: '... and, besides, the wench is dead.'

Cornford's pale grey eyes looked across at Morse with almost childlike innocence.

'Yes.'

'Do you want to tell me about them?'

'No. But only because it would be an embarrassment for me and a waste of time for you.'

'You're a married man, I understand.'

'Yes. And before someone else tells you, my wife is American, about half my age, and extremely attractive.' The voice was still pleasantly relaxed, yet Morse sensed a tone of quiet, underlying strength.

'*She* hasn't been troubled by letters, anonymous letters, anything like that?'

'She hasn't told me of anything.'

'*Would* she tell you?'

Did Morse sense a hint of uneasy hesitation in Cornford's reply?

'She would, I think, yes. But you'd have to ask *her*.'

Morse nodded. 'I know it's a bit of a bother – but I *shall* have to do that, I'm afraid. She's, er, she's not around?'

Cornford again looked at his wrist-watch.

'She'll be coming over to Chapel very shortly.'

'Has there been much feeling – much tension – between you and the, er, other candidate?'

'The atmosphere on High Table has been a little, let's say, uncomfortable once or twice, yes. To be expected, though, isn't it?'

'But you don't throw insults at each other like those boxers before a big fight?'

'No, we just *think* them.'

'No whispers? No rumours?'

'Not as far as I'm aware, no.'

'And you get on reasonably well with Mr Storrs?'

Cornford got to his feet and smiled again, his head slightly to one side.

'I've never got to know Julian all that well, really.'

The Chapel bell had begun to ring – a series of monotonous notes, melancholy, ominous almost, like a curfew.

Ten minutes to go.

> *'Come ye to church, good people,*
> *Good people, come and pray,'*

quoted Cornford.

Morse nodded, as he ventured one final question:

'Do you mind me asking you when you got up this morning, sir?'

'Early. I went out jogging – just before seven.'

'Just you?'

Cornford nodded vaguely.

'You didn't go out after that – for a paper? In the car, perhaps?'

'I don't have a car, myself. My wife does, but it's garaged out in New Road.'

'Quite a way away.'

'Yes,' repeated Cornford slowly, 'quite a way away.'

As Morse walked down the stairs, he thought he'd recognized Cornford for exactly what he was: a civilized, courteous, clever man; a man of quiet yet unmistakable resolve, who would probably make a splendid new Master of Lonsdale.

Just two things worried him, the first of them only slightly: if Cornford was going to quote Housman, he jolly well ought to do it accurately.

And he might be wholly wrong about the second . . .

The bedroom door opened a few moments after Morse had reached the bottom of the creaking wooden staircase.

'And what do you think all *that* was about?'

'Couldn't you hear?'

'Most of it,' she admitted.

She wore a high-necked, low-skirted black dress, with an oval amethyst pinned to the bodice – suitably ensembled for a seat next to her husband in the Fellows' pews.

'His hair is whiter than yours, Denis. I saw him when he walked out.'

The bell still tolled.

Five minutes to go.

Cornford pulled on his gown and threw his hood back over his shoulders with practised precision; then repeated Housman (again inaccurately) as he put his arms around his wife and looked unblinkingly into her eyes.

'Have you got anything to pray for? Anything that's worrying you?'

Shelly Cornford smiled sweetly, trusting that such deep dissimulation would mask her growing, now almost desperate, sense of guilt.

'I'm going to pray for you, Denis – for you to become Master of Lonsdale. That's what I want more than anything else in the world' (her voice very quiet now) 'and that's not for me, my darling – it's for you.'

'Nothing else to pray for?'

She moved away from him, smoothing the dress over her energetic hips.

'Such as what?'

'Some people pray for forgiveness, that sort of thing, sometimes,' said Denis Cornford softly.

Morse had walked to the Lodge, where he stood in the shadows for a couple of minutes, reading the various notices about the College's sporting fifteens, and elevens, and eights; and hoping that his presence there was unobserved – when he saw them. An academically accoutred Cornford, accompanied by a woman in black, had emerged from the foot of the Old Staircase, and now turned away from him towards the Chapel in the inner quad.

The bell had stopped ringing.

And Morse walked out into Radcliffe Square; thence across into the King's Arms in Broad Street, where he ordered a pint of bitter, and sat down in the back bar, considering so many things – including a wholly unprecedented sense of gratitude to the Tory Government for its reform of the Sunday licensing laws.

CHAPTER FORTY-FIVE

I'd seen myself a don,
Reading old poets in the library,
Attending chapel in an MA gown
And sipping vintage port by candlelight
(John Betjeman,
Summoned by Bells)

IN THE HILARY Term, in Lonsdale College, on Sunday evenings only, it had become a tradition for the electric lighting to be switched off, and for candles in their sconces to provide the only means of illumination in the Great Hall. Such a procedure was popular with the students, almost all of whom had never experienced the romance of candlelight except during power-cuts, and particularly enjoyable for those on the dais whereon the High Table stood, constantly aware as they were of flickering candles reflected in the polished silver of salt-cellars and tureens, and the glitter of the cutlery laid out with geometrical precision at every place.

On such evenings, no particular table-plan was provided, although it was the regular custom for the visiting preacher (on this occasion a black bishop from Central Africa) to sit on the right side of the Master, with the College Chaplain on the left. The other occupants of High Table (which was usually fully booked on Sunday evenings) were regularly those who had earlier attended the Chapel service, often with their wives or with a guest; and in recent years, one student invited by each of the Fellows in rotation.

That evening the student in question was Antony Plummer, the new organ scholar, who had been invited by Julian Storrs for the very good reason that the two of them had attended the same school, the Services School, Dartmouth, to which establishment some members of the armed forces were wont to send their sons whilst they themselves were being shunted from one posting to another around the world – in former colonies, protectorates, mandated territories, and the few remaining overseas possessions.

Plummer had never previously been so honoured, and from

his new perspective, seated between Mr and Mrs Storrs, he looked around him lovingly at the gilded, dimly illuminated portraits of the famous alumni – the poets and the politicians, the soldiers and the scientists – who figured so largely in the lineage of Lonsdale. The rafted timbers of the ceiling were lost in darkness, and the shadows were deep on the sombre panelling of the walls, as deftly and deferentially the scouts poured wine into the sparkling glasses.

Storrs, just a little late in the proceedings perhaps, decided it was time to play the expansive host.

'Where *is* your father now, Plummer?'

'Last I heard he was running some NATO exercise in Belgium.'

'Colonel now, isn't he?'

'Brigadier.'

'My goodness!'

'You were with him in India, I think.'

Storrs nodded: 'Only a captain, though! I followed my father into the Royal Artillery there, and spent a couple of years trying to teach the natives how to shoot. Not much good at it, I'm afraid.'

'Who – the natives?'

Storrs laughed good-naturedly. 'No – *me*. Most of 'em could have taught me a few things, and I wasn't really cut out for service life anyway. So I opted for a gentler life and applied for a Fellowship here.'

Angela Storrs had finished the bisque soup, and now complimented Plummer on the anthem through which he had conducted his largely female choir during the Chapel service.

'You enjoyed it, Mrs Storrs?'

'Er, yes. But to be quite truthful, I prefer boy sopranos.'

'Can you say why that is?'

'Oh, yes! One just *feels* it, that's all. We heard the Fauré *Requiem* yesterday evening. Absolutely wonderful – especially the "In Paradisum", wasn't it, Julian?'

'Very fine, yes.'

'And you see,' continued Angela, 'I would have *known* they were boys, even with my eyes shut. But don't ask me *why*. One just *feels* that sort of thing, as I said. Don't you agree? One shouldn't try to *rationalize* everything.'

Three places lower down the table, one of the other dons whispered into his neighbour's ear:

'If that woman gets into the Lodge, I'll go and piss all over her primroses!'

By coincidence, colonialism was a topic at the far end of the table, too, where Denis Cornford, his wife beside him, was listening rather abstractedly to a visiting History Professor from Yale.

'No. Don't be too hard on yourselves. The Brits didn't treat the natives all that badly, really. Wouldn't you agree, Denis?'

'No, I wouldn't, I'm afraid,' replied Cornford simply. 'I haven't made any particular study of the subject, but my impression is that the British treated most of their colonials quite abominably.'

Shelly slipped her left hand beneath the starched white tablecloth, and gently moved it along his thigh. But she could feel no perceptible response.

At the head of the splendid oak plank that constituted the High Table at Lonsdale, over the roast lamb, served with St Julien 93, Sir Clixby had been seeking to mollify the bishop's bitter condemnation of the English Examination Boards for expecting Rwandan refugees to study the Wars of the Roses. And soon after the profiteroles, the atmosphere seemed markedly improved.

All the conversation which had been criss-crossing the evening – amusing, interesting, pompous, spiteful – ceased abruptly as the Master banged his gavel, and the assembled company rose to its feet.

Benedictus benedicatur.

The words came easily and suavely, from lips that were slightly over-red, slightly over-full, in a face so smooth one might assume that it seldom had need of the razor.

Those who wished, and that was most of them, now repaired to the SCR where coffee and port were being served (though wholly informally) and where the Master and Julian Storrs stood side-by-side, buttocks turned towards the remarkably realistic gas fire.

'Bishop on his way back to the railway station then?' queried Storrs.

'On his way back to *Africa*, I hope!' said the Master with a grin. 'Bloody taxi *would* have to be late tonight, wouldn't it? And none of you lot with a car here.'

'It's this drink-driving business, Master. I'm all in favour of it. In fact, I'd vote for random checks myself.'

'And Denis there – hullo, Denis! – he was no help either.'

Cornford had followed their conversation and now edged towards them, sipping his coffee.

'I sold my old Metro just before Christmas. And if you recall, Master, I only live three hundred yards away.'

The words could have sounded light-hearted, yet somehow they didn't.

'Shelly's got a car, though?'

Cornford nodded cautiously. 'Parked a mile away.'

The Master smiled. 'Ah, yes. I remember now.'

Half an hour later, as they walked across the cobbles of Radcliffe Square towards Holywell Street, Shelly Cornford put her arm through her husband's and squeezed it. But, as before, she could feel no perceptible response.

CHAPTER FORTY-SIX

But she went on pleading in her distraction; and perhaps said things that would have been better left to silence.

'Angel! – Angel! I was a child – a child when it happened! I knew nothing of men.'

'You were more sinned against than sinning, that I admit.'

'Then you will not forgive me?'

'I do forgive you, but forgiveness is not all.'

'And love me?'

To this question he did not answer

(Thomas Hardy, *Tess of the d'Urbervilles*)

'COFFEE?' SHE suggested, as Cornford was hanging up his overcoat in the entrance-hall.

'I've just had some.'

'I'll put the kettle on.'

'No! Leave it a while. I want to talk to you.'

They sat together, if opposite is together, in the lounge.

'What did you do when the Chaplain invited us all to confess our manifold sins and wickedness?'

The measured, civilized tone of Cornford's voice had shifted to a slightly higher, yet strangely quieter key; and the eyes, normally so kindly, seemed to concentrate ever narrowingly upon her, like an ornithologist focusing binoculars on an interesting species.

'Parrdon?'

'"In thought, word, and deed" – wasn't that the formula?'

She shook her head in apparent puzzlement. 'I haven't the faintest—'

But his words cut sharply across her protestation. 'Why are you lying to me?'

'What—?'

'Shut up!' The voice had lost its control. 'You've been unfaithful to me! *I* know that. *You* know that. Let's start from there!'

'But I haven't—'

'Don't lie to me! I've put up with your infidelity, but I can't put up with your *lies*!'

The last word was hissed, like a whiplash across his wife's face.

'Only once, really,' she whispered.

'Recently?'

She nodded, in helpless misery.

'Who with?'

In great gouts, the tears were falling now. 'Why do you have to know? Why do you have to torture yourself? It didn't mean anything, Denis! It didn't *mean anything*.'

'Hah!' He laughed bitterly. 'Didn't you think it might mean something to *me*?'

'He just wanted—'

'Who was it?'

She closed her eyes, cheeks curtained with mascara'd tears, unable to answer him.

'*Who was it?*'

But still she made no answer to the piercing question.

'Shall I tell *you*?'

He knew – she realized he knew. And now, her eyes still firmly shut, she spoke the name of the adulterer.

'He didn't come here? You went over to the Master's Lodge?'

'Yes.'

'And you went to his bedroom?'

'Yes.'

'And you undressed for him?'

'Yes.'

'You stripped naked for him?'

'Yes.'

'And you got between the sheets with him?'

'Yes.'

'And you had sex? The pair of you had sex together?'

'Yes.'

'How many times?'

'Only once.'

'*And you enjoyed it!*'

Cornford got to his feet and walked back into the entrance-hall. He felt stunned, like someone who has just been kicked in the teeth by a recalcitrant shire-horse.

'Denis!' Shelly had followed him, standing beside him now as he pulled on his overcoat.

'You know *why* I did it, Denis? I did it for *you*. You *must* know that!'

He said nothing.

'How did you know?' Her voice was virtually inaudible.

'It's not what people say, is it? It's the *way* they say it. But I knew. I knew tonight . . . I knew before tonight.'

'How *could* you have known? Tell me! Please!'

Cornford turned up the catch on the Yale lock, and for a few moments stood there, the half-opened door admitting a draught of air that felt bitterly cold.

'I *didn't* know! Don't you see? I just hoped you'd deny everything – even if it meant you had to lie to me. But you hadn't even got the guts to *lie* to me! You didn't even want to spare me all this pain.'

The door banged shut behind him; and Shelly Cornford walked back into the lounge where she poured herself a vast gin with minimal tonic.

And wished that she were dead.

CHAPTER FORTY-SEVEN

Virgil G. Perkins, author of international bestseller *Enjoying Jogging* (Crown Publications NY, 1992) collapsed and died whilst jogging with a group of fellow enthusiasts in St Paul yesterday. Mr Perkins, aged 26, leaves behind his wife, Beverley, their daughter, Alexis, and seven other children by previous marriages

(*Minnesota Clarion,* 23 December 1995)

IN THE KING'S ARMS, that square, cream-painted hostelry on the corner of Parks Road and Holywell Street, Morse had been remarkably abstemious that evening. After his first pint, he had noticed on the door the pub's recommendation in the *Egon Ronay Guide* (1995); and after visiting the loo to inject himself, he had ordered a spinach-and-mushroom lasagne with garlic bread and salad. The individual constituents of this particular offering had never much appealed to him; yet the hospital dietitian (as he recalled) had been particularly enthusiastic about such fare. And, let it be said, the meal had been marginally enjoyed.

It was 7.45 p.m.

A cigarette would have been a paradisal plus; and yet somehow he managed to desist. But as he looked around him, at the college crests, the coloured prints, the photographs of distinguished local patrons, he was debating whether to take a few more calories in liquid form when the landlord was suddenly beside him.

'Inspector! I hadn't seen you come in. This is for you – it's been here a couple of weeks.'

Morse took the printed card:

Let me tell you of a moving experience – very moving! The furniture van is fetching my effects from London to Oxford at last. And on March 18th I'll be celebrating my south-facing patio with a shower of champagne at 53 Morris Villas, Cowley. Come and join me!
RSVP (at above address)

Deborah Crawford

Across the bottom was a handwritten note: 'Make it, Morse! DC.'

Morse remembered her well . . . a slim, unmarried blonde who'd once invited him to stay overnight in her north London flat, following a comparatively sober Metropolitan Police party; when he'd said that after such a brief acquaintance such an accommodation might perhaps be inappropriate.

Yes, that was the word he'd used: 'inappropriate'.

Pompous idiot!

But he'd given her his address, which she'd vowed she'd never forget.

Which clearly she had.

'She was ever so anxious for you to get it,' began the landlord – but even as he spoke the door that led to Holywell Street had opened, and he turned his attention to the newcomer.

'Denis! I didn't expect to see you in tonight. No good us both running six miles on a Sunday morning if we're going to put all the weight back on on a Sunday night.'

Morse looked up, his face puzzled.

'You mean – you went jogging – together – this morning? What time was that?'

'Far too early, wasn't it, David!'

The landlord smiled. 'Stupid, really. On a Sunday morning, too.'

'What time?' repeated Morse.

'Quarter to seven. We met outside the pub here.'

'And where did the pair of you run?'

'*Five* of us actually, wasn't it, Denis? We ran up to the Plain, up the Iffley Road, across Donnington Bridge, along the Abingdon Road up to Carfax, then through Cornmarket and St Giles' up to the Woodstock Road as far as North Parade, then across to the Banbury, South Parks, and we got back here . . .'

'Just before eight,' added Cornford, pointing to Morse's empty glass.

'What's it to be?'

'No, it's my round—'

'Nonsense!'

'Well, if you insist.'

In fact, however, it was the landlord who insisted, and who now walked to the bar as Cornford seated himself.

'You told me earlier' (Morse was anxious to get things straight) 'you'd been on your own when you went out jogging.'

'No. If I did, you misunderstood me. You said, I think, "Just you?" And when I said yes, I'd assumed that you were asking if both of us had gone – Shelly and me.'

'And she didn't go?'

'No. She never does.'

'She just stayed in bed?'

'Where else?'

Morse made no suggestion.

'Do you ever go jogging, Inspector?' The question was wearily mechanical.

'Me? No. I walk a bit, though. I sometimes walk down to Summertown for a newspaper. Just to keep fit.'

Cornford almost grinned. 'If you're going to be Master of Lonsdale, you're supposed to be fit. It's in the Statutes somewhere.'

'Makes you wonder how Sir Clixby ever managed it!'

Cornford's answer was unexpected.

'You know, as you get older it's difficult for young people to imagine you were ever young yourself – good at games, that sort of thing. Don't you agree?'

'Fair point, yes.'

'And the Master was a very fine hockey player – had an England trial, I understand.'

The landlord came back with two pints of bitter; then returned to his bar-tending duties.

Cornford was uneasy, Morse felt sure of that. Something regarding his wife, perhaps? Had *she* had anything to do with the murder of Geoffrey Owens? Unlikely, surely. One thing looked an odds-on certainty, though: if Denis Cornford had ever figured on the suspect list, he figured there no longer.

Very soon, after a few desultory passages of conversation, Morse had finished his beer, and was taking his leave, putting Deborah's card into the inside pocket of his jacket, and forgetting it.

Forgetting it only temporarily, though; for later that same evening he was to look at it again – more carefully. And with a sudden, strange enlightenment.

CHAPTER FORTY-EIGHT

Is it nothing to you, all ye that pass by? Behold and see if there be any sorrow like unto my sorrow, which is done unto me, wherewith the Lord hath afflicted me in the day of his fierce anger

(*Lamentations*, ch. 1, v. 12)

FEELING A WONDERFUL sense of relief, Shelly Cornford heard the scratch of the key in the front door at twenty-five past eleven. For over two hours she had been sitting upright against the pillows, a white bed-jacket over her pyjamas, her mind tormented with the terrifying fear that her husband had disappeared into the dark night, never to return: to throw himself over Magdalen Bridge, perhaps; to lay himself across the railway lines; to slash his wrists; to leap from some high tower. And it was to little avail that she'd listened to any logic that her tortured mind could muster: that the water was hardly deep enough, perhaps; that the railway lines were inaccessible; that he had no razor in his pocket; that Carfax Tower, St Mary's, St Michael's – all were now long shut . . .

Come back to me, Denis! I don't care what happens to *me*; but come back tonight! Oh, God – *please*, God – let him come back safely. Oh, God, put an end to this, my overwhelming misery!

His words before he'd slammed the door had pierced their way into her heart. 'You hadn't even got the guts to lie to me . . . You didn't even want to spare me all this pain.'

Yet how wrong he'd been, with both his accusations!

Her mother had never ceased recalling that Junior High School report: 'She's such a gutsy little girl.' And the simple, desperately simple, truth was that she loved her husband far more than anything or anyone she'd ever loved before. And yet . . . and yet she remembered so painfully clearly her assertion earlier that same evening: that more than anything in the world she wanted Denis to be Master.

And now? The centre of her life had fallen apart. Her heart was broken. There was no one to whom she could turn.

Except, perhaps . . .

*

And again and again she recalled that terrible conversation:

'Clixby?'

'Shelly!'

'Are you alone?'

'Yes. What a lovely surprise. Come over!'

'Denis knows all about us!'

'What?'

'Denis knows all about us!'

'"All" about us? What d'you mean? There's nothing for him *to* know – not really.'

'*Nothing?* Was it nothing to you?'

'You sound like the book of *Proverbs* – or is it *Ecclesiastes*?'

'It *didn't* mean anything to you, did it?'

'It was only the *once*, properly, my dear. For heaven's sake!'

'You just don't understand, do you?'

'How did he find out?'

'He didn't.'

'I don't follow you.'

'He just guessed. He was talking to you tonight—'

'After Hall, you mean? Of course he was. You were there.'

'Did you say anything? Please, tell me!'

'What? Have you taken leave of your senses?'

'Why did he say he *knew*, then?'

'He was just guessing – you just said so yourself.'

'He must have had some reason.'

'Didn't you deny it?'

'But it was true!'

'What the hell's that got to do with it? Don't you see? All you'd got to do was to deny it.'

'That's exactly what Denis said.'

'Bloody intelligent man, Denis. I just hope you appreciate him. He was right, wasn't he? All you'd got to do was to deny it.'

'And that's what you wanted me to do?'

'*You're* not really being very intelligent, are you?'

'I just can't believe what you're saying.'

'It would have been far kinder.'

'Kinder to *you*, you mean?'

'To me, to you, to Denis – to everybody.'

'God! You're a shit, aren't you?'

'Just hold your horses, girl!'

'What are you going to do about it?'

'What do you mean – "do" about it? What d'you expect me to do?'

'I don't know. I've no one to talk to. That's why I rang you.'

'Well, if there's anything—'

'But there is! I want help. This is the worst thing that's ever happened to me.'

'But don't you see, Shelly? This is something you and Denis have got to work out for yourselves. Nobody else—'

'God! You *are* a shit, aren't you! Shit with a capital "S".'

'Look! Is Denis there?'

'Of course he's not, you fool.'

'Please don't call me a fool, Shelly! Get a hold on yourself and put things in perspective – and just remember who you're talking to!'

'Denis!'

'You get back to bed. I'll sleep in the spare room.'

'No. *I'll* sleep in there—'

'I don't give a sod who sleeps where. We're just not sleeping in the same room, that's all.'

His eyes were still full of anger and anguish, though his voice was curiously calm. 'We've got to talk about this. For a start, you'd better find out the rights and wrongs and the rest of it about people involved in divorce on the grounds of adultery. Not tonight, though.'

'Denis! Please let's talk *now* – please! – just for a little while.'

'What the hell about? About *me*? You know all about me, for Christ's sake. I'm half-pissed – and soon I'm going to be fully pissed – and as well as that I'm stupid – and hurt – and jealous – and possessive – and old-fashioned – and faithful ... You following me? I've watched most of your antics, but I've never been too worried. You know why? Because I knew you *loved* me. Deep down I knew there was a bedrock of love underneath our marriage. Or I *thought* I knew.'

In silence, in abject despair, Shelly Cornford listened, and the tears ran in furrows down her cheeks.

'We're finished. The two of us are finished, Shelly – do you know, I can hardly bring myself to call you by your name? Our marriage is over and done with – make no mistake about that. You can feel free to do what you want now. I just don't care.

You're a born flirt! You're a born prick-teaser! And I just can't live with you any longer. I just can't live with the picture of you lying there naked and opening your legs to another man. Can you try to get that into your thick skull?'

She shook her head in utter anguish.

'You said' (Cornford continued) 'you'd have given anything in life to see me become Master. Well, *I* wouldn't – do you understand that? But I'd have given anything in life for you to be faithful to me – whatever the prize.'

He turned away from her, and she heard the door of the spare bedroom close; then open again.

'When was it? Tell me that. *When?*'

'This morning.'

'You mean when I was out jogging?'

'Yes,' she whispered.

He turned away once more; and she beheld and could see no sorrow like unto her own sorrow.

The keys to her car lay on the mantelshelf.

CHAPTER FORTY-NINE
Monday, 4 March

> I work all day, and get half-drunk at night.
> Waking at four to soundless dark, I stare.
> In time the curtain-edges will grow light.
> Till then I see what's really always there:
> Unresting death, a whole day nearer now,
> Making all thought impossible but how
> And where and when I shall myself die
> (Philip Larkin, *Aubade*)

NEVER, IN HIS lifetime of muted laughter and occasional tears, had Morse spent such a horrifying night. Amid fitful bouts of semi-slumber – head weighted with pain, ears throbbing, stomach in spasms, gullet afire with bile and acidity – he'd imagined himself on the verge of fainting, of vomiting, of having a stroke, of entering cardiac arrest. One of Ovid's lovers had once besought the Horses of the Night to slacken their pace and delay thereby the onset of the Dawn. But as he lay turning in his bed, Morse longed for a sign of the brightening sky through his window. During that seemingly unending night, he had consumed several glasses of cold water, Alka-Seltzer tablets, cups of black coffee, and the equivalent of a weekly dosage of Nurofen Plus.

No alcohol, though. Not one drop of alcohol.

At last Morse had decided to abandon alcohol.

Lewis looked into Morse's bedroom at 7.30 a.m. (Lewis was the only person who had a key to Morse's flat.)

In the prestigious area of North Oxford, most householders had long since fitted their homes with anti-burglar devices, with neighbours holding the keys to the alarm mechanism. But Morse had little need of such a device, for the only saleable, stealable items in his flat were the CDs of all the operas of the man he regarded as a towering genius, Richard Wagner; and his earnestly assembled collection of first editions of the greatest hero in his life, the pessimistic poet A. E. Housman, who, like Morse, had left St John's College, Oxford, without obtaining a degree.

But not even North Oxford burglars had tastes that were quite so esoteric.

And in any case, Morse seldom spoke to either of his immediate neighbours.

'You look awful, sir.'

'Oh, for Christ's sake, Lewis! Don't you know if somebody says you *look* awful, you *feel* awful?'

'Didn't you feel awful *before* I said it?'

Morse nodded a miserable agreement.

'Shall I get you a bit of breakfast?'

'No.'

'Well, I reckon we can eliminate the Storrs – both of 'em. I've checked with the hotel as far as possible. And unless they hired a helicopter . . .'

'We can cross off the Cornfords, too – *him*, anyway. He's got four witnesses to testify he was running around Oxford pretending to be Roger Bannister.'

'What about *her*?'

'I can't really see why . . . or how.'

'Owens could have been blackmailing her?'

Morse fingered his stubbled chin. 'I don't think so somehow. But there's *something* there . . . something Cornford didn't want to tell me about.'

'What d'you think?'

But Morse appeared unable to answer, as he swung his legs out of bed and sat for a while, alternately turning his torso to left and right.

'Just easing the lumbago, Lewis. Don't *you* ever get it?'

'No.'

'Just nip and get me a glass of orange juice from the fridge. The *unsweetened* orange juice.'

As he walked into the kitchen, Lewis heard the post slither through the letter-box.

So did Morse.

'Lewis! Did you find out what time the postman usually calls in Polstead Road?'

'I've already told you. You were right.'

'About the only bloody thing I *have* been right about.'

'Arrghh! Cheer up, sir!'

'Just turn out those pockets, will you?' Morse pointed to the suit and shirt thrown carelessly over the only chair in the bedroom. 'Time I had a change of clothes – maybe bring me a change of luck.'

'Who's your new girlfriend?' Lewis held up the invitation card. '"Make it, Morse! DC."'

'That card is wholly private and—'

But Morse got no further.

He felt the old familiar tingling across the shoulders, the hairs on his lower arms standing up, as if a conductor had invited his orchestra to arise after a concert.

'Christ!' whispered Morse irreverently. 'Do you know what, Lewis? I think you've done it again!'

CHAPTER FIFTY
Monday–Tuesday, 4–5 March

The four-barrelled Lancaster Howdah pistol is of .577 in calibre. Its name derived from the story that it was carried by tiger hunters who travelled by elephant and who kept the pistol as a defence against any tiger that might leap on to the elephant's back

(*Encyclopedia of Rifles and Handguns*,
ed. SEAN CONNOLLY)

FOR THE RELATIVES, for the statement-takers and the form-fillers, for the boffins at ballistics and forensics, the murder of Geoffrey Owens would be a serious business. No less than for the detectives. Yet for Morse himself the remainder of that Monday had been unproductive and anti-climactic, with a morning of euphoria followed by an afternoon of blood-trouble.

Hospital instructions had been for him to take four daily readings of his blood sugar level, using a slim, pen-like appliance into which he inserted a test-strip duly smeared with a drop of his blood, with each result appearing, after only thirty seconds, in a small window on the side of the pen. Whilst the average blood sugar level of the healthy person is about 4.5, the pen is calibrated from 1 to 25, since the levels of diabetic patients often vary very considerably. Any level higher than 25 is registered as 'HI'.

Now thus far readings had been roughly what Morse had been led to expect (the highest 15.5): it would take some little while – and then only if he promised to do as he was told – to achieve that 'balance' which is the aim of every diabetic. More than disappointing to him therefore had been the 'HI' registered at lunchtime that day. In fact, more of a surprise than a disappointment, since momentarily he was misled into believing that 'HI' was analogous to the greeting from a fruit-machine: 'Hello And Welcome!'

But it wasn't; and Morse was rather worried about himself; and returned to his flat, where he took two further Nurofen Plus for his persisting headache, sat back in his armchair, decided he lacked the energy to do *The Times* crossword or even to turn on the CD player – and fairly soon fell fast asleep.

At six o'clock he rang Lewis to say he would be doing nothing more that day. Just before seven o'clock he measured his blood sugar once again; and finding it somewhat dramatically reduced, to 14.3, had decided to celebrate with a small glass of Glenfiddich before he listened to *The Archers*.

The following morning, feeling much refreshed, feeling eager to get on with things, Morse had been at his desk in Police HQ for half an hour before Lewis entered, holding a report.

'Ballistics, sir. Came in last night.'

Morse could no more follow the technical terminology of ballistics reports than he could understand a paragraph of Structural Linguistics or recall the configuration of the most recent map of Bosnia. To be sure he had a few vague notions about 'barrels' and 'grooves' and 'cylinders' and 'calibres'; but his knowledge went no further, and his interest not quite so far as that. Cursorily glancing therefore through the complex data assembled in the first five pages, he acquainted himself with the short, simply written summary on page six:

> Rachel James was fatally shot by a single bullet fired from a range of c. 45 cms; Geoffrey Owens was fatally shot by two bullets fired from a range of c. 100 cms. The pistol used in each case, of .577 in. calibre, was of the type frequently used by HM Forces. Quite certainly the same pistol was used in each killing.
>
> ASH: 4.iii.96

Morse sat back in the black leather armchair and looked mildly satisfied with life.

'Ye-es. I think I'm beginning to wake up at last in this case, Lewis. You know, it's high time we got together, you and me. We've been doing our own little things so far, haven't we? *You've* gone off to see somebody – *I've* gone off to see somebody – and we've not got very far, have we? It's the same as always, Lewis. We need to do things together from now on.'

'No time like the present.'

'Pardon?'

Lewis pointed to the ballistics report. 'What do you think?'

'Very interesting. Same revolver.'

'*Pistol*, sir.'

'Same difference.'

'I think most of us had assumed it was the same, anyway.'

'Really?'

'Well, it's what most of the lads think.'

Morse's smile was irritatingly benign. 'Same revolver – same murderer. Is that what, er, most of the lads think as well?'

'I suppose so.'

'Do you?'

Lewis considered the question. It either was – or it wasn't. Fifty-fifty chance of getting it right, Lewis. Go for it!

'Yes!'

'Fair enough. Now let's consider a few possibilities. Rachel was shot through the kitchen window when she was standing at the sink. The blind was old and made of thinnish material and the silhouette was pretty clear, perhaps; but the murderer was taking a risk. Revolvers' (Lewis had given up) 'are notoriously inaccurate even at close range, and the bullet's got to penetrate a reasonably substantial pane of glass – enough perhaps to knock the aim off course a bit and hit her in the neck instead of the head. Agreed?'

Lewis nodded at what he saw as an analysis not particularly profound. And Morse continued:

'Now the shooting of Owens took place *inside* the house – from a bit further away; but no glass this time, and a very clear target to aim at. And Owens is shot in the chest, not in the head. A *modus operandi* quite different from the first.'

Lewis smiled. 'So we've got two *moduses operandi*.'

'*Modi*, Lewis! So it *could* be that we've two murderers. But that would seem on the face of it highly improbable, because it's not difficult to guess the reason for the difference . . . Is it?'

'Well, as I see things, sir, Owens was probably murdered by somebody he knew. He probably invited whoever it was in. Perhaps they'd arranged to meet anyway. Owens was dressed and—' Lewis stopped a moment. 'He hadn't shaved though, had he?'

'He was the sort of fellow who always looked as if he needed a shave.'

'Perhaps we should have checked more closely.'

'You don't expect *me* to check that sort of thing, do you? I'm a necrophobe – you've known me long enough, surely.'

'Well, that's it then, really. But *Rachel* probably didn't know him.'

'Or *her*.'

'She must have been really scared if she heard a tap on the window that morning and went to open the blind—'

'You're still assuming that both murders were committed by the same person, Lewis.'

'And *you* don't think so?'

Morse shrugged. 'Could have been two lovers or partners or husband and wife – or two completely separate people.'

Lewis was beginning to sound somewhat exasperated. 'You know, I shall be much happier when we've got a bit more of the routine work done, sir. It's all been a bit ad hoc so far, hasn't it?' (Morse raised his eyebrows at the Latinism.) 'Can't we leave a few of the ideas until we've given ourselves a chance to check everything a bit?'

'Lewis! You are preaching to the converted. That's exactly what we've got to do. Go back to the beginning. "In our beginning is our end," somebody said – Eliot, wasn't it? Or is it "In our end is our beginning"?'

'Where do you suggest we begin then, sir?'

Morse considered the question.

'What about you fetching me a cup of coffee? No sugar.'

CHAPTER FIFTY-ONE
Tuesday, 5 March

The overworked man who agrees to any division of labour always gets the worst share

(Hungarian proverb)

'WHERE DO YOU suggest we begin then?' repeated Lewis, as Morse distastefully sipped his unsweetened coffee.

'When we *do* start again, we'll probably find that we've been looking at things from the wrong angle. We've been assuming – *I* have, anyway – that it was Owens who was pulling all the strings. As a journalist, he'd often been in a privileged position with regard to a few juicy stories; and as a man he pretty clearly gloried in the hold he could have on other people: blackmail. And from what we learned, I thought it was likely that the two candidates for the Mastership at Lonsdale were being black-mailed; I thought that they'd have as good a motive, certainly Storrs, as anybody for wishing Owens out of the way. But I never dreamed that Owens was in danger of being murdered, as you know . . .

'There's just the one trouble about following up that particular hypothesis though, isn't there? It's now clear that neither of those two, neither Storrs nor Cornford – nor their wives for that matter – could have been responsible for *both* murders. And increasingly unlikely, perhaps, that any of them could have been responsible even for *one* of the murders. So where does this all leave us? It's a bit like a crossword clue you sometimes get stuck with. You think one bit of the clue's the definition, and the other bit's a build-up of the letters. Then suddenly you realize you've got things *the wrong way round*. And perhaps I'm reading the clue the wrong way round here, Lewis. What if someone was blackmailing *Owens* – the exact opposite of our hypothesis? What if – we've spoken about it before – what if Rachel James came to discover something that would upset his carefully loaded apple-cart? And blackmailed *him*?'

'Trying to climb aboard the gravy-train herself?'

'Exactly. Money! You said right at the start that we needed a *motive* for Rachel's murder; and I suspect she'd somehow got to know about his own blackmailing activities and was threatening to expose him.'

Lewis was looking decidedly impatient.

'Sir! Could we *please* get along to Owens' office first, and get a few simple *facts* established?'

'Just what I was about to suggest. We shall have to get down there and find out everything we can about him. See the editor, the sub-editor, his colleagues, that personnel fellow – especially him! Go through his desk and his drawers. Get hold of his original application, if we can. Try to learn something about his men-friends, his girlfriends, his enemies, his habits, what he liked to eat and drink, his salary, any clubs he belonged to, his political leanings—'

'We know he voted Conservative, sir.'

'—the newspaper he took, where he usually parked his car, what his job prospects were – yes, plenty to be going on with there.'

'Quite a list. Good job there's two of us, sir.'

'Pardon?'

'Hefty agenda – that's all I'm saying.'

'Not all that much really. Far easier than it sounds. And if you get off straightaway ...' Morse looked at his wrist-watch: 10.45 a.m.

Lewis frowned. 'You mean you're not joining me?'

'Not today, no.'

'But you just said—'

'One or two important things I've got to do after lunch.'

'Such as?'

'Well, to be truthful, I've been told to take things a bit more gently. And I suppose I'd better take a bit of notice of my medical advisers.'

'Of course.'

'Don't get me wrong, mind! I'm feeling fine. But I think a little siesta this afternoon ...'

'*Siesta?* That's what they have in Spain in the middle of the summer when the temperature's up in the nineties – but we're in England in the middle of winter and it's freezing outside.'

Morse looked down at his desk, a little sheepishly, and Lewis knew that he was lying.

'Come on, sir! It's something to do with that invite you had, isn't it? Deborah Crawford?'

'In a way.'

'Why are you being so secretive about it? You wouldn't tell me yesterday either.'

'Only because it needs a bit more thinking about, that's all.'

'"You and me together" – isn't that what you said?'

Morse fingered the still-cellophaned cigarettes, almost desperately.

'Si' down then, Lewis.'

CHAPTER FIFTY-TWO

It is the nature of an hypothesis, when once a man has conceived it, that it assimilates every thing to itself as proper nourishment, and, from the first moment of your begetting it, it generally grows the stronger by every thing you see, hear, read, or understand

(Laurence Sterne, *Tristram Shandy*)

'IT WASN'T DEBORAH Crawford, Lewis – it was her initials, "DC". When we found that list in the manila file, I jumped the gun. I automatically assumed that "JS" was Julian Storrs – I think I was right about that – and I assumed that "DC" was Denis Cornford – and I think I was *wrong* about that. As things have turned out I don't believe Owens ever knew Cornford at all, *or* his missus, for that matter. But he knew another "DC": the woman at Number 1 Bloxham Close – Adèle Beatrice Cecil – the ABC lass Owens knew well enough to call by her nickname, "Della". "DC". And the more I think about *her*, the more attractive a proposition I find it.'

'Well, most men would, sir. Lovely looker!'

Ignoring the pleasantry, Morse continued: 'Just consider for a minute what an important figure she is in the case. She's the prime witness, really. *She's* the one who sees Owens leave for work about sevenish on the morning Rachel was murdered; *she's* the one who rings Owens an hour or so later to tell him the police are in Bloxham Close' (again Lewis let it go) 'and gives him a head start on all the other newshounds. That's what she says, isn't it? But she might not be telling the truth!'

Lewis sat in silence.

'Now, as I recall it, your objection to Owens himself ever being a suspect was the time-factor. You argued that he couldn't have gone to work that morning, parked his car, been seen in the newspaper offices, got in his car again, driven back to Kidlington, murdered Rachel, driven back to Osney Mead *again*, taken the phone-call from Della Cecil, driven back to Kidlington *again*, to be on hand with his mobile and his notebook while the rest of the press are pulling their socks on. He could *never* have done all that in such a short space of time, you said. Impossible! And of course you were right—'

'Thank you, sir.'

'—in one way; and quite wrong in another. Let's stick to our original idea that the list of initials we found was a blackmail list, and that *she's* on it – Della Cecil. He's got something on her, too. So when he asks her to help him in his plan to get Rachel out of the way, she's little option but to co-operate.'

'Have you any idea what this "plan" was, sir?'

'That's the trouble. I've got far too many ideas.'

'Want to try me?'

'All right. They're all the same sort of plan, really – any plan to cut down that *time* business you're so worried about. Let me just outline a possible plan, and see what you think of it. Ready? Owens drives out to work, at ten to seven, let's say – and *she follows him*, in her own car. When he's parked the car, when his entry's recorded, he goes into the building, makes sure he's seen by somebody – doesn't matter who it is – then immediately leaves via a side door and gets into *her* car, parked along the street in front of the offices. Back in Kidlington, he murders Rachel James, about half past seven, *and doesn't return to work at all*. He's got a key and he goes into *Della's* house – and waits. At the appropriate time, when the police arrive, a call is made to his own office – he knows there'll be no one there! – and a message is left *or isn't left* on the answerphone. All that matters is that a telephonic communication is established, and gets recorded on those BT lists we all get, between *her* phone and Owens' phone in his office. Then all he's got to do is to emerge amid all the excitement once the murder's reported – the police, the local people, the Press, the TV . . . Well?'

'You make it up as you go along, sir.'

Morse's face betrayed some irritation. 'Of *course* I bloody do! That's what I'm here for. I just told you. If once we accept there could be *two* people involved – *two* cars – there are *dozens* of possibilities. It's like permutating your selection on the National Lottery. I've just given you *one* possibility, that's all.'

'But it just couldn't—'

'What's wrong with it? Come on! Tell me!'

'Well, let's start with the car—'

'*Cars*, plural.'

'All right. When he's parked his car—'

'I didn't say that. I deliberately said parked *the* car, if you'd been listening. It could have been his – it could have been hers: it's the *card* number that's recorded there, not the *car* number. She could have driven his car – he could have driven hers – and at any point they could have swapped. Not much risk. Very few people around there at seven. Or eight, for that matter.'

'Is it my turn now?' asked Lewis quietly.

'Go on!'

'I'm talking about Owens' car, all right? That was parked in Bloxham Drive – "Drive" *please*, sir – when Owens was there that morning. The street was cordoned off, but the lads let him in – because he told them he lived there. And I saw the car myself.'

'So? He could have left it – or she could have left it – in a nearby street. Anywhere. Up on the main road behind the terrace, say. That's where JJ—'

But Morse broke off.

'It *still* couldn't have happened like you say, sir!'

'No?'

'No! He was seen in his office, Owens was, remember? Just at the time when Rachel was being murdered! Seen by the Personnel Manager there.'

'We haven't got a statement from him yet, though.'

'He's been away, you know that.'

'Yes, I *do* know that, Lewis. But you spoke to him.'

Lewis nodded.

'On the phone?'

'On the phone.'

'You did it through the operator, I suppose?'

Lewis nodded again.

'Do you know who she probably put you through to?' asked Morse slowly.

The light dawned in Lewis's eyes. 'You mean . . . she could have put me through to Owens himself?'

Morse shrugged his shoulders. 'That's what we've got to find out, isn't it? Owens was *deputy* Personnel Manager, we know that. He was on a management course only last weekend.'

'Do you really think that's what happened?'

'I dunno. I know one thing, though: it *could* have happened that way.'

'But it's all so – so airy-fairy, isn't it? And you said we were going to get some *facts* straight first.'

'Exactly.'

Lewis gave up the struggle. 'I'll tell you something that *would* be useful: some idea where the gun is.'

'The "pistol", do you mean?'

'Sorry. But if only we knew where *that* was . . .'

'Oh, I think I know where we're likely to find the pistol, Lewis.'

PART FIVE

CHAPTER FIFTY-THREE
Wednesday, 6 March

A good working definition of Hell on Earth is a forced attendance for a couple of days or even a couple of hours at a Young Conservatives' Convention

(Cassandra, in the *Daily Mirror*, June 1952)

Miss Adèle Cecil (she much preferred 'Miss' to 'Ms' and 'Adèle' to 'Della') had spent the previous evening and night in London, where she had attended, and addressed, a meeting of the chairmen, chairwomen and chairpersons of the Essex Young Conservative Association. Thirty-eight such personages had assembled at Durrants, in George Street, a traditional English hotel just behind Oxford Street, with good facilities, tasteful cuisine, and comfortable beds. Proceedings had been businesslike, and the majority of delegates (it appeared) had ended up in the rooms originally allocated to them.

It was at a comparatively early breakfast in the restaurant that over her fresh grapefruit, with Full English to follow, the head waiter had informed Adèle of the telephone message, which she had taken in one of the hooded booths just outside the breakfast-room.

'How did you know I was here?'

'Don't you remember me? I'm a detective.'

Yes, she remembered him – the white-haired, supercilious, sarcastic police officer she didn't want to meet again.

'I shan't be back in Oxford till lunchtime.'

'The Trout? Half past twelve?'

As she started on her eggs, bacon, mushrooms, and sausages, she accepted the good-natured twitting of her three breakfast companions, all male:

'Boyfriend?'

'Couldn't he wait?'

'What's *he* got . . . ?'

*

During her comparatively young life, Adèle had been companion-ably attached to a couple of dozen or so men, of varying ages, with many of whom she had slept – though seldom more than once or twice, and never without some satisfactory reassurance about the availability and reliability of condoms, and a relatively recent check-up for AIDS.

They were all the same, men. Well, most of them. Fingers fumbling for hooks at the backs of bras, or at the front these days. So why was she looking forward just a little to her lunchtime rendezvous? She wasn't really, she told herself, as she parked the Rover, crossed the narrow road just below the bridge, and entered the bar.

'What'll you have?'

'Orange juice and lemonade, please.'

They sat facing each other at a low wooden table, and Morse was immediately (and again) aware of her attractiveness. She wore a slimly tailored dark grey outfit, with a high-necked Oxford-blue blouse, her ash-blonde hair palely gleaming.

Morse looked down at his replenished pint of London Pride.

'Good time at the Conference?'

'I had a lovely time,' she lied.

'I'm glad it went well,' he lied.

'Do you mind?' She waved an unlit cigarette in the air.

'Go ahead, please.'

She offered the packet across.

'Er, not for the minute, thank you.'

'Well?'

'Just one or two questions.'

She smiled attractively: 'Go ahead.'

Morse experienced a sense of paramnesia. *Déjà vu*. 'You've already signed a statement – about the morning Rachel was murdered?'

'You know that, surely?'

'And it was the truth?' asked Morse, starkly. 'You couldn't have been wrong?'

'Of course not!'

'You told me you "had a heart-to-heart" with Rachel once in a while. I think those were your words?'

'So?'

'Does that mean you spoke about boyfriends – men-friends?'

'And clothes, and money, and work—'

'Did you know she was having an affair with Julian Storrs?'

She nodded slowly.

'Did you mention this to Mr Owens?' Morse's eyes, blue and unblinking, looked fiercely into hers.

And her eyes were suddenly fierce, too, as they held his. 'What the hell do you think I'd do that for?'

Morse made no direct answer as he looked down at the old flagstones there. And when he resumed, his voice was very quiet.

'Did *you* ever have an affair with Julian Storrs?'

She thought he looked sad, as if he hadn't really wanted to ask the question at all; and suddenly she knew why she'd been looking forward to seeing him. So many hours of her life had she spent seeking to discover what lay beneath the physical looks, the sexual prowess, the masculine charms of some of her lovers; and so often had she discovered the selfsame answer – virtually nothing.

She looked long into the blazing log-fire before finally answering:

'I spent one night with him – in Blackpool – at one of the Party Conferences.'

She spoke so softly that Morse could hardly hear the words, or perhaps it was he didn't wish to hear the words. For a while he said nothing. Then he resumed his questioning:

'You told me that when you were at Roedean there were quite a few daughters of service personnel there, apart from yourself?'

'Quite a few, yes.'

'Your own father served in the Army in India?'

'How did you know that?'

'He's in *Who's Who*. Or he was. He died two years ago. Your mother died of cancer twelve years ago. You were the only child of the marriage.'

'Orphan Annie, yeah!' The sophisticated, upper-crust veneer was beginning to crack.

'You inherited his estate?'

'*Estate?* Hah!' She laughed bitterly. 'He left all his money to the bookmakers.'

'No heirlooms, no mementoes – that sort of thing?'

She appeared puzzled. '*What* sort of thing?'

'A pistol, possibly? A service pistol?'

'Look! You don't seriously think *I* had anything to do with—'

'My job's to ask the questions—'

'Well, the answer's "no",' she snapped. 'Any more questions?'

One or two clearly:

'Where were you on Sunday morning – last Sunday morning?'

'At home. In bed. Asleep – until the police woke me up.'

'And *then*?'

'Then I was frightened. And you want me to tell you the truth? Well, I'm *still* bloody frightened!'

Morse looked at her again: so attractive; so vulnerable; and now just a little nervous, perhaps? Not frightened though, surely.

Was she hiding something?

'Is there anything more,' he asked gently, 'anything at all, you can tell me about this terrible business?'

And immediately he sensed that she could.

'Only one thing, and perhaps it's got nothing ... Julian asked me to a Guest Night at Lonsdale last November, and in the SCR after dinner I sat next to a Fellow there called Denis Cornford. I only met him that once – but he was really nice – lovely man, really – the sort of man I wish I'd met in life.'

'Bit old, surely?'

'About your age.'

Morse's fingers folded round the cellophane, and he sought to stop his voice from trembling.

'What about him?'

'I saw him in the Drive, that's all. On Thursday night. About eight. He didn't see me. I'd just driven in and he was walking in front of me – no car. He kept walking along a bit, and then he turned into Number 15 and rang the bell. Geoff Owens opened the front door – and let him in.'

'You're quite sure it was him?'

'Oh, yes,' replied Adèle.

CHAPTER FIFTY-FOUR

He looked into her limpid eyes: 'I will turn this Mozart off, if you don't mind, my love. You see, I can never concentrate on two beautiful things at the same time'

(Passage quoted by Terence Benczik in
The Good and the Bad in Mills and Boon)

WITH SUSPICIOUSLY extravagant caution Morse drove the Jaguar up towards Kidlington HQ, again conscious of seeing the name-plate of that particular railway station flashing, still unrecognizably, across his mind. At the Woodstock Road roundabout he waited patiently for a gap in the Ring-Road traffic; rather too patiently for a regularly hooting hooligan somewhere behind him.

Whether he believed what his ABC girl had told him, he wasn't really sure. And suddenly he realized he'd forgotten to ask her whether indeed it was *she* who occasionally extended her literary talents beyond her humdrum political pamphlets into the fields of (doubtless more profitable) pornography.

But it was only for a few brief minutes that Morse considered the official confiscation of the titillatingly titled novel, since his car-phone had been ringing as he finally crossed into Five Mile Drive. He pulled over to the side of the road, since seldom had he been able to discharge two simultaneous duties at all satisfactorily.

It was Lewis on the line – an excited Lewis.

Calling from the newspaper offices.

'I just spoke to the Personnel Manager, sir. It was him!'

'Lew-is! Your pronouns! *What* exactly was *who*?'

'It wasn't Owens I spoke to on the phone. It was the Personnel Manager himself!'

Morse replied only after a pause, affecting a tone of appropriate humility: 'I wonder why I don't take more notice of you in the first place.'

'You don't sound all that surprised?'

'Little in life surprises me any longer. The big thing is that we're getting things straight at last. Well done!'

'So your girl *wasn't* involved.'

'I don't think so.'

'Did she tell you anything important?'

'I'm not sure. We know Owens had got something on Storrs, and perhaps ... it might be he had something on Cornford as well.'

'Cornford? How does he come into things?'

'She tells me, our Tory lass, that she saw him going into Owens' house last Thursday.'

'Phew!'

'I'm just going back to HQ, and then I'll be off to see our friends the Cornfords – both of 'em – if I can park.'

'Last time you parked on the pavement in front of the Clarendon Building.'

'Ah, yes. Thank you, Lewis. I'd almost forgotten that.'

'Not forgotten your injection, I hope?'

'Oh no. That's now become an automatic part of my lifestyle,' said Morse, who had forgotten all about his lunchtime jab.

The phone was ringing when Morse opened the door of his office.

'Saw you coming in,' explained Strange.

'Yes, sir?'

'It's all these forms I've got to fill in – retirement forms. They give me a headache.'

'They give *me* a headache.'

'At least you know how to fill 'em in.'

'Can we leave it just a little while, sir? I don't seem able to cope with two things at once these days, and I've got to get down to Oxford.'

'Let it wait! Just don't forget *you*'ll be filling in the same forms pretty soon.'

Bloxham Drive was still cordoned off, the police presence still pervasively evident. But Adèle Beatrice Cecil – alias Ann Berkeley Cox, author of *Topless in Torremolinos* – was waved through by a sentinel PC, just as Geoffrey Owens had been waved through over a fortnight earlier, on the morning that Rachel James had been murdered.

As she let herself into Number 1, she was immediately aware that the house was (literally) almost freezing. Why hadn't she left the heating on? How good to have been able to jump straight into a hot bath; or into an electric-blanketed bed; or into a lover's arms . . .

For several minutes she thought of Morse, and of what he had asked her. What on earth had he suspected? And suddenly, alone again now, in her cold house, she found herself shivering.

CHAPTER FIFTY-FIVE

To an outsider it may appear that the average Oxbridge don works but twenty-four weeks out of the annual fifty-two. If therefore at any point in the academic year it is difficult to locate the whereabouts of such an individual, most assuredly this circumstance may not constitute any adequate cause for universal alarm

(*A Workload Analysis of University Teachers,*
ed. HARRY JUDGE)

JUST AFTER 4 P.M. that same day, Morse rang the bell beside the red-painted front door of an elegant, ashlared house just across from the Holywell Music Room. It was the right house, he knew that, with the Lonsdale Crest fixed halfway between the neatly paned windows of the middle and upper storeys.

There was no answer.

There were no answers.

Morse retraced his steps up to Broad Street and crossed the cobbles of Radcliffe Square to the Porters' Lodge at Lonsdale.

'Do you know if Dr Cornford's in College?'

The duty porter rang a number; then shook his head.

'Doesn't seem to be in his rooms, sir.'

'Has he been in today?'

'He was in this morning. Called for his mail – what, ten? Quarter past?'

'You've no idea where he is?'

The porter shook his head. 'Doesn't come in much of a Wednesday, Dr Cornford. Usually has his Faculty Meeting Wednesdays.'

'Can you try him for me there? It's important.'

The porter rang a second number; spoke for a while; put down the phone.

'They've not seen him today, sir. Seems he didn't turn up for the two o'clock meeting.'

'Have you got his home number?'

'He's ex-directory, sir. I can't—'

'So am *I* ex-directory. You know who I am, don't you?'

The young porter looked as hopefully as he could into Morse's face.

'No, sir.'

'Forget it!' snapped Morse.

He walked back up to Holywell Street, along to the red door, and rang the bell.

There was no answer.

There were no answers.

An over-lipsticked middle-aged traffic-warden stood beside the Jaguar.

'Is this your vehicle, sir?'

'Yes, madam. I'm just waiting for the Chief Constable. He's' (Morse pointed vaguely towards the Sheldonian) 'nearly finished in there. At any rate, I hope he bloody has! And if he hasn't, put the bill to 'im, love – not to me!'

'Sorry!'

Morse wandered across to the green-shuttered Blackwell's, and browsed awhile; finally purchasing the first volume of Sir Steven Runciman's *History of the Crusades*.

He wasn't quite sure why.

Then, for the third time, he walked up to the red door in Holywell Street and rang the bell.

Morse heard the news back in HQ.

From Lewis.

A body had been found in a car, in a narrow lane off New Road, in a garage rented under the name of Dr Cornford.

For a while Morse sat silent.

'I only met him the once you know, Lewis. Well, the twice, really. He was a good man, I think. I liked him.'

'It isn't Dr Cornford though, sir. It's his wife.'

CHAPTER FIFTY-SIX
Thursday, 7 March

> Is it sin
> To rush into the secret house of death
> Ere death dare come to us?
> (Shakespeare, *Antony and Cleopatra*)

'TELL ME ABOUT it,' said Morse.

Seated opposite him, in the first-floor office in St Aldate's Police Station, Detective Chief Inspector Peter Warner told the story sadly and economically.

Mrs Shelly Cornford had been found in the driving-seat of her own car, reclining back, with a hosepipe through the window. The garage had been bolted on the inside. There could be little doubt that the immediate cause of death was carbon-monoxide poisoning from exhaust fumes. A brief handwritten note had been left on the passenger seat: 'I'm so sorry, Denis, I can't forgive myself for what I did. I never loved anyone else but you, my darling – S.' No marks of violence; 97 mg blood alcohol – the equivalent (Warner suggested) of two or three stiffish gins. Still a few unanswered questions, of course: about her previous whereabouts that day; about the purchase of the green hosepipe and the connector, both new. But suspicion of foul play? None.

'I wonder where she had a drink?' asked Morse.

'Well, if she'd walked up from Holywell Street, there'd be the King's Arms, the White Horse, The Randolph . . . But you're the expert.'

Morse asked no more questions; but sat thinking of the questionnaire he had set for the *Police Gazette* (it seemed so long ago): 'If you could gladden your final days with one of the following . . .' Yes, without a doubt, if he'd been honest, Morse would have applauded Shelly Cornford's choice. And what the hell did it matter *where* she'd had those few last glasses of alcohol – few last 'units' rather – the measurements into which the dietitian had advised him to convert his old familiar gills and pints and quarts.

'Do you want to see her?'

Morse shook his head.

'You'd better see *him*, though.'

Morse nodded wearily. 'Is he all right?'

'We-ell. His GP's been in – but he refuses to take any medication. He's in the canteen with one of the sergeants. We've finished with him, really.'

'Tell me about it,' urged Morse.

Denis Cornford's voice was flat, almost mechanical, as he replied:

'On Sunday just before I met you in the pub she told me she'd been to bed with another man that morning. I hardly spoke to her after that. I slept in the spare room the last three nights.'

'The note?' asked Morse gently. 'Is that what she was referring to?'

'Yes.'

'Nothing to do with anything else?'

'No.'

'She was there, in your rooms, just before Chapel on Sunday, wasn't she?'

Cornford evinced no surprise.

'We'd had a few harsh words. She didn't want to see you.'

'Do you know who the other man was?'

'Yes. Clixby Bream.'

'*She* told you that, sir?'

'Yes.'

'So – so she couldn't have had anything to do with the Owens murder?'

'No. Nor could the Master.'

'Did *you* have anything to do with it?'

'No.'

'Why did you go to see Owens last Thursday?'

'I knew Owens a bit through various things I did for his newspaper. That night I had to go to Kidlington – I went on the bus – the Kidlington History Society – held at the school – "Effects of the Enclosure Acts in Oxfordshire" – seven o'clock to eight. He lived fairly near – five minutes' walk away. I'd done a three-part article for him on Mediaeval Oxford – Owens said it needed shortening a bit – we discussed some changes – no problems. I got a bus back to Oxford – about nine.'

'Why didn't you tell me you knew Owens?'

'I didn't want to get involved.'

'What will you do now?'

'I left a note for the Master about the election.' The voice was still monotonous; the mouth dry. 'I've withdrawn my nomination.'

'I'm so sorry about everything,' said Morse very quietly.

'Yes, I think you are, aren't you?'

Morse left the pale, bespectacled historian staring vaguely into a cup of cold tea, like a man who is temporarily anaesthetized against some overwhelming pain.

'It's a terrible business – terrible!'

The Master poured himself a single-malt Scotch.

'Drink, Chief Inspector?'

Morse shook his head.

'Won't you sit down?'

'No. I've only called to say that Dr Cornford has just told me everything – about you and his wife.'

'Mmm.'

'We shall have to get a statement from you.'

'Why is that?'

'The *time* chiefly, I suppose.'

'Is it really necessary?'

'There *was* a murder on that Sunday morning.'

'Mmm. Was she one of your suspects?'

Morse made no direct answer. 'She couldn't have been making love to you and murdering someone else at the same time.'

'No.' The bland features betrayed no emotion; yet Morse was distastefully aware that the Master was hardly displeased with such a succinct, such an unequivocal assertion of Shelly Cornford's innocence, since by implication it was an assertion of his own.

'I understand that Dr Cornford has written to you, sir.'

'Exited from the lists, poor Denis, yes. That just leaves Julian Storrs. Good man though, Julian!'

Morse slowly walked to the door.

'What do you think about suicide, Sir Clixby?'

'In general?' The Master drained his tumbler, and thoughtfully considered the question. 'Aristotle, you know, thought suicide a form of cowardice – running away from troubles oneself and leaving all the heartache to everybody else. What do *you* think?'

Morse was conscious of a deep loathing for this smooth and odious man.

'I don't know what your particular heartache is, sir. You see I never met Mrs Cornford myself. But I'd be surprised if she was a coward. In fact, I've got the feeling she was a bit of a gutsy girl.' Morse stood beside the study door, his face drawn, his nostrils distended. 'And I'll tell you something else. She probably had far more guts in her little finger than you've ever had in the whole of your body!'

Lewis was waiting in the Jaguar outside the Porters' Lodge; and Morse quickly climbed into the passenger seat. His voice was still vicious:

'Get – me – out – of – here, Lewis!'

CHAPTER FIFTY-SEVEN
Friday, 8 March

Those who are absent, by its means become present: correspondence is the consolation of life
(Voltaire, *Philosophical Dictionary*)

SERGEANT LEWIS had himself only just entered Morse's office when Jane came through with the post: six official-looking letters, opened, with appropriate previous correspondence paper-clipped behind them; one square white envelope, unopened, marked 'Private', and postmarked Oxford; and an airmail letter, also unopened, marked 'Personal', and postmarked 'Washington'.

Jane smiled radiantly at her boss.

'Why are you looking so cheerful?' queried Morse.

'Just nice to have you back, sir, that's all.'

Inside the white envelope was a card, the front showing an auburn-haired woman, in a white dress, reading a book; and Morse read the brief message inside:

Geoffrey Harris Ward
Radcliffe Infirmary
7 March 96

We all miss your miserable presence in the ward. If you
<u>haven't</u> finished smoking, we shall never meet for that G&T
you promised me. Look after yourself!

Affectionately
Janet (McQueen)

P.S. I looked through your old hospital records from <u>many</u>
years ago. Know something? I found your Christian <u>name</u>!

'Why are *you* looking so cheerful?' asked Lewis.

But Morse made no answer, and indeed appeared to be reading
the message again and again. Then he opened the letter from
America.

Washington
4 March

Dear Morse,

Just read your thing in the Police Gazette. How did I know it
was yours? Ah, I too was a detective! I'd have had the
champagne myself. And I think the Fauré Requiem's a bit
lightweight compared with the Verdi – in spite of the
imprimatur of the Papacy. I know you've always wept to
Wagner but I've alvays vept to Verdi myself – and the best
Xmas present I had was the Karajan recording of
Don Carlos.

I know you're frightened of flying, but a visit here –
especially in the spring, they say – is something not to be
missed in life. We'll get together again for a jar on my return
(April) and don't leave it <u>too</u> long before you take your
pension.

As aye,
Peter (Imbert)

Morse handed the letter across to Lewis.

'The old Metropolitan Commissioner!'

Morse nodded, rather proudly.

'Washington DC, that'll be, sir.'

'Where else?'

'Washington CD – County Durham, near enough.'

'Oh.'

'What's your programme today, sir?'

'Well, we've done most of the spadework—'

'Except the Harvey Clinic side of things.'

'And that's in hand, you say?'

'Seeing the woman this morning. She's just back from a few days' holiday.'

'Who's she again? Remind me.'

'I told you about her: Dawn Charles.'

'Mrs or Miss or Ms?'

'Not sure. But she's the main receptionist there. They say if anybody's likely to know what's going on, she is.'

'What time are you seeing her?'

'Ten o'clock. She's got a little flat out at Bicester on the Charles Church Estate. You joining me?'

'No, I don't think so. Something tells me I ought to see Storrs again.'

Lovingly Morse put the 'Girl Reading' (Perugini, 1878) back into her envelope, then looked through Sir Peter's letter once again.

Don Carlos.

The two words stood out and stared at him, at the beginning of a line as they were, at the end of a paragraph. Not an opera Morse knew well, *Don Carlos*. Another 'DC', though. It was amazing how many DCs had cropped up in their inquiries – and still another one just now in the District of Columbia. And suddenly in Morse's mind the name of the Verdi opera merged with a name he'd just heard: the 'Don' chiming in with the 'Dawn', and the 'Carlos' with the 'Charles'.

Was it *Dawn Charles* (Mrs or Miss or Ms) who held the key to the mystery? Did they belong to *her*, that pair of initials in the manila file?

Morse's eyes gleamed with excitement.

'I think,' he said slowly, 'Mr Julian Storrs will have to wait a little while. I shall be coming with you, Lewis – to Bicester.'

PART SIX

CHAPTER FIFTY-EIGHT

The best liar is he who makes the smallest amount of lying go
the longest way

(Samuel Butler, *Truth and Convenience*)

DAWN CHARLES looked nervous when she opened the door of
her flat in Woodpecker Way and let the two detectives through
into the grey-carpeted lounge, where the elder of the two, the
white-haired one, was already complimenting her on such an
attractive residence.

'Bit unlucky though, really. I bought it at the top of the
property boom for fifty-eight thousand. Only worth thirty-four
now.'

'Oh dear!'

The man made her feel uneasy. And her mind went back to
the previous summer when on returning from France she'd put
the Green Channel sticker on the windscreen – only to be diverted
into the Red Channel; where pleasantly, far too pleasantly, she'd
been questioned about her time abroad, about the weather, about
anything and everything – except those extra thousand cigarettes
in the back of the boot. It had been as if they were just stringing
her along; knowing the truth all the time.

But these men couldn't possibly know the truth, that's what
she was telling herself now; and she thought she could handle
things. On Radio Oxford just before Christmas she'd heard P. D.
James's advice to criminal suspects: 'Keep it short! Keep it simple!
Don't change a single word unless you have to!'

'Please sit down. Coffee? I've only got instant, I'm afraid.'

'We both prefer instant, don't we, Sergeant?'

'Lovely,' said Lewis, who would much have preferred tea.

Two minutes later, Dawn held a jug suspended over the
steaming cups.

'Milk?'

'Please,' from Lewis.

'Thank you,' from Morse.

'Sugar?'

'Just the one teaspoonful,' from Lewis.

But a shake of the head from Morse; a slight raising of the eyebrows as she stirred two heaped teaspoonfuls into her own coffee; and an obsequious comment which caused Lewis to squirm inwardly: 'How on earth do you manage to keep such a beautiful figure – with all that sugar?'

She coloured slightly. 'Something to do with the metabolic rate, so they tell me at the clinic.'

'Ah, yes! The clinic. I'd almost forgotten.'

Again he was sounding too much like the Customs man, and Dawn was glad it was the sergeant who now took over the questioning.

A little awkwardly, a little ineptly (certainly as Morse saw things) Lewis asked about her training, her past experience, her present position, her relationships with employers, colleagues, clients . . .

The scene was almost set.

She knew Storrs (she claimed) only as a patient; she'd known Turnbull (she claimed) only as a consultant; she knew Owens (she claimed) not at all.

Lewis produced the letter stating Julian Storrs' prognosis.

'Do you think this photocopy was made at the clinic?'

'I didn't copy it.'

'Someone must have done.'

'I didn't copy it.'

'Any idea who might have done?'

'*I* didn't copy it.'

It was hardly a convincing performance, and she was aware that both men knew she was lying. And quietly – amid a few tears, certainly, but with no hysteria – the truth came out.

Owens she had met when the Press had come along for the clinic's 25th anniversary – he must have seen something, heard something that night, about Mr Storrs. After Mr Turnbull had died, Owens had telephoned her – they'd met in the Bird and Baby in St Giles' – he'd asked her if she could copy a letter for him – yes, *that* letter – he'd offered her £500 – and she'd agreed – copied the letter – been paid in cash. That was it – that was all – a complete betrayal of trust, she knew that – something she'd never done before – would never have done in the normal course of events. It was just the money – nothing else – she'd desperately needed the money . . .

Morse had been silent throughout the interrogation, his attention focused, it seemed, on the long, black-stockinged legs.

'Where does that leave me – leave us?' she asked miserably.

'We shall have to ask you to come in to make an official statement,' said Lewis.

'Now, you mean?'

'That'll be best, yes.'

'Perhaps not,' intervened Morse. 'It's not *all* that urgent, Miss Charles. We'll be in touch fairly soon.'

At the door, Morse thanked her for the coffee: 'Not the best homecoming, I'm afraid.'

'Only myself to blame,' she said, her voice tight as she looked across at the Visitors' parking lots, where the Jaguar stood.

'Where did you go?' asked Morse.

'I didn't go anywhere.'

'You stayed here – in your flat?'

'I didn't go anywhere.'

'What was that about?' asked Lewis as he drove back along the A34 to Oxford. 'About her statement?'

'I want you to be with me when we see Storrs this afternoon.'

'What did you think of her?'

'Not a very good liar.'

'Lovely figure, though. Legs right up to her armpits! She'd have got a job in the chorus line at the Windmill.'

Morse was silent, his eyes gleaming again as Lewis continued:

'I read somewhere that they all had to be the same height and the same build – in the chorus line there.'

'Perhaps I'll take you along when the case is over.'

'No good, sir. It's been shut for ages.'

Dawn Charles closed the door behind her and walked thoughtfully back to the lounge, the suspicion of a smile about her lips.

CHAPTER FIFTY-NINE

Everything in life is somewhere else, and you get there in a car
(E. B. White, *One Man's Meat*)

LEWIS HAD BACKED into the first available space in Polstead Road, the tree-lined thoroughfare that leads westward from Woodstock Road into Jericho; and now stood waiting whilst Morse arose laboriously from the low passenger seat of the Jaguar.

'Seen *that* before, sir?' Lewis pointed to the circular blue plaque on the wall opposite: 'This house was the home of T. E. Lawrence (Lawrence of Arabia) from 1896–1921.'

Morse grunted as he straightened up his aching back, mumbling of lumbago.

'What about a plaque for Mr Storrs, sir? "This was the home of Julian Something Storrs, Master of Lonsdale, 1996 to . . . 1997?"'

Morse shrugged indifferently:

'Perhaps just 1996.'

The two men walked a little way along the short road. The houses here were of a pattern: gabled, red-bricked, three-storeyed properties, with ashlared, mullioned windows, the frames universally painted white; interesting and amply proportioned houses built towards the end of the nineteenth century.

'Wouldn't mind living here,' volunteered Lewis.

Morse nodded. 'Very civilized. Small large houses, these, Lewis, as opposed to large small houses.'

'What's the difference?'

'Something to do with the number of bathrooms, I think.'

'Not much to do with the number of garages!'

'No.'

Clearly nothing whatever to do with the number of garages, since the reason for the continuum of cars on either side of the road was becoming increasingly obvious: there *were* no garages here, nor indeed any room for such additions. To compensate for the inconvenience, the front areas of almost all the properties had been cemented, cobbled, gravelled, or paved, in order to accommodate the parking of motor cars; including the front of the Storrs' residence, where on the gravel alongside the front window

stood a small, pale grey, D-registration Citroën, a thin pink stripe
around its bodywork.

'Someone's in?' ventured Morse.

'Mrs Storrs, perhaps – he's got a BMW. A woman's car, that,
anyway.'

'Really?'

Morse was still peering through the Citroën's front window
(perhaps for some more eloquent token of femininity) when
Lewis returned from his ineffectual ringing.

'No one in. No answer, anyway.'

'On another weekend break?'

'I could ring the Porters' Lodge.'

'You do that small thing, Lewis. I'll be . . .' Morse pointed
vaguely towards the hostelry at the far end of the road.

It was at the Anchor, a few minutes later, as Morse sat behind a
pint of John Smith's Tadcaster bitter, that Lewis came in to report
on the Storrs: away again, for the weekend, the pair of them, this
time though their whereabouts not vouchsafed to the Lodge.

Morse received the news without comment, appearing preoccupied; *thinking* no doubt, supposed Lewis, as he paid for his
orange juice. Thinking and drinking . . . drinking and thinking
. . . the twin activities which in Morse's view were ever and
necessarily concomitant.

Not wholly preoccupied, however.

'I'll have a refill while you're at the bar, Lewis. Smith's please.'

After a period of silence, Morse asked the question:

'If somebody came to you with a letter – a photocopied letter,
say – claiming your missus was having a passionate affair with
the milkman—'

Lewis grinned. 'I'd be dead worried. We've got a woman on
the milk-float.'

'—what would you do?'

'Read it, obviously. See who'd written it.'

'Show it to the missus?'

'Only if it was a joke.'

'How would you know that?'

'Well, you wouldn't really, would you? Not for a start. You'd
try to find out if it was genuine.'

'Exactly. So when Storrs got a copy of that letter, a letter he'd pretty certainly not seen before—'

'Unless Turnbull showed it to him?'

'Doubt it. A death certificate, wasn't it? He'd want to let Storrs down a bit more gently than that.'

'You mean, if Storrs tried to find out if it *was* genuine, he'd probably go along to the clinic . . .'

Morse nodded, like some benevolent schoolmaster encouraging a promising pupil.

'And show it to . . . Dawn Charles?'

'Who else? She's the sort of Practice Manager there, if anybody is. And let's be honest about things. You're not exactly an expert in the Socratic skills yourself, are you? But how long did it take *you* to get the truth out of her? Three or four minutes?'

'You think Storrs did it as well?'

'Pretty certainly, I'd say. He's nobody's fool; and he's not going to give in to blackmail just on somebody's vague say-so. He's an academic; and if you're an academic you're trained to *check* – check your sources, check your references, check your evidence.'

'So perhaps Storrs has been a few steps in front of us all the time.'

Morse nodded. 'He probably rumbled our receptionist straightaway. Not *many* suspects there at the clinic.'

Slowly Lewis sipped his customary orange juice, his earlier euphoria fading.

'We're not exactly galloping towards the finishing-post, are we?'

Morse looked up, his blue eyes betraying some considerable surprise.

'Why do you say that, Lewis? That's exactly what we *are* doing.'

CHAPTER SIXTY
Saturday, 9 March

Hombre apercebido medio combatido
(A man well prepared has already half fought the battle)
(Cervantes, *Don Quixote*)

SOMEWHAT CONCERNED about the adequacy of the Jaguar's petrol allowance, Morse had requisitioned an unmarked police car, which just before 10 a.m. was heading south along the A34, with Sergeant Lewis at the wheel. As they approached Abingdon, Morse asked Lewis to turn on Classic FM; and almost immediately asked him to turn it off, as he recognized the Brandenburg Concerto No. 2.

'Somebody once said, Lewis, that it was not impossible to get bored even in the presence of a mistress, and I'm sorry to say I sometimes get a little bored even in the company of Johann Sebastian Bach.'

'Really. I thought it was rather nice.'

'Lew-is! He may be terrific; he may be terrible – but he's never *nice*. Not Bach!'

Lewis concentrated on the busy road ahead as Morse sank back into his seat and, as was ever his wont in a car, said virtually nothing for the rest of the journey.

And yet Morse had said so many things – things upon which Lewis's mind intermittently focused again, as far too quickly he drove down to the Chieveley junction with the M4 . . .

Once back from Polstead Road, Friday afternoon had been very busy and, for Lewis, very interesting. It had begun with Morse asking about their present journey.

'If you had a posh car, which way would you go to Bath?'

'A34, M4, A46 – probably the best; the quickest, certainly.'

'What if you had an old banger?'

'Still go the same way, I think.'

'What's wrong with the Burford–Cirencester way?'

'Nothing at all, if you like a bit of scenery. Or if you don't like motorway driving.'

Then another question:

'How do we find out which bank the Storrs use?'

'Could be they have different banks, sir. Shouldn't be too difficult, though: Lloyds, Barclays, NatWest, Midland . . . Shall I ring around?'

Morse nodded. 'And try to find out how they've been spending their money recently – if it's possible.'

'May take a bit of time, but I don't see why not. Let me find out anyway.'

Lewis turned to go, but Morse had a further request.

'Before you do, bring me the notes you made about the Storrs' stay in Bath last weekend. I'm assuming you've typed 'em up by now?'

'All done. Maybe a few spelling mistakes – a few grammatical lapses – beautifully typed, though.'

It had taken Lewis only ten minutes to discover that Mr Julian Storrs and Mrs Angela Storrs both banked at Lloyds. But there had been far greater difficulty in dealing with Morse's supplementary request.

The Manager of Lloyds (Headington Branch) had been fully co-operative but of only limited assistance. It was very unusual of course, but not in cases such as this *unethical*, for confidential material concerning clients to be disclosed. But Lewis would have to contact Lloyds Inspection Department in Bristol.

Which Lewis had promptly done, again receiving every co-operation; also, however, receiving the disappointing news that the information required was unlikely as yet to be fully ready. With credit-card facilities now almost universally available, the volume of transactions was ever growing; and with receipt-items sometimes irregularly forwarded from retail outlets, and with a few inevitable checks and delays in processing and clearance – well, it would take a little time.

'Later this afternoon?' Lewis had queried hopefully.

'No chance of that, I'm afraid.'

'Tomorrow morning?'

Lewis heard a deep sigh at the other end of the line. 'We don't usually . . . It *is* very urgent, you say?'

*

The phone had been ringing in Morse's office (an office minus Morse) and Lewis had taken the brief call. The post-mortem on Shelly Cornford confirmed death from carbon-monoxide poisoning, and completely ruled out any suspicion of foul play.

A note on yellow paper was Sellotaped to the desk:

Lewis!
– Just off to the Diab. Centre (3.45)
– Yr notes on Bath most helpful, but try to get Sarah Siddons right – two d's, please.
– Good job we're getting a few facts straight before jumping too far ahead. Reculer pour mieux sauter!
– We'll be jumping tomorrow a.m. tho' – to Bath. Royal Crescent informs me the Storrs – Herr und Frau – are staying there again!
– I need yr notes on Julian Storrs.
– Ring me at home – after the Archers.

M

And on the side of the desk, a letter from the Thame and District Diabetic Association addressed to Det. Chief Inspector Morse:

Dear sir,

Welcome to the Club! Sorry to be so quick off the mark but news travels fast in diabetic circles.

We meet on the first Thursday of each month 7.30–9 p.m. in the Town Hall in Thame and we shall be delighted if you can come to speak to us. We can offer no fee but we can offer a warm-hearted and grateful audience.

During this last year we have been fortunate to welcome several very well-known people. For example our last six speakers have been Dr David Matthews, Lesley Hallett, Professor Harry Keane, Angela Storrs, Dr Robert Turner, and Willie Rushton.

Please try to support us if you can. For our 1996/7 programme we are still looking for speakers for October '96 and February '97. Any hope of you filling one of these slots?

I enclose SAE and thank you for your kind consideration . . .

But Lewis read only the first few lines, for never, except in the course of a criminal investigation, had he wittingly read a letter meant for the eyes of another person . . .

From the passenger seat Morse had still said nothing until Lewis, after turning off the M4 at Junction 18 on to the A46, was within a few miles of Bath.

'Lewis! If you had a mistress—'

'Not the milk-lady, sir. She's far too fat for me.'

'—and, say, you were having a weekend away together and you told your missus that you were catching the train but in fact this woman was going to pick you up in her car somewhere – The Randolph, say . . .'

'Yes, sir?' (Was Morse getting lost?)

'Would you still *go* to the railway station? Would you make sure she picked you up *at* the railway station – not The Randolph?'

'Dunno, sir. I've never—'

'I know you haven't,' snapped Morse. 'Just *think*, man!'

So Lewis thought. And *thought* he saw what Morse was getting at.

'You mean it might make you feel a bit better in your own mind – feel a bit less guilty, like – if you did what you *said* you'd be doing – before you went?' (Was Lewis getting lost?)

'Something like that,' said Morse unenthusiastically as a sign welcomed the two detectives to the Roman City of Bath.

As soon as Lewis had stopped outside the Royal Crescent Hotel, Morse rang through on the mobile phone to the Deputy Manager, as had been agreed. No problem, it appeared. The Storrs had gone off somewhere an hour or so earlier in the BMW. The coast was clear; and Morse got out of the car and walked round to the driver's window.

'Good luck in Bristol!'

Lewis raised two crossed fingers of his right hand, like the logo of the National Lottery, as Morse continued:

'If you find what I *hope* you're going to find, the battle's half won. And it's mostly thanks to you.'

'No! It was you who figured it all out.'

'Wouldn't have done, though, without all those visits of yours to Soho.'

'Pardon, sir?'

'To see the chorus line, Lewis! The chorus line at the Windmill.'

'But I've never—'

'"Legs right up to her armpits," you said, right? And that was the *second* time you'd used those words, Lewis. Remember?'

CHAPTER SIXTY-ONE

Life, within doors, has few pleasanter prospects than a neatly arranged and well-provisioned breakfast table
          (Nathaniel Hawthorne, *The House of the Seven Gables*)

MORSE STOOD FOR some while on the huge slabs that form the wide pavement stretching along the whole extent of the great 500-foot curve of cinnamon-coloured stone, with its identical façades of double Ionic columns, which comprise Bath's Royal Crescent. It seemed to him a breathtaking architectural masterpiece, with the four-star hotel exactly at its centre: Number 16.

He walked between the black spiked railings, through the white double doors, into the black-and-white floor-tiled, high-ceilinged entrance-hall, and then to reception, where he was immediately ushered into the beige-carpeted, pine-furnished office of the Deputy Manager, just beyond.

Sara Hickman was from Leicestershire, a tall, slimly attractive woman in her mid-thirties, with green eyes (just like Sister McQueen) and dark curly hair. She was dressed in a business-like suit; she spoke in a business-like manner; and so very clearly was she part of an extremely business-like hotel, since manifold awards – RAC Blue Ribbons, AA Rosettes, Egon Ronay Stars – vied with each other for space around the walls.

After hesitating, finally capitulating, over the offer of coffee, Morse soon found himself listening very carefully.

Sara had (she told him) been able to re-interview almost all of the service personnel who had been on duty the previous weekend, most of whom, as it happened, were performing similar duties that present weekend. But there seemed little to add, at least in general terms, to the details earlier communicated by the Manager himself to the Thames Valley Police. One minor correction: the room the Storrs had slept in was a Standard Twin, not a Standard Double; and in fact the couple had asked for the same room again, if it was available. Which, by some strange coincidence, it was: the only Standard Twin still available in the hotel that weekend. Registration? She passed to Morse the card dated the previous Saturday, 2.3.96: Guest's Name; Address; Telephone No.; Arrival Date; Departure Date; Nationality; Payment Type; Passport No.; Signature; Car Reg. No. – and more. All filled in with a neat, feminine, slightly forward-leaning script, in black Biro; and signed 'Angela Storrs'. It would be comparatively easy to check, of course; but Morse had little or no doubt that the signature was genuine.

'The Manager told my sergeant, when he rang about last weekend, that we might be able to see some itemized bills?'

Sara Hickman smiled.

'I thought somehow you might ask for them,' she said, and now read aloud from a small sheaf of bills in front of her.

'Last Saturday night they ate at Table twenty-six, in the far corner of the restaurant. He had the Carpaccio of Beef, Truffled Noodles, and Parmesan, for his starter; for his main course, the Sea Bass served with Creamed Celeriac and Fennel Liqueur; Passion Fruit Mousse for sweet. *She* wasn't quite so adventurous, I'm afraid: Consommé; with Baked Plaice and Green Salad for her main course; and then cream-crackers and Edam – the waiter particularly remembers her asking for the Edam.'

'Good low-fat cheese they tell me,' mumbled Morse, recalling his own hard-nosed dietitian's homily in the Geoffrey Harris Ward. And he was smiling vaguely to himself as the Deputy Manager continued:

'Now, Sunday morning. Mr Storrs had ordered breakfasts for the two of them over the phone the previous night – at about eleven, half past – can't be sure. He said he thought he was probably too late with the form, but he obviously had it in front of him – the night-porter remembers that. He said he'd have a Full English for himself, no kidney though, with the tomato well grilled, and two fried eggs. Said his wife would go for a Continental: said she'd like cereal, Ricicles, if we'd got some – Chief Inspector, we've got a bigger selection of cereals than Sainsbury's! – some brown toast and honey, the fresh-fruit compôte, and orange juice. Oh, yes' (Sara checked the form again) 'and hot chocolate.'

'The time?' asked Morse.

'It would have been between seven-thirty and eight. We don't serve Full English until after seven-thirty – and both breakfasts went up together.'

'And last night for dinner?'

'They didn't eat here.'

'This morning?'

'They had breakfast in their room again. This time they filled in the form early, and left it on the doorknob outside the room. Same as before for Mr Storrs—'

'How do you know it wasn't for *her*?'

'Well, it's exactly what he ordered before. Here, look for yourself.'

She passed the room-service order across the desk; and Morse saw the instructions: 'Well grilled' against 'Tomato'; no tick against 'Kidney'; the figure '2' against 'Eggs (fried)'.

'I see what you mean,' admitted Morse. 'Not even married couples have exactly the same tastes, I suppose.'

'*Especially* married couples,' said Sara Hickman quietly.

Morse's eyes continued down the form, to the Continental section, and saw the ticks against 'Weetabix' ('semi-skimmed milk' written beside it), 'Natural Yoghurt', 'Toast (brown)', 'Coffee (decaffeinated)'. The black-Biro'd writing was the same as that on the registration form. Angela Storrs' writing. Certainly.

'I shall have to have copies of these forms,' said Morse.

'Of course.' Sara got to her feet. 'I'll see that's done straight-away. Shall we go over to the bar?'

The day was brightening.

But for Morse the day had already been wonderfully bright; had been for the past hour or so, ever since the Deputy Manager had been speaking with him.

And indeed was very shortly to be brighter still.

CHAPTER SIXTY-TWO

Queen Elizabeth the First Slept Here
(Notice which according to the British Tourist Board
is to be observed in approximately 2400 residences
in the United Kingdom)

THEY WALKED ACROSS the splendidly tended garden area behind the main complex to the Dower House, an elegant annexe wherein were situated most of the hotel's suites and bedrooms, as well as the restaurant, the main lounge – and the bar.

Immediately inside the entrance, Morse saw the plaque (virtually a statutory requirement in Bath) commemorating a particularly eminent royal personage:

George IV
1820–1830
Resided here
1799
as
Prince of Wales

In the lounge, Morse sat down amid the unashamedly luxurious surroundings of elaborate wall-lights, marble busts – and courteously prompt service, for a uniformed waitress was already standing beside them.

'What would you like to drink, sir?'

Lovely question.

As he waited for his beer, Morse looked around him; and in particular at the portrait above the fireplace there: 'Lord Ellmore, 1765–1817', the inscription read, a fat-cheeked, smooth-faced man, with a protruding lower lip, who reminded Morse unhappily of Sir Clixby Bream.

Then he walked through to the Gents in the corridor just off the lounge where the two loos stood side by side, the Men's and the Ladies' logos quite unequivocally distinct on their adjacent doors.

It would have been difficult even for the myopic Mrs Adams to confuse the two, thought Morse, as he smiled and mouthed a few silent words to himself:

'Thank you! Thank you, Mrs Arabella Adams!'

It wasn't that she could have been certain – from some little distance? with her failing eyesight? – that the person she had seen was a man or a woman. Certainly not so far as the recognition of any facial features was concerned. Faces were notoriously difficult to distinguish, appearing so different when seen in profile, perhaps, or in the shadows, or wearing glasses. No! It was just that old Mrs Adams had always known what men looked like, and what women looked like, since habitually the men wore trousers and the women wore skirts. But of course if someone wore trousers, that certainly didn't prove that the wearer was a man, now did it, Morse? In fact it proved one thing and one thing *only*: that the person in question was wearing trousers!

Ten minutes later, as he worked his way with diminishing enthusiasm through an over-generous plateful of smoked-salmon sandwiches, Morse saw Sergeant Lewis appear in the doorway – a Lewis looking almost as self-satisfied as the oily Lord Ellmore himself – and raise his right thumb, before being introduced to Sara Hickman.

'Something to drink, Sergeant?'

'Thank you. Orange juice, please.'

'Something to eat?'

'What have you got?'

She smiled happily. 'Anything. Anything you like. Our Head Chef is at your command.'

'Can he rustle up some eggs and chips?'

She said she was sure – well, almost sure – that he could, and departed to investigate.

'Lew-is! This is a cordon bleu establishment.'

'Should taste good then, sir.'

The buoyant Lewis passed a note to Morse, simultaneously (and much to Morse's relief) helping himself to a couple of sandwiches.

'You don't mind, sir? I'm half starving.'

At 2.30 p.m. Marilyn Hudson, a small, fair-complexioned young woman, was called into Sara's office. Marilyn had been a chamber-cum-kitchenmaid at the hotel for almost three years; and it was soon clear that she knew as much as anyone was likely to know about the day-to-day – and night-by-night – activities there.

Morse now questioned her closely about the morning of the previous Sunday, 3 March.

'You took them breakfast?'

'Yes, sir. About quarter to eight.'

'You knocked on the door?'

'Like I always do, yes. I heard somebody say "Come in" so I—'

'You had a key?'

'I've got a master-key. So I took the tray in and put it on the dressing-table.'

'Were they in bed together?'

'No. Twin beds it is there. She was on the far side. Difficult to miss her, though.'

'Why do you say that?'

'Well, it was her *pyjamas* – yellow an' black an' green stripes – up an' down.'

'Vertical stripes, you mean?'

'I'm not sure about that, sir. Just up an' down, like I said. An' she's got the same pair now. I took their breakfast again this morning. Same room – thirty-six.' Marilyn gave a nervous little giggle. 'Perhaps it's time she changed them.'

'She may have got two pairs,' interposed Lewis – not particularly helpfully, judging from the scowl on Morse's face.

'Do you think it *could* have been anybody else – except Mrs Storrs?'

'No, sir. Like I say, she was there in the bed. But . . .'

'But what?'

'Well, I saw *her* all right. But I didn't really see *him*. He was in the bathroom having a shave – electric razor it was – and the door was open a bit and I saw he was still in his pyjamas and he said thank you but . . .'

'Would you have recognized him if he'd turned his head?'

For the first time Marilyn Hudson seemed unsure of herself.

'Well, I'd seen them earlier in the hotel, but I didn't notice him as much as her really. She was, you know, ever so dressy and smart – dark glasses she wore – and a white trouser-suit. Same thing as she's got on today.'

Morse turned to Lewis. 'Do you think she's got *two* white trouser-suits, Sergeant?'

'Always a possibility, sir.'

'So' (if Morse was experiencing some disappointment, he gave no indication of it) 'what you're telling us is that you're pretty sure it was her, but not quite so sure it was *him*?'

Marilyn considered the question a while before replying:

'No. I'm *pretty* sure it was both of them, sir.'

'Good girl, our Marilyn,' confided Sara, 'even if her vocabulary's a bit limited.'

Morse looked across at her quizzically:

'Vertical and horizontal, you mean? I shouldn't worry about that. I've always had trouble with east and west myself.'

'Lots of people have trouble with right and left,' began Lewis – but Morse was already making a further request:

'You've still got the details of who was staying here last Saturday?'

'Of course. Just a minute.'

She returned shortly with a sheaf of registration cards; and Morse was looking through, flicking them over one at a time – when suddenly he stopped, the familiar tingling of excitement across his shoulders.

He handed the card to Lewis.

And Lewis whistled softly, incredulously, as he read the name.

Morse turned again to Sara. 'Can you let us have a copy of the bill – account, whatever you call it – for Room fifteen?'

'You were right then, sir!' whispered Lewis excitedly. 'You always said it was "DC"!'

Sarah came back and laid the account in front of Morse.

'Single room – number fifteen. Just the one night. Paid by credit card.'

Morse looked through the items.

'No evening meal?'

'No.'

'No breakfast either?'

'No.'

'Look! Can we use your phone from here?'

'Of course you can. Shall I leave you?'

'Yes, I think so,' said Morse, 'if you don't mind.'

Morse and Lewis emerged from the office some twenty minutes later; and were walking behind reception when one of the guests came through from the entrance hall and asked for the key to Room 36.

Then he saw Morse.

'Good God! What are *you* doing here?' asked Julian Storrs.

'I was just going to ask you exactly the same question,' replied Morse, with a curiously confident smile.

CHAPTER SIXTY-THREE

'Why did you murder those workmen in 1893?'
'It wasn't in 1893. It was in '92.'
(Quoted by H. H. Asquith)

'Do YOU WANT my wife to be here as well? I dropped her in the city centre to do a bit of shopping. But she shouldn't be long – if that's what you want?'

'We'd rather talk to you alone, sir.'

'What's this bloody "sir" got to do with things?'

The three of them – Storrs, Morse, Lewis – were seated in Room 36, a pleasingly spacious room, whose windows overlooked the hotel's pool and the sodden-looking croquet-green.

'What's all this about anyway?' Storrs' voice was already sounding a little weary, increasingly tetchy. 'Can we get on with it?'

So Morse got on with it, quickly sketching in the background to the two murders under investigation:

Storrs had been having an affair with Rachel James – and Rachel James had been murdered.

Storrs had been blackmailed by Owens – and Owens had been murdered.

The grounds for this blackmail were three-fold: his extramarital relationship with Ms James; his dishonest concealment of his medical prognosis; and his wife's earlier career as striptease dancer and Soho call-girl. For these reasons, it would surely have been very strange had Storrs not figured somewhere near the top of the suspect list.

As far as the first murder was concerned, Storrs – both the Storrs – had an alibi: they had been in bed with each other. How did one break that sort of alibi?

As far as the second murder was concerned, Storrs – again *both* Storrs – had their alibis: but this time not only were they in the same bedroom together, but also eighty-odd miles away from the scene of the crime. In fact, in the very room where they were now. But alibis could be fabricated; and if so, they could be broken. Sometimes they *were* broken.

(Storrs was listening in silence.)

Means? Forensic tests had established that both murders had been committed with the same weapon – a pistol known as the Howdah, often used by senior ranks in the armed forces, especially in India, where Storrs had served until returning to Oxford. He had acquired such a pistol; probably still had it, unless he had got rid of it recently – *very* recently.

The predominant cause – the Prime Mover – for the whole tragic sequence of events had been his obsessive, overweening ambition to gain the ultimate honour during what was left to him of his lifetime – the Mastership of Lonsdale, with the virtually inevitable accolade of a knighthood.

Motive, then? Yes.

Means? Yes.

Opportunity, though?

For the first murder, transport from Polstead Road to Kidlington was easy enough – there were *two* cars. But the target had not been quite so easy. In fact, it might well have been that Rachel James was murdered mistakenly, because of a mix-up over house-numbers and a pony-tailed silhouette.

But for the second murder, planning had to be far more complicated – and clever. Perhaps the 'in-bed-together' alibi might sound a little thin the second time. But not if he was in a bed in some distant place; not if he was openly *observed* in that distant place at the time the murder must have been committed.

No one had ever been in two places at the same time: that would be an affront to the rules by which the Almighty had established the universe. But the distance from Oxford to Bath was only eighty-odd miles. And in a powerful car, along the motorway, on a Sunday morning, early . . . An hour, say? Pushing it, perhaps? An hour and a quarter, then – two and a half hours on the road. Then there was a murder to be committed, of course. Round it up to three hours, say.

During the last few minutes of Morse's exposition, Storrs had walked across to the window, where he stood looking out over the garden. The afternoon had clouded, with the occasional spatter of rain across the panes. Storrs was humming quietly to himself; and Morse recognized the tune of 'September', one of Richard Strauss's *Four Last Songs*:

> *Der Garten trauert*
> *Kühl sinkt in die Blumen der Regen . . .*

Then, abruptly, Storrs turned round.

'You do realize what you're saying?' he asked quietly.

'I think I do,' replied Morse.

'Well, let's get a few things straight, shall we? Last Sunday my wife Angela and I had breakfast here, in this room, at about a quarter to eight. The same young girl brought us breakfast this morning, as it happens. She'll remember.'

Morse nodded. 'She's not quite sure it was *you*, though, last Sunday. She says you were shaving at the time, in the bathroom.'

'Who the hell *was* it then? If it wasn't me?'

'Perhaps you'd got back by then.'

'Back? Back from Oxford? How did I manage that? Three hours, you say? I must have left at half past four!'

'You had a car—'

'Have you checked all this? You see, my car was in the hotel garage – and God knows where *that* is. I left it outside when we booked in, and gave the keys to one of the porters. That's the sort of thing you pay for in places like this – didn't you know that?'

Again Morse nodded. 'You're right. The garage wasn't opened up that morning until ten minutes to nine.'

'So?' Storrs looked puzzled.

'You could have driven someone else's car.'

'Whose, pray?'

'Your wife's, perhaps?'

Storrs snorted. 'Which just *happened* to be standing outside the hotel – is that it? A helicopter-lift from Polstead Road?'

'I don't know,' admitted Morse.

'All right. Angela's car's there waiting for me, yes? How did I get out of the hotel? There's only the one exit, so I must have slipped unnoticed past a sleeping night-porter—' He stopped. 'Have you checked up whether the front doors are locked after midnight?'

'Yes, we've checked.'

'And are they?'

'They are.'

'So?' Again Storrs appeared puzzled.

'So the only explanation is that you weren't in the hotel that night at all,' said Morse slowly.

'Really? And who signed the bloody bill on Sunday – what – ten o'clock? Quarter past?'

'Twenty past. We've tried to check everything. You signed the bill, sir, using your own Lloyds Visa Card.'

Suddenly Storrs turned his back and stared out of the rain-flecked window once more:

'Look! You must forgive me. I've been leading you up the garden path, I'm afraid. But it was extremely interesting hearing your story. Outside, just to the left – we can't quite see it from here – is what the splendid brochure calls its "outdoor heated exercise plunge pool". I was there that morning. I was there just after breakfast – about half past eight. Not just me, either. There was a rich American couple who were staying in the Beau Nash suite. They came from North Carolina, as I recall, and we must have been there together for twenty minutes or so. Want to know what we were talking about? Bosnia. Bloody Bosnia! Are you satisfied? You say you've tried to check everything. Well, just – check – that! And now, if you don't mind, my dear wife appears to be back. I just hope she's not spent— Good God! She's bought herself *another* coat!'

Lewis, who had himself remained silent throughout the interview, walked across to the rain-flecked window, and saw Mrs Storrs standing beneath the porchway across the garden, wearing a headscarf, dark glasses, and a long expensive-looking white mackintosh. She appeared to be having some little difficulty unfurling one of the large gaudy umbrellas which the benevolent management left in clumps around the buildings for guests to use when needed – needed as now, for the rain had come on more heavily.

Morse, too, got to his feet and joined Lewis at the window, where Storrs was quietly humming that tune again.

Der Garten trauert . . .

The garden is mourning . . .

'Would you and your good lady like to join me for a drink, sir? In the bar downstairs?'

CHAPTER SIXTY-FOUR

Hypoglycaemia (n): abnormal reduction of sugar content of the blood – for Diabetes sufferers a condition more difficult to spell than to spot

(Small's Enlarged English Dictionary,
17th Edition)

'WHAT DO YOU think they're talking about up there, sir?'

'He's probably telling her what to say.'

Morse and Lewis were seated side-by-side in the Dower House lounge – this time with their backs turned on Lord Ellmore, since two dark-suited men sat drinking coffee in front of the fireplace.

Julian Storrs and a black-tied waiter appeared almost simultaneously.

'Angela'll be down in a minute. Just changing. Got a bit wet shopping.'

'*Before* she bought the coat, I hope, sir,' said Lewis.

Storrs gave a wry smile, and the waiter took their order.

'Large Glenfiddich for me,' said Storrs. 'Two pieces of ice.'

Morse clearly approved. 'Same for me. What'll you have, Lewis?'

'Does the budget run to an orange juice?'

'And' (Morse turned to Storrs) 'what can we get for your wife?'

'Large gin and slim-line tonic. And put 'em all on my bill, waiter. Room thirty-six.'

Morse made no protestation; and Lewis smiled quietly to himself. It was his lucky day.

'Ah! "Slim-line tonic",' repeated Morse. 'Cuts out the sugar, I believe.'

Storrs made no comment, and Morse continued:

'I know your wife's diabetic, sir. We checked up. We even checked up on what you both had to eat last weekend.'

'Well done!'

'Only one thing puzzles me really: your wife's breakfast on Sunday morning.' He gestured to Lewis, the latter now reading from his notebook:

'Ricicles – that's sort of sugar-frosted toasted rice – my kids used to love 'em, sir – toast and honey, a fruit cocktail, orange juice, and then some hot chocolate.'

'Not, perhaps,' added Morse, 'the kind of breakfast a diabetic would normally order, is it? All that sugar? Everything else she ate here was out of the latest diabetic cook-book.'

'Do you know anything *about* diabetes, Chief Inspector?'

It was a new voice, sharp and rather harsh – for Angela Storrs, dressed in the inevitable trouser-suit (lime-green, this time), but most unusually minus the dark glasses, had obviously caught some (most?) of the previous conversation.

'Not much,' admitted Morse as he sought to rise from his deep, low chair. 'I've only been diagnosed a week.'

'Please don't get up!' It sounded more an order than a request.

She took a seat next to her husband on the sofa. 'I've had diabetes for ten years myself. But you'll learn soon enough. You see, one of the biggest dangers for insulin-dependent diabetics is not, as you might expect, excessively high levels of blood sugar, but excessively *low* levels: hypoglycaemia, it's called. Are you on insulin yourself?'

'Yes, and they did try to tell me something about—'

'You're asking about last weekend. Let me tell you. On Saturday evening my blood sugar was low – *very* low; and when Julian asked me about breakfast I decided to play things safe. I did have some glucose with me; but I was still low on Sunday morning. And if it's of any interest, I thoroughly enjoyed my sugary breakfast. A rare treat!'

The drinks had arrived.

'Look!' she continued, once the waiter had asked for her husband's signature on the bill. 'Let me be honest with you. Julian has just told me why you're here. He'd already told me about everything else anyway: about his ridiculous affair with that young Rachel woman; about that slimy specimen Owens.'

'Did you hate him enough to murder him?'

'*I did*,' interrupted Storrs vehemently. 'God rot his soul!'

'And about this Mastership business?' Morse looked from one to the other. 'You were in that together?'

It was Julian Storrs who answered. 'Yes, we were. I told Angela the truth immediately, about my illness, and we agreed to cover it all up. You see' (suddenly he was looking very tired) 'I wanted it so much. I wanted it more than anything – didn't I, Angela?'

She smiled, and gently laid her own hand over his. 'And *I* did too, Julian.'

Morse drained his whisky, and thirsted for another.

'Mrs Storrs, I'm going to ask you a very blunt question – and you must forgive me, because that's my job. What would you say if I told you that you didn't sleep with your husband last Saturday night – that you slept with another man?'

She smiled again; and for a few moments the angularity of her face had softened into the lineaments of a much younger woman.

'I'd just hope he was a good lover.'

'But you'd deny it?'

'A childish accusation like that? It's hardly worth denying!'

Morse turned to Storrs. 'And you, sir? What would you say if I told you that *you* didn't sleep with your wife last Saturday night – that you slept with another woman?'

'I'd just hope *she* was a good lover, I suppose.'

'But you'd deny it, too?'

'Of course.'

'Anything *else* you want to check?' asked Angela Storrs.

'Well, just the one thing really, because I'm still not quite sure that I've got it right.' Morse took a deep breath, and exhaled rather noisily. 'You say you came here with your husband in his BMW, latish last Saturday afternoon – stayed here together overnight – then drove straight back to Oxford together the next morning. Is that right, Mrs Storrs?'

'Not quite, no. We drove back via Cirencester and Burford. In fact, we had a bite of lunch at a pub in Burford and we had a look in two or three antiques shops there. I nearly bought a silver toast-rack, but Julian thought it was grossly overpriced.'

'I see ... I see ... In that case, it's about time we told you something else,' said Morse slowly. 'Don't you think so, Sergeant Lewis?'

CHAPTER SIXTY-FIVE

'Is this a question?'
(from an Oxford entrance examination)

'If it is, this could be an answer.'
(one candidate's reply)

APART FROM themselves and the two men still drinking coffee, the large lounge was now empty.

'Perhaps we could all do with another drink?' It was Morse's suggestion.

'Not for me,' said Angela Storrs.

'I'm all right, thank you,' said Julian Storrs.

'Still finishing this one,' said Lewis.

Morse felt for the cellophaned packet; and almost fell. He stared for a while out of the windows: heavy rain now, through which a hotel guest occasionally scuttled across to the Dower House, head and face wholly indistinguishable beneath one of the gay umbrellas. How easy it was to hide when it was raining!

Almost reluctantly, it seemed, Morse made the penultimate revelation:

'There was someone else staying here last Saturday night, someone I think both of you know. She was staying – yes, it was a woman! – in the main part of the hotel, across there in Room fifteen. That woman was Dawn Charles, the receptionist at the Harvey Clinic in Banbury Road.'

Storrs turned to his wife. 'Good heavens! Did you realize that, darling?'

'Don't be silly! I don't even *know* the woman.'

'It's an extraordinarily odd coincidence, though,' persisted Morse. 'Don't you think so?'

'Of course it's odd,' replied Angela Storrs. '*All* coincidences are odd – by definition! But life's full of coincidences.'

(Lewis smiled inwardly. How often had he heard those self-same words from Morse.)

'But this *wasn't* a coincidence, Mrs Storrs.'

It was Julian Storrs who broke the awkward, ominous silence that had fallen on the group.

'I don't know what that's supposed to mean. All I'm saying is that *I* didn't see her. Perhaps she's a Fauré fan herself and came for the Abbey concert like we did. You'll have to ask *her*, surely?'

'If we do,' said Morse simply, confidently, 'it won't be long before we learn the truth. She's not such a competent liar as you are, sir – as the *pair* of you are!'

The atmosphere had become almost dangerously tense as Storrs got to his feet. 'I am *not* going to sit here one minute longer and listen—'

'Sit down!' said his wife, with an authority so assertive that one of the coffee-drinkers turned his head briefly in her direction as Morse continued:

'You both deny seeing Miss Charles whilst she was here?'

'Yes.'

'Yes.'

'Thank you. Sergeant? Please?'

Lewis reopened his notebook, and addressed Mrs Storrs directly:

'So it couldn't possibly have been you, madam, who filled a car with petrol at Burford on that Saturday afternoon?'

'*Last* Saturday? Certainly not!' She almost spat the words at her new interlocutor.

But Lewis appeared completely unabashed. 'Have you lost your credit card recently?'

'Why do you ask that?'

'Because someone made a good job of signing your name, that's all. For twelve pounds of Unleaded Premium at the Burford Garage on the A40 at about three o'clock last Saturday.'

'What exactly are you suggesting?' The voice sounded menacingly calm.

'I'm suggesting that you drove here to Bath that day in your own car, madam—'

But she had risen to her feet herself now.

'You were right, Julian. We are *not* going to sit here a second longer. Come along!'

But she got no further than the exit, where two men stood barring her way: two dark-suited men who had been sitting for so long beneath the portrait of the bland Lord Ellmore.

She turned round, her nostrils flaring, her wide naked eyes now blazing with fury; and perhaps (as Morse saw them) with hatred, too, and despair.

But she said nothing further, as Lewis walked quietly towards her.

'Angela Miriam Storrs, it is my duty as a police officer to arrest you on the charge of murder. The murder of Geoffrey Gordon Owens, on Sunday, the third of March 1996. It is also my duty to warn you that anything you now say may be taken down in writing and used in evidence at any future hearing.'

She stood where she was; and still said nothing.

Chief Inspector Morse, too, stood where *he* was, wondering whether his sergeant had got the wording quite right, as Detective Inspector Briggs and Detective Constable Bott, both of the Avon CID, led Angela Miriam Storrs away.

PART SEVEN

CHAPTER SIXTY-SIX

Twas the first and last time that I'd iver known women to use the pistol. They fear the shot as a rule, but Di'monds-an'-Pearls she did not – she did not

(Rudyard Kipling, *Love-o'-Women*)

(BEING THE tape-recorded statement made by Angela Storrs at Thames Valley Police HQ, Kidlington, Oxon, on the morning of 11 March, 1996; transcribed by Detective Sergeant Lewis; and subsequently amended – for minor orthographic and punctuational vagaries – by Detective Chief Inspector Morse.)

I murdered both of them, Rachel James and Geoffrey Owens. I'm a bit sorry about Rachel.

I was seventeen when I first started working as a stripper in Soho and then as a prostitute and in some porno flicks. Julian Storrs came along several times to the club where I was performing seven or eight times a night, and he arranged to see me, and we had sex a few times in the West End. He was a selfish sod as I knew from the start, especially in those early days, as far as I was concerned. Which was fine by me. He was obsessively jealous about other men and this was something I wasn't used to. He wanted me body and soul, he said, and soon he asked me to marry him. Which was fine by me too.

I came from no family at all to speak of, but Julian came from a posh family and he had plenty of money. And he was a don at Oxford University and my mum was proud of me. She just wanted me to be somebody important like she'd never been.

I was unfaithful a few times after a few years, especially with some of the other dons who were about as pathetic as the old boys in the Soho basement who used to stick the odd fiver up your panties.

I enjoyed life at Oxford. But nobody took to me all that much. I wasn't quite in the same bracket as the others and I used to feel awkward when they asked me about where I'd been to university and all that jazz, because I couldn't even pretend I was one of them. I wanted to be one of them, though – God knows why! Ours wasn't a tight marriage even from the start. It wasn't too long before Julian was off with other women, and soon, as I say, I was off with other men. Including the Master. He needs his sheets changing every day, that man, like they do in the posh hotels. But he was going at last and that started things really, or is it finished things? Julian desperately wanted to be Master and only one person wanted that more than he did. Me!

In London I'd lived a dodgy, dangerous sort of life like any woman on the sex-circuit does. I'd been mauled about quite a few times, and raped twice, once by a white and once by a black, so I can't be accused of racial prejudice. One of the other girls had a water-pistol that fired gentian-blue dye over anybody trying it on. I don't know why it was that colour but I always remember it from the paint-box I had when I was a little girl, next to burnt Siena and crimson Lake. But Julian had something far better than that. He'd kept a pistol from his Army days and after I had a bit of trouble late one Saturday night in Cornmarket with some football thugs, he said he didn't mind me carrying it around sometimes if it made me feel better. Which it did. I had a new-found sense of confidence, and one weekend Julian took me with some of his TA friends out to the shooting-range on Otmoor and for the first time ever I actually fired a pistol. I was surprised how difficult it was, with the way it jerked back and upwards, but I managed it and I loved it. After that I got used to carrying it around with me – loaded! – when I was out alone late at night. I felt a great sense of power when I held it.

Then came our big opportunity. Julian was always going to be a good bet for the Master's job, and we only had Cornford to beat. I always quite liked Denis but he never liked me, and to make up for it I detested his American wife. But this one thing that stood in the way suddenly became two things, because we learned that Julian would probably be dead within a year or so although we agreed never to say anything about it to anyone. Then there was that third thing – that bloody man Owens.

He'd written to Julian not to me, and he'd done his homework properly. He knew I'd been a call-girl (sounds better, doesn't it?). He knew about Julian's latest floozie. And he knew about Julian's illness and guessed he was hiding it from the College. He said he'd be ringing and he did, and they met in the Chapters' Bar at The Randolph. All Owens wanted was money, it seems, and Julian's never been short of that. But Julian played it cool and he went back to the bar later on and had a bit of luck because one of the barmaids knew who Owens was because he'd covered quite a few functions there for the newspapers. We didn't need to hire a detective to find his address because it was in the phone-book!

I knew what I was doing that morning because I'd already driven round the area twice and I'd done my homework too. I parked on the main road above the terrace and got through a gap in the fence down to the back. I don't think I meant to shoot him but just frighten him to death if I could and let him know that he'd never be able to feel safe in life again if he kept on with his blackmail. Then I saw him behind the kitchen blind, and I suddenly realized how ridiculously easy it would be to solve all our problems. It wouldn't take more than a single second. I knew he lived alone, and I knew this must be him. His head was only a couple of feet away and I saw the pony-tail that Julian had told me about. I'd planned to knock on the door and go in and sort things out. But I didn't. I just fired point-blank and that was that. There was a huge thud and a splintering noise and lots of smoke, but only for a second it seemed. Next thing I remember I was sitting in the car trembling all over and expecting to see people rushing around and police sirens and all that. But there was nothing. A few cars drove by and a paper-boy rode past on his bicycle.

It was all a bit like a nightmare I've often had – standing on top of some high building with no rail in front of me and knowing it would be so easy to jump off, and if I did jump off, that would be the end of everything. In the nightmare I was always just about going to jump off when I woke up sweating and terrified. It was the same sort of thing at that window. It was like somebody saying 'Do it!' And I did it. Julian knew what happened but he didn't have anything to do with it.

We planned the second murder together, though. Nothing to lose, was there?

Julian knew someone must have shopped him down at the clinic and he soon found out it was Dawn Charles. So we had the hold on her now and it wasn't difficult to get her to co-operate. She'd got money problems and Julian promised to help if she did what we wanted. Which wasn't much really.

Things went as we planned them. Julian drove down to Bath in the BMW and I followed in my car. He went M4. I went Burford way. He booked in and left his car in the hotel garage. I left my car in one of the side-streets behind the hotel. Dawn Charles went by train to Bath changing at Didcot, so Julian told me. She booked into the hotel as herself of course. After we got back from the Abbey, Julian and I had dinner together, and then I left. Julian rang Dawn Charles on the internal phone system and all she had to do was to walk across the garden. I drove back to Oxford and then up to Bicester where I'd got the key to Dawn's flat. It would have been far too risky to go back to Polstead Road.

Unless Julian persuaded her to sleep in the raw Dawn wore my pyjamas, and the hotel-girl took them breakfast in bed the next morning. Mistake about all that sugar, I agree! Dawn Charles is my sort of height and shape, so Julian tells me, and if she wore something that was obviously mine there wouldn't be much of a problem. The whole thing was very neat really. It didn't matter if she was seen round the hotel or if I was, because both of us were staying there officially.

I'd phoned Owens to arrange everything and last Sunday morning I drove round to Bloxham Drive again. Probably he'd have been more wary if I'd been a man instead of a woman but I told him I'd have the money with me. So he said he'd meet me and have a signed letter ready promising he wouldn't try any more blackmail. I went down the slope at the back like before and knocked on the right door this time. It was about a quarter past seven when he let me in and we went through to his front room. I don't think either of us spoke. He was standing there in front of the settee and I took the pistol out of my shopping bag and shot him twice and left him there for dead.

Angela Storrs
11.3.1996

(As it happened, Lewis was not to read this final version. Had he done so, he might have felt rather surprised – and a little superior? – to notice that his own 'burnt sienna' had been amended to 'burnt Siena', since he had taken the trouble to look up that colour in *Chambers*, and had spelt it accordingly.)

CHAPTER SIXTY-SEVEN

Belbroughton Road is bonny, and pinkly burst the spray
Of prunus and forsythia across the public way,
For a full spring-tide of blossom seethed and departed hence,
Leaving land-locked pools of jonquils by a sunny garden fence
                    (John Betjeman, *May-Day Song for North Oxford*)

SPRING WAS particularly beautiful, if late, in North Oxford that year, and even Morse, whose only potential for floral exhibitionism was a small window-box, much enjoyed the full-belled daffodils and the short-lived violets, though not the crocuses.

Sir Clixby Bream received a letter from Julian Storrs on Tuesday, 12 March. Both contestants had now withdrawn from the Mastership Stakes. At an Extraordinary General Meeting held the next day in the Stamper Room, the Fellows of Lonsdale had little option but to extend yet again the term of the incumbent Master; and by a majority vote to call in the 'Visitor', that splendidly titled dignitary (usually an archbishop) whose right and duty it was, and is, periodically to inspect and to report on College matters, and to advise and to intervene in any such disputatious circumstances as Lonsdale, *omnium consensu*, now found itself. An outside appointment seemed a certainty. But Sir Clixby accepted the situation philosophically, as was his wont ... and the College lawns were beginning to look immaculate again. Life had to go on, even if Denis Cornford was now a broken man, with Julian Storrs awaiting new developments – and death.

Adèle Beatrice Cecil had recently learned that the membership of the Young Conservatives had fallen from 500,000 twenty years earlier to 5,000 in January 1996; and anyway she had for several weeks been contemplating a change in her lifestyle. Morse may have been right in one way, she thought – *only* one way, though – in suggesting that it was the personnel rather than the policies which were letting the Party down. Yes, it might be time for a change; and on Wednesday, 13 March, she posted off her resignation to Conservative Central Office. She did so with deep regret, yet she knew she was never destined to be idle. She could write English competently, she knew that; as indeed did Morse; as did also her publishers, Erotica Press, who had recently requested an equally sexy sequel to *Topless in Torremolinos*. And already a nice little idea was burgeoning in her brain almost as vigorously as the wallflowers she'd planted the previous autumn: an idea about an older man – well, say a whitish-haired man who wasn't *quite* so old as he looked – and a woman who was considerably younger, about her own age, say. Age difference, in heterosexual encounters, was ever a guaranteed 'turn-on', so her editor confided.

One man was to continue his officially unemployed status for the remainder of the spring; and probably indefinitely thereafter, although he was a little troubled by the rumour that the Social Security system was likely to be less sympathetic in the future. For the moment, however, he appeared to be adequately funded, judging from his virtually permanent presence in the local pubs and betting-shops. It was always going to be difficult for any official down in the Job Centre to refute his claim that the remuneration offered for some of their 'employment opportunities' could never compensate for his customary lifestyle: he was a recognized artist; and if anyone doubted his word, there was a man living in North Oxford who would always be willing to give him a reference . . .

On the mantelpiece in his bedroom, the little ormolu clock ticked on, keeping excellent time.

In the immediate aftermath of Mrs Storrs' arrest, Sergeant Lewis found himself extremely busy, happily i/c the team of companionable DCs assigned to him. So many inquiries remained to be made; so many statements to be taken down and duly typed; so many places to be visited and revisited: Soho, Bloxham Drive, the newspaper offices, the Harvey Clinic, Polstead Road, Lonsdale College, Woodpecker Way, The Randolph, the Royal Crescent Hotel . . . He had met Morse for lunch on the Wednesday and had listened patiently as a rather self-congratulatory Chief Inspector remembered a few of the more crucial moments in the case: when, for example, he had associated that photo-

graph of the young Soho stripper with that of the don's wife at
Lonsdale; when the elegantly leggy Banbury Road receptionist
had so easily slipped alongside that same don's wife in a
chorus line at the Windmill. That lunchtime, however, Lewis's
own crucial contributions to such dramatic developments
were never even mentioned, let alone singled out for special
praise.

Late on Thursday evening, Morse was walking home from the
Cotswold House after a generous measure of Irish whiskey
(with an 'e', as the proprietor ever insisted) when a car slowed
down beside him, the front passenger window electronically
lowered.
  'Can I give you a lift anywhere?'
  '*Hello!* No, thank you. I only live . . .' Morse gestured vaguely
up towards the A40 roundabout.
  'Everything OK with you?'
  'Will be – if you'd like to come along and inspect my penthouse
suite.'
  'I thought you said it was a flat.'

Though clearly surprised to find Morse in his office over the
Friday lunch-period, Strange refrained from his usual raillery.
  'Can you nip in to see me a bit later this afternoon about these
retirement forms?'
  'Let's do it now, sir.'
  'What's the rush?'
  'I'm off this afternoon.'
  'Official, is that?'
  'Yes, sir.'
  Strange eyed Morse shrewdly. 'Why are you looking so bloody
cheerful?'
  'Well, another case solved . . . ?'
  'Mm. Where's Lewis, by the way?'
  'There's still an awful lot of work to do.'
  'Why aren't you helping him then?'
  'Like I say, sir, I'm off for the weekend.'
  'You're lucky, matey. The wife's booked *me* for the lawn-
mower.'
  'I've just got the window-box myself.'

'Anything in it?'

Morse shook his head, perhaps a little sadly.

'You, er, going anywhere special?' asked Chief Superintendent Strange.

CHAPTER SIXTY-EIGHT

They fuck you up, your mum and dad.
They may not mean to, but they do.
They fill you with the faults they had
And add some extra, just for you
(Philip Larkin, *This Be the Verse*)

FOR SEVERAL SECONDS after she opened her eyes, Janet McQueen had no idea whatsoever about where she was or what she'd been doing. Then, as she lay there in the green sheets, gradually it flooded back . . .

'Ah! Can I perhaps begin to guess our destination?' she'd asked, as the car turned left at Junction 18 and headed south along the A46. 'B&B in Bath – is that what it's going to be?'

'You'll see.'

As she *had* seen, for soon the Jaguar turned into the Circus, into Brock Street, and finally straight across a cobbled road, where it stopped beside a large magnolia tree. She looked at the hotel, and her green eyes widened as she brought her ringless, manicured fingers together in a semblance of prayer.

'Beautiful!'

Morse had turned towards her then, as she sat beside him in her navy pin-striped suit; sat beside him in her V-necked emerald-silk blouse.

'You're beautiful, too, Janet,' he said simply, and quietly.

'You've booked rooms for us *here*?'

Morse nodded. 'Bit over the top, I know – but, yes, I've booked the Sarah Siddons suite for myself.'

'What have you booked for me?'

'That's also called the Sarah Siddons suite.'

She was smiling contentedly as the Concierge opened the passenger-seat door.

'Welcome to the Royal Crescent Hotel, madam!'

She'd felt important then.

And she'd loved it.

Morse was already up – dressed, washed, shaved – and sitting only a few feet from her, reading *The Times*.

'Hello!' she said, softly.

He leaned over and kissed her lightly on the mouth. 'Headache?'

'Bit of one!'

'You know your trouble? You drink too much champagne.'

She smiled (she would always be smiling that weekend) as she recalled the happiness of their night together. And throwing back the duvet, she got out of bed and stood beside him for several seconds, her cheek resting on the top of his head.

'Shan't be long. Must have a shower.'

'No rush.'

'Why don't you see if you can finish the crossword before I'm dressed? Let's make it a race!'

But Morse said nothing – for he had already finished the crossword, and was thinking of the Philip Larkin line that for so many years had been a kind of mantra for him:

> *Waiting for breakfast while she brushed her hair.*

*

It was late morning, as they were walking arm-in-arm down to the city centre, following the signs to the Roman Baths, that she asked him the question:

'Shall I just keep calling you "Morse"?'

'I'd prefer that, yes.'

'Whatever you say, sir!'

'You sound like Lewis. He always calls me "sir".'

'What do you call him?'

'"Lewis".'

'Does *he* know your Christian name?'

'No.'

'How come you got lumbered with it?'

Morse was silent awhile before answering:

'They both had to leave school early, my parents – and they never had much of a chance in life themselves. That's partly the reason, I suppose. They used to keep on to me all the time about trying as hard as I could in life. They wanted me to do that. They expected me to do that. Sort of emotional blackmail, really – when you come to think of it.'

'Did you love them?'

Morse nodded. 'Especially my father. He drank and gambled far too much ... but I loved him, yes. He knew nothing really – except two things: he could recite all of Macaulay's *Lays of Ancient Rome* by heart; and he'd read everything ever written about his greatest hero in life, Captain Cook – "Captain James Cook, 1728 to 1779", as he always used to call him.'

'And your mother?'

'She was a gentle soul. She was a Quaker.'

'It all adds up then, really?' said Janet slowly.

'I suppose so,' said Morse.

'Do you want to go straight to the Roman Baths?'

'What are you thinking of?'

'Would you like a pint of beer first?'

'I'm a diabetic, you know.'

'I'll give you your injection,' she promised. 'But only if you do me one big favour ... I shan't be a minute.'

Morse watched her as she disappeared into a souvenir shop alongside; watched the shapely straight legs above the high-heeled shoes, and the dark, wavy hair piled high at the back of her head. He thought he could grant her almost any favour that was asked of him.

She produced the postcard as Morse returned from the bar.

'What's that for?' he asked.

'*Who's* that for, you mean. That's for Sergeant Lewis ... He means a lot to you, doesn't he?'

'What? Lewis? Nonsense!'

'He means a lot to you, doesn't he?' she repeated.

Morse averted his eyes from her penetrating, knowing gaze; looked down at the frothy head on his beer; and nodded.

'Christ knows why!'

'I want you to send him this card.'

'What for? We're back at work together on Monday!'

'I want you to send him this card,' she repeated. 'You can send it to his home address. You see, I think he deserves to know your Christian name. Don't you?'

ENVOI
Monday, 18 March

This list is not for every Tom, Dick, and Harry. It's been compiled by Everett Williams, director of the Florida Bureau of Vital Statistics, and on it are the 150 most unusual names he's encountered in 34 years with the bureau. Examples are: Tootsie Roll, Curlee Bush, Emancipation Proclamation Cogshell, Candy Box, Starlight Cauliflower Shaw, and Determination Davenport. But he never encountered a fourth quadruplet called Mo! Williams figures that some parents have a sense of humor – or else a grudge against their offspring

(*Gainesville Gazette*, 16 February 1971)

ON THE FOLLOWING Monday evening, Mrs Lewis handed the card to her husband:

'This is for you – from Inspector Morse.'

'You mean, you've read it?'

'Course I 'ave, boy!'

Smelling the chips, Lewis made no protestation as he looked at the front of the card: an aerial view of Bath, showing the Royal Crescent and the Circus. Then, turning over the card, he read Morse's small, neat handwriting on the back. What he read moved him deeply; and when Mrs Lewis shouted through from the kitchen that the eggs were ready, he took a handkerchief from his pocket and pretended he was wiping his nose.

The card read as follows:

For philistines like you, Lewis, as well as for classical scholars like me, this city with its baths and temples must rank as one of the finest in Europe. You ought to bring the missus here some time.

Did I ever get the chance to thank you for the few(!) contributions you made to our last case together? If I didn't, let me thank you now – let me thank you for everything, my dear old friend.

Yours aye,

Endeavour (Morse)